ROBERT A. BIGNELL

DOUBLE EXPOSURE

busybird
publishing

DOUBLE EXPOSURE

Copyright © 2025 Robert A. Bignell

A Novel Dedicated To

Dawid Sierakowiak, Lodz Ghetto 1942, and A.M.O.R.C.

Published in Australia by Busybird Publishing

Distributed in Australia by Busybird Publishing

Book Design by Robert A. Bignell

Cover Photograph Copyright © Robert A. Bignell

ISBN: 978-1-923216-92-1 (Softcover)

ISBN: 978-1-923216-93-8 (Ebook)

First Edition 2025

BOOK ALPHA

1

"Are yer gunna jump or aren't ya?" the bare-chested tough shouted from the riverbank. Behind him a troop of half-breed youths lolled about restlessly, some dressed only in simple brown loincloths with a Toucan feather behind one ear.

Clinging to a far-reaching bough above the water was the subject of their derision; a pallid, nine-year-old white boy clutching his homemade spear and coil of woven vines. With every passing minute, he was becoming a laughingstock. Those ashore were impatient to join an imminent event downtown; several had already slipped away into the tall swamp grass.

This majestic Fig had once been the Sacred Fishing place of the local Mojo Indians, but today a sickly pale nine-year-old Klaus Hahn was the tree's sole occupant. For a dare, he was preparing to pounce on a Piroruku, the largest and some would say grandest of all fishes in the mighty Madeira. Beneath his bare feet lay a gutter of deep water in which several of the monsters were already gathering ahead of the wet-season thunderheads. The surface nearby was sliced by a golden fin. "Too far away," the boy gulped.

Nothing short of a clean kill would gain him a place in his brother's gang of "River Rascals", some of whom were loitering ashore to witness his first attempt.

"Just shuddup and give 'da kid a chance," elder brother Robert growled, struggling to contain his restless retinue. "I don't remember any o' you bein' too keen either, first time 'round." He cracked his knuckles for extra effect and the pure blue of his eyes took on the glint of grey steel.

Big for his age, Robert Hahn, or "Bobby O Shea" as he preferred the rank and file to address him in private, was doing his best to fend off the cat-calls being aimed toward his white-knuckled sibling, who for the moment was veiled by an eddy of rising mist.

The youngster stifled a sob as he sensed the mood ashore. It seemed that neither his big brother's threats nor flying fists could restrain the others for much longer. After all, at just 13 years of age and rudely robust, Bobby the Irish upstart was noticeably younger than certain of his Mulatto recruits, a fact not lost on several bigger boys awaiting their chance to bring him down a peg or two.

Now it had come to this: the demurring postulant must strike soon or suffer ridicule from every kid in town and worse; Bobby's authority over his Rascals would be weakened. And without witnesses, the attempt would be in vain. Klaus drew a long breath and peered down at the swirling current: a flash of silver! The big fish were rising.

"For Christ's sake, you can tell he's not game to do it …"

At that moment the blast of a familiar steam whistle came drifting through the treetops to announce the arrival of *Madeira Belle* at Main Wharf. A restless buzz ran through the group; alerted to the pending bang and crash of the whole town tripping over itself to turn on a "Traditional Up-river Welcome" for the disembarking batch of well-heeled, if gullible touristas, arriving for three big days of Carnival, each hoping to tread where few white feet had trod before.

River-town gangs are usually "first in-best dressed" types, and here sat the residual Rascals twiddling their thumbs, up the creek without a paddle so to speak, while *Belle's* plush gangways would soon be disgorging new faces and opportunities onto Main Wharf … And still the bloody kid wouldn't jump!

Strains and thumps of the Kriegsmarine Brass Band rolled down from Monastery Hill, marking their route to Oom-Pa-Pa a welcoming bracket for the disembarking passengers. For the next few days and nights Santa Luzia's sleepy boulevards would be alert to every expedient. Such passing influxes, for the most part, were blind to the subtleties of a failing river town that had long since begun choking on its own secrets. They were here for an authentic bush bash featuring Madeira's Biggest Little City's faded opulence and quaint mannerisms.

Captain Streicher had certainly talked it up for days; in fact, few townsfolk begrudged *Belle's* skipper's title as the "Supreme Benefactor" of Santa Luzia; for without fail their Captain Rudy, ex-Kriegsmarine and owner of *Madeira Belle* since the "Stab in the Back" of 1918, was nowadays a major, if not sole underwriter of their wilting metropolis.

They could almost set their clocks by the arrival of his floating palace and to show their appreciation would flock aboard to reminisce and rub shoulders with the mostly gullible, though sometimes interesting visitors. Passengers and locals alike were happy to fritter away their loose change and hard currencies in the "Old Fighters Club" on the uppermost deck behind the wheelhouse.

Captain Streicher, the wise old seadog turned river-cat had, like so many fellow mutineers after 1919, including a certain Hahns of Hamburg, found refuge in far-off South America where he hoped at last to be free of the neverending social convulsions tormenting his beloved homeland.

Given the number of German ex-pats taking over many sleepy riverside settlements all along the great river, his new command was interesting and satisfying, if not profitable. Ever since he'd begun chasing his dream he'd been forced to use every trick in the book to stay afloat, literally, but as far as Santa Luzians were concerned he was nothing short of a True Saviour. His bonhomie and obvious competence endeared him to all who stepped aboard, besides swelling Santa Luzia's populace briefly but predictably every month.

Madeira Belle's layover could always rally a note of repressed merriment in the town's dwindling numbers, which at last count stood at 5,108.

The regal old paddle wheeler was a hangover from the glory days of rubber, now reduced to hauling international adventurers up and downriver on her first-class upper decks, nomadic local traffic on the main deck and much-needed heavy cargo in her broad but shallow hold. He'd had Belle refitted with a tug boat steam engine of great horsepower. "No riverboat afloat will pull a full load in such style as sure and smooth as my Belle," he couldn't help boasting when among fellow ex-pats. And, of course, there were always the unexpected little luxuries tucked away with news and gossip from the outside world.

This morning, Captain Rudolph looked down onto *Belle's* commodious main deck rippling with colourful hammocks intermingled with the bleat and cackle of native voices and livestock. Allocating the lower deck for third-class "locals" was a tradition *Belle's* new owner had continued upon taking command, even though he sometimes received complaints about unpleasant odours reaching the first- and second-class passengers overhead; especially when she was docked beyond the midstream breezes.

"You booked my *Belle* for an authentic Amazonian experience, am I wrong? That includes sights, sounds *and* smells ... I rest my case," he would chuckle.

"W ... Wait! There's something moving," the boy gasped out loud, pulling back. Not every flash of silver meant Piroruku, Piranha too were on the move; through moist eyes, he couldn't make out any shape clearly. Jumping onto one may bring a rich reward; onto the other? He pushed such thoughts to the back of his mind.

Under Robert's watchful eye, the remaining Rascals now pressed forward to witness the fatal blow and help land the catch. A clean kill would not only guarantee young Klaus' place in the gang, but even more importantly provide a welcome feast for the local Mojo Indians long since confined to their rickety bamboo ghetto above the mudflats outside town. Young and old alike were always grateful for a free feed and this would be the boy's first real chance to stand proud in the eyes of the whole tribe.

Within days of setting foot on South American soil, the immigrant half-brothers had heard all about Chief Ticuna and his people being booted out of their traditional hunting grounds, rendering the remainder untenable.

It was general knowledge that huge swathes of the best Indian land had been appropriated by the first Hahns of Hamburg, and now lay behind Grand Kaiser's ten-foot fence and a set of iron gates forged from the finest German steel. Above those forbidding gates, the following words were wrought in iron: "Work means Wealth."

At the stroke of a pen and a plethora of broken promises the entire river basin had been signed over to Hahn Enterprises by the National Government in the guise of a 99-year lease, the fine print of which left much room for manoeuvre.

Almost overnight, the Mojo Indian's supply of wild foods had dried up and the stricken tribe had been quickly reduced to begging and back-breaking labour. Once-proud hunters were reduced to illegal poaching or purchasing basic foodstuffs at inflated prices from the Company Trading Post. Tribal elders found themselves powerless to quell a skyrocketing consumption of sugar and fats by the young.

"Fat Indians were unheard of in our day," lamented the elders. "Before Grand Kaiser came, a porky hunter was the butt of constant jokes."

Chief Ticuna had watched on in tears while his people were abused, his lands plundered and their great jungle stripped bare. One after another the lofty forest giants came crashing down to make floorboards for something called an "Opera House". Indeed, certain die-hards among the ex-pats insist on calling the never-completed building an Opera House to this very day.

Mojo elders had tried in vain to warn the Town Council that every last tree felled made the surrounding air harder to breathe, but none of the elected officials fell for that sort of mumbo jumbo. After all, they pointed out, there was plenty of fresh air for those willing to get off their backsides and do a proper day's work lumping sacks of phosphate from the mine site to the docks.

Wasn't the sign above the gate clear enough?

Klaus' mind again drifted to the praises sure to flow after landing his Piroruku: four or five of Robert's hefty Rascals would carry the carcase downtown while he walked out ahead; he'd hang about for a pat on the back from the Shamans as they haggled over the entrails and choicest cuts and may even catch a smile from Maya, the Chief's daughter, whom he'd occasionally glimpsed at Sunday Mass and guessed to be around his own age. With Indian girls, it was always so hard to tell.

One Sunday morning he and Mutti had found themselves seated in the pew directly behind the young princess and her formidable father in his feathered headdress, the quivering of which was most noticeable during prayers and hymns. On the long walk home, he seemed distracted and could not recount a single moral from the sermon for Mam.

On the second such occasion, he moved up to take the Sacrament and allowed his fingers to "accidentally" brush against her bare brown shoulder, secretly thrilled when the girl did not flinch or cry out. Following that memorable moment there could be no mistaking her almost imperceptible attempts to catch his eye upon entering and leaving Sunday Service. A mere glance or two, combined with her dignified carriage and fine, almost European features, was sufficient to confirm her in his eyes as every inch a chief's daughter.

Yes, today *would* be different!

There! A grey shape slid up from the depths to crack a floating fruit in its vice-like jaws. The great fish looked much bigger up close, playing lazily on the surface, gulping air. *Hit the brain, or else,* the words pounded in his brain. Klaus would have but a split second to plunge his steel-tipped harpoon into the bony carapace: "… between and six inches behind the rolling eyes," they'd stressed.

A dozen times he'd watched Indian kids younger than him leap nimbly from this very branch to strike a fatal blow, and he had even gotten in a little target practice with dead fish carapaces from the safety of a low branch ashore. Mumbling a heartfelt Hail Mary, he took a deep breath and sprang!

For one exhilarating moment, he hung weightless in mid-air, until the plaited cord snapped tight around his ankle and tipped him upside down. As he hit the water his knees came down hard on his face, sending blood pouring from both nostrils and what little wind remained from his sails.

In that instant the great fish exploded from the water in a plume of spray before jack-knifing straight for the bottom; dragging spear, vines and boy down with it. Against such a force struggle seemed useless; in vain he looked up helplessly at the fading light of green and brown, soon becoming all-embracing darkness: the unforgiving cord bit deeper into his flesh and he felt tiny teeth tearing at his leg as he tumbled end over end across the bottom.

All asthmatics fear running out of air and by now his lungs were bursting; a single breath of water and all would be over. Behind his bulging eyeballs, bright stars exploded: drowning was nothing like he'd imagined. So silent, so still.

Little remained but a cool shroud of darkness smothering boy and stars together. He recalled that dying people see their lives flash before them as in a dream, but all *he* could grasp was his own stupidity in accepting Robert's dare in the first place. During those final moments of consciousness, he felt the noose fall free and a sensation of being sucked up into a dazzling silver cloud.

2

"Jeesus, I think he's dead!" a faraway voice peered into the soulless eyes. The body twitched, gave a retch, and began sobbing at the faces lurching in and out of focus.

"Yer bloody fool; ya scared the shit outa me an' the boys, right boys? Yer a bloody embarrassment ta all o' us, that's what you are. It goes without sayin'." Robert's concern turned to anger when he noticed the patches of red flesh where his brother's skin had been nibbled away. "Not a word a dis to Alois or Mam, or you'll wish I hadda let ya drown," he hissed to his sibling before regaining his usual bravado with another round of knuckle cracking and muffled rebukes.

The remaining witnesses, sensing the moment had passed, nodded vigorously in the Rascal's secret sign and hurried off toward the docks. It seemed everyone but the wheezing boy had had a good laugh in the end. "Stop blubbering, will ya? C'mon, get up, *Belle*'s already docked. You're worse 'n a bloody sheila, you are," the re-invigorated leader spat the words over his shoulder and without a backward glance hurried off to oversee the lie of the land downtown.

"W … w … ait," the boy cried, pulling himself to his knees and watching his brother's fine broad shoulders disappear into the undergrowth. He began imagining the ridicule to come, especially from Indian kids around his own age who took such heart-stopping initiations in their stride. At least the blood stains on his pants made it look like he'd put up a good fight; but no matter how he tried to spin the tale, he'd fallen at the first hurdle; despite all his mental preparation and pouncing practice.

He shuddered to even contemplate Robert's third and final initiation, which sent a chill down the spines of even the toughest mulatto boys.

After introducing this caveat for aspirants to endure the so-called Gloves of Happiness, Robert's authority and desire to outshine the Indians at their own game was greatly enhanced.

Ever since witnessing a Mojo coming-of-age ceremony, the Leader had incorporated this final hurdle into his panoply of planned pain. The ordeal involved strapping both hands into woven grass mittens filled with Fire Ants, for the length of time taken to beat out 39 thumps on the village drum. Throughout this interminable torment, would-be Rascals had to remain motionless and suppress any outward sign of discomfort. Only then would recruits be permitted to greet fellow gang members with the secret head nod, as practised by sunbathing skinks on the Fazenda walls.

Weaklings would be sent back to live in the Women's Maloca until brave enough to try on again the maddening mittens. Successful graduates were required to reaffirm their personal allegiance to the Leader during full moon ceremonies every month – "Cross my heart and hope to die if I should ever tell a lie" – allowing them to wear the brown loincloth around town. This was no mean challenge for part-Indian youngsters who feared falling foul of the Shamans. Observing these ancient Mojo rituals had stirred something deep and cruel within Robert.

With the possible exception of the Mojo "Mens Business" Ceremony, when boys showing signs of pubic hair were summarily circumcised with a rusty razorblade, the pulling on of the Gloves of Happiness stood supreme among local customs for the sheer amount of pain inflicted in the shortest period of time.

Henceforth, those seeking to join River Rascals would first need to demonstrate their obedience by submitting for one week to every whim and will of the Leader, culminating in a session wearing the Gloves of Happiness.

Those making it through, Robert concluded, would be invaluable in the ranks, though not unsurprisingly the mere thought of subjecting one's precious pinkies to such torment weeded out many of the faint-hearted before they'd even landed a Piroruku.

Klaus cursed himself at being lured into such shenanigans, especially when it so happened that not one of the gang members or Indian boys had actually seen his big brother wearing the Gloves of Happiness himself. But by now the sidetracked Rascals would be arriving downtown or what remained of downtown in Santa Luzia, eyeing off the milling crowd for a pocket to pick.

He rose unsteadily to his feet; feeling bedraggled, he retrieved his dry shirt from a tree branch and wrung out his begrimed and bloodstained shorts. Then, weaving unsteadily between the green aisles of bamboo he abjured under his breath all the way back into town. Of one thing he was certain: he would never again put himself in harm's way just to prove a point. He didn't care about being part of any stupid gang. Furthermore, the Mojos could stick their "Dream Catchers" made of harpy eagle feathers he would have received for the fish. Gangs and teams were for followers; this wilted sprout had no further desire to be a follower, or a leader for that matter: he much preferred reading the exploits of *real* Heroes of old.

When he finally tottered onto Avenida Santa Maria, he found the entire stretch between Main Wharf and the Monastery's all-seeing bell towers to be a jostle of colourful stalls and touristas attempting to photograph the Spider Monkey Circus. A half mile further downhill, where the rusty tram tracks double back, the town centre snuggled inside its sweeping river bend, the grassy banks of which were sprinkled with bright market stalls sprung up afresh on the hour.

When viewed from midstream, Santa Luzia Del Oro's sloping boulevards appeared as praying green fingers to keep the tropical sun at bay. Beneath in the shade, bygone crafts such as basket weaving, rubber-tapping and target shooting with blowpipes attracted much interest.

Cashed-up visitors were energised by the Pan Flute music as they stretched their legs and browsed the exotic offerings. Endearing, colourful characters shouted out enticements and offered all the jungle had to give: fresh fruits and cool coconut milk, woven fabrics with Indian motifs, caged parrots, stuffed monkeys and Caiman, to name but a few; even stalls stacked high with fine period furnishings from bankrupt estates.

Klaus had seen it all before; these visits from old *Belle* retained a fascination like few others: it was as if the outside world turned up on his doorstep for a few days each month. Thus absorbed, he nearly bumped into a man in top hat and tails carrying a hand-painted blowpipe; the fellow turned his head away and blew his nose.

Santa Luzia's Main Wharf was an engineering masterpiece from the glory days of rubber. The water was now too shallow for year-round access by newer deep-draughted vessels. The use of past tense is apt, because no platform of balsawood logs can stay afloat indefinitely, however large and buoyant it may have been when the logs were first felled a century earlier. Dozens of huge Balsa trees had been purloined from nearby Indian lands, and all able-bodied Mojo had been forced to drag them overland to their present site. Lashed together, the mighty trunks were then topped with a decking of sawn mahogany planks, plundered from their former hunting grounds.

Main Wharf could rise and fall up to 25 feet during the annual floods, and each wet season left more silt behind. For a while, the big-spending tourist boats kept calling, until no more Government funds were allocated for channel dredging.

By the early 1920's the partially waterlogged platform remained Santa Luzia's only remaining link with the outside world, while her remaining life force slowly ebbed away. When loaded up with the usual freight and sawn hardwoods, Main Wharf now barely keeps her nose above high water.

This day, nestled up in pride of place *Madeira Belle* showed off her spacious decks and railings like gilded lily pads: each was decorated with Belgian cast iron that gleamed in the morning sun. She sat ready to service the needs and soothe the nerves of a jaded community. And thanks to *Belle's* tenacious skipper Captain Streicher, she alone continued to negotiate the seasonal shallows long after the others lost interest. Perhaps it could be claimed that it was because of the skipper's deep longing for familiar habits and faces, rather than any likelihood of surplus that kept him returning. With his gruff, commanding presence and attention to detail, this ex-Kriegsmarine looked every inch an old sea dog straight out of the pages of a *Boy's Own Omnibus*.

When he took command of *Madeira Belle* following the Great War, Captain Rudolph established a tradition of bringing together the various German ex-pat communities dotted up and down the river, where he could jolly them into favourable exchange rates over the assortment of little luxuries stored in his cool-rooms below. Yet only Santa Luzia offered him the opportunity to pull on his lederhosen for a few days without fear of ridicule and mix with so many like-minded compatriots; those who could sing along to his collection of sea shanties and martial songs in the Mother Tongue. At least here his nostalgic largesse and plentiful supply of Schnapps were always appreciated. Only in Santa Luzia could he hold forth in his native tongue surrounded by so many genuine Aryan faces and fare.

Grand Kaiser's dispirited mining bosses, many of them ex-Kriegsmarine like himself, would remain yarning into the small hours and often the skipper would proclaim Santa Luzia to be "his very favourite far-flung corner of the Fatherland".

Up and down the mighty waterway in both directions, his beautiful *Belle*, as the last side-wheeler to offer a truly luxurious experience on the Madeira, had long struggled to compete with the newer and faster motor launches. But whenever she docked in Santa Luzia her towering twin blue funnels still dominated the skyline, reminders that she alone retained that level of comfort and elegance once so common on the run between Porto-Bello and Manaus.

Now though, she sat low in the water, her familiar totems just visible behind a patchwork of stalls, fuel drums, bales of tobacco, and mountains of cacao sacks.

As Klaus approached the beaming bow fringed with rows of hammocks and produce, he drew a deep breath of admiration. Wild laughter filled the air as elegant tourists were heaved ashore in flying baskets suspended from a wire rope attached to the middle deck, just as they always had before the rubber price collapsed in '28. Farther out, riding the cocoa-coloured current, a flotilla of dugout canoes circled like sharks around a dead whale, bartering with those on board in a dozen river dialects.

It was clear that the majority of passengers were smitten by the authenticity of their welcome, which often featured a short "war dance" performed by a local group of River Rascals wearing only brown loincloths and Toucan feathers. This could be followed by a "Dance of the Amazons", where topless Mojo girls gyrated in and out through the crowd before spearing a captive Caiman with its jaws tied shut.

Propped against the wheelhouse door overhead, a familiar figure could be seen handing out boiled lollies to a bevy of chattering Muchachas wearing red cotton aprons and little else. Klaus knew that Captain Rudolph was a man of fixed habits: when things were going well he exuded an air of wisdom and jocularity, such as the present moment; otherwise, he had certain well-rehearsed signals known only to the crew to quickly shut things down and throw out troublemakers.

He usually stuck with a proven routine during his three days in port; attending to minor repairs and getting the Kriegsmarine reunion sorted to begin with. As preparations for these essentials were being seen to, he would set the ball rolling for the two other eagerly anticipated events over which he intended to preside: namely, the Flamingo Villa moonlight junket with a few selected guests, and the Gala Ball aboard *Belle* on the final evening. That left ample time in between to regale passengers and locals alike and to settle on freight rates; nowadays it seems everyone wanted his cargo moved faster and farther for less.

Perhaps predictably, there were profits to be made from other than simple haulage of passengers and freight, God knows how little that brought in.

Unbeknown to all who were partial to the charms of an earlier era, Captain Streicher had a trick or two up his sleeve to recoup any unavoidable out-of-pocket expenses. And as usual, it would be the so-called high rollers like Alois Hahn and his fellow Grand Kaiser executives who would end up footing the bill in the enticing atmosphere in the "Old Fighters Club" upstairs.

As the skipper could do little wrong in the eyes of most Santa Luzians because of the life his voyagers injected into the local economy, they in turn showed their appreciation by dressing up in period costume for the whole three days to re-enact cultural high points and early conquests over local Indian tribes.

International passengers especially, never failed to cheer the passing parade of outdated, yet elegant fashions set against a backdrop of quaint buildings and cool narrow alleys. Those sending postcards home were enthused that Santa Luzia was the nearest thing they'd yet seen to authentic Amazonian colonial life.

Some climbed Monastery Hill to imbibe the nostalgic atmosphere and admire the French glass windows in the adobe Chapel that depicted a smiling Jesus blessing a group of neatly attired Indian children kneeling at His feet. Others paid a silver coin to climb the east bell tower, from whence excellent panoramic vistas of both town and river could be had.

In fact, Santa Luzia Del Oro, almost alone among the rubber towns, had remained barely viable because of *Madeira Belle*'s visits and the dwindling output of Grand Kaiser Mines, its principal employer. In the hundred-odd years since the Hahns of Hamburg had launched their first intercontinental foray, much had gone awry: when the rubber price crashed their failing Kaiser Wilhelm Mine No. 1 was left struggling to justify its relevance to the town it was created to serve.

The vein of quartz now ran too deep to be profitable and the remaining phosphate deposits were a good two-hour round-trip on foot from the mine entrance. The once thriving "Biggest Little City Upriver", so the faded sign above the docks yet proclaimed, had once been home to a thriving population of devout Portuguese and German immigrants. Some became fabulously wealthy in a short time and departed but many more latecomers got to glimpse the good life only briefly, if at all. Suddenly, gone were the days when ball gowns and silk underwear were shipped off to Paris to be laundered "properly", and fresh-faced monks spilled ashore from Lisbon to rescue heathen souls. Never again would crates of French perfume or casks of Black Sea Caviar land with a welcome thud onto the floating dock.

Such extravagance had once been common up and down the river, until one by one each township faded away with the price of raw materials. At that time the Brazilian real had become virtually worthless and Santa Luzia only just managed to stay viable. Town Councillors agreed to look the other way when Grand Kaiser announced it was stepping up its exploitation of the surrounding countryside, causing thousands more heavily forested acres to be fed through the Company sawmill. Every promising rock outcrop and gravel sinkhole was blasted apart in the quest for yet more quartz veins or gemstone deposits. Even medium-sized tributaries now ran orange all year round.

Mine management was able to cut day labourers' wages by one-third and increase the number of 50-pound sacks of guano they would need to hump to the surface during a 12-hour shift; the quota jumped from thirty to forty overnight.

The law of supply and demand has no favourites and able-bodied men now scrambled over each for a chance of work at any price. Grand Kaiser was now the only game in town; smart entrepreneurs had long since departed for cooler climes, taking their know-how with them.

Santa Luzian investors found themselves holding worthless stock in a company that cared little about the workers who kept it viable; what little profit it did declare was returned to the Fatherland in exchange for cheap imports. Come what may, the City Fathers would bend over backwards to keep their "Biggest Little City" on the map; there was already talk of an oil drilling project upriver that could, if successful, return prosperity with the first gusher. In the meantime, no job was too dirty or too dangerous in the desperate eyes of management, regardless of the toll on local labourers and the former environment.

This morning, hollow-cheeked peons gathered in small groups at the foot of *Belle's* gangplank, straining their eyes upward for a barely perceptible nod from the overseer guarding Captain Rudy's pile of U.S. Silver Dollars.

These sights and more the boy had seen many times. Now he found himself almost breathless amidst the noise and bustle: behind a mountain of phosphate sacks he came upon a barrier of bamboo cages brimming with colourful parrots and other jungle captives waiting to be loaded. From the stern of the old matriarch, crates of canned goods, machinery parts and liquor thudded ashore with a steady rhythm, accompanied by much yelling and laughing.

Thus distracted, he almost tripped over a bundle of salted Caiman hides before pausing to pet a flock of goats waiting to embark. A rumpus behind the cages caught his attention and he took a few paces for a better view: there, confined in a stout bamboo enclosure crouched a huge male Jaguar surrounded by a group of tourists watching on in horror and admiration. Holding court beside the cage was none other than brother Robert, the inherent show-off, who was performing an Irish jig around the cage and attempting to tweak the twitching tail each time he passed.

While lapping up all the attention and playing to the crowd he tarried a moment too long: with a belching roar, the spotted fury threw itself against the bars, almost splitting them apart and barely missing his fingers in the process. A squeal went up from the womenfolk, who egged him on, drawing in yet more onlookers. Some expressed disgust at the cruel teasing and distress of the great cat as one fellow pushed forward to catch a photo.

Robert was clearly in his element and the females were going wild; even as a boy he'd expressed the desire to become a big game hunter, and this was probably as close as he'd yet come. As the crowd began to disperse he took up his Banjo, upon which he'd mastered the bare basics, to accompany himself in an Irish ballad, dear to his heart: Twang, twang, twang went the Banjo, several people drifting away turned back and the big cat settled with a snarl.

Then, in his sweet warbling voice Robert began to sing:

> "Oh, Danny boy, the pipes, the pipes are calling
> from glen to glen, and down the mountainside.
> The summer's gone, and all the roses falling,
> It's you, it's you must go and I must bide …"

Several women began giggling and wondering what this all meant, but Robert had closed his eyes and continued strumming out of tune. Upon completing the third verse he finally opened them and found he was alone.

The whole spectacle had been enough to disgust his secreted sibling who, ignoring his tattered garments and shortness of breath, kept low and gave the malodourous animal cages a wide berth. At one end of the dock, he descried several mulatto girls baring their tiny breasts for the benefit of the crew members remaining onboard, some of whom called out suggestively in broken Portuguese. Never a dull moment when *Belle* was in town; and much of it on the house too, so many locals believed.

Nothing could be fairer, Captain Streicher figured, than giving with one hand and taking back with the other: everyone felt like a winner.

Night two saw the smorgasbord shut down by 11:00, but not before the ex-pat ladies had the chance to enjoy a flutter on the roulette wheel to risk a few coins of their own. Only afterwards did the skipper and a handful of carefully vetted male passengers feel free to take up Frau Slush-Klunk's standing invitation to join her and her maidens up the hill at 'Flamingo Villa' for a night to remember.

Flamingo Villa, the finest of all the riverine pleasure houses, was just a short stroll away from the docks, the captain assured them, and Madam Slush-Klunk was a stern but obliging hostess. Like so many other German refugees she'd remained fanatically loyal to the Kaiser. Her house served steins of genuine Munich Pilsener and lot-fed beef steaks renowned for their tenderness and flavour. She realised the importance of a belly-full of authentic German cuisine as a prelude to a spell of whoring.

Thus sated, clients could choose from a variety of private rooms designed to carry off a man of means into every fantasy. Certain spaces had been themed after Berlin's finest establishments, and Madam Gertrude boasted that all her guests would experience a real "leg-up" from their bucolic bash aboard *Belle*, when so many ended up being mugged or infected, or both!

Flamingo Villa's stable of mainly blonde and blue-eyed European "hostesses", each selected for her cleanliness and obedience, well knew that only Madam's firm hand and merciless eye stood between their making a small fortune or returning home in disgrace with ruined health. She reserved for herself the tedious but essential task of inspecting each of the masculine members waiting patiently out front. Upon entering the well-lit alcove, each patron was required to approach her respectfully with fly unbuttoned, presenting arms as it were. Sometimes, during these examinations, she would venture an encouraging word or recommend one or another particular hostess to the proud or bashful owner. Be as it may, those found to be unfinancial or unclean were turned around quick-smart by her mulatto bouncer.

During such private sessions Madam Gertrude's entourage looked to be straight out of a Hollywood movie: from Haut Couture through evening wear, right down to topless young wood sprites scampering about in the candlelight, serving drinks and offering various powders to sniff. For a select few river travellers, this invitation to join Captain Streicher's party was clearly *the* highlight of the cruise.

Sometimes, affluent males of Aryan appearance might even find themselves enjoying a return visit on the home run downriver. For those still standing and solvent on the third night, there was the captain's Gala Ball, open to all comers wearing gowns, suits, ties and closed-in shoes. As dusk descended, two Mariachi bands would kick off alternatively on the upper decks, while lesser revellers packed in down below. Crowds always gathered along the docks and long lines began forming outside the "Old Fighters Club", some waiting hours for a flutter on the wheel. It was clear to the ex-pats that Santa Luzia's very reason for existing, perhaps even for holding onto hope itself, would certainly dry up should their benefactor ever pull up anchor for good.

No one looked ahead more eagerly to Belle's visits than Alois Hahn, disillusioned scion of the Hamburg Hahns and shareholder in Grand Kaiser's entire Madeira operation. Oftentimes among the first aboard, Alois would sit debating the skipper for hours, questioning events back home and perusing snippets from the bundles of illustrated magazines sent out from Head Office. On one thing, however, both men agreed: just *who* really was to blame for Germany's untimely and unnecessary "surrender" in November 1918 that plunged the Fatherland into chaos, those Jewish profiteers and their illegitimate Weimar lackeys, that's who "Did you know?" Alois leaned close to his old comrade, as he often did after Schnapps, "… I read where one o' them sneaky Kikes bought up all the unused horseshoes and nails in '17 when he saw we had no chance of winning, sold 'em all over the world afterwards and made his bloody fortune." Alois was resentful of anyone who didn't actually fight in the Great War, particularly those who'd had the foresight and cheek to cash in during the resultant calamity.

He'd conveniently forgotten the fact of his own proud "war souvenir", a wooden foot resulting from a shipboard accident during joint naval exercises in the Irish Sea during the pre-war years, rather than enemy action.

After the Great War, instead of the plum job at Hahn Enterprises Head Office as promised, Alois was banished to the ends of the Earth when his rigid family tradition recoiled at his intention to marry, of all persons unsuitable, an Irish nurse! Marry her if he must; but with the family reputation at stake, he was instructed to keep her and her shame (part of which they suspected to be his) as far away from their own stiff-necked strictures as possible. He should make ready to board the first available Company vessel and take up a newly created position in Brazil. To soften the blow, he was promoted to "Unter-manager" without any colonial or mining experience whatsoever. Failure to submit readily would result in a reshuffle of Grandpa Hahn's Will priorities: he could take it or leave it. There could be no middle ground.

Decades later and half a world away, the failed unter-manager could cast off his worries beneath these familiar blue funnels every month and drink 'til he dropped. He could relive his fondest wartime memories with those who truly understood: for a few days the whole world seemed to lose meaning and he was able to disregard a certain looming deadline.

"Come on up, young Klaus," barked the skipper, twiddling the argent tips of his trademark moustache, "You been swimmin' again with your clothes on, ha-ha?"

As the sorry figure topped the wheelhouse stairs, Captain Rudy let out another loud guffaw and slapped the boy on the back, propelling him uncomfortably close to the quivering fluff-pocked breasts and glistening brown bodies gathered around. Predictably, he reached up to a shelf over the wheelhouse door, retrieving a glass jar filled with brightly coloured blue and green pebbles, which he held up to the light. The Muchachas pushed and shoved each other for a better look as the container passed from hand to hand.

His gallstone collection sparkled in the sun and a little squeal went up when the skipper lifted his shirt to reveal the huge pink scar on his belly. For good measure, he went on to retell how he'd lain wide awake on the operating table sipping Schnapps throughout the whole grisly procedure. No other animal in the jungle could survive such an ordeal, they all agreed. "I'm afraid there are more gallstones than gemstones in the Streicher family," he chuckled at his own joke as if hearing it for the first time.

How these simple native souls and jaded townsfolk revelled in *Belle*'s monthly visits bringing the chance to earn a few reals on the side.

In fact, the entire somnolent citizenry usually turned out for one or other of the captain's free-wheeling saturnalias. Few could imagine life without them. The old steamer was Santa Luzia's essential link with its own glorious past and the entire outside world: of times when Main Wharf rode high in the water and the shaded boulevards were thriving hubs of trade, when the steam tram ran up and down Monastery Hill every ten minutes.

But the boy was beginning to fade, no longer concerned with the "good ole' days". His chest was knotting in spasms from unwanted flashbacks to the drowning experience. The sweet odour of female sweat seemed to stifle his intake of air.

"Now, you girls take good care of this young fella, won't you? He's a special friend of mine ..." the skipper droned on, ignoring his "little mate's" growing discomfort.

Klaus felt faint. What if this turned out to be a full-blown attack and he couldn't make it back home in time for a shot of adrenalin? He really needed to be in his own bed with Mam nearby, but was able to gasp out one last request: "Could the fairy lights aboard please be turned on earlier than usual during this visit so he might catch a special photo of *Belle* silhouetted and back-lit against the tropical sunset?"

The good Captain, by now realising the extent of the boy's distress, agreed quickly to the plea and arranged for two of the stronger girls to see the fading youngster safely home. He helped position one gleaming brown shoulder under each of Klaus' sagging armpits. "Now don't go gettin' all uptight, young mann: no one knows himself until he's put to the test. Doc Wonders will soon have you fightin' fit or I'll be a monkey's uncle, haw-haw," he snorted with a funny little laugh to mask his growing concern.

Once free of the docks with their milling crowds, the two girls chatted away to each other as if the boy didn't exist, pausing only occasionally to let him rest and steady his breathing. The trip home seemed to take an eternity; in the distance the girls spied Frau Hahn standing on the top step of the Fazenda, hands on hips with indurated brow, sensing at once her bairn's distress.

"I'll be blowed, just look at yer! What in the name o' God ha' ya bin up ta? … an' in yer clean clothes an' all." Despite her feigned admonition, Mam wasted no time barking orders to the house girls. "Quick, Ines, run 'im a warm tub, an' send someone to fetch Doc Wonders as fast as their legs'll carry 'em. Tell 'im Klaus is havin' another attack, and be quick about it, girl," she snapped, rolling up her sleeves.

Her spent boy flopped onto the top step of the porch and leaned on one elbow, gasping like a fish out of water. Within minutes his clammy clothes were off and he'd been wrapped in the green blanket, a somewhat superfluous wedding present that Kitty had brought out from the Old Country. Everything was spinning and his cheeks were turning blue.

He heard Mam's voice sending the two helpers packing with a bag of scones. "An' next time git some propa clothes on before you go a visitin' …"

Klaus lost all track of time until Doc Wonders arrived to administer his trademark injection of adrenalin into his patient's flaccid deltoid muscle, and as usual the shot hit like a hammer!

With heart pounding and eyes flashing, he settled back on the cool island of his bed, already breathing easier. And boyo, wasn't the sky the limit for an hour or two? Sometimes after these shots, he worried that his thundering heart would burst clean out of its cage, but Doc reassured him that anything was better than running out of air. From the kitchen, he could hear Mother's worried voice being calmed beneath the other's bolstering baritone, "That leg wound doesn't look too serious, Frau Hahn … and I'm confident we've caught the asthma in time. If I didn't know better, I'd say he'd been bitten by piranha. A good night's sleep and he won't know himself. God knows why he would jump into the river with his clothes on."

Frau Hahn had been deeply indebted to Doc Wonders since the first time he saved her boy from certain asphyxiation. Back then, he too blamed "dust mites and other bugs" lurking in the run-down Fazenda during the periodic onset of the boy's asthma. But after the place had been scrubbed conclusively and the attacks persisted, Doc found himself leaning more towards Alois' theory that perhaps, after all, the youngster's apparent shortness of breath was "all in his head". Doc Wonders had a favourite saying at such times: "Serendipity reigns", which no one in the family actually understood. In fact, few knew just how this laconic Australian had turned up at the mine site around the turn of the century just when it happened that Grand Kaiser's senior medic was breathing his last.

"Serendipity reigns" were the puzzling words Doc Wonders had first uttered in his colourful accent when offered the permanent position: tending to the needs of "tough as nails" phosphate miners sounded simple enough at the time, though he did occasionally resort to unorthodox practices like stitching his patients' ears to the mattress when they wouldn't lie still during a procedure.

It seemed the jungle was forever throwing up ailments that foreign doctors had never heard of; nonetheless, for nearly two decades Doc Wonders had gone out of his way to ease the miners' suffering and remain beyond the fiduciary clutches of his ex-wife in Australia.

Sometimes, when things were a bit quiet he would sit at the foot of the boy's bed and tell tall tales from the ancient continent down under in his rolling nasal twang: kangaroos hopping down the main street of Sydney and how stuffed koala bears were used to decorate family Christmas trees, but the patient remained sceptical. While thus bedridden, Klaus often wondered if his love of literature was a poor substitute for so-called normal outdoor activities. Other kids had no time to waste reading books, they were quick to boast.

As the kitchen conversation lapped against his fading consciousness, he put his volume aside and drifted into all-healing sleep.

He sat bolt upright, at first not sure if and for how long he'd been dreaming: the house shook with loud curses and the slamming of doors. Trembling slightly he felt weak, but his heart rate had steadied and his breath flowed strong and deep. He swung his feet gingerly to the floor and took stock, instinctively crossing himself before Mam's plaster Virgin in the hallway opposite.

Tropical twilights being short and sharp, the boy could see that he'd left his much-anticipated sunset assignment too late for that day. Alois' boozy snarl confirmed his presence nearby, apparently searching for the freshly ironed dress shirt that Frau Hahn had failed to replace precisely between his good dinner suit and collection of naval jackets.

Klaus could hear him grumbling through the thin walls. "To hell with you, woman … If you stayed at home more often like a proper Frau, you'd know where my things are supposed to go. I'm sick o' tellin' the housemaid and I'm sick o' tellin' *you.*"

"It's *yourself* who'll be goin' ta Hell, ya drunken sot," responded Mutti, rising to the affront. "Don't think Oim not a wake-up to you, Alois Hahn, with yer drinkin' and awhorin' down on them boats." Mutti always reverted to bog Irish when she "did her block" or got frustrated. Her baby boy was concerned and amused when he glimpsed her skipping backwards down the hallway, taunting the old man by waving the missing garment aloft.

"Open yer eyes fer once, Alois Hahn; it was hangin' right there on the door in front o' yer drunkern nose. Ahem! Just where you told me ta leave it," she retorted strongly, beginning to tire of the game. Such domestic disharmony achieved little and was likely to stir up Klaus' asthma again.

Later, when she and Klaus were alone together she sighed, "At least 'e's stopped goin' on about 'is 'marital rights' and my so-called 'filial obligations'." Such was the tone of Mam's discourse after the big bust-up; everyone agreed that the unter-manager's wife had led a real "dog's life" before and since.

Not only had river town provincialism undercut the "proper" manners and niceties she'd hoped to cultivate in her new family, but as for the so-called breadwinner, the less said the better. He was consistently obnoxious during the fleeting hours he spent under his "own roof", tortured by the marital misalliance he'd been lured into and by his failure to thrive in the new setting.

How could he not have realised what marriage to a fervent Irish Catholic really meant? Why hadn't he listened to Grandvati? Worse still, the child he'd supposedly sired looked less and less like *him*, mirroring its mother's mousy looks and of less-than-robust fettle, especially when held up beside that blond-haired, bad-mouthed lout overtopping all her other baggage.

Too late he'd been confronted by the power of his new Frau's inexhaustible Faith, quick wit and sheer strength of character that lay behind those flashing eyes, fit to tempt a saint when it suited her.

When emerging from a fog of anaesthetic, Nurse's Aide Kitty O'Shea was the first friendly face Alois saw when he came to, surrounded by strange languages in a foreign land. This crusty German sailor had promptly fallen in love with his angelic caregiver, and was of course not the first patient to have ever made the same mistake. Fraulein Kitty's breezy chatter and infectious optimism certainly helped soften the blow of losing a foot to gas gangrene. After all, it wasn't every day that an eligible Irish lass got to fuss over a strapping German seaman of obvious means.

First, she'd talked him out of his black depression, fretting tirelessly to ensure his new wooden prosthetic fitted comfortably. Those following weeks were the happiest of Kitty's life as the unlikely pair hobbled around Galway together. With great difficulty she was able to coax him onto the back of her bicycle and wheeled him up to the cliff tops outside town; here they could spend a whole day picnicking together and watching the green breakers below. The more they chatted and laughed, the more he came to feel their common Aryan bond. One thing led to another and, as they say, the rest is history.

Alois was now working himself into a proper rage, snatching at the shirt as Kitty danced one step ahead. "I'm warning you Frau, give it here! You *will* do as I say!" he commanded, shambling after her.

"Garn, take it then! We wouldna want you to miss art on yer singsong with yer arld Navy mates nah, would we Klaus?" she chided, winking at the boy.

"You can git yourself right away from us, where you bilong," she said, slamming the door behind him. Mother and son watched through the window as the beaten man pulled on his dress shirt and set off towards town, still fiddling with his tie and mouthing curses. She put her arm about her goosen's shoulder but neither spoke.

3

When it became clear that the rubber boom was over, along with the hundreds of jobs that went with it, the social structure of Santa Luzia began to fall apart. A great unrest arose among the Indians, whose living and working conditions went from bad to worse. The Shamans' voices were raised as one, urging abandonment of their disease-ridden slum and a return to the traditional way of life in the far-off "Land of Streams" of their ancestors. Chief Ticuna was suddenly possessed of great strength in mind and body: always that jagged blue smudge beckoned him from the far horizon.

Up until 1860, prior to the Calamity, generations of Mojo ancestors had thrived atop that distant plateau under the watchful eye of Great Atua. As the designated day of departure drew closer the elders milled about in confusion, not wanting to stay but fearing to leave. After a spate of prescient dreams the old nun carefully channelled their discontent, urging Chief Ticuna to prepare the people for a great journey by gathering together only those essentials they could carry on their backs. It required the combined wisdom and powers of persuasion on all sides to fan the flames of action, and now suddenly the great moment was upon them.

A small group of hot-headed braves pressed for vengeance: sprinting part-way up Monastery Hill they set fires beneath the venerated floorboards of the so-called Opera House. For months they'd been unsettled by the strange music and screeching that issued forth during rehearsals; if birds and howler monkeys could fall quiet after dark it should be good enough for the white man. The never-completed building had long represented a symbol of foreign superiority and was an obvious target for payback; it remained as a slap in the face against everything the Mojo had almost forgotten, and which was stirring back to life.

Foremost was the need to thrive within the vast estranged jungle. The white invaders had shown contempt for the native and disregard for his customs; had pushed him aside under force of superior weaponry and coerced him into clearing away his sacred forests for farmland. Decades of sly-grog and disease had decimated the Mojo, until their legends lingered only in the hearts of the elders. That was, until one otherwise uneventful day Atua's Earthly Messenger came down from the sky via the Monastery and walked among them in her sacred robes.

Delirious at the success of their initial payback, the warriors cut a further swathe of mischief through the centre of town, before disappearing noiselessly into the drowned Varzea to rejoin the tribe; behind them, the skyline glowed orange with their victory.

Each piece of mine equipment they encountered en route received a lump or two of sugar into the fuel tank. Though a mere afterthought, the firebombing of the Opera House signalled clearly that there could be no turning back; they had burned their bridges for good. Chief Ticuna grasped this reality, and it suited him fine: there was no chance whatever of the tribe submitting to serfdom for a second time. It seemed everyone in town had turned out to watch the pyre of angry sparks roaring into the night sky, but Santa Luzia's mule-drawn fire wagon was no match for this crackling inferno.

After an hour or more, the hard-pressed volunteers managed to save only the main marble staircase, the portico columns and part of the stage area, the latter having been fortuitously shielded behind a temporary wall of corrugated iron. While the ruins still smouldered, the mayor faced uproar from the People's Planning Committee, not least for having to call off their first ever and long-awaited production of Wagner's "Ring Cycle" by a traveling amateur group from Belem.

A posse was quickly formed to pursue and punish the perpetrators, but by this time every last one of them had melted away. Howling for blood, the armed contingent swept along the waterfront, gaining in courage and numbers of dirty deeds, before moving on to torch the abandoned Indian village. Drinking heavily, the men egged each other forward, losing volleys of shots into the air and ignoring wiser heads: some took off toward the distant Dragon's Teeth along the only foot trail remaining above water level.

At first, the light held and fleeing footprints were easy enough to follow over the sodden forest floor. Suddenly, the dogs turned off acutely with noses to the ground; the tell-tale human spoor had vanished beyond the banks of an urgent freshet. Ahead, several transpicuous white ribbons of spray poured down from the black cliffs and into the forest below. "I know where they're headed. Believe me, if they make it into those lava caves we'll never catch 'em," declared Gabrielle Medina, trying to instil some order into his fractious deputies.

If anyone knew the 30,000-acre exclusion zone better than most it was Grand Kaiser's Senior Warden. Gabe had always gotten on well with the Indians and was even on a first-name basis with the Shamans. More shots and curses echoed off the rock face to be lost in the roaring falls. At that moment, old Gabe was baffled to see the main tribe had split up into smaller groups; among the bare children's prints, he spotted the distinctive heel marks of Sister Klara's buttoned boots. That old German nun had been nothing but trouble ever since she'd arrived at the Monastery, only to depart soon after to live in squalor among the Indians and adopt their lifestyle as her own. How in Montezuma's name would she be able to keep up with the nimble Indians?

He wondered aloud what could she be wanting with those kids in this God-forsaken no-man's-land, suddenly conscious that many in his roistering posse had lost interest and dropped back when the sun went down.

After dark in this unfamiliar dank gloom, few townsfolk could tolerate the striped leeches that began to plop down from the trees overhead, but Gabe was used to the inconvenience and determined to press on.

Soon, the beam from his miner's lamp began to fade and sputter. Once before, he'd tracked poachers this far, only to lose them in the caves behind the cascades. He took a few more cautious steps until his lamp flickered again and the darkness pressed menacingly. Involuntarily, he recalled the Indian legend of Curupuri, the giant Lizard Man who stalked the Dragon's Teeth by night, supposedly killing and roasting lost or disobedient children. This foul creature hopped about on powerful hind legs with feet and toes pointing backward to confuse his enemies. The unlikely tale sent involuntary chills down Gabe's spine; why would that silly old woman lead the children straight into Curupuri's lair?

Pushing on through the thick undergrowth he became even more unsettled, spurred on by the knowledge of certain punishment if he were to return empty-handed. Any Indian caught hunting or even trespassing on Grand Kaiser Land was fair game, and over time he and old Sergio had hoisted many a bloodied scalp from the flagpole outside the main office as a warning to others.

He went down on one knee to study the prints more closely; it appeared as if the whole group had first waded into the stream only to emerge near the base of the cliffs, before disappearing behind the curtain of white water. Clutching his 12-gauge Hartmann and Weiss tightly, he stumbled knee-deep through the snarling current, hoping for fresh signs, any signs. How could a decrepit old nun even think of undertaking such a journey? His mind struggled with the facts as known: that the Mojo had suffered decades of humiliation and torment prior to her arrival was undeniable, and she had quickly stirred up trouble with all her talk of "Peace Profound" and the necessity for "her" Indians to rise up and regain their "proper place" in the natural order. He'd heard whispers of able-bodied tribesmen training to carry heavy loads and that Chief Ticuna was encouraging them to prepare for a long journey. The very idea of reclaiming their lost homeland and culture after a century and more seemed preposterous.

Gabe stopped dead in his tracks. He had seen many shocking things during his years in the jungle, indeed, perpetrated many himself, but as he peered into the ever-deepening shadows nothing could have prepared him for the deplorable sight that met his eyes: old Sergio had clearly beaten him to the place where the footprints had vanished and among the low branches his discarded clothing had been carefully draped. Something pink and purplish hovered in the spray overhead, at the limit of Gabe's feeble beam.

When he staggered from the forest the next day, no one could get any sense from the torn and bleeding Senior Warden.

After downing a couple of quick rums, he slowly came round and gathered his wits, before recounting his discovery to the stunned onlookers. News of Sergio's demise spread up and down the river like wildfire: every shocking detail of how Sergio had been flayed by an expert hand or hands unknown, and his hide pegged out around the bole of a Hairy Brazil Nut Tree and up above, perched cross-legged on a rock ledge overlooking the scene, was Sergio's blotchy carcase nursing a bamboo basket containing his severed head.

4

Klaus chose his vantage point carefully for the afternoon photo session. Dusk was settling fast and he knew that the whole town would be headed dockside when the oppressive daytime temperatures softened.

Some 200 yards away *Madeira Belle* wallowed contentedly alongside Main Wharf, her brightly lit railings and superstructure splashed a flaccid orange glow along the bustling waterfront. Mariachi players in imposing sombreros and smart uniforms had already begun honking out a few bars from the top deck, while a group of matrons also in large hats picked their way purposefully up the gangway. They would enjoy the captain's repartee and hospitality on board until he closed the Old Fighters Club early and headed off with selected comrades toward his favourite haunt.

The entire horizon lay pink and flushed as Klaus wrestled his brand-new bamboo tripod into position beneath an overhanging limb, hoping the silhouette thus created would enhance his composition. He took a deep breath of appreciation and felt ready to capture the twinkling scene with his cherished Voigtlander Avus. He found himself sweating over his earlier calculations: it came as a shock to find the rolls of Agfa 620 film he'd been allotted were rated at a lowly ISO 19 [ASA 64], certainly not ideal for moving objects or soft evening exposures.

Conversely, the ten rolls of Agfa ISO 30 [ASA 400] sent out by Onkel Fedi and Tante Gretel for his birthday had proven too fast, grainy and quite unsuitable for the high contrasts of tropical sunlight. He'd pored over the "How to Take Better Photos" magazines they had so thoughtfully included when anticipating the dearth of cultural activities in their relations' remote new homeland. From the moment they'd learned of Alois' new family and subsequent exile, they had set out to spoil their new nephews from afar with regular packages.

"Although we've never met you," began the first note on hand-pressed paper with a flowing hand, "… we know that you will treasure this Avus camera and make every shot count. Who knows, one day you may visit us in person and show us your photos of life in Brazil.

"When you grow into a man, our home will be your home and the Fatherland will need your talents. As you will see from the enclosed magazines, modern photography is a far cry from the clumsy craft of yesteryear (with a few notable exceptions) and we hope our little gift may help you prove this to yourself. Please write and tell us which classes you are studying in school and which subjects you most like to photograph."

Such was the tone of warmth and generosity flowing from Alois' brother Frederick and his artist wife Gretel. With no children of their own, they somehow seemed to know exactly what two growing boys would need to keep their minds culturally active in a far-off land. However, it was the neverending stream of books in German *and* English, the latter for Robert's sake, encompassing subjects as diverse as History, Geography, Arts and especially Adventure which brought the greatest joy to their young nephew in particular, so often flat on his back or confined to the compound.

One such cardboard carton, much larger than usual, came addressed to "Master Klaus Hahn, Esq." and contained a second-hand, leather-bound set of *Meyers' Lexicon Encyclopaedias*, in German. He'd never seen anything like it and hardly dared riffle through the pages.

At first, he began tackling the A's, intending to read each volume from cover to cover, but long before reaching B he realised that encyclopaedias were intended more to enrich his existing knowledge of any given topic. He'd already picked through the kleptomaniac collection at the Mine Library, which also included classical gramophone recordings favoured by previous employees. While always hungry for a good read, Klaus suddenly discovered the joy of fine music in several genres, unlike Robert who couldn't care less for either of these time-wasting diversions.

Long before his 12th birthday Klaus had consumed Karl May's "Wild West" stories of Old Shatterhand and Winnetou, along with Kipling's *The Jungle Book* adventures. But above all, it was *Tarzan of the Apes* who made the greatest impression: no one was as fearless as Edgar Rice Burroughs' unlikely hero, who like himself was feted to grow up in a strange land surrounded by wild beasts.

Tarzan's woman, Jane, and their adopted chimp, Cheetah, were always getting into trouble and having to be rescued. To Klaus, it didn't seem quite the same having spider monkeys instead of chimpanzees. While wandering the jungle paths he attempted to imitate many of the bird calls and other sounds that reached his ears, but unlike his hero had no inducement to kill and eat any creature responding. He didn't need to, there was always a bowl of Mam's hearty stew on Ice in the pantry.

All this reading and music, however, was but a backdrop to the pursuit of his new passion: photography.

And dead ahead, under almost perfect conditions, one of the Madeira's more spectacular panoramas was unfolding: a stately old side-wheeler tethered to shore by a glittering harness of coloured lights that filled each corner of the composition with something of interest. *Belle*'s decorated funnels stood defiantly against the sunset and the silhouette of her upper decks became a layer-cake flambé.

He held his breath and pressed the cable release, holding it open for a full second. Then, to be on the safe side he made a second exposure of five seconds and a third of ten, realising that he may well be the first and last to capture such a vanishing scene; a shiver of excitement marked the moment.

Didn't Captain Streicher always complain that none of *Belle*'s photos ever did her justice or encapsulate her true grandeur? Just wait until he saw his pride and joy from this vantage point; no other photographer had attempted to balance the lights of ship and shore against a background of liquid gold. But how would it appear in black-and-white?

For the sharpest results, he settled on an aperture of f/8 and hoped that the wonky tripod would hold steady for the long exposures. When bending down to confirm the composition, a movement in the viewfinder caught his eye: on a scrubby isthmus of land interposing the lower frame he spied two shadowy figures weaving along a rocky ledge jutting out into the main current. The rear figure, draped in the cowled cassock of a Christian Brother, occasionally slapped the other across the back of the head while driving him forward.

A muffled curse rang out as the pair disappeared among the boulders.

Klaus turned back to his subject and prepared to press the cable release for a full ten seconds; surely one of these bracketed exposures would contain sufficient shadow detail for a good print, without over-exposing the artificial highlights? Black-and-white film could never do justice to the vibrant scene before him, but colour processing was way beyond his present capabilities.

Undoubtedly, his rented photo stall had become something of a novelty with the waterfront crowds that gathered when *Madeira Belle* was docked. Postcards of riverside scenes and local characters were his best sellers, and he soon showed a real knack for catching river folk unawares as they went about their business. By way of appreciation, he gifted a postcard in a folder to anyone who obliged him by posing, and for many of Santa Luzia's colourful identities, this was the only likeness they had ever possessed.

He was pleasantly surprised to find that his "freebies" often resulted in extra sales and began to imagine one day renting a shop front in the Avenida Isabella where he could imitate the poses and lighting techniques he'd studied in the German illustrated magazines.

Had not he just captured the most beautiful scene possible?

There was much to feel pleased about. Carefully packing up the equipment he made his way toward the crowded dock with the tripod over one shoulder, feeling strangely satisfied at having immortalised a spectacle that few others would take time to notice or enjoy, let alone capture forever.

The evening certainly had gotten off on the right foot and the future looked rosy, if only he could keep on top of his asthma: imagine if he was booked to do a big event like a Caboclos wedding and couldn't get out of bed?

He would need to give this potential career path more thought before throwing wide the doors of free enterprise.

At the foot of the gangplank, he hung back from a queue of sweltering guests in formal attire, arriving early for the captain's private dinner dance: hordes of the less favoured swarmed up and down Main Wharf and crammed onto *Belle*'s lower deck.

This was surely the pulse of river life as it had been in the good ol' days that everyone kept talking about. He fumbled to steady his tripod, took a deep breath and drank in the surrounding atmosphere. "Is it even possible to catch such rhythms, colours and energy in a single photograph?" he wondered aloud. "Can any single moment in time convey the power asleep in these great wooden wheels?" He straightened his shoulders and thought for a moment, *Well, why not at least have a try?* The clear limitations of still photographs, and especially black-and-white film, plagued the young artist often. Could his piddling little postcards ever hope to capture the realism of life on the river when compared to the exciting silent movies that had screened weekly in the Opera House?

Would his fantasy evaporate at the first whiff of reality? This was his world now, the jungle his studio. And for two whole days he had Captain Streicher's permission to board *Belle* whenever necessary and to position himself anywhere he wished for the best photos. At a nod from the guards, he slung the cumbersome contraption over his shoulder and ascended several more flights with some difficulty, eventually choosing to settle in a wooden lifeboat suspended precariously above the action. From this vantage point he had grand views fore and aft along both upper decks, and even more absorbing into the Old Fighters Clubhouse itself, where ex-pats and passengers alike were already gathered around the gaming tables.

One or two guests broke from the merry crush, looked up from the open windows and threw self-conscious smiles, concerned that he might be waiting to catch their antics on the dance floor. "When can we get a look at the proof sheets, young fella?" one man called, giving the thumbs up.

Most of the revellers, however, took no heed of a camera nearby and began their roistering as only bored travellers and novelty-starved local folk can.

Down below, huddled in a group by the rear railing he spotted Robert's Rascals mingling with two of the Christian Brothers in traditional brown robes and knotted white rope girdles; the shrouded pair appeared to be frisking the boys' clothing after crossing each forehead with a moist thumb.

Following this little ritual, each monk threw back his cowl and took a swig from the confiscated brass hip flask. Klaus recognised immediately Brother Romero arguing animatedly with Robert, while the old priest hung back, nodding assent at the harangue being dished out by his colleague.

Klaus had noticed the crooked spine hanging about the Mission School on previous occasions, without ever seeing him teach a subject. He'd recognised the silhouette as one and the same spotted earlier among the rocks: could that other shadowy figure being smacked about the ears have been his own brother?

Next time they were alone he would ask Robert just what they had been up to out there. Perhaps something would show up on the negatives? That particular ancient's behaviour had always unsettled the students: he usually kept his distance while observing their every move and was suspected of tattling straight back to Father Malone.

Given that many of Robert's mates attended no classes at all, they now looked uneasy in his presence. Behind his back, they referred to him as "the dobber" or "Quasimodo", though he had never been other than friendly towards young Hahn.

Suddenly, a conga line of glistening bodies gyrated into view, headed by a fat-cheeked trumpeter and two prancing drummers. Up the gangway they came to skirt the outside railing, gathering more dancers as they went. Protesting feebly, the two brown eminences were swept up in the reptilian glissade and carried onto the foredeck, soon to be seen swaying in step with the Mariachis performing from their temporary stage in the bow.

Robert, however, speaking on behalf of his Rascals, resisted all pleas to catch hold of the undulating serpent. Once his lads gripped those gleaming flanks and brushed against those glistening brown titties they would be lost for the whole evening. He and the boys had been discussing serious matters before the interruption; they now turned back reluctantly to the leader for guidance.

"What did I tell you? I for one am not goin' up there again at night after the last time when they locked us in and all," one boy piped up. The voice floated clearly upward, alerting Klaus that something was up. The speaker was a boy usually game for anything, one who'd shown great bravery and skill in spearing his Piroruku and wearing the Gloves of Happiness. Now he sounded agitated.

"Just shut up and do as you're told, Billy. Either we all go, or no one goes; an' we all stick together, right?" Bobby responded tersely, knowing that one or two of the bigger half-breeds would never miss a chance to undermine his authority. Though wary of his flying fists and the filthy temper that could erupt in a heartbeat, Robert alone enjoyed the "most favoured" status among the Christian Brother brethren.

As most children are aware, it pays to have the teachers on their side in any schoolyard dispute, and it was preferable that others and not he who copped those "sixers" dished out almost daily in front of the whole class.

On the contrary, the treatment Robert received at home from his stepfather was far from favourable: right until the big bust-up with Mam, Alois would lay into him gleefully with his razor strop for the merest infraction of "duty" or a failure to fulfil his allotted chores promptly and efficiently.

As far back as the *Ladybird* voyage, Alois had vowed to teach the "ignorant little bastard" a few manners if it was the last thing he ever did. At one point he even threatened his new spouse with a thrashing, in a futile effort to instil some decent manners into "this bog-trotting brood I've been stuck with".

Kathleen too had become thoroughly disillusioned with all the rules and regulations and soon refused to have a bar of his pedantry. "Oi'll gi' him what he's entitled ta' as me hoosband, and nary a penneth more," she told Father Patrick during confession one Friday evening, whose own loins tightened uncomfortably at the very prospect.

No sooner had the boys settled into the Fazenda when, after lights out, Alois would sneak up silently and listen at their bedroom door. From the very first night in their own beds, he had insisted that they sleep on their backs with the door open, hands clearly visible above the covers. Woe betide if he caught either of them "at it" under the sheets.

One such night, upon hearing muffled laughter, he tiptoed in and threw back Klaus' bedsheet with a triumphal cry, revealing nothing more sinister than him reading *Midsummer Night's Dream* by the light of a miner's lamp. Suddenly flustered, he gave the boy a clip under the ear anyway for not persevering with approved German authors rather than an overrated English Bard.

Like many domineering husbands, Alois' strict moral code was best imposed upon others. When his fancy led Kitty off behind closed doors to have his way, as it did often in the early days whether she wanted to or not, Klaus couldn't make head nor tail of the strange cries and thumps emanating through the thin walls. Poor Mam's ordeal sometimes dragged on for an hour or more, after which she would emerge dishevelled and tight-lipped.

This was very different from the brief cat and dog couplings, even the red howler mating he'd observed from afar, most of which took only a minute or two.

"I tell yer Bro, he's doin' it to her; you know, screwing!" Robert blurted one day upon noting his brother's bafflement. The youngster was clearly disgusted at the very thought of this bossy booze-hound forcing himself onto and actually doing anything intimate with his beloved mother.

"They're not, they're not," he objected, "… Mam wouldn't do that with any man, let alone *him*." Klaus would put his hands over his ears and run from the room, but Robert followed him onto the porch, enjoying the other's distress. "Come off it, dummy; how do you think we got here? Grown-ups do it all the time, mainly for fun! Wives *have* to do it for their husbands; even Father Malone says so," he replied knowingly.

"B ... But Mam wouldn't, she just wouldn't ..." the youngster offered lamely, before burying his nose in his book.

Robert loved causing trouble, especially whenever the new family looked like settling into some workable arrangement. His growing animosity towards Alois rarely abated; one step forward and two back required daily contortions behind a mask of obedience. He could barely hold his tongue whenever "Vati", as the stepfather now insisted on being called, was within earshot.

This was about the time that Klaus first saw evidence of his big brother's growing cruelty toward birds and animals, even stray pets. "Why shouldn't I trap them? There's plenty more where they come from," Robert responded arrogantly when the other looked aghast upon the growing list of victims. "If they're stupid enough to get caught, then that's just the Law of the Jungle."

Both Klaus and Mam were dead against the baited traps he concealed around the house and yard, checking them over each morning for victims feathered and furry, great and small.

Following a cursory "Trial", Robert would pronounce a "Death Sentence" in a solemn voice before "putting them out of their misery" in a variety of ways.

"You know the Indians kill everything that moves," he responded defensively when Kitty ramped up her criticism of the senseless daily toll.

"Yes, but they EAT them, you don't!" she responded angrily, "... and they dinna make the wee things suffer first." Mam was particularly referring to Robert's habit of hanging birds by the neck in tiny nooses until they either choked to death or were freed soon after by Klaus when his brother's back was turned.

But the cruelty didn't stop there; he shot and skinned one of the tortoise-shell cats from the mine to make a lampshade and bludgeoned to death a whelping bitch from the Indian camp for no reason at all. The inoffensive canine had sniffed out a pile of household scraps behind the Fazenda and had been caught in the act by Robert. When he proposed tanning its hide for a doormat Mam hit the roof, refusing to condone any further taking of life within her line of sight.

Klaus later found its broken body behind the woodshed, near where he himself had been training the luckless thing to sit up and beg.

Mustering every ounce of courage, he'd once fronted his big brother and demanded in no uncertain terms that the senseless killing of innocent creatures must stop only to find himself flat on his back licking blood off his top lip and fighting for breath.

Right now, though, Robert stood proud by Belle's stern rail, unaware of his brother's existence overhead. He was again passing the hipflask among his motley mates, looking every bit the cock o' the walk he saw himself to be. He may have to live at home for the time being, at the whim and mercy of his new "Vati", but sure as hell he was not going to accept chastisement from any other quarter, the Rascals could be sure of that. He vowed to "punch the eyes out" of the very next adult who laid a hand on him. Suitably primed and animated, the gang members sauntered back down the gangway, hot on the heels of a group of giggling Muchachas.

From his perch in the lifeboat, the photographer was in the perfect spot to observe the goings on below. More revellers now joined those aft in a brilliant display of colour and movement; he could wait no longer and opened the shutter for five full seconds hoping to fix the riot of movement.

On a notepad, he jotted down details of the flashing vermilions, greens and yellows, so that later he could hand-paint the eye-catching party frocks and feathered headdresses more realistically onto his postcards. Of course, this would not be as natural as the real thing, but good enough to catch the eye and sell for a higher price.

His knees began to cramp, necessitating a move to the opposite end of the lifeboat, from where he could enjoy an unimpeded view of the dancefloor and lower decks, which by now were bursting at the seams. All two dozen side windows had been lowered to allow the river breezes through and the Dixieland music out. From Klaus' vantage point, it appeared that moderation was already the first casualty; displays of passion were everywhere.

Aloof above the sweating masses and middle class, *Belle*'s top deck boasted six anterior suites with private amenities, whose passengers were always chosen to join the German ex-pats in the Old Fighters Club. It was here the serious money changed hands, private liaisons unfolded, and political arguments reached fever pitch.

On this space Klaus now homed in with his camera, suppressing a snigger at the contrast between the formally attired, obviously uncomfortable guests, and Captain Streicher himself, who sailed between the gaming tables showing off his ivory knees in a crusty pair of lederhosen.

There too, in the thick of things sat Alois, bow tie awry and waving his arms about rabidly. His heavy-drinking compatriots seemed more interested in the line-up of taut bottoms on barstools, the proud owners of which were tossing back one complimentary cocktail after another. The captain would more than recoup this decoy expenditure with a few throws of the dice and a spin or two of the roulette wheel later.

"I tell you, this fellow Hitler heralds a whole new era for the Fatherland," Alois declaimed. "He looks very much like the saviour we've all been waiting for. It says so right here in black-and-white in the *Illustrierter Beobachter*. The man is featured on every cover," he added, waving a magazine in the air. "Mark my words; stragglers will soon follow."

"Who said 'every'?" came a voice through the smoke.

"Ach! Alois is spot on. And this lot is already three months old," Captain Streicher pointed with his sandalled foot towards a bound pile of periodicals under the counter. Such parcels arrived from Head Office each month addressed to Grand Kaiser Management, supposedly to keep them informed of economic and political developments back home, and from getting homesick!

His old comrade suddenly perked up. "Well, I wish I was back there now contributing to the Great Revival. Adolph Hitler is calling on every able-bodied man to get behind his National Socialists. From what I've read, he's rebuilding our beloved Deutschland for generations to come. He says it's time to take back our rightful place as the cultural leaders of all Europe."

Alois paused to let his words sink in, pleased by his own show of patriotism. "Ha! Like the article says: the only way that can happen is if Germany fully re-arms. To hell with the perfidious 'Treaty of Versailles' designed to keep us on our knees forever." His once quadrilateral features again flushed and sagged, as if uttering the word "perfidious" had drained all the fight out of him.

The captain shifted in his seat and gave the roulette wheel a casual spin. "Come on Ladies and Gents, don't hang back, there's plenty more silver dollars to be won," he called, aiming his invitation squarely at the ladies' bottoms, before turning back to Alois.

"Is that so? And what good do you dream of bringing to the great cause, eh? With your pot belly and gammy foot to boot, get it? To boot … Ha!" he laughed into the other's chastened face. "I don't imagine there are too many vacancies opening up back home for the likes of you and me, comrade. These Nazis are looking for younger blood, perfect specimens to carry the Nation forward; after they sweep away that lame-duck Republic they had foisted on them, of course. If you ask me, the likes of us are better off well out of it. You could do a lot worse than Santa Luzia, Alois," he cleared his throat, seeking concurrence … "With regular visits from your friends, of course," he added.

"C'mon folks, time to place your bets; I'm feeling lucky on red tonight," he announced to the crush of players now gathered to watch the steel marble hissing round and round.

Captain Rudy had perfected the knack of overseeing the green tables while carrying on separate conversations without losing either thread. The more he spun the wheel, the keener the crowd became to chance their diverse currencies. "My wheels do all the work," he would often say with a wry grin, referring not only to the giant propellers looming outside, but to the sure-fire money spinner occupying pride of place in his mini-casino. If friend or foe lost their hard-earned salaries playing roulette, that was their bad luck; each loss partly compensated, in his eyes, for the declining volumes of freight.

His carefully chosen "shills" had each been given 20 reals up front, "to get things moving" and were expected to pay them back at closing time.

Few regulars lost larger sums more often than Alois Hahn; never suspecting for a moment that two tiny magnets cleverly concealed inside the spindle of the roulette wheel ensured that the odds always leaned toward the house.

Just as players began to suspect a bias toward red, there would be a run of sudden blacks to lighten the mood. Nevertheless, like any compulsive gambler,

Alois was always hopeful that the very next throw of the dice or spin of the wheel would bring home his lost chickens.

"Thank you sir, thank you madam" the captain purred, raking in the assortment of river currencies, of which there were almost as many as there were languages. Crumpled bank and promissory notes, gold nuggets and uncut gems were swept into his leather apron pouch without fear or bias. Never too greedy, he paid out six or seven winners for every ten who lost; contentedly observing his well-heeled patrons as one by one they threw their hands in the air and retreated to the bar. When drunks become incautious, as they often did, he could relax and pour himself a full-strength Schnapps from the green bottle under the bar, knowing that at any hint of trouble, his hefty enforcers would arrive from below decks at the touch of a button. Otherwise, these three days in port promised nothing but predictable amusement.

Behind the shrewd eyes and silver handlebars, he was content to watch his old countrymen tossing back the Schnapps, and especially to observe the desperate defalcations of comrade Alois trying to win back the missing funds he'd "borrowed" from the Company Pension Fund. These hard-won, carefully labelled bundles of blue-chip securities would surely be found missing at the next audit, not a few of which had ended up in the grateful pouch of Captain Streicher's lederhosen. All's fair in love and war; Heaven knows the Old Girl could do with a facelift. Every contribution was gratefully received if it meant keeping *Belle* afloat for one more season.

And in between visits, there was always Flamingo Villa and the waterfront speakeasies with which Alois could share his unearned largess. The skipper thought it suicidal that a sidelined scion, ostensibly above suspicion, was not only dipping into the Company Pension Fund for gambling but to finance an ill-fated rubber plantation. Alois kept hoping that Providence would miraculously turn things around and restore the lost funds overnight: drink up and ignore the looming deadline!

Such pressures meant life at home went from bad to worse as the Unter-manager revealed a growing disdain for his own feeble progeny and a downright contempt for the elder boy that left a bad taste in Captain Rudy's mouth.

An increasingly combative Alois would roll his eyes whenever the youth ventured a strong opinion, which was often, and more than once called him a "smart arse" in public. In fact, he only stopped beating the boy after he refused to beg for mercy and even began counting out loud each stroke of the strap on his bare backside.

Something had finally snapped in that fateful hour, causing an exasperated Kitty to fly at her husband with nails drawn: "Gi' off him you animal! I swear by Mary, Mother of God, if you ever lay another hand on 'im, I'll cut yer black heart out in yer sleep." Alois had reeled back, speechless and chastened. Mam's trademark twinkling eyes now blazed, leaving no room for misunderstanding.

"Oi'll … Oi'll poison your food, you poor excuse for a hoosband, an' don't think I can't get at yer one way or 'tother." His mouth had flopped open and the strap hung mutely in his hand as Robert smirked thinly and pulled up his trousers. He couldn't wait to dash off and tell his mates about Mam finally standin' up to the old man.

From that day on, the beatings ceased and the captain, too, was secretly chuffed when he heard how Kitty's unexpected show of spirit had called her husband's bluff. "That's two mighty fine-lookin' boys she's given him. Some people don't know when they're well off," he confided to his first mate. He'd always suspected Kathleen Hahn's free spirit, despite her obedience to the Cross on the hill and oft-expressed aversion to life aboard the river boats.

Captain Rudy turned again to his boastful countryman. "With six million men unemployed, this Hitler character will have his work cut out. They say a loaf of bread back home now costs a million marks. But, as you say, it's a damning indictment against that bunch of criminals running the Republic. Lord knows the Fatherland is crying out for change, any change, but I'm not sure it's going to come from this funny little fellow and his band of thugs."

Alois nodded absently and swallowed the last of his drink before venturing his own thoughts. "We Hahns are a proud family. It was our mine that brought wealth and culture to this shitty backwater. Now, just look at us!" He waved his hand toward the crowd at the bar, and pronounced his words slowly and precisely. "Is this the thanks we get after decades of sacrifice for Kaiser and Fatherland, eh? Ach man: did I ever tell you my Great Nephew was the fourth pageboy at the King of Denmark's Wedding?"

"Yes! Many times, comrade," the skipper replied, clearing his throat. Well before midnight he often affected a little more intoxication than he felt; it helped to clear the Clubhouse and free him up for what lay ahead. He could read the tell-tale signs that his companion was preparing to settle into the corner lounge, wrapped in self-pity. That was Alois' usual routine when he'd run out of "readies", a string of tired anecdotes and martial tunes in slow succession; then nothing. There would be no more political parrying tonight, and Captain Rudy was keen to get away. "Come and take your father home, young'un; he's nearly emptied the bar with his repertoire," he yelled up through an open window. "Did you think I hadn't noticed you perched up there?"

The boy was startled by the booming voice from below. "I … I'm just packing up, Captain Streicher. I think I got some great shots, but I might need someone to give me a hand with Papa." He knew that if Alois turned violent or even collapsed entirely, he alone would never handle him.

"Perhaps he's forgotten he's taking a hunting party upriver in the morning, so he'll be needin' his beauty sleep, won't he?" added the skipper, "… and he's probably better off in his own bed."

Santa Luzia Safaris had become a much-touted high point for every voyager and after many boring days upon the brown flood tide, a group of six passengers had booked the promising adventure for their last day in Santa Luzia.

Grand Kaiser's massive estate was renowned for its big game like Tapir and Caiman, with myriad monkeys in the riverside treetops providing excellent target practice along the way. Of course, if they kept the noise levels down, there was always the hope of bagging at least one big cat. In that case, Alois would score an extra 1,000-real "Panther Bonus" and begin repaying the pilfered funds.

He and Robert could pick up an extra 500 real for skinning and salting down the trophy pelt before *Belle* departed the next morning, although the boy seemed more skilled in that department. If all went well, Alois would pay him 100 real and put the remainder back into the Pension Fund.

It was mere chance that found an unskilled Alois leading an expedition into the flooded Varzea, having substituted himself and Robert for the skilled Mojo guides who'd vanished into the swamp with the rest of the tribe.

Previously, Indian braves had been granted "concessions" to guide visiting hunters around their former tribal lands and as payment were rewarded with the resultant fresh meat. No one could quite understand why Alois had been so keen to put up his hand for the job, given his lack of people skills and jungle experience but as the sole nominee, Captain Streicher just had to go along with the compromise and hope for the best. During one or two earlier safaris under Alois' command, not a single big cat had been glimpsed, let alone bagged.

A rattled Gabrielle Medina, previously the logical substitute to lead hunting parties, nowadays refused point blank to wander farther than a rifle shot away from the main compound.

For the moment, more urgent matters beckoned; Kitty spotted a familiar sight through the kitchen window.

Hobbling towards the house was Alois, with one arm draped over the shoulder of his struggling boy fighting gamely to juggle his father's dead weight and keep his tripod from dragging in the dirt. The old man's other armpit was supported by a gaily clad Mulatto girl who, every few minutes, cheerfully brushed away a playful hand.

Grim, but composed, Mutti met them at the front steps and a cry broke from her lips: "*You!* Git goin!" she waved away the girl, who needed no encouragement to turn tail. "Don't bring 'im thru the house Luv, he's liable to chuck everywhere." She ran a scornful eye up and down her estranged Herr.

"May the good Lord forgive him, for I won't," she spoke partly to her wheezing bairn and brusquely at Alois' uncomprehending face with its thin, slack lips, before poking her former lord and master twice in the chest for good measure. "You listen to me good an' proper, Alois Hahn! I told you, I've had enough, and you're not welcome in this house."

He mumbled something about the Fazenda and everything in it remaining company property.

"Yer can stay ternite now yer 'ere, 'cause I'm off to 'elp up at the Mission; the Yeller Fever's back," she said solemnly, emphasising the importance of her calling. "And if you lay a finger on either o' my boys you'll ha' me to answer ta. Oh, and make sure you're gorn by the time I return," she warned.

"He will be Mam, he's goin' out on a Safari first thing," the boy gasped, now supporting the entire weight on his own. She gave a little huff and moved to shore up the unresponsive mass. "Your tea's still warm in the oven, lad. It's up to you whether you share it with *'im*, or not … Gord, let me give you a 'and." She'd suddenly noticed Klaus' other arm buckling which allowed his precious camera equipment to slither to the ground.

Together, they half-dragged and half-carried Alois' deadweight to an outside bunk where he could sleep it off. Then, kissing her baby on the cheek, Mam vanished without another word.

A task still lay ahead for the exhausted boy; first, he removed his father's shoes and socks with difficulty, before spreading a mosquito net over the dishevelled dinner suit and struggling back through the house for his plate of "sausage and three veg". He knew the effects of the adrenalin had well and truly worn off and that his asthma was threatening to return with a vengeance.

With hindsight, he probably shouldn't have gotten out of bed in the first place.

5

Kathleen Mary Hahn, nurse's aide, was weighing up the legalities and implications of reverting to her maiden name, having moved beyond playing the German Frau. On one hand, she had to think of her boys' future; on the other, regaining her independence. Never in her short life had she felt so valued and important as when Father Malone sent for her to assist in the Charity Ward. During daily Mass, Frau Kathleen hung upon his every word and hungered for the Church's blessing over each forthcoming shift.

There were always the usual infectious diseases like malaria, workplace injuries and domestic violence incidents that she could handle with ease. However, today's summons was different: Father's note had warned her to bring along waterproof clothing, a tight bonnet and clean cloth to use as face masks.

The messenger advised that the dreaded yellow fever had arrived in the guts of a billion mosquitos that had cut swathes through the outlying shanty towns. All hands would be needed at the Mission Hospital.

Right from the start Kitty had felt a warm inner glow when attending the Lord's careworn flock alongside Father Paddy, and it had gotten her out of that mouldy old Fazenda. She'd long had a soft spot for the long-suffering labourers who turned up seeking treatment with their thin mattresses under their arms. When fussing and bussing about in the clinic she quite forgot her own problems and became once more the cheery Kitty O'Shea of old. The monks occasionally helped out, but it was her cool head under duress that Father Malone valued so highly and which set her apart. Her nursing skills were basic and effective, while her bright smile lifted the patients' spirits. Most of all, he rejoiced in her Gaelic wit during those long hours they laboured side by side: a single ditty from her lips could make the hair stand up on the back of his neck and transport him straight back to the Old Country, to savour spring wildflowers on the pungent black bogs.

For this unlikely Irish pair, homesickness was never far below the surface.

Distinct among the usual run of snooty European women in his flock, "with faces on 'em like a pound o' tripe", he once let slip, was sweet Kathleen Hahn, or "Kitty" as she preferred. Not a one of 'em could hold a candle to his newfound soulmate: her honesty, sincerity and especially her simple Faith gave him renewed hope that the likes of them both together could allow "Da True Church o' God to carry its Divine Mission to every far-flung corner of dis Gard forsaken place".

They would preach the very Christian values she'd attempted to instil into her boys. And she would have succeeded too if it wasn't for that overbearing husband of hers. Father Paddy was pained to overhear Kitty's boys, especially the elder one, lying his way out of trouble to sidestep responsibility. He knew the big fellow had lied in confession, especially over his refusal to attend regular classes with the monks and his hanging around Flamingo Villa after hours.

Yet, God knows there were earlier times when Father Patrick felt himself an imposter, understanding little Spanish or Portuguese while attempting to minister to the locals. He'd never fitted in among the tight-knit covey of Christian Brothers who oversaw the school curriculum and corporal punishment of the children. Behind his back, they referred to the Paupers Ward patients as "Paddy's Pigs".

One year to the day before the Hahn Family landed in Santa Luzia, Father Patrick Malone had himself bent down to kiss Brazilian soil for the first time.

His head and heart were abuzz with ideas for much-needed reform: he would immediately increase tithing from the corporate sector, encourage temperance among the savages and stamp out misalliances between Catholics and heathens. High on his list were cohabitation and divorce, both damned out of hand.

But how could he have known then that the Amazonian Cultural Tide was all-consuming, dwarfing his own vacuous ambitions just as it had swamped the hopes and dreams of those who'd come before?

Boatloads of carpetbaggers and bible-bashers had spilled ashore to plant their puny settlements on the banks of the mighty river, seeking converts and gold; having to settle instead for rubber and slaves. Most were simply swallowed up by the vastness.

During his first tortuous year at Holy Cross, the old Irish priest had encountered only rebuff and loneliness. His faith hung about his neck like an ill-fitting halter, as one by one his cherished proposals were met with indifference or outright hostility. Most of the white folks were quite happy with things as they were thank you very much, and the Indians were becoming more argumentative over the Holy Message and its continuing relevance for them. "To be sure, they began losing their way after the old sister moved in with 'em," he concluded sadly, commiserating with the younger monks.

So he did what those before him had done, and probably most who would follow: he rediscovered the smell, taste and songs of Ole' Ireland in the bottom of a whiskey bottle. Now, instead of wooing corporate sponsors with his fiery sermons and settling spiritual disputes, he found himself up to his elbows in the pus and blood of the charity ward. That first nip each morning got him going and kept a smile on his face throughout the daily grind when working beside an angel straight out of heaven. It seemed like all his birthdays had come at once.

Why, Peggy O'Neill herself (the only female besides his mother he'd ever kissed) couldn't compare to this little bogtrotter, who as it turned out, had grown up almost next door in the big smoke back home, three hops and a jump from his own hamlet of Ballindooley. He had to pinch himself every day to make sure he wasn't dreaming; by God he did, and often. Feelings he thought he'd long since conquered were stirring again. Emotions long-buried were anxious.

Starved for forgiveness he began travelling downstream to confess in the adjoining diocese, where his sinful musings could not be turned against him. Even there, the zeal of God's house almost ate him up, and he found himself admitting only trifles: "Forgive me Father for I have sinned. I sometimes eat meat on Fridays when the Indians bring in a freshly killed peccary" and that sort of thing.

The confessional always frightens those who have drifted, and he just couldn't bring himself to admit to the chronic drinking and the lustful thoughts that wracked his waking hours. These latter he'd convinced himself were the first pure thrusts of sweetest love so long denied, unlike anything he'd felt before. He saw similarities in his own confessional obfuscations to those employed by that young Robert Hahn, reasoning that Catholic life was nothing more than a succession of sins committed, partly confessed and then forgotten.

Unlike that teenager, his own transgressions could not be so easily dismissed, rearing into immoral thoughts that could only be managed with difficulty. "Kitty, Kitty, Kitty O'Shea. Her name rattled around in his head and the thought of her little sayings could set him chucklin' uncontrollably. Foolish options crowded out all common sense and his sermons became charged with a new urgency … "Repent! Or be lost in the Black Bowels o' Hades farevar!" he thumped his pulpit and glared down into the dwindling congregation. It could be no coincidence that fate and the Sinn Fein uprising had thrown two kindred spirits together in this far-flung backwater, as unlikely as a pair of four-leaved Shamrocks sprouting on the same footpath.

Time and again he vowed to cut back on the grog for Kitty's sake, but God wasn't listening: He'd placed the forbidden fruits within easy reach to tease out his deeper feelings.

Alois, meanwhile, although not entirely oblivious to these developments, decided to settle accounts in a roundabout fashion by cutting back Grand Kaiser's monthly tithes to Holy Cross Mission by 90%.

"Do they think we're made of money?" he responded when his outraged wife pointed out the shortfall in the Easter envelope. "I've enough on my plate already. And you can tell that scrawny-necked Abbot of yours that I'll cut off every last peso if he continues to turn my own wife against me."

Kitty blushed involuntarily and knew it was useless to argue. How much could he really guess? At least she now had a perfect excuse to devote herself to the procession of poor suffering souls who presented outside the ward each morning. Just let him try and stop her. It was so typical, so bloody tight-fisted when it came to God's Holy Church yet tossin' it about like a drunken sailor at gambling parties aboard *Madeira Belle* and elsewhere. Come to think of it, he *was* a drunken sailor.

While the missionaries harped and carped, Alois sought his own salvation in the back streets; whenever he had spare change in his pocket, that is.

6

Secluded, yet easily accessible by land or water, Flamingo Villa was nestled on a shaded embankment between Grand Avenue and the big bend of the river, just a short walk from the wharves and what passes for downtown in Santa Luzia. A single footpath winded lazily up past the front door and on through a copse of moss-draped Cyprus Trees to the private mooring.

At certain times, "Villa Escorts" could be seen lounging aboard an ever-changing flotilla of pleasure craft, or even diving naked for coins to the delight of those on board. Otherwise, "house calls" to Santa Luzia or the mine site itself were strictly forbidden.

It was toward Madame Slush-Klunk's notable establishment that Captain Streicher, having departed early from the green tables, made his way up the said garden path in the company of a dozen comrades and eager tourists.

Predictably, Alois Hahn had been left behind asleep and flat broke on a couch in the Old Fighters Club. "A change is as good as a holiday," the skipper teased the others out loud, looking forward to finding something new and different among the Teutonic trappings of Flamingo Villa. Up ahead, beneath a creaking, life-sized wooden shingle featuring the said Wader, the welcoming party could already hear the plangent strains of Volkslieder long before Captain Rudolph's party hove into sight. Soon, all were exchanging hearty greetings in the foyer.

Then followed Madame Gertrude's customary scrutiny of each proud private part applying to enter: any simple pimple, unexplained swelling or rash showing up in her Jeweller's eye-glass was quickly shown the door, along with its owner. Approved guests then joined the skipper in eyeing off a series of erotically themed alcoves en route to the great salon, each inhabited by an elegant reclining consort murmuring suggestive entreaties in a variety of languages.

43

"No, no … not yet," Captain Rudy chuckled at his impatient entourage, before wading further into the main gallery. "Aha! This'll do …" he said with a sigh, plumping down on a velvet chaise not far from the dancefloor. "Now it's every man for himself." He flashed a generous wink and grabbed hold of the young white girl dressed as an Indian Squaw serving drinks. "Onkel Rudy wants a young one; you youngest?" he grunted, running his eye around the room. The trapped girl fluttered her loaded eyelashes and wiggled about trying to find a comfy spot on his ample leathern lap. Some of the girls joked that being selected by Captain Rudy was like trying to climb side-saddle onto a draught horse, of which there was one only in Santa Luzia. Bare-bosomed, fair-haired "Amazons" fussed about him with a fat cigar and a plateful of Madame Gertrude's celebrated devilled eggs for starters.

"Fill 'er up again girls," he said, tossing down two quick Schnapps. "I'm as dry as a nun's nasty, haw, haw. Have you heard that one before, eh?" he bounced the ersatz maiden up and down until she gave a little squeal and spilt her drink. "Bonsoir Fraulein, or is it bonjour? I can never remember at this hour," he called to the balcony above, ignoring the squaw and knowing exactly just where to toss his mangled greeting in the gloom. A third shot of Schnapps and another pink-coloured drink for the captive maiden appeared on the coffee table. It was still early.

Despite the variety of fashions, shapes and sizes, each white-skinned "Escort Dancer" carried herself with an air of confidence and refinement, quite different from the drab mandatory uniform of skirt and blouse when not on duty. Each stood ready to soothe the world's ills in an evening; and if anyone knew how to train a girl to please a man, not just any man, it was Gertrude Slush-Klunk, formerly of Berlin's finest pleasure houses.

One thing she did not know, however, was as midnight approached, Bobby O'Shea and certain older Rascals would be creeping one by one, like shadows, ready to settle in the spreading arms of a giant Lupuna tree outside the bordello's heavily draped windows to pass the wee hours talking in whispers and passing around Alois' binoculars.

Fraulein Gertie (Captain Streicher being the only person permitted to use that fetching endearment) sipped her mineral water and surveyed the lively scene below, only partly visible through the rising cloud of smoke. She returned Herr Rudolph's bibulous greeting with a barely perceptible nod of her mousy tresses, which meant, "You are not in a common barroom now, boys."

To all others, including her stable of girls, she was strictly "Madame Slush-Klunk". A spare woman in appearance, Gertrude Slush-Klunk was not at all like one would imagine a madam should be. She wore a standard uniform of smart unobtrusive button-up blazer over a plain white satin top and snug skirts in muted tones of modest length. Black leather flatties complimented her tiny feet, or open-toed scuffs during the wet season. Very occasionally, when the Kriegsmarine skipper was in town, she would break out her red-checked dirndl, a treasured 21st birthday gift from her long-dead parents, certain to loosen the purse strings. One other visible concession to the trade she plied so successfully was a black velvet choker featuring a modest emerald at the throat, which picked up the hue of her eyes.

Although Madame's disciplined hands and stoic demeanour hinted at a life of service, any casual observer might take her tight leggings and firm bound bosom crowned with a simple coronet of mouse-coloured braids to be those of a modest alpine maiden out for a stroll. Her taut and shapely thighs had not been violated since her earliest days of setting up the Villa when she'd needed a few favours done in a hurry.

Nowadays she held herself aloof from the rough and tumble of the salon floor, but behind this carefully crafted façade lay her true gift, honed in the aftermath of the Great War. At that time, she could just afford to sweep up pretty, blonde homeless girls off German streets and train them in the arts of discipline and pleasure. Her discerning eye and uncompromising work ethic soon shaped a competent stable of twenty girls ready for high adventure and easy money, well away from the grey horizons of conflict.

She spoke to each girl individually about using her body as the mighty Amazonian Tribeswoman had once used hers, for maximum impact and reward. And pleasure too, if so desired.

Looking back, it seemed an eternity since that first batch of dancers found fame and fortune up and down the river. Now their hard-won savings grew fat in the Grand Kaiser Pension Fund, with a small percentage of the gross deposits being forwarded directly to the "Restoration of the Fatherland" appeal back home. "The German Woman is knitting again," she proudly announced soon after.

Nearly every Villa "regular" had a favourite, whether she be clad in a simple red loincloth or a Parisienne evening gown; hostesses were expected to "put out flat out or get out" at any hour of the day or night when the boats were moored below. Madame Gertie had a profitable knack for pairing her higher-ranking clients with her more adventurous "Jung Madels", as she called them. No protection was required upon payment of an extra fee. This practice, of course, resulted in her having to ply another of her backroom remedies from time to time, after which the said unlucky madel was granted three nights off on half pay. During these procedures, she often speculated as to which of the "little peckers" (as she liked to call them) she'd met at the front door may have done the damage.

But tonight, the place reeked of Cuban cigars and French perfume; mine hostesses became the very essence of alertness and efficiency, flitting noiselessly from room to room, making notes in the gloom of her heady Erebus like an apex predator.

A single word was sufficient to send her shirtless Mulatto eunuch flailing into any trouble spot with his truncheon. Rich or poor, old and young, big

Albert the bouncer sent them sprawling onto the street with no hope of reply. She and her girls had come to make money, and plenty of it, without being roughed up. (Each secretly hoped to return to the Fatherland with a small fortune and an overall suntan.) "Get in and get out quick! It's the long haul that does you in," Madam always stressed.

From time to time, Alois Hahn kept the establishment posted with forecasts from the Pension Fund Trustees and glowing updates on the Term Deposits and Brazilian Government bonds, through which their precious savings grew daily fatter.

He hinted that if things kept on this way, the ladies' nest eggs would probably double over the next three years.

7

The brothers blew out their candles around midnight. Earlier, Klaus had tried re-reading the adventures of his hero, *Tarzan of the Apes,* but the action-filled pages only caused his heart to beat faster. Robert had arrived home early and flopped down on his bunk without a word or sideways glance. He looked dishevelled and out of sorts, straightaway leaning down to engage his formations of tin soldiers on the floor.

The youngster closed his book and propped on an elbow, unable to concentrate. Across Robert's rug, the French and German ranks were springing to life. After a long hiatus, the tin soldiers flew at each other, with sound effects from the Commander-in-Chief firing cannonball percussions from the back of his throat.

At such moments Robert seemed lost in a faraway world. Among the dozen or so senior students attending classes at Holy Cross, he alone refused to take the lessons seriously: he longed for more adventure than any school could offer.

When not out roaming the Varzea with his rifle he would lose himself at home by re-enacting one of his famous European land battles known by heart. Unlike the real bone and gristle combatants cut down in real wars, Robert's armies actually grew larger after each skirmish, thanks to his newly revealed, if nebulous "Onkel" Fedi in the far-off Fatherland.

Alois' brother Fedi had taken a keen interest in his older nephew's martial inclinations from afar. Nestled among Tante Gretel's selected volumes would be one or two brand-new "Stormtroopers" in lead-painted brown, plus a piece of field artillery made from pressed tin.

Robert's Grand French Armee was further strengthened after he successfully swapped his brother a collection of Napoleonic Generals for a set of wooden zoo animals, none of which appeared to be much like those in the surrounding jungle. After his initial disappointment, the youngster soon realised that even lions, zebras and elephants could be easily concealed in the long grass for a pretend ambush on Tarzan and was satisfied.

Of all the surprises Tante Gretel shipped out, none could compare with the Voigtlander Avus folding camera in its brown leather case, which actually arrived one month late for Klaus' ninth birthday. It even had his name and date of birth engraved on the base [6 Februar 1912] which caused Robert to sulk for days afterwards.

"Why would they waste their precious moolah on me? What do I get? A bloody maths book! Oim not good enough, dat's why. Oim not trooly 'their blood' after all, am Oi? Well, Oim bloody glad o' dat, to be sure. Anyway, cameras are fer sissies too weak to get off their lazy bums an' learn how to fire a gun ..."

But Klaus wasn't listening. He could hardly believe his eyes. This was a whole new world of possibility. He poured over the instruction manual for hours before inserting the first roll of film, marvelling at the Skopar F1:45 anti-stigmatic lens and smooth rangefinder action which someone at the mine laboratory told him was first class. Beneath two separate viewfinders, the Voigtlander possessed an optional fold-down leg that would allow him, whenever he wanted, to take self-portraits with the aid of a timer. No more wheezing or confinement to bed with a book; now he had more reason than ever to explore Santa Luzia's colourful byways.

As he began snapping away in the weeks that followed, if somewhat hesitantly, the former invalid felt relieved to find the rough-looking locals friendly enough and soon trained himself to include something of interest in all four corners of a picture whenever possible. He was conscious of the apparent ease with which his idol, Heinrich Hoffmann, caught so many of his subjects off guard for the illustrated magazines, producing a more spontaneous result.

The boy learned quickly to estimate both apertures and focus prior to lifting the bulky Avus to his eye and tried to visualise the final cropping of the print a moment before the camera came up. The trick was to release the shutter before his intended object had time to turn away, protest or pull a face.

One particular Saturday morning he decided to do more than just take happy snaps around the backstreets: alerted by muffled growling and strong smells coming from a pile of bamboo cages, he detoured around the wall of crammed and frightened faces of former wild animals awaiting their voyage of no return.

Later, when he showed Mam his black-and-white prints of the doomed creatures peeping through prison bars, he fought hard to hold back a tear: it didn't help to know that to generations of river-folk, the presence of wild animals on their doorsteps remained more annoying than interesting. Keeping the jungle at bay remained a daily obsession for most.

Klaus had already concluded that Santa Luzians in general were indifferent to the unfolding beauty of the Great River and its surrounding menagerie: was he the only one responding to the jungle's perfect rhythms?

It seemed that for three and a half weeks each month, Santa Luzians led lives of quiet resignation followed by brief spells of predictable excess. Their main leisure-time activity was shooting every living thing that moved; and others like the sloth, that didn't.

More confusingly, tourists were lining up to buy postcards of these very creatures, along with photos of the last giant trees, it just didn't make sense.

Both locals and visitors pored more over the photograph than the creature itself, which only reinforced the boy's plan to become a professional photographer one day. Imagine the money to be made capturing the whole world on film. There would be no need to harm a living creature, ever; surely, a well-composed postcard could serve just as well as an animal tooth or hide as a souvenir of one's travels?

Photography is the art of catching a moment, any moment, for all eternity, and Klaus' pleasure was never greater than when he felt he'd captured the *perfect* moment.

And of course, at that stage the job remains only half done; it was in the developing dish that his real talent sprang to life. Fixing the image onto a sheet of paper seemed so basic and simple; surely no other device had brought such truth and happiness to the world as did the camera obscura and the enlarger.

After cleaning out the cobwebs and mildew from the laboratory darkroom he'd set to work polishing the much-neglected Opemus Enlarger, just big enough to hold a 5" × 4" negative. Management was so pleased with his initial results that they granted him unrestricted access to both materials and facilities. Thankfully, the enlarger lens had not grown whiskers between its elements, one impediment he could not have wished or washed away.

Slowly, roll by roll and sheet by sheet, the youngster mastered the art of producing sharp and snappy prints, until eventually, the quartermaster found it necessary to place a padlock on the supplies of printing paper.

An overhead fan now kept the closeness of the darkroom bearable while he laboured over his chemical trays and marvelled at his improving technique. Even Vati grunted approval when confronted with his own likeness and Father Paddy ordered five extra postcards of himself delivering a sermon from the pulpit – "Ta send back home ta th' rellies, and show 'em Oim still alive and the savages ain't et me yet, haw, haw." His good eye squinted as he perused his likenesses. "Oim glad ta see you captured me doin' what Oi do best, young fella …"

It was soon after Mutti moved to the mission that she received the high-sounding promotion to Deputy Matron of the Paupers Hospice. Father Malone had come hurrying into her cell brandishing an official-looking letter. "Yer in, me goil: it's official! From Belem. Listen ta dis, 'Senora Kathleen Hahn is hereby authorised by the Belem Diocese of the Holy Roman Catholic Church to administer all medical and spiritual aid to the souls of Santa Luzia under the guidance and instruction of Father Malone ...'" – he paused for a breath and beamed – "'... until furder notice.' See, it's soigned by Bishop Da Silva himself."

He searched her expression for a reaction, before adding, "Now you and Oi will be able to get the resources we need to look arter these poor buggers properly." He lowered his voice and leaned closer ... "And each udder Kitty. None will be oible to say we shouldna be spendin' all dis toim together, now will dey?"

The new Deputy Matron flushed involuntarily and took the document from his trembling fingers; she couldn't quite believe that her calling was now endorsed by the highest authorities. The old priest stood rubbing his hands, proud of his initiative. Such elevation may well encourage deeper feelings to grow.

8

In the darkroom a disaster was unfolding, Klaus removed a film from the flask and held it up to the safelight: Nothing! Blank!

His eyes searched desperately for even a faint image, and he felt instantly sick to his stomach. The roll was supposed to contain an official party from Belem inspecting the poppet-head and machinery sheds, in his new "candid" style, where no one looked directly into the camera. In his haste to keep ahead the boy had failed to properly engage the film tongue into the winding sprocket, leaving every frame unexposed.

Thank heaven the remaining three films were perfect, capturing the formal welcomes and group shots of V.I.P.s stepping ashore to meet the Grand Kaiser Executives. Of some consolation, everyone therein was all smiles as they nibbled from a table filled with local delicacies and sipped German wines.

Alois' carefully prepared Sales Prospectus was passed from hand to hand, while dusky Indian girls flitted to and fro performing "traditional" topless gyrations. Between these distractions, each potential investor was encouraged to seize this one-off opportunity to get in on the ground floor of Grand Kaiser's proposed expansion into sawn hardwoods.

Klaus was supposed to turn up later at the formal dinner/signing ceremony to hand out souvenir snapshots taken earlier in the day. Each signatory would receive a small album containing highlights of his visit to Santa Luzia, plus a framed print of himself surrounded by beaming Mojo waitresses.

Alois, for one, would be furious over any slip-up that could compromise the hoped-for injection of capital; this the boy knew as he hurried home along the shortcut by the river, still struggling to settle on a plausible explanation.

Despite his gloomy mood, he could not ignore the evening chorus, pausing to immerse himself in the pulses of sound and watch a gentle moon parting the tree branches opposite. He kicked forlornly at a clump of grass and finally settled on his story: he would blame an uncorked bottle of developer that had "gone off".

"Why didn't you check first? How come the other rolls turned out? Why was that bottle of developer left exposed to the air?" He could hear Alois now, and would need to get his story straight if deflecting blame onto the materials.

Anyway, he didn't care if they never gave him another V.I.P. assignment which had clearly placed him under excessive pressure. He'd prefer to be photographing trees, animals and birds any day; even the local identities treated him with far more deference than these "bumptious snobs" as Mutti called the visitors. Wrestling with these thoughts he failed to notice the approach of a familiar figure striding downhill from the Mission.

A startled Robert was first to speak: "What the hell? Ya scared the bejeesus outa me, jumpin' art from behind those bushes."

"I … I wasn't jumping out from anywhere. You scared me too. Where you been at this late hour?"

"Seein' Mam, what else?" his brother responded defensively, relaxing somewhat as the youngster fell into step beside him.

"I thought you weren't going up to the Mission alone anymore?"

For the first time in ages, they walked together without getting into an argument, each lost for a while in his own thoughts. Klaus persisted after long minutes of silence, but his brother had withdrawn.

"That's sure some moonrise," the youngster tried again to no avail. "How is Mam settling in up there, anyway? Do you think she's happy?" he persisted.

And this time Robert remembered to pass on a message. "She's alright, I spose. She said ta get yer own dinner an' be sure ta take a bath afore bed."

Again the pair lapsed into silence. Perhaps this was more like the wordless camaraderie that should exist between real brothers? As they hurried along the boy grew more confident in the sterling light, closer than at any time since Big Brother had saved him from drowning.

He felt a sudden urge to share details of the failed candids and possibly run the risk, if the bonhomie faded, of Robert blabbing the embarrassing truth before he'd even had a chance to offer up his own version. It wouldn't be the first time that Robert had brought the house down at the boy's expense, the very person who always bent over backwards trying to please him. But the wayward Irish urchin saw only his odious stepfather staring back: Klaus decided not to mention the blank roll of film after all.

Right from the start both brothers picked up a smattering of the eighty-odd river dialects in common use, and even a few of the popular French catchphrases downtown. This enabled them to mix easily, exchange pleasantries and even flirt with the Flamingo Villa dancers as they lolled about on their upper balcony during daylight hours.

Kitty too had undertaken a refresher course in local names of common tropical ailments, which had previously involved lots of head nodding and arm waving using her brand of charades. She boasted that her firstborn was the real communicator in the family and had kissed the blarney stone before he could even toddle; languages came easy to both boys if not to herself.

She was especially proud of Bobby's good looks and quick wit, which initially endeared him to many, though she'd cottoned on early to the cold calculation behind much of his thinking. "Give 'im an inch and 'e takes a mile," she tut-tutted more than once. Moreover, her lad was developing the muscle to back up his forthright opinions and didn't mind who he offended with his throwaway jibes and mocking glances. Behind that baby face lay a certain cockiness and lack of remorse, as if defying the whole world to slap him down.

"He could prob'ly get away wit murder wit those blue eyes o' 'is," Kitty more than once confided to Father Malone. There was simply no explanation as to why such an outgoing child would lock himself away in his room for hours on end, reliving military battles from the past.

Looking back, the whole treehouse incident seemed inevitable and could have cost Klaus his life.

It so happened that one Sunday after Mass, the boy sought and gained permission to walk Chief Ticuna's proud princess Maya home to the reservation. This went on for several weeks and all went well, with the two merely exchanging shy phrases in their own tongues while walking side by side.

As trust grew, he decided to show how easily he could catch her life spirit in the little box around his neck and make her picture appear out of thin air. The simple girl was of course astonished when he arrived at Mass the next week with several postcards showing her in full-length costume and in close-up.

For the first time, she saw her own facial tattoos as others saw them; until that moment she'd only ever seen herself in the faded mirror hanging outside the Shamans' den, the one occasionally adorned with shrivelled human hearts.

Klaus suggested a detour via the nearby lookout platform high in the Kapok tree by the oxbow lake and she nodded shyly. In a flash, she'd shinnied up behind him and they were seated side by side, giggling over a handful of choccy chews that had been going soft in his pocket.

He could tell from her expression that they were the first éclairs ever tasted by this chief's daughter. Separating the remainder into two small piles he began counting numbers slowly across in English.

Suddenly Robert's Cheshire face appeared over the parapet, flanked by several older Rascals, an unsettling intrusion that could be no accident.

"Y … You! Go away and leave us alone," Klaus stammered. "C'mon Maya, Father Malone is expecting us back at the …"

"Shut your face little brudder, you too, greaseball," Robert leered, grabbing Maya's wrist and pushing her against a rear railing. "Well, what have we here?"

he smirked, lifting her loincloth, "baby titties and no panties!" The half-wild creature was already mute with fear as her guardian leapt forward with fists clenched. "N … No! Let her go! You mustn't touch her, I gave my word …"

But he was too weak and too late: first one pair, then half a dozen grubby hands forced him back and groped at the quivering body on the floor. Robert tried later to excuse what had occurred, that he'd intended only "to show off a bit" in front of his mates and the tomfoolery had simply gotten out of hand, arousing baser passions in the older boys. But Klaus knew better: from their first days ashore in Santa Luzia, Robert had voiced the opinion that generally speaking "Indians were subhuman savages, and their womenfolk stank". Now he had one entirely at his mercy.

"What you waitin' for lads?" he urged. "We know what smelly Indian squaws are good for, don't we? Git outa our way, you little shit." One brute came at Klaus from behind and pinned his arms; one by one they took turns with the girl, giggling and smirking, before disappearing over the rail and down the ladder.

Throughout the ordeal, not a sound escaped Maya's lips, but her black eyes spoke volumes.

Then, all was still; the shattered chaperone was left alone with the stricken princess, seized by a black dread. Her nakedness had suddenly become shameful and he tried to cover it with his shirt. She merely stared straight ahead.

There was nothing for it but to help her down the ladder and make straight for the Mojo village. He would try to explain everything. On the outskirts, they were met by a concerned Sister Klara and several elders who could see at a glance what had occurred. Without warning the boy was snatched from Maya's side and hurled to the ground; his mousy curls were yanked tight and a heavy club was raised ready to bash out his brains.

"No! … Not him!" Maya threw herself forward sobbing and bloodstained across his feet and raised a trembling hand. "No! I say. Klaus save Maya. Other boys do this to Maya! Not him." She turned her face imploringly to the old nun, whose eyes darted back and forth between girl and boy and raised weapon. Time seemed paralysed.

"Shamans, peace, be still! Listen to her … It wasn't this boy," Sister Klara declared, placing herself protectively between the cringing Klaus and a quivering Xina, whose thwarted eyes shot defiance.

"There's nothing we can do about it now," she said calmly, "you know those gang members will never own up to something like this, even if we do lodge a formal complaint with the constable. The girl needs care."

There followed a long silence before the war club was slowly lowered. "This boy must be allowed to return to his own home, he has done nothing wrong, do you hear me?" More awkward silence and shuffling followed.

"Do … you … hear … me? Klaus, turn slowly and walk away. No one is going to hurt you." She spoke gently but firmly as the boy felt his tender scalp and rose unsteadily to his feet. Several of the elders pressed forward, vowing revenge, but no one lifted a finger. Once out of sight, he broke into a run, hardly believing this day had occurred. How would he explain the grime and bloodstains again on his best Sunday outfit?

For weeks he kept an eye out for his friend at Mass, and among her favourite haunts by the river, but it appeared she had been swallowed up by the tribe, hiding her shame under sackcloth and ashes.

From that day forward, Chief Ticuna took to wearing a full battle headdress whenever he left the Indian camp, and Robert's rascals took the hint to keep their heads down.

About that time Klaus opened his first Kiosk on the waterfront, displaying a wide range of postcards and portraits of local identities. Actually, he was loaned the window space by an unlicensed bookmaker, who preferred to operate out of the backdoor.

<h1 style="text-align:center">9</h1>

Some months after Maya's defilement the great Indian migration occurred. One night in the heavy hours, before the big wet set in, and while the town slept, the whole tribe simply up and vanished. Only the sobering spectacle of a burning Opera House and a trail of vandalism marking their direction of travel finally stirred the townsfolk into action. It seemed that footprints had been found heading straight for the jagged horizon known as Dragon's Teeth, about which terrible rumours swirled and scalding waters were said to spurt from the very cliffs. Few whites had ever ventured so far beyond the lease.

When the news reached *Madeira Belle*, Captain Streicher was floored; this unforeseen exodus without permission had left his famous Safaris without experienced guides and trackers, and tickets already sold. The brochure clearly stated that only the finest and soberest Indian Guides were employed; what it didn't say was that he hated giving refunds.

Whether motivated by desperation or misplaced bravado, Alois Hahn had put up his hand to lead future expeditions into the Varzea. He would sequester Lotte, the shallow-draughted company launch best able to feel her way through the filigree of flooded waterways. With himself in command, his eldest boy would come along to identify targets and direct the gunfire. For the foreseeable future, most of the profits and all of the tips would go straight into Alois' pocket. He intended to sit back, share in the drinks and swap a few yarns with the tourists while the "useless eater" would be responsible for navigation and spotting prey. Perhaps one day the boy might show himself capable of taking over the day tour operation entirely.

During the first few forays, it became obvious that only a miracle could prevent a mishap: prodigious volumes of alcohol were consumed and the indiscriminate discharging of firearms en route was both nerve-racking and dangerous.

The old man soon showed himself way out of his depth in the watery wilderness and it was only Robert's skill and initiative in bringing *Lotte* back home after a long day upriver "spreading mayhem", as Mutti and Klaus described the shooting of wild animals, that kept the Safari business viable. But it was Alois' own incompetent navigation that would mark the young photographer for the rest of his days.

Looking back to that 16th birthday, had not Klaus received a brand new 35 mm Leica A from his generous relatives in Germany he would never have needed or even desired to go aboard *Lotte* in the first place. If Tante and Onkel had not been quite so chuffed with the selection of postcards he'd captured with the old Voigtlander, he would never have been tempted to follow up on his brother's fateful offer to join a safari.

Robert had been boasting of the wondrous sights upstream, claiming that the boy would have every chance of capturing a hundred roaring waterfalls and more wild animals than he could "poke a stick at".

After days spent poring through the Leica manual, Klaus felt ready to run a test roll through her; clearly, she was going to be much easier to handle than the clumsy Voigtlander.

The season of flooded Varzea was now at hand, a time when the entwined canopy overhead erupted in fruits, flowers, birds and monkeys. Robert would put the youngster ashore close by a clifftop colony of red howlers, and retrieve him later that afternoon when homeward bound; the plan sounded perfect and exciting. He claimed that most of the best hunting areas were accessible only in a flat bottom craft like *Lotte* and that he alone had perfected the technique of sneaking his poaching passengers up the narrowest of channels until they were right on top of their unsuspecting prey, all without getting their feet wet.

For Klaus' maiden excursion, Mam had lovingly packed his favourite banana sandwiches and insisted he wear long sleeves and a huge sombrero made of woven palm leaves. In his knapsack, he carried more than enough victuals for several meals and did not expect to have to witness any of the actual killing.

Come the big day though, as the hunters gathered aboard *Lotte* and downed their first beers from the icebox, there was no sign of their much-touted hunting guide. In fact, there was no crew at all on board.

Klaus sat in the bow fiddling with his shiny new toy; the sun was already up. Mutti had embarrassed him by kissing him fondly in front of complete strangers. He fired off one or two snaps of the docks and was amazed at the slick and silent operation of the Leica.

He then nibbled a banana sandwich before the butter melted, peering impatiently over his shoulder to see, not his big brother but Alois and several mine labourers approaching the vessel; the Acting Commander was dressed in a tattered navy cap and jacket with a hunting rifle slung over one shoulder.

Ignoring one or two muffled jibes Alois clumped noisily aboard and took his place at the tiller, raising a handful of trembling fingers to steady the growing unrest as he kicked over *Lotte's* sluggish motor. With a roar, the engine sprang to life and the unter-manager was once again in charge; nothing to it really, a bit like riding a bike. One never forgets.

When in doubt, a good tour guide entertains with tales of his own family lineage: how great Grandvati Rudolph, an incorruptible Customs Official on the Austrian border, had waved through the Kaiser's escort many times with a mere nod.

Once these clods learned more of the Acting Commander's connection to the celebrated Hahns of Hamburg they'd show a bit of respect. When pressed further, Alois admitted that the regular guide, the one in Captain Streicher's brochure, had failed to return from an all-night sojourn behind the Mission walls and could not be located in any of his usual haunts.

Furthermore, if those aboard wished the expedition to proceed smoothly they would not only need to obey their substitute skipper, but haul the anchor, hoist the auxiliary sail when required and pitch in with other shipboard duties.

Someone grumbled that given the exorbitant fees they'd been charged, there might not be much time left for actual hunting. They were already a full hour behind schedule and lacking the usual buzz of enthusiasm when *Lotte* finally slipped her moorings and chugged out into midstream – several shots were fired into the air.

From his seat in the bow, Klaus could barely contain his excitement; the freedom to do and capture anything he wanted with his brand-new camera. Surely, today would bring a real chance to obtain wildlife close-ups, especially those elusive red howlers camped part-way up the cliffs. If Robert were right for once, it should only be "a bit of a scramble" up one of the many animal tracks. The boy had read somewhere that these big red primates alone viewed the world in full colour, just like humans. But he didn't believe it.

Each dusk and dawn, and sometimes in between, he would tune in to the great monkey acapella filling the forest; he'd tried calling them closer but had never once been able to obtain a natural howler family snap. This was the first occasion he'd been allowed to roam unsupervised beyond the Exclusion Zone, hungry to try out his Leica under actual field conditions.

He had also brought along a simple homemade "hide" rolled tightly atop his knapsack, which he hoped would allow any inquisitive creatures to come within range. After nosing in and out of a dozen swollen tributaries, Alois announced that they had arrived at the drop-off point marked by Robert on the chart. He barked instructions to a fellow with a stein in his hand and proceeded to beach Lotte in a tiny horseshoe bay of black sand before permitting the boy to go ashore.

Almost as an afterthought, he passed Robert's single-shot Deutsche Werke .22 rifle over the rail; "just in case". The gleaming weapon added yet more weight to his bulging load. Several passengers jumped ashore and shook his hand in admiration, jokingly reminding him to keep his eyes peeled for caiman and jaguar, and especially for those Fer de Lance vipers lying undetected in the leaf litter.

"It's more the red howlers that interest me," Klaus called gamely as the tiny vessel backed away with a toot; the hopeful hunters had returned to their drinks and were taking wagers over who would shoot straightest when it came to live targets. Had anyone cast a backward glance, the boy struck a forlorn sight standing alone before the green curtain of jungle. As his last link with civilisation disappeared into the riparian tangle an unwelcome lump arose in his throat.

He decided to sit tight for the moment and pour a hot tea from his flask, remembering to cross himself and mumble three Hail Marys as instructed by Mam. To calm his nerves further he attempted to go over his plan out loud, but his voice sounded thin, drowned out by the rushing waterfalls in the distance. For a moment he longed to hear another voice, any voice in the great loneliness, not knowing that the banal onboard banter he'd so eschewed would be the last familiar language he'd hear for awhile.

Forcing a deep breath he peered into the dense vegetation for possible access to the escarpment, with its scalding steam vents and the colony of howlers overhead … but could see none.

The so-called hop, skip and jump as seen from the comfort of *Lotte*'s deck was actually choked with undergrowth and vines and after several false starts, he'd made little headway. There seemed no option but to lighten his load and stash Robert's rifle in a hollow tree above the high watermark. Shooting with a camera was far more appealing anyway; he doubted if he could ever pull the trigger on any wild creature, including the so-called dangerous ones. No siree, he would leave the killing to others.

With sudden determination, he slung the camera around his neck and the knapsack across his shoulders, before dropping on all fours to crawl stoically towards his objective. A labyrinth of vines and spider webs closed in, clinging and tearing at his face. Gasping stentoriously, all sense of direction was lost; only the sound of falling waters drew him on.

Yard by tortuous yard, doubts plagued his mind: what if Robert's "sure thing" turned out to be fanciful, as so often happened? Had "liddle brudder" again been too eager to take the bait? Was this even the correct waterfall among many? His clumsy progress was enough to send any napping monkey straight back to the safety of the crags.

At last, Klaus wiggled his way past a final thorny barrier and stood up into a sunlit, grassy clearing at the far end of which the force of falling water had scoured a deep pool. A tumbling torrent from above made the boiling surface dance with tiny rainbows in the spray.

Contrary to the despondent light reaching the forest floor, the rearing crust of cliffs overhead was bathed in a vicious glare, making accurate contra-jour light readings almost impossible. At any other time, this would be a splendid subject on its own but his heart sank. This wasn't what he'd come for; the howlers seemed impossibly far away. What had appeared as a simple goal now loomed overhead: a wall of shining black with bleak and barren steep-scarped battlements, broken here and there by clinging tufts of water fern and yellowed cracks that issued hissing steam. He could see no way up for man or beast, doubting even whether monkeys could negotiate that slick surface.

Squinting upward from beneath his sombrero with the torn brim, he finally spotted the family of red howlers grooming each other in the sun atop a lava outcrop but they might just as well have been in Bolivia.

He suddenly remembered his plan, which for the moment seemed far-fetched, and drew from his pack Mutti's former silken scarf, now reduced to a dozen or so brightly coloured strips. This was the very item given her in Galway by a moonstruck Alois featuring "Bavarian Wildflowers in spring" that she'd long ceased wearing.

The young photographer, like others before him, had accidentally discovered that amused responses could sometimes be evoked from shy or stone-faced portrait subjects by waving a bright cloth above his head and sending forth a loud "Yahoo" as the shutter opened.

Perhaps, if secured properly to catch the breeze, Mutti's colourful scarf might well attract some of the cautious or curious monkeys within range. He also had one more trick up his sleeve: choosing a slightly elevated position on soft grass by the water's edge, he erected his "hide" consisting of the moth-eaten green blanket with cut-out peepholes in the middle. It draped nicely over his head and tripod as he settled down to wait … and wait.

He'd set the shutter at 1/125 sec. as a minimum necessary to freeze moving subjects, and when pointing the camera toward the extreme light contrasts above would need to reduce the aperture by three full f-stops.

Had the roaring waters indeed masked the sound of his arrival, as hoped, he could trust the Leica's silent shutter and crisp Leitz lens to do the rest. Like so many amateurs, he struggled to find the perfect balance between so-called fast films, perfect under the shaded canopy but often too grainy for enlargement, and the fine-grained sharpness of slower ISO emulsions which usually resulted in blurred movement.

Fortunately, the Mine Quartermaster had agreed to stock plenty of each, plus a full range of printing paper and chemicals. Under the present circumstances, however, either choice only confused the boy.

Droplets of sweat began to drip from his chin onto the precious camera, the air beneath the blanket was becoming foetid and too heavy to breathe. Outside, cool spray condensed on the restless green blanket, as it did on every other rock, stalk and branch in the glade, rendering all surfaces soggy.

Underneath, the boy was now struggling; minutes felt like hours and his brother's callous canards rattled around inside his head like Lucifer's own rebuke. Should he throw the damn thing off and step out for fresh air? As soon as the howlers spotted movement the game would be up.

He tried distracting himself with visions of a future career in photography, but who in his right mind would willingly undergo such tortures as these for the sake of a postcard? He gulped again and briefly closed his eyes. It was fanciful to imagine nature photography as a profitable hobby, let alone a full-time career. There would be no Doc Wonders in places like this if an attack suddenly came on, one more good reason to stick with human subjects in the future.

"Oh, Gawd, never take the Lord's name in vain ..." He could hear Mam now rummaging through her lingerie drawer in search of "Bavarian Spring Flowers". Then again, maybe she wouldn't give two hoots; perhaps she'd even thank him for plucking her Albatross?

The sodden scarf fragments drooped unenticingly; he was growing tired of raising his camera at every little movement. He began to doubt whether his colourful lures were even visible from the howler refuge overhead and kept glancing impatiently at his wristwatch, aware of the uncomfortable long hours ahead until *Lotte* returned to take him home.

Suddenly, two movements caught his attention through the peepholes: approaching his hide from the forest was a troop of florid-faced uakari monkeys, sniffing the air and chattering excitedly together. He'd never before seen their strange bibulous features up close, but before he could lift the camera to his eye their leader uttered a cry of alarm which scattered the group.

Had he moved too suddenly? Had the uakaris seen through his waterlogged disguise? Frustrated and uncomfortable, his gaze was drawn to the far end of the clearing, where the green wall of jungle had begun to shiver in the gloom.

Sucking at the dank air he looked again and forgot his discomfort. "Holy Mother o' God!" he exclaimed under his breath. "Army Ants!"

Millions of the voracious insects were pouring from the jungle fringe in a moving carpet of black and tan, consuming every living thing in their path.

Everyone had heard horror stories of mile-wide swarms that could overwhelm even large mammals who failed to flee in time. He remembered seeing the pulpy hands of Robert's gang members when their Gloves of Happiness were removed: the poor devils couldn't feed themselves for a week.

Fortunately, the tide of ants seemed to be hugging the fringe in its search for prey, easing his concerns momentarily. Keeping one eye on the moving tide he turned to the other peephole, through which he was excited to see the uakaris again approaching his decoy.

Several of the younger monkeys were having the time of their lives dashing back and forth through the fulminating spray, offering superb action shots.

He slowly raised his camera and made a final adjustment of 1/250 sec. at the maximum aperture of f/3.5. At that very moment, the ruddy old uakari leader let out another sharp alarm cough and dashed back up into the treetops; whatever he'd seen aroused a chorus of angry bird calls.

There! Just a hundred yards away a small hunting party of well-armed Indian braves crossed downstream and melted away in the gloom, luckily not noticing his dewey hide; so far so good. Perhaps less threatening, he watched with racing heart and bated breath as several Mojo girls carrying baskets of fruit and wearing flower coronets spilled laughing from behind the tumbling wall of water and settled down on the grassy bank opposite. Despite his initial apprehension, Klaus was touched by a vague feeling of deja vu when seeing them tease each other above the background noise; almost like that painting of Gaugin's *Tahitian Maidens* in Tante's volume of "Great Impressionists". Was it the way their brown skin shone, or the tittering exchange of little secrets?

Then again he mused, it could almost be that famous scene of Manet's, or was it Monet's, *Breakfast on the Grass* with just one fully-clothed male admirer. Maybe such sylvan scenes really *did* occur among primitive peoples and he was the sole witness? If only he could catch the beauty of the moment on film. Two of the girls rose to bathe in the clear pool and as they waded toward him hand in hand. He could barely stifle a cry of joy.

The slim girl leading … could it be? She was the spitting image of his long-vanished companion. He felt suddenly ashamed at remaining concealed like Robert's mates who hung around Madame Gertrude's after dark: should he break cover and risk an unpredictable reaction? Confused and flustered, he remained undetected to spy upon their perfect nakedness.

10

No one in Santa Luzia believed that Chief Ticuna and his all-seeing Prophet could have lasted more than a week after "going bush", let alone an entire tribe attempting to live off the land.

Decades of decadence had dulled the Indians' natural instincts for setting traps and resisting temptations. Yet assuredly, here stood Maya and her friends looking healthier and prettier than ever. The girls were almost close enough to touch. Should he call her name out loud? He could hardly ignore the fact that she had grown taller and developed larger, perfectly shaped breasts which glistened in the spray.

Or should he remain silently peeping and risk losing her again; or worse, be caught taking pictures of the naked swimmers? If he broke cover and it wasn't who he believed it to be, or if she didn't recognise him and called out in alarm, what then? How far away was that hunting party? Would she ever forgive his part in Robert's vile breach of faith? How could he live with his conscience after being so close to confessing the guilt he'd been bottling up inside?

For long minutes his heart beat wildly and his mind was a log-jamb of fraught alternatives, but before he could settle on the right course of action a sharp pain stabbed at the back of his neck, closely followed by another.

Simultaneously, just as the girls emerged onto the bank opposite, his ears, eyelids, and every inch of exposed flesh were peppered with stabs of red-hot venom. His mighty bellow drowned out the noise of falling water and stopped the girls in their tracks. Dumbstruck, they watched the mythical green creature rise from the grass on the far bank flapping furiously and screaming abuse in its own foul tongue.

It leapt in the air several times, swiping the air and staggering sideways to lose its footing and plunge down the embankment into the water. The panic-

stricken girls clearly saw its backward-facing feet flailing in the foam. There
could be no mistake: "Curupuri! Run! It's Curupuri!" Needing no further
prompting the fleet-footed maidens abandoned their baskets and fled into the
undergrowth.

Since time began, Mojo children shivered and shook when hearing the Legend
of Curupuri repeated, of the cunning Lizard Man who lurked in unexpected
places awaiting disobedient youngsters to wander away from the tribe. Maya
and her companions had immediately recognised the tell-tale feet and bone-
chilling cries and had no intention of hanging around to be roasted alive.

No Mojo child had ever come face to face with Curupuri and lived to tell
the tale.

Blinded with pain and unable to rid itself of the tangle, the green monster
stumbled after them in pursuit: "Maya! Maya! It's me, *Klaus*!" But his voice
was lost in the spray and his throat turned hoarse until he could call no more.

Standing knee-deep in a pool of pain and enmeshed in the sodden blanket
he was being peppered by poisonous pincers too numerous to count. He felt as
if he was being held against one of those steaming sulphurous vents that hissed
from the cliffs.

It was no use … the girls had vanished, leaving him to prod his puffy
eyelids and lament his ruined camera. This was a catastrophe in more ways
than one. Both Indian groups had vanished in the same direction, away from
the crawling carpet of ants. There was nothing for it but to try and drag himself
after them and hope that a village could be found to soothe the angry welts
now covering his body.

Klaus Hahn wasn't too proud to beg for help and would explain everything
from the beginning. The poison was already causing his joints to swell and
his airways to narrow. His breathing was laboured, always the first sign of a
pending attack. What if he stumbled inadvertently upon the hunting party?

Wincing, he hauled his unyielding body onto the bank and grimly began
counting each step forward, determined to make contact with his friend, if
indeed it was the noble one he'd glimpsed and not mere delusion masked in
pain.

To heck with the consequences, he decided, things could hardly get much
worse. The faint track he followed soon petered out with no signs of habitation;
at every step thorns tore his attenuated limbs.

Distant rumbling alerted him to a bank of ominous green thunderheads
approaching fast above the canopy, just as they did every afternoon in the wet
season. He realised now the folly of having dumped his rucksack at the pool.

Nothing seemed to be going right and he wasn't thinking straight. He was a
fool for not having acted more sensibly, regardless of pain. Too late, and trying
not to give in to rising panic, he made the painful but necessary decision to

turn back while mouthing a silent prayer that the ant swarm may have left untouched at least part of his food.

Which way was it? Ill-defined animal tracks led off in all directions. The roar of falling water was joined by a violent crack of thunder and the sun was swallowed up. The dense undergrowth looked impassable, the cliffs unscaleable.

He felt a double fool for having attempted to pursue the girls; as if he could ever hope to overtake Indians in their own lands in such a state.

Suddenly, the first drops of rain splashed his face and within minutes obliterated any surrounding landmarks. Blindly he bumped and groped his way forward between the glistening buttresses and tangled roots. From the dripping leaves above striped leeches began dropping onto his broken skin, enlivened by the deluge and maddened by the smell of blood. Within minutes they seemed to cover the ground, standing up to wave hungrily from every twig and blade of grass. Klaus' attempts to tear them off dissolved in loathing and panic; slippery fingers fumbled futilely, unable to uproot a single one.

This was a final outrage upon his tender skin; sinking to his knees he sobbed uncontrollably, thinking of the salt shaker Mam had insisted he take along for this very purpose. He could do little but labour for breath while imagining the revolting creatures were emptying his veins.

Overhead, the thunder cracked again in censure.

Summoning every last ounce of energy the beaten boy stumbled a few more paces into a clearing, realising at once he was back at the very place he'd started; he had been going around in circles. This was the last straw: he sank exhausted into the mud, past weeping, as all his remaining strength was required just to breathe. Huge raindrops hammered against his skull like pebbles.

When Maya and her raving companions overtook their menfolk, a great and lively pow-wow ensued. It was agreed, with much arm waving and casting of dark looks, that something profound had occurred. She would return alone with three of the best trackers and, despite the cloudburst, search for any remaining evidence of Curupuri's foiled abduction attempt. Clutching their bows and arrows and a heavy machete, the group set off at a brisk trot with the girl at their head. Here and there, she pointed to scraps of fabric clinging to the bushes.

They padded on unerringly through the weeping forest, first to the water's edge where the attack had occurred and then, after warily poking at Curupuri's partly-submerged, discarded garment, she led them back to the base of the cliffs. Something wasn't quite right and the hunters quivered in readiness, mimicking the urgent movements of their guide.

Maya slowed, lifting and placing her feet with the precision of a jungle cat. Cocking an ear she suppressed a little cry and stopped dead, causing the others to bump into her glistening rear end.

There on the ground, curled up among the green mossy roots lay their bloodstained quarry, moaning and gasping its last.

"Kill it!" snarled one brave, leaping forward with the machete raised.

"No! Not yet." The girl's voice was firm. Her keen eye wrestled to comprehend the fuchsine phantasm at her feet. The other hunters backed away, unsettled by the bloodied shreds of a white man's clothing. Curupuri had been known to disguise himself as a white man when handing out lollies.

The downpour stopped abruptly, as it had started; eerie vapours began rising from the forest floor to wreathe the creature's broken head.

Cautiously, purposefully, the girl stretched out a tremulous hand and touched the familiar mousy curls. Peering closely at the lopsided features, her face showed at first alarm, then slowly recognition. Groaning softly, the creature forced open its swollen lids and for a few moments the face seemed frozen. Painfully and deliberately between breaths, it wheezed a single word, "Maya ..." and passed out.

The braves were astonished and fell back as if smitten by an unseen hand.

11

That terrible day, that inconsolable hour when *Lotte* returned home minus her baby boy had driven Kitty's behaviour ever since.

She knew as only a mother can just what the wailing of the dock sirens meant, that funny tummy every morning since waving Klaus off on his first big solo adventure. Now she realised too late the intuition was overridden. She should never have trusted her boy with Alois at the helm.

Dropping everything, she ran all the way down to the docks seeking answers: one after the other, crew and passengers lowered their eyes and turned away, mumbling vaporous excuses.

The errant skipper, in a haze of panic and guilt, was doing his best to look busy; he would blame the boy himself for not listening properly.

In any event, he feared Kitty would stick a knife in his ribs if she got half a chance. Brushing her aside, Alois called loudly for a search party posse of armed vigilantes, having not yet given up hope of relocating the place with Robert's help. The water level had risen; everything looked different under the canopy and no signs of a campfire had been found.

In front of everyone, he deputised his surprised stepson to relocate the tiny beach where he'd dropped off young Klaus. A thorough ground search would then be mounted.

When the rescue armada departed later that evening, Kitty sat huddled in the bow of *Lotte* out front, having successfully demanded that the Tapir and Capybara carcases from the hunting trip be cut loose over the side.

Throughout that painfully slow trip upriver she refused all attempts at conversation or consolation; her rosary beads sped back and forth between unfeeling fingers and her eyes were fixed on the shadows ahead. Over and over she replayed in her head the tragedies of past years as punishments delayed; and now this most grievous blow.

Admittedly, her marriage existed in name only, but why had she bothered to cut herself so utterly adrift from the whole dysfunctional family? She'd not only failed to endear her "two menfolk" to each other but tried to warn them both that she'd had a "gutful" of their bickering and rivalry and she was coming to the end of her tether. What choice did she have?

There could never be peace with those two living under the same roof. Klaus had tried to help by reciting an old adage, something about unstoppable forces meeting immovable objects, but he couldn't remember where he'd read it or what conclusions had been drawn.

Busying herself at the hospice she counted down the days. The minute Klaus was old enough to look after himself (thank the Holy Mother he didn't take much looking after), she would be able to spend more and more time up the hill in the only sanctuary that meant anything at all. And now this!

Fear rarely leaves room for forgiveness, and Kitty knew deep down that there are many times in a girl's life when, in the words of the proverb, it *is* better to seek forgiveness than ask permission. "Da Lord Jaesus looks into ya heart every single day and reports back to 'is Daddy when he spies even the littlest loi tryin' ta sneak out," she'd drummed into her boys, warning of the dire consequences in drifting away from the One True Faith.

Surprisingly, both her goosens had greeted the idea of having her own space up the hill with alacrity, but not Alois, who refused to accept that she would dare to leave at all.

When the time came he berated the boys for not speaking up sooner and limped away uphill to pound on the Monastery doors: No one had seen or heard anything of Frau Hahn. What's more, the hospital grounds were off-limits due to a Typhus alert. Alois had worn out his welcome.

During one of Kitty's heartfelt Confessions, Father Patrick himself hinted that it was no sin to walk away from a civil marriage service performed in a Registry Office. "Gard alone knows where your heart trooly lies Kitty," he assured her as they strolled together in the garden following Mass. "But fer dis old priest," he added with a wink, "hope springs etarnal."

Beggars can't be choosers, she thought to herself.

Father had secured her a comfortable cell above the cloister with a window looking down on the courtyard; for the first time in years, she had time after work to stroll down to the river and count her blessings.

For a while it appeared that things were looking up; she had never felt more privileged or beautiful than working beside such an "Angel o' God". Now what? A certain niggle would not desist. Closing her eyes she saw only the frightened faces of her boys.

Her baby Klaus was already sprouting wisps of hair, "bumfluff" she called it, in certain places, and except for his touchy health appeared to be finding favour in God's eyes. He and those books of his!

On the other hand, her Robbie couldn't seem to open his mouth without descending to the level of the waterfront riff-raff he hung around with.

Nonetheless, he *was* her firstborn and as such held an unshakeable place in her heart. She clung to the hope that there remained good chances for his ultimate redemption and was grateful to the Holy Cross Brothers for dedicating so much of their own time toward his improvement. She vowed that come what may she would not dwell on his faults; anyway, he looked perfect on the outside.

Whether it was his cutting wit aimed at getting under Alois' skin, especially now his growing strength ruled out further corrections with the strap, or his cruelty towards animals and anyone else who tried to get close he exhibited a certain presence of forethought. On the one hand, he attracted others to him; on the other, he took smug satisfaction in keeping them at bay.

There was no denying that when she gave 'im an inch, 'e'd take a mile but deep down she knew it was the old man's beatings that had coloured his nature. It just didn't seem natural for any growing lad to spend days at a time playing with tin soldiers, or when not thus engrossed to be out shooting everything that moved. She realised now that it had done no good at all forcing the boy to apologise to his stepfather so often. As soon as the old man left the house, Robert could be heard muttering to himself, "I swear by all Mam's rosaries I'm *not* sorry and I *won't* forget."

But that was all in the past. Now Kitty was comforted to see him standing on his own two feet, after for so long appearing to stray. If anyone could locate his brother it was her Robbie. Perhaps those private sessions with the Christian Brothers *and* his new career among worldly tourists were finally reinforcing at least part of the "proper manners" she'd striven so hard to instil.

There was no denying that her boys were turning out as different as "two spring days in Derry" to be sure, and she remained confused by the apparent struggle between Nature and Nurture, or was it the other way around?

"Master, Master, meek 'n mild, help me calm this blessed child …" she recited softly to herself with eyes closed, imagining her bairn back safe in her arms.

However she looked at it, her gentle and creative "Longhead", as the Indians early christened Klaus, was a dreamer; the result of her own misplaced compassion for a broken German seaman. Even more unlikely Robert, the "real doer", was conceived of a Gaelic bumkin she'd fallen for briefly at the Galway Easter Pageant, none of which seemed to make much sense now.

How many times would she be forced to confront these two "blind bargains with fate" and always arrive at the same answer, which was really no answer at all? What else could a faded Shamrock have done upon receiving her one and only proposal of marriage? So what if it came from a German sailor upon whom she'd showered more than brief affection? Kitty had often asked herself that very question. At the time, anything looked better than trudging through west coast slush for the rest of her life to do 12-hour shifts. Now, with one child already roaming the streets she would not be able to disguise for much longer a second bun in the oven.

Yes, yes, yes! Frau Kathleen Hahn had had a certain ring to it.

She couldn't believe that she'd thrown caution to the winds and agreed so readily to wait months, even years if necessary, for her accidental fiancé to return from Germany and collect her after he'd "sorted things out" with his family.

According to his grand plan, Kitty would be whisked away to a brand new beginning in faraway South America, a place she had formerly been unable to identify on a map of the world.

Robbie too had been swept up in Mam's excitement, captivated by Alois' tales of real hand-to-hand combat in the Great War and of vast unexplored jungles filled with savage Indians to come. Her thoughts then had not so much focused on what may lie ahead but what she was leaving behind: an unimagined chance to conquer her doubts and flee the incubus of the Emerald Isle and to bring up her bairns free from censure in a faraway land. From her very first day on foreign soil had not she "bent over backwards" trying to please everyone and make a go of it?

Being absent on the fateful day Robert now brought a semblance of methodology to the search. Alois' confusion over the exact spot where he'd dropped the boy had wasted precious hours; after all, every cliff face and tributary looked alike in the rising dark waters. It was decided to split up and allow smaller vessels to work the shallow tributaries, all the while calling aloud and firing off occasional volleys. Here and there at vaguely familiar locations, armed search parties with torches scrambled ashore to fan out and search for clues.

At last, some news arrived back at the flotilla at first light. Robert himself had stumbled upon his brother's belongings in the soaking spray: a sodden green blanket, a fogged camera with a broken strap, a knapsack containing mushy banana sandwiches, and a salt shaker. A broken bamboo tripod bobbed up and down in the nearby shallows. Word flashed back that a thorough search of the area was underway; old timers thought the chances of finding the boy alive were slim.

Pathetic and alone, Kitty had not flinched from her vigil in the bow, pausing just long enough between self-recriminations and heavenly entreaties to accept a cup of hot black tea. News of the find brought a sliver of hope.

When the second day drew to a close, one by one the dejected search parties returned empty-handed. They reported that most of the human footprints had been obliterated in a spate of heavy showers and the roaring torrent at the base of the cliffs.

Robert and his trackers were stumped, coming up against one dead end after another. Bloodstained leaves and occasional snagged clothing fragments had been found over a wide area as if the missing boy were going around in circles. He had been swallowed up by the jungle, certainly not the first to disappear under similar circumstances.

Then, almost obscured by the roaring curtains of water, a cavernous lava tube was discovered emerging from the base of the cliffs and disgorging its own white torrent into the pool. One glance at the unscaleable battlements above sufficed to show the impossibility of gaining a foothold. "Especially for an inexperienced bushbaby like Klaus," they all agreed.

While he carried the rifle there remained the slim chance of being able to defend himself against man or beast, though no one could remember him having ever fired a shot in anger.

As darkness settled over the scene on day two, the convoy turned reluctantly for home. One stark figure now sat staring mutely from the stern of *Lotte*. Mile after dreadful mile, the broken woman rocked slowly back and forth, repeating his name in her prayers and fingering her babe's recovered belongings. Smears of dried animal blood beneath her lace-up boots proclaimed the inevitability and closeness of death. For days afterwards, she sat caressing the water-stained knapsack and refusing to accept the terrible truth.

Why on earth had she relented over a silly camera and allowed him to venture off alone? Her guilt was palpable and potent. She had always known that one day, when she least expected it, the Good Lord would call in His outstanding debts. Despite her aversion to pagans and fornicators she had succumbed outside of wedlock, not once, but twice; sins second only to murder.

Marrying a protestant foreigner not only compounded her long list of transgressions but sealed her fate in the eyes of the Holy Roman Church.

She'd talked herself into believing that marrying a near stranger and attempting penance among savages may provide a slender chance for expunging, or at least alleviating, the worst of God's punishment to come if not in this world then surely in the next. A vengeful Almighty would be denied no longer; He had finally called in his pound of flesh.

Surely, if *her* life was to be ruined in this fashion she would see to it that the person responsible would also suffer, if it was the last thing she ever did.

By the time the sad armada slunk back into port, she had convinced herself that Alois had abandoned the child on purpose. Would this hateful man stop at nothing to repay her transgressions?

Gi' me a good ole Oirish fella any day, she'd concluded too late; perhaps the day would come when she wouldn't have to continually fib and fudge in order to survive.

Later that month, following a three-hour inquest it was pronounced that 16-year-old Klaus Alois Hahn had met with foul play at the hands of wild beasts or persons unknown.

12

The injured boy remembered little of the hours and days that followed his capture. Following Maya's example, the braves overcame their initial reluctance and set about fashioning a litter from bamboo and vines. They would be forced to carry the captive for sentencing at the feet of Chief Ticuna and Sister Klara, the tribe's beloved Saviour.

Lapsing in and out of consciousness the boy felt spray on his torn face and trembled at the roar of strange beasts trapped in the bowels of the earth where they carried him. At times he sat bolt upright gasping for breath, eyes wide with fear and confusion, at other times almost sliding off the makeshift litter. "Help, Papa! No boat! No, no!" Fortunately, each Indian had clearly heard him pronounce "Maya" several times, and that repeated utterance had saved his life.

Slipping and struggling, the hunters pushed and dragged their load up through the winding lava tube, at every step becoming more and more fearful about admitting outsiders to the sacred citadel, let alone a white boy from the hated river town below. But the girl was adamant: she knew who he was and was determined that his life should be spared. Surely, even the Shamans would come around when reminded of his former bravery on her behalf?

For almost a week Klaus lay in a coma, oblivious to the impetrations being undertaken on his behalf by Maya and the old German nun. Thus far, all decisions had been deferred until he regained his senses and could be questioned properly. Gently, twice daily, the girl cradled his delirious head in her arms and fed him thin manioc porridge, assisted periodically by Sister Klara herself with his bathing and hygiene.

Benign or otherwise, his very presence rested heavily on the tribe; Xina the head Shaman and his entourage were calling for the boy to be cast down into

Devil's Gullet without further ado. This plan was rejected outright by the major faction holding sway, namely Chief Ticuna, Sister Klara and those among the elders convinced not only of the boy's life-saving intervention during Maya's ordeal but of his inoffensiveness.

Hour after hour, curious Indians filed past the doorway of his vaulted cell, whispering among themselves and speculating on the significance of his arrival. Was he truly Curupuri's messenger as rumoured, and if so what would this mean for the authority of Xina and his future hold over the tribe? The dumped deity's earthly agent was convinced the boy's presence would bring certain doom upon the whole village. In secret, the Shamans plotted to have his head at the first opportunity and restore their own supremacy.

"The boy is awake and sitting up!" Word spread through the village like wildfire, an ethereal miasma of sweet sound from a dozen throats was reverberating off his prison walls. "Mmaaa, Thhh, Raaaa," repeated over and over.

At first, the groggy captive thought he must have died and gone to Heaven: through half-opened eyes, he was astonished to see a vision of white-robed angels gathered 'round his hammock. They were being led in their chanting by that same old nun who'd absconded from Holy Cross under a dark cloud of heresy. One of her cowled coterie was dabbing at his skin with a whitish lotion, revealing two rows of perfect teeth as she smiled.

Instinctively, he reached up and peeled back the hood, revealing his friend and saviour. "M … Maya … Maya? It *was* you. It *is* you! I knew it all along," he exclaimed, bursting into a garbled palaver mixed with tears. The girl too, was beaming and quivering. "Klaus safe. Klaus stay still and quiet," she purred.

"How did …? Where am I? What is this place?" His asthma had subsided and though lightheaded and weak, his first thought was that he really had died and gone "aloft" to be serenaded by the Celestial Choirs, just as Mam's homespun solipsisms predicted.

The old nun now raised her hand for silence and moved closer. She had been the first to believe Maya's tearful insistence that the boy had done everything possible to pull Robert's mates off her during the rape until finally he'd been felled by a blow from behind.

During her time spent in cloisters, Sister Klara had seen and heard enough to differentiate between this sensitive boy, his bombastic father and contumelious brother. She was well informed of his mother Kathleen's selfless devotion in the overstretched Charity Ward at Holy Cross, where coloureds and poor white trash (as the Portuguese ex-pats labelled them) were treated alike. Sister admired anyone who could side-step the self-serving Missionary dogma in order to perform Christ's work among the poor and ignorant.

Frau Hahn's much-needed skills were more down-to-earth and immediate in the healing process than mere recitations. She began questioning the boy with a keen edge that quickly softened as she confirmed his sincerity: "Why had he been tracking the Indians? Was he not aware of Sergio's fate, intended as a warning to other white pursuers? Why was he carrying no belongings when captured? Hadn't his family caused these people more than enough harm in years past?"

Slowly but surely she probed his motivation and understanding. "M ... my father says Santa Luzia would have died a long time ago without Grand Kaiser ... an' I like all Indians, even Mulattos ... I guess I like most people. Oh, and animals too," he added in a croaky whisper.

She searched his face again with narrowed eyes. "We'll see about that. For the time being you will stay with us until your fate is decided. We have only Maya's word that you are a true friend to the Indian, but that was a long time ago. What sort of person are you now?"

"I'm much better, thank you, and my asthma is gone," he replied courteously. This was the first occasion he could remember recovering so completely without a shot from Doc Wonders. "I ... I can breathe again," he said.

A flicker of a smile crossed Sister Klara's lips when the astonished boy glanced down to see the wounds on his arms and legs had almost completely healed. A few red blotches remained here and there, but miraculously, no swelling or joint pains. Gingerly, he poked and prodded before turning a questioning face toward the old woman. "I don't understand ..."

"For a week you have hovered between life and death and you can thank your lucky stars that those braves didn't finish you off there and then; they joked that there wasn't enough blood left in you to make a decent sacrifice ..." Again, she gave a wry grin. "If you had been carrying a gun I don't believe we'd be having this conversation." His heart leapt at the thought.

"As it is," she continued, "the Shamans want you gone, now that you've discovered our secret, and I mean gone for good!"

"What secret? I haven't learned any secrets. I promise not to tell anyone where you've gone. I don't know exactly where we are, anyway. I just want to go home to Mam. She will surely die of sorrow if I don't return soon." He cast his eyes about frantically. "You see, I'm completely over my attack. Please, please?" he whined.

The old woman slowly rose and motioned to her group of silent songsters, "I'm afraid that's impossible for now. The tunnel will remain flooded until the end of the wet season and even then its presence may never be revealed to outsiders. It would mean the end of the entire Mojo revival, do you understand?"

"B ... But what if I get sick again, or they send out the police to search for me?" He knew he was clutching at straws.

"They'll never find you here and no one ever leaves Atua's Lost City. If Chief Ticuna and I prevail, you will remain living here with us and participate in the Great Teachings."

"T … Teachings? What teachings? What's going on? I already attend classes at the Mission and am studying to be a professional photographer one day …"

She cut him short. "Best to resign yourself to your new situation and strive to excel in new and different ways. Tomorrow, you should be up and about and we will introduce you to the dreaming stories in the Plaza carvings that hold mysteries known only to the Ancestors."

Words, words and more meaningless mandates; yet, Klaus' mind remained fixated on the hidden rifle. If it should be discovered, and sooner or later he knew it would be, no amount of intercession or goodwill would count.

"I shall return tomorrow before sunset with the elders' decision; so far we've been able to hold the Shamans at bay. Until then, Maya will attend to your needs and you will speak to no one but her unless spoken to."

Pausing beneath the heavy stone lintel over the doorway, she shepherded out her flock of singing lambs and turned back to the boy. "Who knows? You may even grow to like it here." And then she was gone.

Cautiously, he took stock of his cavernous place of confinement between two sloping windowless walls made from huge, snug-fitting stones. High overhead a woven ceiling of bamboo and palm thatch cut down the glare and heat, allowing a few specks of sunlight to sprinkle the flagstone floor. There appeared to be but one exit, guarded by a boy around his own age armed with a bow and arrow. His single hammock took up one end of the chamber and at the other stood a tall stone stele almost touching the roof.

He felt not a little embarrassed by the miraculous healing of his naked body; what was left of his torn clothing lay washed and folded beneath the hammock. The whole experience seemed like a dream, from which he kept awakening only to drift off again. *Lotte* was but a distant memory.

The intimidating disproportionate features of the face on the stele sent a shiver down the boy's spine. There it squatted on its haunches with arms folded, chiselled plumes radiating outward from its head like rays of light. It was a terrifying yet intriguing sight that made him feel small, even insignificant.

When his eyes became accustomed to the gloom he discovered the basket of fruit and a gourd of water on the floor nearby, easing his apprehension somewhat. He realised for the first time that he was hungry, and he was happy to try and regain a little strength while he had the chance.

At that moment, squatting together in a circle before the mouth of Devil's Gullet, Xina and his fellow Shamans were deep in discussion, preparing to expose their unwanted guest as a fraud and a coward. While the boy dozed, the old fakir gave instructions for a small oil lamp to be placed at the foot of the stele, where its flickering flame could accentuate the huge nose and protruding tongue, and cause certain shadows to dance across the walls.

Suddenly Klaus was wide awake. Sitting upright and rubbing his eyes, alarmed by the spectre of weaving figures on the walls. The more he tried to ignore the accusing features, the more they demanded attention; one moment the thick lips puckered and teased, at another the great hooked nose seemed ready to leap down and crush the very life out of him.

Instinctively he sensed he was facing some kind of test, with the Great God Atua weighing up his worthiness. There was nothing for it but to summon his courage and force himself to go back to sleep, which of course is the least likely method for achieving peaceful slumber.

Tossing and turning with one eye half open, he watched fascinated as the tongue of stone slowly withdrew and the lips curled back in a snarl.

Again, he started up in shock, unsure where reality and dreaming overlapped. He saw himself in the skin of a male howler rebuking aloud the townsfolks' selfishness, only to be silenced by a leaping Jaguar that sank its yellow fangs into his booming throat sac to render him mute.

Then, as if by secret signal Maya appeared, pinning back the doorway curtain and hurrying to his side in a cordial shaft of morning light that heralded the end of the ordeal. The oil lamp sputtered and died as she wiped the beads of sweat from his brow and lifted a gourd of cool water to his lips.

"Klaus very brave, not scream or try to run away from dreams. Chief Ticuna say you live with Mojo now," she whispered in a mixture of broken Portuguese and river dialect. Still, no sound escaped his lips. "Klaus come."

Pulling on his tattered shorts, he followed meekly behind.

All heads turned as the pair emerged onto the Central Plaza, which he could see was a hive of activity; but no one engaged them. He gasped at the magnitude and design of the ruins: enormous pumice slabs lined a courtyard flanked by two steep sloping flanks of stone.

"For ball games," she pre-empted his question. "Ancestors play many ball games here … and eat many enemy hearts," she added reverentially.

The place had obviously been reclaimed from the jungle with an almighty effort; some areas, like the market square, had been restored to their original purpose. At each corner of the Central Plaza stood a lava stone stele similar to that which had almost stolen his sanity. He noted with some satisfaction that they looked far less threatening in the sunlight and upon closer examination appeared to contain mainly carved scenes of forgotten conquests and simple village life, interspersed with row after row of strange hieroglyphic symbols.

"Sister Klara say stones tell Indian dreaming story," she said proudly, running her fingertips across the ancient markings.

However, it was the great crumbling edifice in the distance, rising through a mantle of moss and green vines that took his breath away: tiers of a seven-stepped Ziggurat were adjoined to a row of stone columns that partially supported the roof of a once mighty Temple. As the morning sun touched its broken apex three mighty blasts rang out and everyone in the open disappeared beneath a canopy of woven branches overhead. A curious pilot flying past may glimpse the abandoned ruins in a seemingly inaccessible location but certainly no visible sign of life.

Maya explained that at the first kiss of sunlight on the great shrine, or any other sign of danger, a huge Conch Shell, the tribe's proudest possession, would be blown three times followed sooner or later by a single blast announcing the "all clear". Any failure to obey this warning promptly was cruelly punished by splashing the offender with scalding water from one of many steaming fissures in the cliffs.

She confided further that Sister Klara's "Magic Prayers" had re-invigorated the whole tribe and that her daily sermons continually alerted them to something within that she termed "Peace Profound". Between one wet season and the next, she had somehow revived their deepest cultural longings by employing techniques simple and mysterious. Within the space of a single year, the tribe was once again living hand-in-hand with Natural Law and mainly free from conflict.

Not unexpectedly, the arrival of a white boy in the mix had upset this balance, prompting Xina's fellow shamans to call for a solution based on traditional voodoo justice.

"Klaus wants Maya help to go home," he whispered when they were out of sight behind the base of the pyramid, but the girl merely looked away and pretended not to hear. She put a finger to her lips and beckoned him to follow through a maze of tree-lined pathways. For some minutes he struggled to stay close upon her heels until they emerged onto a jagged lava outcrop offering grand views of the vast river basin below. Left and right the sheer escarpment walls fell away in the distance, broken only here and there by streaks of white water feeding the boisterous confluence below.

A soft mist bearing the chatter and screech of jungle parlance swept up from the flooded plains below and brushed their faces with cool water droplets. His friend took a contented breath and pointed out various Indian names of the surrounding features. "Klaus see over there? Rolling-Thunder Mountain," she said in a low voice, pointing to a cone-shaped hill in the distance issuing innocuous wisps of smoke. "And down there ... Devil's Gullet," she said, "Mojo bring Klaus through there to Lost City ..."

At first, he saw nothing but the sheer steaming cliffs gashed by ribbons of white water, unscaleable to all but the nimblest primate. Following her finger, he could make out a jet of bright foam spurting from the base of the cliff.

"Maya find Klaus near there," she said and pointed again as he stared dumbly down, barely able to comprehend the extent of his predicament.

Far off on the eastern horizon, a narrow silver serpent wound its way through a checkerboard of clearings carved from the endless green forest, taunting him with thoughts of home.

Through the parting mists, he caught a splash of sunlight glancing off the white tiles of the Great Holy Cross. His sense of smell, so long congested by a dozen allergies, came alive as he drank in the sweet musty odour of his friend: he realised with a jolt how much he now depended on this girl for survival. Turning away with a heavy heart Klaus was convinced he would never see his beloved Mam again.

13

Frau Kathleen Hahn became a different person after her boy went missing, convinced that her disobedient soul was forever damned. The day had finally arrived to pay the piper as she always knew it would, and she went about her duties thereafter with a grim determination. For several Sundays, she avoided Mass altogether and even private confessions in Father Patrick's cell failed to lift the burden of guilt from her shoulders.

For his part, ever alert to Kitty's prescient purgations, the old priest continued to nibble away with a heart full of love and a mouthful of home-spun ditties. Despite her broken heart, or perhaps because of it, she found herself succumbing to the comforting presence of her unlikely new soulmate.

Before long she was back to caressing and praying to her ceramic Virgin, at least twice daily. She could stand the uncertainty no longer, agreeing to take up full-time residence in the cloisters on the hill. "It'll do ya th' world a good me goil to get away to where yer trooly appreciated," said the priest.

After all, he'd often noted, it wasn't as if her "mail order hoosband" was around as much these days to interfere with any of Frau Kathleen's proposed living arrangements.

One evening, she let it slip during confession that given half a chance she'd just as soon "Tear 'is eyes out with me own bare 'ands" if backed by her testosterone-fuelled eldest goosen but Father Paddy granted her absolution anyway.

Down below, the brothers were content to remain around the Fazenda for now, even coming to accept it as home.

Robert for one was determined not to spend one minute more than necessary behind those Monastery walls. Ever since his stepfather's fumbling voyages upstream, he had been pressing his claim to take over as the pre-eminent hunting guide around town. Amazingly, and despite his tender years, his first solo trip as captain and guide aboard *Lotte* bagged a fine male jaguar, two tapir and a half dozen caiman.

Captain Streicher was, of course, delighted and waxed lyrical over the youth's hunting skills to *Belle*'s first-class passengers. The safaris were once again back up and running, and booked out from one month to the next. "Just like in the good old days," he chortled to his new business partner.

Owing to Mam's outright hostility toward the "cruel and unnecessary slaughter" that went with the job, Robert reacted predictably by clamming up and refusing to discuss his further plans. She attempted to balance her heartfelt disgust with his need for praise, fearing that without the right balance she might lose the respect of her firstborn as well.

"Yet, what can any mother do when confronted with a rebellious teenager jus' startin' to feel 'is water?" she lamented to Father Patrick. There was no denying that physically, her Bobby was a real "doer", and his rugged good looks kept her heart abeatin' proud much of the time. He seemed immune to all the usual pestilences that swept through the population, often ignoring her warnings to never leave the house without shoes.

She'd even marched him up the hill one morning to point out the suffering of her hookworm patients in the Charity Ward, with their bellies distended from eating fistfuls of clay. Those unable to afford proper footwear were sitting ducks for the tiny parasites that burrowed through the soles of their feet and into the bloodstream, eventually causing mayhem and death.

Nonetheless, Kitty's warnings fell again on deaf ears. A crack shot with a rifle in hand, Robert was now his "own man", seemingly one jump ahead of pestilence and local authority. He honed his quick lip with incisive observations and backdoor compliments; often, his victims didn't realise they'd been insulted.

For example, on the day of Alois' 50th birthday, when all four of the family were to sit down together at the table for his favourite baked meal, Robert planned a sweet revenge upon his unwitting tormentor.

Forewarned that the family would be mustered to pay full respects to the "Head of the Household" on his big day, the boy had seen his chance. Tradition demanded that a chicken be killed and dressed for the main course, and perhaps his whole sordid prank may have gone unnoticed but for a pile of wet feathers left scattered beside the scalding tub.

When Klaus was eventually despatched to the barn by an over-anxious Alois, he came across stages one and two of the killing process but no sign of either brother or victim. Poking his head around the barn door he could not quite believe his eyes: what he observed coloured his attitude toward sex for years to come.

There in the far corner crouched his big brother with eyes closed, moaning softly; doing something vile and unmistakable to Alois' freshly dressed chicken.

Shocked and disgusted, the boy ducked away and hurried to the kitchen to stammer that Robert had nearly completed the said chore; Mam could go ahead and grease the baking pan in readiness. For the rest of that morning, he suffered recurring visions and didn't know whether to giggle or gag.

Come lunchtime, when the old man sat down at table to receive due homage, he began with a lecture on what he would and wouldn't do if he were back in the Fatherland right now, fighting the good fight.

He paused only briefly to chastise Klaus for refusing to take up a single mouthful of the main course.

"But baby, you luv Mam's baked chicken, Vati's raised 'em 'imself," his mother interceded, "… at least 'ave some stuffin' and roast taities, you especially luv Mam's taities …"

"No! I don't want any … I'm not hungry, thanks." The boy choked on the very thought and had sneaked a glance at his brother standing with carvers raised above the golden carcase and a twinkle in his eye.

"Won't eat this, and don't eat that," Alois grumbled, "it's no wonder you're a poor excuse of an Aryan Jungvolk. What sort of man do you think you'll grow up to be? A weed, that's what!"

"Like you, happy birthday!" Robert fired back in a deceptive, sing-song voice, avoiding eye contact with the already tipsy guest of honour. "Look, Klaus, I'm going to eat all mine," he quickly added, but this barb between brothers flew over Vati's head.

Mam was beginning to think they'd both gone "troppo" and warned them several times to sit up straight and remember their manners. Notwithstanding the importance of the occasion, eat of that plump chicken Klaus would not, even when banished to his room for failing to show "proper respect" for all Vati's efforts in providing "a roof over their heads and the shirts on their backs, let alone a feast fit for the Kaiser himself!"

Through the bedroom door, the boy strained his ears as the dastardly event unfolded. Alois' boozy breath heralded his mood from the moment he sat down and Kitty recited a practised Grace that barely eased the chill. "Once a bastard, always a bastard," he heard the old man mutter into his soup. "And an Irish bastard at that," he added for good measure.

"That's enough of that talk, you know how I hate that B-word," his mother replied courageously. Yet, despite these clear provocations Robert failed to take the bait, remaining strangely attentive. He jumped up and down to steady Mam's chair and insisted on carving every last portion of the carcase, loading Vati's plate with crispy skin and giblets. He even leaned forward to wipe a dribble of fat from the old man's chin with his own napkin. "There, Daddy …"

"Get away, you bloody fool. And don't call me 'Daddy'," Alois grunted, unsettled by all the attention. As the boy fussed about topping up Vati's wine so politely and regularly that "Mutti", as her boys were now required to address her, took it as a sign of a real nice "about-face" in her firstborn's attitude.

When he insisted on clearing the table and washing the dishes her chest swelled with pride. My, my, how he was growing up and could turn it on when he wanted to.

"Alois is always like that when he's hadda skin full," Mam confided later when smuggling a plate of cold veggies into Klaus. "Trouble is, he's always gotta skinful," she said with a muffled cluck of her tongue. But the boy never let on what he'd witnessed behind the chook shed, and it seemed no one was any wiser. Besides, Bobby had always been Mum's favourite, the one who'd held her hand tight during that gut-wrenching day of departure from Galway.

How could any true-blue Irish lass forget the pain of leaving behind nearly everything she held dear? Since then, Kitty's mind often drifted back to those first hours aboard the S.S. *Ladybird*, dreaming of having her chances over again.

"Holy Mother o' Gawd, grant us a home of our own ..." she had begun to pray in earnest over the stern rail, as shouts and streamers were jerked away in the heavy air. Almost overcome by the import of the occasion, her throat had croaked out the Galway Anthem one last time. "... just to hear again the ripple of the trout stream, the women in the meadow making hay, just to sit beside the turf fire in a cabin, and watch the barefoot goosens as they play ..."

She had broken down completely in her little mate's ear, with a voice muffled beneath the throb of *Ladybird*'s engines. Clutching each other silently, they cleared the grey-green harbour mouth, watching Mutton Island's droll mudflats sink behind the gathering swells. At that desperate moment, Robert had flashed his sparkling eyes and crossed his stout heart, swearing to protect his Mam and little brother from any "Indians or savage animals" they might come across.

"But I have a hoosband now, dearest, who will take care of that sort of thing ..." Kitty had reassured him, enjoying the sound of the H-word rolling off her tongue. "A hoosband who I jus' know in me bones is goin' to take good care of us." She gazed at her boy fondly, suddenly filled with new hope, resolving then and there to remain cheery and honest toward her precious goosens wherever possible; excepting, of course, in "delicate" matters of birds, bees and other taboo subjects running counter to her hard-won moral principles.

Perhaps, it may become necessary to tell a little fib or two.

Following Robbie's fourth birthday in their tiny Galway flat, Kitty had insisted that each evening after supper he read aloud a single passage from the Bible, including proper pronunciation of all the hard words.

For long months they had struggled with the task; her so knackered after double shifts, and he was ever more drawn to the streets with his mates. Night after night she overrode his protests, assuring him of the many benefits to flow from studying the Holy Scriptures. Years later, some wit scribbled a slogan on the wall of the Monastery "The road to hell is paved with good intentions", which reminded her that Robert's contempt for book learnin' and schoolin' probably stemmed from those pre-emptive though well-meaning censures. He would grow up almost the opposite of his young brother in that regard, a briar bush amidst wild Mountain Thyme. And within ten years he would profess himself an "atheist", which didn't make Mam feel any better. Once a black sheep always a black sheep, she had to accept.

As *Ladybird* began to pitch and roll on the open sea, Kitty's frail figure clung to the railing while collecting her thoughts.

She lifted her chin and straightened her shoulders. "Don't forget, Herr Hahn is now *your* father too, a real father at last, I 'ope," she went on. "He has given us 'is name, and we must try to do as he says, or give it a damn good try," she added hastily, but the words caught in her throat.

"But Ma, I *like* being called Bobby O'Shea, everyone calls me Bobby O'Shea …"

"Not when your new daddy is around," she said softly, putting her arm around his shoulder. "You must realise we are starting a whole new life in Amazonia, wherever that is, and it's not goin' to be easy at first. When we get there, Alois will introduce you as Robert Hahn and you'll soon get used to it."

"He's not my pa and I don't want 'im for one … my real pa's coming to get me one day. Jus' let 'im try an' make me." But Mother silenced him with a gentle finger to her lips. At length, he squeezed her hand tight and reiterated his intention to be "protector". "But only for you and Klaus."

She turned away and blew her nose into the embroidered lace hanky, a memento from the girls at work. Was she stark raving mad, charging off half-cocked to the other side of the world with two bairns in tow? And sharing her bed with a foreigner she hardly knew?

Her emotions during those long days at sea wavered between fear and hope. "Angels and ministers of Grace defend us," she would whisper to the plaster Virgin propped up on her suitcase, always straining for the strength to face an unknown future.

Captain Ribbentrop and the crew of *Ladybird* were clearly out of sorts from day one. The skipper wasn't looking forward to this outward bound at all, given Herr Hahn's assumed jurisdiction that threatened his own authority aboard.

This inflated scion had already demanded an early departure from Hamburg via a time-wasting detour down the west coast of Ireland, of all the wild seas, in pursuance of a most unlikely affair of the heart.

The object of Herr Hahn's distraction, he had informed the captain over dinner on their first night out, was one Fraulein Kathleen O'Shea, a "Medical Assistant", with whom he had become involved while recuperating from a service wound in Galway.

One thing had led to another, Alois confided after a few drinks, and the unlikely mail-order romance continued to flourish even after he'd been shipped back home on a medical discharge.

There followed fevered exchanges between the pair, especially following his unexpected "promotion" to a Senior Management position with the family firm in far-off Brazil: At last! Hahn Enterprises was recognising his potential. Time was ripe to dangle the ultimate carrot of marriage!

In her prompt and breezy reply, Fraulein O'Shea was clearly flattered, though firm on one point above all others: she wasn't leaving old Ireland without a ring on her finger.

And right now S.S. *Ladybird* remained stuck in a foreign harbour in the depths of a harsh winter: two days behind with her schedule shot to pieces, all over the intended bride's "pigheadedness". No one had ever ruffled conditions aboard the pride of the fleet quite like Alois' infatuation. And had not she in turn "bent over backwards" for months to expedite the legalities, despite few of her workmates believing it would ever come off?

So be it; she'd had gossiped all her life.

Then the erstwhile groom-to-be arrived with great fanfare aboard his own family merchantman, eager to sweep away any remaining obstacles.

Kitty's principles would stretch only so far. She could make do without a full Nuptial Mass, but there was no chance of joining in any mad-cap South American adventure until she'd laid eyes on certain legal papers along with said ring. Outside of wedlock, she hinted, there would be no more cuddles in the big bed or his favourite massages with the "happy" endings. She hadn't spent these past years on her knees in shame, praying and confessing to one after another, only to be impregnated for a third time.

"A promise is a promise," she'd repeated ad infinitum to her sceptical colleagues at Galway Central, all the while dreaming of his return. "So you can stick that in your pipes and smoke it!"

Sure enough, Alois Hahn was a man on a mission and ready to agree to almost anything to be underway in his new promotion. He would soon enough show them who was boss.

Meanwhile, Captain Ribbentrop paced *Ladybird*'s decks cursing the uppity scion as dark clouds gathered seaward. At that very moment, the happy couple having been refused dispensation from the cardinal in Armagh was downtown Galway tying the knot in an anteroom of the General Registry Office.

It seemed for the time being that Kitty's guilt was destined to linger; the fact remained that neither of her bairns had been properly baptised and that meant the B-word would follow them to the ends of the earth. She'd tear the eyes out of anyone who dared repeat it to her face.

As the fairy tale unfolded, the newlyweds sped off in two Hansom Cabs, accompanied by colleague-witnesses and the "two cutest little tykes in County Galway" with their primped faces, tight suits and borrowed shoes.

An informal, though very posh "High Tea" so Kitty thought, had been arranged in the nurse's quarters where she was almost overcome by the belated well-wishes and trepidations of her colleagues. Like "Frau Hahn" herself, few could quite believe she was legally hitched, let alone to a protestant foreigner and a Kraut to boot.

At the bride's insistence, Alois was sent clumping away through the vaguely familiar hospital corridors, cheerfully waving the elusive marriage certificate above his head as if trying to convince all Ireland of his noblesse oblige, rather than the stark necessity, as some whispered, of his having been "bogied" into it. But today even he was elated by his own impulsive derring-do, flying as it did in the face of relentless family objections.

Under the circumstances, a profitable sinecure amidst the mythical perils of Amazonia was probably the best he could have hoped for. This was *his* moment and he was finally receiving the recognition he deserved. As a matter of fact, he had been mulling over a few ideas of his own on how to turn a little extra profit in his new posting, using cheap native labour.

14

No sooner had Kitty settled the boys into their ramshackle Fazenda and the Monastery school, when Robby's petulance again took a turn for the worse.

He continually bifurcated between excessive charm and sarcasm, reverting to outright hostility when the mood took him. Anyone exhibiting the slightest aberration in dress, looks or manner (and river towns being full of such individuals) came in for a humorous jibe or a cutting aside behind their backs, much to the amusement of his Rascals and a bashful brother who would never dare think such thoughts, let alone utter the words.

Frau Hahn had no idea what to make of these sudden outbursts during her over-indulgent attempts at guidance. "Something may well be true from your point of view," she would chide him, "but other people don't have to be hearin' it all da time. You tink with your tongue, dat's your problem. It'll get you into trouble yet, to be sure ..."

Once too often, in front of others, she thoughtlessly dandled his blond curls and flicked them back off his alabaster forehead like she'd always done, but rather than snuggle close he had recoiled like a viper. She began to suspect it was something to do with the secretive Christian Brothers teaching methods, but just as quickly dismissed such thoughts from her mind.

One obvious fact would not go away: that first week of schooling under the monks had changed something in her boy. Mothers just know such things.

Robert began to shrink from overt displays of affection, eschewing hugs or kissing on the lips. Moreover, she noticed for the first time that the sparkle had gone from his eyes, as if they had shut themselves off from further outside influence.

"It's just a phase he's in, I guess ... he jus' wants to appear grown-up. All boys go through stages," she tried to kid herself, "Lord, don't he remind me of meself at times?"

Nurse's aides ceased early seeking perfection in human nature, and Kitty clung to the more important notion that despite her Bobby not settling down like his wee brother, he clearly possessed an extra-large brain in that handsome scone of his; certainly bigger than most boys his age.

He could be a real little charmer when 'e put 'is mind to it.

But many of these insights were yet to dawn.

When *Ladybird* did eventually cast off from Galway, the presence of Alois' barefoot urchins on board, just as Captain Ribbentrop predicted, soon proved more than irritating.

"Square Irish pegs thinking they'll fit into round holes," he confided to his officers, skimming a Skua's eye over the oddly dressed and funny-sounding newcomers; especially that older boy, clattering up and down the ship's ladders slamming doors and touching everything with sticky fingers.

"Just don't let those damn kids anywhere near me," he warned the crew. "It's a pity certain bare feet don't stick to the steel ladders in this bloody weather."

"The younger one looks harmless enough, Chief," responded his first mate. "I haven't seen him so far without his nose in a book, poor little fella. You can't help feelin' sorry for all of 'em, being dumped in the middle of nowhere for years on end; not me." But Captain Ribbentrop was staring straight ahead into the rearing grey-flecked breakers, thinking of how much time *Ladybird* would need to make up.

"*Ladybird*! What sort a name's dat for a big boat like dis?" the elder one had suddenly appeared to shout in the captain's ear. "Why, dat's a stupid name!" he added cheekily, rising on the balls of his feet and trying to jiggle the knobs on the instrument panel. Instinctively, the boy dodged a ham fist whizzing past the spot where his head had been.

"You need a good clip under ear boy!" sputtered the captain, being caught quite off guard by the brash familiarity. Unbeknown to the interloper he had struck a nerve.

Prior to *Ladybird*'s naming ceremony in Hamburg, the "limp-wristed" title chosen had drawn disparagement from all sides. It was downright hurtful to see any oceangoing vessel, especially one being touted as "Pride of the Fleet" so demeaned. These views, however, were not shared by Rudolph von Hahn Snr, Grand Kaiser Mine's tottering founder who, quite out of the blue, decided to name her *Ladybird* after his favourite garden insect.

Captain Ribbentrop sweated on a last-minute change of heart, but no one dared actually suggest an alternative to Captain Rudolph Snr.

"How fast does dis tub sail anyway?" It was the boy again.

They'd not been underway a full day yet and the little pest had pressed the captain's hot button. "Ship, boy! S - H - I - P ... not boat! Not tub!" he grumbled. "And children are not allowed in this part of the SHIP ... Garn! Be off with you, and learn a few manners or I'll have words with your father."

"He's not me father, and he can't tell me what to do neither," the boy shot back.

"What you sayin' lad? Dat's not proper English language! Clear off the bridge or you get a kick up the arse." At that, the first mate attempted a poor Irish imitation of "one-two, one-two" while marching the unwelcome intruder back down the ladder.

"Well, Captain Ribbentrop *can* tell you and everyone else aboard what to do, see? Git out and stay out, you bloody little pest ... and stay right away from the bridge in future." It seemed there was one on every voyage.

Undaunted, the youngster at length won over the rest of the crew with his lilting Gaelic voice and jargon, confounding them into stitches with a neverending stream of jokes and observations. Of course, "Captain Dribble-snot", as he was soon after labelled, would never have dared actually strike the boy without the father's permission. He didn't want any trouble, hated surprises and liked to think he ran a tight ship.

Plying the misnomered steamer back and forth across the equator twice annually he had to admit that she moved well through the water, making direct contact possible between head office and the far-off "Wildernesses", as everyone in the head office referred to Grand Kaiser's operations in Santa Luzia.

At first, exports of gold and rubber returned a handsome profit, and for this important task, *Ladybird* had been custom-built to the highest standards.

She was proud-prowed to override the worst that grey Atlantic storms could throw at her, yet suitably shallow-draughted to access Manaus and other river ports during the dry season. Outward bound, she carried manufactured goods, fashionable clothing, cases of Rheine wine, even bolts of bright fabric and other tradeable trinkets, leaving little room besides for rotating staff family members and their luggage.

For this voyage, all Grand Kaiser employees, with the exception of Herr Hahn's new family, found themselves sardined together in Spartan quarters below decks.

After weeks at sea, and days among the smooth eddies of the mighty Amazonian Estuary, vessels of all shapes and sizes began to swarm about in midstream awaiting their arrival. Honking and signalling, they offered to trade fresh fruits, bush meat and folk art, in exchange for alcohol, motor parts and scarce building materials.

For those with precious gems to trade, *Ladybird's* cool room was a Hamburg delicatessen, dangling knots of fatty smoked sausage and a variety of bourgeois titbits so sought after by the brightly painted ferries that plied the tea-stained tributaries.

Alternately, it could accommodate fifty frozen sides of prime Brazilian beef which often turned out to be the most profitable cargo of all when served in Berlin's finest restaurants.

Return voyages carried mainly low-value phosphate and declining balls of blanched rubber, both of which, since the gold and silver ore ran out, barely managed to keep Hahn International afloat. Local agents scoured the surrounding countryside for more profitable cargos like sawn hardwood, bales of cotton, raw sugar and unusual artefacts.

Sometimes in the dead of night, something else was slipped aboard and straight into Captain Ribbentrop's safe: *Gold ingots! 99.9% pure*, which did not appear anywhere on the ship's manifest. A bar or two, sometimes three, of hard-won bullion secretly extracted with the assistance of a new-fangled contraption brought in to re-work the long abandoned mullock heaps, but mostly by trading with certain shadowy prospectors upriver. Management turned a blind eye toward these little windfalls panned and smelted beyond the vague boundaries of Grand Kaiser's sprawling claim, using a process that polluted the waterways with mercury.

The head office proceeded on the principle that what the Brazilian authorities didn't know wouldn't hurt them.

Almost from their first moment aboard Alois Hahn had attempted to forcibly integrate his new family among the "jabbering Germans" as the brothers dismissively titled their fellow travellers. As unter-manager in waiting, Alois felt embarrassed by their lack of language skills and social graces, realising that perhaps he had more in common with the hired hands than with his own clumsy kith and kin. Once upon the open ocean, his short-lived bonhomie gave way to a coarse and dominant disposition, which Kitty had always sensed but shrugged away. "He is what he is," she repeated over to herself between bouts of seasickness.

There would be numerous times in this new life when she would need to view her own past transgressions and present discomforts as beautiful and holy things, simply in order to survive. "I guess I'm no angel meself," she would confess to herself under her breath. "In for a penny, in for a pound."

To hasten his family's integration Alois refused to communicate in their native, "so-called English" language, demanding instead that they master a list of useful words and phrases with German roots. Then, during *Ladybird's* Southampton stopover, he flexed his muscles even further by posting a notice that none of "his" employees would be granted permission to disembark on

British soil. From their very first day at sea, he commandeered *Ladybird's* saloon bar for group "bonding" purposes.

This snug social space had been decorated at the behest of Rudolph Snr in classic "Black Forest Hunting-Lodge style", boasting an assortment of trophy heads, antlers and tanned hide rugs.

It was here, soon after plunging into the heaving Atlantic swell that he chose to reveal to his queasy wife and anyone else who cared to listen, that it was her "Aryan Heritage" more so than her appearance that had convinced him to choose her for such an important position by his side "despite one or two unfortunate missteps in the past".

Hahn Enterprises would rise again, he claimed, bringing European prosperity and reform to one of the world's darkest corners. When his terse telegram arrived at Galway Central, instructing Nursing Aide O'Shea (who'd never previously ventured much further than Mutton Island lookout on her bicycle), to make ready for departure to Amazonia, wherever that was, in a mere matter of weeks, the whole ward erupted in excitement. It appeared that her years of waiting and hoping were over, though she did remain sceptical of his assurance that the company would take care of "everything" that could not be squeezed into a single suitcase apiece.

Soon enough, and not without reason, Kitty was troubled by ever more uneasy thoughts as to whether her proud Catholic values and sense of humour together could suffice to tame, or even mellow her fiancé's lordly outlook.

How indeed could any parochial bride-to-be grasp the extent of her wounded warrior's ingrained prejudices? As with so many other defeated German sailors who'd served aboard the Kaiser's war-torn dreadnaughts, Alois' lingering hatred of French, British and Jewish "warmongers" was fanned by the plethora of pseudo-scientific pamphlets circulating widely in the aftermath of the Great War. These scurrilous and inflammatory publications vilified "Jews, traitors and other profiteers" for their greed, cowardice and cultural sins over decades; indeed, for losing the war itself!

These were the very forces that had conspired to "stab German soldiers in the back" just as they were on the cusp of victory. Following the army's collapse and a naval mutiny, moderate voices all across Germany had been poo-hooed and violently attacked by political rabble-rousers from Left and Right; Alois Hahn considered it presumptuous for uneducated and lukewarm civilians to involve themselves in politics at all. He raved and vowed that the deaths of two million comrades would not be in vain and that one day they would be avenged.

Throughout the entire voyage, the Irish trio felt they were being "picked on and left out", while their new breadwinner busied himself whipping the German workmen into shape each evening in the saloon bar. While thus assembled, the new assistant manager insisted on placing a "proper emphasis" on what lay ahead, and especially on the importance of the Fatherland's past triumphs before being so cruelly stabbed in the back. After a toast of Schnapps all around, he led them in "Songs of the Western Forest", and especially his favourite, the "Badenweiler Marsch", convinced that rousing martial tunes above all offered a sure path to regaining national dignity and maintaining group cohesiveness. These same melancholy strains wafting nightly up and down the ship's passageways served only to inflame even deeper feelings of aloneness in the bosom of a seasick Frau Hahn and two boys.

"They'll come around soon enough," Alois reassured the other ex-pats. His new family would need to lift its game if ever they hoped to make a go of it in the rough and tumble of a lawless Amazonian outpost. As senior Hahn aboard, he cultivated a commanding air and did not hold back when anyone appeared to be "slacking". He practised daily for his newly created position which, he was assured, lay just beyond the horizon. The voyage was turning out to be full of challenges and responsibilities, not least of which came with the opening of a personally addressed envelope from the head office.

As instructed, and after waiting out the required seven days at sea, the unter-manager with trembling fingers unfolded the single sheet of monogrammed paper and his chest swelled with pride. The official-looking letter, signed in a heavy hand by none other than Grandfather Rudolph himself, authorised Alois and his new team to, among other things, "take control of all Grand Kaiser's Amazonian operations and assist in the 'restoration of profits' within Hahn International's most far-flung [and as it turned out, least lucrative] enterprise."

At last, the black sheep of the family had been thrown a lifeline, one final opportunity to show what he was really made of.

Thus emboldened, Alois commenced spot-checking the staff quarters aboard, shamelessly sticking his head inside doors and portholes at all hours. "You never know what employees get up to when they think no one is watching …" he confided to a chastened Captain Ribbentrop, himself feeling undermined by the other's intumescent influence.

It was galling for Alois too, that his new bride did not seem to be making any credible efforts to pull herself together. As an ex-navy salt, he had little sympathy for landlubbers suffering seasickness … "It's all in the mind, Kitty; everyone knows that!" he repeated through her open porthole. "I must insist you try harder to at least put in an appearance," he added impatiently.

The poor woman, however, was no socialite and no sailor; her unremitting biliousness smacked of the worst days of pregnancy. Incapable of lifting her head off the pillow for days at a time, she refused to take a single bite of the sauerkraut, blood sausage and cool ale delivered on a silver tray at Alois' insistence by her own two rug-headed kerns.

Barely able to raise a smile, she dreamed only of the day when she may set foot once more on solid ground.

Unsurprisingly, Alois' affections cooled with each rejection; long days of missed opportunities went begging. "Kitty" became "Kathleen" and before the voyage ended, "Frau Hahn" was receiving daily reminders of the many solemn duties to which she had, being of so-called sound mind, signed on to. He fumed inwardly: had not *he* stood tall and done *his* bit to legitimise the whole damned misalliance by hanging the esteemed Hahn Family name on the shoulders of her and her brats?

She had sworn "black and blue" that baby Klaus was indeed his own flesh and blood, despite the child's early timidity and pasty complexion. Without exception, the Hamburg Hahns remained unimpressed at the first snapshots of the newborn in his crib. Alois even threatened to have independent paternity tests carried out if and when such facilities ever became available in Brazil. Surely, it was not too much to ask any new wife with a chequered past to fall into line?

Now and then he would sit at the foot of her bunk and attempt to engage her in his plans for the future, but the new bride wasn't having a bar of it. She wished only to be left alone, gulping down salty air and fresh water while praying that the nightmare might soon end … "Before I give up the bloody ghost altogether," she moaned.

"When you are finally up and about," he persisted, "I will expect a more business-like attitude toward both staff and senior frauen following our arrival in Santa Luzia." He would continue to hope that her demeanour at that time would more properly reflect the status of an unter-manager's Frau; someone who now belonged in the family and carried the good name of the owners. He informed her that his first task would be to ensure that everyone on board learned his proper place in the new order.

Weeks later, notwithstanding the harsh regimen to which they'd already been subjected, the brothers were also disbarred from the Belem shore party, their first port of call within the great estuary. When pressed by Kitty he stated that the pair needed to learn a lesson or two in respect, and had arranged with Captain Ribbentrop for them to help out with odd jobs aboard. It would do them good.

Robert especially, the apple of Mam's eye and hungry for adventure in the new land, was already chafing openly at the litany of restrictions and growing more resentful toward his stepfather.

Forced to idle at the ship's rail for one more stinking day while other passengers streamed ashore to explore Belem's exotic waterfront, it was simply tortuous being stuck within spitting distance, constantly stumped by his brother's harping questions. If he must stay aboard he just wanted to be left alone to drink in as much as possible of this exciting new landscape and plot revenge.

Once underway again en route to Manaus, through the calm and vast expanse of jungle, the frail woman was at last able to stagger out onto the foredeck and join her baby in the morning sun. She found him gazing absently at nothing in particular, surrounded by a pile of dog-eared volumes which she noticed, had begun to fall apart in the harsh conditions of the long voyage. They reminded her of her own prematurely aged features when she'd brushed her hair in the mirror.

Yet, for a brief moment, those long weeks of discomfort were forgotten; like the symbiotic joy that follows swiftly upon the smarting heels of childbirth, all Kittys' hardships dissolved when her bairn lifted his slender cheek to hers, as innocent as a new-laid egg. "Mam, you're here. Are you feeling better now?"

For a moment she continued to drink in the scene, speechless; squinting into the glare of tropical sunlight at her feet sat her cherub, pinker in the cheeks and more alive in the eyes after weeks at sea. His skin glowed in contrast to her own flaccid features. His thin, now somehow fuller lips were partly open, revealing a single gap in front; it was almost as if she'd never left his side.

She stifled a sob of thanksgiving. "… forever and ever, Amen."

Perhaps her "pig in a poke" decision may be paying off after all? Grabbing hold of that one unlikely chance had been a long shot at best, a move that had only strengthened her resolve to never again let any man "put it over" her. Surely, all this fresh air, combined with a good old-fashioned Catholic curriculum would guarantee that she and her two babes could flourish in the new land. According to onboard whispers, Santa Luzia's Holy Cross Mission boasted airy classrooms and a structured program overseen by an Order of Christian Brothers. Best of all, Abbott Malone was rumoured to be a dyed-in-the-wool Irishman, an unimaginable blessing for Kitty if indeed this turned out to be so.

She took another deep breath of the fragrant atmosphere and crossed herself three times, restating her commitment to making a fist of it, "So 'elp me God." Why, wasn't this very moment evidence, if more were needed, of Mother Mary's grace? How much proof of Christ's forgiveness could a girl with such a past really expect? Right here and now though it was revealed through a curtain of shining tears, she'd been to the very abyss and back again, or was it just her silly eyes playing tricks in the bright sunlight?

"Mama, I haven't wheezed once for the whole journey. And I've been saying my prayers every night," her baby bubbled on. "Papa says it's the sea air responsible, but now we are in the Amazon it's supposed to be jungle air. Oh look, Mam, it's so wide, I can't see any trees. When are we going to see the big trees up close? And the monkeys, and the birds, and the Indians?" But Kitty just kept smiling, gazing dead ahead and hearing little, allowing herself for the first time in ages to revel in her long-suffering Faith.

During those long lazy days pushing upstream, passengers might feel themselves still upon the broad Atlantic with nothing to see but swirling currents, steamy skies and a dogged retinue of seagulls trailing astern.

New species of freshwater fish began appearing on the menu, often requiring several men to haul on board. Chef, however, preferred to wreak his own brand of revenge upon the schools of easily caught Piranha, serving up platters filled with patties and bony fillets in a variety of styles.

When questioned by Alois as to this preference he told a story of growing up in remote riverside settlements where he'd witnessed a native boy being beaten up by a group of thugs before jumping into the river to escape. The bruised and bloodied Indian didn't take a dozen strokes before being enveloped in a silver cloud of scales and slashing teeth; the boy was stripped to the bone within minutes.

Helpless onlookers ashore could only watch in horror as the water blushed crimson and his last scream fell silent. Chef told how his skin still crawled at the thought of the "little bastards" always lurking beneath their feet. Then and there he'd vowed to eat as many piranhas as possible in a lifelong quest to even the score.

Onward, with nothing to see but sky and water, or so it seemed to the Brothers Hahn lost in dreamy thoughts of their own. It felt like *Ladybird* was standing still, except for an occasional freighter, barge or even dugout canoe heading downstream. Surely Manaus couldn't be too much further?

Ahead and astern, the shimmering horizons were lost in mist and rattled each afternoon by vast thunderstorms. At length, clumps of floating lily pads, grasses and shrubs began drifting by, followed soon by whole mini-islands of forest. With the wet season dumping yards of rainwater upstream, it appeared that whole chunks of the riverbank were being torn away and flushed toward the distant ocean, along with their occupants.

A ripple of anticipation passed through the ship; Captain Ribbentrop now had often to alter course in order to avoid the largest of the hazards, some the size of football fields, harbouring not only stands of mature trees but marooned animals and roosting water birds. A cry went up as passengers spied their first family of spider monkeys feeding noisily in the passing treetops; below, a family of capybara sunned themselves at the water's edge. Klaus recognised these strange whistling beasts at once from his picture books as the largest rodents on earth. Robert informed the other passengers disdainfully that they were, in fact, "giant rats".

Nature was turning on a real show for the youngster's eighth birthday. Ranks of basking Caiman, some with mouths propped open showed rows of wicked teeth; unlike the other island hitchhikers, these were not at all constrained by the swift current. At *Ladybird*'s approach, several slid silently into the water and swam out a short distance to meet the passing ship, anticipating a dump of garbage from the stern.

This distraction dispelled the gloom that had surrounded the boy all morning. He rarely received the gifts he hoped for and this time was no different. Mam had approached Cook for a Black Forest Cake, but the shortage of ingredients and candles turned into a platter of honey and cheese dumplings. Otherwise, his special day passed with a few half-hearted wishes and a nasal rendition of "Happy Birthday" after lunch.

Alois ignored the occasion completely, occupied all day in drawing up rosters and future efficiency targets.

Then suddenly, over the loudhailer came news that Manaus would soon be moving into sight and a collective sigh of relief went up; even the unter-manager appeared relieved.

His new family, by now desperate to please, would be permitted to go ashore while their baggage was being transferred to the paddle wheeler *Madeira Belle* under the command of one Captain Streicher, a retired Kriegsmarine.

That Sunday heralded the most exciting and disjointed birthday experience the boy could remember; the Hahn family finally planted its feet on foreign soil and was eager to join in a whirlwind tour of the city sights. From the dockside throng, a beaming Chinese guide emerged, wearing a Hahn Enterprise logo on his shirt and a huge conical straw hat like a halo around his head. His arrival heralded a welcome change of pace for the wide-eyed voyagers.

"I Chan. You follow, stay close." And then, he was off down the narrow alleyways and broad, tree-lined avenues like a rabbit, barely pausing long enough to suggest a souvenir. It seemed good fortune was finally smiling on them in spades: past troubles melted clean away when surrounded by such exotic sights and warm, happy people.

Alois' incessant calls to "keep together" gradually faded in the distance. For the moment the crowded marketplace offered more than enough distractions.

Then, almost predictably, a wail went up from Kitty and a head count was ordered. A second frantic count followed; the birthday boy was missing!

Resentful cries rang out from fellow travellers when the tour was called off to form a search party. Chan went one way and a cursing Alois the other; smaller groups fanned out through the maze of back street bazaars.

No one it seemed had seen a white boy unattended.

In due course the wayward absconder was located inside the orchestra pit of the Teatro de Amazonas, having no idea of the trouble he'd caused.

From the first moment the boy had stood side by side with the others gazing up spellbound into the soaring cupola, time seemed to stand still. He was captured by the originality of the artist in choosing such an unusual viewpoint of the Eiffel Tower from directly below. Of all the photographs and paintings he'd seen of this famous Parisian landmark, the cupola of the Opera House revealed a very different perspective, appearing to place the viewer at ground level between the tower's four massive cast-iron legs. He could almost imagine the excitement of riding its fancy elevator all the way to the top and looking out over the City of Love. Having spent time alone wandering the upper passageways and balconies the boy concluded that the building was certainly overwhelming, but perhaps a little gaudy; like being inside of a giant birthday cake.

Suddenly, he was torn from his daydream by the sound of approaching footsteps. Alois was flushed and fuming, pausing just long enough to hiss a reprimand and grind a fistful of knuckles into the soft deltoid muscle of the boy's arm. He then gripped his ear savagely and marched him down the sweeping marble staircase into a hooting mob gathered about the forecourt mosaics. There, smothered by Mam's tearful embraces, the shaken boy attempted to brush off outward signs of guilt and embarrassment.

In fact, he spoke nothing of Father's rough handling until the next day, when safely aboard *Madeira Belle* for the final upstream leg. Assembled beside one of *Belle*'s rumbling side-wheels, the passengers were informed by Captain Streicher that the next ten days would be the most enjoyable of their whole trip thus far but most were unconvinced; one or two applauded half-heartedly.

Kitty, by now much restored and relieved, when shown Klaus' bruised shoulder and swollen ear lobe, brushed the whole incident aside as "making a mountain out of a molehill". It was no good trying to blame his father for his own foolishness, she scolded; after all, hadn't he promised to keep up with the group? He was lucky not to have received a sound thrashing from the grown-ups whose day ashore was ruined.

But the boy had seen another side to his father that he didn't like at all, one he feared. That single clandestine act of violence had pushed both brothers into the same camp. For the remainder of the voyage, they agreed to spend as little time as necessary anywhere near the old man.

As the thunder of *Madeira Belle*'s great paddles churned the surface into life, Robert sprinted nimbly up to the wheelhouse and farewelled *Ladybird* at the top of his lungs as they passed, "See ya later Captain Dribblesnot; ha-ha, I hope not," while his little brother remained sniggering below.

Ladybird's first mate returned a stiff finger as the tiny riverboat slid past beneath her towering bridge.

For one whole week, the youngster kept to himself, out of the fierce sun and under cover in the shady bow, enthralled by passing flocks of colourful parrots and other wildlife emerging from the green drapes of the jungle on either bank.

For the first time in many weeks he found little time to thumb the familiar assortment of picture books he'd so carefully squirrelled away in his luggage.

Robert, as usual, endeared himself to the crew by running errands and performing Irish ditties when the workday ended. With his distinct, warbling vocals and animated gestures, he quickly won over the assortment of rough-and-ready types under Captain Streicher's command; even more so when daring to down a swig or two of their throat-scorching home brew under the cover of darkness.

His libertine routine went mainly unnoticed by his preoccupied parents, who fancied the boy stuck in a corner playing tin soldiers, or sulking alone in his cabin. Kitty had her hands full as it was, trying to get a word in edgewise past the flurry of instructions being heaped upon her by her new spouse.

But Klaus knew his brother better. Upon hearing the bawdy repertoire of riverboat songs which he was memorising, a "fricken this and fricken that" in broken Portuguese with an Irish accent began creeping into Robert's vocabulary. As aboard *Ladybird*, his experiments with "grown-up" language reduced the river boat's crew to side-slapping mirth.

At first, he only dared mutter new words under his breath; then loudly enough to distract and disgust some of the female passengers. All this unfolded as his new "Vati" was attempting to enlighten the boys with examples of Aryan superiority throughout history.

Following endless weeks afloat, the sprawling settlement of Santa Luzia del Oro moved slowly into view. At last, a place to start over, where Frau Hahn could surely earn forgiveness in service to these poor ignorant savages and raise her two goosens in a more natural environment. As *Madeira Belle* rounded the great bend and drew near the floating docks, a waft of dank moist air rolled out to envelope the new arrivals.

"Holy Mother o' God," Kitty exclaimed, pursing her lips to apply a dab of lippy and crossing herself absent-mindedly. Just the thought of trying to survive or work in this heat was too much. The closer they came the worse it looked, even worse than the dark and deadly slums she'd left behind.

"What ha' a' got meself inta?" she added softly with a mouth suddenly gone dry. Yet deep down she knew she had no option but to make a go of it, being both unwilling and unable ever to face the rigours of a return voyage.

15

The Irish trio held hands tightly as they followed Alois down the gangplank into a forest of necks straining to catch a glimpse of the new unter-manager and his family.

They were surprised to discover the bustling docks were much more exciting and welcoming than had initially appeared, being soon surrounded by friendly faces of myriad hues and cries.

Alois and his welcoming party surged ahead to board an old yellow bus with its windows painted over. Meanwhile, amidst much chatter, Frau Hahn and her boys were greeted and ushered through the merry rabble by a chocolate-skinned coachman wearing partial livery, who helped them into an ancient upholstered dray drawn by two bony mules tethered in the shade.

The whole scene, Kitty thought, looked straight out of *Adventures of Huckleberry Finn*, or was it *Uncle Tom's Cabin*? Two of the few books she'd ever read for pleasure. Her shrewd eyes darted between the flushed faces of her bairns and the unfamiliar landscape. Then, with a crack of the whip they were off, and the cart turned into a broad boulevard lined with spreading Jacaranda trees, at the far end of which stood Holy Cross Monastery perched on the only knob of high ground for miles around.

Two campanile towers (one of which had had its bell lost overboard en route from Portugal in rough weather) with flaking, pinkish-coloured adobe walls flanked a pair of elaborate wrought iron gates blocking access to the cloistered complex beyond. Through the bars could be seen a colonnaded walkway enclosing a narrow courtyard on three sides, at the far end of which rose the freshly whitewashed walls, almost blinding to the eye, of a proud chapel, appearing just large enough, Kitty guessed, to seat about a hundred worshippers.

Their coachman proudly pointed out in broken English that Holy Cross was the last remaining Christian Brothers Mission for hundreds of miles, boasting living quarters for twenty monks and novices. Several airy classrooms and a Charity Hospice staffed by Father Malone and his volunteers occupied a separate building to one side. Surrounding the Monastery and contained within a crumbling outer wall, now overgrown, sprawled a shady garden in which cowled figures sat reading aloud to small groups of Indian children sitting cross-legged on the ground.

The heart of the nurse's aide jumped for joy. Long before exposure to Alois' imprecations or noting the Red Cross daubed above the hospice door, Kitty had already planned on making herself useful. From her first glimpse of the bell towers from *Madeira Belle* she had felt the pull and energy of the place; perhaps the all-embracing aura of Saint Luzia herself, an eternal symbol of self-sacrifice, was reaching out to calm her tangled thoughts? She was sure of it.

"Whoa there, my lop-ear beauties," the driver pulled on the reins to allow a full appreciation of the huge Ibutu wood cross, covered in a white mosaic that reared above all. "Biggest Crucifix anywhere along the river," he said proudly. "When lit up on Sunday nights and special occasions, our Holy Cross is visible from all corners of the parish; as far away even as settlements on the far bank," he waved his arm expansively over the brown current.

"I hope we can see it from our house," Frau Hahn whispered to her boys.

Further on they passed the imposing shell of the Opera House, with its web of bamboo scaffolding and corrugated iron sheeting tacked onto a façade of marble columns.

Their glistening guide again took pride in relating a from Santa Luzia's glorious past, how circumstances had conspired to prevent the completion of her grandest building.

"Despite the stage mechanism remaining intact, nowadays it is used mainly for silent movie screenings and occasional travelling concerts in the Folkloric style," he informed the wide-eyed newcomers, hinting that "Grand Ol' Lady Opera" may one day return when funds became available. "When rubber prices recover, that is …" he said with a faraway look in his eyes as he lit up a foul-smelling cigar.

Small gatherings of semi-naked mulattos and full-bloods, mostly wearing odd scraps of cast-off western clothing, loitered on the steps beneath the soaring portico, while chattering womenfolk tended an array of market stalls spilling all the way back down to Main Wharf.

Frau Hahn crossed herself again and noted that such wild-looking characters would need to be kept at arm's length from her precious goosens. Niggling in the back of her mind was Alois' grandiose plan to resurrect the district's rubber trade – on the side, of course – which she hoped would not distract from, or even nobble altogether the prospects of her family. "If it is all that easy," she wondered, "how come none of the other Rubber Barons had been able to make a go of it on plantations of their own?"

Faith alone would be her sword and shield; surely, life here couldn't be as tough as it was in County Galway. When the chips were down she was still one resourceful little puck bunny used to getting by on a wing and a prayer.

"Whoa thar ... home sweet home, at last," cried the coachman as the drooping mules plodded to a standstill before an overgrown, once glorious homestead he called the "Fazenda".

Was *this* the "Palace" promised by Alois? A pile of tangled vines inside a fenced compound from which protruded a lopsided weatherboard porch?

Gingerly, Frau Hahn lowered herself to the ground and dusted her hands on her apron. Her boys were off in a flash, running free and whooping like wild things. Taking stock, she noted a separate kitchen area tacked onto the main building via a rickety boardwalk. Peeping inside. she saw a huge wood-burning stove standing heavy with dust and cobwebs in the corner; obviously, it had not been lit for years owing to the oppressive temperatures.

She realised with a shudder that their new home was little more than a gated compound resembling a huge prison yard, nothing at all like the free and open lifestyle she'd been promised.

"To keep good worker in and bad Indian out," the driver volunteered helpfully, noting her furrowed brow.

Like it or not and given half a chance she would make it a place of their own, a home to be proud of. With loads of fresh air and God's House nearby she dared to hope that both her precious bairns would grab the opportunity to grow up straight and true on the path of righteousness.

And being part of the unter-manager's household, she would insist upon them always dressing smartly and for the first time ever, wearing closed-in shoes. Between her long bouts of seasickness, Nurse Kitty had read all about the dreaded Chagas and hookworms that could burrow in through the soles of the feet and break down the most robust of bodies. She'd been staggered to read of a hundred other potentially fatal infections waiting to pounce, fly or creep out of the jungle.

Before sailing, she'd wisely purloined a near-new copy of *Nurses and Everyman's Guide to Tropical Diseases* from the Hospital Library by tucking it down her blouse. "I'll be needin' it a lot more than they do," she confided to her workmates while preparing for the great unknown.

Alois' telegrammed Proposal of Marriage had been precise: exactly 20 kg maximum of luggage for each person, including books, toys, *and* the heirloom altarpiece and Walrus Ivory candle sticks she'd been able to squeeze into the centre compartment of her suitcase between her "good clothes" and clean uniforms. A tiny leather satchel containing precious photos, documents and toiletries comprised the remainder of Kitty's worldly wealth.

"Everything else will be taken care of by Hahn Enterprises," her new man had trumpeted from afar.

Years later, these repressed memories of the upheaval stirred mainly regret; that is, when she gave them any thought at all.

It seemed almost as if life before Santa Luzia had been lived entirely by a stranger in a dream. She tried her best to exist only for the moment, opening her heart to the plight of the local Indians, while simultaneously blocking out the whispers of the resident dowagers.

Further recriminations over Alois' new plantation weren't long in coming. His first, last and biggest-ever investment, using other peoples' savings, had spectacularly flopped and there was talk of legal action. His thousand thriving rubber trees had been smothered and stripped bare overnight by an onslaught of caterpillars.

Perhaps predictably, other tappers didn't have insecticide to spare, especially after having cautioned the newcomer that his trees were being planted too close together. The stooping hidalgo soon became a laughing stock, forced to tap further into the Company Pension Fund to pay his mounting debts.

After months of maintaining a "cheery" front, one single ray of sunshine had slowly and surely penetrated the dolorous void of Kitty's "marriage": Father Patrick Maloney, harried Abbot of Holy Cross Mission and, prior to the scandal that saw him booted out of Ireland altogether, a faithful and partially repentant servant of the Lord.

"Top 'o the mornin' to ya', me little Oirish Flar. Welcome to the ends o' the Oith. Just call me Father Paddy if yer please … Let's take a good hard look at yer," he had gushed on the pier, taking her careworn hands in his own and rocking back on his heels to gaze into her eyes. For long minutes they'd stood face to face on the docks, beaming and squeezing each other's hands till they hurt. Nearby, her two boys were poking sticks into a cage packed with spider monkeys.

The sprightly priest, though past his prime, had gussied up and preened his robes to make a good impression, even clipping the proud black hairs that poked from each nostril. Not for a moment could he have imagined that a kindred spirit could so unsettle his emotions with a single glance; he was finding it hard to conceal his rapture.

The addition of any skilled hand on the Charity Ward was cause enough for celebration, but to come across a "dinky-doi nurse's aide from der auld country" was surely manna from Heaven.

Kitty too was bowled over by that initial filial embrace, quite out of character she assumed, that nearly squeezed the breath clean out of a body.

"Tank der good Lard, me prayers ha bin answered at last. 'Tis little shart of a miracle to be sure. Welcome into the fold, me darlin' goil," he said with a wink.

The startled woman had crossed herself three times, did a little curtsy and recited her practised lines: "Oim here to serve Mudda Choich, Father, and Oil be doin' me best for de naked savages …"

"Faith an' Oi believe Yer, child, we'll make a great team togetha," he chuckled, putting her at ease.

During a subsequent tour of the Monastery, the two dyed-in-the-wool kinsmen found much in common over which to rejoice. In fact, Father Patrick quite swept her off her feet and filled her fading heart with hope. She'd never known any churchman to treat her so warmly or brush aside the usual protocols.

"We'll be seein' a good deal of each other from here on in, Miss Kitty, if Oi moight be so bold as to address yer in future boi der name on yer cap?"

She nodded agreeably.

"Gard's Mercy don't settle over our little Mission House as often as we'd like dese days …" he stammered, before appearing to run out of words.

Right from the start she'd been reminded that her "mail order spouse" was an irreligious protestant, vocal in his declaration of Father Malone as a "lost cause". The strutting scion immediately expressed disapproval over the Church "meddling" in his family affairs, smouldering away publicly behind a mask of civility.

Before leaving Germany, had not Grandvati Rudolph warned him of the ongoing power struggles between Church and State in Brazil or, more importantly, between the Church and Hahn Enterprises? To make matters worse, the eager priest soon slipped up in attempting to intercede between his new nurse and her domineering spouse. "I jus' couldna stand to see her being treated poorly by her hoosband like so much baggage," he declared. At the first occasion, Alois simply turned beetroot from the neck up but held his tongue.

Since interceding in several such exchanges between the newlyweds, the goodly priest began plotting one possible pathway out of the "sham marriage", working quietly to exploit the growing rifts. Slowly but surely he attempted to monopolise her own dear body and soul for God's Charity Mission on the hill, now overflowing with desperate paupers unable to pay.

From the first moment, Father Paddy found himself stuck in God's forgotten corner, his mission was clear, and now that his prayers had been finally answered he planned on easing Nurse's Aide O'Shea away from her unhappy home life and into his own pet project; hopefully without putting her off altogether.

Yet, despite all his conniving, Kitty's initial deference soon gave way to vague feelings of discomfort. She considered the old priest to be overstepping the line with his flowery compliments and casual brushing against her bare skin while pretending to administer a blessing, sometimes under the very nose of the unter-manager. She would blush involuntarily when he leaned unnecessarily close to whisper trifles while on duty in the ward. She had no idea how to respond to these not-so-subtle displays of affection within sight of others, but deep down she suspected it was not only wrong but a cunning temptation from Satan himself.

Then, almost inevitably, he really went too far and confirmed her growing fears. He let slip that "for the first time he could remember he'd come to know troo luv, rather than joost lust".

"Don't talk such rot! Yer know I'm a married woman," she had reacted sharply, brushing off his lonely hands. Neither spoke again for the remainder of that shift.

Despite the shock Kathleen could not avoid being flattered, though it had never occurred to her to betray her marriage vows; that was, until one Sunday following Mass when Father Patrick drew himself up to his full height beneath the stained glass window to announce that there may well be a way out of her "dilemma", perhaps a path acceptable to God and Man alike. "I believe it's a sure path to happiness," he intoned, "free from Eternal Damnation!"

He paused to let his words sink in, knowing her emotions were vulnerable.

"Try ta remember dis, me little Shamrock; yer not *properly* married in the ois o' de Holy Roman Choich, accordin' to my reasonin'," he winked again conspiratorially and tapped the side of his nose, seeming sure of himself.

From then on Kitty's thoughts began to waver between hope and guilt, with guilt predominating during prayer and attempted absolution.

Twice daily, at morning time and end of shift, she knelt with a pounding heart before her makeshift altar to ask her missing bairn be kept safe in God's arms and to give thanks to the Holy Mother for leading her out of loneliness and beside the still waters of a truly understanding colleague. The grieving woman found it easier to forget her loss by immersing herself in the dirtiest and toughest jobs in a ward beset by baffling ailments.

"I guess when all's said and done things ain't that much different to back home," she finally confessed to Father one evening as they sat together on a garden bench, exhausted, "... except for the lack of medicines."

"At least here de poor buggers don't freeze ta death in the corridars."

These little quips lightened Father Paddy's load during his gruelling 16-hour days, but no amount of banter or distraction could fill Kitty's empty void.

Her precious baby was surely gone, yet for months afterwards she doggedly refused to give up hope; at least until his remains or some other proof was located. Fully half her joy and manna had been cruelly snatched away and in the end, she had no one to blame but herself for letting him go.

Meanwhile, ever since the ill-fated voyage upriver, for which Robert had also been held partly responsible, her firstborn goosen, the first ever to suck her paps and crown her emerging womanhood, now compounded her loss by shrugging off all further pretence of obeying instructions.

He went on his own merry way relying upon his mother's protection in times of trouble. In that same spirit, she was obliged to extend an unlimited indulgence to his half-truths and caprices. *Just let it go over your head, dear,* she told herself in growing despair, choosing to concentrate on his fine healthy body, winning smile and crown of soft blond curls. Surely, his keen intelligence would seek out more mannerly methods of behaviour as he matured? Luckily, few Santa Luzians seemed to know what "fricken" meant.

Alois had tried to warn her what the boy was up to, that he was, in fact, "trying to put it all over her and everyone else". He often emphasised his points by poking a forefinger into her chest.

But deep down Mam suspected that Robbie's waywardness was in fact only right and proper retribution for her past sins and omissions, the consequences of which she accepted would dog her to the end of days. When overtired she felt detached from the harsh reality of the hospice surroundings and the back-breaking effort required to keep on top of the workload; it was like watching herself going through the motions from afar, much like how a frog eyes off an approaching snake, indifferent to the looming danger.

One thing, however, she did know: while her remaining bairn continued to struggle through a rough patch his Mam wasn't going to turn her back on him, now or ever, no matter how much hot water he got himself into.

On other occasions, she could imagine that the Blessed Virgin had forgiven her entirely, and those thoughts made light work of the daily grind.

At the commencement of each shift, Father Patrick would lead a prayer session for the soul of her departed bairn, and not a day passed when she didn't shed a wee tear or two in his memory. It was simply inconceivable that the search parties had turned up nothing and that a white boy could just be swallowed up without a trace, wild animals notwithstanding.

Her twinkling eyes now bore crows' feet at their corners, a sure sign of dashed hopes in a woman. Some days she even doubted whether God existed at all.

16

For his first few delirious days of captivity, none but the girl and the old nun approached or even acknowledged the captive.

He was seized with apprehension at the constant throb of drumbeats rendering sleep impossible. From his stifling prison, he could sometimes observe the two of them in animated conversation with a gaggle of elders dominated by Chief Ticuna's feathered headdress and loud counter-declamations from Xina and his henchmen. When at last the tempo calmed down they came hurrying back to his bedside. For the time being Klaus would be allocated a hammock at one end of the large thatched Women's Maloca, surrounded by a handful of other boys about his age. He would soon learn from their fearful expressions and whispered conversations that they were being prepared for some kind of initiation ceremony.

Twice each day after mealtimes, he was allowed to leave the building under escort and approach the edge of the Plaza where a fresh banana leaf parcel was laid out on a stone slab. This usually contained a side of dried catfish and assorted ripe fruits wrapped in manioc pancakes.

Fresh water sprang from the mouths of gargoyles on a hillside nearby, before draining through a series of irrigation canals into the main Igarapé that emptied into Devil's Throat. After eating in silence he was free to stroll for a short time through the village, with all except elders and warriors lowering their eyes when he passed. On the third day, he was joined by Maya, breathless at her first chance to slip away from her sacred duties tending Sister Klara. She found him standing in the Plaza before one of the towering stone steles. On all sides, more broken statues lay scattered in fragments on the flagstones.

Upon closer inspection, many of these reliefs depicted fierce scenes of antediluvian conquest, interspersed with obscure patterns, signs and symbols that had him scratching his head. Almost the whole paved area was woven over with an umbrageous treetop garland that served to conceal any sign of human activity below.

Haltingly, Maya attempted to explain some of the strange moss-filled symbols chiselled into the lava-stone blocks. Above each of the battle scenes, a dominant semi-circle represented the Sun with its long beams radiating downward to become tiny cupped hands. From the weathered stele bases, three figures reached up hungrily to receive the life-giving rays.

A tattooed chieftain in the centre wearing a full-feathered headdress was flanked by a masked witch doctor and a warrior with the lizard head of Atua. One feature of the ancient inhabitants stood out in every scene: their huge jutting noses were far more prominent than any he'd seen among the Mojo.

What could this mean? Were the ancestors so very different, after all?

Other reliefs showed shamans holding aloft the spurting hearts of conquered victims, while lines of sullen shackled captives awaited their turn on the sacrificial stone. The boy shuddered.

Most perplexing, Maya confided, were the apparently visored heads and coats of arms belonging to two mediaeval Knights, whose origins were a complete mystery. Even Sister Klara, with her grasp of Indian history, was unsure of their provenance, convinced that the Sun City's abandonment pre-dated by far the arrival of the murderous Spanish.

From a waist-high, domed sacrificial stone nearby, gouts of dark lichen resembling black blood the boy thought, had somehow survived as downward drools forming puddles of moss on the flagstones below. This could be the very spot, he realised, where the ghastly rituals depicted above had transpired.

Furthermore, the unmistakable motifs served as sharp reminders of his precarious position: he knew that the Mojo had once been cannibals and that the Shamans were pressing for a return to the old ways.

Unlike the Women's Lodge, where baskets of fresh fruit hung within easy reach, the Shamans' Maloca was set apart on the outskirts and adorned with a necklace of shrivelled grey muscles strung together above the doorway.

In shock, he heard Maya point out that these were in fact human hearts guaranteeing immunity from a surprise attack and only recently being returned to pride of place outside Xina's refurbished armoury of charms and potions.

It seemed that each kneeling Shaman had his own special chant when summoning Curupuri from the depths after dark, apparently receiving instructions in a strange tongue understood only by him, so long as Xina was consulted on matters of life and death.

Behind the pillars of a once mighty Temple, Klaus came across the daunting entrance to the lava tube known as Devil's Gullet, partly concealed beneath a crust of buckled magma and tangled tree roots. Into this black hole the fast flowing Igarapé waters disappeared with a sigh.

Hard by, an overgrown quarry indicated the probable site from which the huge stele and stone building blocks for the city had been hacked with enormous effort; using slave labour he guessed. Dominating all else, a crumbling Ziggurat of seven terraces poked its flaking skin of pumice above the jungle canopy.

Yet, it was the mouth of the great lava tube, from whose depths sweet music flowed during dawn's golden gleam that had first pricked Klaus' ears and fired up his curiosity.

At certain times the mountain torrent was diverted away from the Devil's Gullet and over the waterfall, allowing safe return for hunting parties from the floodplains below.

At first light each morning, tattooed warriors brandishing spears manned the tunnel entrance, permitting only Sister Klara in full regalia with her group of vestals in simple cotton smocks to freely enter and descend. Other times, the swift-flowing Igarapé was sent plunging into the black hole via an ingenious sluice gate system that could render its entire length an impassable death trap.

Klaus was desperate to join in the morning tutelage and to learn more, but so far Maya had remained unresponsive to his badgering.

"Sister Klara say Klaus see Rainbow Cave soon," she informed him one afternoon when appearing noiselessly by his side. He had been mooching around the upper terraces of the Pyramid for any possibility of escape. From this vantage point, he could overlook the gaping mouth below and weigh up his chances. "Sister sing out Sun God down there e'ry mornin'," she added in a mixture of Pidgin and Portuguese that had lifted markedly in just a week or so.

Putting a finger to his lips Maya bent low and pulled aside a concealing bush, revealing a narrow niche some yards long terminating in a vertical shaft barely wide enough to allow passage for a single person. She motioned him to follow and took his hand until he grew accustomed to the darkness. She touched her own lips for silence and nimbly ascended the set of corbelled toeholds in the air shaft.

Diverting his eyes from the void below Klaus followed blindly; hand over hand, straining every tendon to emerge inside a tiny square cell situated directly beneath the great capstone. Squatting to catch his breath, he noted a thin light entering through openings in each of its four sombre walls, allowing patches of soft cyan to splash on the flagstones at his feet.

Somehow the strange silence pained his ears. He needed to hear Maya's reassuring voice. The air was filled with a sweet, musty odour. Something in that gloom made him feel uneasy, as if being watched.

Now she was fondling a small round object removed from atop a surrounding lintel, softly humming to herself. Dozens of similar coconut-size objects, some hirsute and others smooth adorned with faded tattoos, came dimly into focus as his eyes adjusted.

Reaching out he took the thing from her revering fingers and recoiled sharply.

It was a tiny human head, neither male nor female and not much bigger than his fist, perfectly preserved with the mouth and hollow eyelids sewn shut. Instinctively he wanted to hurl it from him, but its strange peaceful expression belied the horror of its final moments. He stroked the glossy blue hair, feeling both spooked and moved to be holding an entire human life story in his own hands.

"Xina say enemy warrior heads keep away evil spirits. Eating enemy hearts please Curupuri and protect Mojo from white man magic. Xina want to bring back old gods," she whispered, gently returning the decorated trophy with its long lashes to its permanent home. Despite his initial jolt, the boy felt that this was surely a special moment, a demonstration of her trust.

Reaching out she placed a second swarthy sconce into his reluctant hands. The distinctive ponytail hairstyle cried out for a name, having been worn by only one man he knew. In growing dismay he turned it to the light; there was no mistaking the yellowing tattoos of Sergio the Swift.

"This one new one, this one Mojo enemy, kill many Indian," Maya confided solemnly before returning Sergio to his lintel and turning back to stare at her friend for a full minute. He remained in shock.

Suddenly, she tossed back her hair with a mischievous grin and gave a little laugh. "Xina want Klaus curls. Shamans want Klaus' head for Sun Temple."

He swallowed hard but could think of no suitable response.

Once back on level ground things felt more normal.

Maya revealed that a big dancing ceremony was planned for in two days' time, a Sunday according to Sister Klara, when the boy would be formally inducted into the tribe.

Thus far the Shamans had not been able to shake Chief Ticuna from his stated path of mercy or pry him away from the gratitude he felt he owed Atua's guardian angel and her liberating message. None could deny it was Sister Klara who single-handedly had stirred the breezes of rebirth in the lost soul of the tribal people.

From the day she'd fallen foul of the Holy Cross and removed her meagre chest of chattels to the Indian village, the blasphemous mystic further shocked the City Fathers by encouraging the Mojo to be done with the white man's ways and rediscover their neglected traditions.

"From now on," she informed them from day one, "you will live once more in harmony with the Great Father-Mother God, and with each other. The children will be taught by lofty tales of love and self-discovery."

Suddenly gone from the Monastery was that smouldering resentment her embrace of Indian lore and custom had stirred up among the monks. They were here to convert the heathens, not the other way 'round. She would surely feel God's wrath for her disobedience, they warned her.

Soon after, the whole tribe just up and vanished without a trace.

A dark lethargy descended over the curriculum, and whispers of voodoo and black magic persisted. But generally, it was good riddance to the lot of them.

17

As the weeks passed, the new friends met often atop the Sun Temple's crumbling inclines, where bit by tortuous sentence a lachrymose Maya shared her tragic tale.

Beneath searing sunsets and the silvery night sky, the pair drew ever closer as she relived the details of her grim confinement following the treehouse assault. And long terrible months they were, having to deny her instincts while awaiting the birth of her condemned half-caste bastard. Almost incoherent at times, she recounted how Xina had snatched the newborn from her breast and flung it into Devil's Gullet in a failed attempt to call forth Curupuri. And all without a protest from any voice but Chief Ticuna and his ancient Apostle of Peace, and even she had been blindsided by what unfolded so quickly.

There and then Sister Klara took up the terrified girl as her personal ward and Colombe, promising to protect her for as long as she lived.

Sobbing softly, Maya went on to reveal how, unable to face the looming repercussions she had in despair tried deflecting blame onto Boto, the Pink River Dolphin, a most unlikely culprit who often took the rap for unexplained pregnancies among the river Tribes; but of course, everyone knew how it happened and that ploy fell flat.

There was no escaping the fact or magnitude of what had occurred with the chief's only daughter, or who was to blame: she had been defiled irrevocably by a rabble of impure clods.

She pointed to the growling cavity half hidden by its overhang of fig buttresses, revealing that the Shamans would have thrown her in too if she hadn't been the chief's daughter living under Sister Klara's roof since the first swelling became evident. Every tribe knew well the heartache to be endured when raising mixed-race children, especially those resulting from unwanted advances or worse still, rape. Such unfortunates were usually shunned or killed by an otherwise tolerant society.

That Klaus' own brother could have instigated such misery against this gentle creature was simply unforgivable.

Consumed by grief at the birth and its aftermath, Maya confessed to him that there had been many times when she wished they had indeed tossed her in after her helpless babe. Not one of the Indian boys would so much as look at her now.

She had had to accept that even a chief's daughter was taboo for marriage following such public disgrace. Behind her eyes, Klaus glimpsed a lingering despair, until she brightened visibly when he took her hand during the descent and held it tightly as they crossed the Plaza together.

Once again she disappeared as silently as she'd come, leaving him standing perplexed in the doorway of the Women's Maloca. At such moments the world itself seemed warped in time and meaning. On all sides stretched the ancient weathered ruins beneath their canopy of jungle, prompting him to imagine this very scene long before the present occupants took over.

He knew something of Olmecs, Mayans and Incas in those times of high Indian civilisations from his history books. Nonetheless, the new Wave appeared content occupying humble huts in between the overgrown masonry: still a far cry and a big improvement from the squalid slum they'd left behind.

He even found time to admire Sister Klara's single-minded vision of relocating the entire Indian community after decades of European exploitation.

How on Earth did she know of such a place? Was this really the fulfilment of Chief Ticuna's dream? Was this indeed Atua's Earthly disciple?

Now at last he had some answers to the speculation rife in Santa Luzia following her sudden disappearance, and the whole damn tribe gone with her in the end. Maybe it *was* witchcraft like they said?

But for that unforeseen upheaval, he would probably not now be alive and Sergio dead.

Come Sunday morning, as foreshadowed, fifty painted braves looking determined and healthy, broke from their Sun Dance in the Plaza to come rocking in fearsome ranks towards the place where Klaus sat waiting anxiously.

Stopping just yards away they swayed from side to side, stomping calloused feet in time to the throbbing drumbeats. "Ura! Ura! Ura!" chanted Xina, his war cry picked up and amplified by the others; the astonished boy thought he caught sight of women and children giggling in the distance.

The braves and Shamans were clearly trying to unnerve him and test his courage to the point where he wasn't enjoying the initiation at all, especially when forced to prostrate himself before Chief Ticuna and Xina while both spat several times into his hair. This phase concluded embarrassingly with tribal elders of both sexes closing in once more to rub him down from head to foot with pungent red Urucurum paste. A long line of single girls took the opportunity to pass by and slap him heartily on the buttocks with open palms.

The whole procession then let forth a piercing shout and swept up the initiate for a snake dance through the village. Panting excitedly he enlisted the pulsing rhythms and stamped his tender feet in time to the drumbeat and accompanying melody of reed flutes. Between curling buttresses and thatched walls wound the human serpent, then twice around the base of the Sun Temple, before all collapsed in a raucous heap in front of a sizzling peccary on the main campfire. For the first time since being captured, Klaus wished for a camera, any camera, to record the thrilling assembly of tough tattooed hides and bright toucan feather embellishments. The old nun replied laconically that some things "are better felt than telt".

Following this short break, the menfolk launched once more into their stamping war-like display, making the ground shake as they passed. Nearby, a group of newly initiated boys with porcupine quills inserted through their tender septa, cheeks and lower lips, found cheering a tricky business. Given this "traditional welcome", the white boy would be permitted to take a turn on the ceremonial pipe as it passed between the elders and the group of freshly circumcised youths.

"You too will receive the Yopo, but first you must drink this," said Sister Klara, leading him to the edge of the Plaza and handing over a small gourd of foul-tasting liquid. Within moments of drinking, he was overcome by nausea and vomited violently into the bushes, surprised to see several other boys about his own age undergoing the same ordeal. After washing his mouth out beneath a spouting stone gargoyle he was led back to take his place before the elders, assured by the abstaining nun that he was now properly purified to receive the Yopo pipe.

Calling for silence, Xina made a big show of producing a stone pestle, upon which he began grinding several flat brown beans extracted from boomerang-shaped pods he kept in a bag around his neck. He began chanting incantations heavenward while adding a sprinkle of campfire ash to the mixture.

"First, Xina takes Epena bark", his teacher explained. "He likes to think it opens up favourable channels between the old gods and those taking the Yopo pipe." With that, the Shaman tossed a pinch of brownish powder in the air, placed a bamboo pipe containing the remainder into his nostrils and inhaled sharply.

A long pause followed. The youngsters watched in awe as Xina dropped the pipe and allowed his arms to hang loosely by his sides. Then, suddenly, he leapt into the air with a shriek, his body arching back and forth violently for some minutes as if controlled by an unseen hand.

Gradually he steadied, raised his head and opened his eyes to fix them squarely on the boy. To Klaus, the Shamanic apparition seemed to rise off the ground and float toward him, clutching its decorated ceremonial club with the heavy head matted in hair and dried blood.

Again it contorted fearsomely and raised the terrible weapon above its head with both hands, invoking the spirit of Curupuri for permission to strike.

Instinctively, Klaus closed his eyes in terror and waited for the blow to fall. He would never see his Mam again. Would it hurt?

A great roar went up from the tribe: a roar of laughter!

His eyes flew open! Before him stood Xina, motionless, grinning from ear to ear in his sly, toothless way, proffering the bamboo pipe which he indicated the boy was to place into his own nostrils. With a racing heart and jellied legs, the initiate could barely grasp the magnitude of his reprieve, let alone follow instructions.

The warriors strained forward to scrutinise his reaction. Realising all eyes were upon him Klaus took the bifurcated bamboo implement and inserted one tube into each nostril, while the reddish powder was sprinkled into the far end of the pipe. He inhaled deeply which resulted in a violent coughing fit accompanied by howls of glee all around, before the pipe was snatched from his hands, refilled, and passed on.

Sister Klara had always stressed that the occasional use of "Jungle Potions" was more acceptable if the resultant experience could be conjoined with a worthwhile spiritual purpose rather than merely "sitting around all day staring at one's own navel." Some of the elders doing just that.

Initially, he felt nothing, until a surge of colour and sound enveloped his mind in a tingling glow. For the first time, he glimpsed himself in the future, as a strong and happy individual, no longer alone but a vital part of all Creation … "One tiny cog in the whole heaving Universe," as Sister had described it.

No more important than any other cog but certainly no less.

She cautioned him against the commonplace conception of seeking happiness in the hereafter, quoting Jesus that Paradise could be seen as nothing more or less than fostering harmony with one's own Inner Self, here and now.

Or, to put it another way: a constant striving for "Peace Profound" in all one's thoughts and actions, hardly practical given his present predicament.

The drumbeats rebounded off the grey retaining walls like the beating heart of infinity, but now he faced the way ahead with a glimpse of his own responsibilities in the wider scheme of things: if he could only feel like this every day he might yet make the most of what was to come. Somehow, this ribald ceremony had led him to the brink of atonement. His animal spirits had been aroused and he was hungry for life. He'd tasted that "Oneness" the old nun spoke of and could hardly wait for the Yopo pipe to come around again. For a time he felt his heart would burst with bonhomie for the whole tribe, including the Shamans.

Later, he learned that this "Truth" powder was usually rationed out by Xina for prayer and hunting parties, and by his learned teacher who sometimes allocated small doses to her pupils during certain ceremonies.

"Today you have glimpsed your future as a man: tomorrow you will join my lambs and commence your studies," she said when they were finally alone. "I trust you will find them rewarding. Your bravery in defending Maya has spared you the worst of Xina's scheming for now. Few earn a chance to unlock the Secrets of 'Knowing Themselves'." Her words now seemed to echo from afar.

"As above, so below," she continued, "the mind must triumph over the body's cravings and not be deceived by false idols ..."

But by now he was past caring. His head was fuzzy, and the euphoria was dimming.

"You will come to know the power of these higher Laws and be well placed to participate in Life's hidden mysteries; rather than simply becoming one more babbler ..." she droned on. "Or a clanging cymbal who thinks with his tongue: never forget that you have two ears and only one mouth ..."

Noting his lack of response she again fixed him with a questioning eye until he squirmed and looked away, feeling the need to throw up again.

He just wanted to be home with Mam, not hanging about here imbibing laws and lessons. There were moments when Robert's words rang in his ears: "All talk of religion was nothing but bullshit!"

For the remainder of that day and the 154 that followed his restless mind could neither quash nor conceive of any way down off those forbidding cliffs. However, he was getting ahead of himself with a Damoclean blade dangling above his guileless head and his adventures had scarcely begun. He had more unexpected setbacks to come, especially when faced with the Gloves of Happiness.

18

Since regaining his strength, Klaus' schooling began in earnest, commencing with the enigmatic hieroglyphs in the Plaza that had lain hidden for centuries. Carved into the stonework were scenes from village life at a time of great prosperity, before the coming of the white man.

Owing to their enduring dependence, the old folk had borne for decades a collective "Dark Night of the Soul" while clinging hopelessly to the squalid fringes of Santa Luzia: one by one the old legends had simply faded away. That was the time of forced resettlement and backbreaking labour in the mines, overshadowed by an array of crippling new diseases like smallpox and V.D. All talk of renewal had long since faded.

So may the dreary life of the tribe have continued, until Chief Ticuna, quite out of the blue, disclosed his prophetic dream: he assembled the tribe to divulge that Atua had not forsaken the Mojo. He had descended from heaven in the dead of night to sweep up their leader and reveal the long-lost homeland.

Enthralled, the elders drank in every syllable, begging him to reveal what else he had seen beyond the "Dragon's Teeth". Was this the fabled "Land of Streams" where the ancestors once roamed proud and free since time began? They gasped when he spoke of gripping tight the piebald plumage protruding through Atua's rindy ruff. No amount of tugging or pleading could deflect the great winged lizard from his chosen mission until, suddenly, with the wind whistling through his leathern wings, Atua had lashed his forked tail and commenced a slow-gliding descent toward what appeared to be ruins half-hidden in the tangle below.

The Chief told how he'd strained his eyes … there! … Overgrown terraces? … Part of a wall? Could this really be the Mojo lost city of the Sun? Surely, these were signs that the forefathers had indeed resided here. Perhaps their whole lost culture awaited his coming? He drew a contented breath through his proud nose, set his jaw and tightened his back muscles while examining the scene below.

Here and there the jungle thinned, and the blanket of green gave way to what could only be a network of overgrown thoroughfares crisscrossing the legendary fortress, where the mighty flying lizards were said to have once roosted in their thousands.

With a rasping hiss, Atua had wheeled lower, skimming the canopy on level wing above the tumbled rubble that stretched in all directions; clearly, this had once been a large city. A crumbling pyramid dominated one end of the paved though weed-choked Plaza. At the other stood a vine-encrusted portico and a partially collapsed roof of stone. Could this be Atua's Sun Temple so long spoken of by the elders? His heart leapt. Now there was no doubt that this indeed was the lost homeland of the Mojo; their city, *His City*! And almost close enough to touch.

As Atua slowly circled, Chief Ticuna searched in vain for a pathway up the sheer forbidding wall, for the sprawling complex sat a thousand feet or more above the valley floor. Except on Atua's broad back, no other access seemed possible. The gleaming black face appeared unscaleable, beyond the skills of man or beast.

Such was the conclusion of Chief Ticuna's first tantalising dream, which upon disclosure gradually elicited dark mutterings among the Shamans. To a man, they had been convinced that true liberation, if ever it did come, would be as a result of Curupuri's resurgence; not through Atua.

Days later, it seemed no coincidence when Chief Ticuna laid eyes on further confirmation of Atua's ascendancy. This appeared in the unexpected guise of Sister Klara performing her evening oblations for the first time in full view of the Indian camp. The true meaning of his midnight commute struck home like a war club.

There at the water's edge stood the old nun, alone, bedecked in full habit with arms akimbo, chanting her sacred petition in Latin to a levitating moon. Oblivious to his presence, she prayed earnestly for a miracle, and in that instant the final pieces of the puzzle came together in Chief Ticuna's mind. Oddly, it was neither her wailing nor her words that riveted his gaze. Rather, it was the distinctive plumage of her rarely seen vestments from behind, especially the black-and-white cape spanning head to toe. Spellbound, he saw her batlike wings catch the river breeze, enfolding the spotty globe. Surely, this was the signal he needed to act: it would be as foretold in his dream.

Further proof was not long in coming: a thin mist rolled in off the water to congeal around Sister's head as she prayed in what appeared to be the long-forgotten ancestral tongue. A voice boomed out from the swirling cloud, faster and faster the silver vapour whirled, at first enveloping her garments before lighting up the scene in a blinding light.

Then, with a barely audible "Amen", she vanished into the cloud.

Such a sight had never been seen in living memory as far as Chief Ticuna was concerned. He stumbled from behind a bush to the place where she'd been standing and fell on his face in supplication. "Great Atua, mighty Atua," he cried in anguish with sweat now beading on his brow, "you who created our mighty river and the jungle filled with life, you have returned at last to save your people." Here was *real* voodoo, greater than Xina's empty mouthings to his murderous Curupuri Totem. Sister Klara clearly held the key to future Mojo fortunes. Henceforth, the Shamans' bleating admonitions would be treated with the ill-concealed disdain they deserved.

Soon afterwards, he was astonished to find her in mufti, reading a story to a group of children beside the communal campfire, as if nothing untoward had happened. The indisputable supremacy of Atua's earthly messenger was now signed and sealed; he hesitated no longer in declaring to one and all that she was indeed their long-awaited Saviour, henceforth enjoying his full protection.

At this it became clear that Xina and his coterie were increasingly hostile towards the chief's far-fetched tale; they hastened to see for themselves the very spot where the second so-called miracle had taken place. Like the Holy Cross priesthood before him, Xina recognised the threat that this self-styled messiah posed to his own authority, with her direct appeals to the Almighty and her puzzling, healing hand. To a man, they were trebly frustrated that such exhibitionism could so readily undermine their own long-held customs, with all that talk of "throwing off the shackles of superstition" and suchlike. For now, their endorsement would remain in abeyance while they explored new ways to shore up their waning status.

However, Chief Ticuna had spoken and was himself all ears to Sister Klara's confident directives. She alone had taught him how to *more than dream*; how to offer truly effective prayers for Mojo resettlement:

> "Oh, God's Mighty Sun,
> Whose cleansing beams probe the whole world and all its secrets,
> We weep for our lost homeland
> Make clear your plans for my peoples' return …"

Now, with *His* backing, would not this divine message inspire each and every member of the tribe to seek his lost heritage and return to the ways of Great Atua? It was now or never, he warned the doubters.

Then came the second dream, in which the chief again scrambled nimbly onto the scaly back and clutched the piebald mane, to be whisked high above the treetops with his feathered headdress streaming behind.

Retracing their former course he savoured the whiff of freedom for his people: Atua's great beaked head swayed reassuringly as they soared up and over the weeping black escarpment to again circle the ruins. In vain, he strained his eyes for any sign of a path up the glistening wall, until suddenly, in a terrifying manoeuvre the huge creature folded its parchment wings and plummeted like a stone in behind the foaming waterfall, only to emerge moments later glistening like a Man o' War breaking free from a sudden squall.

Chief Ticuna told how clinging on for dear life, he had glimpsed behind the fury of tumbling spray what appeared to be a concealed tunnel. Below the line of cliffs created when the Earth was liquid fire, several gaping lava tubes perforated the mountain. Could this be a "Devil's Gullet" of Mojo folklore, the sole access to the lost world above?

Atua croaked and gave another mighty flap, wheeling down for a second time through the stinging spray. Sure enough, after lying hidden for centuries, the secret passageway so long denied the Indian and sought in vain by the white explorer beckoned ominously.

When awakening from this second dream, Chief Ticuna harboured no doubts as to the drastic actions required; he wasted no time preparing for the dangerous journey ahead. Mojo adults were sworn to secrecy and instructed to go about their business as usual. Standing side by side with Sister Klara he called for a pow-wow, commanding them to prepare weapons and put aside provisions for several days of hard cross-country travel. Rumours abounded, no one knew quite what to expect. Xina's faction went into a huddle, smelling a trap. At the very least, such secrecy appeared just one more ploy to thwart their own intentions. From the moment the tribe's absence was discovered, Chief Ticuna knew that the town population would rally together and spare no effort to round up their absconded labour force. The departure would need to be sudden and final if the Mojo were ever to be free of the white man's heavy hand.

Come Monday morning at 5 o'clock, Sergio the Swift, as he was waggishly known around town, strode toward the Indian village humming a popular tune, with his dog whip in hand. He often had to give one or two of the lazy buggers a good clout across the backside to get them moving.

Approaching the bamboo boardwalks he sensed something was amiss: no dogs barked and no children played in the mud. A lone mongrel slunk up to sniff his heels. He came to the huts and pushed open one door, then in growing dismay, another. Nothing. No one.

Suddenly alert, Sergio spun on his heels and ran toward the mine office, yelling at the top of his lungs for the siren to be sounded. Within minutes all Santa Luzia was abuzz: their pool of cheap labourers, gardeners, cleaners, cooks and housekeepers had been drained overnight, apparently into the flooded Varzea.

Daybreak found the Mojo pushing deep across the swamp-grass plains, strung out in a long line beside Grand Kaiser's purloined boundaries. Young and old alike struggled through the web of waterways, pressing forward with renewed purpose toward their promised destination.

No longer displaced "savages", they were once more a people united in determination to reclaim their sacred homeland which for decades past was known only as a purple smudge on the far horizon. Word rippled through the tribe: they were making for the place called "Dragon's Teeth", where white men rarely ventured and boiling steam was said to spurt from the very cliff face. Marching night and day without pause, Chief Ticuna called a halt before the forbidding black lava cliffs, allowing his exhausted followers time to gobble down their rations and await the coming of a second daybreak on the run.

Armed braves were posted in a defensive ring at the camp perimeter, in case the posse had picked up their trail. At dawn's first blush, the chief held high his firebrand and with a triumphal whoop led them on behind the great falls and into the mouth of the lava tube.

He commanded that the old woman be placed on a litter for the final ascent, bringing up the column rear with her own lighted torch. Up ahead he knew lay Atua's City, the birthplace of his people where Sister Klara had promised that peace, joy and freedom would forever dwell. It was all he could do to prevent himself from sprinting ahead over the slippery rocks.

However, within the first few hundred arduous yards a pall of gloom descended, thanks to Xina spreading fearsome tales of Curupuri's looming revenge. Perhaps the Shamans were right after all? This was nothing at all like the Promised Land. In addition to the fearful predictions, their feeble lights and pressing blackness concealed many slippery surfaces and hidden dangers, especially for those carrying litters and heavy loads. Any careless step brought pain. Squeaking cave bats rattled past their faces and on all sides the sulphurous walls wept putrid green and yellow tears at their slow progress. From the rear, Sister Klara shouted encouragement and called for patience and courage. "As the ancestors would wish!" she cried out. Occasionally, her bearers were forced to halt and pray for strength and guidance. Thus, the slip-sliding procession proceeded ever upward, through caverns of glittering crystal, past geysers of scalding steam.

Until, at last, a pinprick of daylight ahead. First Chief Ticuna, then two by two, the exhausted runaways spilled out through a tangle of tree roots into the life-giving sunlight; there before them lay a tumbled-down gateway of stone blocks, with more ruins beyond. Following his lead, all fell flat on their faces to repeat his prayer of thanksgiving: Atua had once again proven his supremacy!

All this and more had their supernal archangel delivered, a culmination of all Sister Klara's promises from her first day among them. She had appeared as both teacher and pupil, to share their pains and pleasures.

Then came the astonishing acts of healing with her sanative hands, so different from the overwrought medical procedures practised at Holy Cross, and a far cry indeed from Xina's pertinacious trawling through the entrails of dead chickens. Even sceptics came to fear and respect the old white woman's "Magic Fingers".

Miraculously, as foretold by Atua and Chief Ticuna, the venerable old heretic had led them back to the promised land.

19

"Sister Klara say Klaus jus' look, not speak in Rainbow Cave," Maya whispered as the pair began their pre-dawn descent into the gaping black hole.

As the boy stumbled along behind a dozen or so teenage girls wearing white smocks he recalled his friend's terrible tale of human sacrifice; she alone wore a simple sackcloth garment. The single file of ghostly firebrands threw menacing shadows on the walls that mocked him like omens and did little to allay his nerves. The humid air grew slowly more oppressive until the slope curved sharply upward and opened out to reveal a massive cavern encrusted with white crystals from floor to ceiling. On all sides and overhead, milk-hued selenite formations, ranging from fist-size to more than twice the height of a man, tumbled haphazardly over each other and glowed softly in the torchlight. To the astonished boy, it looked like the innards of the giant "Thunder Egg" in the mine laboratory collection that he'd once examined through a magnifying glass.

Though he vaguely recollected this place from that first terrible ascent, its limits now, as then, were beyond the range of their feeble firesticks. Amidst the rhomboidal chaos, he could glimpse pockets of amethyst and pink surrounding a black pool, a stone's throw across and of unknown depth. Rising from its dark heart was a single pillar of selenite capped with a perfect white pyramid some four feet square that seemed to float upon the meniscus.

Sister motioned to her "lambs", spacing them around the water's edge with Klaus sitting cross-legged beside her. He gulped a breath of the warm humid air that sent a tingle of anticipation down his spine. Each youngster was given a sniff of Yopo and the burning brands were quenched, allowing dawn's first glow to ripen through a fissure in the outer crust.

At the first pure ray of sun, the old nun rose slowly, stepped to the water's edge and dipped her tangled toes into a puddle of quicksilver. Then, stretching her arms akimbo she chanted three times into the pool, "Mmaaa – Ttthhh – Rraaa" … as one by one the white-robes took up the canticle in pitch and intensity until the whole chamber began to quiver. A chandelier of bright crystals crashed to the floor nearby.

Wide-eyed, he observed Aladdin's transmogrification of white crystals into sparkling diamantes that seemed to be scrambling over each other to get at the light. More astonishing was the pellucidation of the imposing pyramid now sparkling like a fresh-cut diamond. It appeared to be floating above a black void of tiny wavelets, scattering light in all directions. An audible sigh rose to greet the spectral coronet radiating from Sister Klara's piebald cowl to splash the children's foreheads as they sang, "Kayyeee, Kayyeee; Mmaaa, Thhh, Rraaa."

At first, the soulful intonations pulsated in thin waves soon swallowed by the vastness; but soon the entire chamber trembled with the swelling purity of their cords. The boy thought it sounded like a choir of angels.

Might the whole ceiling give way under such a riot of pure sound?

The humming continued and no one moved while the piercing beam traversed toward the glittering prism, before it too exploded in a chain reaction of rainbows.

For minutes Klaus witnessed the astonishing secret of the Rainbow Cave living up to its name: single formations and fragile crystal clusters danced together in the spectral panorama lighting the farthest reaches until, all too soon, the chanting faded and the gilding ray passed once more beyond the hidden cleft. Twilight's curtain was drawn for another day and the diamonds again became porcelain pillars.

When the echoes subsided there followed a sated silence, broken only by the sound of rhythmic breathing, in which by sign language the new pupil was encouraged to participate. His own breathing soon matched those nearby and his mind soared; was it the Yopo or the revelation, or both? Time stood still.

Sister Klara softly urged her charges to be aware of the Vital Life Forces flowing into their perfect bodies with every breath, nourishing every living cell; not to mention the additional health benefits that surely follow with the breathing of pure air.

For a moment Klaus wondered if the others even knew what a "Cell" was, let alone a "Vital Life Force". However, judging from the broad smile on every face they were immersed in a trance-like ecstasy of some kind.

Then, inexplicably, his puny chest filled to bursting with a surge of pure joy, and for a time all fear vanished. He wished this feeling could last forever.

When the firesticks were eventually rekindled, Sister concluded with a brief prayer to the "God of our hearts".

Purring softly, Maya helped him to his feet and led him back up the tube and into the glare of the Plaza, where for a moment he was forced to shield his eyes. Through his fingers, he noticed several braves levering the bamboo sluice gate across the life-giving Igarapé that bisected and nourished the settlement.

He looked hard at the forbidding entrance, only now grasping the purpose of this clever device capable of redirecting the flow away from the cliff edge and down into the lava tube. Unwanted intruders could be easily blind-sided, or if persistent, blown away in the roaring bowels of the earth.

Following the midday siesta, Sister Klara's chosen lambs would pull on their white smocks and prepare to learn more about their own dimming traditions. During her years in cloisters at Holy Cross, the disenchanted nun had meticulously recorded Mojo language and songs garnered from all known sources at the time.

Their ancient history now lived on in one precious, careworn volume that was rarely out of her sight. Most afternoons, between the tumbled masonry blocks in the shade, she tried hard to balance her message of "Peace Profound" with their need for boisterous and sometimes violent play. She laboured tirelessly and humorously to entwine her simple proverbs and spiritual exercises within their lost lifestyle.

Klaus learned more in a week than he'd learned in years at Holy Cross.

To celebrate the full moon, she encouraged the whole tribe to re-enact its traditions honouring Atua, the Great God, exempting only Xina and his shamans who begrudgingly sacrificed a chicken to Curupuri outside their lodge.

By now the boy had had his hair cut in the customary basin style and plastered down with the ground-up paste of Urucurum seeds. His head and torso thus adorned in reddish dye and harpy eagle fluff, he was regularly drawn, against his will, into the dancing circle where his ghostly appearance sparked great amusement among the younger girls.

Being a tribe of smooth-skins, they continually snuck up behind him and tweaked the hairs on his slender shanks. As he struggled to master their strange customs there were times when he felt as if Maya were treating him with the same impudent affection shown to the pet spider monkeys that scurried about the village seeking hand-outs. He laboured over the jumbled river dialects made up mainly of pidgin slang, Portuguese and a smattering of German.

During one memorable full moon ceremony and following the completion of the first dance bracket, he sat catching his breath before accepting a gourd of Papunya juice thrust into his hands.

"This one made from, how you say, Peach Palm?" Maya informed him. "Sap bubbles up in belly." For long minutes he had been watching the vessel of vile-smelling brew being passed around and consumed by all. Not wishing to appear ungrateful he forced himself to swallow a large mouthful of the tepid liquid and immediately regretted the decision. Foolishly he'd gulped the fermented palm sap too soon after his snort of the Yopo pipe, which was not customary or advisable.

In short order, the surrounding forest began to spin wildly and dissolve into coloured blobs. Had not Maya cautioned him about mixing potions and powders, even those imbibed by the Indians as remedies for hunger, thirst and fatigue since antiquity?

During these moon rituals, such substances were consumed for their pleasing hallucinogenic effects; potency became more pronounced after purging with a sip or two of Papunya juice.

But now it was too late for regrets; he staggered away alongside several other youths to vomit in the bushes, and soon after this unpleasant hiatus the liberating effects of the Yopo took over. Time slowed to a crawl and he felt grateful that these primitive people appeared to be accepting him as one of their own. Ever since Chief Ticuna had laid welcoming hands on him, the Shamans had been forced to back away from their initial hostility.

Grinning ear to ear, he ogled Maya conveying Sister Klara's instructions back and forth around the village; her unmistakeably lithe movements being quite distinct from the shuffling gait of the other Indian girls. Like them, her upper arms and torso had been tattooed with the juice of a common purple berry applied with a sharp thorn, but when pressed she explained that her traditional designs indicated the degree of spiritual attainments rather than sexual maturity. Sister Klara saw to that.

Klaus was greatly relieved to note her pretty face remained free of the large wooden lip plugs preferred by so many of the women and adolescent girls. These four-inch flapping encumbrances made speech and eating difficult but levelled the nuptial playing field by pronouncing the wearer as now ready for marriage, an estate from which Maya was already denied.

He noticed with dismay that the larger the lip plug the more excited became the pubescent boys, especially when both sexes danced together. Between lip plugs and Porcupine quills he wondered how romance ever progressed beyond the hand-holding stage with these people. Not even the Yopo could convince him to return their tortured smiles.

Each time Maya floated past wearing only her red-frilled apron and the gold crucifix around her neck, which Sister called her "Rosy Cross", he grinned more broadly. Surely, he had never seen a more beautiful creature or enjoyed a more perfect time in all his short life. Perhaps tribal life could be agreeable after all.

The reality, however, was never far away. Emerging from his reverie he began to struggle for breath. Could it be the mixing of potions or an allergic reaction to the spider monkey perched on his shoulder?

Within minutes the old healer spotted his discomfort and moved close to apply her magic fingers to his spine. Unlike Doc Wonder's adrenalin injections, Sister Klara's soothing cures came minus the violent heart palpitations, allowing her patient to remain lucid for the remainder of the festivities; or so he believed.

Several times he'd attempted to penetrate the mystery of her curative secrets, especially her laying on of hands that appeared so deceptively simple. Calling for silence, she had him sit cross-legged on the bare earth with eyes closed, before commencing her now familiar chant: "Mmmaaa – Ttthhh – Rrraaa" … at first barely audible and rising with each repetition.

The energy she called "Nous" was being delivered through her fingertips, directly into the vertebrae at the base of his skull. "Kayyeee, Kayyeee …"

Relief usually came within minutes, and today was no exception. He'd watched her treat fevers, headaches and open wounds; it was rumoured that even birthing pains could be avoided. Sometimes, her treatments culminated in a violent fit of vomiting by the patient, while the tribe looked on in awe.

Klaus was calm and confident again.

"Sister Klara teach us how to shine light through fingers," confided his friend one afternoon as they sat perilously close to the cliff edge, gazing toward the far-off sprinkle of rooftops and silver threads of the river in the distance.

He was always probing, hoping to glean a better understanding of the depth and extent of the old lady's mysterious methods being so freely imparted.

"Sister Klara want Klaus grow strong here," she said, patting his chest, "and wise in head. She say everyone has God in heart and teach us how to find."

This all sounded a bit airy-fairy when compared to Father Malone's sermons of brimstone and blarney that the boys felt were aimed squarely at their own shortcomings. But the evidence of his eyes could not be denied: it seemed hardly credible for adolescent minds to grasp the magnitude of Sister Klara's all-embracing God, let alone commune with Him directly.

This was a far cry indeed from Father Paddy's cramped confessional.

The boy's formerly flimsy faith had been upended almost from the first day he awoke in Sister's presence; she'd somehow banished his aches and pains and shortness of breath with the laying on of soft hands.

What other powers might be flowing through those wise old veins nudging the children relentlessly toward self-realisation?

Occasionally she was forced to intervene with Xina and his soothsayers, who protested to Chief Ticuna that a whole generation of Mojo teenagers were refusing to heed the omens revealed in the chicken gizzards. To a man, they complained that since Atua's rise they were losing face and influence ever since the white boy had been initiated.

Smarting at the chief's repeated brushing aside of their complaints, they resolved to rid themselves of the pale-faced interlopers once and for all.

20

Since witnessing the subterranean spectacle, Klaus was first in line with Maya for the predawn visits down Devil's Throat, eager to see and learn more of the mysterious manifestations.

"It may be too late for the adults," Sister Klara confided to him one morning as they picked their way through the crystal columns. "But not for my innocents. It is *never* too late for a miracle in a pure heart," she said loudly while looking back over her shoulder; and the spit went dry in his mouth.

As before, the semi-circle of white smocks was arranged beside the pool and the lesson commenced with a bracket of soft vowels. Gradually, the children joined in with their own sweet-swelling harmonies and again a discernible tremble shook the crystalline cavern. Unable to resist the dancing rainbows, the boy, too, hummed along with the vowel intonations, discovering an inner confidence he'd never known.

When the light show ended and the twilight returned, their teacher allowed more time for deep breathing, using a specific technique to "awaken the Master within".

She instructed them to close their eyes and imagine a tiny flame flickering in the very centre of their hearts, the beating of which, she assured them, could be readily apprehended with a little concentration. "Slowly you see the light growing brighter," she intoned, "until it becomes like a bright star reaching into every dark forgotten place ..."

If successful to this point, the children were urged to allow the light to burst forth from their chests and envelope the whole group in a golden cloud.

At least that was the theory!

In reality, most of her lambs considered the so-called parables mere amusing vignettes at best, only agreeing to pull on the white smock for the attendant pleasures of the dramatic light show in the Rainbow Cave and the feast that followed.

To the white boy, however, Sister Klara's sayings seemed more profound with each rendition. Her little mind games enabled him to enter a state she called "meditative" when he became of all concerns and the very cells of his body vibrated in perfect harmony with their surroundings. "Afflatus" was the word she used to describe his condition upon exiting the tunnel invigorated and inspired.

He was growing stronger by the day, eager to discern and identify the jungle's many sounds and fragrances. Though easily distracted, his keen intelligence spurred the old woman to persist with ideas and methods that cut through the fear and confusion he'd always felt over matters Divine.

"Treasure is seldom turned up in the first spadeful," she chuckled when he expressed frustration with his lack of progress in concentration exercises. Nonetheless, as he applied his mind to this "Oneness of all Creation" that she espoused, the more probable it appeared, as did his own distinct place within the vast celestial orbit. She described this condition as "Nestling under God's wing" which was rather comforting.

When wandering alone among the ruins, Klaus would attempt to plumb the intentions of his captors: it was all very well for his Guardian Angel to tell tales of tolerance and urge the children to heed an inner Master plucking at their heartstrings, but he now realised that these and her other impieties had not only soured the Monastery monks but increasingly alienated the Mojo Holy Men against further white meddling.

Only Xina the witch doctor could commune with the underworld and offer live animal sacrifices for Curupuri's return. The Shamans were losing the battle against a resurgent Atua and schemed for a way to implant more doubts in the hearts and minds of Sister Klara's burgeoning flock.

"The Indians have their gods in this world and the next," she responded when Klaus pointed out this clash of views. "It's almost like my own orthodox upbringing filled with fearsome bearded saints performing miracles in their own ways. Furthermore, I believe that all paths to knowledge are beautiful if beautifully pursued. And that rules out Xina's voodoo.

"Long ago I came to the realisation that much of the so-called Christian teachings to which I'd been exposed were almost in lockstep with those of the Shamans. They too rely more on fear than love to win and keep their converts, but such methods were no longer acceptable to me.

"From the time of the Pharaoh Akhenaten until our blessed Nazarene upended the money changers' tables, one eternal Truth has trickled down through the aeons: there can be but One Supreme Consciousness encompassing all there is and all there ever will be, an urgent Energy propelling the Life Force through all its sublime variations despite human greed and self-deception.

"Most people out there," said the teacher as she motioned toward the cliff edge, "are consumed by selfishness and ignorance, stumbling along without ever knowing what's truly important ... until it's too late.

"Mother Nature, God, Allah or the Almighty, whatever you choose to call Pleroma, it has gifted Humanity alone with 'Free Will'.

"And if countless millions of Hindus are to be believed, then also with infinite Time in which to seek out and perfect our purpose on Earth. Those who know this will surely be renewed in hope and courage to face whatever lies ahead." She gave a deep sigh and a soft blue haze enveloped her head.

"Everyone should be able to worship in the way he chooses, providing of course this does no harm to others. After all, we are praying to the Same God. I trust you will carry my words in your heart as a guiding light that no one can ever steal," she added warmly, "... even if you *do* forget them until the dark times come.

"Remember, I loff you and God loffs you."

Such talk only confused the boy, and as days turned into weeks his mentor secretly rejoiced at his readiness to practise the simple exercises and come to grips with the underlying Principles.

"The flame within is your guiding light known to no other; it alone can illuminate the path through all eternity. It may only be extinguished by your striking wrong choices."

He was confused; how could he remember even a fraction of all this? No one had ever spoken to him of such things as the divine connection between a single raindrop and the mighty river itself. Or indeed a "silver thread" linking all living things together.

"Don't get too big for your boots," she often reminded her eager pupil. "'Always there are greater and lesser beings than thou,' says the Great Tibetan Dalai Lama. We humans are little more than clever primates wearing fancy dress to hide our shame. Yes, living in crowded cities soon dispels any notions of Homo sapien superiority." The boy gulped again.

"Free Will!" she repeated emphatically. "Free Will stands as *the* single heavenly blessing that sets us apart from all other living creatures, including the primates. At best we are a few evolutionary steps ahead of howler monkeys and don't you forget it!" This was the first time she'd raised her voice. "... but Free Will is a two-edged sword for those with dark intentions."

So saying, she suppressed a quiver of her generous nose and widened her arms to embrace his dazed expression. Such was the tone Sister Klara took when he got ahead of himself. Between daily deluges, her lessons progressed beneath the ruins: "Remember to practise your deep breathing and exercise your vowels daily; otherwise the brain becomes constipated."

He soon realised that by following the simple methods she prescribed he could not only tame his asthma but occasionally enter into that elusive and ethereal state of mind she called "Afflatus". Once or twice in the early days, he thought he'd achieved it, but unwanted thoughts came rushing in to ruffle his short-lived tranquillity.

With practice, his constitution slowly ripened and his emotions took on a more empathetic bent. He no longer saw the jungle as a mere "green mass", but as one enormous living organism wearing a thousand robes and speaking countless tongues.

Neither Tante's books nor the Mission School had hinted at the true nature of things lying *below* the surface, beyond the obvious realities presented by the five senses so taken for granted. Maya seemed puzzled that her new friend had to be *taught* to look into the nature of things, to the place where most Indian children dwell instinctively.

"White man see only skin deep, all time want feel good even if hurt others," she added shyly, flashing her strong wide teeth.

Notwithstanding these worthwhile but apparently superfluous snippets of advice, Klaus could see little chance of ever putting them into practice given his current supernal shore comprised but a few square miles of overgrown jungle and jagged rocky outcrops, with occasional tantalising glimpses of a past life on the far horizon.

Furthermore, Sister confided that there was little chance of his ever being released to reveal their whereabouts and bring ruin down upon the tribe.

"B … But, I wouldn't tell anyone. I really wouldn't," he pleaded, and often. "Why are you teaching me all this stuff if you don't want me to go back out … out there with my own tribe?"

Sister Klara was firm. "This is your life now. True wisdom is not restricted to those in positions of authority. Wisdom and Truth carry their own rewards. Sincerity in your dealings with the natives offers as much opportunity for fulfilment as any pursuit in the outside world," she waved again at the cliff edge. Her narrowed eyes perused him closely and a wrinkle creased her brow.

"There are certain Eternal Laws and Values which once learned cannot be broken with impunity. For the time being, I am prepared to continue sharing them with you, if – and I must confess it's a big 'if' – you desist from your childish ways and demonstrate ongoing worthiness.

"My flock see me as some kind of Sorceress and follow blindly. You alone have the potential to lift your thoughts to the next level, to glimpse those Great Truths sought by so many and revealed to so few. Of one thing you may be certain: you are a vital part of all Creation, here but for a moment in time to share your light with the World.

"God alone knows your full measure and has given you all you will need for your journey."

Klaus sweated and prickled beneath his Urucurum jacket, and during further visits to the Rainbow Cave prayed earnestly to be freed from cowardly thoughts. Thus emboldened and embedded he decided to knuckle down and take each day as it came, surprising himself by going for long periods without even remembering that he was being held captive at all.

21

As the steam rose following the afternoon deluge, the youngsters would clamour up the Ziggurat and sit together by the apex, often holding hands without the need for words.

Once in a while the devoted girl would hum a lullaby in her own throaty dialect with a faraway look in her eyes. Some mornings the curtains of mist crept up languidly from the lowlands, cooling their faces and engulfing their vantage point in folds of soft spray.

Later in the day when the air was clear and the sun was at the right angle, he might even catch a sparkle from the great white Cross dominating the distant settlement. Torn by homesickness he would try to imagine his beloved Mam, "head down, bum up" slogging away in that cramped and stinking hospice. To what end? Private daily confessions and an occasional pat on the bottom from Father Malone. "If t'ings were different, Kitty, oi wouldn't be holdin' meself back … yer can be sure o' dat," and other oft-repeated sweet nothings he didn't think had been overheard. Would Mam have forgotten him already or given up on finding him alive? Would she be too busy to even miss him?

Both innocents could be seen choking back a tear when reliving a certain shared experience, and more than once Klaus was plunged into a dark place, feeling lost and alone for no apparent reason.

At other times Maya could lift his spirits in a flash by tossing back her blue-black hair and teasing with a wide grin just inches from his mouth. Still, he continued to resist her advances, mainly for fear of being found out, all the while struggling to suppress his own feelings beyond the holding of hands.

One evening at sunset they clamoured down from the crumbling terraces and bumped into an Indian hunting party emerging from the tunnel mouth.

Across the shoulders of the braves dangled a brace of lifeless squirrel monkeys and a three-toed sloth clinging to a bamboo pole, the latter gazing about impotently. Stern-faced shamans waved the hunters on, impatient to activate the spillway mechanism and once more flood the passage.

Surrounded, the boy's eye was caught by the dainty nodding faces of the spider monkeys, each fixed in wide-eyed disbelief at the sting of the dart that brought them down. Instinctively, he reached out to caress the dead hands with their tiny nails and fingerprints, perfectly evolved for a long and happy life in the treetops.

Suddenly, he was overcome by a welling anguish and something snapped inside: from his throat came a guttural howl and from his eyes tears streamed.

At first, the braves fell back in astonishment, before smacking him smartly across the shoulders with a blowpipe and raising their machetes menacingly in his face, now barely able to conceal their mirth at his obvious distress.

"Why? Oh why … of all the animals in the jungle? … Look at them. They're just like you and me …" At this, they roared with laughter.

"You really shouldn't be kill—" In a flash Maya saw the danger and intervened, steering him away from the ruckus towards cover in the Women's Maloca where no initiated man could follow.

But Klaus was unapologetic: even prior to Sister Klara's anthropomorphic analogy, he had not been able to stand the sight of monkeys being killed or to hear them sizzling and popping in the coals. Necessary protein or not, he could not rid himself of the belief that a single mouthful of that sweet monkey meat would mark him forever as an accessory to murder.

Come the early hours he woke the hut with his screams: "No! No! Stop! You mustn't … I won't let you …" before the spotted Jaguar sprang forth to silence him with its yellow fangs in his throat.

He sat bolt upright, wheezing and sweating, almost coping the hammock. It took a while to figure out what was real and what he had dreamed. Around his head, a cloud of grey mosquitoes had gathered, though nothing like those he recalled on the flood plain below.

November came and went according to Sister Klara's reckoning, heralding a new wave of malaria. Nearly every dwelling contained at least one occupant laid low in a feverish delirium. The whole tribe observed that the old nun, by now run off her feet, was having far more success with her ameliorating hands and chants than were the witch doctors with their secret spells and potions.

Although bringing relief to many, even she was unable to ward off a growing death toll among the frail and very young, and before long these failings were seized upon by Xina. A whisper spread that the white intruders had themselves brought down the curse upon the tribe, until Chief Ticuna stepped in to remind everyone that they were no longer "ignorant savages", and the sweating fevers always arose with the marsh mosquitos during the wet season.

If it was Atua's will, the weak would die.

Thus empowered, the old healer appointed all healthy members of the tribe as "special orderlies" and even Chief Ticuna did as she directed. The Shamans shuffled noisily about the outskirts beating drums and calling upon Curupuri for a sign. Again and again, their attempts to drive out the malaria demon by administering foul-tasting potions failed.

Miraculously, the boy's sensitive skin remained protected under its layer of red paste, plastered on daily by Maya at the old lady's insistence. When not running errands, he snatched a few moments to pursue the basic breathing exercises set for him in happier times.

Ever since that tearful confrontation with the returning hunters, he'd thrown himself into a daily routine that hopefully resulted in that palpable, if brief tranquillity he craved.

Sometimes, when the tribe was deep in an afternoon siesta, Klaus would sneak a pinch of Yopo and allow his thoughts to range wide and free; well, almost free. Maya always seemed far less affected than he by the pipe and would repine cross-legged nearby, amused by his oohing and aahing at the varying effects of Light among the leaves without which, Sister stressed, Life could not exist at all.

He even went so far as to imagine each scene as an 8" × 10" black-and-white print. Without a camera to capture what he saw, he was given to estimating apertures and f-stops in his head. Sunray, moonbeam or light from a flickering campfire, each generated a mood all its own.

Again and again, Sister pointed out the tiny triangles carved into the stele and temple walls, hinting that this very symbol embodied *the* Holy Trinity described in ancient Hindu Sanskrit *and* subsequent Christian Teachings. "Father, Son, and Holy Ghost; surely Father Malone drummed that much into you?" she teased. "Some things cannot be taught, they have to be learned," she persisted, pointing out that the Sun God's carved corona arms also dangled tiny triangles over the figures below.

"There are no symbols greater than the triangle and infinite circle of our Sun for depicting Universal Principals. Religions and rulers come and go, but Eternal Truths reside in safe hands. Since Babylon first discovered the right angle triangle, few Laws are more profound and easier to remember than this simple shape that unlocks all Mysteries," she added wistfully.

"According to Jung, there resides in each of us another whom we do not know. Your own consciousness is the final frontier; once this is met and mastered, the whole Universe will reveal itself to you." Running her fingers over the worn grooves she explained that such snug-fitting stonework had been perfected during the construction of the Great Pyramids of Egypt, yet within a few centuries the symbolism of the Triangle had spread to the ends of the earth; as far even as the South American Indian Nations. Since then, all sacred meaning was consigned to history's cold ashes by the Conquistadors of Spain.

In the midst of the rainy season the boy witnessed yet another dancing ceremony to mark the apogee of local flooding, and coincidentally the birth of baby Jesus. None but Sister Klara was capable of integrating the Christmas message and Tribal Lore in a manner understood by all. Somehow, she put together a carved gourd in a basket of soft leaves to represent the Christ Child, above whose hand-painted face she had glued a halo of harpy eagle fluff. Dancers were required to approach the makeshift manger and deposit gifts of fish and fruit, before crossing themselves in gratitude for the life-giving rains.

From this point onward, so the singing revealed, the daily deluges would gradually diminish, opening up more of their newly won homeland to further exploration. For the boy, such a time of drying out may hold the key to his dream of escape. For years he had been subjected to Father Maloney's long-winded sermons about Jesus' miraculous Birth and mighty ministry, most of which seemed irrelevant and confusing to the Indians. One thing they had learned to fear, however, was going to Hell!

The old priest also warned of the wrath of the great Chief in Rome, a God waiting to condemn any sign of disloyalty toward the Holy Scriptures or their earthly representatives. Deliberate blasphemy or even a poor joke could result in "six of the best" from Father Paddy's twitch, administered to the offender's bare backside while bending over the communion rail in front of the whole congregation. Three such capital corrections and the wayward parishioner would be excommunicated; "… to wander farevar in a Hell of dere own devisin'," he repeated.

Wisely, Sister never tried explaining the mystery of Easter to the tribe. Raising of the dead was simply a bridge too far for their common wisdom. They knew that once the heart was out then that was the end of it, let alone being nailed to a wooden cross and coming back to life three days later. She kept such incredible tales for her own spiritual nourishment and that of her two most promising lambs.

When the distemper abated, Sister Klara again found time for one-on-one lessons with her brightest pupil; Klaus was always happy to avoid the rough and tumble of the tribal games.

First up, she reiterated the subtle distinctions between actuality and reality, two of life's seeming contradictions which, she said, most people never even suspect. "What seems real to you may not actually be the truth. Discerning the difference is a basic spiritual quest."

"Why Klaus stare so much at tree?" Maya's amused expression showed she could see no need for any such intense scrutiny. "Indian see everythin', not just what in front of nose," she responded to his latest preoccupation.

At first, he'd resented her patronising jibes and his own shortcomings; he was learning to ignore distractions and appreciate the bigger picture. Actuality usually lay behind his own realities, as important as they may be. Five miles may actually exist but in reality, it may only be five inches in a photograph. How soon is too soon? Mostly though, his thoughts were indistinct and unfocused. What was the point of all this, anyway?

22

S itting alone one afternoon, mouthing soft incantations, the boy was aroused by a commotion outside Devil's Gullet. Parting the bushes he watched a group of agitated hunters emerging to a noisy welcome, before dumping two dead peccaries on the ground at Xina's feet. Forays such as these to the flood plains below were dependent on the flow of water being diverted away from the tunnel entrance and over the waterfall.

Immediately, his eyes popped and the colour drained from his face. The Shamans were examining something leaning against the carcases: a familiar shape. It couldn't be! He almost stopped breathing.

Right there amidst dark mutterings, he watched Robert's rifle pass from hand to hand, before Xina called for silence and began scraping off the coating of Verdigris from the gilded breach, revealing an engraved inscription: Robert Hahn – Belem 1922. With a triumphal whoop, he held the accusing weapon high in the air for all to see. "Hahn name, see here? Hahn! Him Hahn," he cried, casting a wild eye towards the Women's Maloca. Before they could respond, through the ugly mob strode Sister Klara. Being the only fluent German speaker she called for silence, and reaching for the rifle read out loud the manufacturer as "Weismann and Hart". A little more rubbing confirmed the initial revelation: Robert Hahn – Belem 1922.

The Shamans cried out as one to be heard. The High Priest had already identified the guilty party; what more remained to be said? They were sick of being deceived and distracted by this Devil Woman.

"This boy not *Robert* Hahn," Sister stated firmly, flapping wide the sleeves of her Habit and motioning to the building behind. "This one Longhead! This one good Hahn, save Maya."

136

Unable to bear the suspense Klaus shrank back behind a mud wall, head spinning as he tried to cobble together a credible explanation. He could not deny his surname, which by now they all recognised; but how could Sister Klara prove that he was definitely not the Robert Hahn inscribed on the weapon? He could protest that he knew nothing about guns and perhaps argue that the search party had somehow left it behind. Now there was nothing for it but to face the music head on. Taking a deep breath, he stepped forward through the blockade of bare backsides: an immediate hush settled over all.

Sister Klara was first to speak, "You haven't been lying to me Klaus, have you?" she confronted him tersely, revealing her serenity was being well and truly tested. Only with difficulty did she hold her ground before the emboldened witch doctor. The shamans were all talking at once, egged on by Xina brandishing the damning evidence and calling for swift justice to be meted out by Chief Ticuna, who had by now arrived upon the scene. "Kill him … this one kill plenty Indian," they cried, before reminding him of their Omens concerning Longhead. Throwing out a commanding arm Chief Ticuna cried, "Be still. Wait!"

The hostile wall of weapons opened before him as he retired with his charges to a nearby hut, intending to find a way through this mess or at least seek a calming signal from Atua. Once inside he stressed that the tentative trust of the tribe had been shattered by the discovery of the weapon; if he could not somehow smooth the waters, retribution might yet claim all their heads. If the Shamans would not be mollified, this would surely mark the end of the road for at least one of the prisoners. Klaus guessed which one.

Upon rejoining the pow-wow, Chief Ticuna, at the elders' insistence, had no option but to agree to accept a Divine ruling from "Great Ticuna", his own desiccated and greatly revered ancestor, the final arbiter in such disputes.

Great Ticuna was ordered brought forth from his resting place within the Ziggurat, the irony of which was not lost on Sister Klara. It was she who had pressed the chief to carry his mummified ancestor on his own back, all the way from Santa Luzia to an empty crypt in the Sun Temple. This desire to restore the ancient customs may now prove to be the boy's undoing.

The jabbering ceased, alerted by a sombre banging on the witch doctor's drum and discordant wailing of Pan Flutes announcing the arrival of the shrivelled and partly bandaged cadaver being borne outside for the first time since its internment. Reverently, Great Ticuna was placed in a sitting position among the elders as a gasp caught in every throat.

"It doesn't look good," Sister Klara whispered. "They aren't likely to be put off by the difference in your given names; you represent the entire Hahn Dynasty they've grown to hate. All the old wounds have been reopened, they seem convinced you've been lying. For both our sakes I hope they can't prove it. I pray we may persuade them otherwise," she sighed before the pair were bundled brusquely once more into the centre of the circle.

"The Gloves of Happiness!" A cry went up from Xina and the Shamans. "Let him be tested by the Gloves of Happiness; the truth will not remain hidden for long," they pressed the disconcerted chief. Few dared defy the High Priest outright, but Sister stuck to her guns. The rifle clearly did not belong to this boy, she insisted. They would have to take her word for it as the only one among them who could read German and decipher the complete inscription.

"She's lying to save him! Both must die!" Xina sensed the changing mood and rent the air with chilling threats.

"Enough!" Chief Ticuna again raised his hand. As was customary it would fall to Great Ticuna to dispense final justice and chart the path ahead. Both sides would put their case to the empty sockets peeping between their wrappings, after which the inviolate verdict would be pronounced the next morning at sunrise. So confident of the outcome were the Shamans that no extra guard on the captives was thought necessary.

Throughout that longest night the accused pair huddled together in the empty Maloca, illuminated by a single candle and not daring to raise their voices above a whisper. In the distance the tribe chanted and danced around in circles of drug-fuelled frenzy; and always the throbbing drumbeats.

Again and again, as if in a normal classroom, she tried to reassure the frightened boy more in hope than expectation, pressing him to repeat those qualities he must commit to memory while awaiting his inner Spirit to reveal itself fully. "Future, what future? I haven't any future. I think I'm going to poo my pants." His sheep's eyes glanced up imploringly but she continued undaunted. "Devotion, Study, Patience and Practice ..." over and over she whispered the words to the thud of drums.

At times he pressed his hands over his ears and snuggled into the sumptuous folds of her skirts, exhausted by the fear of impending pain. She ignored his distress, calmly bringing him around with each assurance. "B ... But, why? What's the point of trying to remember anything now?" he whined.

"You will survive, you must survive", she persisted. "You already have the answers. My words are with you always." She urged him to trust in the God of his heart to ward off the danger that had reduced him to a trembling mess.

Long before dawn's first chorus, Klaus had convinced himself that he knew nothing whatever of the accusing firearm. If all else failed, he'd decided that unlike on that previous occasion, when he'd sat meekly awaiting Xina's blow, he would not go down this time without a fight. If the chance arose he'd make a run for it. But run? Run where? His story had better sound convincing.

Either way, wearing the Gloves of Happiness was unthinkable. He'd heard whispers that the very title hid a devious deception, played out upon pubescent boys by the witch doctors that imposed wide-ranging punishments and humiliations upon any faint-hearted novice who failed to remain silent inside the gloves. For those who failed a second time, sure death was his lot, delivered with a single blow from Xina's decorated war club, the one with the dried blood and hair on the heavy end.

Even more ominously, Xina the High Priest would be both Oracle and arbiter over this particular celestial struggle, via a secret sign from Great Ticuna known only to him.

As the night dragged on, Sister Klara harboured few doubts over the likely sentence. Even Chief Ticuna must obey the Supreme Verdict when it came. Either way, there would be no more light-hearted flirting or pulling the hairs on the boy's legs by the younger girls. Judging from the hostile faces in the crowd his former playmates were now all business.

Suddenly, Sister drew herself up and straightened her vestments, even as Klaus continued to protest his innocence. She knew he would never withstand the fire-ant ordeal, not least because of the likely asthma reaction from the venom on his airways. She had witnessed robust Indian youths fall to the ground in agony, frothing at the mouth as the infuriated ants spent themselves upon the ten defenceless fingers in the bags. A mere whimper would banish a boy back to the women's camp for a further three moons of humiliation and menial tasks. She realised that this would be the end for her charge.

A calming presence now appeared to envelop her and she spoke to him with assurance. "You will have to flee. I'm afraid there is no other way. If you attempt to hide, they will track you down and kill us both. The Shamans won't pass up a chance like this to undermine Chief Ticuna and restore Curupuri."

"B ... But, how? Where? What about you and Maya? Oh ... it's all my fault." Again, his lip began to quiver, "I know I've placed you both in great danger just by being here."

Sister merely shrugged. The decision had been made and she already looked years younger, appearing to tap some inner well of strength and stare him straight in the eye. "We will just have to give it our best effort then, won't we?" He nodded foolishly, elated and terrified both at the possibility of being free.

"Tonight, the menfolk are high on Epena. You must be ready to face great challenges at first light. Dear child, I'm afraid there is only one way out alive. If we can hide you in the tunnel while they are distracted there's a good chance our absence will not be noticed until you have a good head start. Grand Ticuna will not pass judgment until the sun's first rays touch the Temple and my other lambs have entered for their convocation. I trust the Shamans will not dare to stop me or even notice your disguise. At the right moment, Maya will lead you down through the tunnel and out behind the falls. After that, you will be on your own. I'll do my best to drag out the service and keep the waters diverted. And Klaus, remember whatever happens you always carry the light within ..." Her words sounded hollow and distant. He could not believe this was really happening.

During the pre-dawn hours, a group of hooded figures noiselessly skirted the Plaza and paused at the tunnel mouth, while other shadowy shapes hurried to divert the Igarapé stream. The boy was then led, short of breath and almost blind, to a familiar place deep inside the great cavern, where he was instructed to remain hidden behind a cluster of dripping crystals. Sensing his trepidation, Sister Klara took him in her arms and placed several fingers of her right hand on the back of his neck, as she'd done many times before, softly intoning a catenation of soothing vowels. He soon felt as if he were rising to observe the scene, including himself, from above.

When he opened his eyes, she and the others were gone, taking their firesticks and leaving only the steady dripping of water nearby. The heat was becoming oppressive. He tried to ignore the tick-tock of droplets growing steadily louder, reminding him of the carved cuckoo clock in Vati's office, which he doubted he would ever see again.

Would his Mam have given up all hope by now? Drawing several deep breaths he calmed himself by concentrating on his thymus gland. Somewhat proudly, he knew precisely where this and other important glands in the human body were situated from studying the detailed charts in Doc Wonders' waiting room. It had taken Sister Klara to explain the importance of all these glands in general health and spiritual wellbeing, and the effects of repeated incantations upon them. Soon afterwards he began to feel strangely reassured, quite unlike his earlier incontinence, and more accepting of the heat. Oh, if only he'd paid more attention to her healing techniques. It would surely be a long wait.

Suddenly he sat bolt upright, rubbing his eyes. Despite all former apprehension, he must have drifted into a fitful slumber. The flicker of distant firebrands was coming closer and a soft mauve effulgence was peeping through the eastern wall. He watched the white-robed disciples extinguish their flames and take up positions around the pond, to await the arrival of the first sunbeam. Simultaneously, firm hands grasped his elbows and steered him swiftly through the crystal maze and deeper into the forbidding tunnel, which dropped away sharply. He could just make out Maya to one side and Sister Klara continually tripping over her regalia on the other, all lit by a single burning brand held overhead.

Finally they halted, the moment he dreaded had arrived and the colour drained from his face. "Now, my child; I must return to my flock. Maya will see you safely down to the lower falls. You must not try to persuade her to go further, her destiny lies here with her people … and mine now remains in the hands of God." The frail woman sighed, placing one finger over his quivering lips. "You have no time to waste, they will send out a hunting party when your absence is discovered. I'll do what I can to confuse their intentions."

Choking back a tear for the first time in weeks, she removed the white smock from his shoulders to leave him sweating in his original tattered khaki shorts. And, you will need these things," she added, placing a fat string bag over his shoulder, protruding from which was a machete handle and several unlit firebrands. In between he glimpsed an assortment of dried foods and manioc cakes.

"Say nothing," she said in a low voice, drawing a finger across her lips. For a moment more she looked hard into Klaus' eyes with the flickering torch held aloft, "May God's Grace go with you always." Again, she embraced him and put her mouth to his ear: "And remember, dear boy, Sister Klara always loffs you," came those final words he would carry to the grave.

Then, with a rustle of fabric, she was gone forever, leaving the pair standing hand in hand in the hissing belly of the monster. A wink of light beckoned far below, marking their destination. As the incline dropped away, his soft feet were soon slipping off the lava rocks and his fingernails were torn and bleeding. First one, and then another of the precious firesticks slipped from his grip and tumbled away into the depths, just missing the agile girl below. Descending by way of woven vines anchored at strategic intervals, he pursued his fleet-footed friend, trembling and praying under his breath. Boldly, Maya lifted her face to urge him on, keeping one ear to the ground for any signs of pursuit. They had barely covered half the distance and his blistered hands were crying out, and the soles of his feet were raw. Gouts of sulphurous steam spewed from unseen fissures, threatening any careless handhold. "Klaus hurry, water come soon …" she pleaded, as he bumped and slithered towards the ripening patch of daylight. Now they could hear the roar of the waterfall and feel the spray on their faces.

Letting go, he half-tumbled the last few metres until his feet hit solid ground and they both heard it … a distant growling that shook the mountain and could mean only one thing: the sluice gates above were opening sooner than planned.

Within minutes the tunnel would become a raging cataract. "Klaus go faster!" she cried, turning back to drag him through the swiftly rising current. Together they took their final few steps before she exclaimed, "Klaus jump!"

With every ounce of strength in her tiny body, she propelled him sideways as the torrent struck her like a fist of steel. His last memory of his friend was as a flailing red patch entombed in a wall of white water.

When he came to, hanging head down in a tangle of scrub, the deafening sound of the waterfall filled his skull. *Where am I? Who am I? What happened?*

For long minutes he had no idea where he was. His body felt like one long bruise, hands and feet crying out as he gathered his wits and clamoured painfully to the ground. He felt himself all over through the enfilading pain but miraculously there appeared to be no bones broken. The woven bag remained twisted around his neck in a stranglehold, its contents soaked but intact.

Carefully, he unwound the cord, allowing him to breathe easier.

A single thought now pressed itself upon the fog of uncertainty: Maya! Where was she? Did he really see her flying off into the clouds? Struggling to make sense of the unfamiliar setting his first frantic cries were lost in the thunder, producing a stab of loneliness. Peering beyond the spray, he commenced picking his way gingerly along the tumbled rock perimeter of the pool, becoming ever more aware of the perils from loitering too long in that place.

At first, no landmark was recognisable, until he reached the major overflow that Sister had marked on her map, with instructions to follow this waterway toward the main river where he might chance upon a passing vessel; if indeed he made it that far.

Reaching into the dilly-bag he uncorked a tiny gourd of Yopo and took a single sniff to each nostril, feeling immediately invigorated. No part of him seemed more painful than any other. Mouthing a prayer of thanks to his rescuers he contemplated the unknown route ahead and set off timidly for the long walk downstream toward freedom.

Soon exhausted, step by painful step he fought the confusion; but at least he was on the move. Up ahead, his eye caught a slash of crimson high in the moss-draped branches. Could it be a clue? Might one single ruddy fragment mean his prayer had been answered? With growing doubt, he slipped and slid toward the tell-tale red cloth, from which he soon saw protruded a rag-doll figure spreadeagled backwards as if in homage to the cruel force that had blown her fragile life away. "Maya? Please God, no!" A single glance sufficed to show his friend was past all caring. She had saved his miserable hide with that one supreme and selfless act. Pausing guiltily he forgot his discomfort and climbed closer to touch her cold copper flesh one last time, plucking the tiny Rosy Cross from around her broken neck. He pressed his fingers to her blue lips and cried out to Heaven with a beastly howl that was swallowed in the vastness.

Finding himself totally overcome among the rocks, he repeated her name until he could speak it no more. He kissed and confided in the tiny keepsake, before wrapping it in his handkerchief and tucking it into the pocket of his shorts. Unable to bear the sight overhead he turned away for the last time, stumbling blindly over log jams and boulders until the terrible scene was far behind and he lost all track of time. Whenever the rapids became impassable he was forced ashore to crawl along the low-hung animal pathways, slashing wildly with his machete at every shadow. Again and again, he was compelled back into the leechy waters where, partly swimming and often crawling, he dragged one leg after the other toward an unknown fate.

Often delirious he came upon a narrow gap in the green curtain, where he was able to haul himself ashore and avoid being swept out into the main current. All those snippets of jungle lore he'd picked up while captive had long gone; yet, despite all the pain and confusion he'd managed to make it this far.

As if to sheet home his parlous position, a colony of fruit bats overhead became engaged in a bout of orgasmic bickering, showering him with a spray of sweet-smelling scheisse as he crawled on all fours toward the open water. His puffed and smarting eyes failed to spy a low-hanging nest of wasps, causing a swarm of the angry insects to launch upon his bare flesh. Numb with pain he huddled beside the main channel, moaning softly, willing his swollen fingers to locate the remaining pinch of Yopo powder and to force down a few soggy mouthfuls of manioc and catfish. Only then did he proceed to tear away the remaining leeches from his tender parts, wondering if were possible to bleed to death from losing this amount of blood in a single day.

Throughout the entire ordeal he never quite forgot his fleet-footed pursuers, who surely could not be far away. Before him loomed the wide brown currents of the mighty Madeira, which alone held the promise of rescue or doom.

In quelling his nerves he again avowed the two women who had given all for his survival. Precious minutes passed while he mouthed the only healing vowels he could recall. As if from nowhere, a floating island of river grass caught against the nearby embankment, revolving slowly in a whirlpool by the creek mouth. This was no time to speculate whether such a clump might hold his weight or even carry him to safety. The tributary behind had slowed to a trickle, a sure sign that a scouting party was through the tunnel. With one last mighty effort, Klaus threw himself onto the spongey mass, and for a second time that day fell unconscious.

A merciless sun beat down upon the drifting islands of grass; through a delirium of infected wounds, the castaway slipped in and out of lucidity.

During one brief conscious moment, he prayed to the God of his Heart for the torment to end, at another point even falling back on a recitation of three Hail Marys, to no effect.

Worse still, through squinting lids he observed a flock of black vultures circling overhead and eyeing off the certain meal below. Again and again, he was forced to lash out with his machete when the croaking scavengers alighted ever closer; emboldened, they jostled each other as he slipped in and out of consciousness.

His precious blade slipped from his fingers and sank.

23

Frau Kathleen Hahn first heard the hullaballoo outside the Mission walls. Father Maloney came puffing up the hill with spindly shanks pumping beneath his flowing robes, accompanied by an envoy from the mine office.

"They've found him, Kitty me darlin', thanks be to the Lard Jaesus! They've found your boy alive; it's nuthin' short of a miracle, I tell ya; a real miracle."

His words echoed in her head as if coming from a great distance; surely, her ears deceived her. Should she dare to grasp this straw of hope? Her bright eyes had grown dim with prayer and weeping but the jabbering emissary left no room for doubt: in a familiar mix of Pidgin and Portuguese he poured out the tale of rescue; it was her boy alright, just barely breathing, they said, but alive!

"They're caring for him at one of the tappers' outstations, Doc Wonders is with him nah," the old priest gasped, his purplish nose sucking for air.

B … But how? When? Take me to him!" she implored, before falling to her knees. "Holy Father, do not dash my hopes again, I beg yer. I swear I couldna take anudda blow."

"Nar ya jus' settle dahn me goil, they're sendin' a car, one o' them new-fangled T models. They should have carried him out of the bush by the time we get there, so let's not hang abart. Doc Wonders says the boy's very weak but he's gonna pull through."

How Kitty had prayed and pleaded to one day hear these very words. On her knees in the dirt she tearfully kissed the crucifix that hung at her throat on its silver-plated chain; Father Patrick too, had dropped down and cradled her head against his own pumping bosom.

During that frantic fifteen-minute car ride to the outstation, the excited envoy told them everything he knew; how one of the Garimpeiros working the farthest boundary of the Claim climbed out to salvage his canoe entangled in one of the floating islets that clog the jetties during the wet season.

Curious over a flock of squabbling buzzards hopping about their still-twitching prey, he scrambled over to investigate the hapless creature being eaten alive, burnt almost black by the sun and covered in blood and grass.

The thing was rolling madly back and forth, trying to fend off a dozen clacking beaks aimed at its eyes. At first, the half-breed moved cautiously to put the creature out of its misery and maybe carve off a lump of meat for the dogs, but the rest, as they say, became known as the greatest miracle ever performed by Father Malone and the Holy Roman Church in all its decades saving souls in Santa Luzia. The boy's story of survival became richer with each telling.

Apparently, after overcoming his astonishment, the Garimpeiro man-handled the body ashore, firing off three rifle shots into the air as an emergency signal for his wife to come running. She in turn, after first applying a poultice of green banana leaves to the angry flesh, was despatched on foot to the main office, a good hour away along poor jungle trails.

Doc Wonders and his pack horse had been the first officials to arrive on the scene, and though the sunburned face was badly swollen, declared it was indeed the missing boy. Even a sceptical Alois was startled into action when he heard the news and headed straight for the docks to celebrate.

Following an initial shot of adrenalin, old Doc dressed the worst of Klaus' wounds and rigged up a litter to be pulled behind his pack horse. Throughout the arduous, one-hour journey the patient uttered not a word, strapped in safely and smiling wanly through fat lips at the taunting forest, until they reached the rendezvous site beside a road of sorts. When the mud-spattered T model finally bounced into view, he could see Father Malone perched precariously on the running board beside Mam's head hanging out to gawp frantically.

Even as she smothered the boy's broken head in kisses and admonishments she could not bring herself to remain joyous. Something *was* missing; she knew it from that first minute when he'd barely responded to her tearful embraces, or even to the well-wishes from a dozen others. His dark staring eyes looked vacant, seeming to absorb all without focusing, and a foolish grin played at the corners of his mouth. For the first time in many months he felt safe!

But it was soon apparent that something shocking had happened to the boy. He didn't seem quite "right in the head". Doc Wonders said all he needed was "a damn good feed and plenty of rest in his own bed". Father Patrick insisted that Kitty stand down for the next fortnight to keep a close eye on her bedevilled goosen, giving assurance that he would drop by every other day. The patient was prone to awaken in terrifying cold sweats, imagining that his throat was being gripped in the jaws of a jaguar, of all things.

"Once he gets his head back into those books he'll start to remember who he is," Doc had wisely counselled, "... oh, and Frau Hahn, a bowl or two of your special Galway stew will surely put a bit of meat back on his bones, eh?"

Once again, the Fazenda sprang to life as housemaids stuck their heads through his doorway every ten minutes and surrounding settlers brought baskets of fruit from their own tiny plots. For months an air of neglect had settled over the chastened homestead, with Robert and Alois keeping well clear of each other and Nurse Kitty grieving apart in the Spartan confines of the Mission.

All of a sudden, the boy's miraculous homecoming breathed temporary life back into the family; cheerful meals materialised at his bedside and an endless stream of visitors popped in hoping to hear the details firsthand.

However, not a word of the ordeal crossed the boy's lips, adding further to speculation over the alleged kidnapping. One tiny souvenir, however, remained hidden beneath his pillow: the first thing he fondled upon awakening each morning and the last at night, never yet shown to another soul.

Strange humming sounds escaped from behind his bedroom door at all hours, prompting yet more conjecture over his mental state. Physically, the boy made swift progress and the household relapsed into a familiar routine, allowing Mutti to return part-time to her calling behind the flaking walls of Holy Cross.

As visitations inevitably slowed to a trickle Klaus found himself once more alone during daylight hours, a not altogether unpleasant development. This brought time to discover new meaning within the hitherto obscure language of Classical literature and break out Alois' collection of Bakelite gramophone recordings, hardly ever played since the day they'd arrived from Onkel Fedi in Bavaria.

Beauty now revealed itself where confusion once existed. From the passion of Beethoven's symphonies to the perfect balance of Mozart's piano sonatas, somehow he could see, hear and understand more than ever before, without really knowing why. Every so often he took a deep breath and plunged into the broad mysterious strains of a Wagnerian opera: were these the much-promised glimpses of a world "beneath the surface" that Sister Klara had pledged him to forever seek?

Most afternoons he looked forward to Mam's hands-on attentions as she swept in to issue updates regarding his care. Without fail, she would replenish the candles on her shrine before insisting they both fall on their knees before the holy flame and recite three Hail Marys for his deliverance. Yet, deep down Klaus held fast to his own incipient awakening, far removed from Father Patrick's venerated long-winded intercessions, but out of respect for Mutti's faith he prayed anyway.

Alois soon lost interest in the boy's recovery, preoccupied now by a teetering Stock Market and its implications for worldwide commodity prices, especially rubber. What did this all mean for his disease-plagued plantation, now left without much hope of a market even if it ever did one day manage to produce sufficient quantities of the precious white sap? Then there remained the matter of the defalcated Pension Fund which would have to be repaid, and soon!

During this time, the brothers found time to reacquaint themselves with the annoying facts of each other's existence. When the youngster did eventually break his silence and utter a few halting words, before shedding a tear, his brother walked off in disgust. Robert's own incessant boasting had been met with indifference and apparently didn't sound appealing to the boy at all.

Yes! Yes! He got it … Robert had since discovered his real purpose in life, taking wild delight in recounting the lewd and violent shenanigans he'd gotten up to during the other's absence. But the convalescent remained unmoved; nothing could ever compare with his own exploits. He contented himself by clucking and whistling to the birds outside his bedroom window and perusing his library with renewed vigour, even tackling *The Merchant of Venice* in the German translation.

How could he ever reveal what he had been through? It was absurd, simply unbelievable; if it were not for his scars and blotches he may not believe it himself. But something remained smouldering inside his deepest reaches, something profound and unshakeable.

Meanwhile, the rough-and-tumble mine workers had all missed the little fella and his camera. Passing the hat around they'd raised enough to purchase a second-hand Voigtlander from the Company stores and to coax him out again into the fresh air. A great cheer went up when he eventually did totter into the bright sunlight, smiling broadly and holding the precious gift aloft.

Though grateful, Klaus remained tight-lipped, knowing full well what would happen to the Mojo if ever the truth got out. He had lost his dearest friend and that grief would never fade, but he knew Sister Klara must be allowed to continue her work unhindered among the Indians; if indeed she had survived.

Robert and his mates would be up those cliffs "in two shakes of a tapir's tossle", a smutty quip often exchanged between gang members which Klaus didn't think very funny at all. What a coup it would be for the river's youngest hunting guide and Santa Luzia's lagging tourism industry to tack on an "Encounter with Head-Hunters" to their "Once in A Lifetime" hunting Safaris which even Captain Rudy thought sounded enticing.

While the boy digested his inconceivable salvation, the more outlandish became Robert's tales in which naturally enough, he shone forth as the best organiser, best tracker and best shot all rolled into one. Of course, the sickly sibling now saw through all this bluster, suspecting the other of begrudging any white person, let alone himself, having survived for months alone in the jungle.

It grew into a case of speculation versus unsubstantiated proof.

One morning, when they were alone together, Robert revealed that his hatred for Alois had not abated and that he had in fact been able to turn the old man's former scorn "arse up". It was now Vati's turn to keep clear of the short fuse and flying fists of his unpredictable ward, who shared an unlikely tale of how he had twice come across a drunken Alois late at night behind the warehouses and given him "a good thrashing". It felt so good. "He never nu what 'it him …" the disgruntled guide boasted.

Startled from his quietude Klaus fixed dark eyes upon his brother with a determined look the other had not seen before. "I don't think I shall ever forgive you for what you did to Maya …"

"W … What? … Oh that? Her? … You're not still going on about that little grease ball, are you? Anyway, why bring that up now? Is this your idea of brothers sticking together? Anything else you want to get off your puny chest while you're at it?" said Robert, cracking his knuckles. Aggression was never far beneath the surface.

"You know nothing! She saved my life, in spite of what you and your mates did to her." Silence. "I loved her like a sister … and now she's dead." The words tumbled out before trailing off in the knowledge that he'd already said too much.

"Loved her? Good God, brudder, you really are off the rails! What do ya mean saved ya life?" The colour rose in Robert's cheeks. "Now you listen to me, you little turd. I dunna know how long you're going to persist with this silent hero bullshit, but I need ta start showin' you off to my tourists. It'll be a big drawcard for the Safaris; they just luv hearin' tall tales of lost tribes and head-hunters, all dat sort of thing. If ya like, ya can jus' make it up as we go along; don't worry, they'll swallow anytin'. I want you to come work the river with me and make something of yourself. You can take snaps of me wearin' me Coati Mundi cap an' the touristas wit' dere trophies. We can 'ave a bit of fun on the side wit' dere spoiled-brat daughters if you get my meaning."

The boy would not be shaken. "But I don't want to kill anything, ever, and I won't."

"Or what? You still eat meat, don't ya?" his elder shot back.

"Yes, but I don't have to see it being killed."

"Bloody hypocrite! Well, I *do* like to watch it happenin', see? An' the bigger, the better," Robert sneered, "… ever since I had to kill 'is Sunday chickens. That was when I started to enjoy the killin'. Then I started dreamin' that one day it would be his head I sent flyin'."

"Good grief! Don't let Mam hear you talkin' like that. Perhaps it's *you* who is the sick one … after all, you *did* pay him back, didn't you?" Klaus held his gaze, "… I mean, with the gravy and all."

Robert ignored the prompt and went on. "So what if I can make a few real bagging wild animals? There's plenty more where they come from," he added, becoming more animated at the very suggestion. "Not like some I could name, jerking off at home all day and being mamby-pambied by the housekeepers.

You should get your head outa dose stupid books. If you ask me, this whole song and dance about your asthma is bullshit …"

At this the boy yielded, dropping his eyes and letting the rebuff go over his head. His brother obviously held grudges and his pugnacious attitude grated.

Then, in an about-face, he flashed a perfect smile and leaned closer. "All I can say is you are missing out on a lot of fun … but that's your business. Let me know when ya change your mind."

But Klaus did not change his mind. He cringed whenever called upon to record the regular parades of tourist-adventurers holding up their dead trophies to the camera, of almost anything that had crept, climbed or flown in the jungle.

He began to wonder if these waves of holiday hunters would eventually succeed in wiping out the very things they'd come halfway around the world to see, with his own brother adding to the slaughter.

By working the darkroom all night he was able to brush away these concerns and deliver a set of perfect postcards to each proud hunter before they sailed away. And the extra pocket money did come in handy.

Nowadays, confined within the compound perimeter he rediscovered his true passion lay in the deceptive simplicity of still-life photography; a tree root here, a mysterious shape over there wrapped in the morning mist, or a last shaft of sunlight picking out the veins in a single leaf. All became possible during the hour of long shadows just after dawn and before sunset.

He called it the time of golden foliage, when a special light danced off the oxbow surface to splash the underside of foliage.

The entire lease was now off-limits to casual hunting, offering exclusive pickings for Robert's blossoming business and his brother's eager lens.

In this protected space the photographer could observe nature's ancient rhythms at work with a camera in his hands, but how he missed the lightweight ease of the lost Leica.

When alone, he was mindful to practise his vowels and birdcalls, delighting in the sure replies from a dozen unseen throats. At home he tackled the classics one by one with renewed passion, sometimes concurrently: Homer, Sophocles, Dante, and most of all Virgil's soaring descriptions of adventures that rivalled his own; there was even a complete folio of Shakespeare in German.

Such daunting tomes that had for so long gathered dust on Oncle Fedi's bookshelf now filled his head with tales and phrases he longed to repeat and exceed. His interest in ancient wisdom had been well and truly awoken under Sister Klara's mystical wing and he now found himself invigorated rather than daunted by her formerly indecipherable phraseology.

Could his distant mentor really reach out from dark history to illuminate his affairs? It seemed impossible.

Another fascination, now that he was excused from formal schooling, lay between the covers of various German illustrated magazines arriving as part of *Belle*'s cargo each month.

Some, like the *Völkischer Beobachter*, kept him abreast of unfolding political events in Germany as captured by renowned photographers like Heinrich Hoffmann of Munich, whose modern techniques with lighting and design underpinned a certain studied spontaneity he admired. In particular, he pored over the prolific output of Presse Illustration Hoffmann, an adjunct to the master's swelling stable of portrait studios which encompassed everything from formal studies of rising Nazi dignitaries to split-second candids on location at various rallies, meetings and marches where his number one patron was appearing.

To a mere beginner, the variety and precision of Hoffmann's poses seemed endless; though easy enough to imitate, the boy suspected that he would need to blend his own wooden style using more of these avant-garde techniques. Perhaps only then might he hope to earn a living in the exacting profession. Day by day he attempted to assimilate what he was seeing, reading and printing into taking better photos, always mindful of Sister Klara's admonishments to "look beneath the surface".

24

To Kathleen Hahn, the jungle had become the enemy. One way or another it could strike down both rich and poor, but mostly poor, with a litany of crushing ailments. Now she remained over-protective of her baby boy, hoping and praying that his ongoing peregrinations humming meaningless sounds and whistling back and forth to the birds of the forest were somehow residual symptoms that would pass.

Almost daily he could be seen scattering food scraps along the tree line and searching for subjects with his camera. Such behaviour, she confided to Father Patrick was not without good reason but it was far from normal. In between overseeing his nutritional requirements, she had given up trying to coax the story out of the boy, supposing he would get 'round to it when he "was good and ready".

While it was true that his asthma had improved, she was perplexed by the sense of purpose he had somehow suddenly acquired and the hours locked inside that stuffy old Fazenda, which couldn't be good for his health.

Father Paddy, now adored for the power of his prayers, told her to leave such healing in the hands of Jesus Christ the Saviour; and soon afterwards the boy announced he was determined to forge a permanent career from his former hobby. Whenever not occupied taking and printing photos he could be found beneath a tree with a volume of Classics, deep in thought. Whenever they did cross paths, he would throw his arms around Mam's waist and tell her that he loved her more than anything in the whole world.

Of course, she then had to pop by her little shrine to mutter three Hail Marys and kiss her silver-plated crucifix in tearful gratitude. It seemed at last the Holy of Holies had finally forgiven her; but would He forgive for a third time if she ever again allowed herself to taste the forbidden fruit?

Meanwhile, the attentive priest hovered and fussed, striving to share his thoughts and emotions, while she in turn strove to lighten the load of Holy Mother Church. She pretended not to notice when he would flash a merry wink across the ward.

The more Klaus tried to make sense of his expanding consciousness, the greater loomed the futility of ever being able to reveal the details of his ordeal to a prying public. No one could ever know what he had really endured, and there were times when the whole adventure seemed implausible even to himself.

Initially, Mutti had chalked up his "resurrection" as proof of Divine Intervention through Father Patrick, while his own father had let slip that he didn't much care whether the kid had lived or died. Alois' indifference appeared even more heartless when the boy eventually did turn up. Kitty and the whole town believed Father Malone's unceasing evening vespers.

This was the straw that broke her camel's back. She banned her estranged husband from coming anywhere near the sick room and for weeks personally oversaw the boy's every need. It was reassuring to see him propped up in bed each morning simply reading, which gave her a sense of satisfaction she'd not experienced in years. Her baby seemed convinced that everything in existence, even the Universe itself, was one great living organism, whose mysteries could be revealed only by careful observation and study.

Searching frantically in her bible for answers, Mam could find nothing to convince him otherwise. He rambled that all human senses should be developed fully in order to appreciate life in all its richness, but she had no idea of his meaning.

Sister Klara had stressed that certain immutable truths exist, whether he believed them or not, and warned that enhanced sensitivity could be a two-edged sword, bringing as much misery as pleasure to the unwary abecedarian on the path.

Loftier notions of the Great Nazarene such as "Peace Profound" and "Universal Love" would only ever be grasped, she stressed, by a few worthy souls in all cultures. Mother simply shook her head at such nonsense and Doc Wonders believed it was all a carryover from the sunstroke. The boy seemed confused as to whether his own thoughts were actually "original", or merely like "cosmic fragrances", some sweet, others pungent, wafting through space waiting to be inhaled.

How could anyone who wasn't there possibly grasp such concepts, and why had his mentor undermined her own sincerity by urging him to see himself and others as mere monkeys dressed up in rags? If he kept on with such gibberish, Mam threatened to wash his mouth out with soap.

Furthermore, why were the chosen few – like his own family, for example – able to live off the low-hanging fruit, while the majority of indigenous squatters knew not where their next meal was coming from? These and other social anomalies now plagued him continually, and he sensed that a superhuman effort would be required to fit back into family life, such as it was, or even into the society of fancily dressed primates as it presented.

However, he need not have worried, as the parlous state of Hahn family relationships finally imploded without any help, on the very next St Patrick's Day.

Always her favourite day on the Church calendar after Good Friday, Kitty foolishly invited Father Paddy back to the Fazenda for pikelets and tea.

After last Mass the old priest came shuffling down the hill, humming a ballad and concealing a small bunch of paper shamrocks under his robes. These days, despite his reputation for miracles, only a handful of his former congregation remained at his feet, and since the disappearance of the Mojo Tribe, he found himself with more time on his hands for house calls.

Still basking in the notoriety of divine intercession, somehow over the crisp starched tablecloth and baking aromas, discussion between the pair turned to life after death, and Satan's strategic patience awaiting wayward souls.

Shifting uncomfortably in his chair, Father Malone cleared his throat and confided to Mam and the boys that he too suffered from a recurring nightmare that was almost too embarrassing to recount and one which had nearly put him off preaching altogether.

Sometimes, he revealed, whenever he turned away to prepare the Host, faces in the front pews would contort into mocking, horned masks behind his back which, when he attempted to administer the Eucharist, spewed out a vile greenish liquid down the front of his vestments.

Klaus flashed a glance at his brother, before lowering his eyes to the blowfly crawling on the edge of his plate. All chewing had now ceased. He couldn't see why Mama had had to share his personal phantoms with the priest, or why he in his turn felt a need to fill the boys' heads with such unsettling disclosures. Robert, always bored by ecclesiastic speculations, rose to leave.

The banging of the screen door and a string of curses warned of Alois' approach. An awkward silence ensued before he stumbled into the parlour, glaring uncomprehendingly from one flushed face to the other, before collecting his wits at the priest's awkward greeting. "Peace be with you, Alois …"

"*You!*" he bellowed. "Peace be buggered. What are you doing here in my house? Isn't it enough that you've got my Kitty working her arse off day and night in your disease-ridden clinic? And without pay! I see too you're sewing discord among my boys with your mumbo jumbo," he added in words slurred and toxic, before warming to his grievance. "Where is your God now when the whole world economy is collapsing? If He's so all-powerful, why are my rubber trees dying? Answer me that! My Kitty does enough praying for the whole bloody town. It's the likes of you and your damned sorcery that's got the world into the mess it's in now."

"Stop that swearing! You'll not speak to Father like that when I'm around. It's his prayers that brought our Klaus back from the dead." Mother had risen to her feet and moved to position herself between the nervous priest and drunken husband, pretending to rearrange the candles in her ceramic manger.

Her eyes glittered. "We're here to celebrate this special day at home, together … not that you'd know anything about that, you poor excuse for a Christian."

"Yeah, that's right Alois!" Robert had risen to his full height and moved to confront his stepfather, "Why don't you fu … buzz off and mind your own business?" This show of defiance took the old man aback; it looked like matters had finally come to a head. He swung around to confront his tormentor with his mouth flapping open and shut.

"What did you say? You … you traitor! What my family gets up to *is my business*. You always seem to have plenty to say …" he spat out his words to the boy's face. "Just who do you think you are anyway? I'll tell you who you are. You're an illegitimate bastard conceived in an Irish bog, that's who you are."

There! He'd finally said it out loud after rehearsing the words over and over in his head and awaiting the right moment to pounce. The stunned silence was broken by an unexpected source. "You, you leave him alone, you b … bastard!" Klaus stammered, jumping up and raising his fists as he'd seen his brother do, while Mother merely moaned and buried her face in her hands.

"So … you're all against me, are you? I might have guessed as much …"

All signs of intoxication now vanished as he moved intently towards the precious shrine. "Fucking Catholic Church!"

"Nah-nah Alois, there's just no need to be a carryin' on like dis," sputtered Father Malone as he too rose uncertainly to his feet. "Kitty is as loyal and true a wife as is to be farnd anywhere. If ya could get yerself offen the grog, ya'd see it as plain as the nose on yer face man, just what an Oirish jule she really is …"

Now, few actions infuriate a disgruntled husband more than another man (especially one he's already jealous of) telling him how wonderful his wife is. With a low snarl, Alois leapt forward and swept his arm across Kitty's altarpiece, sending most of it, including grandmother's china plate with the Our Father printed in gold letters, smashing to the floor.

"There! That's what I think of your God and the so-called only begotten Son of the Father," he raged, grabbing the wooden crucifix and spitting on it, before hurling it to the floor. "Bah! Messiah! I'll show you a *real saviour*: one who's bringing *practical* benefits to millions of Germans as we speak.

"Adolph Hitler is raising the German Nation from its knees to take its rightful place in the world. It's high time you took a good look at your own miserable flock, Father, a bunch of misfits and cripples as they are. So much for the healing power of your Jesus and his brown-robed lackeys. Or should I say 'lickeys'?" The spittle flew from Alois' mouth, causing Father Paddy to place a restraining hand on Kathleen's arm. She was ready to hurl herself upon the blasphemer with nails drawn. Just to think that she'd once given her heart and soul to this loudmouthed bully, but the tirade wasn't over yet …

"As for you, you little wimp, I'll say what I like in my own home under my own roof," he continued, lurching around the table as if daring the youngster to open his mouth again.

"Home! Is that what you call it?" Kitty stood hands on hips and spoke again, motioning Father Malone and the boys to remain silent. "Home? It's a Godless hovel at best. And you're the only heathen misfit around here Alois Hahn, that's what you are!" she snapped in his tone and thread. "And yer'll surely rot in Hell where yer belong. Mark my words! Yer've done yer dash with me 'n the boys. As the Good Lard is my witness, I'm divorcin' ya here and now. So there!"

"Divorce? Divorce? Remember your place, Frau Hahn. The ink's not even dry on the certificate and you're already walking away from your commitment to honour and—"

"Obey?" she cut him short, now almost speechless with fury. "You?"

"Na … Na … Kitty, ya mustna be hasty," Father Malone intervened. "Dere's more ta marriage in da oise o' de Choich dan mere obeyance. The fool attracts his just deserts as surely as the miscreant. He doesn't know for sure what he's sayin'. 'What de Lord hath joined together, no man must split asunder', Kitty," he pleaded, feeling on safer ground impetrating for marriage in general, rather than the obvious misalliance unfolding before him.

"B … But, it's merely legal in the oise o' the Choich, Father, yer said so yerself; dat's good enough fer me … an' Oim no man, in case yer hadna noticed. It's a heckuva long time since Oi've been made to feel like a real woman by dis misery-guts 'ere. The whole shebang 'as been a disaster from the start; me 'n the boys has had enough. I'll not stay under this roof a minute longer. C'mon nippers, grab your stuff; we're movin' up to the Mission, now!"

"Good riddance to the lot o' ya then," Alois blurted. "But don't think you'll be getting away scot-free. I'll make you regret this day if it's the last thing I do."

Nonetheless, he was stunned. And don't come running to me when you run out of money," he added, upping the stakes. Robert made half a move forward, fists clenched and jaw muscles working.

"Well, I got news for you, Pops: me 'n Klaus *ain't* movin' out, don't think you're getting' rid of us dat easy. You're never at home anyway …"

He turned back to his startled mother. "We're not comin' to live up at the Mission, Mam, and we got ar reasons, see?"

It was a standoff; no one knew quite what to do next. Kitty had regained her composure and broke the silence. "Well, you boys can make up your own minds, but I'm out o' here. Come along Father Pat, help me to throw a few things in a suitcase," she said, turning on her heel and pushing past her ex-hoosband. "As for you, Alois Hahn, just keep outa my way while we're packing; and don't try to come crawlin' arter me, either. Over here Father, there's more pieces under the dresser," she sniffled, pointing to chips of Mary's plaster halo on the floor.

And that was that.

From then on the two boys stuck closer together and locked off the back half of the house for themselves. For hours after the confrontation Robert paced up and down their new quarters cracking his knuckles and muttering over to himself, "I wish me n' Klaus hadda smashed 'im when we 'ad de chance."

Eventually, Alois did grasp the enormity of his transgression and kept well out of their way, while young Klaus, emboldened by his own plucky if futile outburst, was relieved that the whole incident had not come to blows.

He was only too glad to settle back into his simple routine of reading, taking photos and listening to gramophone music. When the light was right he would wander off with the old Voigtlander to see what he could find amidst the web of wonder surrounding the fractious Fazenda.

Grand Kaiser Management, like most other folks in Santa Luzia, soon realised that there had been some kind of breakdown within the Hahn family; nonetheless, they passed a motion allowing the budding photographer permanent access to the company darkroom, including a "reasonable" quantity of black-and-white supplies. Even those scornful of Alois had to admit that his younger son possessed a superior talent with the camera when compared to the sloppy efforts of former employees. Likewise, the whole workforce was chuffed when postcards of themselves wearing period costumes went on sale to tourists along the pier.

Prompted by Doc Wonders, management got together and passed the hat around to raise funds for a new 35 mm camera. When this windfall was added to the profits the boy had put aside, he had sufficient funds to send off to Belem for a brand new Leica A. Six weeks later it arrived aboard *Belle*.

25

No one, apart from the boy's mother, was more dismayed than Captain Streicher by Klaus' disappearance. He'd seen a thing or two during his years on the river, but nothing like this. All attempts to jolly the real story out of the boy, however, were met with silence, and for the rest of that year, speculation was rife along the Madeira. Even Madame Gertrude's girls looked up from their knitting to offer desipient little comments whenever the inscrutable youth passed beneath their cast-iron balustrades. Not unexpectedly, he had become somewhat recherché even among the insular Portuguese ex-pats, who now rerouted their evening promenades to peruse his photo booth display, greatly amused by the action shots of local personalities at work and play.

His "Studio Style" family portraits might choose from one of three coloured backgrounds that he'd painted himself. Almost overnight a framed likeness from "Klaus Hahn Photography" had become all the rage. It seemed everyone wanted to know him and even complete strangers said "Hello" in the street. He hung a wooden shingle out front of his fold-up awning and was amazed by the response.

Secretly though, most of his clients hoped to glean more crumbs of his mysterious tergiversation, and once he had to fight off an attempt from an older woman of obvious means to seduce him on the job. After that, he always insisted that female sitters bring along a chaperone, especially those wanting one of his daring new eau natural poses in the nearby forest. He never quite overcame his embarrassment when women of all ages eagerly cast aside their inhibitions to appear before his camera in their birthday suits. He struggled to maintain eye contact with them at all times, but unfortunately, this ploy only managed to make him look furtive and overly intense.

Masking his secret sorrow behind a self-deprecating banter merely fanned the public interest: how could one so young and modest produce such stunning photographs? Ever more requests poured in for his daring "Tarzan and Jane" poses against real jungle backdrops when he could turn his attention to the effects of forest light on wet skin and primordial poses. He realised he could turn plain-Janes into wild creatures crouching on gnarled tree trunks or emerging otter-like through shallow reed beds, poses that no other had dared imagine, let alone print and put on display. Not even the illustrated magazines contained anything similar.

Robert could not understand all the fuss being made over the sickly kid and his camera when he himself took on the jungle's dangers almost daily. He was becoming fed-up with the totally undeserved popularity of the youngster that threatened to overshadow his own swaggering achievements and did not appreciate having to share the limelight. As the pre-eminent youth leader around town, Robert's position as the gang leader, in which he'd invested so much time and energy, could be threatened.

His attitude toward Alois remained visceral, despite having given him a dose of his own medicine. Occasionally he would see the old man performing his boozy mummery between the waterfront speakeasies, or whenever *Belle* was in town, propped up at the bar of the Old Fighters Club animatedly discussing German politics with Captain Streicher. Since that fateful day when Mam had left them to it, Klaus too had observed his father's imposture playing out beneath gathering clouds of bankruptcy, if not total ruin.

Now it seemed that everywhere Klaus turned, shame threatened; never far in the back of his mind lurked the loss of his beautiful wild companion, snatched away from what he still dreamed might have been. At any moment he could suffer a flashback and relive that tiny smudge of red wedged high above the cruel torrent: and there was never any doubt just who was to blame.

Mutti meanwhile, looked down from her hilltop refuge upon the successes of her lads as a mixed bag; the one showing undeniable bushcrafts and the other an artistry of sorts, impressing all and sundry with his mastery of the latest photo techniques. She would have preferred to see them taking up proper trades and was disappointed further when her Robbie refused point blank to set foot inside the Monastery under any pretext.

Both boys conceded that Mam was enjoying an unparalleled period of contentment behind those flaking walls, within the nimbus (some said arms) of her Irish God. To hell with the anile nattering of the other wives behind her back, she'd waited long enough for a chance at real happiness and by Jesus and Mary was not going to give it up without a struggle. She was as good as any of 'em.

Perhaps this predictable routine would have drifted along indefinitely in like vein, until one day the festering jungle humours crept out to draw a fatal finger across the town's beloved matron, long since reverted to her maiden name of Kitty O'Shea.

The boys' first inkling of trouble arrived with a breathless messenger from the Mission. Their mother had come down suddenly, yesterday, yes, late yesterday afternoon, with a bad rash and flu-like symptoms.

She had at first waved away all concern, refusing to alarm her babes unnecessarily over a likely case of food poisoning. "Nuthin' ta get yer knickers in a knot over," she had assured her carers. Too late, Father Malone realised the misdiagnosis when she suddenly worsened overnight. The runner then uttered the chilling words that all Santa Luzians fear: "Yellow fever!"

Forgetting his former vow, Robert joined his brother in tearing up the hill to her bedside, dashing ahead to wait impatiently for the other to catch his breath. Donning makeshift masks, both boys were shocked by the miserable scene and stench that greeted them inside the hard-pressed ward: rows of semi-comatose patients lay moaning on flimsy cots.

At the far end of the ward, they spotted the sniffling, humped-over figure of Father Malone, who appeared to be administering last rites of sorts to the jaundiced form of their Mam, his beloved Kitty. Klaus was reminded of scenes from Dante.

"Why didn't you call us sooner?" Robert screamed at the shiny round occiput, "She's *my* Mam, not yours!" But the old priest ignored him, continuing to bleat his futile mantra over the wasted woman.

Weakly, she raised her head from the pillow and half-coughed a delirious warning. "Stay away! Keep back wee goosens ..." They were stunned by her appearance: the thin, sallow features almost unrecognisable.

"No! ... No!" Robert screamed again, and the former man of steel, the great white hunter, threw himself blubbering between priest and patient, across the sweaty sheets and into his mother's arms.

"No! Mummy, no! Yer not dyin' are yer? Dey said it's just food poisonin'. Tell me she's not dying ..." His face turned imploringly to the other anxious faces nearby before he was pulled away forcibly by two men in gowns.

Throughout this performance. Klaus remained stunned and stoic until being advised in a whisper that Alois could not be located in any of his usual haunts.

The youngster could never imagine his brother breaking down in such a torrent of sorrow; fortunately for him without fear of ridicule from his detested stepfather. But Robert wasn't finished yet, casting about to point the finger of blame. "It's all 'is fault entirely. That fucking kraut! If 'e 'adn't let 'er work in this shit 'ole in de first place ..."

"No, no, my son, dis is no one's fault but God's volition. Your mother stepped forward to spread Christ's healing touch among dese unfortunates, knowing full well the risks involved. We are all praying for her recovery, and if it be His Will then that will surely happen." Father Patrick spoke with confidence, composed. He was again in charge.

"I'm not your fucking son! And I'm not dat other bastard's neither," Robert blurted, pushing his way back to the bedside and jerking his chin downhill towards the docks. His teeth were gritted, and he was spoiling for a fight.

"Stop right dere! You boys canna stay in here, it's too risky," the revived oblate stated emphatically, ignoring Robert's outburst and shepherding them towards the door. "We're doin' all we can. If it turns out more serious than first thought then be assured I'll send word …"

"But just look at her, she don't look right … and all you do is stand around mumbling Hail Marys."

"The good Lord works in mysterious ways, my son; I saved your brother, did I not? You'll see if she's not up and abart in no time at all," he persisted. The expressions on other faces told a different story and filled the brothers' hearts with dread.

Shattered, they wandered side by side back down the hill, each lost in his own thoughts. Klaus spoke first when they sat down together on the front porch. "W … What do you think we should do now?" he asked timidly.

"Shouldn't one of us go and try to find Papa?" said Klaus. He was numbed by the utter declension of his mother and taken aback by Robert's emotional collapse. All this uncertainty was taking its toll; for the first time in many weeks, he began to struggle for breath.

"Fuck Alois!" Robert continued, "I don't want him anywhere near 'ear. Oh, fer Christ's sake, don't tell me you're startin' dat up again," his brother offered with head in hands. "A fat lot of good you'd be in a crisis …"

"W … Well, you weren't much better yourself!" the boy wheezed out, fighting for breath but determined not to let his brother regain the initiative.

"Alois reckons it's all in your 'ead, and for once I'd 'ave ta agree wid 'im. Ow come now, all of a sudden you go down in a 'eap for no apparent reason?"

Klaus made no reply, suddenly reminded that the old man was probably still ignorant of unfolding events. Neither boy felt motivated to undertake a search along the waterfront. "Sister Klara says it's caused by stress! … whenever I'm upset over something, but I don't want to talk about it anymore. You don't know what it's like not to be able to breathe properly," he puffed, forgetting entirely his vowel sounds and other potential remedies. "He did say she was goin' ta get betta, didn't he?"

Robert hadn't been listening, turning over Father Malone's assurances in his mind and sidestepping his brother's growing distress. "Why wasn't Doc Wonders sent for, even if it is only food poisoning? That's what I'd like to know!" he suddenly exclaimed, jumping to his feet. The fact that Company facilities and expertise were off-limits to Mission patients was of no consequence now. "Well, I'm goin' to get him up there to take a look at 'er, one way or another," he called back, setting off along the rubber track with renewed purpose.

"W … What about my asthma? What about Vati?" Klaus called weakly after him, but Robert was already out of sight, running for dear life.

Despite all the misplaced nosology and prayer Kitty O'Shea did not recover; she slipped into a coma soon after her boys had left the building, without uttering another word. There in the dim dystopia, she drew her last breath, clutching her well-worn Rosary to her withered breast.

She died as she had lived, alone and unforgiven. Not even her own two boys were allowed to approach the body without wearing gloves and gown, or even to kiss her goodbye for fear of the fever. It was the most soul-destroying dilemma they'd ever faced.

A ripple of fear spread right throughout the community; the whispered re-emergence of the yellow plague kept even the vaccinated Europeans on edge and terrified the coloureds. If only Kitty had not spent all that time in the Galway Registry Office and missed out on her needles, but that was irrelevant now.

Due to the oppressive heat, Frau Kathleen Hahn nee O'Shea was laid to rest early the next morning in the unhallowed ground outside the Mission walls. Despite the short notice, a small group of grateful peons, Caboclos and Seringero tappers and even a few of Robert's Rascals had turned up at the Mission to pay their respects.

Several of Madame Gertrude's girls hung back in the distance, mindful of the special services Frau Kitty had provided in their times of trouble, despite her making jokes about "all of 'em goin' ta Hell in a hand-cart".

The smell rising from the open grave kept everyone at a respectful distance, a languid breeze held off while the visibly shaken priest rattled off a quasi-formal service without the Eucharist. He attempted, where possible, to blend and direct his soaring praise and halting apologia – "Fer da life of dis outstandin' God-fearin' sister o' da Holy Roman Church, may her troubled soul rest in peace ..." – toward her two furious sons, even as they stepped forward to sprinkle a handful of red earth into the hole. They'd been overlooked in the planning of their mother's send-off. No one else spoke; in the distance, a shadowy figure could be seen hanging back from the crowd, before it hobbled away without so much as a backward glance.

26

During *Belle's* next stopover, Captain Streicher attempted to drag the details of Kitty's passing out of Alois. Decades of failure and self-abuse had stamped themselves on the features and behaviour of his old comrade in arms, who now appeared devoid of hope.

All he would say was "Good riddance" which made the skipper feel like belting him one. Captain Rudolph had a soft spot for the little Irish leprechaun and her boys, vowing to do what he could to fill their sudden void.

Robert especially seemed able to put the loss of his mother behind him and throw himself back into the safaris as if nothing untoward had occurred. He continued to badger his brother about visiting the so-called "lost tribe", and when referring to Mam at all it was almost always a jaunty recounting of earlier childhood incidents.

Conversely, following an initial outward show of composure, the younger boy spent a week in a mine emergency bed enduring a near-fatal asthma attack. Nothing he attempted could calm the chest spasms, and even Doc Wonders refused to administer further doses of adrenalin fearing his little heart would burst. Fighting for every breath, his mind raced in a diluvian jumble of parables and palpitations that dissolved in a whirling cloud of coloured lights. He drifted in and out of lucidity; what was real and what was dreaming?

"Try to see beneath the surface ..." Was he still inside his own skin ... or actually far out in the Universe witnessing the beginnings of all Creation?

When all else fails turn to the God of your heart... her invocations rang in his ears. *True knowledge is always available to the sincere seeker.* He concluded with a gulp that he had not always been sincere; not really, not always.

If only he could excel at one thing he would surely be happy; he felt ready to promise almost anything to be free of guilt over Maya and now Mother. He would become a master of light, like those in the illustrated magazines he so admired. The camera had been kind to him, why not pursue the dream?

But was he kidding himself? Would he be betraying his deeper desires to create something using his own hands rather than allowing a mere tool to read between the lines, or indeed to see beneath the surface? There were a thousand reasons why such high-blown goals would never reach fruition. The muscles in his chest were tiring and sparks continually danced behind his eyes; if only the bloody spotted cat would pounce and get it over with. There was still so much he wanted to do if only he could master his thoughts and breathing.

When he opened his eyes Captain Streicher was sitting at the foot of the bed. "Hope I didn't disturb you, young fella?" he said tenderly.

Seeing the boy fighting so bravely revived a long-dormant lump in his throat, an unwanted reminder of his own beloved little Gretchen with her long blonde pigtails, taken so cruelly by a cancer of the lung. Her last hours fighting for breath had broken his heart, steeled his character, and destroyed his marriage, finally driving him into anonymity halfway around the world. It seemed so unfair and even now he didn't like to be reminded.

Suddenly, he had an idea. Shaking off the painful recollection, he leaned forward during one of the kid's clear-headed spells and made him an offer: if he was up and about on his feet next time *Madeira Belle* was in port, he would commission a group portrait of Miss Gertie and her girls on the foredeck, no less. He'd spruce her up for the occasion. "*Belle*, not Fraulein Gertie, ha-ha, get it kid?" Furthermore, he would pay for a framed 8" × 10" print of each girl out of respect for the "difficulties" of their profession and out of the profits from his trusty roulette wheel. These would be little keepsakes from a grateful ole' River Trader. What did the boy think?

He sat back satisfied and lit up one of his handmade Cuban El Groucho, inhaling deeply and sending a blue cloud swirling over the patient's head.

But Klaus couldn't answer; his mouth flapped open noiselessly and his eyes popped at the proposal. His benefactor obviously wasn't aware that he'd already had the embarrassing privilege of posing several of the older Flamingo Palace escorts as youngish sylvan maidens emerging from rock pools or draped over mossy tree trunks.

If he had been aware, the captain would have wanted to know why copies of these very prints had not been passed among the crew members for a bit of a chuckle.

But, heck! This would be his biggest sale ever, and he'd always wanted to display Captain Streicher's distinctive profile in his showcase by the pier. He *would* be better soon, the skipper could be sure of that.

Twisting sideways, he struggled to place several fingers from his left hand onto the back of his neck, all the while intoning soft sucking sounds and trying to stay focused on his breathing. He felt like he wanted to vomit into the bucket beside the bed. With eyes closed he visualised the knots in his chest loosening and the iron grip releasing its hold on his rib cage. Or was it just the excess adrenalin lingering? He knew what he should do, and some answers began to flow. He repeated the beautiful vowels while his heart raced on and his lungs struggled for every breath. Could he remember the intonation sequence exactly?

Then suddenly, he vomited into the bucket and felt better for it.

The captain rose silently, not wishing to interrupt the strange performance; whatever the boy was doing seemed to be easing his distress and bringing him some comfort behind those tight-closed eyes. When he reached the door he looked back in bemusement, fiddled his cap up and down a few times and shook his head regretfully. "Damned if I'm not a monkey's uncle," he repeated to himself before strolling briskly back downhill toward the docks. The kid might never again be right in the head or body but he, Captain Rudolph Streicher, would not stand by and watch him suffer needlessly. His unusually generous offer would give the youngster plenty to think about before his next visit.

Doc Wonders too was baffled by Klaus' sudden improvement after he'd given up on all conventional treatments. He could see plainly that the affliction had loosened its grip and the boy seemed taken with determination to get well.

All this nonsense about hands on necks and the repetition of meaningless humming sounds had no place in modern medicine. Notwithstanding, there was no doubting the boy's improved appetite for food and reading material as he recovered in bed or propped up in the shade outside Doc's own office. He spent long hours poring over the latest posing and lighting techniques on display in the illustrated magazines featuring Heinrich Hoffmann's work. From formal portraits of Nazi bigwigs to spontaneous candids on the hop, Hoffmann became an almost mythical figure in the boy's mind, snapping cover after cover for many international publications.

With the gradual return of energy, Klaus began planning a systematic project among the outlying Seringero families, many of whom had such lived-in faces; far more interesting, he thought, than some of the shining lights glaring out from magazine pages.

Also from Hoffmann, he picked up one important tip in the form of a large fold-up square of white cardboard to reflect daylight onto his subjects' swarthy faces and soften their features, while adding highlights to the eyes. This was merely one of several aids he could take into the field for more professional-looking results of his own, but of course, few locations offered the degree of control and flexibility afforded by his tiny studio on the pier.

Regrettably, none of these clever ruses were of much use in catching wildlife unawares; most animals and birds always seemed too far away, even when he crept up practically on top of them. Or they moved too quickly to allow proper alignment of his reflectors.

While nature remained his true passion, he soon figured out that human subjects were much easier to capture, and far more profitable.

One morning, as he crouched in a clearing ringed with trumpet flowers, he caught a flash of emerald wings whirring in and out of these giant blooms like busy bumblebees: star-throats feeding!

He quickly adjusted his new Leica to 1/500th of a second in the hope of freezing their tiny wings in mid-flight, if indeed there was sufficient light to allow such fast shutter speeds. He knew that these rare sword-bills possessed the longest beaks of any hummingbird, longer even than their bodies, which enabled them to reach deep into the trumpets for nectar. He also guessed that no one in Santa Luzia had ever managed to snap a hummingbird in flight.

High above in the treetops a flock of great-beaked toucans were cackling and cavorting back and forth in a stunning and distracting mating display. From practice, Klaus knew the distinctive whistle of toucan wings before he even glanced up. One skill he'd picked up from his time among the Mojo was the wingbeats of various species sounding different through the air.

He loved to sit with eyes closed and try to guess which of his feathered friends was passing and rarely got them wrong. The Indians had pointed out that many of the less-colourful birds often possess the more melodious songs, with insect eaters being the best songsters of all.

He discovered for himself that there was no such thing as a "drab" feather: a single sunbeam could evince beauty from even the most unassuming quill. He rejoiced that nothing was drab about this buzzing swarm of sword-bills with their plum and emerald plumage catching the sunlight. Juggling his reflector between the trumpets he failed to notice a soft tread approaching.

Suddenly his brother was beside him, shotgun over his shoulder, quick to feign interest in the hummingbird project. These few acres surrounding the Fazenda were supposedly set aside for "artistic purposes" with hunting forbidden. Up until now, the cameraman had had it all to himself. Since Mam's funeral, when Alois had moved into one of the foreman's cottages with meals provided, the brothers had been leading more or less separate lives. Occasionally they exchanged banter over the breakfast table, but that was about it.

Now, out of nowhere, Robert had sidled up in full camouflage gear, unslinging his shotgun from his shoulder and showing a little too much of his perfect smile. "Whatcha upta, liddle brudder?" he purred softly.

"What's it look like?" the boy responded brusquely, jolted from his artistic reverie. "What are *you* doin' around here, more like it. There are no jaguars in this neck of the woods, or should I say, no jaguars left. You should know better than anyone." As the words came out of his mouth he remembered there *was* still one jaguar about these parts; that very real incubus haunting his nightmares.

"Why do you always have to be killing things, anyway? You could try just enjoying the purr of the hummingbird's wings or the wind in the treetops for a change ..."

For a moment his big brother looked puzzled. "Nah! I'll leave such simple pleasures for sissies like you. I'm after a couple of keepsakes for someone at Madame Gertrude's," he continued undeterred. The boy now tweaked to his brother's sudden interest in the hummingbirds. These exquisite creatures felled with birdshot and dried in the sun made cute little keyring ornaments. That would be just like Robert.

But before he could move to object, a mighty roar exploded overhead, followed immediately by a second. Deafened and in shock, Klaus looked up to see two toucans tumbling slowly down from the heights, bouncing from branch to branch in a slow-motion descent. In that same instant, the surrounding jungle erupted to the very horizon in alarm; the shooter broke cover and strode forward to collect his prize.

The remaining flock of toucans, however, far from being put off, launched from the heavens like a shower of Thespian Hags and dived at the unsuspecting youth; their huge clacking beaks tore his blue bandana from his head and sent lumps of scalp, hair and flesh flying. The startled poacher cried out in fear, struggling to protect his eyes from the savage wingbeats and preventing his reloading of the shotgun. Robert's head felt on fire as he flailed about, now swinging his empty weapon by the barrel. Instinctively suppressing a grin, the boy raised his Leica and made a single exposure.

It was only fair and just to see Mother Nature exacting revenge upon his brother, who now stumbled around blindly through the undergrowth. From a distance, he could hear Robert's garbled outburst and several bloody wounds were clearly visible.

The inoffensive photo assignment had ended in a blatant act of cruelty and humiliation; Klaus gathered up his equipment and fled toward home as fast as his legs would carry him.

"I ... I thought they might go for me too if I hung 'round," he lamely explained that night to his chastened brother, who stood cursing before the bathroom mirror and applying fresh salve to the angry wounds on his face. After hours of playing cat and mouse, confrontation was no longer avoidable.

"No fucking thanks to you, yer little coward. Take a gander at dis ..." Robert exclaimed, peeling back fresh dressings to reveal several nasty gashes in the formerly translucent skin of his face and neck. The boy winced and immediately felt guilty for having chortled at the time. One particularly deep cut under the left eye appeared already to be infected, and a chunk of ear lobe was missing.

"Fucking toucans, I hate 'em. All I wanted was a few feathers for Trudy, didn't Oi? From now on I'll shoot every one of de bastards I see, mark my words," he muttered, directing an evil eye toward his useless brother and the invisible enemy.

For weeks, he gazed anxiously into the mirror each morning, hoping against hope that the scars and swelling would soon be gone, but as time passed it became clear he'd been marked for life. The perfect lustre of his skin was chipped and dented, causing the determined set of his jaw to appear slightly askew. Thank the Good Lord that Mama hadn't lived to see the damage. Healing was slow, and the resultant weals gave him a distinctive battle-scarred look of maturity. His face now exuded the repellent fascination of an age hard to fathom.

Yet inside, swelling resentments simmered, and with the passing of time, he would convince himself and others that the pinkish welts were actually duelling scars.

Soon after, Klaus was strolling past Madam Gertrude's and lifted his face to return a good-natured jibe coming from the balcony above. One girl in particular leaned over the rail and caught his eye, causing a sinking feeling in his stomach. It was Trudy, wearing a tiara that quivered unmistakeably of bright toucan plumes. Her upper arms were also adorned in like-coloured amulets.

He lowered his gaze and continued toward the docks, mumbling to himself, and for a time avoided Flamingo Villa entirely by distracting his mind with a few ideas on light he wanted to try out before Captain Streicher's pending portrait sitting.

"Do you miss Mutti? ... I sure do," the youngster enquired of his brother during a rare moment together. Robert stared back coldly. "What do you think? Of course I do, but I don't wanna talk about it."

"Why not? If I can't share my feelings with you, then who? You really have no idea what I've been through, do you?"

"Well, take my advice and don't share 'em at all unless you want to spill the beans on where your imaginary tribe of head-hunters is holed up. Nobody's interested in your far-fetched stories; just grow up and face de real world for a change." Robert was in no mood to be reminded of his own loss, let alone another's. "I've just about had enough o' all this God shit you keep goin' on about; there is no God." His voice trailed off and his brow creased. "If you must know, I've heard it all before, up close and personal. I've seen our blessed Christian Brother in action ..." He struggled to get the words out, unsure whether to continue, "How I hate dem sanctimonious pricks with a passion; have you no idea what dey did to me and the boys? Dey knew I was havin' trouble at 'ome, see: 'God dis and Jesus dat' ... an' den, wham! If you ask me, the whole bloody Mission's full of perverts."

The boy looked puzzled, but the floodgates had opened. "Can't you get it threw your tick head? Now I'm free, once and for all!" came his muffled revelation. "All my life I've had Mam's mumbo jumbo ringin' in my ears, then Father Paddy and 'is lot; and now *you*! From here on in I go my own way, and I don't care whose nose ends up out of joint, get it?" He had worked himself up in a moment, looking a little foolish glaring out through his strappings. Since his run-in with the toucans, Robert had taken to wearing the most outlandish outfits scrounged from a variety of sources, possibly to legitimise or distract attention away from his facial blemishes toward his overall appearance.

With curls tied back in a ponytail and buttoned waistcoat over leg-o-mutton sleeves, all the way down to his knee breeches and boot buckles, he looked every inch the swaggering buccaneer. While there was no denying that his superior "kill rate" endeared him to many hopeful tourists, his high and mighty treatment of Caboclos and other "inferior" hired hands left a bad taste in some local mouths. Blacks, browns, or merely "creamies" were referred to as "niggers" or "half-breeds" to their faces. Whispers circulated that the boy was turning "queer".

At that time his charms became more calculated, able to be turned on and off at will. There were occasions now when townsfolk went out of their way to avoid him in the street. Few knew or cared what had occurred behind the flaking mission walls to fan his change of heart. He fired off unprovoked insults to anyone who'd stop long enough to listen, often rounding on his stepfather's culpability for Mam's "murder" and the indignities to which she'd been subjected. "It was 'is stand-over tactics dat drove her to it, we saw it wit' our own eyes," he lamented to his brother for the hundredth time, "... and der loneliness, leaving her alone all day long after promisin' er da earth. You tell me. Is dat de proper thing to do when you remove a person from everythin' dey love, and dump 'em a million miles away when dey can't even speak de language?" He had apparently forgotten his stated intention to change the subject. "It's no wonder she ended up packin' her bags to shack up with dat old fart up de hill."

"S ... She didn't move in with him. She had her own cell and slept among the patients. That's how she caught the fever. It's almost as if she was putting God to the test. There's no point in blaming Vati ..."

"I'll fix 'im if it's the last thing I do," Robert muttered, raising an eyebrow at the prospect of revenge, "... at least I got to fix up 'is Sunday dinners good an' proper. C'mon, I know you saw me dat time. At least I had dat pleasure of watchin' 'im tuck in," he perked up noticeably at the treasured memory. "Yes sir, yes sir, three bags full, sir. Enjoy your big fat homegrown chicken, Vati, sir ..."

Despite his brother's resentments and superficial successes, Klaus could never excuse his shameful betrayal of Maya, having crossed his heart and hoped to die. Worse was his total lack of remorse. How could the very person he'd looked up to stoop to such a shameful act against a mere child, no matter his own alleged misuse at the hands of Brother Romero and his onanistic monks?

As the time for the portrait sitting approached, Madame Gertrude's girls were all abuzz, and the Hahn boys too were excited for different reasons. Captain Streicher had wired ahead that not only was *Belle* going to be spruced up for the group photo, but had on board a small but exclusive hunting party of German military advisors en route from Bolivia to Manaus. He gave notice that several days layover was scheduled in Santa Luzia to apply a long overdue facelift to the old girl, and he had assured his honoured guests that they would have plenty of time to bag a panther or two. He knew of just the young fellow to guarantee them a kill.

Robert was instructed at short notice to prepare for a two-night camp-out in the Varzea, and for days he scrambled about hiring the necessary contingent of camp servants, including of course, a German chef from the mine to provide a truly "Top Deck" experience.

"Regardless of cost," the skipper had stressed. These visitors were obviously in a category all their own, as Captain Streicher rarely went out of his way for anyone, let alone foreign touristas. The new German military was different.

When contemplating the long and specific list of instructions, Robert thought his "booking agent" must be going soft in his old age.

27

The Hahn brothers got their first glimpse of the German V.I.P.s in the Old Fighters Club behind the wheelhouse, where they could be seen breasting the bar and engaging in vigorous discussion with Alois and Captain Streicher.

Their superior officer, a short, stocky man with an obvious military bearing was attended by a lithe, blond-haired valet and two sun-tanned Bolivian orderlies barely out of their teens, both wearing smart white uniforms.

All three were nodding agreeably at their leader's every utterance; in profile, the boys could see the officer's face was horribly scarred, and that the bridge of his nose was missing. There, in the mid-afternoon heat, he was holding forth to a saloon filled with ex-pats and selected big-eyed barflies, the lively background buzz told of a good deal of Schnapps having already been consumed.

"… stabbed in the back? Of course, Germany was stabbed in the back. We'd just begun to turn things around at the front when those November criminals threw in the towel; it's common knowledge. And then out of the blue, we have all those clever fellows who stayed behind to thank for the so-called Armistice, just when my old fighters were getting on top. Look at what we were left with: fucking Bolsheviks and Jews running the show; they're all the bloody same. Don't worry; my stormtroopers and a little rabble-rousing from Adolph will stop these bastards in their tracks. We Nazis are determined to control the whole country and give the Volk a voice."

A sprinkling of applause followed as he puffed out his chest and tossed down another drink. "Death to all traitors, I say: Long live the Fatherland!"

"See, see … what did I tell you?" Alois piped up excitedly to no one in particular. "Fresh news about what's really going on back home, that's what we've been waiting for …"

Well, you may not get it from him, Alois; he's been stuck in Bolivia for the past two years training an army," Captain Streicher countered, "he's probably no more up-to-date than the rest of us."

"You know, Colonel Röhm," added Alois, ignoring the hint and pleased to enlighten the newcomers, "we get the *Völkischer Beobachter* delivered here every month; that's how I know so much of what's going on back home, see?" At that, he leapt off the stool, clicked his heels together loudly and stuck out his right arm. "Heil Hitler!"

A stunned hush fell, before the clubhouse erupted in laughter. The colonel motioned for silence. "There's no need to bother with that sort of thing out here, old chap," he responded, clearly taken aback. Stumbling to attention, he returned the new-fangled obeisance. "As a matter of fact, Herr Unter-manager, I am in constant contact with the leadership by mail and telephone. "Or I was, until we got stuck in this God-forsaken hole."

Alois continued, quite unabashed, "Is it true Colonel Röhm, that Adolph Hitler and his National Socialists get around one hundred thousand souls turning up for a single meeting these days?"

"Tosh! Two and three hundred thousand is not uncommon; with a half million or more coming together for the annual Party Rally in Nuremberg. No one can motivate the masses like Adi. I can tell you that Germany is on the move again, and it behoves every Aryan patriot to get behind the Great Revolution. That's why Marty and I are heading home to rejoin the fray, as soon as this little jaunt is over, aren't we boys?" Again, he looked toward his companions for confirmation. "Parting is such sweet sorrow, aaah."

The Bolivian youths exchanged wan looks.

"I promised Mutti I'd bring back a jaguar hide from Bolivia, but thus far we've not seen so much as a glimpse, have we boys?" he slurred again over his companions, leaning forward to drape a lazy arm around each of their shoulders with far more familiarity than is usual between ranks.

"Yes Colonel, and this time we're going to make a proper job of it, right? Back in Germany, I mean," replied the blond petty officer flippantly, "… after we bag a jaguar or two, I mean." The squat man smiled his crooked grin and nodded approvingly, before gathering himself to address his enthralled audience.

"Since I am an immature and wicked man, war and unrest appeal to me. At last, we Nazis stand ready to fight our way into power, nothing and no one can stand against my stormtroopers. We will rid the Fatherland of every last weakling and traitor who collaborated in the Nation's betrayal. Are you with us or against us?" Some applause.

He fumbled his glass, spilling Schnapps down the front of his dress uniform. "Death to all enemies of the Reich!" he roared. "Heil to the Fatherland, Heil Hitler!"

"Fight, fight and more fighting!" Captain Streicher interjected, thrusting his chin forward. "Why such disputes can't be settled peaceably between so-called civilised peoples is beyond me. Wasn't one World War enough for you and your lot, whether we were cheated out of victory or not?" Silence.

"It's pretty obvious that all this fighting hasn't done *you* much good, Colonel" he added pointedly, referring to Röhm's shattered features. These days he would back himself against all further talk of war, but soon realised he was overstepping the mark.

"Aha! That's where you and a lot of others are confused, Mein Capitan," retorted Colonel Röhm, "… because we Nazis are not so *civilised*, as you call it. We see ourselves as true Barbarians, no less, and will use barbaric methods where necessary to achieve our ends. Adolph has convinced the ranks they must be *proud* barbarians …"

He took a sip of his drink.

"Hullo! What have we here?" his voice faltered, catching sight of the two brothers hanging back awaiting an introduction.

"This is the hunting guide I promised you, Colonel Röhm," beamed Captain Rudolph, clearly relieved, "and his young brother is a photographer of note who will capture your triumphs perfectly on film." He motioned the boys to step forward.

"Tour Guide Robert Hahn, sir, at your service … for the hunt, sir," spoke up the elder boy confidently as he stepped into the light. The others looked him over slowly, bemused by the boy's buccaneer outfit topped off by a sweeping cocked hat with toucan plumes.

Without a word, Röhm spun on his stool to face the youngster in the shadows. "And who might you be sweet pea? A bit young to be a cameraman, aren't you?"

Klaus fiddled with his cap, but before he could respond, Alois again lurched from his stool, cleared his throat and stood to attention, elbowing Captain Streicher to one side. "Obersturmführer S.A. Captain Röhm; may I present my two sons, Robert and Klaus Hahn, of the Hamburg Hahns." It was unbelievable and embarrassing. For the first time, Alois had acknowledged his ill-gotten stepson in public. But the officer ignored the belated announcement and continued to feast his eyes on the boys, reaching forward to give each a brisk, firm handshake.

Robert broke the ice. "I'm sure we're all committed to makin' your trip as enjoyable as possible, Colonel Sir".

"God help us! Just you make sure I bag my big cat, for starters. Oh, and plenty of booze. I already heard this young monkey spent some time among the Indians; see if you can line up a couple of boys from the local tribe who'd like to come along for the ride and keep the mozzies away at night, ha-ha." He winked at Klaus who blushed crimson.

"Oh no, sir, if you don't mind me sayin'," Robert interjected, with his plumes quivering righteously, "Dese Indians never wash and steal everytin' dat ain't nailed down."

"Well, I'll be the judge of that," said Röhm. "You just see to it that we have a good time and you'll be well rewarded. He rolled a gold coin slowly between his thumb and forefinger, motioning towards the boy. "And what about you, sunshine? What do *you* plan on doing for the Great Revolution back home, eh?" he said and winked again.

"Not too much, sir, I suffer from asthma," Klaus responded nervously.

"Asthma? Ha! The disease of weaklings, it's all in the head; attention-seeking," he scoffed, turning back to the bar and accepting a light for one of Captain Streicher's hand-rolled El Groucho. The introductions were over.

He turned back to the guests. "Like I was saying, the masses understand only one language: force! Brutality is understood and respected everywhere. Anyone who thinks differently is a fool and a traitor to everything we Nazis stand for. We were stabbed in the back in '18 and are doing no more than reclaiming our God-given rights on behalf of the German Volk."

They were warming to his theme. "We are battling for the very existence of a new Reich and I've created my stormtroopers out of nothing for that very purpose; we're smoothing the path for the coming German Man." He glared hopefully towards the ex-pats with his tiny porcine eyes flicking back and forth from the others to Robert, who had eased onto a nearby stool, drinking in this yarn of war and revolution. Klaus had never seen his brother so completely captivated; he shrank back into the shadows to study the charismatic Soldier of Fortune from afar.

"Captain Röhm", as addressed by his young valet, was formidable even when drunk; the very embodiment of command. Although short, no more than 5'5", his barrel-shaped torso rippled with muscle and confidence. But the face! It clung like a three-quarter moon to a neckless egg-head atop broad bovine shoulders. The bridge of the nose had been shot clean away and both cheeks carried deep, disfiguring scars. A tiny clump of hair, centre-parted, adorned the crown of his polished skull like a doily.

Now, some sixth sense drew Röhm's attention back to the boy in the shadows, who sat suspecting something terrible may happen if he allowed his eyes to stray. "Go on; take a good look, Jungvolk. This is the cost of standing up for one's Principals," he slurred, "… for defending one's homeland."

Klaus stared back.

"I earned an Iron Cross First-Class to get these scars, storming a machine gun nest with half my face blown away," Röhm lied. "And how about you, Captain Hook?" he spun back to face Robert. "What's your excuse? Did you get your head caught in an alligator's jaws or something?" he guffawed loudly at his blushing guide-to-be and slapped him hard on the backside.

Klaus thought there was something equally fascinating and repulsive about Röhm up close: his double chin wobbled and his tiny schnurrbart "snot-catcher" looked a poor imitation of Herr Hitler's own distinctive black bristles so evident in magazine photos. The attentive youngster had noticed ever greater numbers of these funny little upper-lip appendances popping up in group photos right across Germany; he wondered if the disparaging nickname impeded kissing.

From that day on, Robert looked upon his own disfigurements more easily.

"Ahem, yes Colonel", said Alois, clearing his throat and hoping to change the subject. "One has only to look at the differences between two mighty world rivers, Colonel, the Rhine and the Amazon, of course; yet why only one mighty people?" he probed, wagging a finger and steering the conversation in a direction only he understood.

"Just look at what we Germans have accomplished throughout history: great castles, bustling cities, fine vineyards. Compare it with this disease-ridden dump. Why, the only signs of civilisation for a hundred miles around are those brought in from Europe by the Grand Kaiser. It's the same all up and down the river," he disparaged. "Without German culture and initiative, these untermenschen would still be roaming about half-naked eating each other …"

It seemed obvious that Colonel Röhm was a man after his own heart.

"*If* you overlook the fact that the Portuguese were here a hundred years before us Germans," Captain Streicher threw in sarcastically, "and I suppose you're also referring to the smallpox, the deforestation and the waterways poisoned with mercury. Don't think I'm blind to the real damage being done to these people, not to mention a certain rubber plantation going bust with creditors breathing down a certain neck. We don't have to look too far to find more examples of so-called European superiority over the natives." He stopped himself going on as Alois' mouth flopped open and shut, searching for a suitable response. "Damage? What damage? The forest grows back soon enough; every fool knows that."

The skipper took a deep breath. "Unless too much of it gets burned down too often to grow back, and turns instead into a wasteland of weeds and herds of cattle where the mighty jungle has stood since time began. It *never* comes back the same; even a fool like me can see that". The unter-manager remained silent.

Captain Streicher had watched his embittered countryman fading for years, everything he touched had fallen apart. Now his old comrade in arms was attempting to hitch his wagon to an "Elite of New Men" who would miraculously transform their crippled homeland and hopefully himself along with it. Alois now slumped across the bar, his bubble pricked.

Röhm meanwhile looked bored, again lowering his green eyes from Robert to the boy, who was trying his best to remain inconspicuous.

"I'll ask you again, Jungvolk. What contribution do you intend to make in the New Reich, eh?"

Klaus paused briefly, holding the Colonel's eye. "With photography, sir!" he replied confidently this time, "if I had to choose just one thing."

"Photography? How in God's name do you expect to fight a war with a camera?" Röhm was clearly bemused: a snigger ran through the crowd.

"Perhaps you've not heard the saying, sir, that a picture is worth a thousand words? For years I've watched Photohaus Hoffmann and others using photography in a powerful new way to promote Adolph Hitler and his revolutionary ideas. Heinrich Hoffman, perhaps more than any other photographer, highlights the leading personalities and achievements of the New Movement while also pointing out the dangers of Bolshevism. If I may say, Herr Colonel, I believe I've seen your own image appearing beside Herr Hitler on certain front covers."

"Bolshevism, Photo Hoffmann? Who is this kid hiding his light under a bushel? What the hell do you know about Heini Hoffmann? He's an old friend of mine from way back."

"I study his work in the illustrated magazines, sir, and admire him greatly. I've been hoping to post a portfolio of my work one day for critique by the great Master himself."

"Perhaps when you return to Munich you might consider, er ... Photo Hoffmann publishes more decent photos than all the other magazines combined ... at least so it seems to me, sir." The boy cleared his throat, wondering if he'd already said too much.

"Shades of Wotan! The kid's a political pundit to boot," the broken face beamed. "Come out here and give me a good look at you. Next thing you'll be wanting from me is to line you up for an introduction." The boy stepped out of the shadows, looking spick and span in his freshly ironed khaki safari suit.

"Oh no, sir! I have no intentions of moving to Germany. I love living here by the river. My postcard business is just beginning to take off. I simply could not imagine being uprooted from this world of nature and trying to function surrounded by millions of people ..."

"Nature! What's nature ever done for anyone except bite and sting and burn? The boy's had too much sun," Röhm announced to the room.

"As for art, I'll tell you one thing Jung mann: there's a lot more money to be made in the gutters of Munich than in this so-called El-Dorado, your father's right about that much at least. German Art is undergoing a real revival under the sure eye of Adolph Hitler, returning to the eternal styles of Greek Classicism and better. For us Nazis, there'll be no more of that modern trash that had begun to pop up in German galleries before I left.

"Munich is the heart and soul of the Nazi movement and Heini Hoffmann is flat-out spreading the message; he's opening studios all over the place. Stay here and you end up as just one more dawdler in a straw hat; or shacked up with one of those half-breeds and a tribe of snot-nosed kids under your feet." He leaned back to assess the impact of his words. "Postcards? Bah! Stick with me and I'll teach you to catch real men with that camera of yours; powerful men who are making the whole world quake in its boots. Marty! Where's Marty?" his reddened eyes darted through the smoke. "For Christ's sake, Marty, try and talk some sense into the kid. Good German stock going to waste with no sense of his own destiny ..."

"B … But, I'm half-Irish, sir … my mother is from Ga—"

Too late for excuses, the colonel raised his glass in the air. "Three cheers for the Fatherland, hip hip!" Further protestations were drowned in a roar of consensus.

"Why don't you tell 'im about de lost head-hunters and da flying lizards while you're at it," Robert ventured when the din subsided, nervously flicking his fingernails and trying to remind Colonel Röhm of his presence. "For your information, Colonel Sir, I've studied how Blucher saved Wellington from defeat at Waterloo; against the French, sir …"

But his words had little effect and this time Klaus refused to be sidetracked. "I believe photography is poised to become the most exciting art form of the 20th Century, Colonel Röhm. It is photo-illustration even more than the words in magazines that are informing not only Europe but those of us on the other side of the world about what's really going on these days."

The Humpty Dumpty head gave a thoughtful nod. "Well, you might have a point; I hadn't really considered it. But don't believe for a moment that your glossy magazines tell the *whole* story; things back home have been getting somewhat out of hand without the inspired leadership of yours truly."

All of Adolph's letter-writing and frantic phone calls tell the same story. "Come back where you belong, Brother Ernst, all lovey-dovey when he wants something. Make no mistake, I've been playing hard to get – 'All in good time, Adi; I'm out to shoot a big cat for Mutti' – haven't I, Marty?" The valet nodded sheepishly.

"It seems National Socialism is at last on the cusp of power and Adolph needs Ernst Röhm back on the scene to seal his chances. He's finally realised that without the muscle of me and my million-plus Brownshirts, he might not find it quite so easy to pull off," he chuckled and rubbed his sausage fingers gleefully at the thought of laying down a rosy future on his own terms.

"Who is this man?" whispered the ex-pats; on first-name terms with Germany's rising star and brimming with political theories. Up until now, Captain Streicher had had no real inkling of the importance of his V.I.P. passenger who had arrived on board wearing the uniform of a Bolivian Army colonel and bearing a signed letter of introduction from President Hernando Reyes himself.

He'd booked the whole upper deck of *Madeira Belle* for his private party, paying with gold coins in advance. "And there'll be plenty more after we bag our first jaguar," he promised. The skipper was confident he'd brought them to the right place for an authentic "rumble in the jungle" as specified.

"Well, if you ask me there's no such thing as gratitude," slurred Alois, rejoining the fray. "Take my two boys, for example. Didn't I go out of my way to instil proper discipline in them, and did I get any thanks from their mother? Didn't I go halfway around the world to share the Hahn Family name and fortune with a bog Irish peasant? And what thanks do I get? I get ignored and insulted, that's what."

"Aha! Perhaps if you had acted a little more fatherly, and husband-like for that matter," Captain Streicher interjected, coming to the aid of the brothers, "you just might earn yourself more respect all-round."

"You? Listen to yourself!" Alois blurted. "Fleecing people at the tables and watering down the Schnapps. Don't think I'm not awake to your tricks, comrade."

"Tricks like providing you with all the homeland comforts when we're in port? And keeping you safe from all those who'd like to put a bullet in you, *comrade*!" The skipper had won again, and Röhm resumed his interrupted monologue on the virtues of National Socialism and the essential role of the Monarchy in German Affairs. "It's all about the working classes; they not only respect their rulers but are the real strength of the Fatherland. We Nazis reject capitalism outright as a tool of the Jews. It's time the big estates were broken up among the people. My stormtroopers will stand beside the workers on the picket lines and there will be no class distinctions under a revitalised Volksgemeinschaft. And by the way, under *my* leadership, all essential industries will be nationalised. Our mighty army would never have been tricked into surrender if not for those fat Kikes who stayed behind and got rich while we foot-soldiers were bled white in the trenches. I'm sure you are aware that we were not beaten on the battlefield, but were betrayed by—"

"Yes, yes, you've said that already." Captain Streicher was growing weary of the tale.

A hush fell as Röhm continued undaunted. "Well, why wouldn't we have failed? Those treacherous old fogies in charge of the war effort need lining up against a wall and shot if you ask me! And Adi's just the man to do it. Now, it seems *only I* can pull the stormtroopers back into line, isn't that so, Marty? We're flying out from Manaus to La Paz in a couple of weeks and then over to the coast for the voyage to Hamburg; this looks like the last holiday I'll be having for a while." He stared vacantly for a moment.

"The Movement needs all the help it can get and in return offers adventure, good pay and reliable comrades." He raised his glass. "Who's for the Fatherland!" A roar went up from every throat as the crowd joined in with the former National Anthem, "Deutschland, Deutschland, Uber Alles". Tears mixed with sweat ran free.

Later that afternoon when the sun had lost its bite, Robert offered Röhm and his bleary-eyed companions a tour around town in a horse-drawn wagon, while Klaus slipped away to prepare for his much-anticipated portrait sittings on the morrow. He spared a thought for his impulsive elder brother, who no doubt intended to stay up half the night carousing with his clients. He wondered at the guide's ability to lead a full safari the next morning at daybreak, let alone shoot straight.

Drowsing lightly under his mozzie net, he planned perfect poses in his mind. How would he ever control such a rowdy group? How would he react when confronted with dozens of powerful personalities in such confined spaces? He suddenly flashed back to the Rainbow Cave with closed eyes, reliving recent events, always in the wrong place to catch the horns of sunrise and be lifted up. Compelled to watch on from afar as the rainbows scattered over the others, his legs were leaden and no one could hear him crying inside.

The coloured lights slowly faded away, leaving the boy alone in the darkness. He so much wanted to take a photo of the scene but his Leica was gone.

Only the sweetness of reverberating sound remained between the drips. He dreamed he was awake, struggling to understand why Captain Streicher and Madame Gertrude were pacing up and down together in mounting frustration.

It was as if he didn't exist at all; like he was a mute shadow again observing events from above.

Following that troubled night, he could scarcely concentrate on his mental exercises and deep breathing. In such a fragile state he fronted up dockside and busied himself examining the angle and intensity of the sun which was already searing *Belle*'s port-side planking.

He settled on several good patches of shade aboard and ashore.

Up above on the top deck surrounded by a band of Madame Gertrude's madels, Captain Streicher sat holding court: a squeal went up as Klaus struggled up the gangplank with his camera around his neck and unwieldy tripod over his shoulder.

"Good mornin' Jung mann, or should I say, man of the hour, ha-ha?" the skipper chuckled good-naturedly; so far so good.

Panting nervously, the pristine professional placed his equipment on the deck, faced the milling courtesans and gave a little bow from the waist, at that very moment noting a loose leg on the tripod. Dammit! Of all days.

"We thought you weren't coming, didn't we, Frauleins? Come closer you beauties over there, don't hang back. Well, let's get on with it, boy!" This sudden brusqueness unnerved Klaus further, the whole scene was enveloped in a heady cloud of perfume.

Madame Gertrude clapped her hands and called for order. Slowly, and with some ongoing adjustments he managed to seat the younger, often prettier girls in the front row, while those with prominent bustles looked best standing in profile at each extreme, like bookends. Of course, given his promise to foot the bill Captain Streicher was seated front row centre alongside Madame Gertrude, who blinked uncertainly in the daytime glare.

The skipper wore a double-breasted masters jacket with shoulder boards and braid, the breast pocket of which featured a Kaiser Wilhelm Crown and Anchor Logo embroidered in silver thread. Three bright medals rode upon the other breast beneath his freshly clipped and waxed trademark handlebars. On either flank three diverse rows of fashion stood poised in readiness. "C'mon, what are you waiting for?" he urged. "Don't forget, we're having individuals done after this," he reminded fellow posers over his shoulder. He looked sleek and contented with thumbs tucked into suspenders.

The more the budding artist tried to tighten the sprawling group the greater the mirth he evoked; stragglers pushed and shoved each other on the fringes and several old campaigners were deliberately hiding their faces behind the bonnets of those in front.

"When you're ready ladies; don't be bashful, chests out!" Klaus cried in vain above the merriment. He very nearly lost his temper when a pair of "rabbit ears" popped up above Madam Gertrude's tight-wound braids.

Then, suddenly, magically, it all came together and the job was done; three quick clicks and the girls were off down the gangplank waving their parasols, ready to appear as background extras out of focus during the private sittings. Their turn to shine would come soon, if indeed the young photographer could maintain the gruelling pace.

"Can't wait to see the results, Jungle Boy," one beauty called up coquettishly from a nearby stall selling coconut milk, but his stomach was churning and he blushed in response, fearing he'd buggered up the settings given the severe glare and contrasts in clothing. The company store had been out of flashbulbs for a month, or he would have tried the new "fill in flash" technique he'd read about in the *Illustrierter Beobachter* … too late now.

"Righto then! Where do you want me to stand? I rather fancy over here," Captain Streicher strode confidently to the rail and struck a Napoleonic pose in full glare of the sun. "How's this one?"

"I … er … think it would be better to avoid direct sunlight, Captain," Klaus ventured timidly, trying to avoid a background clutter of hammocks and a herd of goats on the third-class deck below.

"Hell, I could get used to this modelling caper. *Shade?* I thought we needed bright sun for good photos."

"Not these days, Captain. Modern film allows me to capture perfect images in softer, ambient light. I mean, shade is more flattering for wrinkles and blemishes, and that sort of thing."

The artist stood his ground; Madam Gertrude nodded approvingly.

"I thought a couple in the wheelhouse and a couple on the docks to finish up with, sir; showing *Belle* in the background, of course," he added. The imposing subject snorted and straightened his tie. "All right then, but cut the lecture, will you? This collar is killing me."

"Perhaps you could choose to wear something less formal for the afternoon session at the palace. Madame Gertrude stipulated there's no point in us arriving too early," the boy chatted on, trying to manoeuvre Captain Streicher into a less shop-worn pose. "I was hoping that after these formals I could follow you around for a while and catch you going about your usual duties?"

"Ha! Think you'll catch me unawares, do you? Well, I won't be doing too much work in my best jacket, now will I? Then again, I will need to stay half dolled up for Gertie's little prayer group afterwards, ha!"

But Klaus had been thrown by the residual nervous confusion following the group photo, and by the captain's insistence on flitting back and forth between sunlight and shade. "How's this look, Jung mann? I'm beginning to get the hang of this posing business, eh." He plonked his foot upon a lower railing once more and leaned forward with a fist clenched beneath his chin. "What about this, like I've seen the movie stars doin'?"

"I … er, think it looks like you're giving yourself an uppercut, Captain." But before he had a chance to adjust his aperture or focus, the subject changed position yet again, resting his elbows on the balustrade with chin in hands and gazing pensively into the distance.

"I see the great white hunters got away late again," he ventured after a long silence, changing back to himself with a note of sarcasm. "That Colonel Röhm has certainly got your father stirred up, and quite a few others by the looks of it, with all his talk of a New Age back home …"

"Could you place your foot on the rail again Captain, and lean your elbow on your knee, like before … please? Now, tilt your chin slightly toward me, to catch the reflection off the gunnel …"

"Harrumph! I'll be buggered! I hadn't realised there would be this much mucking about," Captain Rudy chortled, but the artist could see he was secretly pleased to be "professionally posed" this way and that.

At 1:30 pm sharp, they arrived at Flamingo Villa for high tea, where a stunning display of high fashion awaited the weary boy: each girl had changed into evening wear and insisted on being photographed separately, as well as on the captain's generous lap.

"After all, I am paying for the damn things," he reminded them shamelessly. "And, in case you hadn't realised, this kid charges like a wounded bull. Git over here you gorgeous creature and don't be shy," he said, reaching for the nearest mannequin.

As each pose morphed into the next Klaus' head began to spin, forcing him to abandon any pretence of revealing individual character and revert to somewhat hackneyed poses beside the only large window in the building. His pleas to work on the upper deck outside fell on deaf ears; none wished to risk their makeup in the pressing humidity. The light indoors remained dim and his subjects lively, a thorny combination to tax even the most accomplished professional.

On the verge of collapse and plagued by doubt, he finally extricated himself and headed for the darkroom with five exposed rolls of Agfa black-and-white tucked safely in his bag. This was by far the largest and most diverse sitting he'd ever attempted in a single day. If only the tripod hadn't fallen apart. Hand-held cameras often result in unsharp portraits, but they are indispensable in catching those candid moments many seem to prefer nowadays. There was no middle ground. When roll #5 finally emerged from the fixing canister, he was able to breathe a sigh of relief and collapse into a comfy chair. He could see at a glance most of the negatives were sharp and properly exposed. He muttered a brief prayer of gratitude to the "God of his Heart" before dozing off.

Upon awakening, he dared to hope that Captain Streicher would also be pleased with the results, sufficiently pleased to pay the full fee of two hundred reals as agreed. A career in professional photography may yet be on the cards after all. Holding roll #5 up to the light he searched hopefully for one particular exposure where a certain bold young lady had momentarily popped out a bare breast with one hand while stroking Captain Streicher's proud moustache with the other. Of course, he would get a huge pleasure on seeing the finished results, having no idea what the girl had been up to when the shutter clicked.

Well satisfied, Klaus dashed home to make a banana sandwich, something less exotic than the smelly cheeses, sausages, olives and caviar usually gracing the Villa's brimming sideboard, every morsel of which he'd been too timid to sample in case he had to spit out into his hanky, like the first time he'd tried pickled artichoke hearts.

What he needed now was a dose of wild simplicity to digest the overwhelming events of the day and may just have an hour or so till sunset. Gathering up an essay on Schmidt-Rottluff he hurried towards his favourite Kapok tree beside the oxbow lake, safe behind the compound wire. At this time of year, the water's edge was receding, though wheeling flocks of honey-eaters still dipped into the clear millpond farther out.

Right on cue came the evening howler chorus, appearing to endorse all his own stresses and frustrations of the day.

The antics of a tiny tree-creeper diverted his eye from the colourful pages as it scuttled up and over the mighty buttresses, tearing off tiny flakes of bark in a neverending search for insects. Overhead turquoise lorikeets spoiled for choice, tumbled about in the fruited foliage. Dragonflies glistered in and out among the reeds, pausing only long enough to deposit their eggs beneath the spikes of a sumptuous Victoriana lily pad. He breathed easier as his spirits rekindled, feeling again the urge to reply to those unseen feathered friends whose melodies he knew off by heart.

Between these conversations he could imagine himself attuned to that same primal energy as Tarzan before him; his one true hero whose fluency in jungle jargon, albeit on another continent, was absolute and enviable. Unlike Tarzan, however, he doubted if he'd ever be brave enough to remain alone after dark in the rustling darkness without a campfire.

Again, the old male howler sent forth a string of impotent arias; equally harsh rejoinders rode back astride the rising moon. Thoughts of blazing sunsets and clifftop campfires with a lost friend came; had those months among the

Mojo *really* taken place as remembered? Alone in the twilight, surrounded by the chattering web of life evoked eidetic fantasies and drew him back inexorably to the Lost City of Atua.

"Maya loves Jesus and his Papa …" he could hear the girl speaking those simple words of faith confirming Sister Klara's deistic detritus concerning the Divine Force that she said fills the Universe with Truth, Justice and especially Love … or, was it Charity?

Breathing deep through clear nostrils he hummed his favourite vowels in sequence, not wishing to burst this bubble of comforting thought. There in the lonely shadows, he sank ever deeper into reverie, entering an elusive afflatus of "Peace Profound". His heart seemed to exude tiny pulses of light and energy which peppered his eyelids, growing into the familiar flickering flame of knowledge.

He knew not how long the atonement lasted, but could again rejoice in Maya's alluring odour and almost taste her purple lips when she smiled. He saw again the blue-black sheen of her hair blowing free in the clifftop breezes; again he was part of All Life, of Creation itself. No more important than any other portion, but certainly no less.

For all their fancy clothes and thick-pasted cheeks, Madame Gertrude's girls could never hold a candle to the childhood sweetheart who had accompanied him through thick and thin to her doom. She had given her life that he might succeed. His head was clear again, clear enough to weigh the big issues barely touched upon thus far. Surely, if he could enhance his *true* self by mixing with good and decent people, he wouldn't go too far wrong. A life serving his Creator and all living things was the only goal worth striving for. Oh! And of course, it was essential to define one's *priorities*, as Sister had stressed. He must learn to disavow distractions and pursue only those interests of greater value to himself and others.

For the moment, however, he felt poised and thrilled to be on the brink of a new career, one not at all out of step with his love of nature and passion for wild places where he could be immune from the cloying entrapments of human society.

Yet a teensy niggle persisted behind his breastbone. Perhaps Colonel Röhm was right after all and he might end up as one more bum frequenting the riverside whorehouses like his father, or hitched to one of the fiery local half-breeds. For a shy and sensitive soul, neither prospect held much appeal as he toyed idly with alternatives. Had not the colonel touted his connections with the great Heinrich Hoffmann? Now, there was a future he could get excited over. Perhaps the returning warrior might carry a portfolio of his prints back to Germany for review by the master himself? Or, was he simply being carried away by "delusions of grandeur", a flaw in the characters of both brothers diagnosed early by Alois?

Who knows, one of these days if he ever did make it back to the Fatherland, might there exist even the faintest chance of an introduction? His mind soared and quickly sank. Here, surrounded by wild jungle, he could at least share in the daily rhythms of all Creation, just as Sister Klara predicted. Half a world away, surrounded by millions of people in a foreign country spoiling for a fight, sure he may turn a profit, but at what cost to his love of wild things and places?

He suddenly felt a fool contemplating such lame-brained urges. No! He was determined. The Hahn family holdings around Santa Luzia all but guaranteed his place as a big fish in a small pond, just the way he liked it. Earning a living beside the great river may be fraught, but he felt certain that that extraordinary encounter with the wise old nun had equipped him with all the necessary apodictics for success in any neck o' the woods. He realised a little smugly that his acquired artistry, however imperfect, was appreciated by the townsfolk.

Upon opening his eyes, the pearly moonlight peppered the scene to catch a snuffling giant anteater waddling by, a clear reminder that the darkness with all of its dangers had fallen. A leathery plop nearby was quickly followed by another, alerting him to a pending raid on his ankles if he didn't make a move.

Tiny shapes hopped clumsily over the grass toward his bare flesh, homing in for a nip of blood. He gave a little shudder and rose to pull on his boots, guided towards the lights of the mine by the rattle of frogs and the distant cough of a big cat.

Overall, the boy felt rather satisfied, and struggled for a moment to recall the exact words Sister Klara had taught him to repeat at times like this: "God's in his Heaven and all's well."

<h1 style="text-align:center">28</h1>

He had been busy in the mine darkroom since well before dawn; right now though, trotting along the Tappers' Track towards town, he clutched a manila folder containing ten sheets of contact proofs and a half dozen 8" × 10" glossy prints with which he was well pleased.

As feared, Captain Streicher had started the sitting hiding behind a variety of nervous grimaces until they'd moved on to the candids when he finally loosened up. He appeared jolly enough with a Madam Gertrude madel perched upon each knee, but didn't stop clowning around while the boy fumbled with exposures. Two shots in particular that stood out were the very first candids he'd taken on the docks with the skipper barking instructions back and forth to the crew, some of whom were busy putting finishing touches to *Belle*'s new paint job. Between ship and shore, a shaft of strong light had fallen across the old man's features at a perfect angle of 45 degrees and he had the presence of mind to fire off several quick exposures.

Still only partially satisfied, he decided on a bold move that would make or break the moment: stepping forth he plucked the old man's El Groucho stub from the corner of his mouth and leapt aside, pressing his cable release to catch the ensuing expression of annoyance. This masterpiece was one of the 8" × 10" samples now under his arm, probably the best character portrait he'd ever taken. Stopping once more to examine his handiwork he noted with satisfaction that the background of vulcanised rubber balls was blurry in the f/8 shot and a goodly portion of *Belle*'s freshly painted gunwales showed over the captain's other shoulder. Against such fuzzy surroundings, his subject appeared almost to leap off the print.

Madam Gertrude's individuals, however, hadn't turned out so well. Unlike the other girls, her expressions were stilted and unresponsive. She had chosen to appear initially in a drab plaid suit with her crowning glory tied back in its usual severe bun. She wore no makeup and had no intention of belittling herself on a certain lap.

It took Captain Rudi's best efforts to convince her to change into something more melodic, "more authentic", for the Villa shoot. Meanwhile, the same cheeky escort who had earlier flashed her breasts unbeknownst to Captain Streicher, now repeated the gesture in front of the blushing photographer while changing from one outfit to another for her own individuals.

While Santa Luzian streets bustled with bare backsides and black and brown breasts of all shapes and sizes, this close-up glimpse of a puckered pink bosom made Klaus' heart skip a beat. He turned quickly away, pretending to fiddle with his lens.

Naturally enough, as Captain Streicher was footing the bill, he insisted on thumbing through each and every proof sheet, here and there grunting what sounded like approval. But it was the 8" × 10" of himself minus the cigar that really tickled his fancy. "There's no doubt about it boy," he bubbled. "How on earth you managed to capture a fightin' expression like that I'll never know … and I must say the others seem nice n' sharp too."

The artist beamed at the compliment; after all, he had managed to retain a full tonal range between highlight and shadow, not easy in the lighting extremes with which he'd been confronted. The skipper seemed eager to order. "Well, for starters, I'd like a group shot and individual for each girl, and a complete set of prints for myself," he spoke thoughtfully. "Oh, and a half dozen enlargements of myself, just in case … that should keep you busy for a while." He pressed a 100-real note into the boy's hand, the most money Klaus had ever seen at one time. "And let me know what I owe when the order's completed."

The captain studied the boy staring at the money in his own hands, then sighed. "You know, son, you're too talented for this crummy backwater. Anyone can see Santa Luzia is as good as finished. Grand Kaiser ran out of precious minerals long ago and everyone but Alois knows the arse has dropped out of rubber. Soon there'll be nothing left but a brothel and a Monastery. What an attraction!

"While you're young there's more to life than scraping ticks off cattle sores. With respect, do you want to end up like your old man? Have you given any thought to Colonel Röhm's suggestion? It wouldn't surprise me if your big brother hasn't already fallen for all his wild adventure stories."

"Y … Yes sir; I mean, no sir, my mind's made up. I love it here by the river …"

"Tosh! So do I. You know what they say: 'Decide in hast, repent at leisure.' Wait until you hear what Colonel Röhm has to say, he's already changed more than a few minds around these parts. I hate to admit it, but your father saw it before anyone. Take it from me boy: there's a big wide world out there, just cryin' out for someone with your natural ability.

"Now, show me those last shots of Fraulein Gertie in her dirndl again …" he chuckled, changing the subject.

The other girls had howled with laughter when their mistress appeared reluctantly in her traditional alpine attire, comprising a checked frock, lace-up bodice and jaunty fedora sporting a toucan plume. Captain Streicher had insisted.

"There!" The boy pointed, proffering the magnifying glass and once more spreading out the proof sheets. The 35 mm contacts were sufficient to again send the old man into something of a reverie as his fingers stroked the tiny images. "Rosie! Where's Rosie? Cheeky bugger, I dare you to get yourself over here and do that again. Ah! … those were the days," he exclaimed wistfully, staring at the girl's microscopic rack in black-and-white.

"You'd better run me off an enlargement of that one as well," he added eventually, wiping away an artless tear and clearing his throat. "Tomorrow night before the hunters return. Can you do it? I'm throwing a farewell party aboard for Colonel Röhm and the Old Fighters. Of course, a few of Gertrude's girls will be attending and it'll be a good chance to surprise them with the finished product to show off your style."

That was it. The race was on.

All that night and the next morning Klaus sweated in the steam bath of the mine darkroom, straining his tired eyes beneath a hot enlarger beam; printing and reprinting until every image came alive. It crossed his mind that Captain Streicher, in view of his martial connections, may well require a keepsake of Colonel Röhm's own shattered features; the boy had glimpsed them but briefly on the day of his arrival and if all went well he may suggest it.

After lunch on the third day little *Lotte* came chugging 'round the bend and prepared to dock alongside the resplendent side-wheeler. Pegged out across her foredeck was the spotty pelt of a jaguar, and from her mast dangled two fresh Indian scalps. By any measure, the safari had been a great success.

There stood the hunters proudly on deck beside their trophies, as Robert gave an impatient tug on the whistle cord to summon his brother for photos. An answering honk from *Belle* reverberated up and down Main Street and coloured streamers fluttered from her freshly painted masts and railings.

After all, it wasn't every day that firsthand news of the Fatherland arrived in any guise, let alone from the mouth of one of its more highly decorated warriors reputedly cheek by jowl with the up-and-coming Nazi leader himself.

Robert seemed a little uneasy after an escapade that had gone way past a simple hunting trip. In three short days, he'd gotten to know Röhm and his companions only too well, and his eyes had been opened by their lack of modesty.

Röhm's principal aide-de-camp, one 20-year-old Martin "Marty" Schartzl was painfully good-looking, having revealed himself as a brilliant painter and sketcher, a graduate of the Munich Academy of Fine Arts.

He now referred affectionately to the Colonel as "Onkel Röhm" and when not tending the other's every whim, lolled about producing watercolour landscapes and character studies. Two young Bolivian Army recruits completed the party, hardly old enough to pull a trigger Robert thought.

Then, at the last minute, several Mulatto boys wearing skimpy Indian loincloths had been bundled aboard at Schartzl's insistence and assigned quarters in the hold. Given his not-so-covert cat-and-mouse experience among the Christian Brothers, and normally one to be raising eyebrows himself, Robert did not at first take kindly to such blatant and overt physicality around the camp. Colonel Röhm notwithstanding, now free of all harness and primed by the splendid onboard refreshments, became ever more ebullient and outrageous.

He would not shut up about the fun to be had by putting aside one's "prudishness", joking that there were more interesting things to be found under the water than piranha. He flaunted his unnatural naked barrel amidst his squealing companions as they cavorted in the shallows, and dogged the shanghaied mulatto lads with barely concealed intent.

"In the coming Third Reich," he assured a doubtful Robert, "all society will be modified to accept homosexuality as a human behaviour pattern of a very high sort, indeed as a completely alternative lifestyle to so-called normal heterosexual activity." Unconvinced, *Lotte's* crew upon setting up camp and tending to essentials, retreated into the nearby bush to sling their hammocks at a safe distance.

The invitations had been hand-delivered. *Madeira Belle's* last night in port would culminate in a dinner and dance featuring Germanic themes and cuisine exclusively. Sweating guests constrained in evening wear filed up the carpeted gangway to be greeted by Captain Streicher and introduced to his honoured guest, both of whom were bedecked in lederhosen and cocked mountain caps.

To a man, the Grand Kaiser ex-pats were fascinated by this battle-scarred and decorated war hero from home. The colonel dominated the saloon bar with his glowing tales of battle and his radical politics, not only regarding the "real truth" about the Great War but also those "commies and counter-revolutionaries" who wandered still in the streets of German cities.

So many astonishing yarns flowed over the packed crowd that sultry evening, and Klaus had difficulty finding a flat surface to display his prints.

Captain Streicher gave the order for one whole buffet table to be cleared of food and drink and announced that anyone wishing to see "real talent" should avail themselves of the wondrous photo exhibition now on show in the far corner. At that, he and several of Madam Gertrude's girls eagerly moved over to examine the collection, shifting the focus away from the charismatic colonel.

"Oh, I just love this one of me," gushed one big-bosomed courtesan, passing an 8" × 10" from eager hand to hand.

"How about this beauty? The young pup has snavelled me at just the right angle, don't you agree?" the skipper intervened, waving his own likeness in the air. "That light makes me look years younger. He caught me off guard with *Belle* in the background, even if she is out of focus. I could have saved myself the trouble of the new paint job, eh?"

"Oh no sir. The background is meant to be soft. Can't you see how it makes you stand out?"

Young Schartzl, attracted by all the fuss, sauntered over to peruse the compilation. "Not bad, not bad … Good God, this is terrible!" he exclaimed, singling out the shot of Madam Gertrude in her dirndl. "It looks like the poor creature has a broomstick up her backside. The outfit totally dominates, and you've failed to catch anything of her personality," he opined cruelly to the deflated boy, who'd already been reminded that his critic was a graduate from one of Germany's finest academies.

"Anyway, photography runs a poor second to painting when it comes to portraiture … or even landscapes for that matter," Marty sniffed, now running his eye up and down the would-be artist.

"Is that so? … well, I beg to differ," retorted Captain Streicher, taking it personally and, feeling put down by the comparison, had drawn himself up looking squarely down his nose. "There's no way you and your fancy paint brushes could produce this many different results in a few hours, now is there?" He was puffed up and sure of himself. "I say this here is *real* art."

"That's exactly my point, old boy; surely, one decent portrait comprising dozens of hours or days of concentration must transcend any so-called artwork produced in a fraction of a second?" he said patronisingly, to which the captain could find no reply.

"B … But there's a lot more work goes on behind the scenes to make a good print; in the darkroom I mean," the lad responded gamely.

"Have it your own way," Schartzl replied, "but I must say the boy's right about the impact photography has had on the current political scene back home. If we had more time I'd show you what a competent painter could do with this coterie of beauties," he waved gallantly toward the band of happy hookers now gathered under the gaze of Madam Gertrude.

"Come on Fraulein Gertie, loosen up a little," jollied the skipper. "We're all here for a good time, aren't we? What would a whippersnapper like him know anyway? This kid has real talent, and the whole collection is a gift from me to you and the girls. What could be fairer than that? How often do we get to enjoy a real slap-up German shindig, eh?"

As if on cue, Colonel Röhm struck up an impromptu recital on the honky-tonk upright behind the bar, from the first notes it was evident that the wounded warrior was in his element, possessing more than average capacity.

Effortlessly, his pudgy fingers skipped across the keys, summoning traditional Volkslieder, rousing marching songs and even soul-wrenching motifs from a Wagner opera or two, until there was hardly a dry eye on the top deck.

Through a cloud of cigar smoke, the great bull-neck quivered and glistened, while his newest recruit turned the music sheets and joined in the harmonies. When Klaus tried to catch Robert's eye across the room he seemed evasive, distant; it was obvious that the colonel exercised an almost hypnotic effect over the whole group, especially the boy in the pirate outfit.

Alois too, stirred by the performance, did his best during the break to convince one and all that he was in absolute lockstep with the colonel's version of contemporary Nazi ideas. "You've been like a breath of fresh air to us, Colonel Röhm, sir ... and not before time. That Versailles Treaty has to go," he slurred. "Germany has always needed a strong man to keep her on top, and it looks like this fellow Hitler is just the man to do it. Germanic blood has always been the purest on the planet, everyone knows that, eh?" He peered about through glazed eyes for support. "Those Yiddish fat cats have had their day and shown their true colours, making fortunes off the backs of our misery: I'm all for a Party that restores Germany to her rightful place in the world ..."

"Yes, yes, Herr Hahn, we all know what's required, but there's more to life than politics; give me a clean young boy anytime," Röhm snorted loudly.

"I've had the clap seven times, so much for the fairer sex," he interjected, shocking his listeners. "Real men will always seek to enjoy the whole range of human experience and it's an obvious fact that the strong will always dominate the weak, that's nature's way. Just look around, the smarties will always triumph over the dummies; ask that old Tom Jaguar pegged out over there, ha!

"As for you," he continued with an eye fixed on Robert, "take my advice and join the fight, there's never been a better time Jung mann. Germany must rise again with a monarch at her head as before, and my stormtroopers will see to it. Our time has come, and yours too, if you've any sense beneath those pretty curls of yours. From childhood I've dreamed and desired only one thing: to be a soldier defending my country ..." His rousing testimony stirred the crowd to a fever pitch, with "hear, hear's!" and "count me in's" almost drowning out the applause. "... Nazism is an idea so profoundly radical and forward-looking," he continued, "It's not so easy for newcomers to grasp."

"Like Blücher crossin' da Rhine, Colonel?" Robert piped up, referring to the many times his tin soldiers had swept across a make-believe river in the dirt to save Wellington at Waterloo.

"Eh? Blücher? What's he got to do with it? No, no ... Nazism is far more than that; it's aiming for worldwide domination. But, I do see what you mean boy about the element of surprise; out of the blue at the last minute and all that."

"I too, have always wanted to be a soldier, Herr Colonel," Robert added, leaning forward in a burst of excessive high spirits, "... a soldier of Free Ireland." Dead silence followed.

"Ireland be damned! They can't even make up their minds which side they're on. Just look at *you*. In spite of that funny accent we're every one of us Aryans when all's said and done, do you hear? I'll wager there's pure Teutonic blood running somewhere in your veins. As a natural child of the master race, you'd make a fine foot soldier in my S.A. Battalions." Röhm was emphatic.

He tossed down another Schnapps and relit his cigar stub, blowing smoke in Robert's face, who was both flattered and confused.

"Sail back to Germany with Marty and me. Once your Vati gives the word, I'll take care of all the arrangements. What do you say?"

"As we say in de old country, Colonel Sir, I dunno wedder to shit or go blind; dat's if you'd not be pullin' me leg?"

"And as for the arty one over there in the corner, I can guarantee him a job interview with the great Hoffmann. He and Marty will be good company for each other; I've no doubt they'll find plenty in common to talk about during the voyage. As for you, my fine feathered friend, I'll pull more than your leg if you're not careful. You will see great things in the Fatherland such as you've never dreamed of *and* you will be getting in on the ground floor. The Movement needs good comrades from all Aryan backgrounds and I want to show you off around my circle of friends. Give me three months and you won't know yourself."

Robert was taken aback by Röhm's blunt suggestiveness. It was inconceivable that such an opportunity could be opening up almost overnight: a chance to be a real soldier, enjoying protection at the highest level. Perhaps his one and only opportunity to leave this shithole behind forever. His head raced, and for once he could think of no reply. From his retreat, Klaus could catch only snippets of their conversation, unsettling at best.

"… and those Berlin bathhouses, ooh-la-la!"

He could see his brother lapping it up and couldn't quite dispel the nagging suspicions in his solar plexus. Searching the faces around he wondered if he was the only one with a knot in his gut, but before he could come to any conclusions Robert bounced from his stool and motioned his brother to join him outside on deck.

"Cantcha see, brudder? 'Tis da chance we've bin waitin' fer," he babbled, almost breathlessly. "Ernst is actin' on behalf of Hitler 'imself. They're offerin' to pay ar fares ta Germany and set us up in good jobs." He hadn't wasted a moment coming to the point, until at last the boy managed to find his voice.

"B … But, I don't want to go to Germany or anywhere else, at least not now. I'm happy here doin' what I'm doin'. So much for you fighting for a Free Ireland, you have no idea what you'd be gettin' into and—"

But Bobby would have none of it. "You don't seem to understand what I'm tryin' to say an' what he's offerin'."

"It all seems a bit sudden to me. What about Papa? He'll never give his permission before you turn 21. He expects you to take over from him one day at the mine so he can go on drawing his pension …"

"Fuck 'im and 'is pension! I'm not goin' ta let a chance like dis go by an' if you've got any sense you'll grabba hold too." He was being irrational, absurd; there was no way the boy would be drawn in by such pie in the sky. Something more than instinct cautioned him to stick with what he knew; best not be swayed from a promising career path, ever.

But Robert seemed as a man possessed. "Ernst says we could take a fast ferry ta Santorum an' pick up de *Mariana* ta Panama. He's already radioed de steamship company; Oi tell ya, Ernst has it figured it out good an' proper. He 'n Marty will be aboard de *Sachsen* comin' tru the canal in October. From what I hear she's even bigger dan *Ladybird*, which might be fun. From dere it's straight on ta Hamburg for a short life and a merry one. Dat should allow us plenty o' time."

He paused, almost imploringly, before catching hold of himself. "Whatcha tink?"

"Ernst now, is it? It all sounds a bit sudden. How do you know all this? What if they're pullin' your leg, man?"

"Well, Oi for one trust everything Ernst says; Oi've never met anyone like 'im. He reckons 'e an' Marty are gettin' picked up in Manaus by a Bolivian Airforce plane an' flyin' back to La Paz. Dat's where he's been trainin' da whole fucking Bolivian Army, would ya believe? Marty's puttin' on an exhibition of 'is paintings before they sail. He actually wants me, and you, of course, to join them as dey come trew the canal. Can't ya see? Dis is de chance we bin waitin' for."

"You, not we; I'm perfectly happy where I am. How do you ever expect Vati to agree, let alone sign any papers?

"Fuck Alois! I told Ernst I could take care of it. He gave his knuckles a crack. "Oi wouldn't need *'is* permission if Oi was 21, now would Oi? Anyway, Marty says dere might be a few of us from Santa Luzia puttin' up our hands for trainin' wit 'is own brigade in Munich ..."

"B ... But you're not 21 until next April," Klaus called in vain to the back of his head; in all the haste he should not have to point out the obvious to one usually so clever with numbers, one who turned back from the doorway and hissed, "... or unless he's dead!"

Leaning on the corner of the piano, Alois was having a whale of a time, accompanying Röhm's splendid renditions among true comrades who echoed his own dream of seeing the Fatherland great again.

Through a fog of Schnapps, he harboured growing reservations over the colonel's shameless endorsement of homosexuality. Such behaviour had never been tolerated by the Kriegsmarine in which *he* had served, and as the loose smutty talk proliferated during the break the unter-manager decided he'd had enough.

"Herr Colonel! This behaviour is neither widespread nor acceptable in nature and I am the father of two young boys. You wouldn't see sheep and cattle coming together as you suggest; the anus simply wasn't designed for that sort of thing." His voice had steadied and risen above the chatter.

Röhm paused and flushed slightly. "Well, you are never too old to try something different, that's all I can say," he giggled wickedly and threw his arm around the shoulder of his blushing valet as if to emphasise the point. "You Tykes are all the same; kicking up a big fuss in public and pointing the finger at others having a good time all the while your priests molest every choirboy who looks sideways." He let out a loud guffaw and Robert squirmed uneasily.

"I'm no Tyke!" Alois protested, offended at the very suggestion. "I made the mistake of marrying one and I inherited that one over there," he jerked a thumb towards his hostile stepson. We Hamburg Hahns are Lutheran through and through; why I even refused to allow my youngest to be baptised or circumcised in Ireland. No sir, I'm no Tyke. My family can be traced right back to Frederick the Great. You may not know that we once provided a pageboy for the wedding of Prince Albert and …"

"Here we go again," Captain Streicher caught his breath, before wandering over to join the small group gathered by the wind-up gramophone.

Alois' polysemous parley could be heard above the music, realising too late that he may have stepped out of line. "Then again, Colonel, we don't want to get too serious over trifles, do we? Let's lighten up. Why, I still remember a limerick from my time in that Irish hospital; now how did it go again?

> "Came a scream from the crypt of St Jiles
> So loud that it echoed for miles,
> The Priest said, 'Good gracious, has Father Ignatius,
> Forgotten the Bishop has piles!'

"Ha, that just about sums it up I suppose," he added as the colonel and his companions sniggered good-naturedly, choosing not to take offence. Röhm, preferring to ignore the outdated contentions of Alois and his Old Fighters, backed away from the moralising to conduct a few passages with the orchestra.

"Believe me, Colonel, like you, I want nothing more than to see our great nation rise again to its rightful place on the world stage and throw off the shackles of that accursed Versailles Treaty." No petty lifestyle issues would be allowed to impede Alois Hahn's admiration for this fellow warrior and newfound comrade. "I'm convinced this fellow Hitler is the right man for the job …"

"Ah! Wagner. Now there's a real master and a great German," Röhm demurred, cocking his ear congenially and ignoring the others' prattle. He showed little effect from the prodigious quantities of Schnapps and Brandy already put away.

"As a matter of fact, I've had the privilege of attending Bayreuth several times, *and* was invited to dine with Adolph and Frau Winnifred Wagner at her mansion. She was the great composer's much-esteemed daughter-in-law, you know? Actually, she has a soft spot for Adi, who's been leading her on for years," he added. "Somehow, I can't see him falling for a big lump like that, famous or not.

"Just listen to those leitmotifs, you Jungvolk? You think you know music? Well, this is the finest there is. Richard Wagner's Ring Cycle goes on for sixteen hours; just show me another composer who could imagine such an opera, let alone construct a purpose-built theatre in which to perform it."

"I listen to such music at home regularly, Herr Colonel; I am fortunate in having many classical records sent out from Germany by my Tante and Onkel," came a voice from the corner, "and once, we nearly had a performance right here in Santa Luzia ..."

"Bullshit!" Röhm exclaimed. "Wagner operas require a full orchestra and a cast of hundreds. Where do you expect we'd find such talent in this bloody backwater?"

"I'd be agreein' wit ya dere, Colonel Sir. Dat was before da bloody Indians burned de whole place down ..." Robert couldn't help himself. "Well, nearly all of it."

"Who knows? Maybe one day I'll take you to see the real thing," Röhm answered the voice in the shadows. Tannhauser rose in crescendo as the valet Schartzl presented several freshly completed charcoal sketches of local beauties which aroused great interest at the bar. Debate erupted as to whether Klaus' photos were more realistic and acceptable than Schartzl's modernist-style sketches, which distorted some of the girls' features and accentuated others. It was generally agreed that the realistic photographs were more desirable as keepsakes, much to the delight of the photographer and the feigned disgust of Marty, who labelled the judges as "ignorant peasants" and gave away his drawings to the girls anyway.

In this suitably inspiring atmosphere, Röhm chose his moment to present a signed copy of his autobiography to both a startled Alois and Captain Streicher.

"It's already sold out the first edition," he beamed, as the grateful recipients fondled the leather-bound covers. "Chose the title myself, *Portrait of a Traitor*, long before the damn thing was completed in prison after the Beer Hall Putsch; Adolph's not the only one who can write a best-seller, you know. That's why they kicked me out of the Reichswehr in '24," he said, sliding Alois' copy along the bar for all to see.

His soulmate almost fell down weeping with gratitude. "I will treasure it as long as I live, Sturmbannführer. You have brought a real ray of hope to our humble community." Alois paused as if searching for the right phrase to follow. "However, I regret I cannot consent to my boys accompanying you back to the Fatherland. Robert will soon be needed here to take over a very important management position in the mine ..."

"First Oi've 'eard o' dat," the boy exclaimed.

"Rubbish!" Röhm shot back. "This whole bloody place is on life support. Just think of the opportunities awaiting him as a true soldier of the New Reich; rest assured, I'll soon drum the revolutionary spirit into him. They don't call me the 'Machine Gun King' for nothing. National Socialism was born in the trenches of the Great War and will only succeed if each and every German family gives up its sons to the great struggle. Mark my words, Herr Hahn, you have a week or two to think it over before he'd need to sail for Panama. However, let's not get too caught up in details at this point, eh?"

At that, he tore off his shirt with a flourish and began to show off the twenty-odd shrapnel wounds peppering his bulging torso front and rear. "See these? I received an Iron Cross First-Class for this lot; go on Captain Hook, put your fingers in the holes." He pointed out each one to a pop-eyed Robert and beat his chest like a bull ape. "These few only scratched the surface; there are still eight or ten shell splinters sloshing around inside somewhere ... and, so what? I'm ready to cop a few more if that's what it takes." He swaggered about so everyone could see for themselves the extent of his sacrifice.

"I too, Colonel Röhm, did not return from the conflict unscathed as you may have noticed," said Alois, vaingloriously lurching from his stool and pulling up a trouser leg. "No sacrifice is too great for the Fatherland." His wooden foot dangled wanly in its shoe.

"And why don't you just shut the fuck up?" Robert muttered under his breath, sensing a great opportunity slipping away.

"All the more reason to reconsider your decision, Herr Hahn. Let's face it, there's nothing to keep your boys here; I've already told them what I think." Röhm went on, "Let me take them to hike the great Watzmann at Berchtesgaden and plunge into the alpine lakes of Bavaria where they don't need to worry about being eaten alive every time they take a swim, ha!"

"Berchtesgaden? Why, that's where Tante and Onkel have their chalet and ..." Klaus began, but neither Röhm nor anyone else was listening.

With all the resentments of the cripple, the old man dug in: his boys were going nowhere, and he was happy to concoct as many new rules as necessary to keep the Irish bastard in his place. So far, he felt he'd only partly succeeded in curbing his strapping stepson whenever he'd kicked against the traces, which was often. The rebellious boy would one day take up his pre-ordained position at the mine in an unbroken family tradition if it was the last thing Alois ever did. Any suggestion to the contrary was dismissed out of hand.

Watching on in silence, Captain Streicher finally leaned across the bar to confront his old comrade. "Still trying to prove yourself a big fellow, Alois? A fanatic like you is always concealing secret doubts, and now you try and railroad the boy into succeeding in a field where you couldn't ... Balls to you, I say!"

For a moment, the unter-manager looked bewildered. "For one, there's my pension to think of ..."

"Well, I'm goin' one way or another, whether *you* like it or not!" Bobby declared, before turning his back on the discussion and moving outdoors to fume at the oily waters below.

"I've said it before, and I'll say it again," Alois called after him, "you're nothin' but a bog Irish bastard and you'll do as you're told." But his threats bounced off the swinging batwing doors.

A nervous silence followed, before the tinkling of glasses and muffled conversation again filled the bar and surrounded Röhm on the piano, when he once more struck up the traditional "Deutschland, Deutschland, Uber Alles" to swell the drunken revellers into a heartfelt refrain.

Hanging back unnoticed, one serious young man had taken in the whole scene and couldn't begin to imagine a way through the impasse. It was probably better, he thought, if things did continue in Santa Luzia as before. Through the cigar smoke, he watched the tipsy revellers throwing back their heads like a troop of howlers. He struggled to suppress a tinge of sadness for his brother, and although the evening proved artistically more successful than he'd dared hope, his chest began to tighten in the foetid air.

Without so much as pausing to say thanks or goodbye, he hurried down the gangplank and made his way toward home, head spinning with all he'd seen and heard during this night of nights. Above all else, he'd come to realise his own perceptions through the lens; without a camera in his hand, he felt shy and awkward. The little Leica somehow gave him a valid reason to mingle in any company as both observer and recorder of their antics. This magic instrument conferred the power to stop Father Time in his tracks and catch real history being made, however insignificant the slice or setting. It seemed everyone these days wanted to gather 'round and ask questions, or try to pop up in the backgrounds of his sneaky candids. He was convinced that the camera made him feel whole and valuable; these were his happy thoughts as he drifted off to sleep.

As daylight's eye opened the next morning, a small crowd of sore heads gathered at the floating wharf to farewell the gregarious warrior who had made such an impression in just three short days. Cheers rose as the old riverboat slipped her moorings and her two great side-wheels began to churn the brown foam.

From the bridge, Captain Streicher barked orders loud and clear, reversing out through the muddy upwell toward midstream. He noted with concern the dry season low watermarks on the timbers, which he suspected may soon deny even *Belle* the capacity to venture so far year-round. He was as proud as punch as he ran his eye over the sleek new paint job and tugged three times on the cord overhead, sending out a shrill farewell for another month.

Waving furiously, the proud hunting guide blew a kiss to the dumpy figure in the bathrobe astern with the Robin's nest on its head, until the grand vessel vanished into the rising mist, leaving behind a trail of swirling eddies.

Suddenly, a straggler on the pier gasped aloud and pointed to something black and shiny bobbing in the water: a wooden foot wearing a dancing pump had popped to the surface, and almost to a man those who came running knew to whom it belonged.

A runner was despatched to fetch the constable, who arrived in due course quite out of breath, with a sniffer dog and a set of grappling hooks to plumb the murky bottom. Almost directly below the bobbing foot, the hooks bit deep into what came up as a dinner suit containing the remains of Alois Hahn, or at least a torso buttoned tight in jacket and trousers. The piranhas had done a job on the face and fleshy parts, leaving little more than a bag of guts and bones to be hauled out and sifted through.

A cry went up to fetch the youngster in order to console the conspicuously grief-stricken older boy, who could be seen sitting to one side sobbing intermittently and running his fingers through his mop of curls.

By the time Captain Streicher received the urgent wire to turn about and assist the investigation, he merely snorted and ordered full steam ahead with the current at his tail. His V.I.P.s had a flight to catch in Manaus and *Belle* was behind schedule already. Anyway, he had the overwhelming feeling that Alois finally got what was coming to him. Only when death revealed the Pension Fund discrepancies days later and 69 I.O.U.s were found in place of the missing valuables did the full scale of the deception become evident.

Captain Streicher called the crew and first-class passengers together and broke the news: "I can't say it comes as a complete surprise. It beats me how he's lasted this long," he heard himself saying, "… staggering up and down the docks addled to the eyeballs while concealing his dastardly secret."

For a moment, he felt a dash of guilt over his own part in the disbursement of funds and subsequent lack of remorse; after all, he did throw the fatal party. But the feeling didn't last. For years he'd been watching his old navy comrade heading downhill and trying to take the whole family with him.

Now it was the two boys he felt sorry for. The manner in which they and their mother had been treated, especially the older one, was way too heavy-handed for his liking. He continued in the same vein. "I'll be submitting a Statutory Declaration to the Enquiry stating that Alois had been seen unsteady on his feet after drinking heavily. No one aboard *Madeira Belle* has anything to add regarding the incident. That should see an end to it."

"Well, Colonel Röhm, it looks like you may have scored a couple of recruits after all," he opined that night after dinner, unaware that Röhm had pressed a wad of reals into Robert's hand during their final conversation together.

"Thank you, Herr Capitan. We'll just have to wait and see what happens, won't we?" Röhm nodded, lighting up a fat El Groucho and settling back to enjoy his last few days of R&R.

29

If most of the townsfolk including Robert seemed unfazed by the drowning, the younger boy was shaken to the core. He suffered a violent three-day asthma attack and had to be pushed to his Vati's funeral in a wheelchair.

"Well, good riddance is all I can say," his brother had whispered in his ear during the wake held in the Company Kiosk, but it seemed the boy alone was beset by shock and grief. Day after day he sat staring vacantly into the distance with his dark brooding eyes.

Local authorities initially surmised, then concluded, that the depressed fracture at the base of Alois' skull pointed to his having fallen overboard while drunk and striking his head on the protruding rudder shaft. He had last been seen urinating from *Belle*'s stern in the early hours by his eldest son. The remains exuded a strong odour of alcohol and an empty hip flask in the coat pocket confirmed their initial conclusions. From the other pocket, a sodden, signed copy of *Story of a Traitor* by Ernst Röhm was retrieved.

There being no way of checking for traces of hair or scalp on the offending rudder; a verdict of "Death by Misadventure" was recorded in the archives and the case was soon after closed.

Klaus wanted nothing more than to sit alone in the forest and commune with his own despondent heart. The sudden shock left little room to reminisce and he wondered if his shattered world could ever again encompass a passion for life or art. His liberated brother was moving fast to formalise their legal documents with the Santa Luzian authorities. He tracked the boy to the oxbow lake, clutching a copy of the Guardianship Agreement concluded between Kitty O'Shea and Father Malone. "I tell you liddle brudder, dere's nothing to keep us 'ere now," he implored where earlier threats had failed to resonate.

At first, Klaus ignored him, staring glumly across the shallow lagoon with eyes fixed on the dipping and diving of distant birds. Overhead, the smooth grey limbs of the fig tree soared into the sky.

Robert snuggled close to his brother between the buttresses, sharing the dollop of shade. He pulled a wad of notes from his pocket and waved them tantalisingly in the other's face. "Look, reals; *real* reals!" More money than either boy had ever seen. "Jus' take a gander at all dis cash, more'n enuff to set us up for a new beginning, or at least get us ta Germany on da boat …"

"Germany? Since when did *you* give two hoots about Germany? You've always hated Alois and his rants about the Fatherland," Klaus exclaimed.

"Fer more dan jus' dat ta be sure! Can't ya see? Now everything's changed. Ernst has promised me a good job wit' 'is stormtroops. It's all Oi've ever wanted to be, a real soldier …"

"Just listen to yourself!" The boy came alive. "Two weeks ago you were setting yourself up as a hot-shot tourist guide with never a thought of going to Europe, let alone becoming a soldier; Mam would die of shame."

He'd been stung into action by his brother's impulsive "volte-face" that threatened to up-end everything he'd worked for. Given the lull, Klaus continued: "I like it *here* in the old house; how many times do I have to tell you? I'm on the verge of setting up my own studio along the boardwalk and standing on my own two feet …" His words sounded hollow as they fell from his mouth, despite the compliments flowing over the Gala Ball collection. Perhaps the knot in his stomach was a reminder that Captain Streicher had not yet coughed up a single coin of the balance owing from the sitting; the artist had little profit to show for all his careful burning in and holding back of certain faces.

"At least yer could appear a bit interested. What if Oi told you dat Ernst is offerin' to arrange a meetin' wit' your hero Hoffmann? Jus' imagine de doors dat could open?" It was as if he had read his own former disappointment in his brother's eyes. "Oi've already sorted art da passports and we can pick up our Visas in Belem, like Ernst says, on der way. C'mon, how about it?"

He was quickly losing patience with his simpering sibling and threw off the cloak of persuasion. "Anyway, it's time ya woke up to ya fucking self. How long do ya tink dey'll letcha live in the Fazenda once Oi've moved out, eh? Or keep payin' Ines to wash yer fucking socks? An' how much profit do yer tink you'll make when yer have ta start forkin' out fer yer own films and chemicals, 'n all dat stuff, eh? Well, yer 'ad better make yer mind up real soon, cause Oim outa here on de next fast ferry as soon as Oi get these last coupla papers stamped."

Klaus' head was swimming; he'd hardly eaten a proper meal since witnessing his father's body being pulled from the river, the only extremity not stripped to the bone was the wooden foot wearing the dancing pump. He could not get the image out of his mind. The more brother Robert enthused, the tighter the knot in his gut, just behind the belly button. Every principle and scrap of knowledge he'd thought settled, vanished in a miasma of self-doubt. Persistent niggles over Vati's sudden demise would not go away.

Arriving back at the empty house at dusk, Robert prepared his brother a plate of scrambled eggs on toast before dragging out his dusty suitcase from under the bed, all the while besieging the other with tales of high adventure to come. "Jus' tink! Not having to put up wit dat bastard sticking is drunken head in the door at any hour o' der day or night. No more of 'is controllin' ways an' an end to da insults …"

"Listen, who's talking?" the boy thought before answering … aware that his powers of perception were returning. "B … But it's ages since we had to put up with all that; not since you thumped him, I mean …"

But Bobby was jubilant, cracking his knuckles to display his newfound freedom. But, from Klaus' point of view, the whole proposal was absurd.

30

The voyage between Santa Luzia and Santorum took a whole week, during which the boy pretended that it wasn't really happening. The only condition attached to his capitulation required a trunkful of Classics to accompany him on the voyage.

Now and again he lifted his head from the page to savour the short and sweet departure in his mind: half the town had turned out to see them off, including most of the Flamingo Villa girls who wailed and sobbed as if the boys were sailing to their doom.

"You will write, won't you, Klaus?" they called from the dock, ignoring Robert, who disappeared below decks in a huff before Santa Luzia had faded from sight. The boy vaguely recalled one other such emotional parting, when he'd feasted his eyes for the last time on Galway's emerald shores. He made the decision there and then to keep his camera out of sight for the duration and concentrate instead on his mental wellbeing. "We are always becoming," the old mystic had chided a lifetime ago.

From Santorum, they picked up the S.S. *Mariana* for the long journey to Panama, stopping for one last glimpse of Belem where the colourful waterfront now looked shabby and alien. The tedious passage up the uninhabited coastlines of Guyana and Venezuela seemed neverending to the brothers.

Despite his earlier misgivings Klaus became more and more energised by his brother's anticipation of rejoining their much-admired liberators. His enthusiasm was palpable following a final stopover in Caracas as he waxed lyrical over an anticipated lifetime of freedom and discovery to come.

On the afternoon of October 15, 1930, two excited brothers stood beside Gatun Locks at the northern end of the Panama Canal; everyone had said it was a true Wonder of the World, one of the great engineering marvels of the nineteenth century. After several false alarms, the S.S. *Sachsen* finally appeared overhead, all 18,000 tons of her, descending slowly down through the jungle walls toward the broad Atlantic. They could almost touch hands with Röhm and Schartzl as they cracked jokes and threw greetings over the starboard railing. The colonel's egg head sported a smile from ear to ear as he urged the boys to run faster beside the great vessel as it slid at last into the ocean.

The two boys were first aboard when the gangway came down in Cristobal. A breathless reunion ensued and they were shown to their quarters.

Despite her relatively modest passenger facilities, *Sachsen*'s 27-man crew had gone out of their way to provide every comfort for their notorious V.I.P. and his travelling companions, with Captain Röhm (who had by now reverted to his preferred rank) and Marty occupying the only first-class suite. Upon entering the dining room, the boys were overcome by the silver service décor and uniformed waiters showering every attention upon them.

Robert seemed to pick up almost where he'd left off, venturing opinions on every topic and eager to laugh a little too readily at Röhm's smutty wisecracks.

Klaus, in turn, had been relegated to a corner table among lesser beings who were also returning to the Fatherland at the completion of their tour of duty.

He added little by way of conversation, trying consciously not to attract attention and practising his peripheral vision. From the corner of one eye, he could see and hear his brother at the head table, conspicuous in the pirate outfit with his hair tied up in a bright bandana.

And by dinnertime that same evening, a complete transformation had taken place in the bold recruit, thanks to the combined efforts of Schartzl and Captain Röhm. He swaggered in for pre-dinner drinks decked out like the other German dandies and at first Klaus didn't recognise him beneath a jaunty Panama hat with his precious locks shorn away in a latest short back and sides hairstyle.

He wore a pair of high-waisted, pale linen trousers and a polka-dot silk shirt with puffed sleeves, rounded off by two-tone tan and cream leather lace-ups. He carried himself proudly and the corners of his mouth twitched in anticipation. The boy watched fascinated as his brother took the transformation in his stride, exuding ready charm and a thick hide. Later, he led Klaus to his cabin to show off proudly the remainder of his new wardrobe, the likes of which he'd seen only in magazines: several colourful silk shirts, stylish jackets and trousers, including a funny-looking pair of bold-checked plus-fours which tucked into the tops of snug-fitting, high-cut leather boots, all hung freshly pressed next to his own drab assortment of tropical wear.

"Hardly been worn," Robert boasted, "an' the boots are brand new, made up fer Onkel Röhm in Bolivia."

Unlike his brother, the boy felt a little overwhelmed by the turn of events, but from the moment Röhm had embraced him at the top of the gangplank,

Robert knew utterly that he had made the right choice in joining the great adventure. He had decided in a heartbeat to do whatever it took to remain in their orbit and to become whatever he needed to become in order to experience more of this fantastic lifestyle.

Conversely, the youngster insisted on retaining his modest wardrobe, and no one objected when he unwrapped the mothballed camera to begin snapping their shipboard interactions. Röhm had labelled him "Jungle Boy" and the others soon followed suit, which Klaus didn't mind at all seeing it was his brother who had supposedly made his name as the big-shot tourist guide.

He kept his mouth shut and out of the way whenever possible, but could not help noticing that most of the homebound stormtroopers were coarse and thuggish, despite their fancy clothes and affected refinement. By comparison, Röhm's elegance was unforced and impeccable, except when he drank heavily, which was often. The brothers now realised the importance of Mam's insistence on proper table manners, standing them in good stead from their very first meal aboard.

Notwithstanding, Klaus came down with diarrhea and shortness of breath when faced with trooper-sized servings of rich food. Noting his absence over several consecutive meals, Schartzl looked in bearing a slice of freshly baked strudel which the boy downed from a sense of obligation and making his bellyache worse.

Between cramping up on his bunk and venturing a few halting words, the boy soon discovered Marty's common interests in life, art and politics. Their friendly, animated discussions caused Jungle Boy to quite forget his discomfort. Although Marty referred often and fondly to "Onkel Röhm", he confided that the older man was very selective in his sexual preferences nowadays, hinting that he himself was a bit miffed that Robert was fast becoming the apple of Onkel's eye. "All the better for us, Klaus; I feel sure we're going to become bonzer friends along the way, free of all that innuendo and tomfoolery others get up to after dark," he giggled.

Following that warm exchange the boy felt comforted, the two met up almost daily in the cleaving bow as it ploughed toward the ever-cooling waters of the North Atlantic. They curled up with their books among the coils of hemp hawsers, plying each other with questions regarding their two diametrically opposed upbringings; returning again and again to their favourite chestnuts of life's deeper meanings and mysteries.

One had gained his passion from books and private tuition and the other from living a life on the edge, yet both with a keen intelligence and desire to look beyond the obvious.

It was Marty who first broached the subject of "The Leader's concept of God" and the boy wondered why he'd not seen this strange epithet enunciated in any of his history books. "Adolf Hitler says that God is nothing more than Divine Providence at work. Some individuals and races are chosen by

Providence to rule over others and it is the unwritten duty of all inferiors to accept this reality of Nature." He paused to watch the other's reaction, before continuing. "He further claims that Fate has decreed Aryan superiority and must be obeyed eventually."

The theory sounded so rehearsed and convincing that Klaus was surprised when Marty, after a short pause, enquired, "What do you think, my friend?"

He had never heard either the word "God" or any similar concept pass the colonel's lips or those of his companions, except when cursing, although he learned later that Röhm often accompanied his aged mother to church when in Munich.

"I … er … have rather conflicted views about such things at the moment," the boy answered evasively, "but one thing I do know is that a God of some sort is always behind mankind's greatest and most beautiful achievements, artistic or otherwise … and that where there is no beauty there can be no God."

"Wow!" exclaimed Schartzl. "Perhaps that's all true, but how do you explain the hunter and his prey? Not too beautiful for those on the receiving end, eh? The strongest rule the rest, hasn't it always been so? Where does beauty fall in that equation then?" The youngster was momentarily stunned by the sharp response and regretted revealing so much of himself at the first prod.

"And who defines beauty after all? Take Picasso, for example: to the untrained eye his paintings are nothing but a series of smears and squiggles, yet he is undoubtedly shaping up to be the greatest artist of this century …"

"You must be joking," the boy retorted, having been repelled by the few prints of that outrageous artist's work appearing in his books. He knew beautiful landscapes and portraits when he saw them, and nothing could beat the beauty of a dewdrop on the petal of a jungle flower. "I'm afraid I beg to differ, Marty; Classical styles have come down to us over centuries and cannot readily be improved upon …"

"Yes, yes, I expected you to say something like that. Stick with me and I'll show you a new language in art that will make your hair stand on end. Expressionism is taking the world by storm, speaking to the heart and soul in a parlance all of its own, far more than the jolt of reaction felt by most."

It was obvious that Schartzl exuded an almost pugnacious superiority when it came to matters artistic and musical. Furthermore, he went out of his way to forewarn life in the Nazi cauldron, where the boy would need to stay on his toes if he hoped to keep his head on his shoulders. As the days cooled and shortened, the boy spent more and more time snuggled up with his classical volumes and avoiding his flamboyant brother, who by now had convinced all and sundry that Alois had been on the brink of giving permission when he ran afoul of Destiny. By voyage's end, the old man's name was never mentioned.

"Do you believe in coincidences, Jungle Boy? We both have older brothers named Robert …" Röhm volunteered pensively one morning while leaning over the bow rail all rugged up and sucking on a damp cigar stub.

"I swear on the Kaiser's left arm I've never seen anyone with their head stuck in a book and more bloody books than you. Then again, I guess you will need to be right on the ball if you are to get a foot in the door at Studio Hoffmann. Heini's supposed to be one helluva taskmaster."

"Yessir … an' I'm ready for it, sir," he lied. "I've even made a list of the famous dignitaries he's photographed before devoting himself exclusively to National Socialism, sir." Röhm turned to look him squarely in the eye. "Well, for now, all you have to do is sit back and enjoy yourself. When we arrive back home, it's going to be one helluva ride … It's your homeland now too, don't forget, Jung Hahn. It would have been a real pity not to have reached your full potential, with all that German blood flowing through your veins."

"And Irish blood too, sir."

"Yes, yes, we'll sort all that out later. For the time being, you'll do as you're told and will be well looked after. I've decided you will be staying with Mutti Emilie for a few days when we arrive in Munich. Then we'll see about this introduction to the Great Master you're so intent on."

"B … But, what about my brother, sir?"

Röhm took another deep drag on his expired stub. "He'll undergo basic training with me in the S.A. barracks. He's about to get the shock of his life. All going well, I have him earmarked for a special position in the S.A. Choir where I can keep an eye on him."

He noted concern on the face of the youth. "You will find my Mutti Emilie the most perfect and precious woman on this earth, I've no doubt she'll enjoy your company and probably spoil you rotten. I'll be required at headquarters immediately, so after I get you settled, you can fill her in all about my exciting times in South America."

The boy gulped. "B … But I know nothing of your time before Santa Luzia …"

"Well then, just make it up as you go along, I'm sure you've plenty of stories about your time among the Indians, and she'll be happy enough just to see me arriving home safe and sound," he added jauntily. "That's settled then?"

He flicked the soggy butt over the rail and strode away.

Captain Röhm's apparent alacrity and concern went a long way toward soothing the youngster's apprehension. He felt even more safe and confident under the protection of this proven warrior. Gazing at the heaving grey horizon he hardly dared imagine what may lay ahead, reminding himself to take one day at a time, recalling Sister Klara's ultimate admonition: "Defer not to the evening what the morning may accomplish." Taking three deep breaths through his nose, he buried his face again in Dante's *Paradiso*.

31

One evening about halfway between Panama and Hamburg, a bored Röhm decided on a sing-along in the bar and ordered everyone to attend. For the first time, he wore a striking swastika on his left sleeve, which immediately caught the boys' attention. He wanted Robert's vocal accompaniment in perfecting the Third Reich's newest battle march, titled "Horst Wessel Song", which so far no one aboard had heard and which Röhm planned on incorporating into the S.A. revised repertoire as an anthem of sorts. After a few false starts, first Robert and then the others warmed to his soulful piano playing, while Klaus thought the lyrics were corny and melodramatic.

Phrases such as "Soon will fly Hitler's banners over every street, our slavery will last only a short time longer, comrades shot by the Red Front and reaction march in spirit with us in our ranks ..." left him cold and bemused.

Good Lord! Is this the best they can come up with? he wondered. After all, he had been rejoicing over Dante's eloquence for months, but he had to admit that the tune itself did engender a certain emotional upwelling. Captain Streicher could have told him that the original melody originated in the Kriegsmarine, long before the Great War, with different lyrics, of course. It had been especially adapted by an obscure Nazi stormtrooper, Horst Wessel, for the coming revolution, shortly before his untimely despatch at the hands of his girlfriend's pimp.

Notwithstanding, Röhm himself was clearly enamoured, pounding the keys during every stanza and insisting on a right-arm salute through the first and fourth. Following several shaky renditions beads of perspiration stood out on his forehead until finally, he led the whole group from start to finish with eyes closed and a smile playing over his lips.

That night in the reeking salon bar, even young Klaus Hahn felt a tinge of patriotism for the land he'd never known. Within days Robert knew the whole piece off by heart, to the delight of his mentor, but Klaus remained uninspired by any of the onboard activities and his camera lay untouched beneath his pillow.

Weather permitting he haunted the freezing forecastle, huddling out of the wind under Mam's knitted comforter with his books and dreams of things to come. Maya's pitiful declarations of innocence haunted him during such solitary moments; even now he'd not been able to fully unburden his guilt to the God of his Heart.

He searched his panorama of memories for relevance, if any, of Sister Klara's wise teachings for the unknown path ahead. If he'd never seen the miraculous Rainbow Cave with his own eyes and felt the healing touch of her fingers on his spine, the "Great Gift" as she called it, he would surely by now have succumbed to the cast-off views of Robert and the Town Council, that his whole account of a Lost City had been but one long diaphanous delusion, although Robert didn't quite couch his own doubts in such kindly terms.

Revealingly, no one could offer any plausible explanation as to how a white boy, alone, had survived a whole wet season lost in that labyrinth of waterways. Only Kitty knew the truth that miracles were not beyond her ceramic saviour and his mama.

Schartzl too, seemed a little disillusioned by the turn of events and often joined Klaus in his sheltered nook, introducing him to the taste of fine Moselles and ever more meaningful discussions on art and life. He treated the youngster almost as an equal; as the two exchanged ideas and opinions Klaus felt grown up for the first time. "Ain't love grand?" the valet said rather snidely when he spied Röhm and Robert walking the decks arm in arm one evening before dinner. "Still, it is good to see Onkel really happy for a change. Up 'til now, he's been so bored with the whole damn South American jaunt. He thought these wild Indian boys would be a lot more obliging, if you know what I mean," he sniffed, snuggling closer under the blanket. "He says I'm to cease referring to him as 'Onkel' when we arrive back home ..."

"B ... But, you don't understand; Robert's not like that, really, he's just being friendly."

Marty leaned back – "Like what?" – and examined the puzzled face closely, before rolling his eyes and changing the subject. "Well, now that we're all soon to be back in uniform, how do you feel about Hitler's treatment of the swastika? Graphically, I mean. I think it's simply superb; I mean the manner in which he's remastered that ancient Hindu symbol into something so powerful, so perfect and so alive. Don't you agree?"

Now it was the boy's turn to look surprised. "I tell you the man is a great artist," Schartzl continued proudly. "... among his many other accomplishments. There is simply no way that this simple combination of black, white and red could ever be arranged to have more impact. This man single-handedly has come up with the perfect insignia of power and hope for all Germans. Surely as a propitious fellow artist, you must agree?"

Marty's beautiful eyes were glowing, seeking concurrence.

Klaus framed his answer carefully, not wishing to dull his friend's exuberance. "I … er … It certainly catches the eye, and I do agree that the colour combination and composition are dynamic … but, and it's a big 'but', I feel the design implies a certain underlying menace, like a wheel with four sharp cutting blades, rolling over everything that stands in its …"

"Of course little man; that's exactly the point. Germany will never again allow anyone or anything to thwart her rightful aspirations. I must say, you really *do* look into things deeply, even when you fail to reach the right conclusions. If I were you, I'd think twice about disparaging the Fatherland's most recognisable and endearing symbol in public. There are those back home who won't take too kindly to your defeatist interpretations."

For years the boy had pored over black-and-white pictures showing swastikas. Now, after sighting one close-up for the first time in full colour, he was firm in his conclusions. "Come on, Marty … Surely, it's the medium of photography itself that has been the prime mover for Hitler and the whole Nazi movement."

He felt himself on safe ground prickling his interlocutor.

"Naturally enough, you are yet quite ignorant of the power of Hitler's oratory and seem pretty cocky for one who's never yet set foot in the Fatherland," Schartzl responded.

"Well, this much I do know," replied the emboldened young man, "if it is indeed the 'natural right' of the strong to dominate the weak, as claimed by Captain Röhm, then God help people like me …"

"What's God got to do with it? God helps those who help themselves; even you must have heard that old saying back in, where was it? Saint Lucille?"

"As … as I was saying," Klaus persisted, ignoring the jibe, "that would mean every member of society is at the mercy of those above, regardless of merit. I mean, by having to conform to rigid prevailing doctrines all the way to the top, there would be no room for protesting or individual expression. How can that be a good thing?"

"But, my poor sweet little fool … can't you see the Volk are already at the mercy of the Jews and big industrialists, even in the so-called democracies, without them even realising it? Under Nazism everyone knows exactly where he stands, including those too stupid to grasp what this will all mean after we come to power … and come to power we will," he glared defiantly.

"As for protests, it's we Nazis who've been protesting over the dirty deal dished out to Germany by the so-called Versailles Treaty. Now that the country is blessed with a powerful leader who believes himself to be divinely appointed there will be no need for protests. Every German will receive his just deserts according to his rank within the Movement. Mark my words: there will be no hiding place for the slacker and the work-shy. It goes without saying that each of us is now under the strictest obligation to give our all to the New Reich.

"Of course, by necessity, Onkel Röhm always has to knock a few heads together, how else does one create a whole new society? But that doesn't mean deep down he's not just a big puppy dog," Marty paused, smiling thinly.

"And so on it goes, right up the ladder to the very top. I know that Adolph Hitler is not merely a great leader and a fine artist, but he adores children. Furthermore, he's quite the ladies' man; a real all-rounder according to Onkel. Most women pee their pants when he fixes them with those piercing blue eyes of his and addresses them in person. Men too! They say the seats have to be hosed down after his fiery indoor rallies.

"So you see? If one's leaders are beyond reproach, then surely all else follows? Your gloomy scenario denies the reality of human nature's desire to do as told, and to leave the decision-making to those who know best. Do you know of a better method, smarty-pants?"

"Yes!" The boy shot back, "Through enlightenment of the individual, regardless of rank."

"Ooh, quite the thinker, aren't we? Pie in the sky, my dear fellow. That's *my* point exactly. If everyone undertook the work to which he is best suited, as instructed by those in charge, surely the whole of society would function more smoothly? ... rather than a hodgepodge of individuals all tripping over each other? Look at it this way: you and I see the world of cause and effect very differently. It is only through the unwavering willpower and raw strength of a great leader that lasting peace will ever be obtained ... And Adolph Hitler is, above all, a man of peace."

Klaus did not reply, balking inwardly at the logic which he could not quite refute.

Immediately the simple triangle came to mind and he pondered for a moment on the likely outcome of all such violent overtones: "Action and Reaction" represented by two sides, resulting in an inevitable third "Effect" manifesting on top of the Sacred Pyramid. This had been Sister Klara's most cherished notion.

"Let's face it," Marty continued presumptuously, "for thousands of years, not a single one of the great religions has been able to create a more tolerant, merciful or humane society; why not give National Socialism a chance to prove itself?"

"B ... But, is that the fault of the basic message, or the weaknesses of human nature charged with putting it into practice? And I mean the clergy, too. Sister Klara says ..." he paused, feeling on solid ground, "it's a well-known fact that even now religious leaders of every stripe and colour are busily re-interpreting the Holy Scriptures to increase their own power and suit their own ends."

"You've just shot yourself in the foot, dear boy. Moments ago you were extolling the virtues of giving every man the right to speak, now all of a sudden it's his own fault for not obeying Church precepts to the letter. And why most great religions are on their knees, pardon the pun. I agree, it probably *is* the fault of the individual and not the message. That's precisely why unswerving obedience to a great leader is paramount for the success of a great people ..."

He paused with a curious stare and furrowed brow. "You really must have had quite an experience with that nun of yours and her tribe of Indians, but it's now time to put all that aside and focus on the road ahead. You are about to enter the *real* world of lies and deception, where dog eats dog and the so-called Rule of Law is but a fanciful distraction. 'He who prepares, then hesitates, is lost.' We have Caesar to thank for that timely axiom. I tell you, we Nazis *are* preparing to rule Germany, and eventually the world."

The young Nazi could not understand how his new friend, otherwise showing such promise, continually failed to grasp the import and direction of modern politics. Surely, this new way of extolling the real "Law of the Jungle" was self-evident; nature clearly favours the strong over the weak and the smart over the dull.

"Don't you think it's time to put some of your airy-fairy notions aside and focus on what's real? Just stick with me 'n Onkel and do as you're told. You won't go too far wrong."

"B ... But how can wisdom and beauty exist amidst violence and chaos?" the boy persisted feebly. Perhaps it was he living the lie. The logic behind Schartzl's arguments was hard to ignore, let alone refute. Klaus the bookworm, of all people, should realise the relentless and ubiquitous reach of Natural Law.

As if to reinforce that point, a bold Atlantic swell thumped into the bow and whipped their hiding place with spray. Marty snuggled closer. "Through our political leaders, dummy. I've found no exclusive connections between morality, or 'Divine Light' as you like to call it, and *any* of the religions. Politics is the only path to glory for a Nation State, and National Socialism is the only political theory that bridges both Divine and Earthly Realms; through the wisdom and strength of our leader, Adolph Hitler."

Schartzl, sensing interest, was unstoppable. His face shone with enthusiastic conviction as he attempted to hammer the message home. "Take Christianity, for instance, with all its bleating over Love and Forgiveness: we've all seen the rabid Catholic Emissary Cortez going through the Inca Nation like a packet of salts, waving a bible in one hand and a cutlass in the other, much like our own Crusader Knights slaughtering the Mahommedans five hundred years earlier.

"Nothing's changed. It's a wonder your mother didn't reveal the goings on over generations of your Irish brethren; like hurling bombs into children's playgrounds. Why, Catholics and Protestants have been spewing revenge over each other on that little island for so long they've forgotten the God they pray to each Sunday. And each to a man calls himself 'Christian', bah!

"This is the way it always will be. Like Hitler says, 'Taken to its logical extreme, Christianity would mean the systematic cultivation of the human failure.' Just look at the treatment being meted out to the niggers in Africa, or indeed in America, that great bastion of Democracy. The story is the same everywhere for native populations, from Hudson Bay to the tip of Tierra del Fuego and as far as Australia: rape, plunder, disease and exploitation.

"Are these the precious gifts promised by Jesus? This is the reality now confronting the master race. So much for the 'Brotherhood of Man'." Schartzl was not holding back. "Following twenty centuries and more of misappropriation, where is your 'Divine Wisdom' now? The time for preaching and reconciliation is over; we Nazis live for action. Onkel believes in permanent revolution," he concluded triumphantly.

Most of their religious discussions ended in similar fashion, with Klaus' head reeling and his own cherished views struggling to survive.

For the remainder of the voyage, Schartzl's rock-solid beliefs remained confusing yet tempting, especially in the matter of the relative merits of painting (true art) and photography (lazy man's art). The photographer, Marty repeated, had merely to be clever for 1/60th of a second, while the painter has to maintain his creativity for days or even weeks at a time.

He boasted that his exhibition in La Paz had netted over 2,000 German marks, while dismissing Klaus' postcard sales as "chicken feed". Fortunately, Klaus hadn't disclosed Captain Streicher's oversight in the matter of finalising his account for the portrait sitting; or Art Graduate Schartzl's contempt for a mere cameraman would have been total.

Nonetheless, it was a shared creative impulse that sealed their friendship and overrode such trifles; Marty was able to fill in many gaps in the youngster's knowledge of German literature, especially concerning Goethe. Klaus also questioned the origins and structure of the Grand Opera for which he found himself developing more of a taste on the gramophone.

As the days became shorter and the rain squalls more frequent the Hahn brothers found themselves confined to *Sachsen*'s cramped lower decks where other than early mornings, when Röhm and his comrades usually slept late, any attempt to read was thwarted by their loud reminiscences and sing-songs at the piano.

Each day their long-awaited destination drew closer, Robert was clearly in his element. His voice and repertoire had improved markedly under Röhm's tutelage, and prior to each meal, he would proudly lead in singing the new "Horst Wessel Song", the puerile lyrics of which continued to grate on Klaus' sensibilities, especially when witnessing the emotions it evoked among the Nazi coterie straining to harmonise the chorus. "The S.A. marches with silent, solid steps, [How could thousands of soldiers wearing jackboots march silently?] Soon will fly Hitler's flags over every street; slavery will last only a

short time longer …" And so, on and on it went in language crude to Klaus'
unaccustomed ear.

As *Sachsen* ploughed on towards Hamburg, he could not deny some sort of pull
from the Fatherland rising in his breast. He felt torn between his former goal
of self-employment and the promise of unlimited art galleries and concerts to
come.

Marty claimed that Munich's extensive parklands were large enough to tame
even the freest spirit and despite the boy's reservations he was being drawn
inexorably into the web of a truly great cause, an experience he'd glimpsed but
once only briefly during his final days among the Mojo. Perhaps he was, after
all, one tiny but necessary cog of a mighty Nation getting back on its feet, as
Vati had so often tried to drum into him.

One afternoon, as he sat conversing with Marty in deck chairs beyond the
reach of a keen north wind, his friend surprised him by reciting a passage from
the great Shakespeare in English, revealing his own calcified interpretations of
Nazi doctrine. "'We are such stuff as dreams are made on, and our little lives
are rounded with a sleep …' See, even the mighty Englishman acknowledges
that as individuals we are less than dust. It's only by the combined thrust of
whole peoples and cultures that mankind's forward momentum is maintained.
As individuals, we count for nothing!"

He would need to come up with more "proof" than this, the boy thought.

"Try to get it through your thick skull that it takes a truly remarkable leader,
a messiah, to lead a people to their true destiny. Anything or anyone who gets
in the way should be ruthlessly exterminated, for the good of the Volk."

Exterminated! There was a word Klaus had not heard uttered until that
moment, and it made his blood run cold. Surely, the writings of Shakespeare,
Goethe and Dante embodied far more concern for humanity than that
contained in Marty's single incongruous quotation to prove a dubious point.
Was his learned new friend just trying to stir him up?

"And, dear boy, that's why military officers make the best politicians, Onkel
has said so many times," Schartzl rambled. "He did spend one term in the
Reichstag, did you know that?" Klaus pretended not to be listening, holding
his book up to his face.

"Just wait and see; Onkel and Adolph will stand the whole country on its
head." No response.

"There will be a degree of discipline and Realpolitik imposed on the
German Volk unlike anything they've seen before. It's the only way to restore
them to their rightful place atop the world order …"

"B … But, aren't most Germans already Christians, either Catholic or
Protestant?" the boy asked, lowering his book, unable to concentrate. "I read
that Hitler himself was raised a Catholic; at one time he even considered
entering the priesthood. Captain Ernst makes no bones about his Protestant

faith; surely these facts alone contradict the basic tenets of Nazism espousing ascendency of strong over weak?"

"Bah! Their piety is all for show. 'Nothing is more disgusting than the majority', according to Goethe. Christianity in all its guises has become flaccid and decadent over many centuries, crippling the so-called majority with superstition. It suits our cause to introduce our changes gradually, weaning away these millions of cramped lost souls onto the one true path."

"Look, Marty look!" A wandering albatross had skimmed across the stern and hovered accusingly above the foaming wake; from his picture books, the boy knew that this was indeed a rare event in such northern waters and was happy to redirect the pugnacious conversation. The graceful creature dipped its wing and peeled off into the sunset, only then did he realise what a splendid photo it would have made. That lost moment stirred something within him and he decided henceforth to keep his camera nearby, just in case.

He had no doubt that the albatross was a good omen. Marty was now leaning over the rail smoking a cigarette with his back to the boy. His relentless criticisms and emphatic rebuttals had quite drained Klaus' enthusiasm for his chosen field, and two nights later, before they docked in Hamburg, he awoke in a cold sweat with the spotted beast again firmly fastened on his throat. For no particular reason, he'd been dreaming he was a red howler.

<h1 style="text-align:center">32</h1>

Few young men have ever stepped ashore on German soil with a bigger lump in their throat than Klaus Hahn. A sharp arctic wind whistled down the harbour and moaned between the buildings, cutting through the heavy jacket he'd been issued on board. His chest began to tighten.

Through flavourless eyes he watched his brother gliding down the gangplank wedged firmly between Röhm and Schartzl, to be immediately swamped by a pressing crowd of uniformed stormtroopers and well-wishers. A brown-shirted brass band soon gathered behind the trio, clearly overjoyed at the return of their long-absent commander.

A large black limousine stood ready to whisk the party to the railway station, where a decorated sleeper train stood ready in a cloud of steam. This was decidedly not what the boy had been led to expect. Throughout the long train journey south he sat quietly with his nose pressed against the frosty glass, straining in vain to spot a familiar landmark beside the windblown tracks.

His troubled heart swirled erratically as Marty drip-fed him yet more promises of exciting times ahead, dependant, of course, on Klaus' own ability to pull himself together and begin acting like a true soldier of the Reich. He wisely concluded that he wasn't going to be treated as an equal after all.

Upon arrival at Munich's Hauptbahnhof, he watched Röhm, Schartzl and Robert hasten down the carriage steps and into the waiting arms of Hitler himself. From this vantage point, Klaus thought the great man looked much smaller than in his pictures. Last to alight and struggling with his suitcase, he passed almost unnoticed amidst the hubbub of brass bands and press of uniformed dignitaries.

Eventually, after barking a string of orders, Röhm strode over and grabbed him by the arm before bundling him into the back of a huge black six-wheeler.

At that moment he longed for only one thing: to be back in the jungle where he belonged.

Almost childlike, the triumphant warrior leaned across to point excitedly at one Munich landmark after another, as if the boy too were familiar with each grand building as they passed. Up and down the drafty avenues and narrow backstreets growled the Mercedes, while everywhere groups of Brownshirts carrying Nazi banners and alerted by the fluttering flags on the vehicle snapped to attention and thrust out their arms with a loud "Sieg Heil! Röhm is back!"

The great limousine gurgled to a halt outside Frau Röhm's apartment where another group of well-wishers was waiting; soon, formal introductions were taking place on the sidewalk. Röhm clutched his mother for some minutes in a tearful bear hug before turning back to the waiting boy. "Mutti, there's someone I want you to meet. I've brought him all the way from the wilds of South America, but don't be alarmed, there's not a mean bone in his body."

Röhm faced Klaus, then gestured towards his mother. "Klaus Hahn, I want you to meet my Mutti, Frau Emilie Röhm. As her youngest I love Mutti above all else, what more can I say?"

Frau Emilie exuded the humble magnificence of weathered velvet and her face beamed. The boy stepped forward and held out a large bouquet to the astonished woman, who quickly regained her composure and met his moist eyes with her own. He suddenly felt the loss of Mam and was unable to prevent real tears from coursing down his cheeks and becoming icicles on the end of his nose.

"Come, come, young man," the kindly old woman spoke, placing her left arm gently around his shoulder and the other around her beaming offspring, ushering them both up the front steps and into the warm parlour. Frau Röhm's somewhat severe black silk frock and tight bun of greying hair belied a warm and affectionate nature, putting the boy at ease almost at once.

"Now, dry those eyes and meet my two best friends, Hermann and Martin," she purred as two fat, shiny dogs bounded forward to greet him. Within moments, Captain Röhm was rolling about on the floor with the exuberant canines, oblivious to his mother's admonishment not to get dog hair all over the clean rug.

"Clean rug?" Ernst cackled. "You can throw that moth-eaten old thing out. "I've brought you a rug unlike any other in Munich, shot the damn thing myself ..."

Frau Emilie rolled her eyes and winked at the boy. "Can you now see, Klaus, why I need some steady and reliable companionship with my Ernst always away fighting somewhere or other? Now Röhm was up off the floor and making straight for the baby grand in the corner, where he began playing softly with a faraway look in his eye.

Klaus had never seen dogs in such sleek condition; his lingering impressions of dogs were half-starved mongrels haunting the docks of Santa Luzia, skulking for food.

"God, it's good to be back, Mutti," Röhm beamed over his shoulder at his mother, before reverently lowering the lid on the ivories. "And, I don't have to tell you how much remains to be done now that Adi is appointing me Chief of Staff over the whole S.A. My first priority will be to demolish the remains of this phoney Republic and smash any lingering shackles imposed by the Versailles Treaty. After that, the sky's the limit!"

"Tearing? Smashing? … And you've not been in the door five minutes dearest. I trust you will find time to accompany your old mother to church on Sunday as usual? The other parishioners have quite forgotten what you look like."

It was a statement as much as a question from Frau Emilie.

"Yes, yes! There'll be plenty of time for private pleasures as soon as I pull the S.A. leaders into line. And Mutti, of one thing you can be sure: Adolph and his puffed-up Party Boys won't be walking all over me this time around …"

"Dear, dear," Frau Emily concurred reluctantly, arranging her gift of flowers into a rare Ming vase, one of many family heirlooms adorning her tiny apartment.

In years past Frau Emilie had thought nothing of running an open house to entertain a dozen or more of Ernst's rowdy companions, but this time it was different.

She wasn't getting any younger and was looking forward to spoiling this sensitive and artistic foundling being foisted upon her from far-off Brazil. She had taken an instant liking to the frail youth and prattled on like an old friend over a brimming plateful of fresh cream scones with homemade jam.

"Come on, eat up. I'll put some meat on those bones; you look like you could do with a good feed. Take my Ernst, for example, he's always struggled with his weight …"

"I'm all right, thanks," the boy replied. "I find if I eat too much in one go it interferes with my asthma."

"Asthma eh? How about my dogs? Are you allergic to dogs?" She looked concerned as Ernst sat back nodding approvingly with fingers clasped across his ample paunch.

"I … er, don't think so. I've never owned a dog, but I must say they're friendly enough. You mustn't worry, Frau Röhm; I know how to keep it under control and anyway, I'll be spending a lot of time reading. Onkel says Munich's libraries are bursting at the seams."

The boy felt suddenly confident and relaxed.

"Between you and me," the old lady leaned towards him and pretended to whisper behind her hand, "my Ernst was never a great reader, or much of a scholar either for that matter. More often than not his report cards began with 'a tendency to chatter in class' and suchlike; isn't that right darling?"

"Aw, Mutti, Jung Hahn doesn't need to know all that kind of stuff," replied the hardened warrior, flushing slightly and fumbling to light a tailor-made.

"And who was it that nursed him back to health after those Frenchies shot him full of holes? Have you ever seen such wounds?" She spoke directly to the dogs.

"Just shell fragments, Mutti. The boy knows all about my time at the front. Anyhow, I must be off; duty calls. I expect by now this one's big brother is safely stashed away at headquarters," he explained, thrusting his tiny schnurrbart in Klaus' direction. "They'll be wondering where I've gotten to. I'm sure you two will have plenty to chat about until I get around to lining up an interview with Hoffmann in the next couple of weeks."

With those few parting words and a lingering embrace from his mother, Röhm was gone. The exhausted boy allowed himself to be led into an adjoining bedroom where, with much clucking and soothing, he was stripped to his undies and tucked under a huge feather doona. He found his head resting on two of the largest, softest pillows he'd ever seen.

Upon arrival at Munich's Hauptbahnhof, Robert could hardly believe his eyes at the assembled reception. Since stepping aboard the overnight express he'd glanced out only occasionally at the snow-capped mountains, castellated townships and groups of torch-lit cheering well-wishers flying by the carriage window, preferring to embed himself in the raucous merriment of his newfound comrades.

Röhm's excitement too had been mounting visibly, reaching fever pitch by the time they finally pulled in at Munich. He puffed himself up to his full 5'3", straightened his tie and strode purposefully down onto the platform through the clouds of steam and into the embrace of Adolph Hitler.

So, this is the Man 'imself, Robert thought, bringing up the rear, *over whom all the fuss was being made, and whose stated mission was to lead the German Volk back to Glory.* He wasn't a big man, though several inches taller than his long-lost "blood comrade", who'd not only commanded Hitler's 16th Bavarian Regiment in the trenches but almost died on several occasions.

Following the initial greeting of heel clicking and outstretched arms, a brass band erupted in a rousing rendition of the "Horst Wessel Song". Robert stepped out in his dandified outfit and joined the soaring harmonies.

But on this dismal November day, Herr Hitler had eyes only for his long-lost comrade, Röhm, who looked tanned and sprightly as the pair strolled toward the carpark locked in deep discussion. From amidst the crowd of cheering civilians, Robert was hauled up with his baggage onto the back of an ancient army truck sporting solid rubber tyres, before clattering away over the cobblestones.

Looking back, he glimpsed his baby brother being ushered by Röhm into the back of a sleek black six-wheeler that roared off in the opposite direction.

"You'll be bunking down at S.A. Headquarters for the time being," one of the new minders yelled in his ear, which meant nothing to the new recruit.

He gripped the sideboards with freezing hands, enthralled by the grand buildings, ubiquitous brown livery and blood-red swastika banners fluttering from every top-floor window. Hitler's grim visage peered from street pole posters.

"We'll soon have you kitted out in your new uniform, ready to crack a few commie skulls before our Blutfahne reunion on the ninth," came through the whistling wind.

Robert felt up for anything, despite his hands and ears turning blue; even more at home on noticing his thuggish minders swearing every second word between themselves. He was emboldened, being among friends. "Wow! … look at the height of those fucking steeples," he exclaimed to no one in particular, and was greatly relieved when the others laughed out loud, one or two even slapping him on the back approvingly.

When they pulled up outside the former Palais Barlow there was no sign of Schartzl, or indeed anyone else from the ship. His companions leapt nimbly down and waded forward to clear a path through the curious crowd.

"Take a good look at this tired old façade, comrade," one shouted proudly. "The Leader has already drawn up plans to tear it down and replace it with something more fitting." The draftee felt thrilled to be part of what was obviously the winning team, determined to make a fist of it, though deep down he retained a little niggle of uncertainty; something from the past he couldn't quite put his finger on. He refused to allow it to take the shine off the moment.

When Klaus stepped out onto the icy Munich pavement the next morning, he was confronted by a cacophony of sight and sound. An urgent, hat-snatching wind tugged at the rays of impotent light creeping between the sunless buildings.

Frau Röhm, already proving herself a wonderful hostess, had warned him not to wander more than a few blocks from the apartment until he got "the lie of the land".

As if to oblige, his shoes felt stuck to the concrete sidewalk and he seemed to be the only one in the whole street without a sense of purpose. On all sides bustling, honking and shouting filled the air on a scale wholly unfamiliar to his gentle sensibilities. Not even the colourful commotion of a Belem or Balboa waterfront market could compare with a Munich peak hour.

With few exceptions, sedulous passers-by in and out of uniform hurried past with lowered eyes, avoiding his tentative smile. Taking the hint, he pulled his collar around his ears and keeping close to the walls set off with head down toward the Isar River, just a few blocks away.

Coming from the land of myriad greens, where everyone exchanged greetings, or at least lifted a chin when passing in the street, he realised that for the first time ever he felt lonely. If this was the way the city folk wanted it that was just fine. Perhaps these people were being urged on by the countless Nazi banners declaring "Germany Awake!" that fluttered on all sides? On street corners groups of stormtroopers loitered, handing out pamphlets and jeering at old men wearing beards. In fact, they seemed to have a snide word for anyone not wearing a uniform of some description, including himself.

Now and again, a squad of helmeted State Police came jogging in at double time to disperse the Brownshirts, flailing wildly with their billy clubs before moving on to the next illegal gathering. The alien scene was one of violence and chaos, despite a glimpse of mighty spires, fountains and statues which he intended to study more closely at a later time. Taking his life in his hands he darted across busy Ludwig Strasser and continued east towards the so-called river, which turned out to be a disappointing chain of mere puddles enclosed by willow-tangled embankments.

Walking dejectedly downstream for a few blocks Klaus turned back along Prinzregentenstrasse towards home, thereby making his first uplifting discovery: the one-and-a-half square miles of English Garden sitting right in the middle of town alongside the river. He made a mental note to return with a picnic at the first opportunity.

Again he darted across a busy thoroughfare when his eye caught a circular newsstand on the opposite corner. There they were at last, a breathtaking array of current illustrated magazines, newspapers and periodicals, flanked by an assortment of "Hitler Postcards" showing the coming man in every conceivable pose.

He turned one over and read with satisfaction: "Copyright, Studio Hoffmann." Many of these publications were unknown to the boy, and those that were familiar had usually taken two or three months to make their way to Santa Luzia.

Hitler's icy scowl glared out from every light pole and wall; posters espousing alternate parties had been partially defaced or torn down.

"*National Socialism!*" The words screamed at him from every headline and article as he gathered several precious periodicals. "I'm all sold out of last week's *Illustrierter*," the vendor announced from his stool, noting the boy's bundle, "but there's a new edition out tomorrow, with Streicher on the cover. He's just been let out of goal, you know?"

"Streicher? Streicher? … it hardly seemed possible. The boy was startled by the coincidence; not so much of a coincidence really given that throughout the length and breadth of the Fatherland, there must be hundreds of Streichers.

Further enquiry revealed that the vendor was referring to one Julius Streicher, weekly publisher of the particularly vitriolic *Der Stürmer* broadsheet.

The man further informed him in hushed tones that *this* Streicher was one of the Nazis' leading lights, who travelled all over the countryside giving hate-filled, inflammatory speeches denouncing "enemies of the state", and all Jews as "Christ killers" and "vermin".

At this point in his education, Klaus had but a scant notion of what a "Jew" actually looked like, one gleaned from previous Nazi publications and the loose talk of Röhm's comrades. Counting out his precious marks, he selected a variety of titles before hurrying back towards the warm interior of Frau Emilie's apartment which, according to her hastily drawn map, lay somewhere close by.

Over a steaming bowl of vegetable broth, he excitedly recounted the morning's adventures, which he felt included more than enough excitement for one day.

On the morrow, Frau Emilie promised to fill out a membership card for the Munich Bibliotech, which she described as one of Germany's finest libraries, containing "more grand volumes than he could read in a dozen lifetimes".

And, that wasn't all she had in store for her doe-eyed lodger, revealing that "big things were afoot in two days' time" when her beloved Ernst was to join his Old Fighters in celebrating the failed 1923 Putsch. It seemed that her Ernst and Hitler, among others, had attempted an ill-fated coup aimed at unseating the Bavarian Government by force. "Perhaps you've heard the story? Sixteen of his comrades were shot down by the police on that occasion," she confided to the boy, "and Adolph ended up in goal for treason, of all things.

"My Ernst was able to hold the whole Movement together while the rest of them languished in Landsberg but only for 9 months or so, as it turned out," she added proudly. "Adolph was supposed to serve five years, but most of the judicial and prison authorities were sympathetic to his cause.

"While inside he lived the high life and even managed to dictate *Mein Kampf* to his secretary, Hess; mind you, I've never been able to make head nor tail of it. I just can't see what all the fuss is about." She leaned closer. "Just between us, it's made him millions." She spoke warmly and confidentially to the boy, who had scant idea of the personalities and events she was describing.

"This will be the first time in three years that my Ernst has been around to celebrate the big day, and I know he'll be looking forward to rubbing shoulders with his old comrades; if the authorities choose not to interfere, that is. He has reserved front-row seats for you and me at the march past; of course, we won't hang around for the festivities afterwards, they do tend to get a bit rowdy."

"That suits me," the boy responded, before excusing himself and heading for his room with a fat bundle of the very latest tabloids under his arm.

Meanwhile, back in Palais Barlow, just off Brienner Strasser, Robert was admiring himself in a full-length gilded mirror. In just a few short hours he'd been transformed into one more stern-faced Nazi warrior, complete with a brown shirt, cap and jodhpurs, held up by a black belt and shoulder strap. A brand-new shiny pair of black riding boots completed the uniform. Perhaps his proudest accessory, courtesy of Röhm himself, was a heavy leather dog whip made from Rhinoceros hide, similar to that carried by Hitler, which he now stood smacking into the palm of his left hand and against the stripe on his trousers. Tilting his cap a little more to one side, he turned his face back and forth, liking what he saw.

When the light fell at a certain angle, the scars on his face hardly showed at all, even accentuating his orderly features. For the first time, he felt they actually imparted a certain mystery to his battle-worn demeanour. So far he hadn't been required to fill in an S.A. application form, being advised that Captain Röhm had taken care of everything. Up 'til now, the sole instructions he'd received stressed only the unquestioning *following of orders*!

That shouldn't be too difficult. He felt as ready as he'd ever be. Slapping the whip one last time against the top of his boot and flashing his perfect teeth at the mirror, he headed off to join his new comrades for a briefing in the canteen.

On that evening of November 9, the brothers Hahn viewed the passing torchlight parade with very different emotions.

Hours earlier, Klaus and a velour-clad Frau Röhm had filed into the Hofbräuhaus arm in arm, where they were shown to a private table overlooking the brass band and speakers' rostrum. The tabletop was dented and carved with initials from countless Nazi gatherings.

"Don't drink it all if you can't manage," she whispered in his ear when the biggest stein of golden beer he'd ever seen was plonked down before him, just one of a dozen or more being juggled around the hall on the stout arm of their waitress. Without having placed an order, the stein and a small glass of Moselle "compliments of the Party" arrived within minutes, and from the neverending well-wishes being shouted from all sides, it was apparent that the regal old lady was held in the highest esteem.

Klaus removed the stuffy duffel jacket that had miraculously appeared at the foot of his bed that morning and loosened his unaccustomed tie, aware of the choking din. Feeling all eyes upon them he took a tentative sip of ale and suppressed a cough, forcing his peripheral vision to take in the scene.

Various swastikas had been cleverly incorporated into the rustic décor, reflected in the chandeliers overhead. Suddenly the music stopped, and a fanfare of trumpets and drums announced the arrival of the Old Fighters, several dozens of whom came striding down the centre aisle holding aloft as many Nazi standards urging "Germany to Awake" from its lethargy.

Out in front strode Captain Röhm, wearing an expression of utmost solemnity and carrying the largest flag of all. The guard of honour stopped and parted, allowing Adolph Hitler, flanked by his SS bodyguards, to step forward and take their seats on the podium.

"That's the precious Blutfahne, Klaus, most sacred of all their icons," Frau Emilie enthused, "There! You can still see the blood stains from the Putsch." She seemed excited and proud.

Röhm mounted the dais and held up both hands to quell the thunderous applause, nodding his appreciation to all smoke-filled quarters. The old lady nudged Klaus with her elbow, "See? See how they adore my Ernst?"

After rowdy minutes an expectant hush settled over the beer hall. "Comrades of the S.A., I'm back!" From a thousand whetted throats came a deafening roar as beer steins beat a tattoo on the table tops. Again, Röhm waited before continuing. "I know that my destiny and that of the German Volk lies here, at the Leader's side, inspired by the ultimate sacrifices of our blood comrades seven long years ago." He grasped the corner of the Blutfahne reverently.

"The S.A. is and remains Germany's destiny. We will eliminate the Red Peril and do away completely with the Old Order ..." Another howl of approval filled the former Royal Brewery. "Let this Blutfahne remind us always of our sacred pledge and the struggle we face, and that the task ahead cannot, and will not, be accomplished without the selfless commitment of every last one of *you*, my beloved stormtroopers!" He again raised his hands and nodded vigorously before continuing, "I foresee nothing less than your devoted ranks, soon to exceed one million strong, replacing the role of the Reichswehr itself in the not-too-distant future." A brown mass rose to its feet as one and burst into the newly minted "Horst Wessel Song".

There was no doubt at all in Klaus' mind regarding the unbridled affection held by these rowdies for their Leader; however, he noticed that Hitler had not joined in the singing and remained sitting stern-faced. Then, slowly and deliberately, he rose to his feet, returned Röhm's ebullient salute and moved to the microphone.

Unlike the former speaker, he neither raised his hands nor uttered a single word for several pregnant minutes, until a total hush enveloped the room.

He spread his notes on a small side table and stood with arms folded, rocking slightly back and forward on the balls of his feet.

"Old Fighters, Party Comrades," he began slowly, almost reluctantly, with a voice both soft and guttural. "Once more our brother Röhm has rejoined our ranks for the struggle ahead ..." – more banging and cheering – "... and at this fateful hour we may hold few seats in the Reichstag, but I tell you the future belongs entirely to us!" he banged his fist on the table as his voice broke. Once more the crowd leapt to its feet with a flurry of "Sieg Heil's" and outstretched arms.

Despite his former scepticism, Klaus felt a curious patriotism rising in his breast as his eyes roamed across the enervated assembly to take in the full import of the moment. Two familiar figures could be seen through the blue haze opposite, yelling and stiff-arming with the best of them: Robert and Marty had taken up positions beneath a gilded archway decorated with humanoid faces fashioned from fresh farm vegetables; a strange sight indeed, he thought.

For the first time, both of them wore caps and matching S.A. uniforms, like two peas in a pod; a far cry from his rakish brother and the elegant, intellectual

Martin Schartzl he'd come to know. For a moment he wondered what Mam would have made of her firstborn, whose mouth she'd often claimed would not melt butter, now decked out in a brown uniform and baying for blood, looking happier than at any time in his life.

"I have decided," the Speaker continued, "that from this day forward, we National Socialists will pursue all legal pathways to power, at least until such power is firmly in our hands." A murmur swept through the hall and one or two dissenting cries rang out. "I am appointing Captain Röhm Chief of Staff over the entire S.A., effective January 1 …" Again, thunderous applause.

"The day will soon come when November 9, our 'Day of Blood', will be celebrated throughout all Germany in honour of those who died as Martyrs. The whole Nation will quake in its boots!" Flecks of spittle flew from the corners of his mouth as he once more banged the tabletop and the room rejoiced.

From the corner of his eye, Klaus noticed Frau Emilie shaking her head involuntarily, but the crowd was on its feet and Hitler had them in the palm of his hand; he'd never seen anything like it.

"And you, my comrades, will follow Captain Röhm on toward victory, enforcing *my* undivided iron will. Amen!"

Braying trumpets and "Heil Hitler's" reverberated against the cavernous walls and out onto the narrow street. As Hitler gathered up his notes and turned to leave, Röhm leapt to his feet and punched the air with his fist. "Comrades! Now the S.A. marches!"

Through the uproar, Klaus felt his eyes and throat stinging, relieved to see Frau Röhm rise and motion him to join the brown crush flowing outside, where her chauffeur-driven transport was waiting.

Once aboard, she instructed the driver to follow Hitler's black limousine as it sped away toward Rosenheim Strasser, ready to launch the annual torchlight parade. Watching on lovingly and quizzically, the old lady grew increasingly concerned at her wheezing charge fighting for breath and softly intoning his vowel sounds beside her on the back seat.

Before they reached the Ludwig's Brucke over the Isar she redirected the driver homeward. "B … but Frau Emilie, what about your reserved seat at the parade?" She returned his look with a knowing smile.

Wheezing uncontrollably, with Frau Emilie under one arm and her driver Johann under the other, they half-lifted and half-dragged the boy up the front steps and into her cosy apartment.

"Settle down, I didn't want to be out in the cold any longer, either. At the moment your health is more important than Ernst's triumph; Lord, your clothes reek of cigarette smoke," she tut-tutted while laying out a clean set of Röhm's pyjamas in front of a crackling log fire and turning her back while he changed.

Before long he was sipping hot broth and listening to a symphonic concert on her huge console radio receiver.

"Of course, my Ernst was classically trained, you know?" she said eventually, noting an improvement in the boy's breathing. "Although you might not think so nowadays when you see him surrounded by that bunch of rowdies," she added with a chuckle. "I do so wish Adolph wouldn't resort to such violent language; it only serves to stir up the others unnecessarily. He used to be so polite and well-mannered when Ernst first brought him home."

"Well, he's certainly struck a chord with my brother, Frau Röhm. It's the first time I've ever seen Robert looking like he belongs to …"

"I suppose all the Brownshirts belong to my Ernst now," she mused. "Although I have a job telling one from the other. Come along, your hot tub is ready. You may have gathered that I'll be doing my best to keep you away from all that Nazi rough and tumble? Regrettably, my Ernst seems to thrive on it; I suppose it all comes down to the atrocities he witnessed during the War," she added pensively.

"He's promised me an introduction to Heinrich Hoffman himself, Frau Emilie; I do hope it's soon. Onkel Ernst told me that Photohaus Hoffman and Nazi Headquarters share a building downtown …"

"Yes, Yes, I suppose so; I can't keep up with them. I hear they are already renovating an even bigger building in Karinenplatz to cater for the swelling membership. Given your state of health you would be well advised to stay right away from those Brownshirt gangs roaming the streets; it seems they turn on anyone looking sideways at the drop of a hat.

"Anyway, I'm hoping you'll be able to stay safe and sound here with me, at least until Ernst's birthday party at the end of the month. I don't want you to breathe a word, it's going to be a surprise, the first chance I've had in years to do him one of my Black Forest Cakes; they were always his favourite!"

Frau Emilie and the broadcast were suddenly interrupted by a radio announcement that the candlelight parade had now reached the Feldernhalle, the scene of the fatal police fusillade in 1923, where more speeches were to follow.

She reached over and turned it off.

During the fleeting days and weeks that followed, Klaus took to the surrounding streets with a happy heart and camera in hand. Frau Röhm had painstakingly drawn a map of nearby city streets and points of interest, including many impressive facades, museums and art galleries, toward which her lodger began to make his way.

Best of all, however, was the comforting open spaces of the previously glimpsed English Garden, where he could breathe easy and wander about uninterrupted and alone. Once, she arranged to meet him in the Japanese Teahouse, located a short distance inside the South Gate, where she plied him with all manner of strange foods while they sat chatting together and observing the passers-by.

Patiently she listened to his excited prattling of the sights he'd seen and the galleries visited, responding more than once that he sounded "like a kid in a toy shop". One discovery he did not share, however, was the willow-tangled sandbank jutting out into the River Isar that was hidden from prying eyes ashore.

He'd already spent one whole afternoon reading beside a tiny campfire of willow twigs. Of all the unlikely refuges this seemingly invisible isthmus offered the tranquillity he craved. Aside from an odd fisherman in the distance, few people strayed far from the web of nearby pathways.

Putting two and two together, he figured that when nourishing spring arrived to clothe the willows in dense green and to swell the trickling current with melting snow, this tiny secluded nook might just turn out to be the perfect retreat from Munich's rat race. Admittedly, the Isar was a poor substitute for the mighty waterway where he'd been raised, but would have to suffice. "Any port in a storm," Mam used to say.

When first he'd stumbled down the steep riverbank, the only other sign of life was a lone grey heron stalking the shallows upstream. In vain, he'd searched the tangled branches for birdlife, before croaking once at the astonished heron and vowing to keep this place as his own special retreat.

As the flames crackled into life only a distant hum of traffic indicated that he was in fact, slap-bang in the middle of a great city. Wisely, he left behind a small pile of twigs to dry in the sun, ready for his next visit. Life in this concrete jungle might not turn out to be so bad, after all.

Come November 28, Klaus' spirits lifted almost to a fever pitch. Not only was he excited to catch up with Röhm, Schartzl and Robert, but he'd received the welcome news via Frau Emilie that his long-awaited appointment with Hoffmann had been arranged for the very next morning after Ernst's party, which now appeared to be no longer a surprise.

Of course, Frau Röhm did not disappoint: the apartment was adorned with streamers and balloons and her extendable sideboard teetered under every conceivable delicacy. At each end sat a steaming roast leg of lamb, triumphantly garnished with mushrooms. In pride of place at the centre sat a two-tiered Black Forest Cake, bespattered with plump pickled cherries. Her gramophone had been squeezed in beside the Bechstein and was already mewing out a selection of modern swing music.

On arrival, Ernst pretended to be surprised by the loud hurrahs from his Mother's hand-picked guests, most of whom were complete strangers to Klaus. At a glance, the array of fur coats and tiaras indicated that the majority of the invitees were, like Frau Röhm herself, definitely "upper class".

In the far corner of the parlour, a handful of Brownshirts stood huddled together.

Scanning the crush he could just make out Robert and Marty in civilian garb, mingling easily amidst howls of laughter. It seemed everyone wanted to hear Robert reciting Irish limericks in German with his idiosyncratic accent;

even pressing him further, with encouragement from Marty, to recount the dangers of hunting wild Indians and jaguars up the Amazon.

Röhm was gesticulating proudly towards a huge spotted pelt with its snarling fangs and glass eyes staring forlornly out from between the piano legs. He protested that his hard-won trophy should instead occupy pride of place in front of the hearth, but Frau Emilie had remained equally determined that the horrid hunting souvenir would stay half-hidden under the baby grand.

But on this special day, her "birthday boy" was resplendent in his plaid Junkers' three-piece lounge suit and Robin's nest hairdo parted to one side. At the rate he was tossing down spirits, it was obvious to Klaus that he would be lucky to remain standing for the later frolic with his S.A. commanders.

From his seat in the corner, Klaus felt a tingle of envy watching Robert move effortlessly through the crowd, casting backhanded compliments here and a winning smile there, especially toward the enthralled womenfolk.

Whenever he loitered too long in one spot or appeared to be getting snowed under, Röhm held up an empty glass or clicked his fingers sharply which quickly brought his adoring charge to heel. At the first opportunity, Schartzl sidled over to Klaus and sat down on the arm of his lounge chair to begin plying the boy with questions. "Oh, do tell me what you think of Munich so far …"

Before he could answer, Valet Schartzl rattled off a further string of enquiries with boozy breath: "Which is your favourite gallery? Have you discovered the Classical Volumes in the Bibliotech? What do you think of the Opera House?" and so on. Receiving but vague and incomplete responses, he parried from one subject to the next. "Isn't Frau Emilie just marvellous?" he asked loudly within earshot of the old lady, who sailed about serenely overseeing the staff and wearing a look of utter contentment.

"Y … Yes, I don't know how I would have fared without her. I simply couldn't tolerate the crowded barracks you boys live in." Klaus had already sneaked a peek through the ground-floor window display on Amalienstrasse and observed the non-stop comings and goings of Brownshirts from their cramped headquarters two flights above.

"It's not so bad when one gets used to it," Marty slurred. "There's the companionship for starters, given we do have to be on call at all hours. By the way, I tried to catch your eye at the Hofbräuhaus, but you were already on your way out the door …"

"Oh, that? My asthma flared up in all the smoke and noise. Frau Emilie thought it best if we went straight home …"

"My dear fellow! I can't begin to tell what fun you missed out on after the parade was over," he chuckled, leaning close and exuding more fumes. "We even had you lined up with one of our 'Young German Madels', a virgin too, ha-ha! Maybe next time eh?"

Klaus' cheeks flushed bright pink in the stuffy atmosphere and in attempting to change the subject blurted to Marty of his pleasure in having located a secluded picnic spot by the river.

"Christ! You must be joking! Braving the high seas all this way to the political capital of the world just to spend your time sitting on a fucking sandbank. "Wake up old boy! – 1931 is just around the corner and Germany's prospects have never looked more promising."

He turned his head away and burped loudly.

But neither his new "best friend" nor anyone else would be able to shake Klaus from the thrill of discovering a private place of his own, and he brushed off the other's dismay. "It's … it's where I feel closest to God," he finally muttered.

"God? God help us is all I can say. Why don't you commune with your Maker on Sundays if you must – in a church, like all the other so-called believers?" His voice was flinty. "And how come every time we get together the subject turns to gods or goddesses in one form or another?"

Marty was visibly annoyed, quite overlooking the intimate spiritual discussions they had shared aboard *Sachsen*. At that moment a tinkling bell announced the commencement of formalities.

Röhm's sister, also Emilie, welcomed everyone on behalf of Frau Röhm, who through her daughter expressed great happiness to have her boy back home from the wilds of South America.

All guests then joined in singing three verses of "Happy Birthday", after which Röhm blew out his 43 candles with one mighty gust. Robert's misplaced initiative in following on with the "Horst Wessel Song" fell horribly flat, with only a few Brownshirts and Röhm himself joining in the first two verses. The other guests looked embarrassed by the whole performance, standing in awkward silence with their eyes lowered. No one applauded.

"Dear me, boys will be boys it seems; play something for us darling …" Frau Emilie said diplomatically, breaking the ice and stepping forward to lift the piano lid, "… something nice, something sweet."

Within minutes, and after a good deal of throat-clearing, a small group gathered around the Baby Bechstein, except for Robert, who, looking a little chastened, moved toward the corner and inserted himself into the ongoing chat between Klaus and Schartzl.

"So, what's been happenin' wit' you, liddle brudda?"

"I … er, I was about to tell Marty of my job interview tomorrow, with Hoffmann."

"Well, good luck! Is all I can say," Marty hissed. "He strikes me as a real arrogant bastard. We all have to go through him for any official photos of ourselves in uniform, and he charges like a wounded bull."

"B … But his portraits of famous people and especially Hitler are the best I've ever seen …"

"Just a minute, Jung mann," Schartzl replied with a sarcastic sniff, "just how many great portraits have you *actually* come across in your wide-ranging career? ... And I'm guessing Hoffman's portraits *would* need to be first-class, wouldn't they? ... given that *he* alone holds copyright over every image of Hitler for the next 70 years." He paused to allow his message to sink in.

"I heard in the early days of the Movement a decent photo of our elusive Leader fetched a whopping $30,000 U.S., you do the maths. It's no wonder your crafty boss is opening studios all over the place; he's even signed up George Phal, the man who published the very first picture of Hitler. I bet Phal himself never received anything like that amount."

"No need to discourage 'im, Marty," Robert interjected dryly. "If 'e wants to play around in the darkroom wid 'is camera, there's prob'ly no betta place to do it. One thing's fer sure, neither the S.A. nor us wants 'im 'angin' around ..."

At this, both men burst into laughter, before sidling arm in arm towards the piano, where a visibly drunk and garrulous Röhm had been finally roused into action.

A ripple of anticipation preceded his long-awaited, supposedly informal, discourse. "Bah! Legal path my arse. There's only one language the masses understand and that's wholesome dread," he spoke with passion to the ivory keys.

"Tut, tut, language dear," chided Frau Emilie, "remember you are not among your soldiers now." She had been selecting various pieces and began turning the pages as he warmed up. Now she turned her back and bent down to caress the ears of her two dogs, bracing herself for what she feared was to come.

Several men in dinner suits cleared their throats and diverted their eyes, feigning interest with ears cocked. It was after all Ernst's party.

From his quiet corner, Klaus lifted the Leica from his jacket pocket and snapped two consecutive frames. These people appeared as very different from the thuggish boors with whom Röhm usually surrounded himself.

The affected squire spun around on the piano stool, loosened his tie, and held forth with his pent-up feelings. The fact of his irreverence, clearly diverging from the Party line, caused more than a few to take notice but the Chief of Staff was off and running. "Come January, all key S.A. positions will be in the hands of my own men ..." he said, casting a glance toward Marty and Robert, "... you can be sure of that!

"As for the so-called 'moral leadership' of the Nation, I'll live my own private life as I see fit and I won't tolerate criticism from any quarter." It was clearly the alcohol speaking. "Take the hypocrisy of Adolph, for example, he gets off by watching peasant girls bending over in the fields so he can see their behinds. Ha! That's *his* sex life!" Several in the group shuffled nervously and Klaus observed one man by a doorway making notes.

"As for the Catholic Church in Bavaria, they are continually erecting barriers against we Protestants; what hypocrites! Slinging mud at my lifestyle when their own ranks are filled to overflowing with the very 'deviants' they so wholly condemn. I'm growing heartily sick of the aspersions being cast against me 'n my boys in the S.A., both by Church and Party.

"Do they think they'll ever stop us? Not bloody likely! ... about as improbable as one of those sanctimonious South American missionaries ever becoming Pope, ha-ha!" He leaned back, furrowed chin in the air, seemingly pleased with his impious thesis.

"Now dear, that will just about do. This is a happy day and you are among friends; I did say no politics over dinner," his mother tried gently, but there was no reining in the new Chief of Staff.

"Adolph seems to have forgotten that I was *his* commanding officer during the war, and it was *me* who introduced *him* to all the right people. Who was it that procured most of the weapons in the Nazi arsenal? *Yours truly*, that's who! Well, things are going to be very different from now on ..."

Klaus was not a little astonished at Röhm's uninhibited braggadocio, among friends or not. He noticed several men in deep discussion heading back to the sideboard for a slice of birthday cake, and the dim figure in the doorway had disappeared.

Later that evening, as he snuggled under the doona for the last time, Klaus' heart filled with dread at the yawning void before him on the morrow.

As things transpired his fears were not without foundation. Tossing and turning into the wee hours, he sat bolt upright with the spotted Jaguar again at his throat. Was this dream triggered by the shock of again having come face to face with Röhm's trophy pelt, or merely a return to the same old incubus? Either way, he elected to remain awake and rehearse his responses for the coming job interview.

33

"Come on upstairs, the chief will see you soon," chirped the modern-looking sales girl behind the counter, before she turned toward the broad sweeping staircase without awaiting my reply.

Following a restless night, I'd arrived early at the corner of Amalienstrasse and Theresienstrasse in order to peruse my portfolio one last time over a cup of coffee at Café Stephanie's on the ground floor. Then, straightening my tie and drawing a deep breath I announced myself at the showroom door at precisely five minutes to nine.

Everything inside Studio Hoffmann looked expensive and overwhelming, from the wide assortment of photographic equipment new and used, to the countless framed portraits of Adolph Hitler and other Nazi leaders glaring down from the walls or out from huge glass showcases. Hurrying to keep up, I noted the slightly crooked seams of the girl's shapely silk stockings, the bold stripes of her loose cardigan and a frozen wave of blonde hair jouncing against her slender neck. Ascending to the first-floor lobby, I was steadily enveloped in a potent pall of fragrance, quite unlike the "Ashes of Derry" that Mam used to dab behind her ears on special occasions. This was quite different, as was the plush floor-to-ceiling pastel décor in blue and apricot.

My head began to swim as I was motioned toward a chaise lounge, deeply buttoned, where I perched panting lightly and clutching my life's work on my lap. The assistant stepped away to knock softly on a glass panelled door marked "Presse Illustration Hoffmann" but receiving no answer, she turned back. "By the way, I'm Eva. It's supposed to be all hush-hush; your arrival, I mean. But we girls soon put two and two together … I'm fairly new here myself. Don't be turned off by the old man; if he likes your prints, you're in." Her eyes were merry as she spoke to the folio now under my arm; I was captivated by her rather severe permanent wave from the front, which reminded me a little of Chief Ticuna's, without the Urucurum paste, of course. "Don't worry, his bark is worse than his bite and Röhm's already had a word in his ear."

"Come!" the sharp command rang out, and I muttered a quick thanks before jumping up to follow her into Heinrich Hoffmann's cluttered den.

"Herr Hoffmann, this is Klaus Hahn … the boy Captain Röhm spoke of."

The bespectacled sharp nose remained pointing downwards, examining a pile of proof sheets on his desk; I cleared my throat nervously and tried not to stare at the bold white streak of hair sweeping back off the partly hidden, high forehead.

"Hahn, Hahn?" He spoke to the pile, before slowly raising his head to fix me with his trademark ice-blue gaze.

"You know, sir … the one Captain Ernst recommended … from South America," Eva added.

"Oh yes. Yes, of course … well, don't just stand there, boy. Give me one good reason why I should waste my time teaching a half-educated savage how to print decent black-and-whites …"

I blushed beetroot and stammered, "Everyone back home says I have an artist's eye, sir."

"Artist's eye? What the hell is that supposed to mean? My workers need to have thick hides and broad shoulders above all else …"

He turned back to examining the proof sheets through a magnifying glass while awaiting my response. I was stunned. This was not the reception I'd expected.

Slowly removing my sample photos from their case I pushed them across the desk and took a step back. I felt like turning around and slinking away; if only I'd had the guts. Two more eternal minutes followed before he spoke again.

"This all your own work, Hahn?" But before I could answer … "Eva! Who's keeping an eye on the front counter?"

"Henni and Herta are both helping out this morning, Herr Hoffmann; I did tell them I'd only be gone for a few minutes."

"I'll take it from here; drop these proof sheets to the darkroom on your way past. Tell them I want the cropping *exactly* as indicated … and for Christ's sake retain more detail in the bloody shadows."

As the great man rifled off-handedly through my best 8" × 10"s, Eva threw me a good-luck wink and turned to leave, easing my tension somewhat.

"Hm … Hm …" He came to the very last one, that of Robert being attacked by the flock of toucans, which I'd always considered one of my best. I had somehow captured the blur of wingbeats surrounding his head like a halo from Hades. Combined with the look of terror frozen on his face it was a perfectly composed moment of action … almost alive.

Of course, I'd never shown it to him for fear of the likely reaction.

"You definitely printed this yourself?" Hoffmann asked again, his jaded features cracking into a half grin of piercing blue and white.

"Y … Yes sir. I took them with my own Leica and printed them in the darkroom at Santa Luzia. For years I've been trying to follow your example, Herr Hoffmann; I mean, by studying your work in the *Völkischer Beobachter*, sir."

His eyebrows creased and rose again as he went back over my samples, finally slapping them down and responding with a terse proposal. "Leica? I'll tell you what I'll do, Jung Hahn: I've got would-be photographers coming out of my arse; there are three million unemployed Germans out there just begging for a chance at anything. You would be undertaking special printing assignments from time to time, as and when I require, quite apart from your usual darkroom quotas. Do you really think you're up to it?"

I nodded dumbly, hope beginning to rise in my breast.

"You will bunk down under the Grand Staircase for now and will be given an allowance sufficient to live on. Bear in mind that *my* orders countermand all others at all times. You should find your quarters comfortable enough, if a little restricted. I used to sleep in there myself occasionally after a big night out; but you don't need to know that, do you?"

"N … No sir."

"Well then, listen carefully: you will be on call 24 hours a day, seven days a week, unless I say different. And no backchat, ever! Is that clear?"

"Y … Yes sir," I stammered, trying to agree quickly. I was excited, yet apprehensive; things were moving fast. What choice did I have? Perhaps with hard work, I could work my way up and make him proud. But at that moment it seemed a lonely hope, not exactly as I'd dreamed nor as bad as feared, something in between. At least I had a foot in the door and a chance to prove myself.

He rang a cowbell on his desk which brought a brawny head and shoulders to the door. "Yes, Chief?"

"Lothar, show Jung Hahn over the place and then to his quarters under the staircase, you know, beside the broom closet … our emergency repose?"

The moon-face in the doorway glared blankly.

"And Lothar," the big man snapped to attention, "see to it that the boy's made comfortable. Or you may have to answer to Captain Röhm, and we wouldn't want that now, would we?"

Lothar thrust out his right arm and clicked his heels with a loud "Heil Hitler!" which forced my new employer to half rise from his seat and respond awkwardly in kind.

The big fellow was almost bursting out of his brown S.A. uniform as he motioned me to follow. He had a neck like a Brazilian Brahman and it was soon obvious he wasn't inclined to go out of his way to settle my nerves. His begrudging tour took in everything on the two lower floors that he decided I needed to know, including the frenzied Press Room and archival storage areas, plus the finishing and framing departments. Most exciting were the several darkrooms adjacent to Hoffmann's own office on the mezzanine, which at first glance appeared to contain all the latest equipment. Preoccupied employees bustled back and forth with a minimum of chatter, few even casting a glance in my direction.

At last, we descended the busy main staircase and stopped outside a low, partially concealed doorway beneath, where he dropped my suitcase with a grunt and motioned me to enter. He reached inside and flicked on an overhead globe that illuminated an adequate, though tiny space, with a collection of buckets and brooms stacked at one end: Just big enough at a stretch, I decided, for a single occupant without much luggage.

"Of course, you will use the staff toilets and shower across the hall," Lothar jerked a thumb towards the signposted doorway opposite. "You will speak to no one unless spoken to, or unless the chief gives permission; otherwise you'll have me to answer to. Is that clear?" he curled his lip and rubbed his hands spontaneously. At last! The veiled threat he'd been itching to utter.

"Your regular hours are 7 am to 6 pm, Mondays through Saturdays, though you may be required for special orders at any time. On Sundays, you will participate in group political discussions with the other staff. Have you got all that through your puny sconce?"

Surely there was no need for such insolence straight off, I thought.

"You will report to Iris Bumke in frames and finishing at 7 am sharp tomorrow morning. She will be your immediate superior for the time being."

I did not wish to address him as "sir" unless specifically instructed and it crossed my mind to enquire after my likely salary. "We will discuss your remuneration when we've had an opportunity to assess your actual capabilities," he sneered, reading my thoughts. "You can count yourself lucky to have a roof over your head at all, or, in your case, a staircase, ha-ha! Better a broom closet in Paradise than a castle in the middle of nowhere, eh?" He guffawed at his own joke as I closed the door in his face.

The single bulb illuminated my new home of about 80 square feet, with a sloping ceiling that rendered one-third of the space suitable only for storage. Placing my bag of belongings at the foot of a narrow but comfortable cot, I took stock.

A small desk had been squeezed in beside the bedhead and a lowboy with limited hanging space divided the storage area from where one could stand erect. Beside the desk was a single power socket, but no lamp, while the seating arrangements comprised a wooden dining chair and rickety three-legged stool, upon which rested a crockery basin and matching jug.

Taking a deep breath, I felt somewhat stifled, but after laying out my meagre wardrobe and sliding my suitcase under the bunk, I realised there remained just sufficient room for my original trunk filled with books, supposedly following close behind. A staccato of thudding boots and creaking timbers overhead assailed my unaccustomed ears as I lay down to gather my thoughts. *How on earth would I ever adjust to this sort of nerve-wracking dissonance?*

With two sharp knocks, the door flew open, my precious trunk was pushed through by an anonymous hand before it slammed shut again.

This single delivery brought more comfort than had the preceding hours; I was able to display some favourite volumes on a shelf against the sloping ceiling. From my bed, I could now rejoice in a selection of embossed titles within easy reach and began to feel more confident at being tucked away in the very heart of Nazidom. Surely, I was well-placed to learn more about my chosen profession and perhaps even to thrive? At that moment it seemed like a big "if" indeed.

As my eyes wandered back and forth over familiar treasures I was again disturbed by a knock at the door, this time softer and more hesitant. Gingerly opening it a crack I was surprised and relieved to see Eva's smiling face.

"C'mon," she whispered, "I'll show you around properly, this is the last free time you'll have for a while. How do you like your little cubby hole?" she bent her back and stuck her head in without waiting for an answer. "Looks like you're making yourself at home? Goodness! What's with all the books? I'll grab you a table lamp from the storeroom if you're so intent on reading," she chatted on as if I were responding positively to every comment. "Oh, and Lothar is having a pad bolt fitted to the inside of your door, so people don't come bursting in at all hours. You wouldn't want the chief climbing in beside you in the wee hours after one of his benders, would you?" She raised a questioning eyebrow at my blank expression.

With that tantalising appraisal, I hurried to join her, happy to draw a breath of fresh air on the ground floor and feast my eyes on the glass cases brimming with shiny new cameras and lenses. Pinching myself, I realised for the first time that I was now part of Munich's largest and most successful photo studio.

On all sides, corridors stretched away like one big rabbit warren, with certain areas given over to displaying Nazi flags, portraits and memorabilia. Other booths featured a variety of coloured portrait backgrounds and homely settings with fixed overhead and sidelight banks. The main showroom and customer service areas were also tastefully furnished in salmon-coloured wallpaper and wood panelling, with soft grey trims and light blue curtains that belied the industrial scale of images being churned out daily.

"As you can see, the chief has not long purchased this building; we simply outgrew the old place. Everything is a little upside down at the moment, but once the Party moves into their new premises at the Brown House, we'll have more space to spread out on the upper floors. The way business is expanding we may have to move again," she volunteered, wobbling along unsteadily on a pair of stilettos with bows on the toes, such as I'd only ever seen in fashion advertisements.

One by one, she acknowledged the 40-odd frazzled staff by their first names as we swept by; one or two returned monosyllabic replies and the remainder ignored me completely.

When once more alone in the corridor I ventured my first impressions. "If you don't mind my saying, Fraulein Eva, you don't seem at all like the others I've seen so far; they seem so … so straight-laced," I attempted to lean close and whisper in her right ear, only to find it partially covered by a curling wave of mouse blonde hair.

"Oh yes, them," she whispered back, "a bunch of old fuddy-duddies terrified of losing their jobs. They're all a little unsure of themselves since I started seeing the chancellor …"

"What I meant was …" I backtracked at her seeming frankness, "that you seem to be the only one I've seen with any fashion sense." I was referring to the bold-striped sweater with the flouncing cuffs which, together with her severe permanent wave, extravagant makeup and teetering heels, set her quite apart in looks and manner from her tight-bunned older women and dust-coated male colleagues.

She suppressed a gummy little smile. "Don't get me wrong; they all know their stuff or Hoffmann wouldn't tolerate them for five minutes … like you, I suppose," she added offhandedly. She stopped herself. "Anyhow, what star sign are you? Herta and I were trying to guess. I thought Pisces."

When I ventured that I knew nothing of star signs and told her my birthday was February 6 her eyes glittered and she gave a little squeal of delight. "Why, that's mine too; what a strange coincidence, another Aquarius!"

She creased her perfect brows for a moment and sized me up and down. "I still say you look more like a Pisces … and, if you must know, I'm dressed like this in case a certain 'someone' calls by to pick up his photos … Herr Hitler, silly," she added, noting my puzzlement.

"Remember? I already hinted at my rising good fortune," she pressed, but did not elaborate further, changing the subject to point out that certain tables in Café Stephanie downstairs were reserved for studio staff exclusively. "The boss runs an account and you will be supplied with a book of vouchers in due course," she informed me. Putting aside her earlier reserve she went on to reveal that she lived nearby with her parents and two sisters, and was desperately hoping for an invitation to Hoffmann's private Christmas party, when she could expect to rub shoulders with the cream of Munich Society and socialise with her "certain someone" beyond the reach of a father's disapproving eye.

She seemed excited to share this part of her little secret with me, a complete stranger, without spilling too many beans in the process. I decided there and then that we should be friends.

What I didn't yet know was that Hitler joined Hoffmann's family for dinner at his villa most nights when in Munich, and that Eva was prepared to spend every other evening poking around the office awaiting his phone calls on the private line. As time passed, I often saw her curled up on the waiting room couch after hours, thumbing impatiently through fashion magazines and continually checking her wristwatch. At other times, I glimpsed her sitting motionless, head in hands, failing to even acknowledge my comings and goings along the hallway.

During that first week, I hardly saw the light of day; printing, printing and more printing on one of the sleek Rolleiflex enlargers in Darkroom 2. "… and when you've finished with that lot, the chief wants reprints of all his old glass negatives from 1923 onwards; that should keep you out of mischief," said Lothar gloating during one of my infrequent ten-minute breaks.

He seemed to come and go as he pleased, popping up when least expected. He oversaw Hoffmann's huge collection of 5" × 7" glass negatives like a clucky hen, many of which featured portraits of the faded aristocracy and Weimar Republican dignitaries, but more importantly, Nazism's own embryonic emergence from the ruins of the Great War. Apparently, the boss had been waiting a long time to find someone with the necessary skills to put in the hours required at minimal cost and I was the obvious choice, being right on the spot and having no inconvenient social ties.

Since the introduction of celluloid roll film, and soon after that the even greater convenience of the 35 mm cassette, Hoffmann's bulky boxes of glass negatives had been pushed to the background collecting dust. My new assignment, while daunting, would allow me to pass many an hour alone with the rise of National Socialism in the darkroom, something I'd long dreamed of doing.

Before long I came across some early shots of Hitler trudging through the alpine drifts or posing self-consciously in a pair of unyielding lederhosen. It was hard to suppress a snigger and I looked around to ensure that no one had heard me examining him up close. Even as negatives, his pale, hairless legs and broad hips appeared quite comical; two thin polished pillars joining socks to lederhosen.

I was to print two 8" × 10" glossies of each for Hoffman's Private Archive, after which the superseded glass plates were to be sent off for warehousing elsewhere. Carefully arranging them on the lightbox I discovered many showed a youngish, energetic man surrounded by his rag-tag gang of Brownshirts addressing some meeting or other. Other moments portrayed him as isolated and pensive, a "Man of Destiny" with only his Alsatian dog for company.

No matter the outfit or the setting, however, there were always the eyes; those blazing, defiant eyes and trademark drooping forelock, knowing and playing to the camera for every advantage. From the very first print, I was captivated by this man's ability to project the force of his personality through his eyes, especially in the early black-and-whites. Hoffmann rarely let us forget that it was he who produced and moulded that chimeric character we think we see before us today.

"Without my photos, Adolph would be just one more face in the crowd," he had been overheard telling one of the newly arrived international pressmen.

"Who was it told him for years to cut off that fucking handlebar moustache? Me! That's who." The younger pressmen nodded agreeably.

With Studio Hoffmann franchises popping up like mushrooms in capitals all over Europe, there were obviously rich pickings to be had from emulating the Master.

Day after day I inhaled the chemical fumes and vapours from open trays in the darkroom, which soon began to take a toll on my health and demeanour. Through Eva's intervention and owing to my prodigious output I was granted one extra day off each week, the continual pressure of being on 24-hour call was affecting my ability to get a decent night's sleep.

"Better that than to have the poor boy laid up in bed with asthma every few days, don't you think?" I overheard her confronting Hoffmann sweetly on the steps one morning. I could not make out all his grumbling reply, merely an odd phrase that "at last someone knew how to print blacks with balls".

Each Thursday hence I would be able to jump onto the studio bicycle with the tray between the handlebars, and set off around town dispensing packets of developed prints to their owners. It looked easy enough.

On my first "official" day off, I was in no hurry, allowing time to take in Munich's sights. Eva, who rode her bicycle to work most days, invited me to ride home with her after work while she pointed out various points of interest along the way.

As we pedalled along side by side, she chatted away and time flew: "There are such and such jewellers" or "down that street is the best beauty salon in all of Germany." She gave little tosses of her perm and seemed happy enough to chatter to one with whom she felt comfortable. She quizzed me again on jungle life among the "head-hunters", and for the first time revealed her secret desire to one day play the part of Tarzan's Jane on the big screen. I hinted at my own boyhood infatuation with Edgar Rice Burroughs, whose name she could not recall.

Through the gardens and along the river we slowly wound our way past her favourite cafés and dress shops until finally, she pulled up outside a generous, five-storey residence in Hohenzollernstrasse. "Well, this is where I get off," she said, panting slightly.

"Wow!" I exclaimed. "This seems a mighty big house for just one family. What does your Vati do?" I could see the well-kept façade rising from a cottage garden behind the high gates.

"My family occupies the third floor only. And as for Vati; why, he's a schoolmaster," she said rather tersely and leaned closer. "And just between us, you know what they're like: always comparing apples and oranges and experts on everyone's kids but their own. Or am I being too hard on poor Papa and schoolteachers in general?" I looked around vaguely, not knowing what to reply.

"As it is, I'm making out quite well on my own, thank you very much. Vati can never know the true dimensions of my feelings for Adol ... Herr Hitler." She gave a little sniff in the air and twirled on the toe of her pretty shoe.

"If you promise not to say anything, he is quite against the Nazis and is being a proper stick in the mud over my friendship with A ... Adolph! There! I've said it in front of someone else at last. I'm just so sick of pretending. If it's not his politics, it's the age difference Vati objects to; a whole generation is too much, he says. When I'm around, Adolph certainly doesn't act as if he's too old," she said with a little giggle. "I don't feel age makes any difference at all when one is in love, do you?"

"I ... er am not really qualified to comment on such things ..."

"Nonsense! A girl should be perfectly free to fall in love with whomever she wishes. Papa would hit the roof if he knew the full extent of it. Don't worry, Mutti will soon talk him around; she's all for my happiness. She senses that Adolph will soon be the most powerful man in all Germany and there I'll be by his side. 'What a catch,' Mutti says! Then we'll soon see Schoolmaster Braun shiver and shake with pride ..."

"Well, I suppose so," I added lamely, thinking for a moment of Maya. "Are you sure Herr Hitler feels the same way as you do? I know we've only just met Fraulein Eva, but I'd hate to see you get hurt ..."

She shifted on her seat and fixed me with a suspicious stare. "Well, aren't you sweet? Ask any of the girls at work if you want proof ... or ask the chief. He's the one who, just accidentally on purpose, lined us up in the first place; thought we'd make a perfect match. Why did he bring Herr Wolf into the filing room when I'm up the ladder in a short skirt? Answer me that. From the moment our eyes met, something wonderful happened and I had no idea who he *really* was. But I just knew he felt something for little ole me. I could have dived into those eyes. At that moment I saw myself floating above this ... this mighty warrior like a guardian angel. Anyway, my mind's made up: I'm going to marry him one day, just you wait and see."

Again there was no avoiding her flashing eyes and I saw she wasn't joking.

"What's more, he's promised to buy me and Gretl a villa of our own, so we don't have to keep on playing cat and mouse with Vati. It can't come soon enough. Adolph needs his privacy too, you know? Surely, then I'll be able to get him away from that fat bitch niece of his and have him to myself for a change. If you ask me, his current living arrangements just aren't healthy and all my girlfriends agree."

"You've lost me," I said, having no idea of her meaning.

"Yoo hoo, Eva?" came a sweet voice from the porch before a pert face poked over the fence. "Papa's wondering where you've been. He wants to see you in his study this very minute … Oh, hello! Haven't I seen you around the studio?"

Eva's younger sister, Gretl, was almost the spitting image of her; if anything, more open-faced and less affected, without the crimson nails and lipstick. She flashed a warm smile and threw wide the gate for her sibling in the tight skirt, quite unsuitable for bike-riding. Eva walked off without a backward glance.

I rang my bell in farewell and turned for the long ride back to town.

34

I suppose I should have seen it coming: my two supervisors soon revealed their displeasure over my newfound freedom and friendship with Fraulein Braun.

Few studio processes escaped Iris Bumke's attention, and with the formidable Lothar to back her up, the pair oversaw a tight ship during the boss' repeated long absences. From the moment I'd reported to Frau Bumke, it was obvious that she begrudged the fact of my being parachuted straight into a much sought-after printing job. She was a dour, thin woman with narrow, colourless lips and a tight bun of silvering hair, always dressed in brown female S.A. attire, right down to the tie. She meant business.

Her roving eye probed every process and oversaw every completed order, all the while compiling daily lists of "incidents" whereby "slackers" were caught falling short. If necessary a word to Gestapo Headquarters saw the hapless staffer hauled in and advised to "smarten up", or in certain cases disappear altogether.

This morbid threat hung over the heads of all Studio Hoffmann employees, especially newcomers like myself, and I was thankful that word had gotten around of my near "untouchable" status courtesy of Captain Röhm's protection and good offices. Everyone had heard that Röhm was soon to take command of all 250,000 Brownshirts with Hitler's blessing: the studio was struggling to come up with a suitable image to mark his political resurrection, owing to his battle-scarred features in close-ups.

The only others besides Heinrich Hoffmann enjoying such freedom of movement, as far as I could see, were the half dozen or so roaming news photographers and stringers and, of course, Eva herself. I wondered how much

239

this had to do with the uncertain chain of command surrounding her alleged "romance" with the Studio's number one client.

When so-called special privileges were conferred on yours truly so soon after arrival, both Iris and Lothar took this as a threat to their hold on power. They saw my venturing forth on the Thursday delivery run as avoiding oversight at best and a frivolous and unnecessary jaunt at worst, even though I usually returned exhausted from pedalling long distances through the heavy traffic. Lothar complained that if I was "such a shit-hot printer" then I should be spending my time doing just that, and it was about time I gave more thought to Party matters, not out "joyriding" with Fraulein Braun.

Throughout that whole Christmas and New Year period of 1930–31, I remained cooped up beneath the crushing workload, almost entirely indoors, and the few times I did bump into Eva she appeared flighty and distracted; I was almost too weary to care.

Notwithstanding, and even if I do say so myself, I received many compliments around that time for the quality and consistency of my professional quality postcards, taken by Hoffman during Party Rallies and march-pasts; but mostly of Hitler himself in a hundred different poses featuring that same blank stare. Apparently, they were selling like hotcakes.

I received no invitations to join in the Yuletide festivities that first year, and except for a single greeting card from Onkel Fedi and Tante Gretel, the season passed unremarkably.

"We're both so pleased you have arrived in the Fatherland," it began in Onkel's familiar jagged hand. "Our home and hearth will be yours when you are free of your obligations to the higher authorities. We shall expect a visit from you in Berchtesgaden next Christm …" the C-word being struck out and replaced with "… Yuletide 1931, if not sooner. Heil Hitler!"

Hardly the warmest welcome, even though I had temporarily forgotten their presence just an hour's train ride away. I fondly fingered the hand-painted "woodsman's cabin" scene on the card and noticed Tante's signature in the bottom corner; a real joint effort. Her sure brushstrokes were certainly easier on the eye than his wording. With a pang I remembered the boxes of books so thoughtfully selected and shipped all the way to South America, to nephews she'd never met. And those cameras had changed my life.

I remembered that Tante Gretel was an artist herself but shamefully could not recall Onkel's occupation. From the card, it was clear where his political loyalties lay. I even felt a twinge of homesickness for a place I'd seen only in pictures, but quickly refocused on the matters at hand.

Belatedly at the very last moment, Eva received the long-awaited phone call.

I put two and two together as she burst from Hoffmann's vacant office.

"Yes! Yes!" she exclaimed, punching the air and placing an unexpected peck on my cheek. "Tonight … tonight! The boss has invited me over to Schnorr

Strasser to see in the New Year with the family, and of course, Adolph will be there," she gushed.

"Oh silly, don't tell me you didn't guess? I knew you didn't believe me. Lord knows there have been enough rumours flying about. Taa daa," she exclaimed and spun around several times, stopping short before my blank expression. "Some are already calling me the Leader's 'girlfriend' and I don't mind one little bit … Of course, nothing is official, yet …"

"B … But what about all those women appearing beside him in the *Beobachter* and throwing themselves at his feet? Might not you be deceiving yourself?" I responded damply. To me the whole business seemed inconceivable: that a senior National Leader would seriously entangle himself with a simple, if pretty enough, shopgirl. Whatever the truth, Eva skipped, sang, and even shed a tear of joy for some minutes. "Oh, oh, what shall I wear? My dark blue silk?" she bubbled.

"No! Polka dots, that's it. *He* says polka dots suit me best!"

I cast my mind back to the swooning women in the Hofbräuhaus and the social pages of the daily papers and wondered why, if things were indeed as Eva hinted, she continued to take Hitler's calls on the work telephone and not at home. Perhaps there was no telephone in the Braun residence, or more likely she was getting way ahead of herself, as teenage girls sometimes do.

For now, my life had become an endless routine of work and study, with brief interludes in the freezing cold outdoors. I began each day by throwing open the first-floor windows and taking a brisk once around the block before starting on my quota, determined to add a daily walk to my Thursday exercises.

I found myself longing for that elusive season called spring that I'd never known, with its promise of bud-burst and lush new life in the rambling English Garden. I was impatient to visit my secret hideaway and strip down to my underpants by the Isar; even cook a sausage over a campfire.

All these rules, regulations and suspicions were leaving me as confused as Lord Greystoke, during his own ill-fated return to "civilisation".

Lothar called it "frivolling" whenever he caught us chatting, or not bent double over the workbench during his irregular rounds. He would often announce his presence with a swift clout across the back of the head. Iris Bumke on the other hand, relied more on cunning and snitching rather than brute force to maintain her authority, especially among the attractive young girls working the front counter.

As several were Eva's girlfriends with time on their hands, the foiled overseer fumed at her inability to discipline these "volunteers" frittering away hours at the boss' expense. Their noticeable infractions included squealing, loud laughing and especially flirting with the passing parade of S.A. muscle-men who shared the building. Sometimes, when the boss was away and business was quiet, Eva's friends would pull out a pack of tailor-mades and puff away the entire shift together.

Over time I was gradually introduced into their conversations, always a little overawed by their confident manner, excessive grooming and fashionable dress sense. Almost from the start they referred to me as "Jungle Boy", tittering behind my back before coming right out loud with the embarrassing nickname in front of others. But I didn't care, really; at least they treated me as some kind of inoffensive novelty.

One beauty, not quite as fashionable as Eva, caught my eye early, and it turned out that she too was a little out of place at the front counter that day, being usually restricted to "Framing and Finishing" upstairs. I say "usually", because during my daily peregrinations collecting and delivering prints in person, I saw no sign of this young Fraulein for days at a time. Despite Iris' hovering presence and insistence on "correct procedures" when visiting other departments, I soon spotted her and discovered her name to be Claudia, as she cast a glance in my direction.

Several times I took longer than usual when discussing mouldings or filling out order forms in her presence, and the first time she actually addressed me by name in her distinctive husky voice my heart danced a little jig.

I was struck by Claudia's serenity and seeming simplicity; the short-cropped blonde hairstyle, feline eyes and high cheekbones suggested foreign origins. Very occasionally a flicker of a smile crossed her full mouth in my presence.

Taken separately I felt her features didn't quite add up to classic beauty, yet somehow together they surpassed the predictable prettiness of Eva's friends. From a distance they imparted an aura of maturity, even mystery, which distracted me further: I vowed to get to know her better.

At the first hint of warmer weather, I parked my bicycle beside the Isar and scrambled down to watch the spring freshet, delighted to discover my favourite sandbar remained proud above the surging current. Searching absentmindedly I uncovered a patch of charcoal left over from my former autumnal campouts, which for a short while tantalised my mind with pleasant memories.

Suddenly acting on a hunch, I clamoured back up the bank and leapt onto the bike, drawn inexplicably toward the English Garden, where slowly and methodically I pedalled up and down the network of gravel pathways until, there on a park bench I glimpsed the familiar bobbed hairdo and turned-up collar of my elusive workmate.

It's easy to imagine my feelings as I skidded to a halt and stood breathless, staring at her shiny boots while scratching up a little pile of gravel with the toe of my shoe. She did not flinch. After what seemed an eternity, I plucked up sufficient courage to speak to her. "H … Hello Claudia. I'm Klaus, Klaus Hahn, er … from the darkroom."

Slowly closing the book in her lap she raised her face and fixed me thoughtfully with a pair of greenish orbs exuding confident repose. Her face appeared more amused than surprised to find me standing there. "Well, hello to you too Klaus Hahn … or should I call you 'Jungle Boy' like the others do behind your back?"

I ignored the jibe with a slight blush.

"What a coincidence; I guessed we might bump into each other sooner or later, if not in Café Stephanie then away from work," she said. "And here we are; why don't you take a load off your feet?"

I sat down beside her on the bench, but not too close.

"I … I'm always pleased to cross paths with you in Framing and Finishing, Claudia, but I don't see you there often. I know it's none of my business, but do you work part-time elsewhere?"

"Ha! Part-time. That's a good one. Some might say I work a combination of full-time *and* part-time!" This pungent response belied her coolness, and why she decided to confide in me at that moment only she knew. "Jungle Boy, eh? It's certainly a distinctive title. Do you like it?"

"I can't say I'm over-fussed. What with Lothar and Iris calling it out at the top of their lungs in front of complete strangers, it is wearing a bit thin."

"Then, how about I shorten it to 'J.B.'? It will be our own special signal when I wish to communicate in private; what do you say?"

"I suppose so … They're only relying on hearsay anyway."

"Ah! Rumours … Sometimes it's best to encourage favourable stories about oneself, especially these days when truth so often leads to trouble. Very few Germans now enjoy much privacy, thanks to the State having a finger in everyone's pie; or haven't you noticed?"

She turned to face me, as if expecting I would jump up and run away.

"To tell the truth, I haven't been out and about that much to form opinions at all …"

"There's that word again! You will do well to adapt to prevailing conditions …"

Strangely, I noticed her green eyes turning grey, perhaps it was the overcast sky now threatening a squall. "Well, I'm stuck in the darkroom most of the time and my accommodation doesn't exactly lend itself to socialising …"

"More importantly, how is studio life working out for a boy with your talents? We've all noticed a big improvement in the print quality."

At that moment I felt a lot depended on my answer.

"Well, it's not quite what I was led to expect. It seems to me that promotion depends more on *who* you know rather than *what* you know. Other than Captain Röhm and Frau Emilie I have few places to turn. I hope I'm not speaking out of place?"

"Is that so? … No, not at all. I have the distinct feeling that your still waters also run deep."

Klaus cleared his throat. "After nearly two months I've been hoping, vainly as it's turned out, to be given a crack at taking photos myself, or even carrying the stringers' bag on assignment, rather than being stuck in the dark for days on end. I do own a Leica, you know? Alas, the harder I work the more my workload increases. I suppose *you* have to put up with Lothar and Iris snooping around, too? I'm finding it almost impossible to relax."

I wondered if I had already said too much, and that my frankness had exceeded her own. She leaned closer and gently took my hand. "Well, that's par for the course around here. The boss knows only too well that there's a hundred more waiting outside to snap up your job, and perhaps even mine. It seems to me that neither of us is really cut out to succeed in this topsy-turvy environment. One day I'll let you in on a little secret; actually, it's a big secret …"

I was surprised to hear her speaking so offhandedly about the man who put food in our mouths, and said so.

"Yes, yes, settle down; it's all a part of your initiation, he likes to know who he can depend on … and so do I," she half-whispered.

"Oops," she said, looking at her watch. "Sorry, but I have to be going. I'm dancing tonight."

"Dancing …?"

She placed her finger on my lips. "No more questions for now. I'm sure we'll have plenty to talk about, J.B.!" She gave a little laugh and was gone.

My whole body remained quivering with excitement, even as I realised she was much older than me, at least in her mid-20s. She was unlike any girl I'd ever met; so down to earth, yet mysterious. I'd seen the patchy spring sunshine playing over her distinctive features and knew that in this single encounter, I'd been swept off my feet.

Pedalling back to work along Prinzregentenplatz I thought of all the clever things I should have said and was certain that I'd managed to conceal my real feelings; which in these early stages of the romance was preferable. There would be plenty of time to disclose my real emotions and to reveal how dear to my heart she had already become. I might even suggest taking her portrait one day in the English Garden, on the bench where we first held hands.

Lying on my bunk that night beneath the creaking staircase I visualised her on stage performing Swan Lake or another of the great classic ballets. I saw the audience rising to its feet as one in applause. Claudia probably would not smile, merely accept a bouquet and return their adoration with silent poise. Our age difference was of no consequence to me; over time I would gently probe the mysterious life experiences that lay behind those eloquent grey-green eyes, while she in turn would coax me into full-blown manhood. Despite the rumble of jackboots overhead, I drifted into glorious slumber, running hand in hand with her along the beach of a desert island.

My project reprinting Hoffmann's glass negatives was turning out to be both more interesting and daunting than I'd imagined. Shots of Hitler around 1923 revealed, naturally enough I suppose, a far less confident and distinctive demeanour. The emerging dictator showed himself as stilted and ill at ease in front of the camera during those early poses. His knuckles gripped the chair arms and his black patent leather pumps skewed awkwardly to one side when seated, almost as one would place the feet of a woman. Already he wore his threatening "Man of Destiny" expression and again I almost cacked myself at the shots of the great man in his well-worn lederhosen: his trademark wide hips, narrow shoulders, chubby white knees and shapeless calves were totally at odds with the scowling expressions. Many of these glass plates had been cracked through careless handling, creating a devil of a task in coming up with acceptable contact prints.

Little did I know that following Hitler's rise to power in January '33, any image of him wearing short pants, or even spectacles, would be banned as unstatesmanlike carrying severe penalties for anyone daring to publish.

For the time being, however, I laboured away putting glass jigsaws back together, earning not only the boss' begrudging accolades but my first ever "promotion" by being placed in charge of the "Hitler Archives" locked safely away in Hoffmann's office. These consisted of one whole wall of small drawers containing negatives or prints of every image taken of the Nazi leader, which totalled thousands. Eva too, I discovered, also had unrestricted access to this collection, occasionally adding informal snaps of her own.

I soon learned that this "promotion" entitled me not only to resurrect the countless boxes of dusty files, but to be awoken at any hour to rush through freshly exposed rolls of 35 mm taken while Hoffmann roamed the countryside with his febrile patron.

I was astonished at the number and variety of poses he continually evoked during such brief engagements in crowded spaces. I studied how he moved about catching each scene from different angles, always managing superior compositions and lighting.

Of course, this "upgrade" inevitably ruffled Iris and Lothar's whip-cracking timetable, as I did not now have to consult either before accessing the confidential collection in the boss' office. The "Brown Bomber", as the front counter girls referred to Lothar, began attempting to exert pressure on me to sign up to the Party and begin paying monthly dues "like everyone else", notwithstanding the fact that I had yet to receive a regular pay packet. I'd been forewarned that once inside the Nazi tent I could find myself performing all manner of unseemly "duties" aside from my lab work.

"Don't fall for it!" Eva warned when I sought her advice. "I have no intention of ever joining the Party, nor have my friends with one or two notable exceptions. The boss is nearly tearing his hair out over the conflicting orders coming from upstairs. He says one thing, and before you know it the powers above countermand as soon as his back is turned. Mind you, he doesn't mind playing off one department head against the other when it suits him, all in the name of greater efficiency. I'm the only one around here who enjoys 100% job security," she pouted, sticking her chest out and checking her permanent wave in the mirror.

"By the way, I believe we both have a birthday coming up soon. Frau Hoffmann has hinted that a party to mark my 19th could be on the cards, but so far, it's all hush-hush. I suppose it depends on the boss' schedule and whether a certain 'someone' will be in town."

I could see her once more "counting her chickens before they'd hatched", as Mam used to say, and if things did go as she hoped, her new love would somehow find time to poke his head through the door of Hoffmann's red-roofed villa.

"And, don't think we're going to overlook *your* first birthday in Munich, either. The girls are dying to get you away from the office and pump a few drinks into you. After all, we only turn 19 once and they are all keen to book a birthday kiss; I'm sure Frau Hoffmann will agree to your tagging along."

I wasn't sure about all the kissing.

With the best of intentions, Eva believed that a joint celebration was appropriate and that it should be a relatively simple matter to coordinate her wishful thinking with mine on the big day.

I held my tongue: she was undermining my carefully thought-out plans to put together a picnic hamper and invite Claudia to share my secret place by the Isar. Sure, it would still be pretty icy, but if we dressed warmly and got a campfire going that may provide ample opportunity to snuggle up without appearing too obvious. I'd been counting the days since our last encounter and had been rehearsing a few of the lines I hoped would win her over.

Myriad questions plagued my every waking moment.

Sadly, however, Eva would not be dissuaded. "Don't you see? I really *do* want you there to meet a few of my *very* special friends," she chortled. "I just know you'll be a real hit, what with your cute accent and all those jungle tales …"

"B … But I don't enjoy talking about that sort of thing, Fraulein Eva; it gives people the wrong idea. You must realise how shy I am in front of crowds."

"Crowds? Nonsense! There'll be just a handful of family and friends, and who knows? You may even get to say 'hello' to the Big Boss. I simply won't take 'no' for an answer."

I knew I was stymied. As far as I could tell, Hoffmann had not yet extended an invitation to Eva or anyone else, let alone to me and the proposed phantom celebration was less than ten days away. Nonetheless, with a combination of charm, petulance and plain old perseverance the single-minded Eva seemed to have lined up all our ducks in a row. Adding insult to injury our joint celebration was being touted around the studio as a foregone conclusion.

When I did manage to wangle a few minutes alone in the hallowed framing department, Claudia greeted me with a note of sarcasm. "Someone seems to be moving in all the right circles, I hear," until I looked her straight in the eye and perceived a deeper twinkle.

"Believe me, it's not my preferred choice of how to spend my birthday," I panted, feeling the need to put her mind at rest. "I had been hoping you and I might have spent the afternoon together by the river … for a picnic, I mean."

She dropped her eyes for a moment, pretending to concentrate on the job at hand. "Yeah, yeah, I bet. It's far too cold for picnicking and anyhow, Saturday is out for me; I'm already spoken for."

Her words hit me harder than I like to admit. I should have known she would probably have a ballet class or be otherwise engaged and I lost my train of thought completely.

"Haven't you figured it out yet?" she continued. "We two have been chosen by Hoffmann for 'special duties', among other things, precisely because neither of us has family ties or other inconvenient distractions."

I looked perplexed as she continued. "You will no doubt be called upon to undertake certain tasks in the darkroom, not only for the chief but the Gestapo and SS, which for you will be particularly distasteful. If you aren't already aware, the boss operates a nice little cash business on the side, providing pornographic and 'snuff' postcards for the delectation of the Nazi hierarchy. I suspect my own fate is probably sealed …"

I stared in disbelief.

"Why am I telling *you* all this? Because there's still time to get out while you can." Her face was flushed.

"Get out?" Did she mean escape altogether? *What was she talking about?*

"Why do you think Lothar and Iris pretend to look the other way at our misdemeanours? They're just biding their time. I've already endured a year or more under their gaze. There's nothing that pair won't stoop to in their quest for power."

Her frankness gave me a head-spin but somehow I managed to look receptive. Sealed fate? What in the Lord's name could she mean? Thus far, I believed our conversations had gone unobserved but I was suddenly jolted when she breezily announced in a loud voice, "These are the last of your frames, Herr Hahn, please sign here." She flicked a glance over my shoulder at the omniscient Iris who had appeared noiselessly in the doorway. Our stealthy supervisor glared suspiciously as I cleared my throat and gathered up my order.

From then on, my printing assignments became more or less mechanical. Claudia's words spun wildly in my head. I played them over and over in the solitary confines of the darkroom and my cramped living quarters. Why had she chosen to trust and confide in me, a virtual stranger? Could she really have plumbed my sincerity and true feelings in such a short time? I believed that so far I'd managed to conceal any hint of romantic intention, merely suggesting a second meeting in the English Garden.

As events transpired, February 6 came and went under a pressing workload, with Eva never giving a second thought to her earlier proposal for a joint celebration.

Apart from a peck on the cheek at work and a tiny rock cake wearing a single candle, the subject did not arise until lunchtime the next day, when I discovered her weeping inconsolably in the corner of the darkroom.

"Oh, oh, how could he do it? Leading me on and then not showing up at all? I just hate him!" she was moaning to herself as I entered.

"B … But what happened? I asked cautiously. "You looked so beautiful and seemed so happy," I ventured further, remembering the bright delirium with which she'd departed towards the Hoffmann villa the previous afternoon.

"Oh, how humiliating; I'd told Henni and Herta and all the girls *he* would be there. I should have listened to Henni, *she* knows what he's really like," she continued sobbing. "Luckily I hadn't breathed a word to Mutti or Papa; it was meant to be their surprise too. And Frau Hoffmann just carried on without so much as an excuse or apology."

"Are you sure you're not making too much of the whole business?" I foolishly inquired. "You know the Leader is in big demand, and going by the Press Room photos he seems to mix in rarefied circles these days."

"Oh, just shut up, Klaus! What would you know, anyway? I bet it was that fat bitch Geli who threw a spanner in the works. He's never too busy to accompany *her* to singing lessons three times a week, oh no! What could be more important than *my* 19th? Given half a chance I'd scratch her eyes out, the way he moons over her in public makes me sick …"

"B … But, she *is* his niece, after all. Surely there's no point being jealous over flesh and blood?" I'd glimpsed Eva's "rival" several times in and out of the studio, and yes, she was rosy-cheeked, buxom and full of chatter, seeming to get on with everyone. Her ample figure and family complications could hardly compare with Eva's petite demeanour and stated willingness to please her man at any cost.

"I tell you, if he's having it off with *her* it's incest, that's what it is!" she fumed. "They say Geli gave Emile the chauffeur a blowjob while driving her back from Obersalzberg; the pair of them were even seen walking together arm in arm around Munich. Harrumph! That's why he was sacked, by the way."

Eva's surprisingly coarse language seemed quite out of character.

I assumed she was referring to Emile Maurice, Hitler's rat-faced, long-time chauffeur-bodyguard who had stood staunchly by him since his earliest days.

Maurice had been the first S.A. leader and had been imprisoned beside Hitler in Landsberg following the failed Putsch, but none of that mattered now. Loyalty had been trumped by jealousy and Hitler's fury had resulted in his hapless if happy friend being banned from all further personal intercourse. Maurice, however, was allowed to retain his SS membership and continue in that organisation until the end of the war.

Predictably, Jewish ancestry was discovered going back to 1750, and Hitler had to step in to grant Emile and his brothers "Honorary Aryan" status so they could remain as members. Both Himmler and Maurice dropped by the front counter regularly to collect envelopes marked "private" and it seemed pretty obvious that neither had much time for the other.

I was sure I'd seen Geli and Claudia in deep discussion outside the boss' office more than once. It had appeared from a distance that the niece's fruitless entreaties were falling on deaf ears. Only in September did I learn the shocking details of these impassioned exchanges.

But Eva would not be comforted and remained cursing all and sundry under her breath, until Lothar pounded on the door to say she was required at the front counter. There was nothing for it but to take a deep breath of the vaporous air and roll up my sleeves. I said a silent prayer for my distressed colleague before returning to my enlarger, still faced with a print run of 500 more postcards to fill the daily quota.

35

As weeks crept into months, I became convinced that Eva was blowing her affair with Hitler out of all proportion, especially when I overheard him discussing with Hoffmann his upcoming appearance on stage alongside a bevy of emerging starlets.

"Oh! And be sure to bring along that little Eva, she amuses me," he'd added offhandedly. I caught his words en route to my broom closet, which didn't sound to me like someone destined for matrimony anytime soon. Then again, who was I to call out the flaws in another's romance when my own was so clearly lacking?

The boss had recently been elected to the Munich City Council, and because of his expertise in organising official functions had been promptly put in charge of future "coming out" events. During 1931, he was often away for long periods, flying here and there at breakneck speeds to capture Hitler's many appearances before parades and Party Rallies.

Gentle spring, the first such I'd seen with my own eyes, washed over Bavaria.

The blush of greens and blossoms lifted my spirits and beckoned me outdoors, eager to capture more of the city sights with my trusty Leica. Only fear of Lothar's brute force and the rat cunning of Iris held me back: If there was to be no escape from my crushing routine then a proper career in photography may yet be won from a system where I was slowly winning a few admirers and wider acceptance.

It seemed my printing skills and natural reticence, the latter generally being misinterpreted as collaboration, appealed to everyone of importance in the Party who possessed a camera of his own: the spontaneity of 35 mm photography was becoming all the rage.

Importantly, my collection of jungle wildlife scenes had been received warmly by the half dozen or so "stringers" working out of Studio Hoffmann, and whose own negatives I sometimes developed. Among them was Herr Phal, the first to ever publish a photo of Hitler, who gave me tips on getting close to one's subject unobtrusively. Also, the visionary Hugo Jaeger was breaking new ground using the latest natural colour films just coming onto the market.

But old habits in photography die hard. Despite the consistent results achieved by Hoffmann with his own Leica, not to mention my portfolio of 35 mm candids, most professionals remained wedded to their tried-and-true large-format cameras. When jostling with each other in their trench coats and gangster hats, the press photographers looked quite comical juggling their cumbersome contraptions.

By keeping a low profile I was letting my work do the talking, tolerated by my colleagues as a somewhat fragile but gifted trainee.

It appeared that National Socialism was making steady gains on the political front following Hitler's recent unexpected declamations: "From now on, the path to power lies not in brute force, but by the exploitation of 'legal' methods and loopholes."

This was a volte-face that stirred great chagrin among Röhm's bristling Brownshirt battalions who were just hitting their stride. Besides the flow of movie footage through the Press Room, I was entrusted with certain rolls of 35 mm from Nazi bigwig amateurs, containing unknown persons and incidents, with strict instructions that they were to be developed and printed by me alone, without additional approval.

When it came to such "special orders", the penny finally dropped regarding Claudia's former caution: one morning, almost offhandedly, the boss produced two rolls of 36 from his pocket and slid them across his desk. "You will tell no one and allow no other person to view or access these images; they are 'top drawer'. Is that clear?" I gulped drily and wondered at the need for secrecy, given the range of risqué images already in circulation.

If I didn't grasp his cloak-and-dagger methods then, I certainly did soon after, blushing to the hair roots as I lifted each roll from the fixing tank and held it up to the light. Unlike Hoffmann's earlier artistic and highly saleable nudes using classical poses and tasteful illumination, these images contained only shameful poses of several young women.

I recognised certain "starlets" who had been induced to reveal all for the camera so soon after their initial introductions to the Nazi dignitaries on the "judging" panel. At first, I thought there must be some mistake; surely, no young madel would allow her body to be subjected to such contortions while still smiling coyly at the camera. Up until that moment, I'd not realised what Eva had meant by "blowjob", and during the whole printing process, I felt shocked and slightly sickened.

Even Fraulein Gertrude had drawn a line that her girls did not dare to cross, unlike these poor misguided creatures cavorting about in my developing dish. With a mighty jolt I had come up against the truth of my hallowed employer's shady sideline: procuring and distributing pornographic images for the delectation of those Nazis "in the know" with a little cash to spare.

Fat envelopes marked "Private" were kept under the front counter and it was common knowledge that he kept a list of certain hopeful "starlets" available at short notice to escort visiting National Socialist luminaries.

By this time I had almost completed my printing assignment with the early glass plates, having been instructed to destroy every last one depicting Hitler in lederhosen or even wearing spectacles; now only a single 8" × 10" glossy remained of such images in Hoffmann's Private Archive. I'd printed the future führer cavorting through the snow in his crusty leathers wearing a jaunty fedora with quill of Grouse. In others, a rhinoceros-hide dog whip protruded from his boot-top with "Wolf", his first Alsatian by his side.

I was having trouble trying to keep detail in both white snow and dark dog fur; Hoffmann had already rejected my first two attempts. Eventually, I succeeded in holding back the shadows and with some difficulty burning in the white drifts, until each snowflake crackled. Holding up the final print I suppressed a chuckle, having no one close with whom to share such a satisfying moment.

Now I understood why those staffers "without connections" were employed as printers: as time went by I overheard many of Hoffman's private conversations between snoozes under the darkroom sink.

Whenever the boss was in town, his Bogenhausen Villa was fast becoming known as *the* hub of art and celebrity among Munich's Avant-Garde Set; ever since that fateful day in '28, when his first wife Lelly, Henni's mother, passed away.

My now world-famous employer, who had already made himself indispensable to Hitler, expanded his business interests into every facet of Nazi culture. In glorious and profitable attunement, he marched in lockstep with Hitler's every move and whim, clearly at a cost to his own private life and residual principles.

I feared that in order to attract adequate wealth and kudos to myself in a new world, I too may find it necessary to abandon at least part of the cardinal dispositions of my own nature. Presse Illustration Hoffmann's monopoly on nearly every "Führer Image" was to have profound implications for my own naive expectations of love and happiness, and the terrible truth was not long in coming.

One Sunday afternoon Eva appeared beneath the staircase in a state of great agitation. "Hurry up Klaus! Get dressed! There's something I want you to see. Today I'm going to have it out with her if it's the last thing I do."

Within minutes I was hustled into the street and piloted along narrow alleyways toward the Café Ostaria Bavaria, Munich's oldest Italian restaurant, often frequented by Hitler and his followers. "I … I was heading back to the studio after Mass," she sniffed, "… and what do I see along the way? Three guesses and the first two are poo!"

Between heavy breaths I studied the sophisticated-looking Fraulein at my side, clattering along in her dangerously high-heeled Farregamos. This was a far cry indeed from the first glimpse I'd had of a young lady posing on the boss' desk in a loud striped sweater and patent leather stilettos, looking like an underage prostitute. Or was it?

Back then I'd winced to see Eva's severe coiffure and gummy little smile that hid her front teeth; and ever since had had a front-row seat in her transformation to high-fashion plaything of the National Leader. These days she exudes a superficial worldliness ablaze with resentment whenever she opens her mouth: "See? See? It's that bumpkin Geli and her Onkel Alf stealing a quiet moment together in public, no less. After he promised me there was nothing in it. I'm sick and tired of his lies."

Taking my elbow, she pulled me closer to the café's huge picture window, where at first, following the direction of her manicured pointer, I could see little of the dimly lit interior. Surrounding tables were obviously excited over something; and there tucked away in a candlelit alcove beneath an ornate gilded dome huddled Hitler himself, engaged in a serious tete-a-tete with Eva's hated rival.

"Just look at her! She … she's nothing but a fat frump," she sputtered, causing heads to turn. To me, the poor girl looked like she was getting a dressing down, nodding dumbly now and then throughout Onkel Alf's monologue.

Eva's face was flushed and she gritted her teeth. "Has she no sense of decency? Keeping him away from those with whom he *should* be spending more of his free time."

"Like you, I suppose?" It just slipped out.

"Why not commune with him at home over the breakfast table if she must?" Eva continued, ignoring my faux pas. Her jealousy seemed petty and unnecessary as the niece Geli appeared overweight and none too affectionate toward her Onkel Alf, showing few of the lively traits with which she was often credited. Now and again she tossed her soft curls defiantly as Hitler tapped his dog whip menacingly on the side of his boot.

I whispered to Eva that they were, after all, blood relatives and Geli's mother Angela was Hitler's live-in housekeeper. She glared at me in disbelief. "That's just the bloody point, you fool!"

More sharp glances came our way. "Well, don't make a fuss or the boss will surely hear about it. I think you're working yourself up over nothing," I whispered while taking in the scene and smiling stupidly.

"Oh … oh dammit. C'mon, I need a drink." She spun on her heel and pulled me back from the crush. Head down, she headed straight for the Hofbräuhaus where I insisted on a table close to the door away from the smoke and thump of the Oom-Pah Band. "What on earth does he see in her, that's what I'd like to know?" she repeated as soon as we sat down, tossing back a glass of Moselle. That I could not answer, nor even guess as to why seemingly sophisticated Frauleins confide their inmost thoughts to men with little more than platitudes to offer in return.

I shrugged, thinking perhaps it was true that staff were being deliberately rotated to minimise the chances of their getting too cosy. My aloneness may be turning out to be a blessing after all.

Something over Eva's shoulder caught my eye in the far corner and sent a chill down my spine. A group of Nazi bigshots were boisterously toasting an off-duty topless dancer, who moved lightly from lap to lap. The girl was being tugged this way and that by hairy hands across her lithe body; some tucked paper money into her panties. I struggled not to cry out, but somehow held it in and sucked for air.

My next thought was to rush into the fray and drag Claudia free, but something inside warned me off. I turned to Eva who was lost in her own thoughts. "You know, both of us have a right to feel cheated today."

"What on God's earth do you mean?" she said, with her back to the action.

Taking out her makeup mirror she peeped at the scene behind while pretending to pat down her eyebrows. "Oh, that? That's pretty standard fare for the topless dancers, but don't breathe a word; I believe that's Claudia Schicklegruber. In fact, I know it is. Who knows what she gets up to when the boss is out of town?" She leaned back and fixed me with a quizzical stare before the penny dropped – "Oh no, not you too? You're kidding me?" – before suppressing a little snort of laughter.

"Surely you can't compare the pain I'm suffering with your pathetic puppy-dog crush. Hoffmann had better not find out, that's all I can say." There was a hard edge to her voice I'd not encountered before. I lowered my eyes so as not to be recognised and attempted to leave, but she grasped my forearm firmly and nailed me to the spot while draining the last of the Moselle.

Once or twice I saw her lips move. When parting ways on foot we were swamped by our own regrets. I decided to take the scenic route through the English Garden and hopefully clear my head along the way; fresh air was still a valuable commodity for me.

Suddenly, I found myself caught up in a parade of Brownshirts marching down Koenig Strasser, and there witnessed my first close-up encounter with senseless Nazi violence. Two or three free-spirited youths, probably young communists, stood hurling jibes at the passing hobnailed columns, whose reaction was swift and well-rehearsed.

With a "C'mon comrades, smash the commie rabble", several beefy thugs broke ranks and waded into the crowd swinging whip and baton, felling all before them with the thud of hardwood on the cranium.

I stood dumbfounded as the drumrolls faded in the distance. Surely, if National Socialist dogma stood sufficiently convincing, the so-called masses would gravitate into their ranks without this need for gratuitous thuggery. I found my way back to the Studio and crawled with a heavy heart beneath the staircase, therein to ponder peace of mind and possible solutions.

While thus attempting to focus on calm breathing and straightforward chanting, the screen behind my eyes rippled with groping hands and bloodied boot-prints; what sort of void have I fallen into? How much did I really know about the dark politics of these people upon whom my fate depended?

However I tried to rationalise and see the bright side of my predicament, predicament it surely was, my attitude would need enormous adjustments to cope and survive. I'd always considered myself a quick learner but such violent shocks to my understanding sometimes took days or weeks to digest.

Soon after, my faith in human nature was partly restored when I was called to take a phone call in the boss' office. "Hello, Klaus? Is that you?" said the thin sweet voice on the other end.

"Y … Yes, it's me … Frau Emilie? … I think of you nearly every day. I do so miss your cooking and companionship … but not in that order," I said.

She gave a little chuckle. "Well, it sounds like you haven't changed a bit. I wish I could say the same, but the aches and pains keep coming. Still, I guess that's better than the alternative …" she added with another chortle.

"Now, where was I? Oh yes. About next Sunday: might you be free to join myself and the family for lunch? I've seen so little of Ernst since he returned, and with spring in the air, I simply had to put my foot down … You will try, won't you, Klaus? I'm so keen to hear how you are enjoying Munich. Well, that's wonderful; don't bring a thing. We'll expect you at 12:30." I was about to enquire about dress but she had hung up; her hearing was not improving.

The "family" turned out to be Ernst and his brother Robert, their sister Emilie, and Frau Röhm's two dogs. Marty Schartzl and my brother Robert were also present, both a little menacing in their official brown stormtrooper uniforms.

The moment I stepped through the front door, clutching a modest bunch of snowdrops I'd picked from a nearby garden, the dogs came bounding toward me in recognition, enveloping me once more in the warm homely smells of a real household. The old lady seemed genuinely pleased to be finally surrounded by "her boys", and demonstrated her usual grace by calling for another vase in which to place my meagre offerings alongside the huge bunch of Arum lilies presented earlier by Ernst.

I looked nervously about: her favourite son was resplendent in a three-piece herringbone suit and tie, with his shattered visage groomed to perfection. Apparently, Ernst had arrived in time to accompany his mother to the morning service at the nearby Lutheran church and was now looking forward to catching up on all the family gossip.

The conversation continued apace before turning to Röhm's recent promotion and my good fortune in procuring a trusted position in the darkroom of Studio Hoffmann. I felt a little embarrassed at her obvious pleasure in seeing me so "settled" in the job she felt suited me "down to the ground", courtesy of her Ernst. Marty seemed his same old self, yet also daunting in full Nazi garb.

I guessed that he alone plumbed my newfound "prosperity" as not quite what it seemed.

While the drinks flowed, the home-cooking and other goodies appeared in quick succession, revealing brother Robert's readiness to dominate the conversation with his endless litany of jungle tales and humorous anecdotes. At one stage he overtalked before receiving a swift kick under the table from Marty.

Robert Röhm, on the other hand, showed little interest in war stories or the political manoeuvrings at Party Headquarters, attempting to steer the conversation toward more general and aesthetic themes. I don't think Frau Röhm cared much what we spoke of, even when things became a little boisterous; she clearly gained great pleasure from the sheer enjoyment of having us all together.

The afternoon passed quickly and joyously, with me being treated as part of the family. When the party disbanded at sunset we left a frail, black-draped figure sitting between the fireplace and baby grand with her dogs, already lonely.

During our stroll back to Headquarters, I took the chance to fall back and caution Robert over his lack of decorum in Frau Emilie's home, concerns he brushed away with the wave of a hand. "Bullshit! Everyone loves a bit o' blarney ta be sure, and you may ha' noticed I bin takin' German lessons ..."

I looked at him in astonishment and saw Marty glance over his shoulder.

"Damned if I'm not. I'm movin' in a whole new circle now, liddle brudda ... Anyways, puttin' a few noses outa joint is what we Brownshirts do best."

"Well, all I can say is there's no need for it in front of Frau Emilie."

Following a dismal pause, I ventured to ask for his impressions of the higher Nazi leadership with whom he'd come in contact; his responses at first were terse or monosyllabic. His jarring new German accent, unlike my own forged in the fires of Vati's carping, had been clumsy and guttural since Alois' very first attempts at Teutonic tutelage. In fact, for years my brother had taken special pride in *unlearning* the new tongue that Alois had been so anxious to instil.

Then, suddenly he opened up, betraying a fierce loyalty to both Hitler and National Socialist philosophy, in which I was surprised to hear he seemed well-versed. Naturally, he subscribed to the mantra of Aryan superiority, before settling on the thrills and spills associated with time already spent among his very own squad of brown bullies: Robert's Sea had finally found its shore.

I admitted that so far I'd not managed to catch on to the overall goals of the Movement, at least those not involving violence and mayhem. I soon felt hours of home-spun contentment dissolving beneath his inclement arrogance; this was as the talk of a stranger who left my blood cold and my mood in free fall. Sure, we'd both been quick learners like Mam said, but now it was impossible to ignore that our experiences in the new land were heading in very different directions.

I wondered if I had already overheard and learned too much for my own good. There was no reasoning with him and no other possible worldview besides Hitler's. It seemed nothing for it but to pull my head in and "follow orders" like everyone else; not exactly a formula for fulfilment.

Meanwhile, Hoffmann was stepping up his volume of "foreign orders" while at the same time certain high-ranking Nazis and their wives were asking for me by name, to personally print their "private" snapshots. My reputation as a trustworthy, taciturn printer was gathering steam, though my embarrassment when dealing with such a lack of inhibition among the upper echelons may well be imagined.

With almost every roll, it seemed I was witnessing the mating habits of Munich's ruling classes. Many of these "personal" films featured uninhibited, even vulgar acts, with copies of anything "interesting" being carefully catalogued in Hoffmann's Private Archive. Of course, I was forbidden to discuss this sordid aspect of my work with another soul.

"Little Evie", as many of the staff now chided behind her back, finally bowed to the inevitable and popped her head under the stairs as I lay reading.

Breathless, she held out a roll of 35 mm film for me to print. "Promise you won't tell anyone. I set the camera on a rock and used the ten-second timer," she bubbled. "It's a big surprise for Ad … the Führer's birthday."

Before long we were leaning over my developing dish in a fog of perfume. Her overdone fragrances tangling with darkroom chemicals created a heady brew, as the first prints sprang to life, revealing a pair of tiny puckered breasts emerging through a waterfall, causing my breath to catch in my throat. I caught a sudden vision of my beloved Maya almost too terrible to bear.

As Nazi nudes go, Eva's self-portraits turned out to be quite tame, but I guess I was more embarrassed because I knew the subject personally. The last time I'd conflated nude bodies and waterfalls was as sad as any day I'd ever lived. Once I'd steadied my nerves I began to have second thoughts. *Eva, you of all girls, shedding your clothes to impress a forty-something-year-old man; famous or not. Yuck!*

Whatever happened to her convent schooling? A young woman, not yet come of age, casting all modesty to the wind for a virtual senior citizen, who as far as I could tell showed little reciprocal interest. At first, it seemed the height of folly, until my Master within whispered that I was being judgmental and prudish.

"Oh, Klaus; do you think I look too fat? You must tell me honestly …" But before I could answer she blurted, "D …Do you think my titties are too small?"

"N … No! Not at all," I replied a little too quickly, rocking the tray back and forth before carefully lifting each print with my tongs to place in the drying cabinet. "Most people have a little spare tyre or two," I added, attempting to soothe her doubts. I needed to smarten up, and fast!

For a long moment, she glared. "You are not to mention a word of this to anyone at work. This year I'll give him a gift like no other. Oh, I do love him so."

I realised then that I knew little of German ways and even less of life itself.

That evening beneath the staircase I reflected on what might have been, once upon a time in a faraway land, and silently mouthed Our Father several times before dropping into fitful slumber. At some point I dreamed that I blabbed Eva's secret within earshot of Lothar and found myself facing a firing squad, waking with a gasp as the bullets slammed into my chest.

<h1 style="text-align:center">36</h1>

Following my rude awakening at the Hofbräuhaus, I went out of my way to avoid Claudia, until in early April we were thrown together over a customised framing order.

"I can't help but feel you've been avoiding me. How about that picnic by the river you promised?" she said softly when Iris had passed by on her rounds. Those few moments sufficed to realise that I still cared about her dearly, irrationally. My animosity melted away that same instant I understood Eva's own improbable infatuation with Hitler; it had nothing to do with evidence or common sense.

I drank in every word from her full lips. "Name any weekday and I'll do my best to get off early," she purred. All pain and admonition wilted under the warmth of those kind words; I was stripped of resolve.

"Th ... Thursdays are good for me," I stuttered meekly.

Her very presence caused my heart to pound and I longed to be alone with her in a private place; I felt I could handle anything with Claudia, alias Sissy, at my side. I could endure any and all future shocks.

"I'll try my best to give you plenty of notice ... and I believe that completes your order, Herr Hahn," she spoke up smartly as Lothar's shining skull cruised past the doorway, pausing just long enough to take in the scene. She gave me a knowing wink as we both suppressed a snigger. The resident bully, like so many other Nazi sycophants, now sported a brand new schnurrbart under his nose, the recall of which kept me in high spirits for the rest of the day.

Photographers, printers, S.A. Brownshirts, office and counter staff, not to mention customers, were all tripping over each other in the beehive atmosphere of Studio Hoffmann. With new sales staff turning up for training almost weekly, Eva and I found ourselves together often in the darkroom.

She remained troubled, keen to tell of her repressed family life and the inadequacies of a convent education; and above all else her unrequited love for Adolph Hitler. In some ways I now pitied her hopeless plight; my own feelings for Claudia gnawed at my innards as she opened up.

Eva's banter helped lighten my grinding schedule as she counted the days on the calendar out loud until "her Adi's" looming 42nd birthday bash.

Following past practice, April 20 would be a day filled with all the usual formalities and appearances of the Big Chief before his adoring followers, after which Eva hoped to snaffle him for herself later in the evening, safe in the privacy of Hoffmann's Bogenhausen retreat.

Yet unsure of her ground, she carefully unwrapped the gilt-framed 8" × 10" we'd printed together and sat it on my workbench. "Well, what do you think of the finished product?" she asked, beaming. Of course, I had to admit it was a stunning and perfect, if bold, gift for any middle-aged bachelor.

"Look here! You can see the droplets of water sparkling on my skin. I must say the freezing water didn't do my boobies any favours."

I tried not to stare too closely. "You have a lovely petite figure, Eva. I'm sure he'll love it."

"Well, he'd better! I spend at least an hour after work each day on the parallel bars and, as you know, I ride my bicycle to work every morning." She gave a long, wistful sigh, then continued. "I think I've mentioned previously that I'd like to star in a Tarzan movie one day … wearing only a loincloth of course," she giggled self-consciously.

"Have you forgotten that Tarzan is *my* hero too? I blurted. "… ever since my childhood in …"

"South America? Pooh! I want to make my movie in the darkest part of Africa where there are real lions and tigers."

"B … But jaguars have the most powerful bite of any of the big cats," I replied a little too quickly, "and furthermore there are no tigers in Africa."

She glared for a moment. "Says who? I just know I'll make the best Jane ever, and I'll choose one of those tall, handsome SS guards for my leading man."

Her mind seemed set and I made no further reply, thinking she possibly had the body for it. All that time spent on the parallel bars may make it a little easier to swing through the treetops.

Since gaining access to the "Hitler Files" in the boss' office, I occasionally overheard snippets of conversation revealing the degree of propaganda being pumped out in Hoffmann's name.

Lothar was instructed to oversee the removal of certain persons who had since fallen out of favour with the Leader, by "doctoring" early Nazi group pictures. He usually brought these "special orders" to me and hovered about until each erasure with Ferricyanide was successfully completed.

One morning, he confronted me on the staircase with a package of prints under my arm, en route to Framing and Finishing, and stuck out a polished jackboot to bar my progress. He then accused me of "smirking" and pushed his face into mine. "You're getting a little too big for your boots, Jungle Boy," he snarled, dousing me in a breath heavy with drink.

"The boss seems quite happy with my performance," I dared reply, "and Fraulein Braun herself asked me to deliver this batch upstairs."

"Don't try to hide behind her skirts, you little weed. It seems to me you've been ducking my authority since the day you arrived." Eva, as noted, seemed immune from all censure, and I enjoyed sidestepping the chain of command when in her company.

"N ... Not at all, Herr Sturmführer, I'm just trying to be friendly ..." My well-worn excuse had worked fine in the past, but not this time: he grabbed my shirt front and almost lifted me clean off the step.

"Don't think I haven't heard you and those Frauleins poking fun behind my back. I'm warning you not to get too cocky," he fumed as his new schnurrbart quivered indignantly. "From now on, all 'special orders' go through me, got it?"

"T ... The boss has entrusted me with confidential tasks and says that no one is to interfere," I boldly responded, feeling not half so confident as my words implied.

"Leave him alone, you great oaf!" Lothar's head spun round to confront Claudia half crouching on the top step with her eyes breathing fire.

For a moment he was too stunned to speak. "What's it to you, Polack whore? Don't think I'm blind to your past either ..." he spat out the words and slowly released his grip on my throat.

"It might mean plenty when I tell the boss you're getting into the booze at this hour, don't you agree? I know you've had ample warnings."

The bully's tone softened visibly. "Aw, keep your shirt on. I was only having a bit of fun with the kid ..."

"Well, next time have your fun at someone else's expense, you *buffoon*!" she shot back, purposely taking me by the arm and ascending the stairs. My breath was coming in heavy gasps, unnerving the big man who stood transfixed, confounded by her audacity. "In the future, you lay off the kid or I'll be having a word in Sturmbannführer Röhm's ear ..."

At this, Lothar turned ashen and spun on his heel, muttering inaudibly under his breath as he clumped away. "I heard that!" she called to the back of the bull neck, before helping me slowly to sit close on one of the salmon-coloured settees outside the boss' office. Her body pressed against my thigh. "Don't worry; I've got plenty on him if he gets out of line again."

"I didn't know you were such good friends with Captain Röhm and the Nazi leadership," I wheezed.

She looked at me long and hard. "... I'm friends with everyone who's anyone in this fucked-up system; the boss sees to it that I get to meet them all."

This was the first time I'd heard her swear, and thought back to the bunch of rowdies in the Hofbräuhaus with whom she'd been flirting so shamelessly.

"D … Do you really think Captain Ernst would intervene with Lothar if you asked?"

"Intervene! Röhm would have his guts for garters if I so much as lifted my little finger. He's one of the few real 'gentlemen' I can trust to defend a lady in distress, and I'm sure you know why."

"Did you know it was Röhm's idea that my brother and I came to Germany in the first place? He made all the arrangements and singlehandedly lined us up with work when we landed." I wanted to tell her of my friendship with Frau Emilie also but ran out of steam. If memory serves true, I shamelessly dragged out my asthma attack that day, wallowing in the touch of Claudia's sure hands and cool flannel applied to my forehead and chest.

"My, my, what a softie you are. You are going to need to toughen up if you hope to survive around here. It's about time you stood up for yourself, or mark my words: these bastards will walk all over you." I could manage only a weak smile of gratitude.

Later, as I limped down the stairs, it seemed that all eyes were upon me and that Lothar had been given the message, loud and clear. Still trembling, I flopped onto my bunk and replayed the staccato events over again in my head.

My insights into those around me had somehow morphed into ambiguity. While Sister Klara's admonition to see myself as just one clever monkey among others was intended to simplify life, it seemed to me that success in Nazi Germany depended rather on "Monkey see, Monkey do". Calming my chest with a series of soft chants, I resolved yet again to face all future threats with a stouter heart.

As the big day drew near, Eva spent night after fruitless night on the waiting room settee gazing into the distance, where we sometimes exchanged a few words.

Being continually in and out of the boss' office, I observed her on more than one occasion winsomely fondling the birthday gift; but she rarely looked up when I passed. I wondered again if she was doing the right thing in presenting such a provocative image to a man who allegedly covered his eyes during newsreel footage of Göring's autumnal stag hunt.

What's more, it was a given that Hitler's morals were beyond reproach; that he kept himself aloof from "all physical temptations" and pure for the Fatherland.

This myth, while perhaps comforting for Party Members, proved crushing to poor Eva; after all, what hot-blooded maiden knowingly chooses to spin her web of allure around a man with so few vices?

I had chosen not to disclose that Robert's birthday also fell on April 20, until I received an invitation to join him for a "drink or two" following the S.A. march-past, and Hitler's speech at the Felderrnhalle.

Studio Hoffmann, except for the Presse Illustration Newsroom, had shut down for the celebrations, so I decided like so many others to witness up close the proposed rumpus in the city centre and afterwards take up my brother's invitation. When the festive dust settled, I may even have time to take my camera for a stroll through the English Garden and light a campfire beside the river; I felt suddenly free.

With Claudia nowhere to be found, I accepted a lift on the handlebars of Eva's pushbike and we headed off unsteadily toward the tumultuous downtown din. As usual, she was overdressed and embalmed in French perfume; I was relieved when she suggested we dismount and walk the last few blocks. A modest crowd of well-wishers had gathered in the cobbled plaza and Eva waved her press pass to allow us closer access to the decorated podium flanked by two huge couchant marble lions.

"What a spot to make a speech," I thought, flanked by cameras, microphones and sheer atmosphere. A temporary press platform had been erected on either side and it was evident that not one jot or tittle emanating from the great man would be lost.

I followed close behind Eva up onto a mighty plinth beneath the big cat's belly, from where we had a perfect view. "A press pass is more important than a pistol for these occasions," she gleefully confided above the clatter of jackboots taking up positions below in the front rows. On all sides, people pressed against each other, many with small children on their shoulders.

Right on time the parade arrived, preceded by lorries packed with Brownshirts handing out tiny Nazi flags on sticks. These were closely followed by drums, flutes and trumpets, each striving for supremacy. Smart grey ranks of Reichswehr foot soldiers headed three black, custom-built convertibles, which slid to a stop at the bottom step.

From the leading Mercedes stepped Hitler, followed by his SS bodyguards, who lightly mounted the trail of flowers up several steps between the big cats. Thanks to Eva, we enjoyed an unimpeded view of what followed.

Solemnly, the guest of honour stepped up to the microphone and waited for what seemed an eternity; until we could hear a pin drop. Then, in a soft, rasping voice he thanked the Party Faithful and German People for their well-wishes and gifts. Soon, the tempo increased, and he reminded one and all that there yet remained much work to be done if ever they hoped to be freed from the clutches of the despised Versailles Treaty. "The Nazis are marching so that Germany can take back her rightful place at the head of Nations," he reminded them.

Then, he proposed that Christ's actual birthdate should rightfully be April 20, even if the year remained uncertain, and that it had been changed to

December only later by meddling clerics. From the corner of one eye, I saw Robert in the front ranks squaring his shoulders and jutting his chin at this suggestion.

"… and I have been sent as your Führer to complete the work begun by Jesus Christ Himself."

At this the crowd could no longer contain its joy, fixing 10,000 eager eyes upon its Saviour while gulping down the mighty blasphemy. Waves of "Heil Hitler" now washed over the diminutive speaker, until he retracted his outstretched right palm across his lanyard with a flourish.

Sitting just yards away, Eva too, was clearly smitten, waving her scarf in a wild attempt to draw attention and almost tumbling from the plinth and into the crowd below. How she hungered for a single glance; but none came.

What did come pouring forth was the Leader's birthday rant. I closed my eyes for a moment and felt the words hammering my skull in slow staccato: they were demotic and deranged, or such sounds as I imagined such beings might utter.

"There will be no second revolution!" he snarled, thumping his fist on the table and rolling his eyes heavenward. "Democracy is nothing more than mob rule! We will show these snivelling gentlemen just who holds the real rising power in Germany today."

Yet more hateful and rousing phrases spewed forth, bringing the mob to its climax. They screamed and jostled for a chance to be part of the New Awakening and to play a part in "Making Germany Great Again". The violent crescendo ended with a loud "Amen", I could hardly believe it. He looked drained, soaking up the Heil Heil's rolling up from a sea of hoarse throats.

Slowly he became aware of his surroundings and I noticed a funny little smile flicker across the spittled corners of his mouth before he patted them dry with a clean handkerchief.

And then it was over. With a final outthrust of his arm, the whole entourage descended the steps and filled the waiting limousines. "Did you see that Klaus? Oh, I might as well not exist at all. How I wanted him to look up, or even blow me a kiss in public."

But he didn't. Only the SS guards were left to sweep the crowd with their steely gaze. In a roar of blue smoke, the great machines were gone. Eva gave one or two deep sighs and helped me down to the pavement; the crowd was dispersing and already the press stands were being knocked apart.

Could this inciteful demon be that same bashful Bohemian who flirts so awkwardly with the sales girls behind the counter? I wondered, still rattled from the barrage of heresy. What might such conviction achieve if directed towards *real* peace and creative ends?

"Did you happen to catch any of the action?" she asked, walking beside her bicycle in the general direction of the Gardens. "In all the excitement I forgot I had my camera in my purse. Whenever I'm near him I forget everything but my own desires."

"Sorry. I too was swept up in the experience. Your 'fiancé' seems to have had the same spellbinding effect he exerts on the Press Gallery. The crowd certainly were fired up."

She pretended to be light-hearted and chatted away irrepressibly. "It really doesn't matter that he didn't see me, he has so much on his mind. Anyway, he'll see me tonight at Hoffmann's, one way or the other." She winked slyly, referring no doubt to her special gift. Would he open it in front of everyone, she wondered, or in private with just the two of them present? Would he kiss her cheek in gratitude at the perfection of the moment?

"I've told you Papa doesn't approve of my affair with the Herr Hitler, but too bad; if only my parents knew him as I do they'd soon change their minds."

I wasn't surprised when she began referring to her lopsided infatuation as an "affair", though otherwise puzzled as to why she continued to confide her innermost thoughts in me. "I *will* marry Adolph, you know? He doesn't realise it yet. Just you wait … By the way, I will be seeing you tonight at the boss' place, won't I? For just one 'Führer Toast'? Surely."

"I … I don't think so. I wasn't invited."

"Nonsense! Absolutely *everyone* will be there. August, Willy and Max are dropping by, and Herta too. In fact, Henni will be introducing her new fiancé around, thanks to a little string-pulling on Adolph's part.

"Oh yes, I'm *so* jealous … And, surprise! Surprise! Captain Röhm let it slip that he's bringing along your brother, whom I hear is also turning 21 today. All my girlfriends are simply dying to meet him. I do hope he doesn't try to steal Adolph's thunder with his wild jungle tales, ha-ha," she chortled.

With a sudden pang, I realised I'd clean forgotten to catch up with Robert after the rally and was now blocks away, on the verge of climbing down the river bank to light a campfire.

"Well, I simply won't take 'no' for an answer, so don't fall in and that's final! If you haven't turned up by 8:00, I'll send out a search party."

With a merry jingling of the bell she gave a toss of her head and pedalled off through the park. I eagerly jumped the fence and pushed through the willow thicket to the water's edge. When safely alone, I once more felt the pull of freedom; scratching a few twigs together I made ready to enjoy the last few hours of daylight.

37

"It's alright Bertha, he's with me," Eva's party voice rang out past the prissy maid barring the front door to the Hoffmann Villa. "Come in through this way Klaus and I'll introduce you around." She was extra bubbly that evening and dressed to kill in a dark blue silk floral frock.

Feeling awkward, I hung back fiddling with my bow tie, a parting gift from Frau Emilie, before Eva took my hand and led me into the tastefully decorated drawing room. We headed straight for a huddle of beautifully coiffured young women sipping champagne around a full-size grand piano.

"Henni, Henriette, actually, Herta, Gretl and Traudl; I want you to meet my workmate Klaus, I'm sure you've all heard his amazing stories and have seen him ducking in and out of the darkroom. Oh, and here comes our hostess, Frau Hoffmann," she exclaimed, turning graciously to greet a beaming though plain woman approaching with her hand extended. "We meet at last, Herr Hahn. I too have heard of your thrilling childhood at the dark end of civilisation ..."

I managed a weak smile and "Hello" to each in turn, lifting the glass of bubbles that had been pressed into my hand. "Er ... here's to ... to friendship!" I offered, realising later that all other toasts proposed during the evening were directed towards "Our beloved Leader, Party and Fatherland".

While the girls went on chatting and casting sideways glances in my direction, I watched Frau Hoffmann floating easily from group to group, putting every guest at ease. Across the room sat Röhm with an immaculately groomed Robert by his side, surrounded by a group of Old Fighters in bemedalled uniforms and several party bigwigs I knew only from photos. They were engrossed in animated conversation and had not acknowledged my arrival.

A small, swarthy man with slicked-back hair was berating the group in a powerful voice that spilled beyond his listeners. "It's a proven fact! No propaganda is too crude, too low or too brutal for the masses; so long as it's repeated often enough. I tell you, they *want* to be bamboozled!"

As the raconteur spun around to emphasise his point to Röhm, I spotted the slow foot in patent leather pumps dragging slightly, confirming him as none other than Joseph Goebbels, newly appointed Propaganda Minister, who was making quite a name for himself.

In the opposite corner, a gathering of refined matrons was examining a table loaded with brightly gift-wrapped packages.

"I said, what do you think of Putzi's playing?" I felt a tug at my sleeve and found "Little Sunshine's" pert mouth close to my ear. I was flustered by Henni's natural beauty up close; blue eyes twinkling with expectation above a fine angular chin and high rosy cheeks crowned with a mop of soft curls.

"I … er, yes, it's wonderful." I then admitted that the only other person I'd heard mastering Wagner's pulsing chords live on piano was Röhm.

"It's Onkel Adi's special music, you know?" she chirped, clearly a little under the weather, "and nobody, but nobody plays Wagner like our Putzi. So far it seems his entire recital had been wasted; Onkel and Papa are not even here yet, typical! Did you know that sometimes Onkel Adi gets Putzi out of bed in the middle of the night to play for him when he can't sleep?" I admitted I did not.

"'Putzi' means 'little baby' in Italian, by the way: don't you think that's funny, given the size of the great lump? Actually, his real name is Ernst, but everyone calls him 'Putzi' so as not to confuse him with Captain Röhm. Between you and me, Onkel is supposed to have a crush on his wife, Helene, but I don't believe that for a moment. Onkel's usually turned off by older women, especially those with political views." She paused for breath and I thanked her for the history lesson, which went part way toward easing my discomfort.

At each brisk ingress of the housemaid, all eyes moved to the front door, thus far yielding no sign of either my host or guest of honour. Following Hennie's prompt I turned back to the great man astride the piano stool, who played with his head thrown back and eyes closed in a sort of trance, fingers pounding the ivories like pudgy ballerinas in one overture after another.

Putzi was pouring forth a pseudo-orchestral style I've never heard before or since. His great square head with the prognathous lower jaw thrust forward seemed oblivious to anything else occurring in the room, absorbed in the stirring mood of his own creation.

Eva, Henni and the girls had almost to shout to make themselves heard above the swelling cords, while graciously attempting to include me in the conversation. "Hello Klaus, I'm Herta," one of them mouthed in my face before taking a nervous sip of champagne. "… I just can't wait to hear all about your time among those head-hunters." Caught off guard, I was thankful that Marty Schartzl and Robert had appeared out of nowhere to pull me aside. Surprisingly, they both seemed rather chuffed to find me in attendance.

"H … Happy 21st, Big Brother," I said belatedly, "Sorry I didn't have time to get you a gift. I really must apologise for standing you up at the Hofbräuhaus …"

"Good ol' Klaus, always getting' sidetracked; nuttin's changed. Forget it. Come wit' me, dere's sometin' I need to tell you." I was already beginning to feel faint from the constant din and cigarette smoke, as Eva too had lit up right beside me, something I'd not seen her do previously in public.

Frau Hoffmann was in deep conversation with Henni's new fiancé, Baldur von Schirach, who was hanging on her every word. Like most, I was aware of Schirach's meteoric rise through the ranks of the Hitler Youth as an unmistakably modern Aryan, and that like Putzi, he was half-German and half-American.

Having somehow missed out on an introduction, I took stock of Henni's unlikely beau from the corner of my eye; a pudgy, effeminate-looking fellow altogether unbecoming who, when he wasn't nodding vigorously, looked bored with the whole show. He appeared to be doing his best to attract the attention of Röhm and his coterie of Old Fighters in the far corner.

Meanwhile, Robert and I passed through a set of concertina doors into the spacious, candlelit garden, where he stopped abruptly and peered into my puzzled face. "You do know it was me, don't yer? I mean, who did the Old Man in?" His voice trailed off as my mouth dropped open incredulously … He surely couldn't mean what I thought he meant. Clearly, he was desperate to get something off his chest.

"I king-hit the bastard from behind while he was taking a leak; he never knew what 'it 'im. Mind you, I didn't mean to kill 'im; just give 'im a bit of a fright if yer know what I mean." He paused and gazed at me intently, unsure whether to continue. "Not that I'm sorry for a minute. No one liked 'im. It was jus' as I thought; they were all so damn sure he'd fallen overboard all by 'imself an' banged 'is 'ead on the rudder blade."

"B … But why? When we were getting ready to leave anyway?" I said.

"Dat's what you tink, and you can go on believin' it if yer want. Right from the word go 'e 'ad no intention of lettin' me off the 'ook. Sheer bloody mindedness, I say; all ta prop up 'is own miserable 'ide. Well, dat's all behind us now … an' good riddance, I say."

"B … But Robert," I protested lamely, "that's *murder*!"

"It's only murder if anyone says different to the coroner's findings. An' that ain't gunna happen, is it?" His intent was clear, so sure of himself, as if such bogus conclusions were the most natural thing in the world.

I was, of course, almost speechless.

"Well, don't try and tell me the mongrel didn't deserve it. I did it for Mam, too," he said. "Let sleeping dogs lie, I say."

"B … But Alois was *my* real father for all his failings," I gasped, thankfully distracted by the trill and pop of a garden cricket hopping into a nearby candle flame. Like the fixated cricket, I simply could not accept what had just happened.

Robert would not be shaken from his self-abrogation, becoming visibly agitated by my failure to "get on board", as he called it.

"Aw, just get over it, liddle brudder. Look at this new world we Nazis are creatin'. Surely you don't believe we'd a bin better off stayin' behind in dat shithole, eh? As far as der police and everyone else are concerned, it was an accident. It says so on 'is death certificate. Did ya really wanna spend de rest o' yer life watchin' rubber balls go floatin' past yer bedroom winda? Course not! I believe jus' like Hitler says; everything comes from Providence an' we should grab every opportunity when it comes," he offered self-servingly.

"It's only natural dat a few skulls get cracked along da way. An' I'll tell you why: 'cause millions of us Aryans are risin' up to keep the White Race in its proper place by puttin' our muscle where our mouth is." He rose to his full height of 5'11" and gave a little twitch of his shoulders, smug in his conclusions.

"Us? … Us?" I was flabbergasted. "You haven't a drop of German blood in your veins, yet here you are sprouting patriotic slogans about so-called Aryans."

"Oh yeah? Well, for your information, neider does da Adolph Hitler, he's *Austrian*! And Aryan, like us," he added, which came as quite a shock to me.

In a flash, I made the connection between Hitler and Bonaparte, that other great opportunist, perhaps the most memorable Frenchman of all time yet Corsican by birth.

"Come on Robert, you talk too much," Schartzl called, stepping out of the shadows. Neither of us had noticed his approach. "Klaus has had enough surprises for one night. Let's go back inside and listen to Onkel Röhm demolishing the black dwarf. By the way, Klaus, Eva Braun's been looking everywhere for *you*. Have you been cheating on me, you slippery rascal?"

Robert gave a nervous cough before the two of them disappeared into the musical haze, leaving me blushing and bewildered. If the truth ever did come out I might even be classed as an accessory. With the benefit of hindsight, all the signs were there and I should have been more attentive to the prodding of my small voice within. Up till this moment it had suited me to seek favour by playing a less-than-robust orphan in a hostile foreign world.

That night in the garden among the fairy lights and crickets my thoughts flickered between fear and guilt: guilt because I hadn't delved deeper into Vati's accident and fear because one day I may find myself implicated up to the neck.

I wished then and there that Robert had never let me in on his dark secret: my own brother, a self-confessed and godless parricide at best, or step-parricide to be more precise. If the truth came out would I ever be able to live down the shame?

It seemed that all of Robert's childhood rebelliousness and resentments had converged in that single act of revenge, unveiling now a leaden lump deep in my gut where order had so recently resided. My naive future plans had become ashes in my mouth and I was past caring.

"Yoo-hoo, Jungle Boy, they told me you were out here. Come on, the guest of honour and host are just pulling up …" one of Eva's friends was gesturing frantically through the French doors. Numb and unsteady, I rejoined the party, where the music had been replaced by eager waves of "Heil Hitler", clapping and heel-clicking.

The boss arrived fawning beside the Great Leader, who was moving slowly with cap in hand and casting a leery eye over the assembled well-wishers. While all were distracted I noticed Eva switching her gift to the back of the pile and feared there was simply no way out for the remainder of the evening.

How could I avoid drawing attention to my dark mood, maybe even from the "cause célèbre" himself; I was trapped. A piercing glance from Hoffmann left no doubt that I'd been admitted under sufferance, despite his wife's earlier gracious attention: I would probably not make the shortlist in future.

By now Hitler had dabbed his schnurrbart damply onto every proffered female hand, before settling into his favourite chair beside the piano and gesturing for Putzi and the guests to resume as before. Eva and her friends scurried to take up positions in a semi-circle at his feet, chatting excitedly over star signs in general and Taurus in particular.

On a previous occasion, I'd mentioned to Eva in passing Sister Kara's theory concerning the Seven Year Cycles of Life, which had immediately caught her interest. Now, following one or two faltering attempts from herself on the topic, I found myself jostled down among the girls to explain the theory further.

Nearby, Hitler lolled back cross-legged in the armchair with eyes closed, absorbed in Putzi's playing. In hushed tones and struggling to be heard over the fortissimo, I revealed that the Leader was entering a particularly exciting period; from 42 to 49 years, and furthermore, how every seven years almost every cell in our bodies, except for the brain, was completely renewed.

This disclosure set their heads wagging. "Oh, Eva," one said calculatedly, "you have three more years until all *your* existing cells are replenished." The suggestion threw them into a giggling fit. I saw Hitler open one eye briefly, before he settled back to conduct one particularly stirring passage with his right hand.

"Oh Klaus, that theory may not even apply to *me*," she half-whispered mischievously, "because Adolph says I'm very mature for my age." More tittering followed. For the next fifteen minutes or so the banter continued on the plusses and minuses of Taureans, while I searched helplessly for an opportunity to depart.

"Actually, Klaus and I are both Aquarians, right on the cusp, aren't we, Jungle Boy?" Eva said, sensing my unease and attempting to draw me further into the topic. "That means we are mostly passive and pure of heart …" – she glanced at me again for confirmation – "… and definitely great lovers!"

At this, a howl of approval went up and all eyes fell on my blushing countenance; I felt like crawling under the piano. Hitler shifted in his seat and I dreaded that he too might be alerted to my disruptive presence. Here we were, supposedly celebrating *his* birthday, and Eva was choosing to focus on her own horoscope; and mine with it. "We Aquarians are naturally most compatible with Aries, but in my case," she paused and cast a loving eye towards her drowsy Idol, "… it's definitely Taureans!" Another titter followed, causing Hitler to finally sit up and open his eyes as the music stopped.

Frau Hoffmann took this belated cue to clap her hands and announce that a finger food buffet was now being served in the adjacent dining room.

"Aha! My little sunshine, I hear that big announcements are in the air," Hitler exclaimed, rising to bypass Eva and clasp both Henni's hands in his, gazing affectionately into her eyes before offering an elbow to escort her toward the sideboard loaded with dainties.

Baldur, the new fiancé, was left to fend for himself, and Eva, with a dejected pout, took my arm promptly to follow close behind the official party, muttering under her breath. It appeared that her night too was going from bad to worse, as was my own.

The Man himself was excused from partaking in the rich fare, after explaining to a disappointed Frau Hoffmann that that he had already consumed a large bowl of vegetable dumplings with Geli, before leaving home. He did, however, allow himself a glass of his favourite mineral water and a small plate of "melting moments" while the other guests fell upon the heaped offerings with gusto; none more so than Eva, who piled her plate high and gobbled down her food in full view of her finicky fiancé.

Worse, she tossed back flute after flute of champagne and laughed loudly at his every utterance. Two more chairs were brought in to settle the boss on one side with Röhm on the other, allowing the guest of honour to once more rest his head between his shoulders and launch into a critical appraisal of the latest movie *Mountain in Flames* that he had already viewed several times in the Berghof theatre. "That Louis Tronker is undoubtedly one of Germany's finest actors," Hitler announced, wiping back his drooping forelock from his eyebrow. "What a man, what courage and what scenery," he enthused, sitting up straight again. "I'm not surprised he has women falling at his feet." He cast an approving eye over his own chortling coterie, which had somehow managed to wiggle even closer.

"It's a well-known fact that to the greatest warrior belongs the most beautiful women," he continued, "… but alas, not for me: my bride is and always will remain Germany …" I noticed that he often repeated such self-serving aphorisms in the presence of company. "One can only imagine the uproar and disappointment if I took a wife; I'd lose half my following overnight. And anyway, it's been proven that the offspring of geniuses often turn out to be imbeciles." At this pronouncement, all the women except Eva nodded approvingly while the Great Seer paused to consume a butterfly cream cake.

Suddenly, the lumbering Hanfstaengl sprang up from the floor where he had been rolling around with the dog and doing impersonations of leading Nazi officials; much to the amusement of the womenfolk and annoyance of Hoffmann. At a given signal from the kitchen, he thundered out a piano roll announcing the arrival of a richly decorated, three-decker birthday cake being carried in by the boss on one side, with a beaming Schwartz and shuffling Goebbels on the other.

For once, Onkel Röhm had been caught napping, forced to watch on as the grand offering was placed reverently before the birthday boy.

Probably alone among guests I was taken aback by the kitsch assortment of swastika flags, plastic tanks, edible field artillery and party comrades mired in chocolate icing, all topped off by a stiff-armed Hitler made of marzipan and 42 fizzing sparklers. Our thoughtful hostess had personally devised this clever tribute in full knowledge that Hitler nowadays refused to blow out birthday candles in case he failed to extinguish them with a single breath.

Somewhat shyly he took the proffered SS dagger and plunged it into the middle layer, narrowly missing a marzipan Röhm and a platoon of chocolate soldiers. The following applause was lost beneath the strains of "Happy Birthday" and a rousing rendition of the "Horst Wessel Song", with Robert's warbling tenor again standing out. When it came time to open the presents, a buzz of excitement filled the room. Hitler motioned his aides to commence the unwrapping and, of course, the colourful pile had been vetted beforehand. In no way represented the discarded thousands of hand-crafted dainties that had poured in from all corners of a grateful nation, items such as home-fired vases, knitted sweaters, scarves and even bed-socks bearing the swastika logo had failed to make the cut.

After handing around trays of strudel, toffees and individually wrapped chocolates to the guests (none of which ever crossed his own lips for fear of being poisoned), the guest of honour paused admiringly before a Spitzweg landscape above the mantelpiece and turned with a grunt of approval to Hoffman, lately risen to the rank of Chief National Socialist Art Curator. Besides running his chain of studios, Hoffman found himself charged with procuring a collection of the finest paintings, sculptures and even photographs, to grace a proposed super gallery in Hitler's nearby hometown of Linz.

Apparently, neither he nor the recipients of all this largess saw anything amiss in passing on the (admittedly slight) risk of an agonising death to his guests, and even I found myself reaching for a bag of delicious-looking éclairs to take back to the Studio. It seemed the tasting team was being pushed to the limit during such times of plenty.

At last, the apogee of Eva's woes arrived with the completion of the unwrapping ritual, when she could contain herself no longer. Reaching across with a little curtsy she placed her own special gift into Hitler's hands. With a look of surprise, he glanced at the cryptic message on the card: "For your eyes only with undying love. Yours always, Eva."

"Nonsense!" he exclaimed brusquely and tore off the colourful tissue wrapping before she could utter a word. He seemed to freeze, while she hung back breathlessly. Others shoved and craned for a peek.

"Of all the cheek," one matron whispered loud enough for those behind to hear. I hunched my shoulders and lowered my sconce, overcome with foreboding.

"Er, yes … thank you, Fraulein Braun," the recipient finally spoke and glanced about stone-faced, before handing the offending object over his shoulder to bodyguard Schwartz, who was already loaded up with unwanted gifts for the forthcoming charity appeal. A long silence followed.

"Well, good on her," exclaimed one of Eva's friends, "I wish I'd had the guts to do it."

This brief showing of the framed 8" × 10" occupied much of the conversation that followed. "Well, it's art if you ask me," someone else added. "I'm sure it was taken at Königssee, I recognised the rock formations below the falls," said another.

And so the evening progressed, with no thought given, or mention made of Robert's own big milestone; thankfully without my being pestered again to recount my adventures among the head-hunters of South America.

"W … Well, he didn't *exactly* say he didn't like it," I finally ventured to my crestfallen colleague during the long walk home. "And, from what I saw there were just as many for as against."

"Oh, pooh! Just shut up, Klaus; he hardly looked at it. I'm just so embarrassed. I'm in for it if Papa finds out. Your brother and his pals certainly took a good gander." We walked the next few blocks in silence before Eva spoke again, "… and as for those gossiping old social climbers, I don't give a fig what they think." She was sounding more feisty with every step and suddenly gave out a harsh, metallic laugh. "Dammit! I wanna dance!"

She grabbed my hand and pulled me down a side street in an unfamiliar part of town. Ahead on both sides flashed gaudy nightclub foyers, each guarded by a brace of thugs. Without hesitation, she led me into "Salon Pussy". Protest was pointless.

"B ... But I'm exhausted, Eva. You have no idea of the mental strain I've undergone this night; I tried to leave hours ago except ..."

"Rubbish! I feel like drowning my sorrows, and if I'm not with a man I might just end up biting off more than I can chew. These places can be pretty rough so I'm told."

From the moment we stepped through the door, the differences between Salon Pussy and the Hofbräuhaus, the only other public house I'd visited in Munich, were immediately apparent. Gathered around circular tables as far as the eye could see, which really wasn't very far at all, were huddled groups of Brownshirts and top-hatted dignitaries, many with naked girls on their laps sipping expensive-looking cocktails.

After being seated at a mid-level table, Eva nervously confessed that she'd never actually crossed the threshold of such an establishment in all her 19 years, and at that moment I couldn't see the point of our being here now. The waitress gave a funny look when I ordered a small glass of Moselle for myself and a double Schnapps for Eva; I guessed she'd seen it all before.

As I slowly sipped my wine Eva tossed down her Schnapps in two quick gulps and pulled a face, before grabbing my hand and heading for the dance floor, which, strangely enough, was enclosed within a ring of potted palms, tangled vines and bunches of green raffia leaves.

"You should feel right at home here, Jungle Boy," she sniggered, clutching me tightly and whirling about in a series of foreign movements. Thankfully, in the dim haze, neither she nor any other of the blurry-eyed couples could see my beetroot blush and tiny, hesitant steps; I was hopelessly trapped.

What was it that Sister Klara had taught me on the hard Plaza flagstones? "Practise and practise some more; the Indians have their own rhythms," she had demonstrated hilariously, more than once twirling her Habit to expose the trademark lace-up boots. "In civilised society, it suffices to hold your partner gently cheek to cheek, like this ..." – she'd drawn me into the smothering black folds – "... while listening to your inner music. See how easily you are picking up the steps?"

And, that's exactly what I did now; taking the lead to whirl Eva around and around as she attempted to hang on and follow my moves. She gasped that if I didn't slow down she would throw up all over the other dancers.

Obligingly, for I had begun to enjoy the heady abandonment despite my shortness of breath, I eased off and settled into a sort of meaningless shuffle. For a while, neither of us spoke, lost in our own thoughts, rolling gently to the five-piece orchestra. I had to admit I was becoming a little aroused at Eva's provocative proximity, never having embraced any girl for such duration. It was as if she was clinging on in need of affection I didn't possess.

I deliberately distracted myself by taking in the surroundings which featured an inordinate number of hostesses/waitresses gliding purposefully from table to table, teasing and topping up drinks. Those who weren't completely naked wore fishnet stockings and skimpy g-strings. Others doubled up as dancing partners, all the while skilfully fending off the clumsy advances of their bibulous patrons. Again, I was reminded of Dante's dark days in the underworld.

In hindsight Flamingo Villa seemed positively tame, even respectable; there, at least, the majority of girls remained properly attired in the public areas, and the jungle lay beyond the outer walls.

"They say that for those with money or influence nothing is out of bounds in these places," she said finally, noting my discomposure. When she brought her face closer I noticed the tear streaks down her powdered cheeks.

"I wouldn't be surprised," I agreed, gliding in and out between the potted palms. "Are you sure you wouldn't like me to walk you home?"

"Of course not, silly. I feel much better already holding on to you. Anyway, the floor show is starting soon. It could be good for a laugh."

At that moment, a funny little man wearing a top hat and obviously false schnurrbart, hopped onto the dance floor and blew a long blast on a pink conch shell, before urging all the dancers to take their seats and charge their glasses.

The overhead lighting dimmed, leaving the make-believe patch of jungle lit up like a desert island floating in space. Following a suggestive joke or two equating the size of a man's hands with his private parts, the orchestra struck up a kind of tom-tom jungle rhythm as each "waitress" in turn emerged from the gloom wearing only a feathered headdress and a coconut shell shard just big enough to cover her pubic mound.

Following the beat they formed a conga line of swaying bodies, weaving in and out of the jungle props. "Herren and Frauen, we're approaching the climax of the evening – climax, get it? – when our beautiful young madels will perform for your delight a traditional ceremony brought all the way from the wilds of South America. For the first time ever in Munich, Salon Pussy is proud to present the long lost 'Dance of the Amazons'!"

At this blatant imposture, I nearly choked on my drink, realising that Eva must have had wind all along of the programme. She came alive. "Oh, how I'd love to go out and join them. At least *here* my body would be appreciated," she mumbled into her drink. "Perhaps, I'm more qualified to work in a place like this than Studio Hoffmann?" The Schnapps were clearly elevating her mood.

Meanwhile, the feathered chorus line, now brandishing facsimile spears, bows and arrows, emitted a discordant howling of "Indian War Cries", arching backwards and forwards and patting their hands over their mouths for effect.

As I watched in dismay, the conga line circled every table, offering lewd gestures toward men and women patrons alike, nimbly bucking and squealing to avoid those groping hands attempting to "pluck a pullet" as they passed.

At almost the same instant Eva and I both locked eyes on one particularly petite "Amazon", who, despite the overdone feline makeup, we recognised at once as our very own Claudia Schicklegruber. She wore a huge smile, a sliver of coconut shell and little else. As we watched spellbound, she circled and teased the uniformed patrons especially, her sinuous body paint moving like a snake. For the second time that evening, I felt like crawling under a rock. Eva noticed my extreme discomfort.

"What's wrong with you? This could hardly come as a shock: you surely know she's Hoffmann's whore for hire?"

Before I could respond, the chorus line in unison tore off their coconut shells and hurled them into the crowd before kicking each leg high in the air three times, sending the audience wild. Then, flapping their arms like swans they flew into the centre of the jungle patch and the whole room was plunged into darkness.

Moments later when the lights flickered back on, several drunken Brownshirts could be seen rummaging through the pot plants, only to come up empty-handed. The entire flock had vanished in a puff of smoke. From behind each column and archway, scantily clad waitresses now re-appeared, carrying trays of drinks as demurely as ever, to a clatter of applause, catcalls and whistles.

I was again the only person in the room unimpressed by the spectacle, but Eva was in stitches upon discovering her workmate in the tasteless thick of the floor show.

She almost slavered over my distress. "Come on Klaus, where's your sense of humour? Well, I guess it's time we called it a night … don't you think? I've changed my mind, Sir Galahad, you may have the honour of walking me home if you please," she pouted, and burst into a giggle.

I stayed miserable for three long days, aware that my work was suffering and blinded by the thought of my Claudia swanning about with that horrid false smile on her face, teasing and tempting those low-lifes. Iris had to warn me twice about leaving chemical bottles uncorked and not switching off the enlarger lamp, but even she eventually seemed to soften at my wretchedness.

"I hear your girlfriend put the wind up Lothar good and proper? Well, if you ask me he's had it coming, don't you agree?" She had caught me at a weak moment, and I knew I was out of order.

"Oh, I don't want to talk about that, if you don't mind." I had real misgivings over her sudden interest in my opinions and hadn't been able to confide in anyone for days. My heart felt close to breaking point.

"You know …" she clucked, "if you ever need to get anything off your chest you can always come to Iris Bumke. I'm sure that deep down you know my bark is a lot worse than my bite, don't you?"

"I just don't understand what's going on around here, that's all …"

"Why? Whatever do you mean?" She pricked up her ears; her usual penetrating gaze softening by the minute.

"This whole system just doesn't make any sense to me," I foolishly continued. "Everywhere I see the weak being trodden underfoot while National Socialist fat-cats enjoy every perk at the cost of their hard labour; that doesn't seem fair to me."

"Whoever do you mean? If you know of anyone on staff not pulling their weight you come straight to me. I am the best judge of what needs to be done. Between you and I, Lothar's methods are proving to be a little old-fashioned."

I apologised for speaking out of turn and confessed that my hopes appeared to be fading on all fronts. Claudia was clearly engaging in some kind of double life and Eva had been distant and aloof since the night of the party.

My supervisor nodded warmly and placed a comforting arm over my shoulder; I began to doubt my own instincts. That day, and in following weeks she shared my doubts and suspicions about the so-called Third Reich; lamenting everything from the boorishness of its leaders to the inevitable failure of its violent methods.

"Those who live by the sword die by the sword," I shared my cherished mantra from Matthew, "... yet here we find ourselves part of the most warlike machine ever imagined."

"Ever? My goodness, that does sound dire. Be assured, I shall forward your concerns to the appropriate authorities. And by the way, you were wise to show Fraulein Claudia the door when you did."

I didn't know whether to smile or object. What exactly did she mean?

I just wanted to keep on doing what I did best. At least I had gotten lots off my chest.

38

On May 5, 1931, a great hubbub erupted at Photohaus Hoffmann when Julius Schaub, Hitler's fawning adjutant, hobbled in for wedding portraits with his new bride Wilma on his arm. Once again Hitler was sequestered as best man and the whole staff were on tenterhooks. Hoffmann himself made a great show of recording the occasion.

I and several others took up discreet vantage points to watch the formal shoot from afar, being careful to remain beyond the line of sight of either the camera or the bridal Party. I was keen to see how the boss would deal with the groom's bulging eyes and awkward stance, the latter resulting from frostbitten toes suffered in the Great War. In the huddle, I suddenly noticed myself pressed between Claudia and Eva, who were also keen to observe the session.

To the best of my knowledge, the Salon Pussy incident had somehow been kept under wraps, quite an achievement given Eva's usual bitchiness towards the other female staff. "Oh, I do wish Adolph wouldn't look so stern and stuffy in photos; it is supposed to be a happy occasion," she remarked to no one in particular.

I was distracted by the unexpected and unwanted proximity of the woman who had again broken my heart; her bittersweet smell was causing my scalp to tingle. By the time I refocused on the wedding party, Hoffmann's formal session was well underway.

Immediately, I felt sorry for Frau Wilma, sandwiched as she was between a beaming husband and a scowling Hitler; she came across as drab and overawed. Both men stood proud in white tie and accessories, dominating the bride's simple understated gown.

Hoffmann directed the main light to be set at a high angle, throwing Schaub's pop-eyes into partial shadow, before going down on one knee to direct the groom's non-existent toes toward the camera. Eva, never one to be outdone, was clicking away over my shoulder in the hope of catching her beloved in an unguarded moment.

However, one presence only dominated my thoughts as we watched the bridal party filing out to their reception at Hitler's apartment in Prinzregentenplatz.

I found myself alone with the "Last Amazon", switching off studio lights and packing up props. I had rehearsed a hundred times what I would say when we inevitably crossed paths, but after an awkward silence Claudia was first to break the ice.

Lighting up a forbidden cigarette she purposely blew a smoke ring in my face and took a seat on the adjustable posing stool. "I thought you said you wanted to take a portrait of me? Well, now's your chance," she said calmly, catching and holding my eye.

"I … I didn't mean a studio portrait; that's far too formal for a free spirit like you, Claudia." Speaking her name again was like music in my ears.

"What exactly did you have in mind then?" she teased cruelly.

"Well … I envisaged something more natural; either in the English Garden or by the river … or both, if you prefer." I could hardly believe how she waved away my doubts and revived my pusillanimous heart with a single sentence.

"Well, why not tomorrow afternoon?" she continued. "I can skip Mass, and your Sunday workload is usually flexible." It was all happening too fast; after the countless hours I'd spent trying to wipe her from my mind, could she be just having a bit of fun at my expense, leading me on like she had those other men? I couldn't care less. None of that mattered now.

"Why don't I put a hamper together and meet you by the Prinz Carl Fountain at 2 o'clock sharp? If you're not there by ten past, I'll assume you've gotten cold feet," she added capriciously, blowing another smoke ring into the air above my head. The whole unfolding sequence seemed like a dream.

Sunday morning found me hard at it in the darkroom processing the Schaub wedding. I was a picture of energy and efficiency, humming away as I worked.

Up came the boss' formal negatives, perfectly exposed as usual, with several rolls of candids taken afterwards; I hung them carefully to dry and planned on returning to them that evening after the picnic. I would work right through Sunday night if necessary.

The appointed hour found me pacing in circles around the fountain pool with no sign of my date. Every minute seemed an hour. At five minutes past two precisely, Sissy alighted elegantly from a shiny cream Maybach Zeppelin Cabriolet, blowing a kiss to the driver over her shoulder; she approached with a welcoming smile.

"Here, carry this," she said, handing me a cane basket from which protruded the pink neck of a rosé bottle. "It's just so good to spend a little private time together, don't you think? Before I could reply she had taken my arm, leading me across the road and into the English Garden where we paused to draw in the fresh summer air, loaded as it was with bright sights and fragrances.

Clearly, hundreds of others had the same idea, and after being jostled by bike riders and promenaders, I watched in dismay as they spread out in every corner of the sunbathed manicured lawns. Claudia insisted on treating me to an "appetiser" at the Japanese Teahouse, after which we would search for a more private place.

"Blow this!" I exclaimed. "There're too many people here for my liking, come on, I know somewhere nearby." I took her hand with the picnic basket and we half-ran, half-skipped the several hundred yards toward the Isar's welcoming willows. Plunging down an embankment I pushed through the bright green foliage to emerge on my favourite sandspit, which I noted had changed shape during the spring freshets. We were alone at last, hidden from the public gaze and surrounded by water on three sides.

"Oh, how exciting, I've not been here before; never even knew it existed," she exclaimed breathlessly, obviously impressed. "How on earth did you discover such a place? It's so close to all the hustle, yet so remote …"

"Just the way I like it," I purred proudly. "I've been busting to share it with you, Claudia. When I first stumbled upon it in winter there were no leaves on the willows at all, something I'd not seen before. Now look at them!"

The willow tendrils nodded and dipped at the surface, brushed by a soft breeze. I spread my jacket in the sun and scampered to collect an armful of kindling. Soon the first thin wisp of smoke was rising in the air, I was surprised and pleased to have her all to myself. She seemed alive to the situation, humming an unfamiliar folk tune while carefully laying out a mini-feast of sourdough bread and cheese, sausage and berries. Two large slices of strudel rounded our fare.

We clinked glasses and I skewered several slices of sausage on a twig over the flames, evincing little squeals of delight. "Oh, dear Jungle Boy; it's true what they say, there's certainly more to you than meets the eye." Again I blushed, and for a while, we chatted easily about nothing in particular. I was determined not to allow any past doubts to muddy these tranquil waters.

After a second glass of rosé, I saw a cloud darken her brow and she fixed me with a straight eye. "I know in my heart that you would never say or do anything to hurt me Klaus, but there are certain things I cannot share." I had already stilled my expectations, not wishing to revive painful ghosts from the past.

"I know you suspect something of my double life away from the studio, but it's not what you think it is."

"Why? Why do you go along with it?" I blurted, "What sort of hold do these people have over you? I saw you at the Hofbräuhaus and then that sordid display at Salon Pussy … Eva saw it too!" I blustered. "Surely, you're too good, too special for that sort of …"

"Just shut up for a minute, will you?" she said, pressing a finger to my lips. Her high cheekbones glowed, and her eyes narrowed to green slits; it seemed minutes before she appeared to relax and take a deep breath … "There is something I will share, but if you ever disclose it both our careers, if not our lives, will be over." A pit opened up in my belly.

"Disclose what? What could possibly compel a girl with your strength of character to debase herself so?" My backhand compliment was ignored, as she leaned forward again to refill my glass, giving a sigh. "So … Eva knows too? Well, she's in no position to pronounce judgment on others, given her own stupidity in falling for a bastard like Hitler …" Again, I was surprised by her frank views of Eva's so-called affair, which somewhat coincided with my own, especially in daring to call Hitler a "bastard" out loud.

"That's no life, stuck beside the phone every night, dodging her father and waiting for calls that rarely come. And, all by choice! Unlike my own unsavoury entanglements …" She stopped herself mid-sentence. "Maybe I'll tell you all about it one day."

At that moment I knew I would never doubt her again. Perhaps unintentionally, she leaned her head against my shoulder and stared upstream, occasionally sipping on her wine. I hoped those moments would never pass, and despite my best intentions, words spilled out to fill the drowsy silence; there were just so many plans for the future I needed to discuss.

"You know, I'd do anything for you, Sissy? You just have to ask."

"Anything? I don't think so, I've heard it all before."

"Well, what I really mean is I care far more about you than those other oafs ever will …"

"Oh Klaus. I'm sure you mean every word you say, but you don't know shit from clay. You have no idea what you are up against …"

"B … But, I think I love you!" There, the words were out and there was no way I could take them back.

Her response was clear and definite; holding me off for the moment while still leaving room for hope. "Shoosh, little man; such talk of 'love' must be kept for another place and time. Let's just remain best of friends for now. I believe we share a special trust that goes beyond mere appearances, don't you? Do I have your word not to mention it again?"

Few sentences so completely crush a lovesick swain as when his intended declares her desire to "remain good friends for the time being". Claudia's honesty had once more left me high and dry as I imagine it had shattered the hopes of so many others before and since. That first picnic beside the Isar undoubtedly marked a turning point in our relationship, but not in the manner I'd hoped.

During the summer months, we sometimes slipped away together, safe in our secret sanctuary engaged in long discussions about work, politics, and hopes for the future. I discovered we shared a deep interest in Religion and Philosophy, and was astonished by her knowledge and curiosity regarding all things spiritual.

While she appeared to know little of Catholicism, despite attending Mass regularly, she seemed particularly enamoured by Sister Klara's "Whole of Universe" approach, and how it differed so markedly from her traditional upbringing. "In one way the Church rituals remind me of a God somewhere; they enable me to focus on Him while I'm going through the motions," she explained when I pressed her further.

"Ah, yes! But God is much more than mere ritual," I ventured, trying to sound convincing. "He is the motivating energy contained in every single atom, and the inter-connectedness between all living things." I had not been able to express myself so completely since those wonderful hours spent with Marty in *Sachsen*'s bow.

"Mind you …" I continued emboldened, "just when I thought I had it all figured out, along comes Einstein with his Theories of Relativity to throw a spanner in the works. For example, we might say that our Earth is spinning clockwise *and* anti-clockwise at the same time, depending upon whether you are standing at the North or South Pole. Is that 'Relativity'? I've also noticed that here in Germany the moon rises on the left and sets to the right, the very opposite of Brazil."

"I must admit I've never thought of it that way," she replied.

"So, you see? Nothing is *absolute*. It all depends on one's vantage point," I pronounced beaming. "Except for God that is everywhere and everything simultaneously. All religions have their preferred pathways toward Divine Atonement, 'At-one-ment', get it? And along the way, there are many traps and pitfalls. In the final analysis, each must discover the Truth within *himself*, with or without all those fairy stories being bandied about in Church."

I was flattered by her continued attention. "For this great task, we alone of all living things have been gifted with the so-called blessing of Free Will, which in my opinion, most of us misuse … that's my understanding of Relativity."

"Good heavens, that's quite a mouthful, and quite a theory; not a little daunting," she replied after a short pause. "Nonetheless, I'll take all the help I can get if it offers hope of one day being free. In Church they teach that 'Truth' will set us free, but where sits Truth here and now in a National Socialist world?"

"B … But, what about your family? Don't you have anyone in the Church you can trust or turn to?"

"Dear God, is he serious?" she said, rolling her eyes. "Can't you see? I can never be a part of their precious 'Aryan' family, bottle blonde hair or not. Studio Hoffmann *is* my family, and whether you know it or not it's your family too. National Socialism *is* Germany's new Religion. I've tried explaining Hoffman's sinister and wide-ranging motives but still, you don't seem to get it. People like

you and I have nowhere, and I mean nowhere, to turn. They are using us just
as they misuse every other person without connections …"

"B … But I've seen your influence around the studio, with Loth—"

"You've seen what they want you to see! Make no mistake, your turn will
come. Nazi disregard for individual expression runs right through society; and
I'm sorry to say, directly counter to your high-blown concepts of Life and the
Universe, as much as I'd like to agree with you …"

At this, she covered her face with her hands and stifled a sob.

I moved closer, feeling foolish and helpless, putting my arm around her
heaving shoulder. At that moment I loved her more than ever.

"Before long, Nazism will be the *only* religion in Germany," she sniffled,
"then every other form of worship, including yours, will be outlawed; it's just
so sad and inevitable." She dried her eyes and blew her nose on the clean hanky
I always carried in my left pocket. As long as we were close I didn't care.

One afternoon, following a particularly gruelling work session, we again found
ourselves on the sand spit in front of a crackling campfire, with time on our
hands.

We were exchanging frank opinions on our workmates, and National
Socialism in particular, when her voice trailed off and she moved closer. "I feel
so sorry and confused when deceiving you," she said at last, "so you might as
well know the truth."

Her brow knitted as if struggling to find the right words to begin. "When
I first arrived in Munich and met Hoffmann in '29, I thought I'd really landed
on my feet. The studio work was interesting, and he started introducing me to
the Nazi hierarchy, most of whose intentions soon became clear. When I began
protesting, he loosed his bloodhounds to flesh out my background … and that
was the end of my freedom, I fear forever."

I looked puzzled. "How? Why? Schicklegruber is a traditional Austro-
Germanic name, like Hahn." Again, there was a long silence, with only the
soft rattle of breeze in the branches overhead and the distant clamour of city
traffic. The resident grey heron landed nearby, eyeing us warily as I rose to
throw a handful of sticks on the fire.

"Yes, but Schicklegruber is only my married name; a good Austro-Germanic
name, granted, and for a while I got away with it. Believe me, there's more like
me that the boss has gotten his hooks into. There's poor Eva, the biggest fool of
all: she really scored the jackpot, or so she thinks … all thanks to Hoffmann's
scheming."

"Married name? What do you mean by 'married name'? Where is your
husband now?"

"He's dead! And a good thing too. At least he gave me a name I could live
with in Germany; for any Jew that's a golden asset." Her disclosure nearly
floored me, but the floodgates had opened. "It didn't take our wily boss long

to sniff out my secret, and now he has me right where he wants me. In case you haven't noticed, there're close to five million unemployed in Germany. Just try finding a job with a name like 'Globocnic', not bloody likely! Anyway, I'm already in too deep, I know too much."

As she relayed an account of her childhood growing up on a small Polish share-farm outside Lodz the facts she recounted were harsh and predictable, almost too painful to hear, let alone repeat. Her elderly parents were devastated when their precocious blonde, bright-eyed daughter was swept off her feet by the handsome German tourist holidaying next door, even more so when she married him in a civil ceremony just weeks later and moved away for a "whole new life" on his Family Estate in East Prussia.

Of course, the affair turned out to be a shocking misjudgment all around, when she soon found herself being treated little better than a serf. Unable to meet the family's strict Teutonic standards and loaded down with back-breaking chores, the new Frau was quickly put and kept in her place while Herr Schicklegruber, far from being the jolly adventurer, became violent and derisive toward his "Polish whore".

Two years later, when he was killed in a pub brawl she chose not to hang around and seek settlement but cut her losses and flee as far away as possible. She told her wide-eyed friend how she had landed in Munich with a single suitcase and a precious German Passport, where she was singled out with two other pretty country girls from the busy Bahnhof crush by one of Hoffmann's "talent scouts".

"Before I knew it I'd been allotted shared accommodation in a nearby apartment block owned by the Studio and gained a position at Presse Illustration Hoffmann under my married name." She closed her eyes for a moment and took a deep breath, "At first, we were decked out in the latest fashions and assigned as 'Escorts' for visiting Nazi dignitaries, and after what I'd been through it wasn't too bad. I soon learned to adapt. Thanks to that devious pig Göring and his Gestapo, Hoffmann now had his hands on my unfortunate ancestry. The rest, as they say, is history; from that day forward my 'duties' became more specific and less palatable. Now are you beginning to understand my situation?"

I felt sick and guilty, unleashing more pent-up emotion from my heart. "Dearest Claudia, none of that matters to me now; I will take good care of you. You could learn to love me as I love you. We could run away together and start over somewhere fresh, a long way from here, where we would never be found."

From her expression, I realised how foolish my desperate appeal must have sounded almost as soon as the words left my mouth, but I continued anyway. "I have relatives down south in the Alps, no one would know us there."

Again she raised a finger to my babbling lips. "Oh Klaus; you are the sweetest boy in all Germany but I'm afraid it's not that simple. Once you come to their attention they'll hunt you down like a dog. Running off with even a 'privileged Jew' would only compound your problems. Nowhere is safe; when are you going to get that through your soft, thick skull?"

It's impossible to describe my state of utter hopelessness at that moment.

With no clear way out, perhaps if I knuckled down and devoted myself to my printing something may yet turn up, as Mr McIver had taught me to hope: circumstances might take a turn for the better. But as usual, my discombobulation came to nothing.

39

It turned out that both Claudia and I were well wide of the mark in our assessments of Eva's true relationship with Adolph Hitler.

Sometime in late summer, sleek Mercedes convertibles began arriving at the Studio front door a few minutes before the knock-off bell sounded. Eva would skip downstairs in a fresh new outfit before boarding the chauffeured vehicle for the short ride home. By early autumn our doubts were further dispelled when enormous bouquets began arriving at the front desk, with Hitler's savage scrawl across the accompanying cards.

She adapted quickly to her new role as the "Führer's Girlfriend", strutting about filing her nails and now answering only to Hoffmann. Her elevated status soon became clear for all to see. Claudia and I sat beside the Isar one afternoon, discussing the obvious problems Eva seemed to be having with her father, who up until that point had been a rabid anti-Nazi. As we talked, I attempted to catch a snap of my friend unawares, against the festoons of golden foliage draping the riverbank.

"I'm telling you, when Fritz Braun found out the other afternoon that Eva had left early in a chauffeur-driven limousine no less, he hit the roof and demanded to see Hoffmann. I had to lie about the boss' whereabouts and pretend that the car had been sent to take them both on assignment. Herr Braun stormed off muttering something about no daughter of his getting mixed up with that bunch of murderers. Apparently, Eva had told him that her new film-star wardrobe was a bonus payment for all the 'overtime' she'd been working in recent months, but I could see he wasn't convinced."

Claudia shifted her position a little at my request, surrounding her head with more of the flaxen halo.

"All I know is she's grown three inches taller with her nose in the air," I added, "and I don't see the studio phone dancing off the hook as often as she likes to pretend."

"It's no wonder her father is spitting the dummy; some mornings she's still sound asleep on the studio couch when I clock on for the early shift. Surely the old man is awake to the number of nights she doesn't return home at all."

"Now, just lift your chin a little and turn your nose slightly left … Ah, perfect." My Leica flickered once and she pretended not to notice. In Claudia's company, I too was becoming a bit of a gossip.

When a bank of dark clouds threatened from the north, she suggested for the first time that we retreat to her apartment and complete our "makeshift meal" on the balcony, to which I replied that that might not be a very good idea.

"W … What about your roommates, won't they be put out? Will they assume things? Should we be seen together away from the workplace?"

She looked suspicious, but regained her verve. "What? Don't tell me you're getting cold feet already? Once Hoffmann found me out he became a very different kind of 'boss', even setting me up in a place of my own. He soon decided that casual arrangements were useless; he and his pals needed somewhere they could 'drop by at any hour' for a little cheering up. I feared the worst, but mostly I have the place to myself mid-week. I told him right from the start that I don't do gangbangs, but I don't mind being first prize in a raffle now and again; if that's what it takes to go on living in a place like this."

We had arrived outside a tidy three-storey but otherwise unremarkable terrace block and climbed a set of wooden stairs to the first floor. As Claudia reached for her key I saw a movement from the corner of my eye in the doorway opposite; a small, strange face whipped back out of sight.

"Hello," I said to the empty doorway, trying to look nonchalant despite my rising concern. Claudia looked up and gave a little laugh. "Oh yes, that's Pauli. He lives here too with his Mama. We're friends. He's frightened of strangers."

She unlocked the door and took my arm, brow creasing. "Please don't judge me, Klaus, that's how it's been for me ever since. Tonight, I've told them I'll be having a headache, so I'm not expecting any calls."

I'm not sure just what I expected, but the simple, tasteful décor set me immediately at ease; as we talked away it was easy to forget the underlying reality of her situation.

That night she made me feel like a king; we yapped our heads off on the balcony and lounged on the soft cushions within. By candlelight she looked even more ravishing, as do most of us I'm aware; I was transported back in a flash to another clifftop far away, and another special sunset. Her voice carried me off like music in sunshine and she became for a time almost a goddess to me.

"... and that arrangement provides many other benefits and protections, cementing my favourable position with the upper echelons of the Party," she was explaining. "What else could a girl do? Corruption is rampant at every level, with the boss himself leading the charge. He bows and scrapes shamelessly when Hitler's around, all the while filling his coffers at our expense ..."

Just then, a soft but urgent knock came to the door and she motioned me to remain silent, a slight look of annoyance crossed her face as she rose and moved swiftly to open it slightly. I could hear an animated male voice but couldn't make out the words. When she returned ashen-faced I knew it was serious. "Geli's dead! She's shot herself with Hitler's pistol."

"You mean his niece Geli, Eva's archrival?" I said stupidly, remembering that ebullient face and shock of curls I'd glimpsed from afar.

"I knew she was becoming desperate when I walked her home from singing lessons two days ago," Claudia muttered. "But this? Oh God, how many more must there be?" Her voice trailed off and I knew my time of reverie was at an end. I rose to leave.

"I'll find out what I can and let you know, this is really going to throw a spanner in the works," she said from the doorway, and once again I glimpsed a pair of tiny slits following my progress down the stairs.

Within days, Geli's "suicide" was all over the front pages, with many dark rumours surfacing over Hitler's "unnatural" relationship with his half-niece and his involvement in her actual death, given his own gold-plated Walther pistol was identified as the weapon involved.

Meanwhile, both he and Hoffmann had gone to ground; I found out only later of the agonising hours and days that followed. The boss had whisked him away from prying eyes to his own holiday villa, where the formerly unshakable Leader prowled up and down for days without sleep, muttering dark threats of revenge against persons unknown. He raved about giving politics away altogether and even of shooting himself.

The studio was abuzz with gossip over Hoffmann's absence, until the following week when I received a note from Claudia under the darkroom door, stating that she could meet me on Thursday afternoon following my delivery. "You know where!" it simply read.

By starting early each day I was able to wangle my workload and get away as arranged, finding her beneath the swaying willows warming her hands.

"Well, you certainly are a quick learner," I began, admiring my chuckling fire of twigs.

"I would not have survived this long if I weren't," she whispered, embracing me for several glorious minutes before turning away to stare at the embers. "In the end, there was absolutely no one Geli could turn to. She told me even her own mother sided with Hitler in his attempts to dominate her every move. Little else has been talked about in the days since."

"What did you mean when you implied there were others?" I ventured, curious to know more. A wisp of mist mingled with the campfire smoke rising in the autumn air.

"The word is there may have been at least two or three others previously," she replied, poking at the coals. "One actress, Renate Mueller, I think, threw herself out of a second-storey window after a brief encounter with our illustrious Leader. And look at those disgusting antics he had Henni, his 'little sunshine', perform. She blabbed about it non-stop to everyone, until Eva came on the scene, little hot-arse that she is. Teenage girls are rarely discreet. Then again, I'm sure there're plenty who would say the same of me …"

"B … But you're being blackmailed into it; you have no choice."

"And all with her father's blessing, I might add," Claudia continued, "it's no wonder the boss is trying to get his precious Henni married off to that faggot Schirach in a hurry. Oh, poor Geli, all she wanted to do was get out and have a bit of fun; Onkel Alf wouldn't even allow that. 'The things he makes me do, you wouldn't believe,' she confided on more than one occasion. If only I'd paid closer attention, but what more could I have done? Should I have tried harder to retrieve those pornographic sketches from Hoffmann's safe when she asked? Maybe that would have helped."

Responding to my blank expression, Claudia explained that Hitler, soon after "Geli" (given that affectionate nomenclature to distinguish her from her mother Angela) had moved into his Munich apartment, had produced a series of pencil sketches of the nubile young woman, some showing close-ups of her private parts as she squatted astride a glass-topped coffee table. The hapless teenager had further revealed that such intimate delving aroused Onkel Alf, and he would ejaculate without further contact.

When the envelope containing the drawings was stolen from the back seat of Hitler's limousine, he was forced to send one of his bodyguards to pay off the blackmailer; that was how they'd come to end up in Hoffmann's safe.

My friend was obviously troubled by the death of Geli. "She came several times to the studio, begging me to get them back but I failed to realise the extent of her distress. Oh Geli, poor Geli, having to be chaperoned by Hoffmann and those other Nazi boors every time she wanted a night out. And then, just when she finds true love in Vienna, she's suddenly dead!" Claudia seemed to be struggling to come to terms with Geli's failings, even seeking forgiveness for her own lack of resolution in the matter.

For a while the newspapers had a field day, stressing the point that Hitler's pistol had fired the fatal shot into her lung. There was speculation that she had been murdered and the gun planted beside the body, until certain newspaper editors suddenly disappeared behind Dachau's hungry walls.

My friend had no doubt that Geli herself had pulled the trigger, having hinted as much during their final meeting. Anyway, Hitler was supposedly hundreds of miles away when his car was eventually pursued and overtaken by Hess with the grim news. Apparently, discovering Eva's love letter in Onkel Alf's coat pocket was the final straw in pushing Geli over the edge.

"It's all very well for Putzi Hanfstaengl and his ilk to write her off as 'cheap and easy', but Eva Braun is in for a shock if she thinks she can ever fill Geli's shoes in Hitler's eyes. She'll be stepping into a void that no one's ever likely to fill. He was reportedly too distraught even to attend her funeral in Vienna, sending Röhm in his place. He told Hoffmann he is setting up her room in the apartment as some sort of eternal shrine," she gave another sniff, "… in a final rush of crocodile tears." Claudia was not holding back. "It's *his* jealousy pure and venal that destroyed her, make no mistake!"

She lit up a cigarette with shaking fingers and for a while, we both sat staring into the flames. My mind was once more overloaded.

When nightfall approached I walked her slowly back toward her apartment, all the while pondering the depths of her compassion. "You know, there's one question I've been dying to ask," I said, trying to lighten the mood. "However did all those Amazons vanish into such a tiny patch of jungle right before our eyes?"

40

As 1931 slipped again into winter's grip my workload increased accordingly, providing little time to frequent Munich's Art Galleries and other attractions.

One exhibition, however, drew me back several times to ponder a "modernist collection" featuring Franz Marc, Wassily Kandinsky and Max Beckman among others, with one whole wall devoted to the cutting incisive caricatures of Otto Dix. These artists, of whom I knew nothing from my art books, demonstrated to me for the first time the power of colour and line as emotional forces in themselves, open to differing interpretations from each viewer.

During one such visit, I was standing in awe before a huge Kandinsky, contemplating his seemingly unrelated blobs, dashes and daubs of colour, when it suddenly occurred to me that the whole painting was somehow perfectly balanced.

Nearby I overheard a group of Brownshirts berating the curator over the "pathetic, puerile and anti-social" nature of the exhibition which, they sneered, could have been done by "any six-year-old with one hand tied behind his back". They warned that the day would arrive when all such "degenerate" works would be consigned to the scrap heap where they belonged, or better still, "burned in the street".

I had read a plaque in the gallery that told how Marc, creator of some of the most beautifully coloured abstract horses I'd seen, gave his life for Germany in the Great War. I was deeply moved, imagining such a sensitive and creative soul huddling in a mud-filled trench, awaiting the inevitable. For a while the stormtroopers looked like they would tear the canvasses from the walls but thought better of it; contenting themselves with spitting on the polished floor and congratulating the jittery curator because he "wasn't a Jew".

Otherwise, my artistic and literary pursuits were confined to Studio Hoffmann's fine library, augmented daily by a copy of every German political publication and dozens of major overseas newspapers courtesy of the Foreign Press Bureau. Most nights, before retreating into my tiny den I flicked through the foreign news and was shocked by the many alternate views.

Besides keeping the Private Archive up to date and churning out countless postcards depicting the shenanigans of the rising brown tide, I was finally able to tackle the boss' "foreign orders" without blushing.

He had recently commissioned a series of bronze and plaster busts of the Great Leader, copyrighted of course, which were selling like hot cakes; while leather-bound, gilt-edged copies of *Mein Kampf* were also flying off the shelves; with over four million of the "must have" tomes already sold. As an extra personal touch, married couples would now find a facsimile stamp of Hitler's signature inside the front cover of their own edition.

Soon after moving into my cramped quarters I too found a volume outside my only door, but after several attempts gave up trying to understand what all the froth and babble was about. It seemed like one long rant and clearly, the author was no Homer.

I was learning to trust my own judgment in matters of art and literature, accepting the evidence of my own eyes when dealing with humans as mere "apes in fancy dress", as Sister had pointed out. Indeed, to this day I'm unable to witness someone eating a banana or a handful of peanuts without feeling a tinge of nostalgia.

It was about this time that Hoffmann went off the rails with jealousy, believing for the first time that his position as Official Reich Photographer was under threat. We had all heard the story of how he'd gained the Führer's undying trust in the earliest days, by voluntarily smashing a glass plate containing a "Hitler image" obtained surreptitiously at a time when the world's press was offering huge sums for a single photo, any photo, of the rising superstar.

The sneaky Hoffmann had snapped one without his patron's knowledge during a private function in his home, and by refusing to release it without Hitler's permission he endeared himself forever to the rising dictator. Or so he thought.

Now, out of the blue, Putzi the acting press secretary had arranged a private sitting for Hitler with Edward Abbe, one of the many famous photographers being despatched to Germany by the Western press. Adding insult to injury, Putzi made it known that he wanted to get away from the "ranting poses" of Hitler being churned out by Studio Hoffmann.

As things turned out Hoffmann's "ranting poses" were preferred by Hitler himself, and try as he may, Abbe could not get Hitler to relax, though he did manage to grab one or two profiles while his subject was distracted.

"I don't look like that!" declared the Führer upon examining Abbe's results, and of course Hoffmann too was dismissive. Poor Putzi, believing he'd shifted the tone of publicity to a higher, more approachable level, received nothing but scorn for his efforts. Heinrich Hoffmann, after that setback, soon resumed top billing in the eyes of the one opinion that mattered.

Meanwhile, our Munich Studio continued to expand and modernise; it seemed everyone who was anyone in Munich, or simply visiting, was lining up to be immortalised. For the first time, I was allowed to assist during indoor portrait sessions under Hoffmann's watchful eye, moving props, lights and backgrounds precisely as instructed.

His temporary dethronement seemed to have softened his tone, and he went out of his way to explain to me the techniques of photo-montage, where various images were masked off and superimposed to create more powerful and interesting covers for the *Illustrierter Beobachter* and other publications. Although not saying as much, he seemed pleased with my months of solid dedication to darkroom duties and "lack of distractions", as he put it.

In October 1931, he had me accompany him to a huge Nazi Rally in Brunswick, where 40 trains and 500 trucks had just deposited more than 100,000 loyal stormtroopers alongside ranks of newly outfitted SS Blackshirts.

During the spectacular event that unfolded, my doubts and cynicism over Hitler's stature were soon dispelled: the march-past took almost six hours, most of which time he stood with his right arm extended.

Later, he boasted to Eva of his ability to keep his arm extended and erect "almost indefinitely".

At a twitch from Hoffmann's silver horn, I scurried from each vantage point to the next, handing over one freshly loaded Leica and quickly changing film in the other. Not for a moment did I allow our camera bag out of my sight, and by day's end was "mother-henning" twenty rolls of 36. Never had I imagined that so many exposures could be fired off in such short order.

Afterwards, during dinner in the hotel dining room, I observed Hitler sitting back in an armchair with eyes closed, obviously exhausted after the extraordinary emotional spectacle performed in his honour. His adjutant Schaub and Hoffmann scurried about tirelessly, the former grinning excessively and the boss cracking smutty jokes designed to amuse and revive his expended chief.

Now and again Hitler would wipe away his runaway forelock or raise a teacup to his lips with a feminine-like wiggle of his little finger. I had heard that he was still in mourning over the loss of Geli, although this did not quite square with Claudia's revelations. Nonetheless, two hours after entering the darkroom next morning I placed ten proof sheets on Hoffman's desk, over which he briefly hovered before expressing his satisfaction with a grunt. The pressure was briefly off.

Not much later, Claudia and I were curious to visit Röhm in his new office, situated in the renovated Brown House off Königsplatz. At last, the Party could consolidate all its Munich portfolios under one roof, no longer having to squeeze in and out through the rear courtyard or front office of Photohaus Hoffman. Each of the top Nazi functionaries now boasted his own suite in the renovated three-storey building, thus eliminating most of the former foot traffic I'd had to endure overhead while trying to sleep.

As we strolled along together mainly window-shopping, Claudia took my hand for the first time in public and I was in no hurry to mount the two steps leading into the grand new Headquarters. Eventually and with great ceremony, we were shown into the Chief of Staff's highly decorated den, where it appeared we had taken a step back in time: there sat Röhm behind his huge oak-panelled desk covered in bric-a-brac, illuminated by a gold-plated desk lamp with fringed shade.

High walls behind him and to one side were completely covered in Renaissance tapestries, depicting Watteau-like scenes of elegant ladies wearing gleaming fabrics in shady glades. Poor Ernst's square face and full-dress uniform were almost swallowed up by the baronial scale of his surroundings; but the warmth of his smile as he rose to greet us, was unmistakeable.

"Well, what do you think? Some command centre, eh?" he exclaimed proudly, puffing up to his full height with arms akimbo. "Adi's responsible for the overall design, but I insisted on expressing my own personality in here." He waved his arms to left and right. "Anyway, how are you keeping, my little Polack beauty?" he moved toward Claudia and patted her playfully on the backside. "I hear you haven't lost the fire in your belly," he beamed.

"And I hear you haven't lost your bad habits either, Captain," she shot back, "despite all your fancy new surroundings." Röhm appeared briefly miffed, before giving a little snort through his shattered nose and squaring his shoulder boards. He fixed us both with a mischievous eye.

"Yes, yes, well enough of that: I've never yet won an argument with you, Sissy, and not likely to win one now. You know you can always turn to Onkel Röhm if you are in trouble, eh?" Her lips broke into a knowing smile but she made no reply. "And you, Jung Hahn; I hear you're winning all the medals in the photo factory."

"I ... er, not exactly ..." I stammered but was secretly proud he held this opinion. "If it wasn't for you, Onkel Ernst, I could never have obtained such a trusted position at the studio ... and, more importantly, I would never have met Claudia."

For a moment he looked puzzled, before holding up the newspaper he'd been reading. "Take a look at this headline: 'CATAMITE AMONG THE PIGEONS'? If it's not bloody Himmler spruiking the 'purity' of his SS, it's these bastard editors who'll stop at nothing to pull me down and spoil my fun."

A further glance revealed the offending article mentioned "certain letters" written by Röhm to a friend soon after his arrival in Bolivia in '28, lamenting "the shortage of suitable boys" which had only now surfaced. The article went on to describe his "well-known orgies" in Berlin's notorious bathhouses which were increasingly being viewed askance by the population at large, and by the many Party rivals who were jealous of his hallowed status under Hitler's wing.

"I know that Adi will always look after me: he'll see to it that things don't get too far out of hand. No one should forget that I've got a quarter million men backing me, every one of them just itching for a fight. I haven't come all this way to give up now on the Revolution." I noticed that he was still parting his toupee on the left and was possibly dying his schnurrbart dark brown.

When Claudia pressed him on the details of Geli's funeral in Vienna he sounded somewhat ambivalent, brushing over the details and grumbling that Hitler should have attended in person. "After all, it was him that drove her to it …" His voice trailed off and he avoided further questioning on the details of her death, or whether she'd been pregnant.

"Well, I've got work to do and no doubt you have also, unless I'm mistaken," he said, cutting us off short and rising to show us into the corridor without further ado, where I noticed again that the general décor of the Brown House was far more Spartan overall than his own bedecked bailiwick.

Later, both Claudia and I agreed that it was a little sad to see our proven warrior weighed down by such pseudo-opulence, "almost like a second-rate Napoleon". Nonetheless, we were pleased for him and grateful for his overarching protection, reminded that having a Nazi benefactor in high authority was a necessary surety these days. We further agreed it would be wise to allow our broader association to roll on much as before.

Shortly before Christmas, Hoffmann had to hurry off to Berlin for the marriage of Joseph Goebbels, the new Propaganda Minister, to one Magda Quant, a society divorcee.

Once again Hitler had consented to stand as best man and later, when Hoffman stuck his head in the darkroom to direct the printing of enlargements for the bride's album, he wanted to see if his clever ruse of hiding the groom's deformed foot in the fulsome folds of Magda's gown had worked. "You see my boy, how one can save the day with a clever pose here and there," he pointed. "Let the light be your friend."

I was flattered by his good humour as if a load had been lifted. Perhaps unwittingly he had echoed the words of Sister Klara; so prosaic yet so profound.

Eva joined us in the darkroom, eager to comment on Magda's outfit rather than those finer points of lighting I was struggling to grasp.

It was well-known that Hoffman's father before him was a renowned photographer of European nobility, even royalty, and that young Heinrich had grown into the job surrounded by the rich and famous. With the advent of National Socialism, he quickly saw his chance to move out from under his father's shadow.

While other press photographers struggled with their cumbersome large format cameras to grab a shot or two, young Heinrich and his 35 mm Leica were prowling unobtrusively about the fringes, catching dozens of candid moments. Because of my shy nature, this was an approach I greatly admired.

But for Eva, wedding photos were all about the latest fashions and accessories. She pressed for details of the colour scheme until the boss produced small swatches of material for the hand colourists to imitate. He contemptuously dismissed other "freelancers and their new-fangled colour films", whom he said were hounding his every public assignment.

"Oh, I think that style suits me too," Eva sighed, poring over Magda's gown. "Personally, I think long hair is more appealing on an older bride who's trying to look sexy, especially when she's a full six inches taller than her betrothed. I'm not at all sure about the wrap though; it makes her look like she's trying to protect herself from something or someone. I wonder who?"

She went on to reveal how Putzi had once glimpsed Goebbels' naked club foot on an occasion when he was changing his boots. Giggling uncontrollably she recounted the graphic details. "Putzi said it looked like a little pink hermit crab emerging from its shell, yuck! Hardly the Aryan role model he's always on about."

In the red glow of the safelight, I saw Hoffman smile. His sharp features looked positively demonic.

"Anyway, in my opinion, they deserve each other," Eva concluded, shuffling bottles of chemicals as if on a mission.

So far, I'd not yet formed a conclusive opinion of the Propaganda Minister, despite hearing his cynical pronouncements on a whole range of issues. That was until later when I heard him address a live audience with his powerful baritone voice dominating the diminutive figure behind the microphone. He waved his little fist and rolled his black eyes in a series of booming condemnations and appeals towards Heaven's great powers of destiny.

As a podium speaker, I quickly concluded that Dr Goebbels was second only to the Führer himself. None of this deterred me from producing two leather-bound, gold-embossed wedding albums featuring thirty sparkling 8" × 10" prints in each, one for the Minister and one for the Nazi archives. This was the first of many sittings I printed for the Goebbels family over the years, as one after another six delightful blond children arrived upon the scene.

At the approach of a second Munich winter, I was feeling more resigned, if not reconciled, to the vagaries and realities of my not-so-new occupation. My position in the darkroom seemed secure and I had discovered one or two more friendly faces among my colleagues; it's amazing how one can feel at home when receiving a smile now and then.

My photographs of notable buildings and scenic spots were well-received and Hoffman agreed to pay a small sum for the reproduction rights of any selected for postcards. Eva too was now receiving payment for her prolific candids showing Hitler's entourage and guests enjoying lighter moments of recreation. Her beau had recently presented her with a key-wind 8 mm movie camera "with which to amuse herself".

However, I began to notice distinct changes in her behaviour coinciding with the length of his absences and spasmodic attention. She would begin a conversation in which she had no real interest, or ask a flippant question before butting in with "Oh, it doesn't matter anyway" prior to receiving an answer.

She began throwing her weight around in all departments, especially when Hoffman was away. She was chain-smoking behind the front counter and I saw her pacing up and down after hours, awaiting the Christmas invitation that never came.

Finally, at 10 pm on December 24, Eva could delay no longer, picking up the direct line to Hoffman's house. "Frau Hoffman, it's me …" She nodded silently several times before slamming down the receiver and bursting into tears.

"Good God, what do I have to do? That bitch haunts me from the grave …" she moaned as I tried to comfort her. Through the sobs, I learned that "her Adolph" would not be attending Villa Hoffman or sharing in the Yuletide celebrations this year. He would be spending his Christmas Eve alone in Geli's bedroom at his own apartment.

"How long must I suffer this uncertainty? It's killing me. He's continuing to worship her like Madonna. He knows I love him more than anything on earth, yet he still sails along his merry way without a shred of commitment." Her voice had an urgent edge. "I tell you Klaus; if something doesn't change very soon I'll … I'll do something drastic, I swear, if that's what it takes to be noticed," she said before again dissolving into her handkerchief.

I knew she was referring to Geli's suicide. "Why? Oh why won't he call? I know I can make him the happiest man in the world, if only he would let me."

I had run out of platitudes.

That festive season Hitler rubbed more salt into her wounds by sending out distinctive black-edged Yuletide cards in memory of his departed niece. When Eva's family received one of these she was plunged into even lower spirits, given her father Fritz remained firmly anti-Nazi and flatly refused to allow her to spend a night at Hitler's apartment.

His schoolmaster mannerisms and strict discipline hung heavily over his three daughters, while Eva and Gretl being the youngest attempted to kick back assiduously against the traces.

Early in 1932, somewhat belatedly, Hitler embarked on a charm offensive in order to win over the Braun parents, sending enormous bunches of roses to Frau Franciscka (known to all as "Fanny") via his personal chauffeur, and urging Hoffman to include the pair in more functions involving studio staff.

Eva dared to hope that things might be turning around.

Around that time a pall settled over grander Nazi ambitions, when Hitler was narrowly defeated by Hindenburg in the Presidential elections. Furthermore, someone had the temerity to fire several shots at his motorcade as it sped through lower Bavaria, with no suspects being so far apprehended. Naturally, Eva was beside herself with worry at this turn of events, while Hitler merely brushed it off as "part of the job". Now she was spurred to capture his every private moment with her new movie camera using the latest Agfa colour film.

As the dreary winter of 1931–32 loosed its grip, Hoffman reluctantly installed a semi-automatic colour printer to cater for the burgeoning Nazi numbers and functions. As none of the existing staff had a clue about colour processing, he was forced to hire Hugo Jaeger to operate the complicated contraption.

Upon viewing the initial results Hitler declared that colour was the "future" of photography, though Hoffman himself was loath to cast aside the traditional methods. Eva had no such compunctions in deriding "single images that capture only one moment at a time" while snuggling up to Hugo with her undeveloped colour footage containing her beloved's private moments.

"Ah, yes, but doesn't that depend on *which* moment one chooses to capture?" I shot back when she tried to browbeat me with her latest results; alas to no avail. From now on it would be movie film, preferably colour, that would occupy her attention, and I saw less and less of her at the developing dish.

For his part Hitler continued running hot and cold with his affections; one minute showering the poor girl with gifts and attention, then foiling her presumptions with lengthy periods of absence and indifference. Predictably, she reacted with ever more flippant and frivolous behaviour, often changing her outfits and hairstyle several times each day.

No one but Hoffman dared rein her in, hoping to distract her by naming her "Project Organiser" for the annual staff picnic. This year it was decided that a full-day excursion to Lake Königssee would be a nice change from the boring nearby parks he usually chose in case something urgent cropped up at the studio.

As the day grew nearer Eva was delighted that we would be within a stone's throw of Hitler's holiday house, referred to by her as "Magic Mountain", perched as it was on a high undulation overlooking the village of Berchtesgaden and part of Lake Königssee. At the boss' insistence, she fired off extra invitations to Hitler himself, Fritz, Fanny and her sister Gretl, plus Ernst and Emilie Röhm, the latter declining because of her lack of mobility and her "wanting the young ones to be able to kick their heels up and enjoy themselves".

"That's just like her, always thinking of others," I told Eva when she popped her head in the darkroom door to advise me I would be in charge of "keeping everyone's glasses filled". I could see that she wanted the day to be a huge success and that Hoffman's ploy had not only had the desired effect but kept her out of our hair in the interim. The new man Hugo told me that he'd just about had enough of her pestering him to develop her colour footage, but had been warned by the boss to "just put up with it".

Eva wasn't really interested in anyone else's suggestions; if things went well she could claim all the credit and a certain person could hardly fail to notice.

During the six-hour excursion, I also was hoping to grab more than a few moments alone with Claudia. Most I spoke to had already put their hands up to hike the slope up to Lake Obersee for a light picnic, from there to take in the magic of the distant Röthbach Falls.

I could tell that Claudia was excited too; she whispered that the boss was turning on "a real Bohemian feast" while allowing Eva to believe it was all her own doing. Hoffman, Hitler and most of the older staff members would remain at the Alpengastalle Tavern, a short stroll from the ferry terminal, while the more energetic would take in the extra beauty spots. It all sounded very exciting.

Then, during the countdown Eva suddenly changed tack and began seeking input from one and all, in case there was something she had overlooked; I supposed it was all part of her coping mechanism. No one had any further suggestions given most of the details had remained "hush, hush" until the last moment.

The drive to Berchtesgaden was bathed in summer sunlight and I covered most of the one-hour journey with my nose pressed against the car window.

Throughout the launch voyage between the soaring grey walls of Lake Königssee, I tried to jockey closer to Claudia, in the firm belief that she would be as keen as I to share a quiet moment. Unfortunately, the constant "oohing and aahing" along with an incessant barrage of announcements over the loudspeaker precluded any meaningful conversation. I had a chance to take her elbow as we explored the cupolas of St Bartholomew's en route, but she pulled away when others came into view. I barely managed a dozen words before our steamboat sent a series of mighty trumpet blasts bouncing off the glaciated walls, to demonstrate their amazing acoustic qualities.

Back aboard, astern, making more noise than the rest of us put together, Röhm lounged. Instead of bringing Frau Emilie, he'd turned up with none other than Marty and Robert. I noticed my elusive brother chatting up a certain dancer from Salon Pussy and there was little I could do about it.

Hitler too was getting fidgety by the time we docked at the head of the lake beside a lush meadow rippling with wildflowers. I'd noticed through my lens that he'd remained tight-lipped in the bow for most of the voyage, gripping the handrail and staring straight ahead.

Once ashore, Eva announced that an ebullient Röhm would lead the 15-minute stroll to Lake Obersee, and soon the more lively among us were strung out enjoying the scenery. Several clicked away with cameras, aware that Hoffman and Hitler among others had remained behind at the tavern. At that point, there was no sign of Robert or Claudia who had gone on ahead.

Soon we arrived at a sumptuous buffet table laid out beneath a copse of shady trees and mossy boulders by the water's edge. Through the haze, a distant ribbon of waterfall waved back and forth in slow-motion, almost like a scene from a fairy tale.

I say *almost* because the day was balmy after a run of unseasonably hot weather, and before the rest of us had taken a bite, Röhm and his mates stripped off and charged into the freezing waters, hallooing loudly for the womenfolk to do likewise.

Alone among the straight-laced studio Frauen in their sun hats and high collars, I was shocked to see Eva and Claudia tear off their blouses and shoes with a wild yell and plunge in to join the three men sunning themselves on a floating pontoon offshore. With much laughing and splashing they taunted me to come on in, but I knew that the icy meltwater would have a catastrophic effect on my ability to breathe. How embarrassing to be rescued in front of everyone should I be foolish enough to even attempt it.

I took a plate of sandwiches and pretended to read my book, calling on all my resources to ignore the muffled squeaks and giggles emanating from the pontoon. Eva's feigned attempts at modesty caused much merriment and once or twice I caught the word "prudish".

The uniformed staff on hand kindly spared me the task of keeping everyone's glasses filled as I hummed a few vowels softly to myself and attempted to concentrate on my well-thumbed copy of the *Iliad*. Suddenly, I was tapped on the shoulder. "Come on old chap, this is not the time or place to be reading a bloody book!"

It was Marty, who'd towelled off and pulled on his shorts before dragging me reluctantly to my feet. His eye had a mischievous twinkle. "Let's grab a bottle of Chablis and take in the sights together." I rummaged for my camera and caught up with him farther around the narrow path, but not before glancing back to see Claudia having her back dried by Robert. Both were laughing as they dressed and she appeared to be having the time of her life.

I wondered briefly if Marty's invitation was a deliberate ploy.

"I've been thinking about what you said regarding the so-called 'Sanctity of all Life' and how it stacks up against National Socialist ideals," he began, as we strolled beside the wave-lapped gravel shore sipping our wine.

"Remember how we'd sit together in the bow of *Sachsen*, just the two of us, and try to solve the problems of the world?" He put a reassuring arm around my shoulder and steered me out onto a flat, protruding boulder, from whence we gained a perfect view of Röthbach Falls in the distance. I began feeling a little less peeved and clamoured down to include the mossy waterline as the foreground in a full panorama.

Marty raised his voice to continue. "I mean, your notion may be correct in an ideal world, but until we get Germany sorted out it will be one long struggle rooting out those cancers gnawing at the body of the Volk; by that, I mean anyone not giving his all to the Movement."

"I daresay that includes the Jews then," I prodded. "They seem to be persecuted simply by being born into that particular religion."

"Religion, don't you see? It's more than mere religion; they're a whole bloody race of parasites. It's all about the *differences* between races and how the scourge of Judaism has corrupted mankind's progress for long enough. At last! Germany has provided a saviour to lead us forward and rid us of wrong thinking." Marty's eyes were aflame, and I was hard-pressed to counter his zeal.

"But he's *Austrian!*" I blurted. "What gives him or anyone else the right to condemn a whole race of people who have existed for millennia?"

For a moment he looked stunned; I knew I had him.

"Th … That's just the point," he stammered, "Enough is enough!

"If the Leader *sees* himself as Aryan, that's good enough for me."

"Many of these Jewish families also see themselves as German. They've lived in Germany for generations; thousands died defending this country in the Great War. Are these well-known facts irrelevant to you Nazis? Surely you can't …"

"Don't try and muddy the waters. *Now* is the time for all Germans to rise and do something under a leader who's not afraid to make the hard decisions. Of course, everything is relevant; we are just lucky to have been *born* Aryan."

"Speak for yourself, I'm half-Irish. It's funny how you are happy to bend the rules when it suits your argument. Any of us could have been born so-called 'inferiors', and then I daresay you would hold a different view."

"Well, at least the Irish are true Aryans in the making," he replied without conviction.

I paused to let my own words sink in. "Try looking at it this way Marty, what time is it?" He looked at his watch, puzzled. "Half past twelve."

"Are you sure? Are you quite sure?" I was emboldened and could see that Marty was annoyed by my pedantry. "As sure as I can be about anything," he answered as shot a glare.

"Well, how about Paris or London? What about Rio or Sydney, Australia? At any given moment, the planet experiences all 24 hours, all 1,440 minutes of each day, *simultaneously*. So it all depends on just where one stands in space as to how one experiences time. It's all relative, right?"

"I guess so, but *I'm* dealing in the here and now; I can't see the point you are trying to make?"

"I'm simply attempting to highlight that National Socialism's 'One Size Fits All' mantra merely abets the hateful vision of a single man, and a non-German at that, being shoved down the Nation's throat. The entire concept as I see it can only triumph if those perceived as weak or of lesser merit are forced to blind obedience, trampled underfoot along the way. For what? The benefit of a few clever bullies? We both know that most of mankind's maladies could be healed overnight if everyone acted according to conscience ..."

"I know no such thing! Until all foreign influences are expunged from the National Body, Germans can never be free. Hitler is promising to purge the Reich of all impure influences and return the Volk to ..."

"Blarney!" I blurted. "How is this so-called perfect society to be achieved without imposing untold misery on millions? It seems to me that your 'Germanism' is only a convenient label denying the *relative* values of anyone who's different by birth or desire. By ignoring the relativity between individuals, you are ignoring Einstein's greatest discovery ..."

"Einstein? Give me a break! Just one more Jewish Bolshevist trying to bamboozle us with fake science. Then there's Freud, Marx and that whole black tribe coming at us from all directions. Well no more. Good riddance, I say! The Americans are welcome to him; we'll deal with the rest ourselves."

I'd never known Marty so vehement and single-minded, and hesitated for a moment before venturing. "Remember that light is invisible until it bounces off something solid; a bit like God's whispers, I guess."

"What's that supposed to mean?"

Just then the lunch bell tinkled in the distance and under the circumstances I felt it useless to pursue Sister Klara's metaphor of reflective minds generating their own light in the darkness. By the time we rejoined the party, Ernst was tucking into a platter of pickled quail's eggs and I was disheartened to see Claudia daintily nibbling at a bratwurst, the other end of which was firmly held between Robert's perfect teeth. The city Frauen had loosened up considerably, charmed by the combination of scenery and Chablis.

I hung back, picking listlessly at the loaded table, glancing about now and then but otherwise relying on my peripheral vision for amusement. I spent the remainder of the afternoon in low spirits; otherwise, it was a merry group that wandered back over to the tavern in time for formalities.

"For God's sake Klaus, grow up; there's nothing to it. I'm sick of you spying on me," Claudia whispered through gritted teeth when joining me in a patch of mountain daisies as I photographed the cliffs in the distance. I made no answer.

"Can you ever imagine you and I not being friends? ... I bumped into Bobby at the club and he just wants to get to know me better, that's it in a nutshell; he is your brother, after all. There's nothing wrong with that, is there?"

"Half-brother," I replied. "And did he?" I asked forlornly.

"Of course not, silly. No man gets to know *me*," she added as we briefly crossed glances. "Now come along and join in the fun, it's the biggest night of the year for all the staff." She reached to help me to my feet, her grip was firm and sure.

"B ... But, you don't know what he's really like," I said petulantly. "H ... He *hates* women ... and he's deceptive. Like today, getting me out of the way with Marty so he could have my girl all to himself. And ... and he's a murde—"

"Your girl, ooh la la! Whatever gave you that idea? Just know that we are friends, special friends, but that's all it will *ever* be. Meanwhile, I'm going to have all the fun I can in this shitty world. Don't be so judgmental towards your only brother. I'm quite capable of deciding who I spend time with ..."

"W ... What about *our* plans together? I mean making art together. Don't you feel that one day you might want more than friendship with someone like me? One who adores you and worships the very ground you walk on ...?"

Her green eyes popped. "Just talk. You see what you want to see. I do love you in my own way, poor sweet thing, as I love many others, but there's love and then there's Love ..."

Up ahead strode the tweed-wrapped barrel of Ernst, with Marty and Robert in lockstep. Robert, like his mentor, was fashionably attired in plaid knickerbockers with bright red braces and socks, sporting a game-keeper's hat.

"Those Frenchies need to be put in their place," I caught a snippet of their conversation, but Claudia hung on tightly for a while as we strolled.

"Your brother is quite a character. Tell me, why is it you two don't see eye to eye?" she probed. "I can't see why the three of us shouldn't spend more time together."

But I had decided to keep deeper feelings to myself and was glad when we melted into the crowded tavern, just in time for dessert and speeches.

Those staying behind had enjoyed a meal of local fish, game and produce, being entertained with non-stop folk dancing in the beer garden. I noticed Eva too had slipped into her dirndl for the occasion and was doing her best to catch Hitler's drowsy eye.

He sat stiffly at the head table with Fritz and Fanny on one side and Eva and Gretl on the other. As hostess and "sole organiser", Eva was trying to put on a brave face before her family and colleagues, but it didn't take Claudia long to discover the source of her apparent distress. Sometime during the afternoon Hitler, within earshot of all, had loudly proclaimed that a great man should always take a foolish and simple woman for a mate so that there would be no possibility of her impinging on his thought patterns. He'd then compounded the slight by repeating his claim that Germany Herself was his one and only bride.

I held a mental picture of poor Eva cringing under such utterances before her family and the staff, having to go on pretending that it was all just so much talk.

Another glass tinkled; one by one Lothar, Iris and other Department Heads rose with much hand-wringing to laud the achievements of their "famous boss", and to further state what a pleasure and privilege it was to see "our number one patron" joining in the staff picnic today.

Then came Hoffman with a bleary but practised response, thanking his "Great Leader" and "this loyal staff" before reminding them that this was only the beginning of the great successes we shall all reap under the Führer's guidance.

Then, to Eva's great relief, someone outside pointed to the dark clouds forming on the surrounding peaks, and a phone call came through warning of deterioration on the morrow. It was decided that the sleepover should be cancelled and that we would be heading back to the pier sooner than planned. Excess baggage would be forwarded on the next available ferry. A rousing rendition of the "Horst Wessel Song", led by Robert, echoed from the sheer grey walls as one by one the stragglers headed downhill.

Being first through the door, I strolled the last few hundred yards constantly distracted by patches of scenery that caught my eye. Shafts of afternoon light broke through the thunderheads to splash fiercely off the rumbling grey rock walls. For scale, I chose one angle showing two tiny human specks on the pier in the lower frame, where even the launch looked like a toy bobbing on the black water.

I sat down on a wooden bench, waiting and hoping for one supreme moment to take my photo. Behind, I heard the crunch of heavy footsteps on the gravel path and the lilt of conversation: it was Obersturmbannführer Röhm, cap askew and clearly under the weather, flanked and propped up by Marty and Robert, both of whom were also stepping high. Claudia tagged along behind, barely giving me a glance. I pretended to be adjusting my camera but could not help feeling foolish and rejected.

Röhm was slurring and appearing to enjoy his beefy supports. "… I've been trying to tell them for years, but the bloody fools won't listen … Röhm. The Law is an ass, and I'm gunna change it. Boys are great fun to play with; who says I shouldn't? Everyone should try it, eh?"

I imagined that both men had heard all this before, nonetheless surprised that he was endorsing the topic so publicly. Then, he went even further, and I looked around hastily to see if anyone was listening. "I'm awowed to play with Wobbie's little pee-pee," he lisped, "but the Law says I'm not awowed to kiss it. What sort of Law is that? Thank God for bathhouses!" At that moment Robert's eye caught mine and he flushed; I knew that Claudia had seen him, too.

"Don't worry, Goebbels is the expert in such matters. He says that if you repeat a big enough lie over and over it will eventually be picked up and accepted by the masses. Mind you, I can't stand the little bastard; wouldn't trust 'im as far as I could kick 'im …" Their words faded as they continued downhill toward the jetty.

Lastly, after settling the account from a pocketful of cash, Hoffman came hurrying along the path looking much refreshed, in deep conversation with Fanny and Fritz Braun, ever the schoolmaster. Eva's father was nodding constantly and taking notes, while Fanny, a picture of dutiful Germanic motherhood, followed one step behind in a huge sun hat trying to catch snippets of the men's conversation. A further step behind, and my heart sank to see, was the drooping figure of Eva shuffling along, being consoled by her sister Gretl.

At the five-minute whistle, all but me picked up the pace: I was hopeful that the newly conquered sun may break through one more time for a postcard.

At the two-minute whistle I gave up and scurried toward the anxious craft, clamouring aboard between thin lips and glares of reproval from Iris and the other senior Frauen already seated, only to discover that the one remaining vacant seat was between Marty and Lothar.

I squeezed in as we pulled away from the shore; an announcement was made that the fortune-telling astern had been cancelled. Further along, Röhm could be seen stretched out, snoring his head off and taking up a whole bench. In a far corner, Robert and Claudia had again ended up side by side.

I tried in vain to attract her attention, standing up to lower a side window and pretending to catch the evening light. This drew savage protests from those who "felt the cold", meaning my snaps had to be rushed. I returned to find Lothar's briefcase occupying my place and had to ask permission to sit there.

A whisper passed around that Hitler had left straight after the speeches on a high-speed SS vessel. From my stuffy position, I could see only the back of Robert's animated head and Röhm's heaving torso. When we finally pulled into the main wharf, I was in no mood to capture the quaint wooden boatsheds opposite.

Dragging my gear to the waiting vehicles a few heavy spots of rain peppered the back of my neck. Later, climbing into bed, my last memory of the staff picnic was having witnessed Claudia kissing Robert on the lips as we disembarked.

Yet miraculously, it seemed not all was lost: my photos of Lake Königssee found favour after publication in the staff newsletter, and Hoffman offered 50 marks for the reproduction rights. Eva, in true Eva style, came bouncing back into our lives as if nothing more could possibly go wrong. No one but me suspected that she had one foot in Paradise and one in Hell. Her footage of the Führer's private life was taking the pressure off Hoffman to be always in attendance.

Both she and Claudia soon stopped making fun of my accent and seemed to be treating me with more respect. At last, my photos were finding a wider audience; this took my mind off the hopeless longing for something I could not have. The staff picnic had marked that last link in a chain of hindsight realised only later.

Word spread quickly that Hitler in a fit of rage had sacked his half-sister-housekeeper Angela, and she in turn let fly with her opinion of Eva Braun, whom she labelled as among other things, a slut. She blamed her half-brother for Geli's death and immediately foresaw Eva's moves to enhance her own role in trying to fill Geli's shoes. The pestering late-night phone calls had driven Angela to distraction and a deep desire for revenge. Without her cuddly daughter around as a foil, things were bound to come to a head.

Eva, for her part, felt that a great obstacle had been removed; with both women now gone, the way ahead seemed clear. She wore different perfumes to work each day and made the stringers guess which was which. In fine weather, she would pedal home to change outfits during extended lunch breaks, "in case you-know-who drops by later". In fact, she considered herself something of an expert on odours and attempted to pinpoint wayward fragrances and colognes; look out if anyone exuded an unpleasant body odour. She even badgered me into wearing a French anti-perspirent.

Despite these many distractions, the coals of jealousy glowed bright behind Eva's eyes, on some occasions more intently than others. Full of hope she'd jumped at the chance to join Hitler's Party for the Bayreuth Festival, only to watch on as he was seated beside Frau Winnifred Wagner herself during every single performance. Worse, Adolph alone was the personal guest of Frau Wagner in nearby "Wahnfried", the great composer's former family home. Gossip had them walking together in the moonlit gardens, after which "Winnie and Wolf" was touted in the gossip columns as a possible item. Other photos appeared of Hitler with the starlet "Mimi' Reiter on his arm and someone pointed out the imposing English interloper, Lady Unity Mitford, who made no secret of her infatuation and intentions for the Great Man.

Eva fumed that the British blabbermouth was everything she was not: tall, aristocratic, long-legged, socially adept and politically attuned. She had arrived in Munich with her sister and glowing letters of introduction to the very highest National Socialist leaders. More rankling was the heavy makeup she plastered on, including heavy eyeshadow, the very opposite of what a "pure and natural" Fraulein should be aiming for.

Strangely enough, and counter to stated Nazi ideals, Hitler seemed fascinated by Fraulein Mitford's distinctive demeanour, having long dreamed of an alliance with Great Britain.

She towered over him as he offered her the choice of four apartments and a pistol for protection. When settling on one nearest the English Garden she had a tearful interchange with the Jewish owners, whom she scolded mercilessly – "What horrible curtains. They will have to go." – before unpacking her considerable baggage train.

Adding to Eva's woes, Henni started bringing in every newspaper clipping relating to Hitler and other women. Perhaps these were veiled warnings from the now-married Frau von Schirach concerning the regime's "Rising New Man".

Although Henni's wedding had been a low-key affair (and Hitler and Röhm were both witnesses), it boasted an Honour Guard of flag-carrying Hitler Youths. When printing the photos I couldn't help noticing that Henni looked a little less vivacious beside her aristocratic and supremely confident, if slightly effeminate-looking husband, now Head Boy of the entire Youth Corps. She lost no opportunity to tease Eva with gossip and a flash of the rock on her finger.

I never knew whether this teasing was the key that opened the floodgates just a little, but the irrepressible "Little Evi" began hinting that her own relationship had moved beyond the platonic stage. Soon after she confided that she and Adi had "gone the whole hog". She seemed resolved to do whatever it took to hover in the rarefied air of her hero and was convinced that if he could, Hitler would one day tie the knot.

When revealing all this to me over a tray of developing prints, I was concerned about her naive lack of restraint, as if she had nothing at all to lose. It was a complete about-face from her lament weeks earlier when she'd regaled my ears with a teary recital of her lover's "many bad habits", such as lack of punctuality or not turning up at all.

Since then, when rocks were thrown during a "Führer Speech", one even grazing the side of his head, these sins were soon forgiven.

It no longer mattered that he "worked 20-hour days, seven days a week for weeks on end", or that he rarely kept his word. So long as her man was safe my anguished workmate seemed prepared to "cop it on the chin".

One afternoon I found her in deep discussion with the new Frau Goebbels at the front counter on the merits of reincarnation, a subject clearly dear to the Propaganda Minister's elegant wife.

"I daresay one would not wish to come back as a frog," Magda was saying, "But, then again, when one looks over the ranks of the S.A. one may have second thoughts …" she sniffed at her own joke. Eva went on gift-wrapping the framed wedding portrait, already resenting Magda's superior attitude and social standing. When Frau Goebbels implied that from now on she would be personally attending to the Führer's Social Programme and other cultural engagements, Eva had a job controlling her temper.

The elder matron continued to boast that her husband was enjoying great success in whipping up the masses and redirecting the storm of S.A. violence against perceived political enemies and anyone else who did not immediately bow down. "Why, one traitorous young 'Bolshevist' has been trampled to death in the street in front of his mother, until finally, Hitler was forced to call for a halt to the excesses," she said without regret. As the story went, Hitler had stormed down the corridor of the Brown House to deliver a two-hour rant on Röhm's tactics and conduct.

The "machine gun king", however, was not so easily cowed and loudly ridiculed his former subordinate for "going soft" on the revolution and seeking too much power for himself. "Don't forget who put you there," Röhm had reportedly warned the uppity former corporal, and in so doing sealed his own fate. According to Robert who was nearby, Hitler exploded over Röhm's "perversion" now being out in the open and giving a free kick to all the major news outlets: he would not stand for it!

It appeared that Hitler's pretence of gaining power through "legal avenues" was clashing head-on with his old comrade's tried-and-true tactics of mayhem and atrocity, the more the better.

His newly minted prudishness over Röhm's sexual peccadillos in the ranks had exactly the opposite effect to that intended. The S.A. Commander dug his heels in defiantly and refused to commit to toning down his behaviour. An uneasy truce ensued, setting the stage for further discord down the track.

Meanwhile, Hoffman, in a belated attempt to jolly Eva, installed her in a new office next door to his own on the first floor and placed her in charge of the sacred "Hitler Files". I was commandeered to help her move the bulging filing cabinets from his office into hers, and to explain the cataloguing system fully. Here it was hoped she could rifle through the historical records of her fiancé's achievements, enjoy privacy on the telephone and be able to sleep over on her own settee when necessary. From this office, she could project more power during the boss' long absences.

At first, the move appeared to be working; Eva came and went at a frantic pace, relishing her new freedom and authority. She found some distraction during Octoberfest, but it was obvious to all that her every waking moment was consumed by unrealistic expectations of the life ahead by *his* side. I now saw her far more often, given we were now neighbours much of the time, especially since the onset of cold weather rendered the Isar unappealing. I'd not heard a word from Claudia in weeks; all my enquiries were met with blank faces or knowing smirks.

One evening at closing time, Eva called down for me to join her in her new office. Putting aside my book I bounded up the stairs and through the open door, where my senses were once more assailed by a toxic haze of cigarette smoke and strong perfume. There she reclined with stockinged feet up on the desk, a half-empty bottle of champagne and a plate of strawberry pastries from Café Stefanie downstairs. I was transported immediately back to Flamingo Villa. By her manner and the size of the desk, a stranger might well have taken her to be the owner.

"Sit down!" she ordered without shifting in her chair. "Have a cigarette," she said, slurring. "Oh, I forgot, you don't smoke, do you? We're so fucking pure, aren't we?" She stared blankly, as if waiting for a response, then reached forward to fill a second glass; I could see her makeup was smudged from crying. I too was keen for a bit of company and hoped she would soon get over her initial cattiness. We clinked and toasted the Führer with a faraway look in her eye, before tossing down the remaining Dom Perignon '24.

She flitted from subject to subject and I pretended to be interested before we settled enthusiastically on photography in general. I commented on how the winter light was better for portraiture, owing to the low angle of the sun. She wanted to know why the sun casts fainter shadows of objects closer to it. "You can easily prove the phenomenon to yourself," I suggested, "by observing any telegraph pole or tall tree."

"What the hell does that mean?" Clearly, she wasn't listening, rolling her eyes and forcing a clown smile while playing with her hands in her lap. Suddenly, she looked up and asked, "Tell me, Klaus. Would you still love a woman who couldn't satisfy you fully?"

I blushed and thought of Claudia. "I ... I guess it all depends on the woman and the circumstances," I stammered evasively, not at all sure to whom she was referring.

Another cork popped and she leaned closer to refill my glass. "If I tell you something just an itty bit personal, will you promise not to laugh?" I squirmed a little, aware that her confidence had a lot to do with the Dom Perignon. Her expression softened to near pleading. "H ... Have you ever heard of a 'Mouse's Ear'? No?" She paused uncertainly.

"Well, it's a condition when certain girls have a particularly small opening in a certain place, if you get my meaning." She gave a little giggle. "They aren't able to do *it* properly. Mind you, that doesn't mean they don't *want* to, but it's just not physically possible without considerable pain." She sat back munching on the last strawberry tart, awaiting my response.

Now it was my turn to fidget. I assumed she was referring to herself as one of those madels with a "small opening", and wrestled with the knowledge that it seemed no time since she'd been boasting of "going the whole hog" with Adolph. Both versions could hardly be true.

She lit up another cigarette and I felt myself getting quite lightheaded. "If it makes you feel any better Eva, I know how you are suffering. I too am unlucky in love, unable to consummate my own desires with a special lady ..."

"What? You're not still on about Sissy the Heartbreaker, are you? Yes! That's her nom de plume; every horn-bag in Munich knows it, except you."

She noted my astonishment and gave a nasty little laugh. "Don't tell me you haven't heard? Don't you know anything? Your lady-love may well enjoy Hoffman's protection, but she doesn't fool me. How dare you compare your tawdry little infatuation to *my* suffering?" she snorted.

I confess I was stung by Eva's callous attempt to twist the blade of her own jealousy between the ribs of my emotions, almost firing back that she should be the last person on earth to claim the moral high ground.

Nursing my chastisement I rose to leave, glancing back to see only an image of unrequited despondency: there she sat frozen in place with chin in hands; beside her sat a second empty bottle and an unlit cigarette hung from the corner of her mouth.

Thinking back, I both pitied and detested her at that same moment. As I lay in my bunk at the end of another crushing day, my breath came in short gasps, probably from breathing in all that smoke.

41

"Eva's dead!" The cry raced through the studio like wildfire. "Shot in the neck!" It seemed impossible; who would dare to shoot the Führer's girlfriend?

And then came the whispers: Eva herself had pulled the trigger using her father's revolver. With relief all around, we learned the slug had missed her heart and carotid artery, nonetheless forming a large pool of blood when her sister Ilse had found her on the bedroom floor.

Has she allowed her envy of Geli and the others to turn the gun on herself? That was my first thought upon hearing the shocking news. We'd exchanged greetings only the day before, October 31, when she'd appeared normal enough.

Nonetheless, the doctor declared that she had indeed intended to kill herself, and the note she left had spelled out her despair.

Hitler came racing to her bedside bearing huge boxes of handmade sweets and making all sorts of promises; it appeared that her dance with death had paid off. As her wound slowly healed he bought her a pearl necklace to cover the scar, and indicated that his new housekeeper, Frau Winter, would be more amenable to her telephone calls in future.

Furthermore, he had already despatched Hoffman to purchase a suitable cottage for the exclusive use of the Braun sisters, a task soon accomplished.

Hitler now insisted that she spend fewer hours behind the counter and more time with him at his mountain house on the Obersalzberg.

An astonished Eva was assured that she could pursue her hobby of photography and be perfectly free to come and go as she pleased. He would build her a suitable darkroom with the finest equipment and she could call on whatever assistance she required from Studio Hoffman.

How could any young madel say No to an offer like that?

There was but one tiny hiccup in the perfect scenario, one so crushing as to send Eva again spiralling into the depths of uncertainty. In blunt terms, Mountain Gauleiter Bormann laid down the law that she would not be permitted to appear at the Leader's side during any public function, and her discretion at all times on Magic Mountain must be absolute. During V.I.P. and Party functions, she would confine herself to the upper floors.

To ease her loneliness and pass the time, she would be permitted visits from girlfriends and Hitler enquired if she would like a cute little dog. It seemed she had survived only to find herself in a gilded cage, or in her case a choice of gilded cages, all linked to the whims of the man at the top.

By December '32, all Germany was looking for a saviour, and a goodly portion of the population believed they had found him.

Hitler was again railing against "Rotten Parliamentarianism" and vowing to stamp it out employing all necessary modern tactics. He was helped along by a besotted Dr Goebbels and his thundering Propaganda Department. Every home and workplace could now afford a "People's Radio" receiver, through which Nazi mantras of ridicule and revenge reached into every kitchen.

Rival publications were shut down or smashed up, and Party polling indicated that electoral success was just around the corner. Events were unfolding quickly as the Nazi juggernaut rolled on. It seemed that every time I poked my head around the darkroom door I was playing catch-up in a miasma of confusing demands struggling for supremacy.

Above all else loomed one doughty doppelganger calling the shots and pulling the strings; with his personal photographer tagging along to record each glorious moment. As a consequence, not much of the supposed "new order" rubbed off around Studio Hoffman; if anything, my workload was becoming more hectic and disjointed. Two more photographers of growing note were hired, August Kling and Otto Wurm, but no extra printer to handle the plethora of parades, speeches, and inductions, over most of which the boss held worldwide publishing rights.

Robert had returned from a two-week course at "Nazi Speakers School" with half a plum in his mouth and was now conducting his own classes of up to a hundred stormtroopers. He acted coy and evasive when I caught up with him in the Brown House, insisting that he'd not seen Claudia "in weeks". I left dissatisfied, taking grudging comfort alone by the Isar every chance I got.

It was a new Eva, much recovered, who moved back into her own office where she could hardly wade through the bouquets and stuffed toys surrounding her desk. Refusing to discuss details of the shocking deed, she instead prattled on about her high hopes for a career in the movies.

Such a step would require the acquiescence and dubious support of Joseph Goebbels, who did not yet hold quite all the reins of German film production. Eva felt she had a foot in the door since discussing her chances with the "Goat of Babelsburg's" wife, already pregnant with the first of his five children. This nickname, together with "Black Dwarf", was well-entrenched among the litany of starlets who had unsuccessfully auditioned for a starring role on the Propaganda Minister's casting couch.

Frau Magda, not to be outdone, was rumoured to be overly friendly with a certain blond and blue-eyed SS officer, all the while consolidating her position as Hitler's "social secretary". On one occasion she demonstrated her absolute loyalty to the Cause by mounting the speakers' rostrum beside her husband and declaring, "The worst German Prostitute is better than any so-called 'respectable' Jewish mother."

Eva fumed when recounting Magda's public tirade, adding cruelly, "Well. I guess that lets *you* off the hook."

The Goebbelses weren't the only high-level Nazis to notice Eva's growing influence, those selected few on Hitler's staff who even knew of her existence thought her uppity, scatty or froward, whereas many of the studio clients saw only sweetness and light, especially following "the incident".

Bruckner, Hitler's looming man-servant, called her a "quiet, stupid cow" behind her back, only to fall all over her like a puppy when he found her and the Chief together. By now, I felt I'd probably witnessed and survived more of her moods than most. It no longer seemed to matter that her true love was mostly away in Berlin, so long as he phoned every night and took her on slow drives through the countryside when visiting Munich, although, of course, he didn't get behind the wheel himself.

In fact, it was during one of these late-night calls that Eva encouraged him to face up to certain unrest brewing in Berlin. "It is always darkest before the dawn: Things always look better in the morning."

I overheard her reminding him on the telephone, hinting that it would be "cowardly" to avoid his customary swift and decisive response. "It's better that ten thousand others should perish than a single hair of your head should be harmed," she told him. She was certainly gaining in confidence, and together with Gretl was becoming a hot item on the dance floor. These days there seemed to be one social event after another, although Eva particularly had to take it easy under the watchful eye of Himmler's liaison officer.

All this Nazi socialising gave her a chance to show off her burgeoning wardrobe and jewellery, which she then passed on to the younger Gretl. The sisters appeared to be having a wow of a time, safe in the knowledge that none of the handsome SS men would dare step out of line with the "Chief's girls". After a few drinks, both could be seen flirting shamelessly.

Eva's wayward bullet was indeed a shot "heard 'round the world", at least her world, and for a while attracted considerable attention for the aspiring actress. Unlike Hitler's other lovesick wooers, she had survived her suicide attempt, and when the hubbub eventually died down, she accepted my offer of a stroll through the English Garden.

She had begun chain-smoking again and I felt a walk in the fresh air could assist in her recovery. As we strolled she rattled on about her proposed new career on the big screen, before berating me with reasons why movie film trumps still photography any day of the week.

As I listened to her blowing hot and cold between topics, I could not fail to think that the more things changed, the more they stayed the same. "Yes, of course, I'll be joining the Hoffmans for Christmas, *and* for the New Year! It so happens I've been invited to accompany Adolph and the boss to a performance of *Die Meistersinger*, here in Munich on New Year's Day," she sniffed. "It's a Wagnerian opera, you know?"

I nodded, smiling inwardly at the thought of her fidgeting throughout the three- or four-hour performance. I retrieved a sudden vision of Captain Streicher's squeaky old gramophone in a bygone era.

"Oh, look!" she suddenly exclaimed, "… the things you see when you don't have a gun." In the distance appeared none other than her "British rival", Unity Mitford, jogging resolutely towards us in the company of two other women wearing skimpy tops and shorts, despite the winter chill. Unity's post-like legs were pumping bravely and in between gasps, she was trying to carry on a conversation. This looked nothing like the over-rouged vamp I'd seen in magazines, but Eva quickly pulled up the sable hood of her jacket and lowered her eyes as the trio thundered past. We caught words including "Führer", "genius" and "bachelor" that boxed Eva's ears like a prizefighter, and she came out swinging when they were beyond earshot.

"She and all the others like her can go to hell for all I care. The 'English Rose' didn't look too hot today, did she? I wonder if Adolph has seen her without all the usual trimmings."

"Certainly not! I mean, I can't see a woman like that being much competition for you, Eva …"

"Oh, I do so wish I were more up on history and that sort of thing. They say that *she* is the only one Adolph allows to discuss politics during mealtimes; I can't see why he's so taken up with the English aristocracy," she sniffed again with undisguised envy.

A threadbare Gypsy organ grinder wandered by and I dropped two marks into the monkey's cup. For a moment, the hapless creature held my gaze before scampering away at the sound of the coins hitting the tin. This was the first macaque I'd seen; a monkey without a tail!

When I revealed my plans to visit Tante and Onkel over Christmas she pricked up her ears and remarked that their location was "just a stone's throw" from Hitler's mountain retreat, where she too would be spending much of the festive season.

We loosely promised to send each other smoke signals across the valley and I shared my concerns at the thought of Onkel Fedi hiking me up and down the snow-capped Watzmann trails, asthma or no asthma … but I might as well have been talking in a foreign language; Eva had already changed the subject and moved on.

42

"For the life of me, I can't see why we shouldn't be friends, like other brothers." Bumping into Robert in the studio foyer, I had decided on the spur of the moment to bite the bullet and put aside our recent friction.

"I'm prepared to make more of an effort if you are," I offered forlornly, driven as much by loneliness as desperation, aware that he probably would have brushed past had I not spoken first. It seemed every acquaintance I'd made in Munich was preoccupied, or like Claudia, absent altogether.

Making a superhuman effort to let bygones be bygones, I had been toying with a bold idea. "How about joining me for a Christmas visit to Aunt and Onkel's chalet overlooking Berchtesgaden? It should be very beautiful at this time of year. I know they are looking forward to meeting us both, what do you say?"

For a moment he seemed to look right through me before his eyes narrowed. "Me? Visit them? They're not my fucking relatives; I want nothing to do with them. I bet the first thing they do is start sniffing around with questions about Alois. As for you, tell them nothing about me. You know nothing! Got it?"

"Th ... they only want to show us their beautiful mountain; you remember the big jagged peak we saw on our way to Lake Obersee?" Robert looked puzzled as to why we were even having the conversation. Foolishly, I pushed on; he hadn't actually said No.

"L ... Look at it this way, according to Tante, Onkel Fedi is also a zealous Nazi, just like you. To secure any real promotion, don't you need to produce proof of your connections? Having the Hahns of Hamburg on side can't be a bad thing, can it?"

He studied my face more closely. "Well, so far the boys upstairs have accepted the word of the German Consul in Belem, and anyway, I have contacts in the SS now and I rather like the look of the black uniforms. *They* are the real elites these days."

"From what I've heard, they are also a lot fussier about who *they* allow to join," I countered, "although you've the build and looks for it."

As he smiled, I noticed his facial scars had been powdered over. "I can't stay under Comrade Ernst's wing forever you know, liddle brudder. And now I'm talkin' proper German I should be a shoo-in."

"Well, whatever you choose to do it doesn't mean we can't remain friends, does it?" I almost pleaded. "This is an alien world we're in. Back home everything somehow seemed to fit together; here I'm frightened most of the time. All the normal rules of decency that Mam taught us have gone out the window. I have no one to fall back on but you!"

For a moment he looked touched, until I continued, "… and all this time you're lapping up their propaganda more than anyone …"

"You bet I'm lapping it up! My memories of the jungle back home are somewhat different to yours and will always remain so. It's about the survival of the fittest over there, or anywhere else I guess. National Socialism embraces the real message of Social Darwinism.

Over here I'm near the top of the food chain and part of the greatest revolution in history; keen to share in the spoils. I'm going all the way and don't care who I have to walk over. My role models have fearsome reputations and will stop at nothing. These are new men, real men, who take what they want. All your talk of decency: you think that if people *like* you they won't harm you; if you ask me, that's a pretty weak argument. To survive we need to use their affection as a weapon against them."

"There's no need to hurt me too, is there?" I implored. "After all, we are still brothers."

"Brothers my arse! Half-brothers and that's bad enough." He rose as if to leave. "Every time you open your mouth I hear that bastard Alois. You always were his pet; even Mam's too toward the end. Now it's my turn to be top dog," he barked, "and I've no intention of letting this chance slip away. I belong *here* in the ultimate gang, where I've a chance to be *somebody*."

I opened my mouth to respond, but his pent-up juices were running free. "All this mayhem suits me just fine. I'm quick enough on my feet to survive, just as I thrived in the Amazon. You can shove all your namby-pamby about God and the Universe; this is *my* Universe now and Adolph Hitler is at the centre of it. As far as I'm concerned everything he says makes sense, and in the coming age everyone will be equal; no more social distinctions! It won't matter that parents don't hang together long enough to get married, the State will take care of all its new-born citizen warriors, like in Sparta in the olden days."

"Good luck then," I muttered under my breath, choosing not to contradict the evidence of my own eyes.

"I've always dreamed of belonging to a greater cause with plans for the future; National Socialism is almost too wide-ranging to grasp," he continued, and his eyes glazed over when he spoke.

"I'm a part of the moral certainty setting things right, whose true path forward lays in the destructive dynamism taught by Rosenberg. The Führer believes that we are all savages at heart and that he's proud of his soldiers being looked upon as 'savages'. The SS will polish up my social skills and I will be mixing in the highest circles; at last, someone wants me for who I really am …"

He seemed possessed, and at that moment looked more God-like and perfect than any of the recruitment posters adorning Munich's lampposts; except of course, for his scars, which now glowed purple. I could see he intended "going places", whatever the cost.

"W … Well, if you don't care for my approach at least think of Claudia," I threw in, still feeling I needed to defend her in spite of the rebuff.

"Claudia? That silly bitch! She actually thinks I'll marry her one day."

I was stunned.

"But, it's you she loves, not me. Can't you see what a wonderful girl she really is? I … I'm prepared to step aside if that's what she really wants. I can't believe you would set out to deliberately hurt her like this."

His face twisted in a sneer. "Hurt her? That's a good 'un. As the comrades say, there's only one way you can hurt a woman," he paused for effect, "and that's by treading on her face when you're getting up, haw-haw!"

I recoiled at his crude maxim; to think that my own brother carried such apparent disrespect for females since childhood made my blood boil. I would save Claudia from this lethal dalliance if it was the last thing I did.

Yet, there was something about Robert's single-minded confidence that I begrudgingly admired: what if he and the Nazis really were onto something, and Herr Hitler was heralding not only a new age but a whole new Religion for today's world?

On the surface it seemed simple enough: an infallible Leader and a few hand-picked enforcers with sufficient crudity to carry out his orders. It appeared to me that the main membership requirement was obeisance absolute, though that all sounded a bit stifling and simian for someone with my imagination. The pull of belonging to such a heady enterprise was hard to resist.

"B … But, you've had your revenge, haven't you?" I surprised myself by referring to his dreadful deed from another life. "What's happened to your own free spirit? You of all people; who knew no boundaries and brooked no master …"

"Listen up, boofhead! There's a reign of terror coming against anyone who doesn't conform, or who continues to speak out; we Nazis just don't care, being on the verge of real power, so I suggest you get busy learning the ropes and playing the system. Take my advice and join the Party, for your own sake, before it's too late." With that he was gone, leaving behind more questions than answers.

43

During my train ride to Berchtesgaden, I replayed our conversation over and over in my head, searching for flaws in the Nazi argument. Did I need to continue all this fruitless jousting when common sense told me I was surely on my own?

He had certainly dampened my enthusiasm for meeting the relatives known previously only from letters, gifts and snapshots, and I held doubts about the wisdom of exposing myself to further complications with virtual strangers.

As the train rattled on through deep cuttings, past snowdrifts and bare-boned copses, I began to feel a tiny tingle of excitement despite my earlier misgivings. Peering through the steamy windows I could feel the landscape closing in as I neared my destination; again I resolved to make an effort to fit in.

"Take a good look Jung mann: that's the mighty Watzmann standing guard over our little valley, as it's done for a million years." Onkel Fedi was as proud as if he had built the mountain himself, and Tante Gretel held my arm as we exited the platform and climbed aboard a gaily decorated sleigh. The whole scene was almost a facsimile of Tante's hand-painted cards from Christmases past, apart from the brown-shirted Santa holding the reins.

Onkel had almost shaken my shoulder loose during his long and formal handshake. I was stunned by his resemblance to Papa in speech and manner, and a little unnerved by his piercing scrutiny. Tante was everything I'd hoped for, smothering me in a heartfelt embrace and tucking a blanket under my chin for the spectacular ride to the plateau above. The whole scene was a fairy tale, and the higher we climbed the more beautiful it became.

"See that wisp of smoke across the valley, Jung Klaus, that's the Führer's mountain; we feel honoured to have him as a neighbour."

Onkel had turned around to make sure I didn't miss the important landmark, and I could see his nose turning bluish-pink.

"Hitler this and Führer that; I'm afraid there will be plenty more such talk before your visit is over," Tante whispered in my ear. "It's the scenery I'm so keen for you to photograph and enjoy, certainly Bavaria's finest. But I guess we might be a little biased, eh?"

Higher and higher we ascended through the powdery snowdrifts, with bells jingling and shouts of "Heil Hitler" from groups of neighbours along the way; for some reason, I recalled the old saying of "blood being thicker than water".

"The boy's obviously done in, can't you see?

"Don't worry, we'll soon have you tucked up in front of a warm fire, little man," she purred, as we plodded to a halt before the enchanting Chalet Hahn. I hated that term but smiled anyway. "We've prepared a traditional strudel for our long lost nephew, who no doubt is starving?" she chortled.

"Who prepared it?" Onkel glared over his shoulder, awaiting a correction.

"Oh well, if you must know, your Onkel Fedi does most of the cooking and domestic duties these days, ever since he lost his job at the ski factory. I'm much too busy with my art to bother about home affairs.

"Of course, that attracts a good deal of tongue-wagging from the surrounding Frauen."

From the porch, I drank in the twinkling township below, while every now and then a jagged peak emerged through the surrounding mists. The story-book residence clung precariously to a grassy shelf beneath a soaring rock wall, which in about 200 yards, dropped away again onto the fairy lights below. In the fading twilight, Onkel pointed out the black depths of Lake Königssee, and I just had time to squeeze off a single frame before Tante hurried us inside.

From Onkel's rocking chair he had an unimpeded view across the valley to the Führer's own domain and from the moment he opened his mouth it was clear that he saw the Nazi Leader as Germany's last hope.

During subsequent visits, I watched this enthusiasm slowly wither and die until it reached its tragic finale, but for now, Onkel Fedi was as pious as any Brownshirt in Germany.

Tante Gretel, on the other hand, had not been fooled for a moment by the emerging "New Order", dividing her lower floor with exquisite Japanese folding screens. "Nazi paraphernalia on that side, I told him in no uncertain terms, and this side is for art, ta-daa! What do you think?" She gestured grandly as I peeped behind a screen.

Sure enough, the place boasted two separate decors: on one side every conceivable swastika banner, flag, trinket and Nazi trophy surrounded a framed and numbered 8" × 10" profile of Hitler taken by Hoffman and printed by myself.

Before I had a chance to point this out, Tante steered me into the vibrancy of her private gallery where my mouth dropped open in astonishment. Here, every inch of wall space was covered with prints by Rembrandt and other eternal Masters, more surprisingly with certain abstract modern originals that I completely failed to recognise.

She bubbled over the dynamics and balance of her collection of "modern" Kandinsky, Kokoschka and Matisse prints, works that in ignorance I had previously shunned. Squeezing between a carved African mask and a Yukon totem pole we came to a huge stone fireplace set in a side wall, throwing heat equally into both areas. Three easy chairs were arranged in a comfortable semi-circle before the crackling flames. One end of the mantle contained stone axe-heads and the other a framed certificate signed by Hermann Göring, lauding Onkel's selfless service to the local Party Chapter.

Almost immediately I fell in love with the place, being my first exposure to authentic German country living. Each time the mist cleared another stunning view snatched my breath away. "Not bad heh? For an unemployed factory manager ..." Onkel quipped as I sat tucking into my slab of strudel and whipped cream. "But not for much longer I trust. There's a new day dawning and I can feel it in my bones."

"It will want to hurry up then, I'm sure," Tante chimed in. "We can't live on an artist's income for much longer. Your precious Leader sits across the valley at Haus Wachenfeld with his feet up, while the rest of us are having to tighten our belts."

Aunt confided that the only work she'd found in three months was proofreading for a Munich publisher. She was feeling more and more frustrated as her artistic impulses became swamped by necessity.

"So much for the Hahn Dynasty, the so-called bastion of the Weimar Republic; where did that get us when things got tough?"

Her Angora beanie quivered as she warmed up. "With Deutsche Bank writing off our last 60,000 marks of savings, that's where! We received a terse letter saying that inflation had eaten it all up; such a sum 'wasn't worth keeping on their books', they said. It's reached the point where folks are taking wheelbarrows filled with cash downtown to buy a loaf of bread."

I realised for the first time that working in Studio Hoffman had insulated me from much of the suffering being felt throughout the land. Tante – just call me Gretel – was nowhere as confident as her husband about Nazism offering any real solutions to the runaway inflation and other social maladies.

In fact, I felt that many of her leftist views were not altogether dissimilar from those expressed by Claudia, much to Onkel's disgust.

Each in his own way had a different take on Germany's emerging position on the world stage, which they relished when relating to a long-lost relative.

During the next 48 hours of near-blizzard conditions, we had a great opportunity of getting to know each other. Gretel seemed pleased that my Leica A remained in sound condition, bringing out a framed postcard of *Madeira Belle* I'd sent over years before. I smiled thinly as I gazed at the view of Santa Luzia's waterfront in my hand, hoping she'd never discover the truth.

Each of them enquired after Robert, and Onkel expressed great pleasure when I related how both of us had been taken under the wing of Captain Röhm. As expected, they probed for more details concerning Alois' "accident".

"Tell me honestly, was Alois drunk when he fell into that damned river?" Onkel enquired out of the blue as we sat staring into the flames.

"It appears so," I cleared my throat. "That was the official verdict."

"What? What do you mean by 'official'? Do you have reason to believe otherwise?" He was being persistent, as Robert had feared.

"Actually, when I saw Papa earlier that evening, he was already a little worse for wear, that's all."

"Hmm, bloody fool. He gets the cushiest job in the company and still can't make a go of it; buggering about with rubber plantations and taking his eye off the main game. If only he'd concentrated on the phosphate like he was supposed to, I might still have a decent job today."

"It's not his fault Fred, and the boy has lost his father …"

"Yes, yes, of course. I'm sorry, Jung fella. As soon as this storm clears, I'll point out the hiking route we're going to take to the summit."

But the storm didn't clear; at certain times around the middle of each day, they left me to my own devices browsing the scattered book titles or admiring Gretel's modernist collection.

Occasionally, I dozed off in the middle armchair.

I had brought along an English translation of Dante's *Divine Comedy*, to be once more smitten by the brilliant phrasing and mental acuity conjured up so effortlessly. Tante disappeared behind her clutter and Onkel tended his hot-house vegetables, leaving me to re-evaluate my prospects.

Christmas Day came and went with little ceremony. It seemed both had become disillusioned with Christianity for different reasons: Onkel through his re-acquaintance with the ancient Aryan concept of Yuletide, and Gretel after seeing her Lutheran pastor hang swastika flags alongside the church altar.

Nonetheless, I presented each of them with a set of my recent postcards showing Munich and Lake Königssee, and in return, I received one of Gretel's framed watercolours and a Chamois leather knapsack from Onkel. "Shot the damn thing myself, you know, but don't tell anyone. Göring's let a small herd go here in the high country, but I can't see *him* doing too much chasing around after them, given his bulk. Now and then one of his special goats pokes its head over the hill looking for greener pastures, and bang! I guess there's plenty more where he came from, eh?"

He tried to convince me that traditional Germanic culture pre-dated and transcended both Christianity and Modern Art's disjointed apologia. This was a time for real men to stand up and be counted, he insisted.

"I hear the Führer has received messages of support from Pope Pius himself, not to mention a host of other world leaders including Lloyd George of England. "'In admiration for your courage, determination and leadership', that esteemed Statesman apparently wrote in dedication across his own head and shoulder portrait; that's good enough for me!"

Onkel seemed as proud as if the praise had been directed toward him personally.

"Tell me, Jung Klaus, have you read *Mein Kampf* yet?" he asked, changing the subject. "No? Well, me neither. To tell the truth, I find it hard going, but everyone else I talk to seems to be in rapture. Mind you, I don't doubt for a moment the breadth of Hitler's vision," he quickly added. "He points out the dangers and corruption of worldwide Jewish Bolshevism *and* so-called Christianity, I might add."

But he'd lost me.

Onkel Fedi's position as a minor official in the Berchtesgaden Nazi Party filled him with a great sense of importance, so much so that he'd wangled a week off during the holiday period. When we did manage to finally tackle the serried drifts it was on snowshoes for the first couple of kilometres, a stint that left me gasping for breath.

I felt a little better when Onkel said it would do my asthma the world of good to breathe in more of the Obersalzberg air. We paused at one magnificent view after another, where I clicked away and drank in my freedom.

"Why didn't you speak up boy?" he chided when I pointed out the sight of the staff picnic in the distance. "I could have shown your workmates around some of the real sights around here, not those tired old chestnuts frequented by the average tourist. They say Barbarossa himself watered his horse in that very stream and that his spirit still lives over there on the Untersberg," he said proudly, pointing to a massif on the Austrian border.

"I ... er, I find the whole area inspiring, Onkel, and that's coming from someone who'd never seen a real mountain before."

As we sat chewing our blut sausage, it was clear that he, like millions of average Germans, had thrown in his lot with Nazism as the only way forward. He listed all the national disasters, travails and other misfortunes that Hitler was poised to sweep away, and urged me to get more involved in the struggle while I still had the chance.

Below us stretched a panorama of field and forest punctuated by shining ribbons of ice, and around us lay a blanket of sparkling white powder. I told how Robert had been swept up in the movement and my concerns that this had stifled his independence of thought.

"Don't you see lad? When you have great leadership, you don't have to figure things out for yourself. All the hard thinking has been done and handed to you on a platter, so to speak. We simply have to carry out our orders without question for the whole system to work perfectly."

There seemed no point in arguing; Onkel Fedi, like Robert, had a ready response for all my doubts and I didn't want to offend his hospitality. On the other hand, Tante Gretel proved to be inquisitive and open-minded, enthralled by my tale of captivity among the Mojo. Her bright, intelligent face lit up when I recounted our childhood growing up in Santa Luzia. For the first time, I did not have to suffer sceptical looks when expounding Sister Klara's Spiritual Principles. When I got around to admitting that I'd lost the original Leica in the deluge, she wasn't at all upset.

"They're only *things*, Klaus. One can always acquire more things. It's not the camera, but the man behind the camera that counts. Of course, the great René Descartes revealed that thoughts, too, are *things*, and we are living in times when one's own thoughts can be turned upside down or against one."

I thought I understood what she was getting at.

"Unfortunately, this is a truth that Frederick doesn't seem able to grasp, and in my view, it's only a matter of time before his happy-go-lucky attitude lands him in hot water; not that he listens to anyone outside of headquarters."

She picked up on my explanation of Time being both absolute *and* non-existent, at least on this planet where every moment was being experienced simultaneously. As we chatted she dabbed away at her canvasses, pointing out how a single dab of colour in the wrong place could make or break any artwork. She speculated as to whether my theory of time might well apply throughout the whole Universe and wondered out loud if any single moment captured in a painting or photograph actually proves or disproves my concept.

"Say, for example, that I hold an image of a burning candle in my mind. Does this mean that I am recreating that past flame as a *thing*, here and now, as suggested by Descartes?"

In such a vein we mused and giggled over many wild and foolish speculations; how I loved having my mind stretched. Each tried to outdo the other in quoting philosophers or artists to prove a point. She again noted my well-balanced compositions and drew attention to hitherto unnoticed tensions existing in the best modernist prints.

But of course, the vacation couldn't last, and by New Year's Eve, I was beginning to experience butterflies in my stomach at the thought of returning to Munich. Sure enough, the mountain air had done wonders for my asthma and the three of us saw in the New Year sitting by an open window gazing at the fairyland below.

On the stroke of midnight, great blunderbusses boomed out in a time-honoured ritual and I confided that this was the best holiday I'd ever had, which pleased them immensely. For the first time, I felt as if I belonged, and I realised that I was the nearest thing to a son they'd ever known.

When I departed from the Hauptbahnhof on New Year's Day, Aunt Gretel refused to let go of my hand and I was sure I'd noticed a tear in the corner of Onkel's eye. "Next summer we'll sleep over in one of the high huts. How would you like that, eh?"

Once aboard the puffing billy, my homesickness abated; I was no longer alone in an alien and terrifying world. I had blood relatives of my own and could hardly wait to process the two rolls of 36 in my pocket.

44

From the moment Adolph Hitler became Chancellor on January 30, 1933, workloads in the studio doubled overnight. My darkroom was swamped by celebratory images from one end of the Reich to the other.

Hoffman too was being pushed to the limit, as trained staffers were again in short supply to assist with the burgeoning assignment list.

Eva appeared to be running her own race and soon got over her bout of depression after not being invited to the Berlin Inauguration.

Stoically, she never ventured far from the telephone, and when the call finally did come she was stunned by its magnitude. Yes! Her Adolph was now Chancellor of all Germany, and she was *his girl* at just 20 years of age.

Little wonder we all noticed it going straight to her head. At last, she appeared to have her man, and Henni's only comeback was to chide her over not yet becoming a Party Member. Like a handful of other dedicated "Hitlers" Henni and Heini both prized their low membership numbers, which could never be usurped by the Johnny-come-lately's now queueing up in their tens of thousands to join the Party.

In a supreme act of hypocrisy, Eva began hounding any staff members not displaying a party badge; she was liable to pop up anywhere as First Lady of the manor. We were relieved when the boss returned from Berlin and gave her a few days off to prepare for her 21st birthday party on February 6. He too seemed filled with a new vigour, but also more touchy; at least we knew where we stood. Our usual 24-hour film processing blew out to 48 and I found myself unable to get sufficient sleep because of the ever-creaking staircase by night and the jingling of cash registers by day.

I'd the bright idea months ago of rigging up a temporary bed beneath the sink in the darkroom, where I found I could rest warm and quiet at any hour.

Outside in the streets and all across the nation, celebrations were erupting in one continuous triumphal parade. Hoffman and his stringers were run off their feet capturing all for posterity, filling my in-basket to overflowing.

I was astonished by the huge crowds forming before my eyes: Old Volk, Jungvolk, uniforms and women of all ages with faces contorted in joy and desire, right arms forming forests of fingers.

The quality of the 4" × 5" negatives of traditional press cameras soon became apparent in the crowd scenes, and a rivalry erupted over the superiority of these images when it came to enlargement or publication. Naturally, the boss took umbrage at such suggestions and simply forbade anyone but printers and editorial staff to pass comment on the finished product until he'd had the final say.

Owing to Eva's absence I was allocated a temporary assistant, which turned out to be none other than Iris Bumke, which immediately created a clash in the chain of command. Although instructed to help out "as required", she did not exactly explain her full brief which, coming hot on the heels of Claudia's warning, I suspected involved more than just printing photos. Long hours together encouraged more civility than either of us might have preferred, and she even laughed at one or two of my jokes. She asked about my Christmas vacation and seemed pleased when I reported on Onkel's status in the Berchtesgaden Nazi and his collection of Party memorabilia. She expressed regret that after more than a year, I'd not made more friends among the staff.

"At least you have Eva and Claudia, whenever they bother to turn up, that is." Her tight lips looked like purple earthworms as she watched closely for my response. I held her gaze and replied that I could use all the friends I could get.

Together, we whittled away the backlog of orders and I began to feel that perhaps I'd been too selfish in keeping her at arm's length.

Looking back, one little niggle did persist when she laughed too hard and long over the crack I made concerning Göring's latest uniform. I had noted that he looked like "a ringmaster in a circus". Spurred on by her approbation, I hinted that from behind, the Reichsmarschall in his full-length fur coat looked like "two brown bears making love", causing us both to burst into laughter.

It felt good to share a lighter moment. "You should have seen him when Hoffman refused to allow his pet lion cubs into the studio. He threw off his fur coat defiantly and revealed, like I said, a ringmaster's outfit, a jolly big ringmaster at that, right down to the whip," I said. "It was all the boss could do to keep a straight face as he searched in vain for a suitable 'Man of Destiny' pose…"

Again, Iris smiled warmly. I felt relaxed, seeking to wind up my observations with a flourish. "In the end, the boss managed to come up with one or two side-lit, rather contrasty chestnuts that suitably conveyed the subject's slenderised authoritarianism," I said rather pompously. She slapped her thigh and invited me to make similar observations on other leading Nazis, which I proceeded to do until she was called away.

During those turbulent winter weeks, I found little time or inclination to visit the Isar, and even less to celebrate my own coming of age. On the other hand, Eva was spoiled rotten by Hitler when he did arrive back in Munich; they were both swept up in a new round of celebrations which she viewed as an extension of her big day rather than his.

On the first occasion, he visited the studio after gaining power, it was as if we were seeing him for the first time, despite his appearing in trench coat and dog whip.

The "Bohemian Corporal", as Hindenburg described him, had a new spring in his step and held his head high. He nodded politely to "Fraulein Braun", who curtsied back graciously before they were both escorted through the craning sightseers to roar away in the back seat of his six-wheeler.

More priority jobs kept coming in, forcing me to grab forty winks whenever I could in my makeshift hideaway. Once I stretched out under the sink between the plumbing, I noticed a strange phenomenon almost immediately: my head lay beside a tangle of pipe coming through a small gap in the wall of Hoffman's office. Through this gap, I could just make out snippets of conversation, which I realised were coming from Hoffman's kitchenette next door. That's how learned of the Reichstag Fire in Berlin before any of the other staff.

"Yes! Burned to the ground and totally gutted," Hoffman's voice sounded shaken. "Hitler's there now; Goebbels called as soon as he was sure it was the Jewish-Bolsheviks behind it ... Say nothing until I give you the O.K." I could hear only muffled comments from the other party before a toilet flushed and a sink plug was removed, sending a rousing gurgle past my nose.

Within a half hour, however, "deliberate arson" was being shouted from the rooftops. Hitler now had his mandate to save German Volk and Industry from the ravages of the "Reds" who were unquestionably behind the brazen act. At a stroke the new Führer dissolved the Reichstag and ordered coordinated attacks against every left-wing district in every German city, vowing to "annihilate the Marxist world".

"There will be no second revolution!" he again assured the big industrialists when the dust finally settled, at the same time poking a finger in the eye of Röhm and his baying Brownshirts who thought they'd seen their hour approaching. Both leaders had recently appeared in double profile on a December cover of the *Illustrierter Beobachter*, where I felt Hitler appeared to have a bad smell under his schnurrbart. Röhm too was clearly disgruntled by this most recent blow to his long-held vision of bringing the "authorised" German Reichswehr of 100,000 under his command.

"Then we'll see who's calling the shots," he had boasted to his comrades in the bathhouse, so Robert informed me later.

Meanwhile, street violence was increasing all over Munich; sometimes, we even witnessed bashings through the studio windows. This unsettled the staff, especially those without a Party badge, but I continued with the view that if it were good enough for Eva to remain above the fray then it was good enough for me.

Hoffman arranged for each of us to receive a yellow press card, which offered some measure of protection when at large. These stated that we were bona-fide employees of the official "Reich Photographer and publisher of National Socialist Images", exempting us from any interference whatsoever as we moved about the city.

Roving gangs of stormtroopers and newly deputised "Auxiliary Police" were systematically raiding pubs, meeting places and opposition office blocks, hauling away "enemies of the people" and especially "work-shy" males to the newly opened concentration camp at Dachau.

Thanks to Goebbels' rabble-rousing, Jewish businesses in particular began to feel the heavy hands of boycott and abuse. Any orthodox Jew caught on the streets would likely risk having his beard hacked off or receiving a severe beating. I was confronted with a very different scene when I eventually stepped out onto Amalienstrasse for the first time in weeks.

All opposition posters had vanished from pillar and post, to be replaced with Hitler's ubiquitous grim visage glaring down from a black background. The war of pamphlets was over; huge red banners bearing swastikas fluttered from every building, casting a simultaneous air of festivity and menace. Citizens hurried about their business in small groups, keeping a wary eye on the pugnacious S.A. thugs loitering on every corner.

With a press card firmly pinned to my jacket, I made my way through the tasteless sunshine, heading via the English Garden to see if my sandbank had survived the early thaw. I need not have worried, as the winding willow roots had, if anything, trapped an extra layer of soft sand, making it easier to build a discrete campfire.

Soon after completing a series of chants and breathing exercises, I was startled to hear the sound of voices and the crunch of approaching footsteps. Suddenly, Claudia burst out of the foliage, half-supporting and half-dragging someone spattered in blood. We stood speechless, staring at each other; her face wore a mask of fear. "Klaus! … Are you alone?" Her eyes darted nervously as she eased her burden to the ground.

"Yes! Of … of course," I stammered. "Are you being followed?"

"Not any more. Here, soak my blouse in water and be quick about it," she thrust the garment at me and turned to the moaning figure at her feet. "Oh Hans, my poor baby; let's get you cleaned up," she muttered, while I did as instructed and plunged my hands into the icy current.

Tenderly, she wiped away the blood, revealing the once handsome face of a youth around my own age. His blackened eyes were almost swollen shut, which didn't prevent him from casting nervous glances in the direction they'd come from. "It's all right, we're safe here. Klaus is a friend," she assured him before suppressing a forced giggle.

"I guess you won't be trying that again, anytime soon?" She continued sponging his head and shoulders before removing his bloodied shirt to be soaked in the freshet. "You're damned lucky I knew of this place," she said to him in her kindest voice. "Although I wasn't expecting to find *you* here," she added, lifting her face. I remained silent, expectant.

Finally, the figure spoke through puffy lips to no one in particular. "Conventional wisdom states that we can't make an omelette without cracking a few eggs. I guess the same goes for trying to make a revolution without spilling blood. But, I've always hoped it would be our lot dishing it out; by the way, I'm Hans," he said, sticking out a swollen paw and grimacing. "Claudia and I play in the same orchestra together," he explained, casting a sideways glance as if he'd already said too much.

I had no inkling that apart from the dancing routines she had a musical bone in her body and thought little more of this disclosure.

As it turned out, most of Hans' blood loss came from a broken nose, received when he not only failed to return the pervasive "Hitler Salute" to a group of passing Brownshirts but responded with a stiff index finger. Following my initial shock, I was somewhat comforted to observe that their relationship seemed more platonic than romantic, tempting me to re-establish my own nyctalopic relationship with the oft-absent girl of my dreams.

It was agreed to stay put until sunset, and while Hans dozed fitfully I was able to plumb something of his relevance. Without revealing too much, Claudia confided that I was still her truest friend and that her unexplained absences and other perplexing behaviour were being conducted with the best interests of Germany at heart; I would just have to take her word for it. This whispered confidence raised more questions than it answered, failing to explain her attachment to Robert and their shameless exhibitionism around high-level Nazis.

I can't say I fully believed her, but for no logical reason, I still believed *in* her. I could stand being hurt so long as I had the chance to remain in her presence, at least during work hours. She warned me straight out that if I truly cared I would never mention Hans to anyone unless she herself raised the topic.

"Oh, and especially don't trust Iris or Lothar as I've warned you many times. You are becoming quite the gossip." I felt a guilty niggle that perhaps I'd already allowed Iris to get a little too close. Not to worry, it had all been in good fun.

"…or we could all end up in the scheisse. This regime doesn't approve of freethinkers like Hans and Sophie. That's why it's so important you don't let anything slip; everyone is being paid for spying on everyone else." I couldn't imagine that I possessed knowledge of any importance at all to the ruling powers.

"'Divide and rule; a sound motto. Unite and lead, a better one' … so Goethe tells us," I declared proudly, sounding slightly conspiratorial.

As we sat huddled over the tiny flame, Hans kept one puffy eye trained on the escape route, while my own bosom burned with rekindled affection. Tasting Claudia's breath and perfume mixed with wood smoke encouraged me to string out the chance encounter for as long as possible, but she did not let her guard down for a minute.

"One wrong word is all it takes, and you could end up sampling the joys of Dachau," she whispered. "You have no idea of the horrors being perpetrated just up the road, in the name of the New Order," she said, not knowing that I'd heard the word "Dachau" mentioned but once in conjunction with some "re-education" programme or other. Surely it couldn't be that bad.

"Can you believe it?" she continued in hushed tones, "… all the good-looking single girls, including the Bund League maidens, have been ordered, *ordered* mind you, to make themselves 'available and amenable' for the pleasure of the graduating 'warrior class' of SS.

"As if it weren't bad enough last year when hundreds of 15- and 16-year-olds returned pregnant from the Party Rally in Nuremberg; I tell you, Klaus, they're turning Germany into one big brothel. When the parents dared to protest they were threatened with a stint in 'protective custody'. Plans are already afoot for a chain of so-called lying-in hostels called 'Lebensborn' where unmarried girls can bring these poor little bastards into the world as future cannon fodder."

I had forgotten how animated Claudia could become in private.

"To top things off, they've suddenly announced that sex between Jews and non-Jews, even husbands and wives, is now verboten. Oh, if only those sweating Nazi pigs knew the half of it, they're happy enough to cough up the marks after a session with this pure Aryan beauty," she smirked ironically and leaned closer. I always felt a touch uncomfortable when she referred to her auxiliary obligations.

"All this hatred emanates from one man and if I had been in any doubt over the extent of his virulence it was dispelled yesterday at Café Heck." She had my attention. "A well-dressed Jewish woman holding her small son by the hand paused beside the cashier and fumbled for coins in her purse. At this, the boy aged about three or four broke loose and ran between the tables filled with Hitler's entourage and groups of society ladies hoping to be noticed.

"'Don't worry,' Hitler declared in a loud voice, as the child scurried back into the folds of mother's skirt, "we won't have to put up with this sort of thing much longer. We intend to do away with the lot of them. See that boy over there?' he nodded towards the cheeky face peeping out, 'I would like to squash him flat like a bug on the wall.'

"I'm telling you, Klaus, I saw his look with my own eyes, aimed at a small child, and I heard those crawlers all around him snigger in agreement. Some of those men I've known for years and they weren't particularly anti-Semitic. All of a sudden they're happy to pile onto a mere Jewish child."

"Howling with the wolves, perhaps?" I reflected. "In fact, Herr Wolf was one of Hitler's earliest pseudonyms. How many times before has it popped up in history and religion?" I attempted to philosophise.

"Well, not like this! I can assure you," she cut me short.

By now Hans was well enough to join in and moved closer to the warmth. His voice was soft but intense: "Sissy's right! We're well and truly in the age of steel production, and when any tyrant's resentments are backed up, as they are now, by real industrial might, human suffering will know no bounds. Believe me, it's mass warfare this fellow is planning ..."

"But he speaks so often of peace. It seems to me it's the stormtroopers who're the ones looking for a fight, and Röhm talks of taking over the entire armed services ..."

"This is mere localised jousting; the real danger lies in Hitler's maniacal desire to rule the whole world. Anyone who's different or holds contrary political views is being singled out as a 'commie' and locked away; this is only the beginning.

"The Brownshirts have taken violence and humiliation of law-abiding citizens to new levels. Make no mistake, once the opposition is quelled at home, Hitler will surely keep going. No one and no country will be immune." I gulped.

"Our new Führer is personally defending and calling for the release of two of Röhm's S.A. thugs now behind bars; they've admitted to murdering an innocent Communist bystander. If it's them today, it'll be the rest of us tomorrow."

"Not if the majority strive to do the right thing at all times ..."

He looked at me incredulously. "Is that so? Take a good look at the 'majority', they're sheep. Do you think any amount of 'Führer this and Führer that' will save your cowardly arse in the long run? Nor will that piece of paper pinned to your chest like a medal of honour."

"Oh, come on Hans, give the kid a break, everyone's not as game as you and your orchestra," Claudia spoke up once more in my defence. "Klaus is entitled to his opinion. That's what we're fighting for, isn't it?

"I've seen the man up close, sipping his mineral water and blowing over a spoonful of vegetable broth. Having to watch him devour a whole plate of cream cakes nearly makes me sick and I have to keep on smiling." She gave a deprecating laugh. "Such is the life of a Polish whore in Germany today. Then again, I have to admit that the average German is also having his rights curtailed. What sort of government is this?"

"The bludgeoning of the people by the people for the people," she spat out the words, answering her own question. "Klaus needs to hear these things." Her face now looked drawn and disillusioned in the flickering firelight.

"So much for Christianity, which Hitler had the nerve to describe in a recent speech as 'the unshakable foundations for the moral code of the nation', ha! He claims to be a pacifist and has struck a concordat with the Vatican, no less. After all, he nearly had *you* convinced."

At that moment it seemed like she had taken upon her shoulders a mighty task, at a time when panic was setting in across all levels of society. "He thinks that all Europe will be grateful to him for cleaning up the mess; the mess he's creating. And all the while that pack of sycophants grovel for crumbs at his feet."

"B … But, how do you manage to maintain your different roles and avoid a slip of the tongue to betray your true feelings?"

For a moment she was silent, thinking. "Concentration, more or less. We Jews know that it's now or never; the moment we let our guard down there'll be no second chances. Whether churning out picture frames, sitting on Nazi knees or dancing topless, it all comes down to staying right in the moment, and not letting one's mind stray. God knows I've had enough practice. Sooner or later our day will come," she looked towards Hans for reassurance, but the expression on his face suggested liberation was a long way off.

"Omens! She's always looking for bloody omens!" he interjected. "You Jews are masters at spotting the Divine Hand in every burning bush."

"B … But God is omnipresent in every Natural Law that surrounds us," I chipped in, missing his point entirely.

"Omen or superstition? Take your pick, it's all the same to me. I fail to see the hand of Divinity in the means and methods of National Socialism," he added.

"Klaus taught me it all comes down to free will, and Man's misuse of it," Claudia interjected, before going on to relate another incident outside Café Heck on March 15, which she had taken as a definite omen.

When Hitler stepped outside onto the footpath, a wizened old lady in rags had burst through his security cordon, shrieking and waving a large scroll in his face, claiming that it contained messages from the "other world". Claudia had glimpsed the horror on the Führer's face as he scrambled to push away the Harpy. "Get her off! Get this crazy person away from me," he had screeched, visibly unnerved.

Although his bodyguards pounced on the mad woman immediately, Claudia and others saw sufficient momentary fear in the Leader's eyes to take heart in their struggle. It was one thing for a stout-hearted Hitler to direct threats and curses at a small Jewish boy, and quite another to see his instinctive response to a tirade from a deranged fortune-teller.

Claudia said that it was these two incidents that gave her the courage to continue, although Hans didn't quite see it as a chink in the Nazi Leader's defences. Little did I know when we parted that evening, the next time we exchanged confidences would be under very different circumstances. And, I would be a very different person.

After Nazi headquarters moved into the Brown House, just a few blocks away, Studio Hoffman suddenly found itself with far more space and much less traffic. With some relief, I was able to move a mattress back under the staircase.

Work became more interesting than the usual cleaning of enlarger lens elements, printing countless postcards and tidying up everyone else's mess. Certain party officials had been given permission from Hoffman to use the darkroom facilities, throwing my routine into disarray.

I was diverted to make printing plates and layouts for the boss' latest venture, an album of titillating nude studies for the Balkan market. Of course, all his models were beautifully lit, though I thought posed rather predictably after the great masters. The "Herr Professor", as Hitler now bestowed his old friend, also turned his hand to supplying yet more bronze "Führer Busts" in a variety of sizes; these were snapped up in their thousands for desks and mantelpieces.

Given that most photographers are opportunists by nature, usually copying either Renaissance Masters or each other, it seemed there was nothing Hoffman could not achieve; film and fortune kept pouring in.

He'd not only struck a deal to buy all of Eva's private "Führer moments", but offered Hitler's pilot, Hans Bauer, a lifetime of free processing for his own family snaps in exchange for publishing rights on anything of interest that Bauer might click during the Führer's travels.

Bauer had been given a Leica by his number one patron, Adolph Hitler, whom he addressed as "father". His absolute commitment to his master's earthly ministry was heartfelt and necessary, given Hitler's demand for total loyalty trumped all other desirable attributes.

Without exception, each member of the inner circle fell over each other to appear most loyal of all. Even Hoffman, who single-handedly created Hitler's "Man of Destiny" oeuvre through his carefully constructed poses and lighting, seemed shameless to bow and scrape to stay in favour. After all, it was in the privacy of the Hoffman family parlour where Hitler's flirtatious inclinations toward a young shop assistant had first ripened.

Even now in power, Hitler often turned up in trench coat and jackboots, usually clutching his dog whip which I felt made him look quite comical. When he announced that Jews would no longer be tolerated around the studio, Hoffman hastened to comply, erecting signs highlighting the new rules and penalties.

Claudia alone remained below the radar, kept safe from close scrutiny for the time being with her future lying entirely in the Herr Professor's slippery hands. Despite commitments on a hundred fronts, the boss still found time to sue non-Nazi publications for breaching copyright.

We all noticed that by mid-summer he was packing a spare tyre or two that made him appear even shorter and ruddier; his orders arrived on a breath ripe with strong cigars and private bin wines.

One afternoon he was berating the darkroom staff over wastage. "Waste! This is what I mean by waste," he roared, kicking over a bin of rejected prints I'd been meaning to empty.

"Money doesn't grow on trees, you know. There're millions of unemployed out there, I could teach any one of them how to print in ten minutes," he slurred, but we were getting used to his throwaway insults.

"What's this?" he said, stooping to pick up a crumpled 8" × 10" of Eva dangling from a low branch beside Lake Königssee. "How many bloody attempts do you need to make a good print, eh?" he thrust his sharp nose into my space and I recoiled from his exhalation.

"Er … Eva wanted me to feature her smile, but the strong background glare blew out the highlights and left almost no shadow detail on the negs; there was just too much contrast," I attempted to explain.

"Call yourself a printer? It should take no more than two attempts to make a perfect print; I'm the one footing the bills around here. It's never any different; give her an inch and she takes a mile. Someone should be paying for all this wastage." His voice trailed off in frustration; there was no point reminding him that the part-time printers caused most of the waste and that none of us now held any sway over Eva's whims.

Hoffman's intemperance, however, seemed not to affect the quality or output of his "Führer Images", which flowed back to me in a steady stream from spending countless hours by the Leader's side. I studied proof sheets of the 'Big Chief' turning sods and training his Alsatians, paying particular attention to the lighting and bracketing chosen.

When it came time to produce a set of portraits showing Hitler as the newly minted 'Führer,' Hoffman opted for a setting in the Brown House Headquarters; but as usual, these attempts to show Hitler as an 'approachable' leader, perched on the corner of his huge desk came to naught.

The subject's choice of a stiff, cream double-breasted suit and customary stare had quite the opposite effect; bending over the developing tray I wondered if there was a photographer alive who could somehow crack that practiced visage. For now, it was sufficient to reprint the chosen pose in countless thousands, ready for the expected rush.

Rumours were already rife over the extent of debauchery being permitted in the Brown House mess room, where certain women were commandeered to perform lewd acts for the delectation of the foot soldiers.

Following the nationwide boycott of Jewish stores in April, just three months after the Nazi takeover, stormtroopers set about mopping up the remaining "commie" enclaves and seizing the last left-wing publications from city newsstands. When encroaching the "Red bastions of resistance", the Brownshirt hordes were met with flying bottles and spitting, shrieking women, who not only bared their buttocks but emptied chamber pots over the invaders from the upper floors; all to no avail.

Even the most heartfelt resistance melted away beneath the hail of billy clubs and hobnail boots as suburb after suburb was "pacified".

Gratuitous violence could now be meted out to anyone not wearing a brown shirt, party badge, or waving a safe-pass signed by the blockälteste.

Behind the scenes, Jewish public servants were being sacked without notice or compensation. Unsurprisingly, the majority of Munich citizenry responded to all this violence with barely disguised enthusiasm, even gaiety. After all, the heavy hand was falling mainly on Jews, beggars, homosexuals, communists, Jehovah's Witnesses, gypsies and other misfits, none of whom were seen as a great loss to the New Order.

The nation breathed a collective sigh of relief upon learning that nearly 1,700 paedophiles had been summarily castrated.

Throughout that summer most cafés, bars and bistros erected outdoor dance floors, where decent citizens could fraternise at all hours. Party panegyrics and martial music continued to blare from loudspeakers, interrupted regularly for important announcements. Hateful slogans such as "No German is a full-blooded Nazi until he has spat in the face of at least one Jew" were disseminated widely. Law and order had become a mockery.

Around the time of Hitler's 44th birthday, I witnessed my first book-burning outside Munich University. It seemed the world-class library was being purged of its "un-German" authors: as each name was called aloud in an "Incantation of Fire", the corresponding heretical volume was hurled into the flames.

I witnessed the contorted faces of students lit by the glow and howling with glee. The distant danger and violence of the streets had now arrived on campus, much to the chagrin of the "Snivelling gentlemen of Weimar" as the Führer referred to his dethroned predecessors.

They were as shocked as anyone by this turn of events, having wrongly believed that if they could raise the former corporal into office they could surely control him. In hindsight, it seemed but a short step to lay blame for these excesses at Röhm's door, where the brown ranks had now swelled close to four million. Not only had the "Machine Gun King" defeated the "Commies", but somehow he'd convinced thousands of them to switch sides and march alongside their former enemies.

Shaken, I hurried back toward the Studio; a proliferation of huge red banners fluttering from every lamppost and tall building dominated the city streets. The brilliantly accented black swastikas revolving in white circles were, of course, Hitler's own particularly potent incarnation of that ancient Mystical symbol, motivating me to seek out its true origins in the State Bibliotech.

Next free day, on a back shelf overlooked by the book-burners, I discovered a trove of timeworn tomes, several of which contained swastika variations throughout history. The symbol appeared in Buddhist Zodiacs and Asoka inscriptions, even among certain American Indian tribes and the Mayans of the Yucatan peninsula: it was the sectarian mark of the Jain Religion centuries before Christ and appeared in the Irish Book of Kells in the 8th Century. Even earlier versions were unearthed in the catacombs beneath the streets of Rome, their origins lost in pre-history. It was a sacred symbol in the Monasteries of Tibet and among other secret Brotherhoods, *but* with one important difference!

Almost without exception, the early swastikas spun *clockwise*, in the direction of wisdom and faith; in a flash, it came to me that these were the very same marks carved into the stele of Atua's Lost City. Since time began it seemed that one man only had dared to roll the wheel *backwards*, denoting force and obedience.

Adolph Hitler, the frustrated artist, had single-handedly resurrected the time-worn symbol and turned it on its head in a blaze of vivid energy impossible to ignore. Undoubtedly, his choice of Black, White and Red are the most potent colours ever combined in a single image.

Being surrounded by these symbols in the streets was meant to be intimidating, their primary purpose; there was no doubting just who was in charge. It was impossible to escape the pull of a New Order that left little room for individuality.

For those who did buck the trend, consequences were swift and brutal, often in full public view. Although I kept my own head down, it was impossible to avoid random acts of violence in the streets. All I wanted was to retreat to my "green cathedral", the one place I could perform my mental exercises and vowel sounds in peace.

One Sunday afternoon I was returning through the English Garden and paused again to drop a coin in the cup of the organ grinder's monkey.

At that very moment, two small groups of Brownshirts approached from opposite directions; upon spotting the hated Gypsy beggar they let out a simultaneous whoop and fell upon him raining blows and curses.

I raised my camera and took a single exposure, before fumbling for my yellow press card.

The hapless macaque was sent flying on the toe of a jackboot, snapping its chain; when it came to its senses it scurried up the nearest tree, wounded but free and cursing volubly. His master, however, could find no tree of his own to climb and was dragged bruised and bloodied to the canal and hurled in, organ and all. I had risen shakily to my feet and stood awaiting the likely repercussions.

"As for you, arsehole, press card or not," their leader snarled, cracking his knuckles and bringing his face just inches from mine, "it is forbidden to consort with Gypsy scum in any way, you will be reported."

"B ... But I caught your actions on film, for the official Hoffman Archives," I stammered, pointing to the camera around my neck. His bloodshot eyes flicked between camera and press card as the others regrouped noisily, congratulating themselves on a job well done. His expression softened. "Studio Hoffman, huh? Do you think we might make it into the newspapers?"

"Hey!" another shouted before I could respond, as the bedraggled organ grinder hauled himself out on the opposite bank. "The bastard needed a good wash. It'll be a while before he shows his face around here again."

"Come on!" shouted another, "... all this racial cleansing has made me thirsty, there's a rally on at the Bürgerbräukeller; fall in comrades!" As a final gesture, one threw a sod at the wide-eyed monkey high in the branches.

Shaky, but proud that I'd managed to talk myself out of a beating, I left my half-eaten sandwich at the base of the tree and headed toward the studio. On the way I narrowly avoided two public whippings, further reminders that a new dawn had indeed risen over Germany. A Black Prince had risen from the ashes of the Great War to lead his eager subjects towards that which rightfully belonged to them all.

Turning into Amalienstrasse I was confronted by an even more sickening sight than that of the previous hour: a pack of Hitler Youth were being egged on by two SS officers; the jeering, uniformed youngsters aged between 10 and 14 were leading around an old Jewish man dressed only in underwear with a collar around his neck.

A mob of rabid onlookers chanted, "Jew perish, Jew perish; make him pay! Make him pay!" Again I was reminded of Dante's *Inferno* which for this old man was real and terrifying. His pleas for mercy were met with kicks and taunts and his silver beard was flecked with spittle.

At each blow, the boys became bolder, and the sight of blood set them baying like beasts. They spun him round and round like a dancing bear amidst the menacing crowd; I was almost overcome with fear and nausea.

I had heard of stormtroopers forcing Jews to eat grass on the footpath and scrub cobblestones with their toothbrushes, but witnessing such scenes firsthand was very different from seeing photographs and hearing rumours. At the sounds of fists smacking flesh and knuckle on bone, I wondered how long I could hold out without losing my senses completely.

All of a sudden I was back in the jungle; the old man became indeed a dancing bear, just like the one outside the Opera House in Manaus, and the crowd a troop of howlers hurling abuse at their perceived enemy. Two younger boys rushed in to grab a handful of his grizzled whiskers and yank them out by the roots. The old man screamed in fear and pain while the beasts squealed with delight. My head spun like a bolas entangling my senses, and I fell to the ground, unconscious.

"Apparently, he didn't get a single decent photo of the sort of things I like to publish …"

"I tell you the boy has a weak stomach and he's asthmatic." I recognised the second voice as Hoffman's, the first a muffled baritone. A door slammed and my head was splitting. "Oh, I see you've come round, it's about time. Remind me never to send you out as a street stringer." The boss was peering into my half-opened eyes.

"W … What happened?"

"You took a turn while they were beating up some old Jew. Luckily someone recognised your press card and dumped you back home on the doorstep. Can't stand the sight of blood, eh? Well, you'd better get used to it."

"I … I'll never get used to seeing innocent people being treated so cruelly in public, no matter their religion."

"Religion? It's the whole bloody race of Jews that's bled Europe white for centuries. You can surely understand the Volk wanting to get their own back?"

"What I saw was far more than mere 'payback'. In the end, I have no doubt that such methods will consume us all," I ventured.

"Well, that's not your worry, now is it? I'm confident that the Führer has things well in hand. Your main concern now should be keeping me happy." There was a hard edge to his response, exacerbated by his florid features and bloodshot eyes. I searched in vain for any softness, but he looked far from a man contended; as if caught up in a fool's freedom.

In the corridors, all the usual bustle and gossip continued, now and again a gangster hat or a tight bun would poke through the door and give a little chuckle. It seemed like the studio was an oasis of denial amidst the carnage.

Through the open window drifted the sound of trumpet fanfares, drums and occasional screams; at least in here I would be seeing only facsimiles of the horrors unfolding outside. For weeks I couldn't bring myself to tackle the Munich streets again, devoting myself day and night to the troubling images to which I was exposed.

When at last I did pluck up the courage to risk a day beside the Isar, I hoped it would bring a chance to reconsider my list of dwindling opportunities. A cramped broom closet hardly offered sufficient room or inspiration to achieve real afflatus, without which I could see no way of holding onto my ideals.

Bang! The door flew open. "Gestapo!" I'd received the dreaded summons: "Get dressed, you're coming with us." My heart nearly leapt from my chest as I fumbled to pull on my trousers.

The alarm clock read 4 am, and my mind raced to imagine what the authorities may have against me. I kidded myself that it would all turn out as a silly mistake and reached for my camera. "That won't be necessary where you're going," said one huge fellow with hands like toilet seats. "Schnell! Raus! Raus!" yelled his trench-coated offsider in my ear as we stumbled through the pre-dawn darkness to a waiting car.

Wedged between both agents in the back seat I tried to think clearly of just what I should own up to. Who had dobbed me in? How much did they know? Driving through the deserted streets I drew in deep steady breaths, resolved to retain my composure at any cost.

"Where are you taking me? What am I supposed to have done?" I asked in my bravest voice, as the pair looked straight ahead with hats pulled low. I decided to try again, this time using every ounce of authority. "I am a valued employee of Heinrich Hoffman. He won't take too kindly to—"

At that moment, a toilet seat slammed into my face and everything went black.

45

"We know all about you and the Polish whore. You're going to tell us just what she gets up to in her spare time." My head was aching; I was dripping wet and pinioned upright in a wooden chair. "You will provide a list of everyone who visits her at work, and what you know of her private activities. After you tell us what we want to know, you'll be free to go about your duties."

The harsh import of their actions was tempered with the carrot of betrayal, but I could see little through swollen eyes and my throbbing nose was surely broken. "It seems Herr Hahn is not quite the simple patriot he's making out to be …" came another voice from behind the blinding light, "… he won't be going anywhere until his memory improves." Another bucket of ice water was tossed in my face, followed by a barrage of questions.

"What do you know of Röhm's intentions for a 'second revolution'?"

"Why are you searching for banned volumes in the Staat Bibliotech?"

The questions came at me like bullets but I was too frightened to answer.

"So you think the Reichsmarschall looks foolish in a fur coat?"

My face was being slapped at regular intervals and piercing screams nearby added to my confusion; apparently, I wasn't the only "suspect" being interrogated that morning.

"Have you read *Mein Kampf*? Which holds the most meaning for you? We've heard that you often express doubts about the Nazi leadership; now is your chance to explain your political views …"

On and on they went for what seemed like hours. I repeated the only passage I could recall verbatim from my attempt to wade through Hitler's whole turgid tome: "In Vienna, at age 18, wherever I went I began to see Jews, and the more I saw the more sharply they became distinguished in my eyes from the rest of humanity.' That's all I remember."

This quotation caused my interrogators to pause; I was aware of protecting my friends. Following a brief discussion among my captors I was dragged off down two flights of stairs into a foetid corridor lined on both sides with metal doors.

"No hurry, Herr Hahn; we've got all the time in the world. Perhaps a spell in here will improve your memory?" With a parting shove for good measure, I was propelled into a tiny dark cell reeking of urine and vomit. The door slammed shut.

I had never considered myself particularly brave, but somehow I had withstood the initial onslaught. Gingerly, I tried to peep through the gloom with swollen lids and felt my tender nose, which by now had stopped bleeding. I groped my way onto a low wooden plank with no mattress, which served as a bed, although I couldn't imagine much sleep being possible in such a place.

A low undulating moan, punctuated by screams, blows and clanging doors echoed up and down the corridors. As my pain gradually abated, I stilled my frantic thoughts and tried to assess the predicament, unable to block out the sounds of suffering on all sides. I was vaguely aware of nearby breathing as I drifted in and out of lucidity for I knew not how long.

My thirst grew into a raging fire, and by the time I was dragged once more before my inquisitors, I was prepared to admit to anything for a sip of cool water. One of them began again in friendlier tones. "Tell us about the Polish whore and those higher-ups she meets with. We want names and aliases."

"S … She is but one of many colleagues and I know nothing of her private life. You should be asking Hoffman; I need water," I wheezed through fat lips.

"And what of your brother; does he discuss Röhm's future ambitions with you?"

"H … He sees very little of Röhm these days. He's in the final stages of joining the SS Cavalry Division, as a sniper, first-class," I explained. "He's being sponsored by one Lieutenant Fegelein if you wish to verify my statement." My interrogators ignored this red herring.

"What have you heard of the so-called second revolution?" said one as I clutched my throat and again begged for water. A full-blown asthma attack was now threatening as I sucked at the foul air.

Thankfully they must have concluded that nothing of value could be gleaned under such conditions. The remainder of the ice water was thrown in my face and I was dragged back downstairs to be cast into another putrid cell occupied by two zombie-like figures. "Next time we might not be so forgiving," sneered one guard as the door clanged shut.

Lying there on the cold concrete, I struggled to repeat the healing vowels in my head and focus on the flickering candle flame in my breast, becoming slowly aware of the zombies whispering. We were almost on top of each other in a cramped space that did not permit any normal-sized person to stand erect.

I established that my cellmates were in far worse shape than myself and through ringing ears I heeded one addressing me in hushed tones. In the gloom, I could see that the front of his trousers was heavily stained and as he spoke he rocked slowly back and forth clutching his groin. "And, what sort of 'socially undesirable' might you be, friend?" he asked, gaining slightly more composure. "I see you've already been introduced to the Reich Guardians of truth and justice." His voice quivered with defiance.

"I really don't know why I'm here; I think they suspect my friends of wrongdoing ... but I didn't tell them anything," I hastened to add. The other man pressed even closer, "You can tell us, friend. We're all in this together." He sounded expectant, exuding comradery and motioning toward a pitcher of water on the window sill, upon which I fell greedily. "Go easy!" the first spoke up again, "... that has to last the three of us all day."

I willed myself to stop drinking, and for the first time noticed the strange silence. "That noise, all that moaning I heard; what's happened to it?"

"They've gone! They've all been shipped out to Dachau," the eager man confided. "Twice a week they send them off, and they'll send you too if you don't tell them what they want to know."

"Why don't you shut your mouth, you damned snitch ... Don't listen to him, boy," interjected the other, rocking back and forth in pain.

Through my thumping skull, I took small comfort from this older man struggling against his own torment to offer a word of caution. Crowded together as we were, privacy was impossible. He turned his back on his cellmate and leaned close to my battered face, "Whatever you do, don't tell them anything. If they had any evidence against you, you would have been sent straight on to Dachau."

"B ... But I haven't done anything. I've been working at Studio Hoffman for years now and I rarely set foot outside the office. Maybe I have cracked a few jokes about the leadership among colleagues, but certainly nothing to deserve this kind of treatment."

I was searching for reassurance. "Anyhow, what about *you*?" I asked in concern. "You look like you've been in a car crash." I cast my eyes again to the bloodied black patches caking his front.

"Jew-lover!" the cellmate piped up. "He won't be doin' too much lovin' from now on; without the family jewels," he cackled, wringing his hands like a harbinger of Hell. Ignoring the jibe, my confidant squeezed closer and for the next two hours shared his own horrific experience; my own beating seemed trivial by comparison.

He was indeed a Jew-lover, a Jew-loving University Professor who had foolishly fallen in love with a Hebrew female student for which transgression both had paid a terrible bounty. He told of being forced to watch on helplessly while the Brownshirts stripped her naked and beat her with truncheons, before putting the boot in as she lay on the floor. "Oh, my poor sweet Sarah," he wailed softly.

"Then," he paused to steady his voice, "they made her pull on her bloodstained underwear and wander up and down the quadrangle with a placard around her neck: 'I am a filthy Jewess who has defiled an Aryan man.'

"At first I thought I might get off with only a beating, but I was wrong. There was this one Brownshirt ringleader who stood out, calling for blood, my blood. After having punched sweet Sarah senseless, he turned his attention to me. 'So you like screwing Jews, do you? Don't you know that consorting with untermenschen brings shame upon every German? Perhaps we should convert you in the most obvious way.'" Again the shadow paused to stifle a sob, "With that, he and two others threw me to the ground and pulled down my trousers in front of the mob, before the young bastard hacked off my foreskin with his dagger, crowing triumphantly as he held it aloft for all to see.

"Oh, how I'd like to get my hands on that blond-haired mongrel with the scar-face and funny accent." He raised encrusted hands to cover his eyes, before sobbing out the final details of those indignant agonies he'd undergone. Unable to gain his signature on the trumped-up 'confession', his interrogators decided to finish the job begun earlier. For good measure, they'd attempted to castrate him in his cell, this cell!

"I won't die. I'm not going to die," he repeated the words over and over into cupped hands and I could not help reaching out to put an arm around his shuddering shoulders. For a moment I forgot my own despair until I recalled his description of the blond assailant. Could it be, surely not? Robert was supposed to have moved into the SS. How quickly I'd been reduced to an even lower ebb.

All the while our third cellmate feigned indifference.

The clatter of approaching jackboots roused me from my stupor and the cell door was thrown open. Once again I was dragged up the dreaded steps, this time into the foyer rather than an interrogation room. There before me stood a smiling Marty Schartzl and a scowling Lothar Shultz. "You can count yourself lucky, this time," the desk officer said, looking up. "You will say nothing to anyone of your stay with us, is that clear?" He was examining the signed "release orders" from the "Highest Authority" while Marty anxiously ran his eye over my battered features. "It looks like you are going to live. It's nice to see Röhm's authority still holds some sway in Gestapo headquarters."

"I would have been prepared to confess anything to get out of that place," I responded through thick lips. Lothar clutched a second signed authority from "Official Party Photographer Hoffmann", stating that I was engaged in an "essential occupation". I was subsequently dropped off at the Hoffmann Villa on Schnorrstrasse, to be greeted by a tearful Frau Hoffmann waiting to bathe my wounds and change me into a fresh set of clothes. In all the confusion I'd not thought to exchange details with the wretched professor. Strangely, no one at the villa questioned me as to how or where I'd received my injuries, and I certainly did not volunteer a single word. In her wisdom, Frau Erna suggested that I explain away my bruises as a "workplace accident", to which I happily consented. Despite her kindness, I asked to be returned to my lodgings, where I hoped to spend a few hard-won days recovering in bed with my books.

"My dear boy, it's all been a terrible comedy of errors when certain people exceeded their authority; Iris felt she was only doing her duty," Hoffmann counselled later from the foot of my bunk. "And of course, one of the librarians dobbed you in for fishing around after books on black magic."

"Swastikas?" I probed.

"Swastikas? What have they got to do with it?"

I was merely looking up their history which is quite fascinating. Do you mind if we talk about it later?"

"Good, yes, of course. First things first. Let's get you back on your feet and into the darkroom, eh? We're getting quite a backlog and I have to admit, nobody else has your touch."

He turned but stopped at the door …

"By the way, it's good that you retain your habit of being outspoken at times. I want you to continue with your silly little jokes and report back to Iris on any of the other printers showing a lack of respect for the Führer. I'm counting on you to help ferret out any rats in the ranks; anyone not committed 100% to our great National Cause. You will be well rewarded for your troubles."

I gave a dry gulp and thought immediately of Claudia. "So, you want me to become a snitch, is that it?"

"I want no more than a demonstration of your loyalty, that's all. Names and addresses at a minimum, and that's an order!" Before leaving, he tossed over a booklet of meal vouchers for Café Stephanie downstairs. When my broken head finally hit the pillow, I reflected if indeed it was Providence or Nature's own Divine Order of direction that I had been spared once again.

Upon resuming full duties I found the workload remained pressing; I was surprised to learn that the "Horst Wessel Song" had been elevated not only as Germany's "Official Anthem", but to be sung aloud in Sunday church services henceforth, including Catholic Mass. With lyrics such as "Soon our banners will fly over every street" and "Millions full of hope look at our swastika, our slavery will last only a short time longer", I wondered who on earth among the Christian community would look willingly to such nonsensical utterings for salvation. I recalled Father Malone's admonition that all Christians need to look no further than unswerving Faith in Jesus and his Blessed Mother for their prayers to be answered.

Yet by the mid-1930s, with one or two exceptions such as the courageous and much-maligned Pastor Niemoller, it seemed devout Germans were now being offered a slicker, more contemporary Saviour in the form of an infallible Leader, who walked among them and spoke in the "here and now", rather than mere echoes from the past. The German Volk was destined for greatness under his leadership.

Well, I haven't seen much evidence of that, so far, I thought, before glancing behind. The truth was slowly dawning in a brain that did not want to know; there was simply no way out for the average citizen being monitored by Gestapo informants in the streets and at work. Prying blockältestes offered bribes to his neighbours to spy on him and each other.

Whether they knew it or not, both supporters and detractors were in this together: in lockstep on a runaway ride towards power, glory, and almost certain doom.

But, and it was a big "but", there was still much work to be done until then, and "slackers" putting a foot out of place were now clearer targets for Iris and her Gestapo contacts. It was made clear that not all of us were destined to share in the spoils. Claudia and I, and so many hundreds of others were utterly beholden to Heinrich Hoffmann and the machinery of a burgeoning empire that churned out Nazi likenesses on demand. He insisted that my naive assessment of photography as "the privilege of catching an important moment forever" was utter pie in the sky, and when next confronted with a suitable Party function he proved it by firing off a whole roll of 36 in a few minutes. The sheer weight and volume of success seemed somehow to be diminishing his aspirations from at least partial artistry to mere making money.

As I was to discover in time, Photohaus Hoffmann and subsidiary sales rocketed from RM 700 thousand in 1933 to RM 15.5 million a decade later. Yet somehow, these bulging coffers brought him scant acclaim outside National Socialist circles and little relief from the pressures of a business empire that now straddled much of Europe.

Hoffman's plans were continually thwarted by Hitler's indulgent Bohemian lifestyle. Visibly tipsy at all hours, his baggy eyes, florid features and pot belly betrayed a secret life of ebriety and excess. With money to burn and no time to strike the flint, Professor Midas was turning his attention to the acquisition of paintings and related fine arts for a pending "Super Exhibition".

One of the first oils he acquired, a Spitzweg landscape that I considered mawkish, could be seen years later hanging in his office, between all the awards and diplomas. Amazingly, Hitler these days deferred to Hoffmann in matters of high art, although he of course gave the final thumbs up or down. In one sense, I felt the boss was as securely bound to the Führer as Claudia and I were to him; by fear and necessity.

Even then Studio Hoffman persisted with black-and-whites. "I didn't learn all these tricks just to toss them away on a fad," he persisted, even though the new direction was clear to everyone. I alone could keep his hopes alive in the darkroom, and sometimes he tapped me to act as "bag man" for certain assignments.

He never stopped reminding me, "It's not the camera but the man behind the camera that counts." And although he had appeared to soften somewhat following my brush with the Gestapo, whenever printing was concerned his instructions remained harsh and incisive.

On assignment, I admired the way he slipped so confidently from one vantage point to another, his roly-poly figure darting furtively below the crowds' line of sight. His proof sheets revealed most subjects captured off-guard, a total contrast to residual Network stringers bumbling along with their large-format cameras and tripods.

In a crowd, Hoffmann's tiny Leica went almost unnoticed, and he had designed himself a smart new uniform replete with a swastika armband, behind which I had to follow at a discreet distance, always displaying my yellow press card on my chest and ready to dash forward with fresh film or a backup camera at the stab of his silver forelock.

Sometimes, he used a long cable release to squeeze himself in on one end of a group photo. At others he encouraged me to fire off a couple of wide-angles from afar with the spare Leica; I guess he liked to show up in certain crowd scenes like an omniscient savant, proving that he'd really been there.

Owing to the explosive success of colour film, Hoffman's once-exclusive photos of Hitler at work and play were suddenly swamped by a host of international freelancers with telescopic lenses. Royalties from such plagiarism, he lamented, came straight out of his own pocket. Ironically, his coffers were to swell again when Martin Bormann hit upon the idea of using the Führer's head on German postage stamps in August '41, thus creating bountiful perquisites for subject and photographer alike. Each bound copy of *Mein Kampf* was illustrated with Hoffmann photos.

It was about that time when Hitler's newest doctor among several, one Karl Brandt, turned up at the studio for an official engagement photo with his fiancée, Anni Rehborn, formerly an Olympic swimming champion.

Fraulein Anni, although somewhat plain, possessed a taut, even spindly figure that hinted at a higher calling. It was apparent from the way Hoffmann fussed over the snooty couple that Dr Brandt enjoyed the Führer's full confidence; ever since he'd stepped in to save the life of Adjutant Bruckner when he was severely injured in a road accident.

For the next five years or so, until Dr Karl too was consumed by a higher calling, he was rarely out of Hitler's sight, either chatting with the inner circle or riding close behind in the second limousine.

In a further shake-up, Dr Goebbels took over control of all the nation's publishing, propaganda and media from the lumbering Putzi Hantzfangel, who had outlived his usefulness as the Party's voice of conscience.

The diminutive doctor now began to flood the empty air-waves and movie theatres with non-stop propaganda, urging on the hounds with messages of hate best reflecting his master's ambitions.

Eva too took a keen interest in the Goebbels' elevation, sensing instinctively that wife Magda, her hated rival "Hostess", was far beyond reach in Berlin and would also be elevated in Hitler's eyes just when Eva felt she was making real progress in Munich.

However, at this time Hitler's vengeful eyes were focused elsewhere; on one of his former primary school teachers no less, who had allegedly dared chastise and even cane his malevolent pupil in decades past. He'd been tracked down in retirement and a movie of the poor old man "dancing" at the end of a piano wire noose was brought into the studio for stills to be run off for the archives. The gloating student had commissioned the grisly footage that played over and over in the Brown House theatrette for the amusement of fellow Brownshirts.

I can't say one ever gets used to printing violent or pornographic pictures, but they were just two of many unpleasant "special tasks" now coming my way. When Hoffmann ordered two sets of 8" × 10" glossies from a secret Gestapo file marked "Erna Gruhn: Private" which contained the usual gyrations of the said Fraulein, I could not know then how they would have profound implications for the future political landscape.

I was familiar enough with the boss' brand of eroticism, but this file of Fraulein Gruhn's revealed a woman clearly enjoying a whole range of activities with a variety of capable men. I kept the darkroom door locked until the prints had completed their journey over the polished rollers; I knew better than to offer any comment when placing the finished prints on his desk, suspecting even then that my good work may be put to dark purposes.

As 1933 drew to a close I tried to push all such complicity to the back of my mind, feeling a bit like Dr Faust hunched over my chemicals in the subterranean gloom of the darkroom but the year had thrown up one or two more surprises. On October 15, I heard Hitler was to make an appearance in Prinzregentenstrasse, beside the English Garden, to lay a foundation stone for Munich's brand new "House of German Art", where the finest examples of coeval Aryan sculpture and painting would finally be brought together under one roof.

I had already decided to pass that way en route to spending my day off among the autumn colours by the river and had brought a few fruit treats in my lunch pack for the liberated macaque, which had since become notorious for raiding picnic hampers in the gardens.

As Hoffmann himself had been charged with curating the first exhibition, I wasn't surprised to find him clicking away as usual when I approached the colourful pageant. I had no intention of drawing attention by flashing my press card on a day off, and after examining a scale model of the imposing neo-classical building I came to the rear of the crowd, hoping to catch a glimpse of the march-past by slowly working my way forward.

Soon, the thump of drums and the blast of trumpets heralded the approach of the brown legions, tramping in time past the reviewing stand and thrusting their right arms stiffly towards their Führer. Lifting the camera to my eye, I recoiled from the sight in the viewfinder.

Row after row of faces was devoid of flesh and features, transformed into mere grinning skulls crying "Sieg Heil" in unison. Instinctively I clicked the shutter; what I had seen was impossible. Looking hurriedly about, it was apparent that neither Hitler nor anyone else in the crowd had witnessed a like phenomenon. I felt my knees buckle and struggled to catch my breath, incapable of moving closer.

All was ready for a "Führer Blessing" on the cornerstone, by striking it with a silver hammer specially crafted for the occasion. With a look of triumph Hitler slowly raised his gavel high, paused for a brief moment and brought it down sharply, with a dull clunk!

The force of the blow had shattered the shining tool in his hand and its head flew off to an audible gasp from the assembled dignitaries.

For a moment Hitler was taken aback before his brow knotted in rage.

Whispers of bad omens rippled through the crowd.

According to Eva, Hitler brooded over the providential implications for days afterwards. A second omen struck just months later when architect Paul Ludwig Troost died suddenly and left his wife, Gertrude, to step in and complete the build.

Once more the rumour mill ignited and I was reminded of Tante Gretel's memorable discourse on the importance of omens in art, and how this tendency had carried over in ever more inventive ways to the present day. Tante knew more about art than I ever would.

Sure enough, into the darkroom strode Hoffman the next day and brushed me aside. With a masterful touch, he set about doctoring the pre-published images to create a perfectly intact hammer for the final press release.

When I got around to holding my negatives up to the light I was dismayed to find that participants in the march-past now looked "normal". I reflected on whether the apparently real apparition was indeed an omen of some kind. I'd never had to worry too much about omens in the past.

My colleagues were clearly focused on what they wanted to see: the fact that Jews of all persuasions were fleeing the country in droves minus their wealth and property did not seem to bother the average Fritz. Many welcomed the return of their "rightful" inheritance and the removal of "unfair" competition in the professions. Even children in the schoolyard could be heard chanting, "Don't punch you, don't punch me, kick that Jew behind the tree …"

The common man now went about his business with a spring in his step and a sense of purpose; "working his way toward the Führer", he called it. So long as he kept his head down and toed the Party line he had little to fear.

Fighting-age men felt needed again and youngsters were jostling for leadership positions within the burgeoning Hitler Youth. Here at last was a chance, after years of humiliation and exploitation beneath the hated Versailles yoke, to once more join the winner's circle in a shower of Sieg Heil's.

Dr Goebbels berated the nation at large with daily announcements extolling the virtues of the New Order. He proudly proclaimed that "the German Man of the future will no longer be a man of books, but a man of character." Was I as immune as I'd come to believe?

If the population as a whole appeared to be falling into line, behind-the-scenes rivalries for Hitler's favour were getting out of hand and threatening to undermine the entire Party structure.

In the pressroom, rumours emerged of Reichsmarschall Göring having gathered enormous power to himself by devious measures, creating a clash of authority between the various arms of his Secret State Police and Röhm's own restive brown battalions, now close to four million strong.

Tensions flared again in December when Röhm and Hess were nominated as "Cabinet Ministers without Portfolio" in Göring's newly formed "Council of State", a concocted institution designed to do away permanently with the Reichstag and cement the Nazis in positions of permanent power.

When Röhm appeared beside Hitler on the cover of the *Illustrierter Beobachter*, I could see at once the chemistry between the two old comrades was far from chummy. The Führer appeared to have a bad smell under his nose and Röhm appeared defiant as ever.

The pugilistic S.A. Commander had just thumbed his nose at Göring's grandiose plans for a lavish Council of State Opening Ceremony, describing them as "too flashy". He then forbade his stormtroops to march in ranks or provide music for the formal launch. I'd heard whispers that such antics may be on the cards and was excited when Hoffman tapped me as "bag boy" for the big event.

Given Hitler's refusal to attend, a resplendent Göring had placed himself at the visible centre of his creation, and witnessing the look on his face as a slovenly conga line of stormtroopers straggled past the review stand was a sight I shall remember forever. All present knew that one man alone was responsible for this humiliation: Ernst Röhm. And to make matters worse he was technically superior to Himmler, who was jockeying with Göring for control of the Gestapo.

This man alone was responsible for the brown rabble openly mocking the Reichsmarschall in front of the invited dignitaries; neither they nor their leader in his opinion, were fit to be called soldiers of the Reich.

As I raised my camera and looked into the eyepiece I saw Göring ashen-faced with fury, overseeing a bare-knuckled troop of howlers loping down for a drink. The SS had also been ordered to attend, and through my viewfinder, I glimpsed Robert's rows of tin soldiers with not a single hair out of place.

Various other groups followed until eventually the Reichsmarschall regained his composure and managed to raise his jewel-encrusted ivory baton with the authority of Nero.

I looked over at Hoffman who also was suppressing a snigger; Röhm's snub seemed forgotten amidst the ensuing pomp and din.

I managed only a single exposure before the boss signalled for fresh film. While reloading the spare Leica beneath the review stand, I overheard the Reichsmarschall referring to Röhm with gritted teeth as "that twisted soldier of fortune". It was a declaration of war.

Röhm meanwhile remained unfazed, announcing that he would continue to "assert the S.A." and never forsake his dream of absorbing the depleted Reichswehr into his own command, all while implementing "True Socialism" throughout Germany.

He continually poked fun at both contenders, especially at Himmler's religious cultism and exaggerated racism, and more alarmingly, let it be known that he was writing a book. According to Robert, whom I met occasionally for coffee at Café Stephanie in between his speaking tours and new life among slick SS companions.

He'd seen little of Röhm since absconding with Captain Fegelein; even sounding a little dismissive of his former "best friend". He said that Röhm was spoiling for a fight with General Blomberg, the most recent "Minister for War", who could be seen almost daily snuggling close to Hitler. Blomberg was an "old school" officer who could hardly miss the threat posed to his one hundred thousand career officers from Röhm's boisterous brown hordes.

In cunning deference to his Führer, Blomberg promptly made the Hitler salute mandatory as Army Protocol while requiring all Wehrmacht soldiers to swear an oath of personal loyalty on their very lives, not to God or to Germany, nor even to the Nazi Party, but to Adolph Hitler personally. In return, their new Supreme Commander vowed that "the German Reichswehr will be the sole bearer of arms in the new Germany".

Röhm's disgust upon hearing "the ridiculous little corporal" being openly addressed as "Your Excellency" now reached breaking point; when his deputised "Protection Squads" overseeing the Führer's security were ordered back to barracks, to be replaced with a brand new unit of black-shirted SS bodyguards, the scene was set for a monumental clash of wills.

But, I am getting ahead of myself as 1933 had yet more dramas in store before it drew to its climactic close: Robert had shrewdly sensed which way the winds were blowing; Captain Fegelein's beguiling recruitment drive had not only riled Röhm but seduced my rugged Aryan brother into cutting ties with all his rowdy brown comrades.

I too, realised that I had some pretty serious thinking to do if ever I was to survive the gathering storm. Freezing temperatures aside, I decided to camp overnight beside the Isar and gather my thoughts: if I could not find solace and meaning while gazing into the flames of a cheery campfire, surely all was lost.

Loading my bicycle with warm blankets and a bag of framing off-cuts for the fire I half-pushed and half-rode towards the English Garden, stopping just long enough in the frosty air to slip a note under Claudia's door advising her of my intentions. It seemed an eternity since the two of us had spent any meaningful time together and I hoped against hope that if she were indeed living at home she might take the hint. Throughout that short and bracing afternoon, I huddled in deep contemplation before the crackling flames. There was much to consider.

"Boo! I could see your smoke a mile off …"

My heart was thrilled at the familiar voice blowing tiny puffs of steam while emerging from the bushes. My Sissy moved swiftly to sit beside me on the soft sand, first kissing me on the cheek and holding her fingers out hungrily to the warmth.

"I … I'm so glad you've come. I've never felt more alone in my life. I know I've taken a risk that one of the Block Wardens might spot the smoke, but otherwise, I'd freeze to death. Being here has allowed me a chance to sort a few things in my head; I don't believe I'm breaking any laws. Anyhow, they would have to go out of their way to find me here, there's so much smoke in the air and fishermen light fires all the time."

"There are so many new laws being rammed through at the moment that it's almost impossible not to be swept up in one or another," Claudia said matter-of-factly. "Just look at you, a bundle of nerves. You really must learn to take a more disciplined view of unfolding events and let things go over your head.

"Spare a thought for us Jews being purged from every profession, banned from public parks and swimming pools, even kids from attending school. Many of these so-called 'good Germans' are happy to look the other way while their Jewish neighbours are being kicked out onto the street; squabbling over their possessions before they're out of sight.

"I'm telling you, now the genie is out of the bottle it may be the Jews and 'untermenschen' today, but it will be the rest of you tomorrow."

"Calm down, now who's uptight? It's not me you should be warning, but those brethren of yours who are trying to stick it out in the hope that the storm will soon blow over. I'm just trying to survive as best I can. At least the boss is rock solid behind *you* I would have thought, correct me if I'm wrong."

She merely rolled her eyes in exasperation and poked at the flames.

As if in response to my hopes, a waxing moon peeped over the rooftops and through the willows, glancing shards of silver off the black surface. I snuggled a little closer and whispered, "I do miss you, Claudie, you know that, don't you?"

I received no response other than a slight pressure from her shoulder. A grey heron croaked toward its mate upstream and my soul filled fleetingly with contentment.

Throughout that long winter's night, we talked and joked together like brother and sister, without a worry in the world. We exchanged our differing observations of the same phenomena while warming our bellies with Schnapps straight from the bottle. For me, nothing Claudia could ever say or do as part of her double life would diminish the respect and love I held in my heart. I was astonished at her knowledge of the inner workings of the Nazi Regime and the mindset of many of National Socialism's top players; she certainly wasn't taken in by the sophisms at the heart of their affairs. She assured me she could handle herself capably, given the knife edge she walked among the violent and volatile characters in her world.

When the Schnapps kicked in she confirmed my worst suspicions in rather blunt terms: Robert alone held the keys to her heart, and she wanted him above all others. I guess deep down I'd always known it, opting to bide my time until she discovered his true nature.

"I believe your brother jumped the S.A. ship just in time, given the tone of Ernst's braggadocio these days," she said casually after I'd tiptoed around the subject of how often they'd seen each other since Robert's ascension into seraphic SS circles.

"The word is out that Ernst needs to pull his head in," she continued. "Outside of the S.A., his reputation is everywhere on the nose and he makes no effort to conceal his outrageous sexual adventures. He is openly contemptuous of the entire political leadership, including Hitler." Her eyes twinkled as she shared her observations. "Then again, who am I to talk?"

"Oh yes, but you're being coerced," I reminded her. "In one way, it's Hitler's own fault: I can see Ernst's reasons for being piqued. As the old saying goes, 'No man is a hero to his own valet', to which I would add, 'let alone to a former commanding officer like Captain Ernst Röhm of the 16th Bavarian Infantry Regiment. Poor Ernst has realised with a jolt that his so-called 'Cabinet Minister' appointment was a hollow ploy to get him out of the way."

"I think I get what you mean, but I owe him so much."

"We both do! But who will shift him from his course? He has millions of men marching behind him. What can Hitler do other than to go on portraying himself as the long-awaited Messiah?"

"I'll always be indebted to Ernst and the kindness of Frau Emilie …"

"That may be so, but I can never forget that he is the leader of three million Jew-haters who won't rest until they rid the world of every last one of us …" She stopped herself and her eyes shot greenish daggers into the flames. I could sense the sadness behind her anger: who could she trust?

Her conscience glittered between bouts of reality as we exchanged points of view on many topics. Occasionally she would give a short laugh and lean over to touch my arm lightly. Yet, for all her hard-won acumen she couldn't see through Robert. If only she knew how poorly he had treated other women, especially those who fell heaviest over him. I couldn't swallow the frog in my throat.

She expounded her theory of why so many Germans, an otherwise cultured and enlightened people, could so easily have been led to vent their pent-up animosities against anyone who was different, especially toward the Jews. She believed that such behaviour indicated a massive inferiority complex of some kind, perhaps carried over from the humiliating defeat in the Great War. The "Stab in the Back" theory was alive and well and she described Nazism as "Society's pummelling fists of revenge".

"You once told me that ignorance is the only sin," she said softly as the firelight caught her cheekbones ... but you are wrong. For some of us, being born at all is turning out to be the greater misfortune, far greater than those we commit every day just to stay alive." She seemed to be talking to herself and I decided not to tell of my hallucination concerning the ape-men and leering skulls at the march-past.

Instead, I repeated the oaths that Eva had uttered upon hearing Unity Mitford had taken a villa opposite the English Garden, and furthermore, had attended the Nuremberg Party Rally as Hitler's personal guest. My friend rolled her eyes. "Evi the fool is dancing with the Devil. Where does she think all this is going to lead?"

"Believe it or not, she actually thinks the Führer is going to marry her one day if only she continues to hang on; he has as good as told her so," I offered.

"Be careful what you wish for is all I can say. Eva, Eva, I'm sick of hearing about Eva Braun! We all get what's coming to us, even when pretending to be Alice in Wonderland; let's change the subject.

"I must say it's good to see your face looking more normal, I doubt you could stand too many beatings like that. At least Robert has sussed out which way the chips are falling; he's been designated an 'Honorary Aryan' you know, in order to be inducted into the SS or hasn't he mentioned it yet? After all this is over he's going to take me back to Brazil where we can settle down on a little farm somewhere, he's told me more than once."

"After *what's* all over? Now who's playing Alice?" I asked incredulously. "You of all people should know better. I thought you were *the* hard-nosed realist around here; yet you continue to fall head over heels for his bullshit.

"I'm telling you he'll never return to South America; he *can't* go back after what happened ..." I blurted, before stopping short, aware that I may have put my foot in it. Should I go on to reveal how Robert murdered Papa in cold blood? Surely, that would bring her to her senses. But I didn't.

She sighed. "I guess each of us is entitled to our dreams, and here I am criticising little Evi. 'We are such stuff as dreams are made on, and our little lives are rounded with a sleep' ... so says the great Englishman."

"But, how do you know such lines from Shakespeare ...?"

"Because I was once in a play at school whose title I no longer remember," she cut me off brusquely.

"*The Tempest*," I offered meekly, "Prospero—"

"Oh, do shut up! You and your book learning ..." My heart gave a little skip though I knew she didn't really mean it.

I gazed intently at the light on her face. "You will never be diminished in my eyes, Claudia; you know that, don't you?"

"And you, sweet friend, should by now be aware of the penalties for consorting with Jews. Should Hoffman choose to blow my cover, then both you and Robert will be sorry you ever laid eyes on me."

"D … Don't talk that way. Why would the boss ever do such a thing? And, I certainly would never be sorry," I shot back.

She paused for a moment and gave another sigh. "If and when the time comes you might turn out like all those other faceless millions of Germans who look the other way when it suits them."

"Not me! You *are* my business," I gushed, and saw her brows knit briefly. "At least most of the time. I mean, when you are around," I added with regret.

That night beside the river, despite all our toing and froing, or maybe because of it, our differences only added to our closeness. The flickering firelight and the moonbeams dancing through the willow fingers made a lasting impression on both of us.

I was able to concede that I couldn't quite see things in the vein she painted or the conclusions she drew. I revealed that in order to preserve my sanity I must continue to strive for excellence in the current moment, regardless of all seeming evidence to the contrary. I begged her to remain positive, hoping to keep my foot in the door by inviting her to accompany me next spring for a visit to the Hahn Chalet at Berchtesgaden, but she merely looked perplexed and poked at the coals.

Sometime after midnight, she insisted on tucking me into my Luftwaffe-issue sleeping bag beneath a leaning tree trunk, "Just to see how you look." Then, pressing a finger to my lips she melted away.

Though cosy I didn't sleep much that night, reflecting on the reality of my existence between a rock and a hard place. On the one hand, Robert held all the cards without really trying; on the other, if I could possess Claudia and keep her safe, everything may yet turn out well. She was the one and only girl since Maya in whom I'd somehow found the female animal spirit so attuned to its surroundings and free of airs and graces.

Puffing little clouds of fog I drifted off dreamily beside the embers until I thought I heard "Ole Stumpy", the one-handed howler and his troop, casting hoarse volleys across the great river. Their bellowing took on the distinctive throb: "Sieg Heil, Sieg Heil," louder and louder, until I had to cover my ears. From out of the ashes rose a burning swastika, rolling toward me: I tried to look away. There was Maya's tiny broken body lashed to the spinning spokes, and she was alive, calling to me in a voice I could not hear over the mindless mantra. Convinced she was mouthing my name I reached out a hand to touch her cheek one last time … but was frozen in place.

When I came to, weeping uncontrollably, a feeble stab of sunlight revealed the hoar-frost rim on my hood glowing golden and the tears on my cheeks as ice. The cold had penetrated my kidneys and the first task would be coaxing a little life from the embers. I'd scratched a crude hole for my hip in the sand and snow, only to find my body warmth had allowed the melting crystals to seep into my bivouac, causing my joints to lock fast.

Perhaps it was as much the fear as the sadness of the dream that had evoked such deep-plumbed emotions. Freezing or not, I was excited at the prospect of spending a whole day alone, practising my exercises and reshuffling my thoughts. No breeze ruffled the ring of bright snowflakes surrounding my campsite.

For long minutes I revived my extremities with a warm mug of tea in my hands, as my thoughts wandered inexorably back to the Rainbow Cave, where I could almost hear Sister Klara's intonations above the bustle and squeak of Munich's morning traffic. Closing my eyes I recited the Our Father, substituting the word "breath" for "bread", and reminding myself to savour every lungful of life force while I had the chance.

I added a final line of my own to the great supplication: "God in heaven, God in me; thank you for these truths I see."

Then, with a twig I drew a perfect equilateral triangle in the sand, to remind myself of its role in problem-solving. Had not Sister said that the Great Pyramids themselves were the ultimate expression of this Divine Principle and that those heeding the message would be permitted to approach the higher Truths of body, mind and soul?

At that time I'd failed to grasp her meaning, but here within the throbbing heart of a great city, my quiescent mind received a long-overdue glimmer of understanding.

Softly chanting, I felt myself blending into the landscape, becoming one with the air and river currents. Bathed now in the morning glow I recalled Amenhotep IV, the first to conceive of the rising sun as a perfect symbol for the singular consciousness of the one true God reaching into every corner of the Universe thirteen centuries before the Master Jesus Himself strode the dusty streets of Palestine.

At a stroke, Pharaoh Akhenaten had put the entire Egyptian Priesthood out of business; his subjects could henceforth make the connection between God and their own consciences without the necessity of an "intermediary".

Long after Sister Klara had stirred my interest, I'd unearthed Munich Bibliotech's splendid and as yet intact Egyptian collection, poring over its many hidden mysteries and Natural Law all the while regretting I'd not paid more attention to her words when I had the chance.

The spell was broken when my teeth commenced chattering and I realised the campfire had dimmed. Scratching about for dry kindling I imagined what it must have been like for the foot soldiers in Napoleon's doomed Grande Armée grinding to a halt in the Arctic blasts outside the gates of Moscow. I had read that a freezing body simply goes numb all over before the last breath departs. Under the circumstances, it wasn't difficult to imagine myself facing such an ordeal, to feel life slipping away with each degree of body heat.

As my fire crackled back to life I realised I still had a good 300 minutes more before reporting back for a scheduled night shift. If indeed it were true that no person can concentrate on more than one thing at a time, forming a logical plan would not be so easy.

Nazi culture had clearly unleashed the demons in otherwise reasonable folk, much as alcohol does with certain drinkers. How could any society evolve safely when built on foundations of violence, greed and envy?

Such thoughts should not be concerning me: my former lycanthropy was no substitute for positive thoughts and sound actions. Sister Klara made it perfectly clear that God did not want us to approach Him on our knees, but standing tall to claim our rightful evolution. I was a damn good printer, everybody said so, and therein lay my best hope of salvation.

In the lead-up to Yuletide, Claudia appeared briefly in the newsroom once or twice, when she allowed me to hope that we might see in the New Year together. She hinted that I would be in for a surprise of sorts and for weeks I stewed and rhapsodised over the possibilities.

At the same time not nearly so elusive, Eva suddenly seemed to be everywhere at once, darting between the counter and darkroom neurotically. She made no secret of her jealousy over Henni's accepting a part-time secretarial position in Hitler's office, especially given the persistent rumours of his earlier clumsy attempts at intimacy with Hoffman's only daughter. She feared that despite Henrietta's recent marriage to the effeminate Schirach, her Adolph may still be harbouring more than a soft spot for his "little sunshine".

Furthermore, that "great horse", Unity Mitford, had returned from England with her sister Diana, only just married to the British fascist leader Oswald Mosley; together they were being spotted more often in Hitler's company.

According to the gossip columns, Unity had delighted her aristocratic parents, Lord and Lady Redesdale, by showing off 8" × 10" prints of herself being chummy with the new Führer; photos developed and printed in Studio Hoffman by me, under Eva's feline gaze.

Both Mitford sisters flaunted their adoration of and loyalty to the new regime and its outstanding Leader.

Unity in particular continued to cake on the makeup in a most un-germanic fashion. Whenever in Hitler's immediate proximity she showered him with penetrating glances of unmistakable meaning. Most of her competition had been craftily sidelined by bribing the head waiters of the Carlton Hotel, Cafés Ostaria Bavaria and Heck, *simply not to notify* Munich's other moonstruck matrons whenever *he* crossed their thresholds.

Suddenly, Lady Mitford was being quoted and admired for her rallying cries and channel-spanning sentiments. "The dream of National Socialism still means something," she would exclaim to the gathered media upon emerging from her Munich villa beside the English Garden.

She foresaw "a great future alliance between Germany and Great Britain, standing as one against the subhuman Communist hordes from the East". Unity's mother, Baroness Redesdale, was even more enthusiastic than her husband and daughters over National Socialist Germany, publishing in London's *Sunday Sun* an unqualified endorsement of Hitler and the society he ruled.

Rhapsodising over her recent visit to Germany, she said she had gone to visit Unity "full of prejudice and imbued with antipathy", but that what she had experienced had "swept away such feelings".

Recounting her meeting with Hitler she "beheld a man of arresting personality; a man with wonderful, far-seeing eyes". She believed herself to be in the presence of one truly great, "he is simple, dignified and humble; a leader of men." She had been, she wrote, "greatly impressed by this simple man of action, beloved of modern Germany for his frankness, sincerity, and great desire for friendship with the English People."

Evidently pleased with her outpouring, she despatched a copy to Ribbentrop in London, which was unnecessary given that all major foreign publications were channelled through our Press Room as a matter of course.

Fume as she may, Eva was powerless to thwart the finger of fate.

"He can always find a sharp reprimand whenever I get a little too dolled up," she lamented to me in the darkroom. "Yet, he thinks nothing of appearing in public besides that … that lanky, painted *thing*!"

She now spent much of her time beside the telephone in her office, drinking heavily, chain-smoking and re-arranging the stuffed toy collection on her desk; once confiding to me that they eased her incessant loneliness.

"No, Miss Eva, I'm afraid the Master has not yet returned," frazzled Housekeeper Frau Winter would reply patiently into the mouthpiece on the other end, up to a dozen times each day. "Yes, Miss Eva, I'll be sure to tell him you called … And that it's urgent."

For imagined revenge, Eva and sister Gretl began arranging to meet with selected SS officers in the homes of friends, thereby flirting shamelessly into the wee hours and hoping to trigger a spark of jealousy from afar. But all to no effect!

Every time she turned around there was yet another female coming between herself and the man of her dreams. She agonised over Magda Goebbels' now total control over the Führer's social engagements, especially when in Berlin, which was increasingly often.

"Little Sunshine", who often accompanied Hitler on the road with his other secretaries, rubbed it in at every opportunity.

Eva, not to be outdone, snidely repeated rumours that Baldur, Henni's new husband, actually preferred boys to his petite new spouse, which would explain why he was so often away with his young charges splashing around stark naked in various mountain streams and meadows. Eva said out loud that any other husband would be furious to see his new bride swanning all over the countryside in the company of older men.

On the few occasions when Hitler was in Munich and could find time for a leisurely motoring picnic in the nearby woods, Eva was quite unable to claim him for herself, other than a brief curtsy or two. She was forced to watch her lover behaving just like "one of the boys", wandering around handing out sandwiches to the others with the briefest of glances in her direction.

"He so much looks forward to his moments of relaxation," she fumed upon returning to the studio. "Playing the waiter should have been someone else's responsibility." Despite appearances, Eva's position was actually far more secure than she imagined.

From the first day that Fritz and Fanny Braun tasted the good life, and despite receiving no response to yet another "headmaster admonition" said to the Führer, among other things, "Young German women can't stick to principles." Eva ensured that never reached Hitler's desk, they too were hooked.

They swallowed their objections and granted permission for their convent-educated, middle daughter to occasionally "sleep over" and "comfort" the harried Leader at his second-floor Prinzregentenplatz apartment.

Furthermore, they agreed she could spend all Christmas week at Obersalzberg, which would be her first and much-anticipated visit to the legendary Magic Mountain.

In any case, it wasn't as if Fritz and Fanny's own marriage had been all smooth sailing or bourgeois respectability; they'd divorced each other in 1921 and remarried in 1922.

Now they were ill at ease over their eldest child, Ilse, continuing her employment under the Jewish Dr Marx, more so since the Nuremberg laws now forbid her "cohabitating" in his rooms. Every day until 1937, when Dr Marx emigrated after being struck off, loyal Ilse ran an increased risk of being charged with "race defilement".

The family breathed a collective sigh of relief when she reluctantly accepted employment under the recent "Führer Edict" granting near-unlimited powers to Architect Albert Speer in Berlin.

Hoffman further assured them that during Eva's visit to Haus Wachenfeld, she would be helping to plan a fully equipped darkroom "somewhere in the basement" of Bormann's grand guesthouse conversion into a fortress. "Something more befitting the all-seeing warrior of a Great Nation," Bormann had stated.

There were yet one or two obstacles along the path to absolute Nazi control, which once overcome, would free up the newly appointed "Mountain Gauleiter" to expand Hitler's "Private Estate" right around the mountain.

"What's more, I shall have a whole apartment to myself," Eva bubbled, trying to busy herself in the darkroom while counting down the days. "On the top floor too, opposite Adolph's," she added for effect, glossing over my beating by the Gestapo.

For days following my "interrogation", she had trivialised my black eyes and battered features with the flippant admonishment that in future I "had best leave humorous observations of top Nazis to those less fragile". Stung by her callous rebuke, I shrank for days afterwards.

Try as I may there was no avoiding contact in the intimate nooks and corridors around the darkrooms. "Do you still believe that prints are better than movies?" she probed one day after backing me into a corner. An awkward silence followed until she knotted her perfect brows and asked petulantly, "You're not still sulking, are you?"

I stared back, swamped by the perfume and chemicals. Under the red safe light, her eyes and jewellery threw off tiny daggers of flame; I suddenly felt faint.

"Well, yes or no? Which is it? Surely by now even you've come to realise the superiority of movie. Wait until you see my latest routine on the parallel bars," she persisted. "Adolph loves it when I bend over backwards."

"Stills can be savoured, alone, for their own sake," I gasped out gloomily, not really in the mood to return to the old contention.

"Yes, but movies are alive … and they tell more of a story, don't you think?" She was like a dog with a bone.

"Not necessarily, 35 mm stills allow us to focus all our attention on a single moment that speaks for many …" I decided not to allow her to override my belief in the force of a perfect point in time and space summing up an incident or era.

"Whenever, and I concede it's rare, I focus my attention on a great photograph, memory and imagination do the rest. The captured moment in time replays in my head; surely a sounder repository than any theatre," I quipped. She did not reply.

I then reminded her of the pleasurable hours we'd spent putting her albums together. "Oh, that's different; they're just simple snapshots," she demurred.

"Even holiday snaps and other special events can evoke powerful recurring emotions. Every day we see Aryan faces filled with joy when they come to collect their wedding pictures".

I felt I'd won the debate, at least for today.

Despite my early mood I'd stood my ground. Suspecting that her pugnacious manner was really no more than a cover for loneliness and insecurity, which no opulent exterior could disguise, I gradually softened my responses over time.

That first "Yuletide", as Dr Goebbels insisted that Christmas now be re-titled, caused dissention throughout the length and breadth of Germany.

From now on, National Socialism would champion a much older and prouder tradition than mere Christianity: a celebration lauding the eternal winter solstice and return of longer daylight hours with its origins stretching back to pre-history. Henceforth, Germany would resurrect her ancient customs. After all, "Who needs a Christmas King when we have our own Messiah?" was the unspoken thought for many.

Eva didn't much care what it was called, so long as she could spend her vacation in the company, perhaps even the arms of her "poor overworked Adolph".

One day in the darkroom I foolishly suggested she read *Mein Kampf* during his long absences, "in order to retain his presence nearby and familiarise yourself with His thought patterns".

"*Mein Kampf? Mein Kampf?*" she snapped. "Why would I want to waste my time on that when I have the real thing?" She was blinking a lot and waving her hands about. "And why can't those horny old Munich socialites just leave him alone for once? They sit there on their fat bums sipping tea on his red velvet couch, not having a clue about its ups and downs and other secrets the apartment holds ..." She gave a forced giggle.

"But I can talk to you in confidence, can't I, Klaus?" she said in her little girl's voice with a slight lisp; "I get moody when alone."

I was surprised by this change of tone. "Sure, you can confide in me, Fraulein Eva, if it makes you feel better, but I'll have the boss on my back if I don't get these orders through."

She ignored my caution and continued unfazed. "Adolph says our affair must remain a State Secret for the time being. I can tell you there won't be too many 'State Secrets' after this Christmas holiday if I have anything to do with it. Or should I say Yuletide holiday?"

She rolled her eyes at our shared confidence.

Up until then, Eva had shown no interest in my alpine visit to Tante and Onkel the year before, peppering me instead with her hopes and intentions for a place she'd not yet actually been to.

I kept my nose down while she prattled on, "The Führer has incorporated a large, south-facing sun terrace into the plans, big enough for me to have a dog and maybe even a pool in summer. He has taken over from Bormann in designing the whole complex himself. Did you know that architecture is one of Adolph's pet hobbies?" I nodded and took another breath of the suffocating air.

"I can't wait to try out the ski slopes at this time of year, but he's just so protective ..." she sighed, and I thought of my clumsy efforts on snowshoes.

"He is afraid that I may break an ankle or something and is insisting that I be accompanied by SS bodyguards at all times. Don't worry, I'll soon lose them," she bragged while lighting up under the "No Smoking" sign.

As I struggled to focus on the task at hand she blew several smoke rings past my burning eyes. As I recall, her first visit to the "Magic Mountain" turned out as no more than a cherry on her glittering casket of trinkets, a far cry yet from the gilded cage it was to become. There was no talk of a Berghof Darkroom.

When the new job sheets were pinned up on the noticeboard, I again appeared at the bottom of the page, rostered on for ten days straight across the main vacation period. When I plucked up enough courage to plead before Lothar and Iris I was reminded of the many disadvantages which logically flow for non-party members. They reminded me of the unemployed millions still roaming the icy streets of Germany and queuing at soup kitchens, begging for work, any work, "even printers …" summed up the warning.

There was nothing for it but to bide my time and notify Onkel and Tante of my revamped schedule, if indeed this would be still convenient for them. "Of course, my dear," Tante's reply began. "Just let us know the day before and we'll be waiting at the Bahnhof, Love Gretel. PS I have a couple of new paintings to show off, G."

46

It seemed that up until now, Studio Hoffman had been in a state of constant modernisation, with the installation of several colour printers, specialist operators and a long line of Henrietta's girlfriends with time on their hands to fill in behind the counter.

Then there was Hugo, Walter, George, Willie, August and Max, Hoffman's expanding bevy of "stringers" all adding to my workload with impatient demands of their own.

Nonetheless, black-and-white developing still comprised the bulk of our work, especially for publication, and films kept pouring in from all corners of Bavaria. Updating and tending to the "Hitler Files" while processing a growing volume of "special orders" now occupied most of my working day. By Christmas Eve, I felt sufficiently caught up to set out for Frau Emilie's apartment bearing a large bunch of hot-house tulips.

"Happy Yuletide!" I cried from the hallway as the new maid showed me through into the drawing room, and I'm not sure who received the greater shock. For a moment, Frau Emilie could not see my beaming face hidden behind the bouquet, while I in turn was distracted to see Ernst and Marty at the keyboard of the baby grand serenading the regal old lady.

Her two dogs leapt up in welcome, and in a flash Emilie too was on her feet. "Please don't use that ridiculous expression in my house. I'm Christian and proud of it; so is my Ernst, if only he'd slow down long enough to remember it. Do come over here Jung Klaus and give us a good look at you," she immediately softened at my chastened immobility in the centre of the room.

"My, my, how you've grown. Oh! They're just lovely, aren't they boys? Beautiful tulips? So early in the season, too," she said, moving lightly to hug me in a warm embrace.

"Come on, Ma," Ernst protested. "How about the bunch I brought?"

"Yes dear, but you probably beat the man over the head for them."

"And aren't I staying back to accompany you to the midnight service …?"

"Yes, yes, of course … Sophie! Put these in a vase of water and bring master Klaus something to eat. He must be starving."

Within minutes, Röhm's chiselled features had softened a little and Marty had thrown an arm around my shoulder.

"What jolly luck, meeting up with you here. I dare say you've been keeping your nose clean since your run in with the Gestapo. Seriously, old man, I bet it was a nasty business. We hear good reports of your work with Hoffman, though Ernst is still dirty over Robert jumping ship to join the SS; there's no denying it, Ernst."

"That brother of yours only ever seems to learn the hard way," Röhm chimed in. "It beats me why he'd want to associate with that bunch of dandies."

I noticed a hint of jealousy in his voice, even though he retained "technical authority" over most of the SS "pretty boys" he so eschewed.

"Well, at least you've still got me," I volunteered to smooth the waters, puffing out my chest and drawing myself up to my full 5'7½".

Did I detect a note of resignation from the S.A. Commander-in-Chief as we moved toward the groaning sideboard filled with warm pastries?

Between dainties Frau Emilie wanted to know all about my job in the darkroom and whether my accommodation was satisfactory, to which I responded in general terms.

"My Ernst was so pleased with his last portraits sitting; he could barely squeeze the new 'Blood Ribbon' onto his chest, could you dear?" she said proudly.

Reaching for an unfamiliar framed 5" × 7", Frau Emilie wiped it lovingly with her sleeve. "See here? He has no room left above his heart; he has to wear this latest one on his right breast, don't you dear?"

I was aware that several Old Fighters (Alter Kämpfer) had recently booked in to be photographed wearing their most recent decorations from Hitler's own hand, a solid silver medal dangling from a ribbon of red and white with black trim belatedly struck to commemorate the failed Putsch of '23. One face depicted the Nazi Eagle clasping a wreath, and the other showed Feldernhalle, scene of the fatal police fusillade that followed.

"Aw, Mutti, put the damn thing away and don't go on about my medals," Röhm said, slightly embarrassed. "I've said it before: if that ridiculous Corporal thinks he can buy me off with a seat in a toothless cabinet and the handing out of baubles he's got another thing coming. My new book will blow the lid off all this 'Messiah' bullshit!"

"Dear, dear, language Ernst. Do you wish more bad habits on the boy?"

But Röhm had triggered his theme. "Knock it off Ma; how many times do I have to say it … the German Revolution is being fought not by Philistines, bigots and sermonisers wearing medals, but by revolutionary fighters. It's all the S.A. knows." I gulped and took a deep breath; Marty and Frau Emilie looked as if they'd heard it all before.

"But Ernst, you are not without victories," Schartzl attempted to mollify the florid face. "You have achieved the near impossible in having our swastika incorporated into every Wehrmacht uniform …"

"Bah! Mere tokenism; that gutless fool Blomberg and his Officer Corp are going out of their way to undermine my position. The S.A. Army of the future will hack its way into power if necessary, straight through all his laws and mazes. Mark my words, heads will roll before I'm done."

"That's quite enough dear," Emilie scolded gently; "After all, this is the season of goodwill towards all men. Didn't you tell me that Adolph was striking a deal with the Vatican? Surely that will guarantee a more united front against the Bolshevist threat?" She sounded a little alarmed.

"I'm afraid there's more to it than that, Frau Röhm," Schartzl responded. "Adolph has been overly influenced by the philosopher Nietzsche and his belief in the so-called Superman. He wants to breed a nation of perfect human specimens and is now holding up the actress Leni Riefenstahl as the ideal Aryan woman. No doubt you've seen her in those mountaineering films; she leaps from crag to crag like a mountain goat." Frau Röhm shook her head.

Marty took her silence as an invitation to continue. "It seems every time the pair of them appear in public together the rest of the 'imperfect population' is required to practise 'obedience unto death'. She does nothing to dispel these romance rumours and such displays run counter to everything the S.A. stands for …"

"It's true Mutti," Röhm added. "Adolph's become a swine and is answerable to no one; his old friends aren't good enough for him. He's even gotten himself a tail coat and wants to sit on his mountaintop pretending to be God. *I'm* the nucleus of this new army and it's about time he accepted it."

"He's right, Frau Röhm," Marty continued, "I know you aren't much interested in political matters but we resent the SS now being sent in to clear venues and secure areas before Adolph speaks; without even consulting Ernst. All I can say is the man must be living in constant fear if he has to surround himself with droves of Blackshirt bodyguards supposedly honed to much higher standards than our stormtroops."

Given my place at Frau Emilie's side, I felt the import of their candour and squirmed a little uncomfortably as Röhm continued. "If the enemies of the S.A. are nursing the hope that we won't retaliate, we are content to let them enjoy this hope for a short time. At the hour and in the form which appears to be necessary they shall receive the fitting answer …"

"Goodness gracious, dear. Surely things are not so dire as you imagine? Must I re-read Adolph's congratulatory letter over to you again …?" she asked, reaching for an opened envelope resting against the sugar bowl.

"He leaves no doubt in my mind of the esteem and affection he feels for you." With trembling fingers, she unfolded the monogrammed letterhead and commenced reading out loud, like an old schoolmistress giving a history lesson.

"My dear Chief of Staff," it began, and I felt like an invisible voyeur privy to the soothing words of the very person being lambasted just minutes earlier. "When I summoned you to your present position, my dear Chief of Staff, the S.A. was passing through a severe crisis." Frau Emilie's voice rose and fell melodiously, with obvious pride in her baby boy. "It is primarily due to your services if after a few years this political instrument could develop that force which enabled me to face the final struggle for power and to succeed in laying low the Marxist opponent."

She cleared her throat and continued. "At the close of the year of the National Socialist Revolution, therefore, I feel compelled to thank you, my dear Ernst Röhm, for the imperishable services which you have rendered to the National Socialist Movement and the German people, and to assure you how very grateful I am to fate that I am able to call such men as you my friends and fellow combatants. In true friendship and grateful regard, Your Adolph Hitler."

She carefully folded the precious document and placed it back in the envelope, before smoothing her frock front and settling in her chair. For a few minutes no one spoke and I thought both men looked a little sheepish. A flickering self-satisfied smile hovered on her lips and at that moment I was in no doubt that Ernst's grievances were no more than a storm in a teacup.

"Now, shall we get ourselves ready? I've been so much looking forward to the evening service," Frau Röhm purred. "Klaus, would you care to join us?"

Eva's long-anticipated first visit to Haus Wachenfeld turned out to be an exercise in mixed blessings.

Before departing she'd had to spend Christmas Eve at the Hoffman family villa, but disappointingly Hitler chose to brood alone with his memories in Geli's bedroom at the Prinzregentenplatz apartment.

After the exchange of gifts on Yuletide morning Eva climbed excitedly aboard a large black tourer at the behest of "Travel Marshall" Schaub, for the nearly two-hour journey to Magic Mountain, a trip over which she had fantasised so long and hard.

"Good God, I thought we'd never get there," she grumbled to me later. "Manned roadblocks and guard houses every few hundred yards past Berchtesgaden. In spite of my pass signed by the boss, it seemed no one had ever heard of me; then there were more delays while each guard house telephoned back to Himmler or ahead to the house. By the time we arrived, I was ready to scream."

This was our first exchange since her return to work in the New Year and she did not arrive empty-handed. Flitting from room to room, she handed out huge boxes of candies and chocolates. "Mind you, they may turn out to be poisoned," she half-joked to each recipient in turn, finally revealing that they were but a tiny portion of the 10,000 or so unsolicited gratuities that had arrived at the front gate of Haus Wachenfeld during Yuletide week.

"Of course, they've all been opened by the guards in case there's a bomb or something," she explained, as I cautiously lifted the lid of my box to catch a whiff of chocolate ginger. "Naturally, Adolph can't eat them himself, just in case … and that leaves all the more for us," she said gleefully, popping one of my chocolate gingers into her mouth.

"Unfortunately, there's one of those stuffy Gestapo fellows stationed with the 'tasters' in the kitchen up there; every morsel has to be examined and nibbled between garden and plate. It's just so frustrating not being able to add my own little touches to the Führer's meals."

I decided to take the risk and bit down on a crunchy peanut brittle; my Yuletide treats may be a little late in coming but they were certainly scrumptious.

"What do you think of these?" she asked, not of the peanut brittle but the hand-made Italian high-boots she thrust under my nose.

"He'll stop at nothing you know, to see me as Germany's best-dressed Fraulein," she said, turning her ankles from side to side. "He even squirrelled a pair of my old work shoes away to Mussolini's bootmaker as a pattern; I just love them."

Personally, I felt the tan leather clashed with her new black sequined frock, another of Hitler's extravagant Yuletide offerings.

"Might I guess what else was in your stocking?" I asked pointedly, drawing in a draught of her latest fragrance. "Oh, nothing much; more underwear and French perfume. A movie camera was what I was really hoping for but no such luck. Sometimes, he just ignores the most obvious hints." She sighed.

"In the meantime, run these few rolls through for me and I'll pick them up tomorrow. Papa's been such a pain since my first week away. Perhaps when he sees my pictures, he'll come around." Eva's responses convinced me that all had not gone quite according to plan or desire. "If only I could do something about those parochial pilgrim cows bearing their udders outside the front gate every time Adolph drives by or shows his nose on the balcony."

I could see her growing frustrations. "And, no radios permitted for staff or visitors, would you believe? Bloody Wagner thundering away over the loudspeakers all day long; Adolph himself has the only radio in Haus Wachenfeld, one that he says can receive and transmit anywhere in the world, although for the life of me I can't see what good that does when he speaks only German." She seemed peeved and proud at the same time.

"And table tennis! Don't talk to me about table tennis; I barely got to see the ski slopes at all." I saw her flush. "At least the boss is going 50-50 with me to publish any of the snaps I took. He even hinted he might use a few of my 'behind the scenes' moments on the mountain in his next publication, *The Hitler Nobody Knows* ... but he never gives anyone else credit. Not that I had Adolph to myself anyway up there; it turned out to be meetings and more bloody meetings during every waking hour. Are you even listening?" she raised her eyebrows capriciously.

Clearing my throat I reassured her that my fondness for the breathtaking beauty of the Southern Alps was well-established, and prompted her to recount the more positive aspects of her visit, such as the scenery and other notable visitors; or any little intrigues on the side.

"Positive? You must be joking. I was stuck upstairs and saw nothing. Adolph doesn't get out of bed until lunchtime, when the best part of the day is over. Even his daily stroll down the mountain usually degenerates into a private discussion with one or two chosen admirers, while the rest of us end up strung out behind in single file like geese.

"Then there's the half-dozen or so armed Blackshirts front and rear; hardly conducive to holding hands or sneaking a kiss," she said, then pouted and sighed. "I suppose all this security is necessary, even in such isolated surroundings.

"While I was there they apprehended a would-be assassin carrying a pistol inside the perimeter fence. The fool tried to disguise himself in a stolen S.A. uniform, which of course, was a dead giveaway among the Schutzstaffel. The swine got what he deserved before he'd gotten very far. It's prompted Bormann to speed up his evictions of the last remaining farm houses so that security can be tightened."

I was a little surprised at her indifference toward the forced removal of families who had occupied the verdant Alpine slopes above Berchtesgaden for generations. These were the same rustic folk who had garnished the Führer's table with flowers and produce since his earliest days among them.

"The sooner they bulldoze those ugly old barns the better," Eva sniffed, "... they are spoiling the view from the new terrace. Would you believe there's a local photographer with a studio nearby who's digging in his heels and refusing to move on? Hess has been sent over to make him see reason. We thought of making him an offer to help out in the new darkroom when it's completed, but the arrogant fellow is set on retaining his independence. Anyway, I doubt if he'd receive the proper security clearance," she added imperiously. "By the way, that's why I've put your name on the shortlist to liaise between Obersalzberg and the studio here in Munich ..."

"Me? Why that's wonderful; I'd give anything to escape from the city ..."

"Hold on! I didn't say 'escape', I said liaise ..."

My adrenal gland gave a little squirt, soon tempered by the thought that Chalet Hahn may well fall within the newly declared "Security Zone", though Tante hadn't mentioned any such concerns in her Christmas letter. No doubt Onkel's status at the local Nazi Party Headquarters would render them immune from any forced acquisitions; after all, they were miles away on the inverse slopes.

"If you hang around for another half-hour I can give you a peep at your negs," I offered, feeling a little sorry for my mutable colleague while sharing her confidences. "Hopefully, this time your exposures will be within printable range," I quipped without thinking, referring to her previous efforts when a setting of ASA 400 had been wrongly paired with a much slower, fine grained setting.

At once I realised my little joke had added to her insecurities, she spun on her Ferragamo heel and swished her sequinned backside, slamming the door loudly.

I felt like kicking myself for allowing such a cheap shot to jeopardise my chance of expanded horizons. I turned my attention to producing the best set of black-and-white 8" × 10"s possible, hoping that by the time of delivery, my unintended slight would be forgotten or forgiven.

About then I received an unusual and tricky retouching request from Putzi Hanfstaengl, who was returning home through Munich from an unauthorised, "semi-official" visit to Mussolini in Rome. The ebullient and highly-talented former "advisor" was attempting to regain favour with the Führer, who it seemed no longer sought or appreciated his old mentor's shrewd guidance. Putzi felt that if he could somehow arrange a meeting between the pair of opinionated dictators, his fortunes may yet be restored. He planned to present Hitler with a signed photograph of himself beside "Il Duce" outside the Colosseum as a token of his warm intentions, but one mighty impediment stood in his way.

Mussolini's gleaming sinciput sported a gross carbuncle, which only professional darkroom skills could retouch from the finished print. I accepted the challenge with alacrity.

The next day, when I presented Putzi with the finished 8" × 10" in a silver gilt fame, minus the offending pustule, he waxed lyrical to Hoffman over modern darkroom techniques, and one particular young printer, before rushing off to Berlin on the last leg of his journey.

Hoffman, however, did not take kindly to accolades being afforded individual staff members; we all came under the one big Studio Hoffman umbrella. He simply grunted his response to the big man that echoed Hitler's own coolness, and soon afterward confronted me not with compliments, but rebukes. He and Lothar ambushed me outside the toilet door, where I had lingered a few minutes too long re-reading Frau Emilie's kindly, handwritten note thanking me for the flowers and expressing regret that I had had to return to work, missing the evening service.

"In future, you will kindly refer ALL foreign orders to Lothar, if I'm not to be found," Hoffman hissed savagely, stabbing his whetted nose and horn of silver hair in my face. I could smell the luncheon wines heavy on his breath and at that moment felt my fate was once more precarious, but answered nothing. Over his shoulder, I could see Lothar's yellowing teeth leering and the folds of his neck heavy on the collar of his uniform. He was enjoying the confrontation.

"Well?" Hoffman demanded. "Do you obey orders or do I toss you back out onto the street?"

"I'm so sorry, Herr Hoffman. I knew Putzi was a friend of the Führer's and I thought you'd be pleased." I was justifiably proud of my efforts and beads of sweat dotted my brow. "After all, it was *you*, sir, who showed me how to remove such blemishes …"

"That's not the point. It's not for you to decide who is and who is not a friend of the Führer's."

"And why haven't you yet joined the Party?" Lothar interjected over the boss' ear.

"Fraulein Braun says that really isn't necessary, nor is she herself a member," I shot back, fixing him with a stony glare that caused him to shrink back.

Hoffman seemed startled at my response. "Leave Fraulein Braun out of this!" I could almost see his shrewd calibration in the costs of training another obedient and proficient darkroom technician. With the cash registers singing as never before, he hesitated. It may not be so easy to find someone prepared to work night and day for a measly 50 marks per month. Who else would be content to remain under his stuffy staircase in voluntary self-denial?

I dared now to give as good as I got. "Herr Hoffman deducts regular Party 'donations' from my paychecks, don't you, sir?"

"Well yes, the boy's right, Lothar. He does pay his way and contributes towards most regular appeals. You just do *your* job in future, and make sure that people don't wander in willy-nilly off the street to solicit *my* darkroom staff … Or anyone else for that matter," he bellowed across the empty waiting room, before doubling back to snatch the opened envelope from my hand. "What's this?" He ran his eye briefly over the monogrammed sheet and thrust it back roughly.

"You fool! Are you trying to end up in more trouble? I'm ordering you to stay away from this woman, Frau Röhm, if you know what's good for you."

"Yes sir," I nodded meekly, quite unable to comprehend what possible reason he could have for warning me off such a sweet and generous friend as Frau Emilie. Within a few short months the reason came for all to see, "… and if you ignore my instructions again I shall alert the Gestapo to your ongoing fraternisation with the Jewess."

I looked at him incredulously and noticed Lothar slavering wordlessly with ears pricked. "I'm sure you know what that means …" he paused to let his words sink in. "Don't play dumb with me, Hahn; I'm not completely blind as to what goes on when I'm away. Just do your job, that's all … And stay away from Frau Röhm and the Jewess."

With that, he vanished, with his enforcer at his heels. Heinrich Hoffman was once more a ruthless, successful capitalist, to whom art and skill took second place after profits. A little shiver ran down my spine, and I took a moment to thank my lucky stars before plunging into the overflowing basket of films awaiting my attention.

Eva was thrilled with her holiday shots from Magic Mountain: so far, so good. This time her focus and contrast were spot on, but I winced at every shot of her wearing the dirndl. She must have set them up using time delay. This rather predictable peasant outfit was indeed a far cry from the designer collections she flaunted at work and I had to look twice to confirm it was her.

"What's with the mountain maid outfit?" I joked upon presenting the proof sheets and selected enlargements.

"If you must know smarty-pants, I decided that if I can't beat them I might as well join them. Given that Adolph is so enamoured with the hordes of peasant bitches flashing their tits at the front gate, I wanted to show him that I too am prepared to appear in traditional costume if that's what turns him on. But, I do draw the line at baring my boozies in front of the guards …"

Poor Eva, it seemed that brazen females were popping up everywhere trying to lure her man away.

"I don't know why I waste my time and money impersonating all those Hollywood creations, he takes no notice anyway …" she slumped slightly, glancing sideways for my anticipated reaction, "… except of course, when I'm wearing my feathers!"

"Good Lord, feathers?" I exclaimed. "Whatever do you mean?"

"That's none of your business, Klaus Hahn!" she shot back petulantly, assuming superior airs. "I would even dance naked for him should he ask. That would soon take his mind off all those other 'would be's if they could be's'," she spoke defiantly. I could not help feeling for her, being continually pushed aside while the Führer featured in countless publications alongside movie stars, cabaret dancers and other female "notables".

"At least he doesn't smile in their photos either," she mused.

Even when Eva did have him to herself at Villa Hoffman he would often repeat his crushing assertions that "great men should always choose simple and stupid female companions" and that "Germany is my only bride" just when Eva had felt she was making inroads.

For this reason, I tried to make light of any such painful moments she cared to share but "feathers" … this was a first!

Before I could regain our former geniality, the darkroom bell sounded and the red light over the door began flashing; the next batch of prints was coming off the dryer.

"I must say I really can't imagine you in your Farregamos wearing only feathers," I threw out this last remark when rising to depart, fully expecting a light-hearted rejoinder.

"How dare you pass judgment on the Führer's judgment," she rebutted, "… and don't presume because I share confidences that you can poke fun at my relationship."

"I … I thought because of … I wouldn't hurt you for the world, Eva …"

"Well don't! … Or you'll be sorry. And, by the way, it's 'Fraulein Braun' when there are others within earshot." Her last word was cut short as I hastily retreated behind the darkroom door, wondering if I should ever gain the knack of mixing business with pleasure.

Come January 30, 1934, Munich's streets were awash with colour and anticipation for the Anniversary of Hitler's accession. Studio Hoffman was inundated with requests for roving photographers and processing services.

I hardly snatched a wink of sleep that week, as huge rallies and jubilant speeches resonated from every corner of the land. Ordinary Germans poured onto the streets, deliriously expressing their approval at being "Great Again", able to hold their heads high once more among the nations.

But not all were enveloped in this bubble of joy, more likely enveloped *by* it. "Politically unreliable" Lord Mayors, Town Councils, Police Chiefs, Judges and other public officials had been swept aside in the preceding twelve months, to be replaced by loyal Nazis possessing little skill or knowledge of the task at hand.

Widespread beatings were still being meted out by Brownshirts, SS and Auxiliary Police targeting dissenters, non-conformists and indeed anyone in a position of power who refused to resign or join the Party.

It was no longer possible to ignore the evidence in my developing dish; too many petty officials possessed cameras, each trying to outdo the other by producing irrefutable evidence of their excesses. I was rocked by the incongruity of such baseness playing out side by side with the festivities.

Most painful for me was the purging of the art scene and the music world, with "degenerate" compositions from both disciplines being banned out of hand.

But it was upon the helpless Jews that the zealous hand of "renewal" fell most heavily. We learned that the Hamburg Philharmonic Society set the pace in announcing that no more Jewish musicians were required; renowned Jewish conductors nationwide were summarily sacked.

Great composers like Mendelsohn and Mahler were struck from repertoires in favour of inferior, though thoroughly "Germanic" substitutes blaring from loudspeakers. Stoic Jewish residents hoping that things might "blow over" were now banned from riding public transport or using public parks and baths. Highly qualified Jewish doctors were no longer permitted to treat "Aryan" patients.

At any moment, the unmistakable tramp of jackboots on the stairs could herald yet another superfluous Jewish family being given 30 minutes to vacate their luxury apartment in favour of covetous neighbours. The night air was filled with curses, blows and screams as one household after another was kicked into the frozen streets. Those unlucky enough to be on the blockälteste's "special list" were literally dragged onto waiting lorries and packed off to Dachau.

More "hellholes" were rumoured to be springing up across Germany, to cater for the swelling numbers of "useless eaters" requiring "protective custody", much of the violence being dutifully recorded on film. I could not ignore the frightening reality emerging in my trays.

Tante Gretel, judging from her lengthy birthday greetings, had also marked the sad and sudden turn of events affecting the art world, which she expressed in veiled misgivings.

She reported that the "new friends" I had met in her parlour had fallen out of favour with the local stuffed shirts and would soon be "vacationing abroad". Many oils had been "placed in storage" and sunnier climes would be "beneficial for their health".

I took this to mean her modest but treasured collection of avant-garde paintings, so perceptively acquired against the flow of common taste and so revealing for my own understanding. I had indeed noticed Munich's galleries now removing works by Klee, Kandinsky, Max Beckman and other contemporary "dabblers" who had failed to meet the "representational" style of the day. Nazi-appointed curators knew full well what great art was and what it was not.

"Herr Professor" Hoffman had now become the Reich's leading art authority, whose opinions on all matters artistic just happened to coincide perfectly with his Führer's. Apart from Gretel and I, it seemed that the absence of the "Moderns" had been barely noticed by the common Volk, who rushed to embrace the more heroic, neo-classical styles now finding favour within the regime.

Thanks to Tante's planting her seeds on the charms of Modernism I had made a point of seeking out and studying Munich's diminishing collection of contemporary masterpieces, always striving to discern the hidden forces at work beneath the surface. Imagine my surprise to discover that my boss now headed up a selection panel charged with drawing up a list of "degenerate" works considered "unsuitable" for German eyes. In fact, I learned that Goebbels was busily planning an exhibition in which all these confiscated works would be placed on public display for the purposes of ridicule.

If it were not for Tante's hand-painted card, my birthday may well have gone unnoticed. I rose extra early, determined to get through my workload and spend the last hour or two of daylight enjoying the fresh air beside the river.

By the time I'd broken away from my claustrophobic work atmosphere, my mood had sunk to an uncharacteristically low ebb, exacerbated by rowdy street corner demonstrations and roving groups of Brownshirts spoiling for trouble.

Fortunately, I'd figured out a low-risk route between Amalienstrasse and my river hideaway on the sandy spit of land between the Eisbach canal and the main channel downstream. Dodging the worst trouble spots I arrived without incident and in no time had a fire crackling.

I consoled myself by wolfing down two of Café Stefanie's famous strudels and a half bottle of dry Riesling to warm my innards.

Where to from here? I mused, disappointed that I'd not had the courage to push back effectively against the enveloping zeitgeist. After all, attaining 22 years of age was no mean feat given my fragile health and precarious surroundings.

I hurried through a series of soft chants and breathing exercises, keen to rekindle contact with my elusive and often ignored Master Within: inhaling through the nose and out through the mouth several times brought relief. From my rucksack, I produced a tattered copy of *Divine Comedy*, and while sipping the remainder of the Riesling lost myself in Dante's exquisite phrasing and vivid mental images.

Having spent many weeks immersed in Homer's *Iliad* with its blazing tales of adventure, I'd hesitated in choosing a suitably inspiring successor. But within the first thirty tercets of "Purgatory" I realised my choice of Dante was both wise and appropriate.

Looking up, I found I'd been reading by firelight in the evening gloom, but my mood had lifted. On vacillating legs I broke through the bushes into the English Garden and took stock of the night sky; overhead dark clouds threatened rain or a late snow squall. Humming softly I pulled my cap down around my ear and wandered back towards the Studio, refusing to be off put by the cheerless grey light shrouding much of the streetscape.

Birthday or no birthday, I was aware that the "Hitler Files" had to be brought up to date each night before I retired. The predictable outpouring of commemorative celebration during the week had required the addition of yet another five-drawer filing cabinet in the boss' office, towards which, upon shedding my coat, I made my way up the stairs.

Somebody said "Huh?" very loudly and made a scraping sound of chair legs; startled, I peered in to see Eva slumped behind her desk in the dimmest lamplight.

"W ... What on earth are *you* doing here? It's your birthday too," I said. Why aren't you celebrating with your family or ... or with girlfriends?"

"Come here you! Come and share a glass of champagne with a lonely Fraulein," she slurred, crooking a finger and dropping her stockinged heels to the floor. Carefully, she drained the last of her bottle into an empty coffee cup and pushed it toward me. "Finish that off and I'll grab another," she insisted, weaving unsteadily towards the boss' bar fridge next door.

Being myself three parts under the weather, I judged from the empty bottle on the desk that she too must be well on the way. "I did not wish to spend my birthday with my boring family," she answered upon returning, plonking down a second bottle of Dom Perignon '26 on the desk.

"I just know Adolph will phone sooner or later; I can't understand what's taking him so long," she said, squinting at the telephone. "He calls nearly every night, you know?" she said, as if trying to reassure herself, "… and I don't want to miss him, tonight of all nights, now do I?"

She gave a forced giggle. "I know he won't be able to keep my birthday gifts a secret."

I tried to protest that I'd already consumed a whole bottle by the river, but she would have none of it. "Oh, come on Klaus, don't be such a wet blanket; it **is** our special day, after all," she said, giving a little whoop as the cork banged against the ceiling.

Following our previous fraught parting I felt there could be little harm and some advantage in bending to her will. I was anxious to know if she had confirmed my nomination as darkroom liaison "runner" between Studio Hoffman and the Berghof extensions.

But it was to herself and her woes that the conversation quickly turned when I mentioned the English Garden. She launched a spiteful tirade upon Unity Mitford, who had just decided to stay on at her Parkside villa in order to "polish up her German language skills".

Like many of Eva's circling rivals, Unity's bold play for the Führer's affections had been scuttled, as we later learned, by her own sister Nancy. Nancy had forwarded a family tree from their father, Lord Redesdale, directly to Heinrich Himmler, who was now tightening his grip on Germanic genealogies.

The doctored certificate falsely claimed a distant Jewish ancestry in the otherwise impeccable aristocratic lineage. Whether out of spite or belated sibling concerns, Nancy Mitford's bombshell may have emanated from her disgust at both her sisters' unseemly pursuits of "Men of Destiny" on both sides of the channel. Nancy was miffed that their other sister Diana had not only hunted down but recently married Oswald Mosely, leader of the British Fascist Blackshirts, almost before his first wife was cold in her grave.

One could not be too careful in the face of such determination, but Eva need not have worried; any whiff of Jewish scandal within the Führer's cherished coterie was enough to see him run a mile, or more precisely, to set the alleged corrupter running.

However, at this point the Mitford scandal had not yet broken and Eva had her hands full with concern for her own elder sibling Ilse's continuing employment and rumoured dalliance with the Jew Marx. Ilse not only refused to forsake her employer but defended him passionately around the Braun dinner table. She "didn't give a damn" about implications for the whole family, nor for Eva's position when the facts became more widely known.

It seemed Hitler, in excusing Röhm's outrageous homosexuality, was also prepared to overlook Ilse's own "ill-considered" employment, at least for the time being. I wondered if he also knew of Claudia's dark secret and Hoffman's motives for keeping her on the payroll.

Sitting there in the twilight, Eva rehashed the dangers posed by her three principal rivals, Unity Mitford, Magda Goebbels and Leni Riefenstahl, growing more unsettled as she rattled off their growing list of dirty tricks. Personally, I felt she should be more concerned about the numerous "starlets" that Hoffman paraded through the halls of power, most prepared to do almost anything to be photographed on the arm of the Great Leader.

Beginning to nod off, I dragged myself away from Eva's soliloquy, blurred irretrievably by the Dom Perignon, and after clumsily reshuffling the "Hitler Files", I stumbled down the stairs and flopped onto my bunk. Through a fuzzy mind, I couldn't help thinking that although Eva's problems were many and varied my own birthday hadn't turned out a complete flop.

Springtime edged closer with the smell of damp soil that heralds winter's end. Indoors, a welcome breath of fresh air also arrived in the shape of Claudia, who suddenly reappeared in Framing and Finishing looking more beautiful and serene than ever.

I dared not speculate on her absence, quixotically dreaming of the hour when I might once more lay my head against her fragrant breast. That chance came in March '34, when Hitler's Dr Brandt married his fiancée, the lithe and likeable Anni Rehborn, who clearly hadn't wasted much time dog-paddling her way into Dr Brand's cold heart.

Naturally enough, the private ceremony was witnessed by Göring and Bruckner, with a sombre Hitler once more standing in as best man.

I had been dragged along by Hoffman as a "runner" to return and develop the exposed film post-haste to the darkroom. Once processed, I was instructed to select the best thirty shots and bind them into one of our custom-made, pig-skin wedding albums. I was also to oversee the framing of one 16" × 20" enlargement of the bride alone, and another full-length of the pair together. The completed package was to be placed on the boss' desk before 10 am the next morning, allowing sufficient time for any "adjustments" he may deem necessary before the bride and groom called in en route for their brief honeymoon.

Of course, this meant I would again need to stay awake half the night printing, binding and mounting. Just as importantly, I was to oversee the final frame selection.

My excitement can be imagined as the wee hours dragged on. Peeling the final enlargements from the dryer I bounded up the steps two by two and knocked boldly at the door marked "Photo Finishing" where a certain girl had also been ordered by the boss to fill in during the dog-watch shift.

Seeing Hoffman had not long warned me off Claudia altogether, I suspected a trap. For weeks I had been wrestling with the uncertainty of revealing his threat if the chance presented, and also the Gestapo's growing interest in Sissy's associations. But all that was forgotten when the door flew open and I was greeted with a Mona Lisa smile and a slightly extended embrace; or was I just imagining?

"My, my, let me look at you. I doubt if your nose will ever regain its original shape … and you've let your hair grow longer. Oh dear, is that a little pot belly I see?" She playfully jabbed her forefinger into my navel as I quickly pulled in my stomach and tightened my belt a notch to allay any such impression. At her touch, a squirt of adrenalin fired up my passion.

"Let's get this framing taken care of first and we may even have time for breakfast at one of the all-night cafés," she continued sensibly, reaching for the roll of prints under my arm.

"Er … yes, yes of course; golly I've missed you, Claudia," I stammered, rolling my eyes at her suggestion. "Or if you prefer, we can go back to my place for a coffee; we have so much to catch up on."

"If I like?"

All tiredness vanished and I nodded vigorously, much relieved that we might enjoy more privacy away from the public eye.

"What are you staring at?" she asked finally, aware of my drinking in her every move as she went about bevelling cardboard mats and chopping the wooden mouldings to size. I clean forgot about the likely hidden cameras and microphones.

"I'm doing just fine. I want to know everything *you've* been up to; you look really wonderful," I gushed. "But not yet," I added, putting a warning finger to my lips.

She paused briefly from her task and fixed me with her greenish gaze. "You don't really mean that, do you Klaus?" she mouthed her words softly. "We all know of certain things that cannot be shared, even if we wanted to. I'm sure we'll find plenty of common ground to enjoy …" she said, brightening visibly, "… that's if you're not too tired of course. It's nearly 4 am , way past your bedtime."

"Not when I'm on dog-watch, Claudie. Wild horses couldn't drag me away now," I enthused, "… although we do need to be careful." I lowered my voice again. "We shouldn't be seen leaving the building together, I'll tell you all about it later."

"Good God! Why ever not? Don't worry about the surveillance in here; I stacked empty cartons in certain places as soon as Lothar's back is turned."

"Does this have anything to do with our secret?" her brows knitted slightly.

"N … No! Well, sort of, but it's not what you think. The Gestapo have been sniffing around and asking questions, Lothar may have tweaked to something the boss let slip."

She continued to concentrate with her head down. "I've always known it would only be a matter of time before Heini opened his big mouth; fine wines invariably loosen tongues and enliven the conversation," she sighed resignedly, "but it always helps to have friends in high places."

Now it was my turn to be silent. This was exactly how I *didn't* want our friendship to resume; yet, in these times there was no room for complacency. Since the boss' reprimand, I'd become more suspicious of Iris and Lothar's feigned amiability, which just as quickly could degenerate into dark threats.

"Don't forget I'm S.A. too," I recalled his last attempt to loiter about the darkroom but I was becoming a wake-up to his little games.

It's not knowing just when he's likely to jump out with a threat or an attempt to win me over; it's hard not to throw up in his face," I ventured.

"And I've discovered that it wasn't Lothar but sneaky Iris who dobbed me in to the Gestapo; I've been walking on eggshells ever since. They told me I was lucky to get off with a warning as they called it, although at the time it was rather scary," I added with a shrug, attempting to downplay the ordeal and not alarm her unnecessarily.

"That pair of toad-eaters," she cursed to the bride and groom on the workbench, "they'll be first in line for their just desserts if my friends in the Orchestra have anything to do with it. These Gestapo 'show and tell' sessions are hauling in thousands of innocents every week. I hardly need reminding that, like you, I too exist from day to day under the permanent cloud of Hoffman's fancy."

I had no answer, alerted by her frankness.

"He's well aware that I know all about his notorious clique of deviants and those orgies involving so-called 'respectable' high rollers. I think it's called a Mexican standoff; whoever spills the beans first is the game we're playing now. I'm not fooled at his pimping those star-gazing hopefuls around the upper Party echelons," her voice died away.

"It seems a lifetime since I was 'elevated' to my present status … and make no mistake, I could be gone in the next gust." If these disclosures were true and I had no reason to doubt them, surely nothing was as it seemed.

"The greed of our illustrious boss knows no bounds," she continued, "I'm ready for your signature, just here," she said unfazed, giving a final rub to the non-reflective glass and thumbing off the frame corners with silver paste.

"Only last week he oversaw the confiscation of yet another premises in Frederickstrasse from its Jewish owners; I tell you, his contempt for the Jews runs a close third behind the black dwarf and Hitler himself. One need only glance at the shape of our very own petty tyrant wallowing in his plunder; he must have put on 30 pounds since Christmas."

Again, I was rocked by her forthrightness and looked around to ensure we were alone.

Then, with a flourish, I signed "Copyright: Heinrich Hoffman, '34" in the lower right-hand corner of the mat. Most framed prints these days received only a facsimile gold stamp guaranteeing their "authenticity" while special clients like the Brandts received a handwritten fake signature from yours truly, and a final inspection from the professor himself.

As signing photographs personally was no longer necessary, among other things, the boss was busy finalising the printer's proofs for his latest picture book, *The Hitler Nobody Knows*, all the while his well-oiled factory churned out likenesses of newly promoted Nazis for substantial sums.

The chain of franchised Studios Hoffmans Inc. had become instant money-makers, running to a tried and proven formula. Everywhere his brand was supported by Nazis great and small, from the very top down.

In addition, there was his lucrative sideline distributing salacious postcards into the insatiable Balkan market. While certain assignments required his appearance in the flesh, such as Hitler's speaking engagements and the Brandt Wedding, most were avoidable.

The world-famous Professor Heinrich Hoffman needed only to pop up briefly behind the lens with a practised air and a cunning wisecrack, to put his sitters immediately at ease, after which the developing, printing and finishing were handled by the studio machine.

As Claudia and I strolled together toward the tranquil dawn, a few fleecy stars lingered over the western horizon.

Not a Brownshirt was in sight as I reached out to place my arm around her waist. She gave my fingers a single hurried squeeze before pulling away on the pretext of locating her keys, well before our destination moved into view. Nonetheless, that brief touch was enough to make my heart beat faster and dispel fatigue as we paused outside her doorway on the first-floor landing. The jingle of keys brought a tiny wizened face to the narrow opening opposite.

I followed her inside to be greeted by the calming fragrance of incense. "I'm afraid that aside from a hot coffee I can only offer you a cold beer and sausage; I rarely eat at home these days."

Before I could reply she snapped the lids off two bottles and flopped down in a cosy armchair opposite; it seemed like we'd never been parted.

At first, she peppered me with questions about other staff and particularly my reasons for such secrecy. What had I heard and witnessed during her absence? Avoiding specific references to other men, I gradually steered the conversation to Robert and his stated new role as "Honorary Aryan" in the SS.

She took the bait. "He only comes crawling these days when he's short of cash. It appears he's become quite a high flyer since joining the Cavalry Regiment. Naturally enough they consider themselves superior to all others."

"That's a good one. Robert's never ridden a horse in his life … though I must confess he is a crack shot."

"It seems to be the lifestyle rather than the horses he's more interested in. Those Cavalry fellows strut about with women falling for them; it beats me why any girl would want to date someone smelling like a sweaty saddle. I'm sure it says somewhere in the Bible that 'Bad companions ruin good character', although in this case, I'm not sure who will be ruining whom …"

I gave a false little laugh. I still held hopes that Claudia may not be completely blind to Robert's faults; if only she knew the half of it. She checked a sneer …

"These gambling debts will bring Himmler's wrath down around his ears if he's not careful. He should know that all forms of gaming are strictly verboten among the SS ranks of pure breeds, as is homosexuality, not that he listens to me. He'd come down a peg or two if he realised just who it is keeps bailing him out, or even polluting his pure Aryan blood when the mood takes him."

"I know nothing of a gambling habit; he used to have a bit of a flutter on the *Madeira Belle* when we were just kids … do you mean to say he's been borrowing money from you?"

"Borrowing? The very word implies that one intends to pay it back. He's as good as cleaned me out, including the tidy sum I'd put aside to visit my family back in the Motherland … Oh Lodz, beautiful sleepy Lodz, what I'd give now to stroll through her tranquil streets and markets … maybe one day?

"No matter my obsequies or successes in the eyes of Robert and our esteemed Professor Hoffman, I remain just one more immiscible commodity to be used up and thrown on the scrap heap. However, until that day comes I won't stop loving your brother. And I won't stop trying to give something back. Surely, you of all people realise that love transcends the evidence of its own eyes?" she said, shooting me a sharp glance. "The trick seems to be to stay alive until cooler heads prevail, but I wouldn't count on that either."

There followed a long pause. "And of course, life's a damn sight tougher without savings," Sissy muttered darkly, peering into the near-empty refrigerator.

Her sudden disclosure and change of mood caught me by surprise. "B … But, why do you let him get away with it? Why do you let him use you so?" I blurted.

"You said yourself that he's moved on to broader horizons with his new friends. You should not have to endure this sort of treatment; there are caring people out there who would treat you with the respect you deserve … Like you, I suppose, Klaus? I'm sure we've had this conversation before … and that's all very sweet. Look what he's bought me, an SS diary of all things; I suppose it's his way of showing affection."

"Say, maybe I could help out with the rent now and again? But …"

"But what? Then I'd be obligated to you too, wouldn't I? Doesn't it also say somewhere in our Bible that man cannot serve two masters?"

"W … What I mean is, I want nothing in return. Only, I would not like to see my hard-earned contributions going into Robert's pocket," I said, staring at the floor. At that moment I felt only shame.

"Poor diddums; still jealous of big bwother?"

Despite this ribbing, it was clear that my friend felt deeply over the plight of her own "leprous Polish brethren" as they were now referred to in widely circulated rags like *Der Stürmer*, needing to share her revulsion at the gratuitous brutality she was witnessing firsthand.

"I must remain above the fray, indifferent yet supportive, while thousands of panic-stricken Jews are being brutally evicted from their homes in every quarter. It's nearly killing me," she confessed.

"First up they were forbidden to keep pets; now whole families are given 30 minutes' notice to hand over their apartments and belongings. And they're considered the 'lucky ones'; many more are simply being murdered in the streets. Those 'fortunate' Jews with international visas are stripped of their assets before being booted out of Germany altogether. As the refugee numbers swell, one nation after another is slamming shut the borders in their faces."

With a faraway look, she muttered almost to herself ... "Don't worry, our day will come. All hope of cutting off the snake's head now lies in the hands of a few courageous souls."

Then, out of the blue, she delighted me with an incisive Goethe quote I'd not previously come across: "'National hatred is something peculiar. You will always find it strongest and most violent where there is the lowest degree of culture.' That just about sums up our current situation, don't you think?" She looked pleased as the lamplight caught her proud cheekbones and threw her eyes into shadow. For now, the boot was on the other foot and I dug deep for a rejoinder, expressing some pleasure in my reply.

"Goethe also said: 'Nothing is more disgusting than the majority!'"

"Damn! I knew you'd find a comeback, albeit backing up my own," she said before downing a third beer without pause.

Two snappy ones of my own had the desired effect, and I felt my shyness slipping away. "You know, Claudia?" I said, beaming. "There are times when I think you and I share the same soul between two bodies. I feel your pain and I know you feel mine. Can we agree on that at least?"

I saw her spine stiffen and anticipated the sting of rejection.

"Klaus! I've told you a dozen times; let's keep so-called romance out of this. You're just a kid and have no idea who I really am. In spite of everything my affection for you as a special friend will never die, but I've already decided to take my chances with Robert. I would follow him into Hell if need be: I can't be any clearer than that."

Few words crush a swain so utterly as to be informed by the girl of his dreams that he is a "special friend".

"I'm over 21, aren't I?" But my response was weak. "I might as well come straight out and say it; I've never met anyone like you before, Claudia," I whispered to the goddess of my dreams.

"Oh, come on, pull the other one. Don't tell me you didn't ping that smelly little Amazonian flower you are always going on about. You don't have any secrets from me do you, Klaus? You can tell your Sissy ..."

"I ... I didn't, I couldn't ... Oh, I don't know what I mean." I was stung by the very idea of her coarse suggestion. "But, that was different, very different," I floundered, "Maya saved my life. I thought you knew that."

It was on the tip of my tongue to blurt that it was Robert, not me, who had violated her innocence and incited the impregnation of a mere child.

But, I didn't. There was no point. She was hooked on my parricidal brother. It's easy to imagine my feelings: common sense should have told me that in her eyes Robert's failings were way down the chart of Nazi atrocities, and I realised then that most women do seem more attracted to men of action rather than of thought, regardless of their other failings.

For the rest of that day, she regaled me with humorous tales of bumbling within the highest levels of Nazidom, predominantly from incidents she had observed firsthand or overheard from her "escorts". Much of it involved misery as well as mirth, usually devolving into lower ranks or sworn enemies.

She told how 'Fat Herman', decked out in a loud brown hunting jacket, breeches and knee boots, had hurled insults at Marinus van der Lubbe in the People's Court. This half-witted Dutch Communist "suspect" was arrested inside the burning Reichstag soon after the first flames were noticed. Claudia was able to relate her disgust at the courtroom laughing out loud when the luckless fellow was sentenced to death. She had watched Lubbe being led away in chains with bowed head, as if in readiness for the waiting guillotine.

She told how at that moment another of Goethe's quotes came immediately to mind: "Men show their characters in nothing more clearly than what they think laughable." She hinted it was more than a rumour that Göring's Gestapo had lit the first match.

I learned in detail how Goebbels the "black dwarf" had come a cropper while trying to bed the actress, Leni Riefenstahl, allegedly after threatening to deny her future access to starring roles or directorships. This time his usual modus operandi fell flat: "Perhaps you should check with the Führer first," came Leni's concise and sobering rebuttal, according to Claudia.

It seemed a campaign was underway among the top German generals to appear friendly toward Poland, in order to keep that country off guard during the massive arms build-up now underway; all in defiance of the discredited Versailles Treaty.

Hitler, since day one had openly derided that "onerous document", which he saw as nothing more than an attempt to subjugate the Fatherland in perpetuity. I could tell from the passion in Claudia's voice that these deliberate deceptions strained her loyalties and heightened her frustrations. I tried to imagine how it must feel knowing that one day the axe may fall on her own neck or that of her vulnerable family.

Astonishingly, she saved her greatest calumny for the Führer himself, reeling off a long list of allegations I could never have imagined, let alone believe.

First, she labelled him "inbred", the result of a misalliance between his brutal father, Alois, and one Klara Polzl, the Customs Inspector's much younger half-niece.

She pointed out the eerie similarities with Hitler's own unnatural infatuation with the teenage Geli and we all knew how that had ended. Adding to the intrigue was a further rumour that Alois himself was the illegitimate offspring of a Jewish grandfather, which Claudia believed may account for the Führer's aberrant and much-discussed sex life.

When I probed further she confided, "What he did with one of my Jewish girlfriends is rather typical. The S.A. dragged her into the Brown House and made her perform degrading acts for Hitler's delectation, at the conclusion of which he slapped her violently across the face and walked out; probably to jerk off when no one was looking," she sniggered. "Malfa was threatened with Dachau if she opened her mouth; that's Germany's Saviour for you.

"And then there's the tale of him swooning at the feet of Hanfstaengl's wife Helene soon after they were introduced. Apparently, poor Putzi returned to find the slavering swain on his knees declaring his undying love for the stunning Helene's feet, right there in Putzi's own parlour, to the extreme embarrassment of both husband and wife who found it difficult keeping a straight face."

Claudia swore she heard this story from Helene's own lips and I wondered if this incident had anything to do with Putzi's ejection from the inner circle, where it appeared even his rousing Wagner recitals couldn't save him.

To all this I listened spellbound, flattered by her trust in my discretion. Apparently, I had passed a huge test by not revealing anything of our "relationship" during my "enhanced interrogation" by the Gestapo.

Later on, we learned that Hitler's festering resentment over this incident almost resulted in Putzi being parachuted into Spain behind Republican lines at the height of the Civil War on a "special mission requiring great loyalty". He had been tersely informed under the pretext of "observing the state of play". Such a vague and dangerous escapade would have resulted unquestionably in Putzi's demise, leaving behind a desirable and grieving widow at the mercy of her jilted admirer.

Thanks to the compassion of a friendly pilot the devious plan was thwarted in the nick of time, and the former confidant was able to escape with his wife and children to the United States, there to take up a much safer position in the Hanfstaengl family's substantial art reproduction business.

Years later, in a twist of fate following America's entry into the war, Putzi became an advisor to President Roosevelt who, like so many other Western leaders, was attempting to plumb the murky mind of the Nazi leader.

At the sound of evening peak-hour traffic outside I was alerted to obligations elsewhere, and prior to my departure made Claudia promise that she would join me for the much-anticipated nationwide holiday marking the Führer's 45th birthday, coming up in less than two weeks' time.

We knew from experience that most of the studio employees, apart from a few die-hard, freelance photographers in the Press Department, would be given the day off to ensure their full participation.

As I closed the door gently, I caught a glimpse of a wide-eyed Pauli noting my stealthy departure and forced a foolish grin in his direction. Stepping into the bustling street, a wave of exhaustion swamped my every fibre.

When Dr Brandt arrived at Studio Hoffman the next day I had the chance to study his initial reactions. Naturally enough, Hoffman took credit for the whole "package" containing the bound album of 8" × 10"s and the pair of framed enlargements. Hitler's tall, gaunt though obviously intelligent personal physician lingered over my flowery gold prose on the title page.

"To Herr and Frau Brandt with congratulations on your special day," it read, "I trust your presence will bring comfort to the Führer as I stand ready to be of service throughout your long life together, Heinrich Hoffman; Official Nazi Photographer."

Brandt wore his slick dark hair swept smoothly back off a high forehead, but it was the bottomless gaze towards anyone other than Hitler that sent a shiver down my spine. Most dark eyes give off a sparkle when pleased. This good doctor, however, betrayed not a flicker of emotion as he sniffed the air and flipped cursorily through the pages.

Then, he nodded once and a thin smile played at the corners of his mouth, before Hoffman instructed me to gift-wrap the three items individually. The boss then showed him to the door, with much head-nodding and hand-wringing. So much for my labour of love.

At least I could look forward to the approaching public holiday, and the days passed quickly enough in the darkroom. Most nights I was too tired to read before sleep carried me off. Secretly, I hoped Claudia too, would be counting the hours until she could show me around some of the "real" Munich sights, as promised. Maybe it was a mixture of fear and the shenanigans we'd laughed over so heartily, or perhaps the result of my printing marathon and a whole day in Claudia's company without sleep, but my mind became affected by a nightmare more troubling than usual.

I dreamed I was outside the Shamans' Maloca, surrounded by a circle of accusing, painted faces egged on by Xina himself. As I watched in horror, his features contorted into those of Adolph Hitler, screaming out a litany of accusations; his eyes blazed and his putrid breath was overwhelming. In vain I tried to cry "Sieg Heil" and attest my loyalty, but my mouth flopped open and shut and no sound came.

"Tell me you swine, tell me now! I want a list of all her friends and associates," Hitler demanded. "What is she planning? Tell me and you can return home to your mother."

A small voice warned me not to say more and I knew that Mutti was not at home. It was a trap! "Admit your part in the Orchestra and all this will be yours," he hissed through yellowed teeth while stretching his arm over the river basin below. "All of it!"

Suddenly he was Xina again, wailing at the heavens in an unknown tongue. He raised his ceremonial club and tapped it three times against the decorated door jamb, calling the garland of shrivelled organs back into life. Slowly at first and then more powerfully, each heart swelled and began to beat, shooting jets of black blood in the air.

"This is my curse! This is your lot! Give them what they seek," Xina hissed to the throbbing muscles as the warm blood splashed over my naked body. I was stuck ankle-deep in the sticky red liquid and opened my mouth again to cry out.

Somehow I broke free and bounded high into the canopy, swinging easily from branch to branch; for a few moments, I was safely delivered. Nothing could ever bother me again. There ahead, parting the wall of bamboo a familiar incubus crouched with teeth bared, blocking my path. I watched fascinated as the great Cat launched toward me in slow motion and resignedly offered my throat.

"What in the Führer's name is going on in here?" Iris' head was poking through my doorway and I found myself sitting bolt upright in bed, instinctively feeling myself all over.

"I … I was having a nightmare; gee, it's good to see a friendly face, Iris."

She gave a little grunt as I stumbled to the open door and sucked at the vernal sunshine. All around was the reassuring bustle of a working studio. She strode off mumbling something under her breath, and while the kettle boiled I sat on the edge of my cot with head in hands, recovering.

April 20, 1934, dawned bright and clear; "Führer Weather", they called it. As I hurried along Munich's flower-strewn streets, I could see that others had arrived even earlier to take up vantage points along the main parade route down Königsplatz. Some perched awkwardly in roadside trees or suspended themselves from lampposts. High above the gathering masses huge red swastika banners emblazoned every building, and a jubilant festive chatter rained down from upper balconies and top-floor windows. I thought how easy it would be for someone to take a potshot from such places, provided of course that the would-be assassin was prepared to forfeit his own life in the process.

It was through fear of such attempts that Hitler's schedules were rarely disclosed in advance, but today was his 45th birthday and it seemed the entire population was turning out to honour their Saviour.

Passing through the gates of the English Garden I spied Claudia in the distance, reclining on her usual bench beside the canal, but as I approached I could sense her wariness; she motioned me to keep walking.

I lifted my camera to record the scene and without a sideways glance strolled on towards the Isar, where we'd discussed having a sunset picnic at the completion of formalities. Before ten minutes had passed, her smiling face popped out through the bushes to plant a little peck on my cheek, quite catching me by surprise.

"Er … what was that all about?" I enquired.

"Didn't you see that woman with the camera walking the dog?" she asked. "Well, she's a snitch."

I had to admit that my normally sharp eye had been fastened on a single subject before being batted away, but later on, when developing the film I could see a shadowy figure coaxing a small terrier in the background.

"We can't be too careful these days," Claudia continued. "I've noticed that woman speaking with Iris on occasion, her yellow scarf is a dead giveaway. Anyhow, I've given her the slip. Come on, let's not waste this chance to join in the fun; all the restaurants are serving free meals until midnight. No one is to go hungry on the Führer's birthday, can you believe it? Apparently, the Party is hosting nationwide festivities of parades and public feasting in every village, right down to folk music and traditional dancing."

We climbed up the riverbank and passed by dozens of temporary viewing stands, with S.A. bands whistling, blaring and thumping away in the background. Helotic ranks shuffled into regimental formations behind their standard bearers.

Some had waited for hours for their turn to parade past and salute their beloved Führer. Brownshirts in the front rows jostled for seats with families attired in traditional period costumes featuring all possible combinations of knee britches, lederhosen, feathered alpine hunting caps and, of course, colourful dirndls on the Frauleins.

It seemed to me that every last Bavarian Gau had sent a uniformed delegation of some kind, wherein the regime's strict pecking order was laid bare at a glance. Woe betides any Party Member (now some seventeen million strong) who mistook those who he was free to push around and those to whom he must in turn submit.

This hierarchy of reward and punishment ran all the way up to the top of the pyramid, to Hitler himself; the only person in Germany not having to ask permission.

Claudia's mood that day, like much of Germany's, was buoyant and infectious. We quickly forgot our unwanted stalker.

"Knowing your brother as I do," she said in a low voice, "he probably believes all the hoo-ha is for him; fancy his birthday falling on the same date as Herr Hitler's. No doubt he'll be riding alongside his new Cavalry chums …"

"Or, riding side-saddle, more likely," I threw in off the cuff and we both suppressed a snigger. Her eyes twinkled. "I left word for him to meet me in Café Heck for a birthday drink around 10:00 tonight, all the excitement should have died down by then."

"That's *if* he's still standing, *and* after he's worn out his welcome everywhere else," she added wryly.

Why does his *bloody name have to come up every time we're together?* I asked myself, thinking it best not to betray any outward sign of disappointment. By now we had turned into Ludwigstrasse, where a great roar announced the imminent arrival of Hitler's motorcade.

We caught sight of him in the distance standing erect in a great open tourer, right arm outstretched above his adoring congregation. Thousands screamed, wept and returned his salute from every possible outlook, the pageantry was overwhelming.

We waited for the leading fanfare to come to a halt nearby, before crossing the petal-strewn streetscape and flashing our yellow press cards to enter a review stand almost directly behind the speakers' podium.

Busily snapping crowd scenes, I hadn't noticed Claudia falling behind to pause alongside a vaguely familiar face in the crowd; one I soon realised belonged to the young rebel known only as "Hans" whom I'd encountered previously. I waved furiously to catch her attention, and within moments she'd bounded up to the top tier where we had an excellent view of the Führer alighting from his vehicle and ascending the Feldherrnhalle steps.

For some minutes he stood motionless, basking in the glow of adulation, before the marching band started up again and the parade resumed its forward momentum.

"I saw you talking with Hans, what's he up to?" I yelled, but she ignored my question and continued to click away at the unfolding spectacle. At first, things seemed to be going to plan, with endless ranks of Brownshirts kicking up the dust and thrusting out their arms in unison, until it came time to receive the adulation of the Old Fighters, Hitler's favourite comrades in arms.

Out front this time was Victor Lutze and Reichsmarschall Göring, the latter almost bursting out of his S.A. uniform. "Fat Herman's" short legs pumped up and down, not at all used to the stresses of parading in formation; both men fired impeccable salutes toward their cherished Leader.

But where was Röhm? Claudia too, had noticed the Chief of Staff's absence and put her lips to my ear. "Ernst must have thrown another tantrum and it doesn't look like he's being missed."

I nodded vaguely. It was plain that no one was going to put a dampener on this Birthday Parade. Wave after wave of stormtroops rocked past in unison, their tesserated knapsacks swaying away into the distance.

Unlike the January 30 parade just three months earlier, when Röhm had ridden a magnificent Bay Stallion at the head of his legions, nodding and saluting like a Roman Emperor, horses had been banned today.

During the earlier event, Röhm's steed had dropped a trail of steaming dung in front of Hitler's review stand: today there were no horses and no Röhm, just an ominous feeling in the air.

I studied the Führer's gestures and demeanour for any changes, but his face remained impassive and his arm rigid. I'd reinforced my view that not a single one of his idolaters, despite their enthusiasm, saluted with quite the same aplomb as the Leader.

Firstly, his right thumb remained folded under his palm in a precise and studied manner, while the arm was outstretched. Every so often, when his arm retracted against the left collarbone in a measured gesture, he formed a fist over his heart at the last moment.

There was no doubting the infectious hysteria generated by the man; I caught sight of Claudia waving a miniature swastika flag on a stick, but when I looked again she certainly was not cheering.

Next, the blond battalions of Schirach's Hitler Youth pranced into sight behind their pear-shaped ring-master wearing lederhosen; adoration written all over their shining faces. From youngest to late teens, their passion for this mysterious man without breeding, education or inherited means was unmistakable.

Seated behind the speaker's podium and pair of marble lions were several rows of bodyguards and bandaged street fighters confined to wheelchairs: Adolph Hitler now reigned supreme! I had to admit to myself that his achievements over a mere decade, outwitting and beguiling German politicians, military leaders and the population at large, were indeed remarkable.

Moments later and out-performing all others came the resplendent black SS ranks in goose-stepping precision, headed by a mincing Heinrich Himmler. Through my binoculars I watched his rhythmic formations tramp past with neither hair nor step out of place. The newly elevated Reichsführer's arm shot out and his feeble eyes twinkled behind thick lenses: his own limp schnurrbart quivered triumphantly and his pride was plain to see; this was Heinrich Himmler's moment, too.

Before the dust had settled, Nazi acolytes pressed forward to shower their dispassionate Führer with birthday tributes. An SS contingent returned to take up reserved seats at the foot of the Feldherrnhalle steps.

At last, the moment they'd been waiting for: Rudolph Hess stepped up to the microphone, unable to contain his excitement. "The Führer Speaks," he shrieked, to be immediately drowned out by a thunder of "Heil Hitler's".

The great man stepped forward to place his notes on a table beside an array of microphones, rocking back and forth on his heels while awaiting absolute silence. He adjusted his belt and covered his lips momentarily as if suppressing an indelicate burp.

Slowly, the words emerged. "In the days when it was difficult to be a National Socialist, when the Party had only seven members, I put forward two guiding principles: namely, a true Ideology, and that we would become the one and only power in Germany." A spontaneous roar erupted, one of many to follow, as he held up a restraining hand.

"We were proud to be a minority, the racially best of the German Nation." Spasmodic cheering. "In proudest self-esteem, I claimed leadership of a fractured Reich and Volk who subordinated themselves to the leadership in ever-growing numbers …"

Now he was becoming more animated and his brow showed beads of perspiration. "Whoever feels himself a carrier of the best blood and knowingly uses it to obtain leadership will never relinquish it …"

More howls rent the air. "The German people are now happy that their ever-changing situation has been replaced by a fixed pole …" He beat his chest with a clenched fist as the assembled audience leapt to its feet as one, reaching out to touch the hem of his aura with outstretched fingers.

Enveloped by the uproar the speaker raised his eyebrows and nodded approvingly, lightly patting his moist forehead with a small white handkerchief while the row subsided. Again he rocked slowly back and forth on the balls of his feet with arms crossed defiantly.

During this hysterical interlude, I motioned to Claudia and threaded my way through the forest of waving arms to a vantage point vacated by Hoffman; a prime position between the two great marble paws providing an unrestricted view. National Holiday or not, there was the boss in person below, darting through the crowd snapping candid after candid.

Fascinated, I watched him firing away with his tiny Leica. Of course, none in the audience were more enchanted than Göring, Hess and Goebbels in the front row, continually nodding and prodding each other in response to the Leader's claims.

"I have called this movement of millions to life," Hitler bellowed, "to fight for the German resurrection. A new State can't simply fall down from the sky, but instead has to grow out of the people …"

"Yes! Yes! Zig Heil," they hollered through yet another standing ovation before order was restored.

"… I will remove the underlying causes of our decay and eliminate those afflictions which would in future foil any real recovery. The method of individuals terrorising the movement has cost more than 350 dead and tens of thousands injured …" he gestured toward the broken Brownshirts in wheelchairs. Those with both legs intact clicked their heels together and several Army Generals applauded.

"The lying [lugen] Press, particularly outside of Germany, will rue the day it fraternised with the interests of Communism. The salvation of the German peasant who wishes only to live in peace with the world must be achieved at all costs. I will cultivate the spirit of a Will for Freedom in the German Volk."

"Hear hear!" the masses shouted with applause.

"In future, high treason and betrayal of the Reich will be ruthlessly eradicated!"

The plaza rocked with approval, and from my vantage point I followed Hoffman's every move, admiring his effective yet unobtrusive technique. He fired off half a dozen before I'd decided on one. I swear at that moment I could have stripped off and stood on my head, and still not been noticed; all attention was focused on the message flowing from the Führer's lips, a message of salvation and empowerment.

He held up both hands as the last throbs of Sieg Heil faded away.

"For all time to come the Party will be the source of political leadership for the German people. In its organisation, as hard as steel yet malleable in its tactics, this organisation will become a training school, like a Holy Order for political leaders." Now he was hurling the words at the microphones in rasping commandments, and with eyes fixed upward he stretched both hands towards heaven. "… all upstanding Germans must become National Socialist, but only the best are true party comrades.

"Once, our enemies worried and persecuted us from time to time," he said as he punched the air and then lowered his tone ominously, "but from today we must examine ourselves and remove from our midst the elements that have become bad; they do not belong with us." The audience was now mad with excitement. "It is our wish and desire that this State and this Reich last for a Thousand Years, and we can be happy to know that the future belongs entirely to us."

With hands raised again to receive God's blessing, Hitler's eyes rolled around in their sockets as if on another plane. Now he was indeed their Führer, with arms akimbo he nodded and prodded the air while his audience brayed for more.

"When the older among us falter, the youth will stiffen and remain until their bodies decay. Only then, with our most obedient dedication we become the highest embodiment of thought and being," he continued, but was drowned out in full-throated ovation for a full fifteen seconds.

"Then, our glorious and laudable army, that proud old standard bearer of our people, will champion the political leadership of the Party; these two institutions together will equally educate the German Man."

General Blomberg was on his feet saluting his new Commander-in-Chief with tears in his eyes. Swept up in the enveloping hysteria I thought it a most extraordinary performance; perhaps I had been wrong all along and this truly was the way of the future. Could all these millions be wrong? Maybe it *was* true that Hitler himself was unaware of the atrocities being perpetrated in his name.

"The rights of the churches will not be curtailed: even the Reich's bishops know it's simply not enough to say 'I believe!' … Rather, to affirm 'I fight!'"

I could barely hear him now. "… and therefore strengthen and carry on their shoulders the German State, our German Reich, as a symbol of eternity." I could see at that moment he was living the dream, with eyes glazed messianically. He pounded his fists on his chest and shoulders: faith in his mission was absolute.

"And then the people will be engrossed anew, happy and inspired, for the Idea and the Movement live on in our Reich. Long live the National Socialist Party! Long live Germany!"

At this conclusion of the tempest he turned abruptly and walked away from the podium, leaving Hess to scream out a farewell staccato of Sieg Heil's and stiff arm salutes: "The Party is Hitler! … Hitler is Germany and Germany is Hitler!"

"Ja, ja, Sieg Heil!" Many were weeping openly and some older women were standing in puddles.

What a show! I swallowed hard and stood dumbfounded as the Führer descended the stairs to cut his monster birthday cake topped with candy swastikas. Hoffman directed him toward the best angle for holding the knife. Following the ceremonial dismemberment, slabs of the said cake were to be dispatched to children in nearby orphanages.

"Come on, let's get out of here; I've seen enough for one day," Claudia yelled in my ear as I jockeyed for a candid of the boss swinging from a lamppost. Effortlessly, he dropped to the pavement and shepherded the besieged Führer toward his open-topped Tourer for the short drive to the Brown House, where he could change from his sweat-soaked uniform into a double-breasted suit for the "official" birthday portraits. Nearby, mountains of gifts were being loaded onto the back of a lorry brought in for the purpose.

"I must say, Hitler's a very convincing speaker in person, don't you agree?" I ventured, as we cleared the crowd to the strains of the "Horst Wessel Anthem" and turned toward the English Garden. She did not reply and her brows were knitted. I prodded half-jokingly, "Well, I saw you waving your little flag along with the rest …"

She caught my smirk and narrowed her eyes in exasperation. "Sucker! That's what you are. That's what they all are; suckers!

"That speech surely sums up Hitler's intentions; it's just so obvious that his whole system of government is a house of cards dependant on the whim and caprice of a single misguided individual; no one will be spared in the end," she spoke matter-of-factly, dampening my enthusiasm. "When all's said and done, we do what we have to do."

I swung the camera bag over my shoulder and slipped an arm around her waist as we strolled amidst the riot of colour and spring fragrances. This time she did not pull away. Continuing in silence we pushed through the willows obscuring my sand bank.

A kingfisher skimmed low across the water as I scraped out a hollow in the sand and gathered together a pile of dry leaves. I'd been buoyed by our close contact and within minutes a blanket was spread with fruit, sandwiches and even a small slice of swastika icing which Claudia had slipped into her pocket while taking close-ups of the monster cake.

Her pack must have weighed a ton, disgorging two bottles of Pilsner and a French rosé. For the first time, I realised I was ravenous, after bypassing all those eateries handing out free meals. I considered my secret retreat to be the best restaurant in Munich by far. Our campfire smoke was soon rising lazily through the foliage overhead and a heron croaked nearby.

"Come sunset we don't want to find ourselves the only sober citizens in Munich on a day like this, do we?" she asked matter-of-factly, snapping open both beers and placing the rosé in the icy shallows.

We clinked bottles and toasted "absent friends", lost for a while in our own thoughts. The fire crackled at our backs as we sat gazing into the oily spring currents, still overawed by the spectacle we'd witnessed earlier. "A penny for them," Claudia said eventually, bringing me back to earth.

"Er … We'd better not drink too much if you intend showing me around the night life later on," I attempted to sound sensible but came across as feeble.

"Holy Mother, grant me Grace! Why do you think I've lugged these bottles all this way? Not to toast Herr Hitler, that's for sure. Funny, isn't it? You pester me for weeks to come on a picnic and when it finally happens you waste our valuable time together lauding his oratory skills.

"You really must come to your senses regarding this whole horrible mummery and see it for what it is. My friends in the Orchestra say he's a maniac out to destroy the world, and now, you of all people sing his praises." Her voice had a hard edge, but I was oblivious.

"As a matter of fact, I was thinking of how much I miss the morning chorus of cicadas in the wet season, and the jungle air crackling with bird calls. Did you know that birds build their nests in circles and worship the same God as I do?

"I've never felt more alone than when surrounded by huge crowds and their cloying pomp. In the jungle there is no pretence or treachery, only deception; every creature gets his natural chance, but here all three are intertwined. I feel foolish saying this, but it's as if the Führer speaks to the emptiness we all feel inside much of the time; as if he alone lays bare my lack of purpose. Yet, when I'm with you, Claudie, or meditating on Sister Klara's words, my common sense returns and everything becomes clear again; I can't believe I fall for it every time."

"Don't worry, you're not alone; we all started off wanting to believe. If I hadn't seen the inner workings up close I might well have remained just one bleating sheep in the flock. The trick for you and me, *and* your stubborn brother, is to stay alive a little longer and hope that somehow this storm of steel will pass us by." Her eyes moistened.

"But even I know that's a lie … Hitler has his tentacles into every guild and cranny. Wasn't it Goethe who said, 'Live dangerously and you live right'? Perhaps we *can* take heart and hope that the intense rivalry within the Party may cause them eventually to do each other in…"

But she didn't sound at all convincing. "You say Hitler is a farce; maybe I agree. But, who else can possibly counter that performance we witnessed today?"

"Well, Captain Ernst for one, if he's as popular as he thinks. You saw the Brownshirts straggling along behind Göring and Lutze, it makes you wonder whose side they're really on … and of course, Hitler always has his glorious Reichswehr to fall back on; God knows he's put in enough effort to keep them close. Did you see that fool Blomberg nodding his head like a lamb with a tear in his eye? He's on the verge of pledging unconditional obedience of the entire Reichswehr to Hitler alone; not the Fatherland, not the German Nation, only Hindenburg stands in his way."

"The cure might be worse than the disease," I replied.

"You're probably right. Don't forget the all-embracing vagaries of National Socialism contain a lollipop for just about everyone; well, not quite everyone," she added quickly. "You're not alone in thinking Hitler's words are directed specifically toward your own insecurities, that's part of his genius."

"It strikes me that his message is a bit like wind and light, and even Life itself …" I ventured.

"What on earth do you mean?"

"I guess I'm trying to say that words are mere vibrations, like wind and light; they only become visible when they strike something. Whether it's Hitler's hate-filled speeches or Jesus' Sermon on the Mount, no message can gain traction without a willing ear."

"I wouldn't be comparing them both in the same sentence …"

"But, can't you see? The principle remains the same. It's rather like radio waves passing through us every moment: they can hardly be imagined, let alone apprehended, without a receiver. Each of us chooses which wavelength our thoughts are tuned into; hence the signals we receive, at least in theory, should reflect the best interests of society. On the other hand, the People's Receivers that Goebbels is churning out like sausages don't permit any worldview other than the official Party line. Do you see what I mean?"

"Well, sort of, but you seem to be drawing a long bow, to use your own term." I could tell I was boring her.

"Do you remember I've spoken of the Great Pharaoh Akhenaten and his 'Law of The Triangle'? All stuff I learned from Sister Klara?"

"Not really. Look Klaus, whenever we spend time together you always try to avoid the obvious realities of modern life as they are, harping on instead how you wish it to be. You can save your breath about 'extra dimensions', besides those under my nose each day."

"They're not so much other dimensions as other realities, depending on how we see the same things differently; from a slightly altered perspective, I mean like spectators at the Colosseum, for example."

By now we had consumed the two bottles of beer and half the bottle of rosé with our sandwiches, and my tongue was loose to continue.

"Each of us listened to Hitler's speech and came away, at least initially, with quite different impressions. It's almost as if our 'inner receivers' were attuned to two different stations. In other words, I was initially taken in by the emotional appeal while you remained aloof, even cynical, at hearing the very same words. From what I've seen , that makes you part of a tiny minority, despite the flag waving."

"I should hope so! That's the nicest compliment I've received in a while. Even Goethe would agree. Are you suggesting that the vast majority of Germans are now 'tuned in', as you call it, to Hitler's wavelength?"

"Yes! That's exactly what I'm saying. Radios cannot pick up more than one station at a time, and every one of these starving souls chooses to stay tuned to the wavelength that feeds them on hope, prestige and boundless plunder; now there's a threesome for you. Each true believer has convinced himself he's a vital cog in the vast machinery of National rebirth.

"Sister Klara taught me to trust in the 'God of my Heart', yet I continue to be deceived on so many fronts. You, on the other hand, with no special training are deceived by none of it. Your conclusions are of a different stamp."

"It's called 'the school of hard knocks', Klaus. I'm afraid it leaves all your fancy book learning for dead."

But my mind was racing, encouraged by the spring air and crackling campfire. "Perhaps you're right. I'm guessing that both methods may turn out to be equally fatal in the long-run, but today, I couldn't care less." I was besotted with my own revelations.

"Well, if one little man can build this whole edifice using bullshit and brutality it may take only one other of equal skill and willpower to pull the rug out from under the whole rotten structure," Claudia rejoined.

"Oh yes? Do you have anyone in particular in mind, someone who can deliver an alternative message with equal conviction?"

She paused for a moment and fixed me with her quizzical feline gaze, unsure whether to continue. "They're all in jail; or dead … I guess there's always Captain Ernst and his three million street fighters. I don't know how much longer he's going to take all this intrigue lying down. Not to mention my friend Hans and his boisterous band of students, who I believe have gotten their hands on a clandestine printing press …"

"A single printing press against the whole might of Goebbels' propaganda machine is a bit like peeing into the wind, as Robert says, though he doesn't say peeing. Captain Röhm is in some ways a far more cultured person than Hitler, but the government under his bunch of bullies may not be much better than what we have now. As I said earlier, the cure may turn out to be worse than the disease, don't you think?"

"Well, anything would be better than this hierophant, who behind all the smoke and mirrors offers himself up as no less than an 'Intimation of Christ', preaching his fresh alternative to the falsehoods of the past. Give me a break! To a Jew and no doubt many others, his mantra is hollow!" She spat out the words.

"We have a 'Messiah' leading the country whose main loves are gossip, movies, bright colours, fast cars and circuses. Incidentally, the Messiah never misses a circus in Berlin, even taking along flowers for the trapeze artists and tipping them generously."

She paused for a few moments, obviously wound up, before leaning closer and continuing in hushed tones. "Putzi believes Hitler is a chronic masturbator; can you believe that? Despite all those lovesick females baring their breasts and hurling themselves at his feet."

I was almost too shocked to speak. "How in the world would Putzi know such a thing?"

"Putzi knows more than most. He's the only one with brains, wit and talent who's had the courage to remain original; and look where that's landed him. The beautiful Helene apparently picked it, and Putzi told me he agrees wholeheartedly."

We were now facing each other over the embers and I saw her eyes twinkle. "How about you Klaus? Are you a masturbator, too?"

"O ... Only when absolutely necessary, Claudia," I responded, blushing obliquely and trying to laugh it off before changing the subject.

"Hoffman says that sometimes, after a particularly rousing 'Führer Speech', the seats in the women's stalls have to be hosed down, and even Frau Emilie agrees that all modesty and self-restraint have quite gone out the window. Well, I guess I can't talk, can I? But, I wouldn't believe everything the boss says, either," she slurred slightly and leaned forward to pour the last of the rosé.

I had rarely felt such contentment, watching pale pink sunbeams slip in and out through the river mists. Claudia was resting on her elbow with her back to the water and continued languidly.

"And, while we're at it, I'll tell you what else I think of our esteemed Führer. Some find it hard to swallow that any man who's surrounded himself so strategically with that bunch of perverts hasn't once or twice dipped his own toe in the water, if you get my meaning? You just have to watch the newsreels to see how he wipes back his forelock and cocks his little finger when sipping a teacup; very feminine gestures, if you ask me."

Up until that moment I'd not really equated these simple hand movements with any particular sexual inclinations, but had to admit that in Hitler's case, her bibulous speculations did make sense. Again, I tried not to overreact.

I recalled Robert's alacrity to 'roll over', to use the vernacular, for Röhm and his mates while sussing out the lie of the land was almost excusable but ... the Führer Himself? Then again, there were all those little aberrations Eva complained of. "What about it, Klaus?" Her feline eyes reflected wickedly in the glowing coals. "How many times did you dip your toe in the water, eh? Spending all that time with Ernst and Marty ..."

"N ... No, never! Neither of them ever attempted to force me ..." I was surprised and shocked by her inference.

"Just checking; it so happens I believe you. They never forced me either and that's why we're still friends. Actually, the thought of intercourse with a woman is repugnant to Ernst. He labels such behaviour 'unnatuwal'," she lisped in mimicry, before draining her glass.

"Then again, these days what is natuwal?" At that, she rose unsteadily to her feet and with a step or two was behind me with those glorious fingers exploring my shoulder muscles. "Oh, come on, Klaus; life's too short. This is the surprise I promised," she purred, "and I don't usually do it for free. In your case, I'll make an exception."

I sat cross-legged on the cool sand and closed my eyes, briefly transported.

When we entered the noise, lights and festivities around Schwabing, Claudia explained that here in particular was at the heart of Munich's celebrations. Socially and artistically she promised a grand night ahead; already we could see bands playing in the street, and everywhere dancing couples in period costumes twirled and glided between Röhm's loitering battle groups.

Strolling arm in arm she pointed out various streetwalkers by name, most appeared in merry mood; their differing coloured accessories alerting potential clients to each girl's specialities. Actually, they came in all ages, shapes and sizes, with yellows taking cripples, greens ready to be whipped, and other shades making calls to hotel rooms. I found it a rather eerie scene, as many had fashioned their clothing on movie stars like Garbo and Dietrich, lounging against lampposts in feigned indifference, cigarettes hanging from painted lips.

One or two Hollywood facsimiles reminded me of Eva, who was not past pilfering her own designs off the big screen.

Suddenly, we were confronted. "Heil Hitler! … Come on young sir, how about it? Only five marks for the Führer's birthday! We street-girls too, are happy to make sacrifices and spread the goodwill."

And less desirable consequences, I thought quickly to myself.

The woman who'd approached was well past her prime, wearing heavy lipstick beneath faded blueish eyelids. Atop her head sat a coiffure of pink fairy floss, which Claudia informed me later was a wig.

Like everyone else in the street she wore a spray of Edelweiss, the Führer's favourite flower pinned to her bodice, and tonight her hard eyes sparkled indulgently.

"No? Then, how about a threesome for six marks? A young man like yourself should be eager to learn all the tricks of the trade. Maybe to try out on your little girlie here? – although she looks like she might be capable of a fast shuffle or two on her own," the repulsive creature said cruelly, running a glance up and down my friend. I raised my hands and backed away, sputtering "How dare you, madam!"

"No Klaus! She's right," Claudia rebutted, "… about me I mean. Goethe says, 'If you don't want the ravens squawking around your head, then don't climb to the top of the steeple.'"

"I'm not sure that's relevant under the circumstances," I blustered indignantly.

Meanwhile, the puzzled Demi-Monde backed away dejectedly, tossing a fox-stole over her bare shoulders and sauntering off to join her co-workers among the Brownshirts.

"Oh Klaus, you just don't get it, or worse, you don't *want* to get it. You really mustn't take offence when others call me out in public, it's just part and parcel of my predicament. I'm quite capable of defending myself."

As we passed beneath the illuminated sign of Salon Pussy, she took my arm again and tugged her hat a little lower, not speaking until we were past the bouncers manning the doorway:

"I don't dance there now," she stated matter-of-factly. "Let's just say Hoffman got me a 'promotion'. I work exclusively under his direction these days."

"Gosh! That's great news. Perhaps now we'll see a little more of each other?"

"What's that?" she yelled, cupping a hand to her ear against the increasing din.

"Follow me, I know someone in here," she yelled, descending a set of stairs into a dimly lit basement cabaret. A hurly-burly of packed tables sat half-hidden in the smoke haze, each boasting an imitation Tiffany lampshade with a "Meeny Miny Moe" logo embossed around its rim; giving off just sufficient light to see the person opposite if both leaned forward.

A word from Claudia to the maître d' saw a drunken couple move swiftly on, and we settled on the still-warm seats between the dance floor and stage. All eyes were on the final moves of a lone stripper, who I was informed was the famous Lola Epp, an old friend of Röhm's. She acknowledged Claudia's arrival by blowing a sweaty kiss our way, before slinking away between tables when the music stopped, twirling her brassiere over her head and bunting her buttocks up against the eager patrons.

"See that woman over there?" My friend leaned forward into the splash of light and motioned toward the gloom. "If I'm not mistaken, that's Ada Klein, another of Hitler's alleged sweethearts: I daresay she would have a tale or two to tell about what we spoke of earlier."

"Sweetheart? What a quaint term to use amidst all this fast-living," I thought, wondering if Eva had any idea at all as to the full extent of her "boyfriend's" rumoured intrigues on the side.

And so the die was cast for our night of "adventure", ambling from club to cabaret downing a beer or a riesling wherever we could grab a vacant table; pausing just long enough to explain the ins and outs of Munich nightlife. Before long, most venues looked pretty much the same to me, and the smoke left me short of breath.

When we eventually arrived outside Studio Hoffman, my head was spinning with excessive drink and desire.

"Well, this is where you get off my fine feathered friend; birds as brothers, indeed," she gurgled in my ear. "Tomorrow we'll have more films coming in than we know what to do with."

"B … But, how will you find your way home through this lot?" I muttered, forgetting that she intended to finish up at Café Heck.

She guided me gently through the front door, and as I turned to pucker for a goodnight kiss that never came I glimpsed her two grey eyes twinkling in anticipation of the fun ahead.

For weeks after the birthday celebrations Studio Hoffman was inundated with record processing orders, many of them "private" films containing the antics of party bigwigs whooping it up in their own crass bailiwicks.

Summer was approaching fast, and try as I may I had barely caught a glimpse of Claudia since her "promotion"; or Robert either for that matter. I spent every free moment by the Isar, sometimes catching a small fish in a woven trap of willow branches and roasting it on the coals; losing track of the hours as I hummed and meditated my free time away. Slowly, my asthma improved in the fresh air and I began to reap the rewards of insight, able to enter that state of Divine Atonement Sister Klara labelled "Afflatus" almost at will.

However, as is well-known, insight is a two-edged sword capable of good or evil. While I printed myself nearly cross-eyed and plotted shady picnics, the Machiavellian fist of National Socialism slowly tightened its grip across the land, eventually coming to rest at the shiny boots of my treasured saviour, Ernst.

According to Homer, "Delusion brings Mankind to Grief", and in retrospect, the events leading up to June 30, 1934, had been obvious for anyone with eyes to see. Earlier that month word had leaked of a tumultuous five-hour meeting between Röhm and Hitler in the Brown House when the S.A. Chief of Staff, amidst mutual ultimatums and threats, attempted to resign from all his posts. A frustrated Röhm was then accused by Hitler of "shameless blackmail", and it was reported that the louder Hitler screamed, oppugned and hurled accusations at his old comrade, Ernst responded with insults of his own.

The Führer pushed the case for retaining the Reichswehr as "one of the two pillars of the Reich, in case of future conflict", while a furious Röhm pressed for a merger between the two martial bodies with, naturally enough, himself in overall command. His last recorded utterance penetrating the Brown House walls was that "His stormtroops were ready to die for the Swastika".

"The S.A. is and remains Germany's fate," he had added, words sadly to be proven true in the broader context. When the meeting concluded, Hitler issued orders for the whole S.A. to "stand down and stand by" on extended summer leave until the end of July, and furthermore, forbade them "to wear uniforms or participate in any gathering".

Röhm abruptly took "indefinite sick leave" and retreated with a select few of his younger stormtroopers to "Guesthouse Hanselbauer" in the nearby

Bavarian Alps, where they could lick their wounded pride and take the waters together.

For all intents and purposes, Hitler then embarked on a hectic round of official and "Public Duties", which included his first-ever meeting with Mussolini in Venice and the reinterment of Göring's first wife Karin's remains in a purpose-built Crypt in Berlin with full-blown Nazi honours. On June 28, to further muddy the waters, he took off in the tri-motor "Führer Plane" accompanied by Himmler, supposedly to attend the wedding of Gauleiter Terboven in Essen, and while there to inspect the Krupp Steel Works and a chain of adjacent labour camps.

Unusually, this time he flew without Hoffman, who was away sightseeing with his wife in Paris. Hitler's pilot Bauer told Hoffman later that during each stopover Himmler was in constant contact with the SS in Munich and Berlin, spending considerable time briefing his subordinates on the other end of the line.

Those of us remaining in Munich were enjoying an unaccustomed lull when I was surprised to receive a summons from Röhm, via Lothar, instructing me to bring my camera and plenty of film to the guesthouse in Wiessee.

It appeared that, upon reflection, Röhm had decided to show off the "softer side" of his S.A. comrades relaxing lakeside, and required a series of photos showing himself and his men "at leisure". Perhaps by releasing a little propaganda of his own, he may counter the "scurrilous and irrelevant" rumours appearing almost daily in the newspapers, and also mollify societies' growing distaste for the S.A. "leadership rabble".

So it was on that brisk Saturday morning of June 30 that I kicked over Studio Hoffman's brand-new Sachs motorcycle-side car and roared off in high spirits toward Tegernsee. Lothar himself had tried to thwart my assignment by putting in a long-distance call to Hoffman, fortunately without success, and now the road to real adventure stretched out ahead.

With a road map taped to the fuel tank between my knees, the throbbing Sachs growled steadily along the winding, forested drive toward Austria's blue Alps. The stability afforded by the sidecar, plus the wind in my hair, lulled me into a sense of false security, which eventually shattered when I began my descent and rounded a sharp bend, coming face to face with an SS roadblock.

Two black guards, one carrying a submachine gun, stepped forward to demand my business as I scrambled to produce my press card.

"Let him through," one eventually motioned after conferring with his superior. "Hoffman will need something to publish ..."

"And for the archives, sir," I promptly volunteered.

With that, he stamped a white paper pass and taped it to the cycle headlamp. Idling toward Gasthaus Hanselbauer it became obvious that some major operation had recently concluded. SS guards stood strategically positioned around the building and small groups of staff were huddled together in fright.

A second roadblock barred access beyond the front gate, and after my papers were examined for a second time I was forced to park the bike and proceed toward the main building on foot.

I was rather surprised that Ernst would choose such bourgeois surroundings for his recuperation; the pseudo-rustic Sanatorium looked as if its layered balconies had been tacked on as an afterthought.

At first, no one would meet my querulous eye, and whispered conversations ceased at my approach; once inside the lobby I was drawn to the sobbing manager behind the desk and someone said, "Don't you know? They're gone, all gone! Heinze and his boyfriend were shot dead right there in the garden. Captain Röhm and the others were arrested in their beds and taken away in handcuffs."

I was too stunned to speak; images flashed before my eyes. I felt my chest tighten in an iron grip as the manager spoke up. "… Hitler himself arrived just after dawn, accompanied by an SS motorcade …"

He seemed to be trying to make sense of things by reliving the fateful hour. "The Führer pushed past me with pistol drawn and rushed up the stairs with his bodyguards, banging on doors and yelling 'Open up!'"

Poor Captain Röhm and his 2.I.C. Karl Ernst thought at first it was some kind of joke; Ernst remained jovial throughout the whole proceedings. He knew that Hitler had phoned Röhm the previous evening to finalise details of the 10 am conference; obviously, there must be some mistake."

So far, the newly revived manager had directed his outpourings at me, before pointing out a group of SS men beating the bulrushes at water's edge. "See! See that? One or two stormtroopers jumped off the balconies and made it to the lake shore; they won't get far."

I tried as best I could to pull myself together, vaguely aware that the scene needed to be recorded for posterity, regardless of the ultimate outcomes. I fired off a couple of quick shots in the foyer, then in Röhm's empty room on the first floor, trying to focus my scrambled thoughts.

Once outside I snapped the building from all angles in its idyllic surroundings. I could see groups of S.A. officers arriving for the scheduled meeting being brusquely redirected back to the Brown House by SS guards, where I suspected an uncertain fate awaited.

Not wishing to push my luck I avoided the foyer and hurried to kick over the Sachs and hightail it back to Munich. Several times I nearly lost control of the big machine as my mind fixated on the terrifying scenario I'd come so close to witnessing. If Röhm's unceremonious arrest was true… arrested for what? I struggled to believe it.

There could be no starker contrast between my own former delusions and what had just occurred.

Several days later my friend Ernst was shot dead in his cell in Stadelheim Prison, after refusing to do the "honourable thing" and shooting himself with a pistol left for the purpose. But the whole barbaric purge was just getting started.

Not yet labelled "The Night of Long Knives", its full extent only became clearer with time. That week saw hundreds of S.A. leaders and other "enemies of the state" gunned down where they stood, following brief and brutal interrogations. It seemed that anyone who'd ever trodden on the Führer's toes suddenly found himself before a firing squad.

Former Chancellor Schleicher, Hitler's hated predecessor, was shot dead beside his wife in the hallway of their home when she answered the doorbell.

When Robert, still white as a ghost days later, arrived outside my broom closet, he was wearing a not-so-spick-and-span SS uniform. He said he'd been on standby for 48 hours without sleep and I'd rarely seen him so rattled.

He revealed his anguish at being forced to participate in the deadly reprisals against Röhm and many of his old comrades. Here beneath the staircase, he could at last show some rare emotion. "I tell ya liddle brudda, it could ha been me! Ernst had invited me to join the boys for a night or two in the hot tubs at Bad Wiessee. Christ! Now I've had to stand by helplessly while the SS butchered the entire S.A. leadership."

He shuffled through several of the Reich Press Office releases on my bed, which stated among other aspersions, that Röhm's "unfortunate proclivities generated such unwelcome pressure as to impose grave conflicts of conscience on the Führer himself".

A special edition of the *Völkischer Beobachter* noted Röhm's "removal as Chief of Staff", along with a list of those already executed, supposedly for "planning the overthrow of Legitimate Authorities". It went on to describe his "utterly intolerable behaviour" amidst a "nest of vipers", and that the iron-willed Führer would address the Reichstag to seek a decree legalising the killings retrospectively.

Later comments by Eva revealed that Hitler, along with her and other selected guests, was actually attending a tea party in the Chancellery garden at the very moment SS Colonel Theodore Eike and one other were emptying their pistols into the chest of their former friend and mentor, after he refused to put a bullet through his own head.

"If I am to be killed, let Adolph Hitler do it himself," the intrepid Ernst had allegedly declared.

After sleeping on my bunk for several hours Robert further enlightened me on the shocking wider details of the counter-coup.

Gregor Strasser, another of Hitler's early "blood comrades", whose two sons referred to their revered Godfather as "Onkel Adi", had been despatched with dozens of others during the first wave. He said that more than 1,100 "suspects" had already been detained, many of them still not comprehending their fate.

Some shouted "Heil Hitler" as they were cut down by the SS firing squads. Among those killed were Röhm's attorneys and his chauffeur, Johann Koenig.

"God forbid! Who else is on that list? Is Marty safe?" I asked anxiously. He revealed that Marty and several others had been dragged off to Dachau for "further questioning", though he remained hopeful that they at least may get off lightly.

But July 2 brought the terrible press release: "Obergruppenführer Martin Schartzl has been shot in Dachau Concentration camp after being found guilty of treason."

My first response was to burst into tears; Robert should have prepared me. He later revealed that a Hitler decree forbade burials of "enemies of the state" in marked graves, and how Röhm's body had been hastily interred on top of his own father's coffin. My thoughts immediately flew to Frau Emilie and I vowed to go to her side.

It took a full week for Hitler's brilliantly crafted Reichstag speech to hit the airwaves. "The boil has been lanced!" he began righteously, sprinkling his sentences with irony and sarcasm that evoked laughter in the chamber.

"This 'apostle of sodomy' has committed a 'string of unfortunate abuses' and 'we have seized evidence by the hundredweight'. A conspiratorial clique of personal ambition and homosexuality mistook my tolerance for weakness while promoting those same rampant proclivities that destroyed ancient Greece. Furthermore, these Bolshevist Pests were planning a great uprising, even going so far as to poison the water in our reservoirs", he lied.

Reichstag members hooted and stamped.

I and other staff had been ordered to gather by the "People's Receiver" outside Hoffman's office; unlike most other workplaces in Germany, we were not usually forced to put down tools during Government broadcasts owing to the importance of our mission. I could see at a glance the impact these words were having on my colleagues. Who would *not* want to rid the National Body of such a nasty cancerous growth? They hung on the Führer's every word while avoiding eye contact with each other.

"In this hour," he continued, "I was responsible for the fate of the German People. If anyone raises his hand against the Reich, certain death will be his lot." Several of my colleagues gave a little cheer. "Only when one takes on the mantle of hero can he fully implement the new intellectual order sweeping Germany."

He further urged every German to "practice obedience", and repeated his claim that "Providence had provided both he *and* the German Volk with this opportunity to complete the work begun by Jesus Christ". The Reichstag was uproarious when he concluded with a rousing "Amen!"

None of us spoke when a hand reached up to turn off the martial music that followed; the spell was broken.

We each slunk back nervously to our respective duties, passing by Lothar who cast a stern eye for potential slackers. "Things will be different from here on. Don't say you haven't been warned," he spoke with a renewed air of confidence.

Before long, however, some staff members shared their thoughts of Hitler sparing his eyes at the sight of having his old friend killed before him.

Between newsreels, the printed media and visits from Robert, I gained a more complete picture of the June 30 bloodbath: in one fell swoop a massive organisation had been decapitated and disarmed.

Newspapers featured pictures of Hitler and the Nazi elites doing their rounds of social activities with various actresses in tow as if nothing of consequence had occurred. Hitler even dashed off to a performance of Wagner in Berlin.

To the dismay of Hoffman's own Press Corps, one Paris-based newspaper went beyond the worldwide storm of protest, claiming that the "would-be dictator" had "gotten rid of those initiates privy not least to the private life of their Führer, who is himself homosexual".

Of course, no one in the Press Room had the courage to repeat these allegations to Hitler's face, preferring to dismiss them as "gutter gossip". Any staffer foolish enough to spread such claims would suffer the direst repercussions.

Reichsmarschall Göring, with trembling lip, referred to "The Führer's terrible hours of sorrow", and vowed to assist the SS in stamping out every last vestige of overt homosexual behaviour in the ranks: those who had hitherto enjoyed the permissive morays of the Röhm years were suddenly pilloried and brutally "outed" for their "abominable vice". Many hundreds were placed in protective custody or packed off to Dachau for "re-education".

At first Eva, like so many of us in the Studio, was shocked by the published lists of those "eliminated", yet after a few days, her tone changed when she calmly disowned Röhm to my face.

We were together in the darkroom and she'd just lit up the first of her morning cigarettes. In hushed tones, she blithely revealed her conclusions. "I happen to know the truth: they were trying to betray him and Adolph had every right to defend himself for the good of Germany. No one can deny that it was my Adolph who slashed the unemployment rate and restored order on the streets. Of course, you only caught the tail end of the Jewish Republic." She blew a smoke ring and gave a sigh of self-pity. "All these distractions. Oh, it's hell to be too much in love, I simply can't talk about it anymore."

But Eva was only one of many to dismiss Röhm's vital contributions and brutal murder with the wave of a hand. The ailing President Hindenburg, having formerly dismissed the aspiring chancellor as "that Bohemian Corporal", sent a congratulatory telegram lauding Hitler's "forthright and necessary actions" against Röhm and the S.A.

Likewise, any lingering doubts within the armed services were soon dispelled by General Blomberg's base and grovelling panegyric extolling the Führer's "soldierly resoluteness and exemplary courage" in ridding the Reich of "these traitors".

"Mutineers and homosexuals are out!" Blomberg snorted sanctimoniously. "Re-armament is too serious a business to permit participation by drunkards, peculators and perverts." He lauded the imminent restoration of "proper State order" and hailed the return of a "normal, healthy lifestyle" right across the land.

Terrified homosexual and bi-sexual men saw the axe fall swift and heavy among their peers. As events unfolded, arrests for this offence increased tenfold, from three to thirty thousand over the next five years.

Meanwhile, Propaganda Minister Goebbels ruminated venomously in the wings, appraising all other responses before launching a radio tirade of his own, replayed several times over successive days. He vowed that "we would clean out rumour mongers, idlers, saboteurs and agitators from every last suburb and village while trampling down reactionaries and alarmist criticasters".

While he was at it he took the chance to banish Putzi from the Brown House in Munich and the Berlin Chancellery, citing his "disruptive influence". The brilliant international raconteur's opinions were no longer required.

As I sat glued to my People's Receiver I could only shake my head in disbelief; if Mephisto did indeed carry through on his threats there should be scarcely left a living soul in all Germany.

It was further reported that warm opprobria was pouring in from Church leaders around the globe, most notably from Cardinals Borcini and Pacelli in Rome; the latter toning down his enthusiasm for Nazi methods following his elevation to the papacy in 1939.

Hitler gloated that he had the Vatican "over a barrel", there being no real choice between his regime and that of the "atheistic Communist hordes from the east", who, since their own revolution, had murdered millions of priests and turned centuries-old Russian cathedrals into pigsties and barns.

For the Vatican the choice was clear: either go along with National Socialism's palsied version of Christianity or face possible annihilation. I knew that both Eva and Claudia attended Mass occasionally, when not playing "escorts" for their respective masters. From what I'd seen each had plenty to confess.

Some leading Protestant pastors, most notably one Dr Althaus, encouraged swastikas to be flown from church flagpoles and actually draped over altars beside the Holy Crucifix. At best, Nazism's shortcomings would just have to be overlooked; after all, the movement seemed to have achieved a certain resurrection of pure Volk values and traditions.

I could not help but wonder why the Führer (who at one time in his youth aspired to the priesthood) had pretended to encourage the participation of the Christian church at the very forefront of his social revival. With Heil

Hitler's now resonating from pulpits across Germany, remaining doubters were "guided" inexorably toward the new true Path to Salvation: National Socialism!

Increasingly, sermons now included phrases such as "Our Protestant churches have seen the year of 1933 as a Gift and Miracle of God." However, despite these errors, not everyone in the wider congregation was convinced.

"One day, we want to be in a position where only complete idiots stand in the pulpit and preach to old women," Hitler had been overheard boasting to his inner circle. Even I had to admit it was becoming more difficult and less inspiring to find a church without the Nazi trimmings. I found some solace in Sister Klara's recitation of Master Jesus' truism: "The Kingdom of God is within."

$$47$$

"The man is mad!" I overheard Herr Braun responding to Hoffman's platitudes regarding the Führer's many virtues, how to many Herr Hitler appeared as a "Saint bringing to life the words of the True Saviour".

"Well, he's no bloody saviour to my Christian values," Herr Braun had rebutted, "I want it to stop!"

This confronting scene took place in Hoffman's office after Eva's father had stormed in to confront her complicit employer. He demanded that Hoffman cease encouraging "these liaisons between Hitler and my virgin daughter, either at your private residence or on the so-called Magic Mountain."

Following the exchange I crawled out from under the darkroom sink to find Eva standing over me with hands on hips, looking quizzical but troubled. "I feel like a prisoner. I thought Papa was coming around but then he goes and locks my bedroom door. He's in there now with the boss trying to ruin my life."

I did not let on that I had "accidentally" overheard something of their earlier conversation. She didn't know whether to cry or curse.

"It's bad enough that Magda the nymphomaniac has been appointed 'Official Nazi Hostess', but that bitch Leni Riefenstahl, Adolph's so-called ideal example of Aryan Womanhood, has flattered him into making an official documentary of the Party Rally in Nuremberg; with herself as director, of course. All the while here's me rotting away behind closed doors; I could just scream." She stamped her foot.

At the sound of voices outside I turned off the red light above the door and emerged to witness the two fathers shaking hands in the waiting room; both looking pleased. "Then it's settled, Herr Hoffman? Now that Henni has moved out of home, Eva may stay overnight at your Villa, so long as you or Frau Hoffman are present." Fritz was going over the details in schoolteacher fashion, tapping one finger against his other palm, "… and if she is visiting Haus Wachenfeld it will be on official Studio Business only. You well know that my daughter is convent-educated and we Brauns have our reputation to think of."

His balding Rhesus-head glowed with righteous colour as he confirmed the relaxed strictures. Hoffman nodded agreeably while ushering Herr Braun toward the door. "You have my word, Fritz; your daughter will be well taken care of."

When they caught sight of Eva she was already halfway across the room. With an embarrassing flamboyant gesture, she leapt upon her father's neck, "Oh Papa, thank you. I do so hate deceiving you," which caught him quite off guard.

"And Chief," she turned teary-eyed toward the now sardonic Hoffman, "without your support, none of this would be possible."

She waved her arm airily, as if all her problems had suddenly melted away.

When I passed her later taking the stairs two by two, Eva was humming the popular tune "Red roses are for you". From what I could see, her apparent change of fortune came at a time of great misery to countless others, during that coordination of forces designed to further isolate the Jews.

While she pored through the pages of the latest Ferragamo catalogue, her elder sister, Ilse, was confronting the reality of Jewish ostracisation, forbidden from further involvement with her long-time employer, Dr Marx, of whom she was very fond.

Dr Marx, like so many thousands of his Jewish colleagues, was now banned from practising on Aryans. When Ilse protested and begged her sister to "do something", Eva urged her to "disassociate herself from the trouble ahead" as she was already doing with her own Jewish friends. "It's best for all concerned," she said imperiously.

Many of Eva's former classmates had already emigrated and now her personal jeweller had been taken into "protective custody". The ban on Jewish participation in "normal" city life extended not only to Armed Services and Civilian Offices but even public swimming pools and parks.

Claudia was clearly disturbed when I eventually cornered her in the darkroom and we managed to exchange a little news. "I thought you said you had received a promotion?" I asked, alluding to her concern over Hoffman's wavering support for her new position.

"Would you believe," she began haltingly, "he's wangled his way onto the Block Committee drawing up lists of Jewish families and businesses to be evicted? The sly bastard has an eye on several shop fronts and has joked more than once that everybody 'has to die sometime'."

"I'm just so sick of these insatiable Party bigwigs with their stinking breaths and pot bellies," she added, as if trying to jolly herself ahead of the gathering storm. She reached over and squeezed my hand hard.

"I suppose this should come as no surprise but the Black Dwarf has just uttered another of his chilling one-liners: "Germans can live without the Jews, but they can't live without us.""

I felt helpless observing her anguish.

"You are no doubt aware of how lucky your brother was to escape being shot?" she continued. "And that was only because his pal Fegelein spoke up for him and settled for a demotion. As things stand, Robert is filling his tailor-made trousers now that Himmler's new offsider Heydrich is sniffing into his background. Urghh! That fellow's been dubbed the 'Blond Beast'; he's brought a whole new level of systematic ruthlessness to the SS."

"Apparently, he's setting up a 'police force within the police force', charged with rooting out potential traitors and slackers *inside* the Party. Incidentally, I'll try to catch up for another picnic while everyone is away at the rally in Nuremberg," she said, forcing a smile.

That night I tossed and turned on my bunk, plagued by a bad dream in which Iris repeatedly hid my work camera and then reported my failure to complete my assignments to Hoffman. I tried calling for Claudia, but no sound came. Her face appeared to hover over Röhm's topless torso as SS Obergruppenführer Eicke's bullets slammed into his chest.

I awoke in a panic, more aware than ever of my hopeless predicament.

I resolved then and there to defy Hoffman, whatever the cost, and pay a visit to Frau Emilie, whose own bitter suffering continued to haunt my thoughts.

The next day, I set out with camera in hand and my hat pulled low. "I'll be somewhere around the English Garden if anyone's looking for me," I fibbed to the counter staff before striking out with set jaw into the lazy summer heat.

Dodging the S.A. street-corner gangs, who seemed to me every bit as pugnacious as under their former leader, I finally mounted the steps to Frau Röhm's apartment and rang the doorbell.

A red-eyed Sophie greeted me warmly but bade me wait outside while she informed her mistress of my presence. Every minute proved a torture as I tried to avoid being recognised by curious passers-by.

Since her loss, Frau Röhm had been receiving no one but family, so I was greatly relieved to be ushered into the parlour where I found the frail old lady sitting beside an open window, engaged in earnest discussion with her two surviving children. All three seemed genuinely pleased to see me and I could not suppress a tear while moving to embrace her bony black shoulders.

Ernst's brother, Robert, was first to speak, even as his mother held both my hands tightly and gazed into my wet eyes. "Klaus, you've come at the right time," he began, almost pleading. "Perhaps you can shed light for us on some of the missing details?"

Hesitantly, I disclosed what I'd heard, sparing the worst particulars but, before I'd finished, Frau Emilie sat bolt upright and addressed me directly. "I won't accept money from my son's murderer!"

Robert Röhm explained that Hitler, via the Party Treasury, had crassly offered his mother a lifetime pension of all things, as if nothing untoward had occurred. "My Ernst always looked and smelled so nice," she ventured, before stifling a sob into cupped hands.

"My brother was a brave and fearless soldier," Robert added, stating the obvious, "Yet, he never lost his zest for life or sense of humour. We simply can't understand it; Adolph always backed Ernst against media vilification and right to the end made a big show of assuring him he was indispensable. They were his very words."

The gutted family Röhm had obviously gone over the evidence many times. "Why, it was our Ernst who helped him into his boots and got him started. Almost from day one, it was my beloved brother who made Adolph what he is." The floodgates of pent-up resentment had opened. "Who was it that set him spying in 1919, right after the War, and propped him up during the '23 Putsch?" The two women nodded in agreement. "Who came back from Bolivia in '30 to save the mighty Leader from the stormtrooper revolt in Berlin?" he asked bitterly.

"What's more, Adolph even copied Ernst's warlike expressions and martial poses for the camera," said Sister Sophie. "Klaus, you of all people would have noticed that in the photos ..."

"Well perhaps, but the studio gets hectic at times and I just try to keep my head down."

"That man has betrayed and discredited the whole S.A. leadership," Robert declared. "Why no trial before the bloodbath? This is nothing short of lynch law." I could think of no response.

"Ernst was never happy following rules, but not once did we ever dream it would come to this. What went wrong with a straightforward movement? They say all revolutions devour their own children ... I read that somewhere."

Sophie too kept raking over the coals, trying to make sense of their loss. "Sure, Ernst made many enemies, because he saw through the double standards of Bourgeois morality. My brother detested any woman who pursued him with love, except for Mama and I, who loved him for who he was. He felt that too many Bourgeois wanted to share in the spoils of power without incurring any obligations. Although Ernst was far from unhappy over his homosexuality he ruffled plenty of feathers with his blunt views on the subject. He made no bones demanding that 'windbags must shut up and men alone make the decisions'... after all, Mama taught him. I suppose that sort of thinking is acceptable in the Brown Army."

I reiterated my belief that the plot allegations against Ernst were surely fabricated and that the whole affair was a most violent injustice. I said that one day there would be a Cosmic Reckoning, at which they dipped their eyes politely while I mumbled my reasons.

"Oh, how my baby loved parties and how he loved Bayreuth." Frau Emilie perked up slightly. "And how he played Wagner so beautifully on the piano, this very piano ..." she waved emptily at the baby grand, where two amber glass eyes glowered wanly from the shadows.

"All he wanted was the ideals and spirit of the German Combat Veteran to count in the running of the country," Robert said. "It's simply shocking that he was betrayed from within his own ranks; that viper Victor Lutze was the first to plant doubts in Hitler's mind. He just couldn't wait to step into Ernst's shoes.

"In the end, he was even complaining about Ernst's 'gluttony' and the stink of his Havana cigars; while Hitler, who detested the smell of tobacco smoke anyway, fell for it. I'm afraid in the end these things all add up.

"Of course, Ernst didn't do himself any favours standing up to Adolph like he did, but he only wanted the best for his men and the Nation. No one imagined our self-appointed Führer would stoop so low as to order the murder of his best friend while sipping tea in the chancellery gardens. I'm afraid the genie is well and truly out of the bottle now."

"It was jealousy, if you ask me," Sophie volunteered.

They went on to warn me not to approach the family gravesite, into which Ernst's body had been so unceremoniously dumped atop his father's coffin. She said that she had seen the Gestapo secretly photographing other mourners.

At our parting, there were solemn vows of friendship all around and I noticed again the permanent tear in Frau Emilie's eye. Little did I know this would be the last time our paths would cross: just months later, on January 6, 1935, she took her greying hair with sorrow to the grave.

Besides the ad-hoc Studio expansions, Hoffman's "modernisation" programme was proceeding apace, with assembly line processing now modelled roughly along the lines of Henry Ford's auto factory; at least, that was the theory.

Each department was required to slide its output through a trap door to the next, starting with rolls of film from the front counter and progressing through the darkroom and Framing and Finishing, before ending up back at the front desk ready for collection, with a minimum of "talking and time-wasting". Owing to the dilemma of creating lightproof trapdoors for the darkroom, my hand deliveries of fresh prints continued more or less as before.

An enormous number of orders were received for framed 8" × 10" copies of Hitler's "official" 45th birthday portrait, the one taken by Hoffman of the Führer wearing his light-coloured, doubled-breasted suit with the flamboyant lapels, while perched on the corner of his huge desk in his 400 square-metre office at the Berlin chancellery.

Both he and Hoffman agreed that this pose, of all those taken on the day, presented the Führer in a more "approachable" light than usual; and despite his "Man of Destiny" glare the orders kept rolling in.

I managed to find excuses to meander in and out of the Press Room and stations en route to the front counter, gaining a greater understanding and, dare I say appreciation, of how the place actually functioned.

The more I learned the more I marvelled at the breadth of Hoffman's stranglehold across the industry. Occasionally, a colleague shared a kind word during my rounds, yet aside from Claudia, most of the others saw me as something of a harmless novelty that turned out damn good prints. Actually, that skill too was played down when Studio Hoffman or the stringers themselves took the first bite at the credits.

My residual accent and dispassionate demeanour did not altogether fit the rumours of a jungle upbringing; behind the boss' back, Lothar remained openly hostile. That bad blood triggered a chain of mixed blessings and liberation of sorts.

I had slipped into Framing and Finishing hoping to catch a certain eye and instead came up behind a burly brown hunk in the far corner. At once I could see Lothar had someone pinned against the bench between his bulging thighs. "Isn't it about time you joined the Party, you elusive little Polack whore? Don't you think Adolf Hitler is the most splendid Leader ever?" He was leering close to her mouth.

"No, I don't. Let me go, you big ape." It was Claudia! I could now see her struggling vainly to slip out from under the commanding embrace. For a moment I stood rooted to the spot, too startled to act, before my fear gave way to anger.

"Stop right there! You have no right," I heard the words jump from my mouth as if from a stranger. The great blob stiffened and the bovine neck twisted slowly around. "Who do we have here? Come to save the damsel in distress, have we? Well, get lost!"

With a wild cry, I sprang forward to cover the distance in a bound, and swung a single clumsy punch toward Lothar's jutting chin, catching the big man off-balance more in surprise than the strength of the blow.

In so doing, his feet remained entangled with Claudia's flailing legs and in slow-motion he toppled sideways, like a forest giant before the woodsman's blade. The scene converged in a split second as his temple caught the workbench corner with a loud crack and he collapsed to the floor with a sigh.

For a few moments, my eyes darted disbelievingly between an apparently unharmed Claudia and the beefy carcase lying at her feet.

"A … Are you alright?" I stammered, lifting her to the floor … and she nodded, obviously shaken but seemingly intact.

All this commotion brought a rush of staff to the door, jostling wide-eyed before the scene. "It's Lothar," someone yelled, "Klaus's knocked him cold."

Within moments it seemed everyone had come for a look. Several even slapped me on the back and offered congratulations, while another tossed a pail of water in the unpopular Sturmbannführer's face when he began snoring. All now knew that Brownshirt's influence and authority had been greatly undermined, and real power had shifted to Iris and her Gestapo connections.

While many expressed approval, and even admiration, at this turn of events, my apparent victory had come at the painful cost of two broken knuckles. As I stood holding my skewed fingers Iris sidled close enough to whisper in my ear, "You'll pay for this, Jungle Boy. There's no Röhm around to look out for you now."

Within minutes Hoffman came blustering into the room, just as three strong men were juggling a wobbly-legged Lothar toward the infirmary.

"Wha … what happened?" the big man was grinning foolishly and staring at the blood on his fingers. The lump on his temple was the size of a duck egg and twice as shiny. Out of the corner of one eye, I noticed Iris hurrying off to write her report.

The boss turned back to hear Claudia's animated account of the incident, noting the disarray of materials on the corner bench.

"He what? Well, I'll be damned; out cold you say? Tell Lothar to report to my office when he comes to his senses," he shouted to the men shepherding the dead weight through the door.

"As for you, young fella, I'll have no fisticuffs under this roof." He tried to look severe but for once let a flicker of mirth play over his pursed lips. "Sissy! Take the boy off to the hospital in my car and have that hand looked at," he barked the order while taking a closer look at my two fingers poking out obliquely.

He gave his driver curt instructions and closed the rear door on the two of us; together at last in the back seat … and me in too much pain to enjoy it. I wound the window down with my good hand to thank him, but as the big Mercedes pulled away he was already making the announcement. "Who would have imagined such a thing? Talk about a dark horse. Wait until I tell the Führer."

Of course, wearing a cast for weeks only served as a visible reminder of my glorious feat, far beyond those who had witnessed the actual incident. Many of my female colleagues now smiled shyly or whispered behind their hands when I passed. Even the stringers looked upon me with a more respectful eye. Snide remarks over my accent vanished overnight.

Although I continued to pursue the policy of "live and let live", it was obvious that Iris and Lothar were cooking up something behind the scenes.

The powers of this conniving duo had been considerably curtailed under Hoffman's new system of departmental responsibility, whereby pronouncements on the way forward would be issued by him alone.

Our future modus operandi would be to fall into lock-step with Hitler's own management style, which could only succeed if the leader is all-knowing and constantly available. But neither Hitler nor Hoffman discovered the secret of being everywhere at once, which left some wiggle-room between certain departments.

The boss was now absent for long periods, and when he did show up he looked to be in continuing decline, packing ever more kilos onto his rotund waistline. His eyes were troubled and it seemed to me that no man could properly do justice to the myriad baneful tasks he'd set for himself. Was it greed alone that drove him? ... Some ambitious itch?

Or was he merely swept up in the heady triumphs of the Great New Era?

Captain Streicher had often declared "dead fish rots from the head" and various other aphorisms concerning leadership; I wondered if Nazism was becoming just one more alternative to smug Religionism, whereby a pecking order of high priests pronounces necessary steps required to remain on the one true path. Was there now a need, or even space for other gods besides the Leader himself? Boundaries between Christianity and Churchianity seemed blurred by a light brighter and more urgent than all others: National Socialism!

My mind pondered these and other developments as I hunched over my chemicals, especially when studio employees were suddenly required to sign a paper stating that they "believed in God" and were "giving up Religion". Which parts? What did that mean? Did they actually believe they could stop me from talking to myself?

President Hindenburg, the Old Bull's much-anticipated passing came in August, and with it went our last remaining freedoms. Hitler now assumed the revered warrior's mantle of authority overnight, becoming the "Absolute Dictator" demanding "blind obedience" and "unquestioning discipline" from the stormtroops under their servile new commander, Victor Lutze: there would be no more "grey areas".

Army Chief Blomberg doubled down on the requirement for all Wehrmacht personnel to take an "Oath of Absolute Loyalty" to Hitler's person as Führer, and it was reported that a few kind words from his risen "Saviour" could bring a tear to the general's eye. The general stated that a friendly handshake from his Commander-in-Chief had cured his head-cold.

Following the "Blood Purge" of June 30, as it was now widely known, the numerous murders became "listed in law" and retrospectively "legalised". Martin Bormann baldly announced that National Socialism was now simply, "The Will of the Führer; no more, no less."

For added measure, Hitler reiterated that "National Socialism is a Movement of Barbarians" above all else. There would be no more "pussy-footing along with one leg on either side of the fence", he announced, sending a chill down many spines.

As the screws slowly tightened across the land, Iris Bumke, Gestapo informant No. 2645 moved to spring her trap, with near-fatal consequences for both Claudia and myself.

It all began routinely enough during one of the boss' many absences when our supervisor summoned everyone to a "staff briefing" in the reception lounge. When the announcement came over the loudspeakers I was loitering around the "Hitler Files" in Hoffman's office, mainly because Claudia was in attendance, tidying the hallowed precinct off limits to all but a trusted few.

As we entered the crowded room, my heart sank; I heard Claudia catch her breath. There stood Iris and Lothar flanked by two sallow, unsmiling strangers in trench coats and hats, who didn't waste time getting down to business.

"Which one of you slandered the Führer and the Nazi Party?" one Gestapo agent demanded as the colour drained from nearly every face and you could have heard a Leica shutter. The practised eye of the man who spoke slowly scanned the crowd, before resting his gaze on Claudia. "You! Step out," he commanded, and I saw Lothar nodding assent from a distance. Then, it was Iris' turn to deliver her own blow. "Fraulein, do you have anything on your conscience?"

Upon receiving no immediate answer she stepped forward and slapped my friend hard across the cheek. "Fraulein, turn out your pockets, now!" she ordered the usually dauntless girl, who fumbled to obey. I shuddered to recall my own brush with the Secret Police and swallowed a rising fear.

"All of them! Including those pockets under your smock," the hard-eyed Iris persisted. Reluctantly, the girl reached beneath her apron to produce a handkerchief, comb and polishing cloth; at last a crumpled sheet of note paper.

"Aha!" the snitch snatched the "evidence" from Claudia's hand, smoothing it out on the coffee table. For a few moments, there was silence as the secret policeman slowly perused the note and fixed his eyes on my hapless friend.

"Is this not a part of your employer's private correspondence, Fraulein? How do you come to have it on your person?"

"It … It was on the floor when I was cleaning, beside the waste basket; I was going to throw it away," she stammered.

Iris took a deep breath and looked to her two agents for support.

"Frau Bumke has long suspected that you have been prying into affairs that don't concern you. After informing us she placed a harmless scribbled note of Hoffman's where your loyalty could be tested."

Claudia stood silent and defiant.

"It appears Fraulein that you have failed the test and will come with us to Headquarters."

"And him, Herr Officer! He's the one who assaulted a Party official," Lothar moved quickly to shove me with his great paw, which I deftly side-stepped before addressing the agents.

"Herr Hoffman fully investigated the matter, Herr Official, and determined that I had no case to answer."

The fellow looked hard at me as he tightened his grip on the resigned girl, replying coldly. "No! Not you … for now," before he brushed Lothar aside. "Brownshirts must shut up and do as they're told."

I watched helplessly the back of Claudia's head with her feet barely touching the ground, being bustled into a low-slung tourer. My insides were churning and my breath came in short gasps at one last glimpse through the rear window sandwiched between two dark hats. I knew what she was in for, if it hadn't already begun.

The Gestapo's methods were equally draconian against malefactors of both sexes and all stripes, with special attention being paid to Jews. Did they even know she was a Jew?

The Studio quickly returned to normal. Everyone returned to their duties and the incident was swept under the purloined Persian carpets; except for me, bedridden beneath the staircase in a state of despair.

Upon his return, a furious Hoffman summoned his former Pox Dr Morell to my bedside, who immediately eased my distress with adrenalin injections at six-hourly intervals. My relief was tempered somewhat by the immediate antipathy I felt for the medic himself, who gave off a powerful body odour in the stuffy air of my cramped quarters, almost causing me to gag.

Furthermore, he insisted upon prematurely removing the plaster caste from my hand and prescribing a return to regular duties within 48 hours. I nodded weakly, meeting his hard eyes behind thick horn-rimmed glasses. This was my first encounter with Berlin's scurrilous Dr Theodore Morell, who was to play such a defining role in the downfall of the Third Reich.

During my truncated convalescence my mind alternated wildly between turmoil and despair, requiring every ounce of Sister Klara's wisdom to steady my nerves. Rumours over my relationship with Claudia and her probable fate were spreading like wildfire; little did they know that her deeper fealty and affections belonged to Robert. Disappointingly, our own friendship had never progressed beyond a lop-sided mutual admiration, and of course a challenging exchange of ideas.

Finally, Eva could contain her curiosity no longer; following Dr Morell's third visit she stuck her capricious face around the door clutching a bottle of cold champagne in one hand and a box of chocolates in the other. "Taraa!" She paused for a moment before flouncing her new hair-do and twirling around once in her polka-dot sun frock; she seemed willing to embrace any distraction to ease her frustrating routine during Hitler's long absences.

She plonked down on the foot of the bunk and gazed quizzically into my sallow face.

"C ... Can you sit on the chair over there Eva? You are taking all my air," I pointed falteringly, not wishing to reveal the extent of my adrenalin trembles.

"Well, is it true?" she began breezily, "I mean, you knowingly consorting with a Jew? You're lucky the Gestapo were looking for something specific."

She popped the cork and added a chocolate crème to each of the fizzing tumblers. "You should talk!"

I clinked in response before sipping the cool concoction. "The word is that your own sister is encountering a few problems of her own," I said curtly, not intending to allow her slights to go unchallenged.

"Ilse's situation is quite different," she stiffened. "Perhaps a stretch in protective custody will bring your 'sweetheart' down off her high horse. Anyhow, the boss won't let things get too far out of hand before he rides to the rescue," she demurred.

"Whatever happened to the former justice system, where suspects were properly tried in court before being punished?" I enquired.

"Oh, courts take forever and they'll never get through the backlog. Adolph does like to run his eye over the lists, but he can't be everywhere at once," she sighed, suddenly draining her glass and looking defiant. "What's more, I will tolerate no criticism of him from you or anyone else."

It was an awkward moment.

"I'm just searching for reasons behind all these violent arrests and injustices, that's all," I said lamely, "especially against Claudia and Captain Röhm ..."

"You heard the Führer's address on the radio along with the rest of us; what more is there to know? I already told you I was initially shocked by the purge, until it became clear that Röhm and his clique of Bolshevist pests were leading the Party off on a dangerous and perverted tangent ..."

"This doesn't sound like the Eva I know who was always so chummy with Röhm and the Old Fighters ..."

"Oh, do shut up! I told you that I don't wish to discuss the matter again. Drink up, I'll leave the chocolates for later. I have an important engagement," she sniffed patronisingly and departed.

Upon hearing of my "breakdown" Robert also made his way to my bedside, albeit reluctantly. It seemed that since the massacre all his swans had turned to geese, he was putting as much distance as possible between himself and his remaining S.A. comrades.

Although reprimanded and demoted from his public speaking role, his friendship with SS Cavalry Captain Herman Fegelein had kept him above the fray, if not above suspicion.

"Would you believe liddle brudda, I'm being blackmailed," he announced unexpectedly in response to my enquiries about life in the much-feared SS.

"One of Hoffman's cronies got wind of my connection to Claudia and I'm going to need her to sign a Statutory Declaration. The stupid girl has always seen our affair as more than just a little fun on the side … I suppose that's partly my own fault …"

At that, I exploded: "How dare you put her through something like that! As we speak she may well be undergoing torture or God knows what else at Gestapo Headquarters."

The colour drained from his face causing his facial scars to stand out starkly against the white shirt collar. "Come on, old chap, how was I to know," he spoke somewhat more affectedly than in the past, angering me even further.

"Keep your shirt on, what's this all about anyway? So far I've managed to avoid the worst of the purge, and I did call it off with her at Café Heck the night of Hitler's birthday."

"Do you have no shame?" I almost shrieked. "Turning your back on the man who got you started and the only woman stupid enough to fall in love with you. What do you mean 'called it off'?"

"I wouldn't say the only one, old chap," he said smoothly, ignoring my question and regaining his composure, "but without doubt the hardest to shake off …" He paused for a moment and picked nervously at his fingernails, something I'd not seen him do since we'd left South America.

"It's like this: there's no point in your mooning around Claudia like a little goody two shoes. For some reason, she has now become toxic. And if anyone asks, you and I bunked together during the voyage aboard *Sachsen*. I was only ever alone with Röhm in barracks, got it?"

"B … But, you know full well I boarded with Frau Emi—"

"Since Himmler took over from Göring," he said, "the Gestapo have launched further enquiries into my 'Germanic' credentials and it seems the whole Hahn lineage. I'm afraid that means you too. So far the consulate in Belem has been stalling; they're claiming that many of their documents suffered water damage during the big wet of '32. Thanks to Göring, I've been getting by as an 'Honorary Aryan'; it seems he had a soft-spot for my bushcraft and hunting skills.

"Don't worry, I'm under no illusions: last week I heard fat Hermann chatting with Hitler, as cool as you like. 'Mein Führer, I've just had to sign twenty-two more death sentences for your approval,' holding out the list of condemned in his pudgy fingers. Hitler had barely glanced at it before nodding approval.

"I can tell you it sure left a nasty taste in my mouth: this fellow Himmler will be no pushover. I might have a jaguar by the tail, but I'll be hanging onto the Nazis through thick and thin; there really is no other choice. We both know everything is pre-ordained by Fate, you as good as said so yourself … What was it Mam used to say when we were kids? 'Not one Toucan feather falls to the ground without God knowing.'"

"That's not the same as pre-ordination," I replied, "and anyway, I don't believe that Fate has much to do with it."

"Well, so far Mam's God has been on my side and I intend for Him to stay that way. Ernst pushed his luck too far in the wrong direction. For now, this ambitious Oirish recruit intends to remain at the pointy end of the Movement. The SS has no more obedient warrior than Robert Hahn aka Bobby O'Shea, no siree," he snapped out the words with a long suppressed twang. I wasn't sure if he was trying to convince me or himself; either way, it felt like a cop-out.

"Tell me," I enquired, "did you really punch a Jewish woman in the face and knock her unconscious? Several people have mentioned it ..."

For a moment his face clouded over, as if wrestling with his inner demons. "Aw ... sometimes I can't explain the rush to violence that comes over me, and after all, we do have to keep things in perspective; 40,000 or more lost their heads in the French Revolution ..."

"What's that got to do with the current situation? Hitler is just getting started. We can always look to history to find someone worse than ourselves, and I've seen your SS partners in crime strutting about as if they owned the planet ..."

"The best part is, we soon will! It's only a matter of time. *You* just keep an ear to the ground and let me know if anyone quizzes you further over Alois or Mam ... or, if Sissy blabs to the Gestapo."

I was gaining strength and feeling cocky, suddenly reminded that even God refrains from overriding a man's free will once he's decided on a course of action. "Maybe some of us are just born bad, right from the word go," I ventured, "and, as for free will, I believe it's mankind's second greatest legacy after Life itself; a two-edged sword that's routinely prostituted."

For the moment I was proud of my inspired suppositions.

"Christ, you do go on. By the way, I'd get rid of that signed copy of Röhm's autobiography if I were you; the remainder have been withdrawn from sale and any person caught even reading the thing will be punished. You don't want to end up like my S.A. mates languishing in Dachau, do you? – not even knowing the exact nature of the charges they're facing. Apparently, the guards are not aware either; such was the size and scope of the dragnet after June 30.

"Mind you, that doesn't save them from regular beatings and all the other degradations of camp-life. I'm just so lucky I got out when I did; we handful of SS initially under a cloud got off lightly, ordered to simply loaf about for a few weeks in barracks."

He went on to hint that he'd met the actual men who'd pulled the triggers to despatch his former "disgraced" comrades, but I'd had enough of his smug superiority. "What's done is done! There's been no word of Claudia. Are you sure you can't do something to help?"

I could see the very idea of getting involved was anathema to my brother. "I won't be taking any further risks for her sake, cockhead, and if you have any sense, neither will you." From his point of view the subject was closed.

Notwithstanding, he was right about one thing: the SS was now the dominant and, alongside the Gestapo, most feared power throughout Germany. Their brutal efficiency was more effective than anything achieved, or even aspired to, by the once ubiquitous S.A.

He bragged that all Jews and even faint-hearted countrymen now found it prudent to step from the footpath into the gutter at the approach of Blackshirts. He reminded me that all the best positions, promotions and accommodations were reserved for either SS or Party Members with the lowest membership numbers, lambasting me for my "lack of ambition" and "overall apathy".

I smiled to myself at Tante Gretel's quoting Oscar Wilde, that "ambition is the last refuge of the failure" and refused to be drawn further until he departed.

48

Claudia's return to the fold was as low-key as her arrest had been dramatic, yet not without sadness. Several days after my own resumption of duties, a note was slipped under the darkroom door advising that "Sissy" would be "recuperating under her own roof" for another week or so, and that she would be pleased to receive "Jungle Boy" in order to clear the air.

Slipping out after dark I ascended the staircase in her building, still searching my mind for the meaning of her cryptic message. A tiny, squinting face across the hall responded to my tread, mouthing a greeting in the dim light. My collegial knock brought the worried face of Hans to the door; over his shoulder I saw my friend sitting up in bed contrary to expectations, looking remarkably unscathed. There was no smile as she waved me to a bedside chair, behind which Hans positioned himself.

"Good Lord, I've been worried sick, this is like a dream," I said excitedly, reaching out to stroke her cheek. "I never imagined finding you looking so well, after all, you've gone thr—"

"What did you tell them?" The voice from behind lacked its usual friendly lilt, halting my enthusiasm in its tracks. In the soft light without makeup, Claudia's tormented eyes burned fiercely; there was no mistaking her intent.

Deliberately, without smiling, she addressed me for the first time. "I want you to think carefully before answering, Klaus; have you told anyone about The Edelweiss Orchestra or my affiliation with Hans and Sophie?"

For a few moments, I remained speechless, realising that a great deal depended on my answer. "Certainly not! I've never discussed our times together with anyone; they're special, just between us …"

"That's not what the Gestapo implied. What else did you reveal during your three days in the cells?"

"Nothing! I swear." I was emphatic.

"Well …" I felt the tips of my ears flushing pink, "… maybe once or twice Eva has brought your name up; she's always up for a bit of gossip. But, I've never revealed anything of our private times outside the studio. Anyway, your private life has always seemed a little too inscrutable and painful for my liking …"

"Don't patronise me, Klaus," she snapped back. "What about Robert? Have you discussed any of these recent events with him? What did he have to say about my arrest?" And then she added in a softer tone. "Oh, I do wish he'd come to his senses." There followed an awkward silence.

"Someone's blabbed about the Orchestra; facts known only to a handful of outsiders, of which *you* are one!" Hans emphasised, gripping my shoulders more tightly and maintaining a firm pressure.

"What Orchestra?" I asked, not attempting to turn around. "You were once introduced to me as belonging to the 'same orchestra' as Claudia, but I had no idea what she meant. I've never known her to play an instrument …"

"For God's sake Hans, let him be. The leak could have come from anywhere and I'll stake my life on him."

"You're staking all our lives," Hans responded coldly. "We have too much to lose."

Claudia glared up at him for a long moment. I sat half-expecting a garrotte around my neck. Finally, he released me with a shrug and came around to sit at the foot of the bed. When she attempted to change position I saw a splash of pain on her face. For the first time I realised she was concealing real injuries as a result of her imprisonment. "Why don't you just show him?" Hans urged.

Slowly, she rolled over and pulled up the back of her nightdress, revealing a patchwork of dressings and ichorous welts across her buttocks and lower back, the sight of which caused me to recoil. Since her release she had been plagued by violent headaches and neck pain from repeated beatings atop her head with Munich's heavy phone book. I winced further when leaning forward to examine the baton bruises on the soles of her feet.

"Great for a dancer, isn't it?" she lamented, before rolling back slowly and pulling the covers back up under her chin. "Apparently, the boss intervened as best he could, threatening that all hell would break loose if they damaged my face, but even he couldn't prevent the rest. They told me that next time no one would be able to help me, that I would die in Dachau …"

"They told me the same thing, Claudia. I guess that only makes our times together all the more precious."

"Twenty-five across the bare backside with a dried ox-pizzle is no fun," she continued wryly. "They say that's the welcome awaiting every new arrival in the camps. I suppose I can count myself lucky this time that I'm still in one piece and will soon be able to walk again; not so sure about dancing, though."

She gave another wince, reiterating her belief that everything is hard before it is easy. Hans whispered something in her ear before letting himself out.

Sitting there by candlelight I felt in those moments that our mutual trust had been restored. She went on to reveal a few more guarded details about the Edelweiss Orchestra, the resistance group ironically named after Hitler's favourite flower. So far they had confined themselves to pamphlet printing and low-level espionage, given the Gestapo had planted informers in every guild and building.

Yet somehow, she proudly informed me, the Orchestra continued to operate with broad insight, amassing considerable information on the entire governing mechanism, and more importantly, on how it may be thwarted. Above all rode the hope that one day they would strike a meaningful blow against the hated dictator himself.

We discussed the gangs of Hitler Youth that continued to rampage through the streets, abusing and assaulting passers-by at random. She had heard that Schirach even encouraged them to inform on their own parents' dinner table conversations.

Regrettably, our talk turned again to Robert, forcing me to backpedal slightly. I shared his concerns that she may have let something slip under interrogation.

"That shows how little he knows me. Then again, he barely knows himself, does he?" she opined with a roll of her eyes. I just can't understand it; I've always made myself available at his beck and call; yet, nothing in return. Does he have someone else? You would tell me, wouldn't you Klaus?" she almost pleaded.

Although shunning confrontation, I plucked up sufficient courage to bite the bullet. "I'm going to tell you point blank and I want you to promise that it will never go any further." She nodded.

"There are certain things about Robert's upbringing that you cannot know, nobody knows. It has coloured his behaviour and made him indifferent toward affection. He is repelled by lovestruck women, just like Röhm, but perhaps for different reasons. Rightly or wrongly, he believes that man alone must woo and pursue. Can't you see? The more you chase after him the more you frighten him away. I'm merely trying to explain what he's really like and why he acts the way he does."

"Oh, rubbish! Are you sure you're not just making this all up? Why ever I can't imagine. I know he wasn't seriously trying to break it off because he's told me more than once he loves me, and that one day when things settle down he's taking me to South America."

I noticed a hint of desperation in her voice, as if she could no longer be certain. "I find it hard to believe that joining the SS with all its intrigue and Jew-baiting is what Robert really wants or needs ..." she said, leaving little room to expand my assessment.

"But, violence is in his nature; he actually enjoys the street-brawling. Reason and restraint are the first casualties when his dander's up; anger and ambition have always blinded him to life's real pleasures ..."

"Is that so? Now you're setting yourself up as an expert on my happiness, too. Well, I'm going to prove you wrong, Klaus Hahn; I'll get him back, you'll see, if it's the last thing I ever do."

Regrettably, my comments evoked another rush of tears, and when I finally rose to depart in the early hours she sat determinedly brushing her hair and staring into space. I was simply too discouraged to offer more than a cursory wave to the wizened face across the hallway before I closed the door behind me.

Following her reintegration into studio life, few of Claudia's colleagues dared mention a word of her arrest for fear of Iris, keeping her at arm's length. Beneath this umbrella of new efficiencies, I still found opportunities for visiting the Framing Department despite having been sequestered for a stint on poster layouts promoting the *Illustrierter Beobachter*.

It was decided that Hitler's face should appear on the cover of each weekly edition, and I was set to work printing an 8" × 10" of recent candids from the good professor's burgeoning collection.

Of course, there were shots of the Führer in every conceivable position and from every possible angle, expression and surroundings. I continued to pore over the boss' proof sheets, in awe of his skill and to practise his signature, yet despite my best efforts a dark melancholy settled inexorably. Barely able to perform my duties satisfactorily and robotically, I searched within and without for solutions to the trap I had fashioned for myself.

Sometimes, to keep ahead of the workload I remained all night at the enlarger, thus freeing up the daylight hours to wander the galleries or picnic beside the Isar, where I could bury my head in a book and be transported without disturbance.

I missed the thrill and challenge of the modernist exhibitions which I had barely begun to appreciate before Minister Goebbels, now Minister for Arts and Culture, began stripping them from gallery walls. Hoffman too bowed to the Führer's plebeian tastes and began scouring the collections of disenfranchised Jewish families for traditionalist masters, proffering bargain-basement prices on a take-it-or-leave-it basis.

When questioned over these new acquisitions he simply parroted Hitler's view that "art is a sublime mission demanding fanatical devotion". Such a perspective seemed to me rather arbitrary and extreme, surely ignoring art's primary function of imparting pleasure.

Now that the boss had been tapped by Hitler to amass a "collection second to none" for a proposed new gallery over the Austrian border in Linz, the Führer's actual birthplace, I could only wonder at his cheek given Austria was yet a separate and sovereign country.

On the rare occasions when I observed Hitler and the boss together in the studio, my view was confirmed that Hoffman's attunement to his master's views was almost instinctive, except in matters of art.

While appearing to acquiesce in the actual selections, I noticed him gently steering Hitler toward works which previously would have been dismissed out of hand. Almost overnight, Professor Hoffman's position as Reich Art Curator became unassailable as he continued on his way tickling the Führer's funny-bone with a neverending litany of pilfered oils and spicy jokes in his thick Bavarian accent.

Many snide remarks, Goebbels', were often shared behind the backs of friend and foe alike and I grew pained upon hearing them, knowing full well that none of us were immune. I forced myself to suppress a rising tide of doubt; at such times there remained one final remedy via Sister Klara's wise counsel: "Monkeys! Just see them as monkeys in fancy dress scurrying about for food on the forest floor."

Her words were as fresh as yesterday; how could I have overlooked them so readily? My sagging spirits lifted slowly through prayer. "Listen to me, Lord of my heart and Universe: wherever you are, I am but a simple monkey among monkeys. But you are everything and I love you." My oft-repeated theme was heartfelt and simple: slowly and surely, my woes dropped away and once I even laughed out loud.

"I thought I'd find you here; so sorry to startle you, I've come to say sorry."

I jumped at the distant voice penetrating my meditation. My eyes took a moment to adjust to the soft autumn light and the smiling face just metres away. "Claudia?" Was this a dream? She was beside me, stroking my cheek.

"My dear Klaus; you are the only one ..."

"Of course, Claudia, I'm so glad you finally ..."

"You are the only one not to take advantage of my distress and I repaid you with doubt; I want you to forgive me, please say you will."

She seemed her old self, settling down next to me on the sand beside the water, restored and even playful. "Me, forgive you? Of course, what is to forgive? I've been so hoping you'd come to your senses over Ro—"

"Stop right there, mister! I understand your need to fill me in about your brother's shortcomings, but you might as well save your breath. There's nothing you or anyone else can say will change my mind. Rationality or even Truth hold no sway against a woman's love; please try to understand.

"Oh, Klaus, when I'm with you, our friendship reigns supreme; only to crumble away at his approaching footsteps. Call it simple chemistry, or even insanity, I'll never understand why those we love so utterly don't reciprocate in like manner. God himself would have a time figuring it out."

"I ... I know what you mean, Sissy," I said. Her ears pricked up.

"You see, I know more than you think of your secret life. It's just that I can't bear to see you being used and misled, especially by my own step-brother ..."

She dropped her head and gave a sigh. "That's the way things are nowadays you hopeless romantic, so you'd better get used to it. I'm a big girl and I can take care of myself ..."

"W ... Well, what about Lothar? Where was Robert, then?" For a moment she seemed lost for words.

"If you must know, I've seen a fortune teller. She was adamant that I will end up with someone whose name begins with 'R'. Now it's so obvious and such a pity that he hasn't realised it yet ..." She was calmer and more assured.

"B ... But, I know for a fact that ..."

"Shoosh up, will you? ... and don't spoil this perfect afternoon," she said firmly, placing a finger over my lips. "My friend, you may know something of men and gods but sadly, nothing of women. After all, you did hint that you were still a virgin, is this so?" She looked mischievous, but I didn't care; my heart beat happily and I gazed upstream so she would not see my cheeks flush.

"Come on, let's go for a dip," she suddenly cried. "Last one in's a rotten egg." Within a moment she had stripped off and flung her garments over a willow branch, while I stood uncertainly staring at the pinkish weals across her buttocks. Turning away and quickly removing my trousers, I covered my private parts with my hands before tippy-toeing in gingerly, up to my chest.

"I suppose you've heard our all-mighty Führer can't swim a stroke," she began, slowly gliding back to join me in the shallows and grazing me with her thigh. If I'd ever known a more glorious moment in Germany it was now forgotten.

She circled, squirting jets of water through puckered lips, every now and then allowing her silken skin to brush against my goose-bumps. I was beside myself with excitement and joy, unsure whether to reach out and touch this whole new chance at intimacy. Around us, autumn gold reflections danced over the surface, and despite being half-mad with a desire that threatened to overwhelm my self-control, I distracted myself by concentrating on the network of billowing spider webs in the branches overhead.

Sure, I'd encountered half-naked women in the clubs and printed up Hoffman's output of pornography, even having had a hand in Eva's dashing birthday gift for the Führer; but this was a whole different level.

Claudia was driving me wild as I stood shivering in the icy current, gliding past underwater she took on the form of Boto, the pink river dolphin. Slowly she circled just out of reach, sometimes dog-paddling and at others revealing her glistening gluteus maximus when she dived.

My teeth were chattering and I was beginning to cramp, too embarrassed to follow, when she finally stood up laughing in the shallows to reveal two firm pink breasts and her triangular love-mound beneath.

Striding confidently ashore she mounted the sandbank and sat down on the rug with a sigh: I could stand it no longer; hauling myself out of the water and trying to look nonchalant I swaggered towards her with my shameless member jouncing at half-mast. Within moments a shaft of setting sunlight burst through the clouds, overlaying our hideaway with an auric glow as I stood drying my hair perhaps too vigorously.

With a little laugh, Claudia took two steps and fell on her knees before me, softly murmuring, "We'll soon fix that; now close your eyes."

Of course, I obeyed without question, rubbing at my hair even more enthusiastically as I felt her warm mouth close over my throbbing manhood, causing me to nearly take off. Slowly and knowingly she proceeded to commit an act of supreme affection upon my virgin body. For the first time ever, I felt fully alive as the beast raged within my loins. Then suddenly, without warning, my ecstasy exploded and I wanted to shout out my joy to the heavens.

I sank to my knees, groaning softly like a wounded animal, reliving the kaleidoscope of colours behind closed lids while reminded briefly of the Rainbow Cave.

"Klaus … Klaus? You can open your eyes now," she whispered as I sat slumped and quivering, almost forgetting she was there.

Then, inexplicably, I laughed out loud. "Dear God and dearest Claudia; my happiness is complete!" Grinning foolishly I realised my shyness had vanished. As she reached up with both arms to pull on her sweater I leaned forward and gave her puckered nipple a little tweak.

"Well, that was certainly a sight I shall never forget; I'm so glad I was able to take you to a place you've never been, and to help you get a load off your chest, so to speak," she said, a little coarsely.

"In Poland, we have a saying: 'A slice off a cut loaf is never missed.' Why can't you see that I'm that cut loaf, dear Klaus, however much *you* may wish otherwise? You can keep your airy-fairy mystical concepts of so-called 'atonement'; there's nothing quite like a good orgasm to smooth out the wrinkles, especially if it's your first with someone else," she teased and drew little hearts in the sand.

"That's one I owed you for being such a loyal friend, so long as you don't expect more of the same anytime soon, agreed?"

"I must say, you are being a little cavalier with my affections, Claudia. You don't seem to understand that for me it was far more than physical; it was d … divine!"

"I'll let you in on a little secret: the heavens shook because of who you are. For most of us working girls the act of sex, which many pretend to be love, is a far more calculated business; or if you prefer, a meal ticket. We do what we can behind the scenes and resort to every tool at our disposal, if you'll pardon the pun. You must pretend too if you are to remain one jump ahead of the monster's jaws. Nazi traps are manifold and unforgiving.

"Unless we freethinkers continue to act with courage we'll see our God-given rights snuffed out one by one. The Edelweiss Orchestra is but one brave resistance group among many, but like any chain it is only as strong as the weakest link. Now it's your time to step up and show what you're really made of, time to join with those of us who treasure freedom above all else." I was both terrified and inspired by her trust.

"We've seen how Hitler brutally silenced Röhm, the one critic he could not bamboozle or dominate, along with hundreds of others who dared question his right to rule. Even Robert is coming to realise he's on thin ice; I just know I could sort him out if only he would let me get closer. There's still time to get out if you know the right people. Perhaps we could fight on from another country," she said, pondering absently. "Given a new start, I know I could make him the happiest man on earth."

I fought hard to choke back tears and in a steady voice replied. "For now, how do I best play my part in the Orchestra without being spotted? I'm not much for confrontations."

"Just keep your eyes and ears open, that's all. Studio Hoffman is a hub of loose talk and revealing photos of what's really going on; between the two of us, we cover a wide range of possibilities. Who knows what may come of your efforts?"

Later that night I lay reflecting on two stanzas from Dante's "Paradiso":

> Nobility, a mantle quick to shrink!
> Unless we add to it from day to day,
> time with its shears will trim off more and more …
>
> … My soul is overflowing with the joy
> that pours from many streams, and it rejoices
> that it endures and does not burst inside.

No wonder that star-struck lovers throw all caution to the wind, I thought.

This lonely, much-afflicted girl was now the source of all my future pleasures and possibilities, even if I was blindsided now and then by an ambitious brother. Was Claudia that much different to an irrational Eva and her chums sunbathing on the Berghof patio wall, willingly casting their soft strawberries at swine?

Even Adolph Hitler occasionally paid lip service to his mistress in private, whereas my brother Robert showed up at Claudia's apartment only when scrounging for money or sex. But to me, none of that mattered now. For the first time, my heart was ripe with contentment and every cell in my body continued to tingle at the thought of those few exquisite moments by the Isar. That amazing afternoon had not been a dream.

Surely, sooner or later Sissy Claudia would figure out which brother was the better bet, though there remained a little niggle in my breast. Why would this otherwise rational woman place such store in the flimsy predictions of a fortune teller?

In recent times though, I did have to concede, there'd been a veritable explosion of fortune tellers, clairvoyants and astrologers around Munich, with many desperate folk seeking answers outside Nazism's all-pervading mantra.

SS Reichsführer Himmler himself was said to be not only enthralled but motivated by the avalanche of heavenly predictions now circulating; even Hitler had supposedly moved a full-time astrologer into his proposed rooftop planetarium above the Berghof.

Speaking of Magic Mountain, Eva poked her head in to remind me that I would be accompanying her within days to run a final eye over Bormann's grandiose extensions to Haus Wachenfeld, including the fully equipped darkroom adjoining the main garage in the cellar.

She was eager for the inspection to take place while the brilliant autumn colours still flushed the high country.

"We will have to move quickly then," I agreed, "judging by the Isar willows. They are already a blaze of yellow and beginning to shed." The very thought brought a smile of such joy within a stone's throw of the bustling Ringstrasse.

When she'd gone I realised I'd read two whole pages of my book without remembering a single word.

Hoffman was quick to note my fresh and breezy attitude, which he attributed to the new time and motion efficiencies recently adopted; nonetheless, I was surprised and delighted when he agreed to my joining Eva on her fact-finding foray.

He saw a chance to lighten his own load by arranging for both Eva and I to share the responsibility for this new printing facility in conjunction with the Munich studio. Attempting to conceal my expectations I remembered another of Sister Klara's wise sayings: "If you change your attitude you change the world."

However, prior to this assignment, I had one more pleasant task to perform: we were invited to accompany Hoffman and Frau Schaub to a private screening in Munich of "Triumph of the Will", Leni Riefenstahl's full-length movie depicting the 1934 Party Rally in Nuremberg.

He wanted me to note the effectiveness of Leni's lighting techniques for concealing baggy eyes and pot bellies, and particularly the low camera angles she preferred for presenting Nazi Grandees as seeming taller and more imposing than they really were.

"… and where do you suppose she picked up that little tip?" the boss boasted when the curtains finally closed and the small audience leapt screaming to its feet with arms outstretched.

I should have known that Eva would find fault with her rival's creation, noticing her hand over her mouth in a suppressed yawn, right from the opening scenes when Hitler's tri-motor descended through the fluffy clouds and into the crush of his adoring followers.

Likewise, the social climbing Frau Schaub, always ready to assert her position as wife of First Adjutant, assuaged Eva's resentments by asserting that the whole tedious production had been nothing more than "Two and a half hours of seductive propaganda".

I figured she should know, having recently faced accusations of procurement and prostitution. I thought it remarkable that Frau Schaub was one of the few people trusted by Hitler to "chaperone" Eva socially, an arrangement that seemingly suited both women given Herr Schaub's self-styled title as "Führer Shadow and Travel Master", guaranteeing him ready access to the Leader's ear more often than most.

Besides Eva, many of the other staffers were repelled by Herr Schaub's effusive buck-toothed grin and obsequious bowing and scraping toward any visitor deemed suitably important. The "Travel Master" hobbled about the Berghof on two crippled feet, the result of frostbite in the trenches of the Great War. His gratitude and loyalty towards the man who had pitied and plucked him from obscurity was absolute.

Eva later informed me that Schaub, despite being a founding member of the SS, was a regular obnoxious drunk behind Hitler's back and never missed a chance to lord it over her and other guests during his Führer's frequent absences. Furthermore, he always seemed to keep popping up in the backgrounds of many "Führer Photos".

When Hoffman complained, Hitler just shrugged and fobbed it off. "What can I do? He's been with me for so long."

Predictably enough, the newly-crowned Demagogue was ecstatic over Leni's grandiose rendition of his leadership of the vibrant and seemingly unstoppable movement. For her depiction of the Nazi Party's "relentless destiny" so perfectly, Hitler showered effusive accolades upon the lithe Director's shoulders.

Relegated to the background for once, Propaganda Minister Goebbels was mad with jealousy. Whenever Leni and Hitler appeared side by side in public, more gossip spread about their "true relationship"; she, of course, coyly denied all such rumours with a little titter which not only fanned further speculation but infuriated Eva.

The following year, when Leni's movie went on to win an Academy Award for Best Picture, against Walt Disney's *Snow White* no less, Eva and Frau Schaub clung stubbornly to their initial verdict, refusing to see it for a second time.

I, on the other hand, had been caught up in her powerful compositions and unique camera angles, especially the expressions of hysteria, joy, determination and submission shaping the faces of the 200,000-strong attendees.

How could any man generate such a national focus on his own singular vision? Leni's choreography and forethought in portraying Adolph Hitler as nothing less than a "True Messiah", presiding over the spiritual rebirth of a new Germany; and I wondered what would happen if someone amidst the serried ranks was suddenly taken short.

By day, attendees were entertained with parades and war games; after dark, the torchlight processions snaked almost out of sight before congealing into a mighty revolving swastika below the speakers' stand. Every branch of the movement had its brief moment to parade in step and sing along to the martial music.

Bringing up the rear, an immaculate Himmler again pranced out ahead of his goose-stepping SS legions, raising dust from the cobblestones. Since taking over the Gestapo there could be no doubt now just who was the rising force of Nazism.

Each morning, in one corner of the huge arena, red-blooded Nazi Youths raced, wrestled and hurled each other to the ground, proclaiming themselves to be "standing ready as the Reich's young men and soldiers of the future". Nearby, 52,000 willing labourers were drawn up in ranks, shouldering their shovels with military precision and roaring their oath of readiness: "One people, one Führer, one Reich."

Martyrs from the Great War were then resurrected individually by name, with an accompaniment of sombre music amidst a forest of erect Battle Standards. Cavalry regiments, some hauling field artillery, thundered around the arena in mock battle, while their commanders stepped up to the microphone one by one to utter stirring progress reports.

As I expected, there was no sign of Robert through clouds of dust from the flying hooves.

Acres of variegated folk costumes suddenly gathered together, nodding their bonnets and stomping the handles of their pitchforks as one, beneath a nasal tirade from Hans Frank, Hitler's former lawyer and now Chief Nazi Legal Officer who assured them that "workers conditions, lives and civil rights will be fully protected under National Socialist Law". During these scenes, Eva whispered pointedly that such visual displays would have far more impact in full colour.

For four whole days, not a moment passed without something going on: bonfires, fireworks and "educational displays" added authenticity and excitement to the programme. When the Blutfahne from the '23 Putsch was reverently unfurled to consecrate all fresh formations mustering for the first time, the spiritual solemnity was palpable.

Of course, these fiery speeches of the Führer contained something for everyone, winding up every session. He reiterated that National Socialism's dictates were "given to us by God, not by men", powerful stuff indeed coming from beneath Albert Speer's mighty papier-mâché eagle that hovered over the sea of burning brands. At that moment it was easy to see why, to a man, those present concurred so lustily. He declared that his beloved Hitler Youth must be "peace-loving", going on to qualify, "and also courageous" to howls of approval.

By day and by night the spectacle unfolded in the main arena, down Nuremberg's narrow streets and into nearby fields. Everywhere, validations of Nazi readiness dominated the landscape. A scowling Führer promised his pupils that "the world was theirs for the taking" and for the umpteenth time swore them to an "Oath of Obedience".

Eventually, Röhm's apple-polishing successor, Victor Lutze, had his turn at the podium, avowing with full-lung capacity, "The S.A. has only ever stood for one thing: undying loyalty to Adolph Hitler!"

In reply, the Führer spoke with a veiled reference to Röhm's effrontery. "No one should dare to sin against the S.A. because we all stand together for Germany." Then, to the boom of cannons, he saluted his "old, loyal S.A. and SS men, who had stood firm and weathered the dark shadow that fell over the movement a few months ago", extolling those remaining as "the best of the best".

Denying there was any "crack in the movement", he assured them their positions were now secure. "Only a madman or wilful liar could think that I would have the intention of breaking up that which took so long to create." From across the S.A. ranks came a collective sigh of relief.

Alternating between birds' eye views, vast panoramas, fervent individual expressions and marching shadow patterns being swallowed up by mediaeval arches, Leni Riefenstahl's celluloid masterpiece left no doubt in the public's mind about the magnitude and importance of events now playing out among them.

Hitler's final keynote address to the rally was almost drowned out by swelling waves of Sieg Heil's from the choir of croaky throats, culminating in a rousing rendition of the new "Horst Wessel Anthem".

Like those on the big screen, I too was suffused with inspiration as I rose to leave the theatre, flanked by the nattering duo that had barely shut up for the entire two hours. To my surprise, Hoffman too seemed underwhelmed by Leni's achievement, although attentive as I rattled off the many observations I'd made regarding her bold lighting and editing. I hinted that my own black-and-whites would be "more informed" in future as a result of what I'd seen.

When heading home, Eva's evening was further diminished when she accidentally stepped into a puddle and ruined a brand-new pair of Ferragamo high heels.

Back at the Studio, the boss quizzed me further about the manner in which the Führer had been presented. "After all, it was supposed to show the greatness of a single man who has built this mighty movement from the ground up."

"Oh, yes, Herr Hoffman; in my opinion, it certainly did that."

I further expressed admiration for Hitler being able to stand erect in his big black tourer, with his arm outstretched for hours on end.

"Never underestimate the power of editing, my boy," he said dismissively, before belittling a bulging Göring who, by contrast, had looked comical when taking the salute in a resurrected S.A. uniform and cap that appeared to be at least one size too small.

Flattered by the boss' attention, I commented that the evening bonfire scenes had reminded me of the Mojo ceremonies back in Brazil, and he seemed amused by the analogy. I told of a similar atmosphere having been created when dozens of small fires were lit around the terraces of the Sun Temple. In those days, I noted, Chief Ticuna had only to withstand the adoration of hundreds, not hundreds of thousands, speculating on how any mere mortal could fail to be confirmed in his beliefs in the face of such lusty adulation.

But by now the boss was bored with the subject and cut me off, enquiring as to whether Eva and I had completed our preparations for the darkroom unveiling on Magic Mountain, to which I re-affirmed my commitment and enthusiasm. Eva had felt it necessary to remind him that between she and Bormann the matter was well under control, but he appeared sceptical.

Nonetheless, he was prompted to allow me a third night visiting Onkel and Tante, whom I'd not seen in months. "Remember to tell Bormann exactly what we need to finish the job properly," he instructed, "with good ventilation, a guaranteed power supply and ample drainage. It's up to you to see that Eva doesn't get carried away with unnecessary clutter."

"I don't think she'll take much notice of me, Herr Professor," I replied.

But as usual, Bormann was taking instructions from no one as he drove forward the renovations at breakneck speed. Darkrooms were way down the Mountain Gauleiter's grand scheme reshaping the entire mountainside.

49

From the moment Eva's chauffeur-driven tourer was waved through the third and final SS guardhouse, we were in another world. Everywhere was the pace and clutter of builders and wreckers toiling side by side.

There was Bormann striding about in jackboots, at times hunched over plans in concentration or barking orders. From the photos I'd seen, not much of Haus Wachenfeld's original façade remained, though fortunately staff quarters had been thrown up nearby as a priority.

When Eva and I were hustled off to adjoining dormitories, I overheard her complaining that she was supposed to be accommodated inside the main building.

Later that afternoon, when we crossed the brand new threshold together she stopped dead in her tracks with a little snort: directly overhead, in pride of place, hung a Ziegler oil of Geli Rubaul gazing down on all who entered.

"That fat slut haunts me wherever I go," Eva hissed, unable to restrain herself from cursing Geli's lingering influence from the grave. She took a deep breath and affected a jaunty stance, before proceeding to lead me on a guided tour through the closed-off wing.

"Adolph says I may keep a dog for company up here," she informed me breezily as we stepped out onto the terrace overlooking the splendid sight of the Untersberg crags. "On a clear day, you can see all the way to Saltsburg." Some distance away we could see lorries full of rubble being driven away from the former site of Pension Moritz and the earth being smoothed over.

"That was a Lutheran church, Fraulein; been there for centuries. Gone, completely gone; like every other building that spoiled the view from the very spot you're standing," replied a workman in response to my query.

"Well, pooh to you, workman! The Führer deserves the very best view this nation has to offer, I'm sure you'd agree on that?"

"If you say so, Fraulein, but many of my neighbours were given just two hours' to pack up and leave homes they'd occupied for generations." I looked away, embarrassed by his sincerity; Eva continued to glare.

"He simply asked where the rubble came from, not for a history lesson," she chided, aware of her growing power. The man wheeled his barrow away with head down, as we continued our informal tour, frustrated that Bormann had not yet decided on which corner would be best suited for our darkroom aspirations; he appeared in no hurry to do us any favours.

"I thought you said that you and Bormann were working together on this thing," I puffed, after climbing yet another set of stairs and sensing an opportunity to put Eva on the spot. "You'll see. He simply *must* recognise my authority in this matter," she fired back.

While wandering about we decided to snap some before and after shots of the surrounding landscape from different vantage points, after which Eva took the chance during his absence to demonstrate her familiarity with Hitler's brand-new quarters.

She took my hand as we tiptoed along an upstairs corridor before halting outside one of several bedroom doors, beside which hung one of his freshly cleaned uniforms and brown peaked caps with the burgundy band. With a little giggle, she placed the cap on her head where it flopped down over her ears.

"See, see what a fulsome size Adolph's head is? That means he has a bigger brain than almost anyone else; go on, you try it," she insisted, thrusting it into my hands. "Don't worry silly, he won't be arriving for another day or two."

I glanced nervously over my shoulder, fearful of being sprung, but resistance was futile. She gave a gasp when the cap fitted perfectly, before snatching it away and stating glibly that there were "obviously other contributing factors" denoting genius besides mere head size.

Two days later, with Hitler's hard-won consent over the telephone, Eva was buzzing about in readiness to receive her sister Gretl, Henny Schirach and her "best school friend", Herta Schneider, as house guests with the intention of hiking and sunbathing together in the fading autumn glow. Sure enough, Murphy's Law had intervened late on the preceding afternoon, when Bormann had suddenly arrived with his floor plan for the allocated darkroom space, to be situated behind the motor garage. "I need your agreement by morning," he growled at Eva, "or we proceed without you."

Through that long night, we argued and wrangled, revising our own plans to fit into the tiny space, where ventilation was poor.

Besides the usual photo chemicals, there would be additional problems from petrol fumes and dust and we were still at it when the time arrived to dispatch a car and driver to collect her guests from Berchtesgaden Bahnhof, stymied by Eva's last-minute demand for a cumbersome colour processer to be somehow squeezed into the very spot required for the black-and-white print-drying cabinet.

"You know that colour is the coming thing, and coloured movies are the most exciting medium of all; surely you can see that?"

"My feelings about colour haven't changed. We must have a dryer beside the enlargers for maximum efficiency," I countered, pointing out from the brochure that the unit was "light tight", enabling it to be operated through a hole in the garage wall.

Following a quick chat with Schreck, head of the driver pool, it was agreed that the machine itself could be fitted among the spare parts shelves in the garage where it could be easily accessed for chemical replenishment. When she returned, chuckling over Schreck's schnurrbart, which she estimated to be twice as bristly as Hitler's own, she was clearly buoyed. "I don't know why I didn't think of locating the colour printer out there sooner."

Dog-tired, we were both relieved when the throbbing limo pulled up below the fresh-laid stone steps and her three attractive girlfriends hastened toward us. "Ladies, you all know my assistant Klaus, I'm sure. We've just spent the whole night together."

With that, all four burst into laughter at the very thought.

"Remember, nothing leaves this building," Herr Herbert Doering spoke bluntly to my face after scanning his clipboard, while Eva with the four of us in tow ran her eye over the huge new kitchen.

Herr and Frau Doering were the Berghof's new housekeepers, freshly recruited from Hitler's favourite Berlin restaurant, and they clearly intended to put their own efficient stamp upon the mountaintop routine. Straight off Herr Herbert took umbrage at Eva's proprietorial airs when, cigarette in hand, she sniffed the air and recommended certain changes to the layout.

"… then, I take it Fraulein you have warned Herr Hahn and the ladies about repeating anything they overhear within these walls?"

"That goes without saying, Herr Housekeeper; I can vouch for all my friends and fellow employees," Eva snapped back, "… and may I take this opportunity to remind you that I am answerable only to the Führer?"

"Perhaps when he is in residence Fraulein, but surely not at other times, if Mountain Reichsleiter Bormann is to be believed?"

The girls found it hard to suppress a giggle.

"Come on girls; Klaus wants to show you his equipment for the new darkroom," she joked as I squirmed with embarrassment and the Doerings barely concealed their annoyance.

Meandering along, Eva filled us in on the house rules and requirements which had been printed up and placed prominently on dressing tables and dormitory doors, leaving little room for misunderstanding:

1. SMOKING is forbidden, except in this bedroom.
2. GUESTS must not talk to servants or carry any parcel or message for any servant.
3. AT ALL TIMES the Führer must be addressed and spoken of as such, and never as Herr Hitler or other title.
4. WOMEN guests are forbidden to use excessive cosmetics and must on no account use colouring material on fingernails.
5. GUESTS must present themselves for meals within two minutes of the announcing bell. No one may sit at table or leave table until Führer has sat or left.
6. NO ONE may remain seated in a room when the Führer enters.
7. GUESTS must retire to their rooms by 11 pm unless expressly asked to remain by the Führer.
8. GUESTS must remain in their appointed wing of the house and must on no account enter the domestic quarters, the offices or quarters of the SS, nor the offices of the Political Police Bureau.
9. ON LEAVING Berchtesgaden, guests are absolutely forbidden to discuss their visit with strangers or to mention any remark made to them by the Führer. The conveying of information about the Führer's private life in this way will be visited by the severest penalties.

Eva's girlfriends did not know what to make of my reticence and I noticed the exchange of certain little gestures behind my back. Henriette, pretty as a doll, had of course grown up under Hoffman's roof surrounded by all the trappings of Nazi power and appeared the more self-assured, while Herta Schneider, the now married childhood friend, never quite adapted to the intimidating surroundings.

She struck me as a guileless and modest woman, more interested in her two small children, yet happy to be going along for the ride. On the other hand, Eva's young doe-eyed sister Gretel, whom I'd already bumped into several times at the front counter, went out of her way to return glances and exchange greetings with every SS guard we passed along the way. This was the first extended period I'd spent with the girls in such heady surroundings and I struggled to fit in.

All that changed the next afternoon when Hitler's limousine swept up the winding mountain road amidst his security convoy, and the whole tempo of the place stepped up a gear.

The girls quickly retreated to the staff dormitories via the rear staircase, while Eva, armed with a set of blueprints, resolved to put her own stamp on the proposed fifty-seat indoor movie theatrette and adjacent winter-garden aviary.

Upon failing to attract the Führer's furtive eye she gathered us together and tramped off uphill to inspect the rustic, 200-bed Platterhof "guest hotel", where unsurprisingly, I noticed identical "house rules" displayed in prominent locations.

She pointed out the "Dietrich Eckhart" room, which she said held many fond memories for the Führer since its earliest days. There were already rumours that Bormann planned to tear down the whole building, retaining only part of the façade and the Dietrich Eckhart room itself, for "sentimental reasons".

From there we climbed an alluring gravel path, past the fresh foundations of the planned SS barracks, to the sight of Göring's proposed mansion sitting just a comfy stone's throw from his Führer's burgeoning fortress. She then led the way downhill, past concealed machine-gun emplacements through open meadows to a lookout, where she paused just long enough to swing upon a wooden fence rail and show off a few gymnastic moves as we chatted.

Nearby could be seen workmen, laying fresh turf over patches of bare soil. "Some view, huh?" She waved expansively and took in a long breath of the crisp mountain air. Without waiting for an answer she added, "Well, it's only fair that some make way for the greater good," before any of us had time to speculate on the fate of the former inhabitants.

By now it was becoming obvious that the other girls were bored with all the ups and downs of the grand tour, and my offer to treat "cold beers all round" at the Hotel Zum Tuerken, just a few hundred yards away, was greeted with relief. This traditional alpine watering hole, where Brahms had once spent a few days, remained the sole local establishment permitted to retain most of the original façade and décor. Its newly renovated wing had been promptly requisitioned for Heydrich's S.D. Security Force Headquarters, with the remainder serving as adjutant and temporary tradesman's accommodation.

Perhaps more importantly, the location did not interfere with the Berghof's 180-degree unimpeded view of the surrounding panorama. Such harmonious arrangements, however, did not endure for long when the owner, Karl Schuster, after enduring an earlier Nazi boycott, was shuffled off to Dachau after refusing Bormann's purchase price of 165k Reich marks.

The Mountain Gauleiter, always zealous in fulfilling his Führer's wishes, forcibly acquired the property regardless.

"Tell me, Klaus," Gretel Braun was the first to speak when we sat down, "is it true that you grew up among the Indians in South America? Eva has told me so many tall tales I don't really know what to believe ..." She paused to nod assent as five steins of beer were placed on the table beside the window of the gloomy parlour.

I kept my head down, soughing "sort of" between bites of strudel. I could see the others were keenly awaiting my response, while Eva held herself aloof and commenced filing her nails. I went on chewing purposefully, hoping the delay would offer a chance for the conversation to drift in a different direction.

"Papa says you have already become one of his best printers," Henni warbled. "Wherever did you acquire such skills growing up in the jungle?

"My Baldur is a keen amateur too, you know; I bet you've printed plenty of his boys getting up to their little antics." It was more a statement than a question.

"I ... er, all the Hitler Youth films arrive together in one satchel and I'm never sure who takes what."

"Is that so? From now on I'll make sure Baldur's films are clearly marked, so I can also obtain a set of prints for my own family album. As we speak he is camped not far from here, with a group of his H.J. Leaders. During this bivouac, he's been having his films processed by a local photographer; won't it be super when our own darkroom is up and running?"

"Let's have no more talking 'shop' if you please. We're here to have fun: F. U. N." Herta finally spoke up to the annoyance of Eva and Henni who were trying yet again to coax out my story.

"If not 'shop', then may I remind you that Adolph detests fat women," Eva exclaimed cattily, glaring at Gretl's empty pie plate.

"Oh yes? Well, he should talk," Henni jumped in again, "given the way he used to gobble down Mama's cream cakes; of course, that was before he developed his so-called nervous stomach."

Eva could not forgive Henni's flippant familiarity when referring to Hitler, resenting not only the Hoffman families' long association but also Henni's adoring and submissive behaviour in the great man's presence.

Even now, after virtually railroading his "Little Sunshine" into marrying the effeminate Schirach, Hitler demonstrably favoured her above most other women in public.

Worse still, it was Eva and rarely the boss' daughter who was sent out to procure "beer and sausages" like a common shop assistant, she complained to me on more than one occasion.

She bitched that her father had reneged on his commitment and continued to crack down on the home front; it was only when she agreed to have Gretl tag along on dates and after secretly duplicating the key to her bedroom door that Eva regained any measure of independence. But it was sweet Henni for the time being who held sway over all of us on the mountain, even as Eva strove to assert herself.

"Little Sunshine" persisted in regaling us with anecdotes from bygone days growing up in Hitler's presence, even hinting that he may have attempted to "touch her up" once or twice while her parents were distracted.

"If you ask me, Onkel Adi will always remain a bachelor; Papa says he prefers the bohemian lifestyle," she teased, trying to keep a straight face.

We each looked at Eva, who appeared to be fighting back tears. "Well, don't just sit there, you lot," she sniffled. "You might at least stick up for me in the face of these deliberate insults … I even have Himmler now prying into my family history," her small teeth flashed a forced grin and her lachrymose eyes darted from Herta to Gretl and back again, before settling on me.

"You know the truth, Klaus; go on, tell them! It's me Adolph wants above all others. And when things are arranged we shall be married," she pronounced in feverish tones.

Herta gave a nervous cough as I held Eva's desperate gaze, unable to think of a suitable response.

"Oh Henni; why do *you* take such pleasure in my insecurities?" she said in measured tones. "You make me feel like a pawn in a game I don't understand, while all around, my friends appear to be basking in happiness."

"Don't say you weren't warned; I'm merely relaying my own experiences," Frau Henni replied, rolling her dolly eyes. "Perhaps you really *are* a prisoner, Eva; a prisoner of your own delusions …"

"Henriette Hoffman! I expect nothing less than unconditional loyalty from my friends, or you can turn around and get straight back on the next train to Munich."

An uncomfortable silence followed, before Gretl leaned forward undaunted to note the approach of several off-duty SS guards. "Check out this trio, girls; looks like a little excitement closing in."

"Heil Hitler! Fraulein Braun, I believe," said the first officer, clicking his heels and snapping out a stiff arm above our heads.

"I am Captain Hermann Fegelein of the First SS Cavalry Division, at your service. May we have the honour of being introduced to your friends?"

There followed more heel clicking and hand kissing until Eva announced my name almost as an afterthought, "… and this is my laboratory assistant, Klaus Hahn …"

"Hahn, Hahn? Surely not the elusive brother of our regimental sharpshooter, Robert Hahn?" I blanched with embarrassment, before snapping "Yes sir, none other." Captain Fegelein ran his eye up and down icily and without another word turned back to the ladies who were already tittering at the attention.

"Well, I'd love to," said Gretl. "How about it, Sis? The boys say Zum Tuerken has a dance band tonight and every Saturday, we have plenty of time to duck up and change."

"Why yes, Captain, as a matter of fact, this is my first trip to Magic Mountain. How did you know?" She gave another snicker behind her hand. "I am so much looking forward to dancing with some of your handsome SS boys."

"You shameless hussy, you might as well have just jumped straight into his lap," Eva hissed as the men strode away, but not before they'd snapped to attention, shot out another still-arm salute and expressed a desire to chaperone the ladies should they wish to attend the dance that evening.

"Believe me, I won't say No; did you see that Bratwurst in his pocket?" Gretl exclaimed defiantly before all four collapsed in a high-spirited huddle.

"Well Sis, are you in or out?" She had thrown all caution to the winds. "Your Adolph won't stir much before lunchtime, you said so yourself," wiping the tears from her eyes. "Did you see the way they looked at us? … and their manners are impeccable. How about you, Klaus? Do you want to tag along? I'm afraid my dance card is already full, ha, ha!"

"No way, José. I prefer to leave you to your own devices," I said quickly, glad that she didn't insist, "… and my asthma plays up in those smoke-filled spaces. By the way, aren't you forgetting something? Like house rules."

"Rules? Oh, those … rules are made to be ignored where possible. There's no good reason why you can't join us for dinner beforehand and retire early for your beauty sleep, now is there?" Eva called over her shoulder as they rose to leave. I had the distinct impression that she was desperate for a familiar male face beyond suspicion to be present, in case her sometime-lover took exception.

I ordered another drink and moved out into the bracing evening chill of the beer garden, where groups of workmen and uniformed SS had gathered earlier, seemingly oblivious to the breathtaking panorama. For a while I looked around casually, taking in the other patrons using my peripheral vision. The nearby workmen, though obviously tired, drank together in a group of easy familiarity, while the SS elites, both in and out of uniform, sat erect in twos and threes, conversing in undertones.

Every now and then an eyebrow was raised at the boisterous labourers and I hastened to pin on my yellow press card. After draining the second stein I felt lightheaded, even emboldened; wandering up the hill I pulled out my camera to catch the day's last golden beams wiping the valley floor and climbing the Untersberg beyond.

Come tomorrow, I knew things would be very different, from the moment the Führer's feet hit the floor, and I counted myself lucky that my mission so far was without incident. I felt ready to undertake the gruelling five-kilometre cross-country trek to Chalet Hahn, with nothing but my camera, a light snack and a bottle of water in the pack on my back. This would be my only three-day break since starting work in Munich.

Naturally enough, Eva and the girls would be staying on at the Berghof throughout the Führer's visit, but first, before I could gain permission to depart, there was the small matter of arranging a Sunday morning champagne breakfast for them on the grassy slope between Zum Turken and the "Berghof", as "Magic Mountain" had now been officially re-titled by most.

At daybreak on Sunday I was up and ready to perform my allotted task and be off. The whole mountainside was like a ghost town set in a movie, with those few up and about speaking to each other in hushed whispers. "He didn't turn in until well after midnight," went the word. The whole area had temporarily settled into a forced tranquillity.

Given the hour I decided to breakfast alone in the staff kitchen and had no sooner sat down, to be roused by a soft, cheerful voice.

I looked up into the attractive face of a uniformed housemaid with a starched white bonnet pinned tight to the back of her head. In a welcoming expression, she leaned over the chair opposite, a pot of fresh perked coffee in her hand.

"Herr Hahn, my name is Pauline Kohler and I'm on my break too." She moved around to pour a second cup of the steaming brew. "Last night I overheard the studio girls, as did everyone else in the dormitory, arriving home from Zum Tuerken," she said, pulling her chair closer.

"Of course, I'm aware of the penalties for gossip, but as your reputation precedes you I did so want to welcome you to the high Alps in person, and to let you know that your secret is safe with me. I gather you will be operating the darkroom from time to time? Still photography is also a passion of mine, you know?"

I nodded, a little unnerved and perplexed by her over-familiarity. *What secret?*

After a little more polite conversation, I discovered that behind this confident approach was a rather apprehensive village girl eager for a sympathetic ear.

I replied "I hoped we'd see more of each other during future visits" when she leaned nearer and whispered, "You will never guess in a million years what my job as 'Führer Taster' entails."

In response to my puzzled expression, she explained how she and several other "volunteers" received modest bonuses and privileges for putting their lives on the line three times daily, whenever the Führer was in residence.

In fact, wherever he travelled, a "Führer Taster" always joined the entourage and a stomach pump was carried in the trunk of the six-wheeler.

I gave a little shudder at her description of the weekly "Kitchen Duty Roster" that entailed several long and terrifying days in which it was her turn to sip and dip Frau Schaub's vegetarian concoctions, at least one hour before Hitler himself put spoon to lip. I said this sounded to me a bit like Russian roulette but a whole lot more protracted. She gave a nervous giggle and asked the meaning of "protracted", before turning up her nose while relating the Führer's usual mealtime omnibus of ingredients: onion, celery, chopped parsley, potatoes, turnips, carrots, nut compound, apple slices, flour, water and salt.

She said that sometimes, if in a good mood and his stomach wasn't playing up, Hitler would round off with one or two additional ladles or a fillet of grilled trout in butter sauce.

"Worst of all," she exclaimed, pulling another face, was his option of baked potatoes with curd cheese soaked in raw linseed oil which almost made her gag at the first mouthful.

The tension only began to ease when it came time to finish her shift by nibbling a corner from each pastry without spoiling the frosting, able to breathe easy again for another few days.

She also remarked on the contrast with the typical SS barracks menu of braised beef with two salads, marinated in vinegar and herbs, with creamed potatoes and young beans followed by apple strudel and yoghurt. "Oh, how I wish I could be a taster up there," she sighed wistfully.

Once again I felt privy to unnecessary and possibly dangerous information, but Fraulein Kohler seemed relieved to be talking to someone on her own level, getting the burden off her chest.

I concurred that a Führer's diet, by comparison, would be hard to swallow day after day, and knew also that Eva was contemptuous of Hitler's vegetarianism, at least behind his back. She showed her own free spirit in matters of food, drink and tobacco smoking, the latter mostly during his long absences.

I knew she worked hard on the parallel bars to keep herself trim, well aware of her Beau's manic aversion to "fat women", often reminding her little sister of this fact in front of others.

"Fraulein Pauline, you will report to Reichsleiter Bormann immediately," Frau Schaub had appeared in the doorway; how much had she overheard? The girl looked hastily at her watch and rose to leave. "Yes, Madame, right away."

She leaned close to my ear for a moment and whispered again. "Don't worry; your secret is safe with me. Hope to catch up in the darkroom sometime." My stunned expression said it all; I figured I'd probably been lucky to engage in such a frank and unexpected exchange with someone on the inside, so to speak.

Hurrying back across a patch of meadow, I wondered if the ice in the tubs would be melted before certain people rose from their slumbers to enjoy the twice-delayed champagne breakfast.

"Don't worry, Adolph won't arise until he's well rested …" Eva's voice alerted me as she drew nearer and headed for the picnic rug in the sun. Close by, a demi-wine cask bobbed with ice-cold champagne bottles, which I'd lugged up in my backpack from the Zum Tuerken beer garden below.

"… probably around 1:00 or 2:00, I should think. Poor dear's been positively overwhelmed." I could see Eva and Gretl both looking worse for wear, with makeup and grooming dishevelled.

"Oh, Klaus! You really should have stayed on for the dancing," Henni announced, before sitting down with the others.

"There were even a few leftover local Frauleins without partners, poor things. Can't say the same for this pair," she said with a smile. "Please do join us for a few minutes, I have a favour to ask." I glanced pointedly at my watch before settling on a nearby log.

"Herr Hahn! Please note that staff breakfasts cease precisely at 10:30 am," Eva parodied Frau Schaub's officious nasal twang and all four broke into a giggle. The party was on again.

I moved swiftly to the cask with a napkin draped over one arm, and with a loud pop fired the first cork away downhill. Without further ado, the girls began tucking in, reliving the evening's highlights with mouths full of tepid food.

Other than being summoned to refill glasses by a theatrical click of Eva's fingers, I was left sitting on my log. I had declined champagne, conscious of the effect it may have on my cross-country navigation skills.

"What an insult, expecting us to rub shoulders with those … those whores! The good Captain Fegelein didn't mention the fact that a menagerie of Munich prostitutes is brought in every weekend to relieve the boredom of SS officers. Obersalzberg guards are committed to a six-month tour of duty, it's no wonder they're so keen to make real friends," she glared at Gretl. "How I hate the stink of morning-after perfume …"

"Oh, don't be so stuck up Sis; we were danced off our feet, and you have to admit we were showered with plenty of attention."

"*They* didn't seem to care that Henni and Herta were wearing wedding rings. By the way, does the Führer know *you* are wearing your dress ring on *that* finger when he's not around?" Gretl still looked a little flushed and spoke boldly. Herta began filing her nails.

I cleared my throat.

"Klaus? What on earth are you doing here? You're supposed to be halfway across the valley by now." A little flutter ensued. "Only joking, everything looks satisfactory; you might as well be on your way. Don't wrestle with any wild bears or anything … and don't look so glum. Henni's going halfway, or had you forgotten?"

"That's precisely the favour I was going to ask," Henni said sheepishly, fluttering her eyelashes, "I do think I'd be bored walking all that way to Baldur's bivouac alone."

"Er … yes, of course," I agreed, surprised and delighted at this last-minute change of plans. I had rarely, if ever, spent much time alone with the boss' daughter, who now proceeded to throw another spanner in my schedule.

Unbeknownst to me, Eva had arranged for the girls to join Hitler on his afternoon stroll downhill, to the proposed "teahouse" site, which would offer unparalleled views of the looming Watzmann Massif and valley below. She insisted that Henni and the others at least "put in an appearance" before the two of us set off across the country.

I realised that this might ruin any chance of my covering such a distance in the remaining daylight hours, which I protested to Eva. "I had planned on calling in for a little shop talk with Herr Brandner, the local portrait photographer; such a delay will not allow sufficient time," I tried to explain, but she would have none of it.

"Oh, pooh! What's one more day? You can always set out on your journey first thing tomorrow morning, with no distractions. And you'll be a lot fresher! Say girls, how about we duck home and slip on our dirndls? It will be such a pleasant surprise for Adolph."

"I guess it doesn't make much difference to me," Henni wavered. "Baldur will get a big surprise anyway, whatever time I arrive."

"B … But, I'm already running late to do all the things I want along the way. Sticking to the road it's nearly five miles to Chalet Hahn; this will be the longest hike I've attempted since arriving in Germany."

"Nonsense! It's all settled. Who would pass up the chance for a stroll with their Führer? Give me one good reason why you both should not set out nice and bright tomorrow morning."

I fumed inwardly that my plans had been thwarted yet again by Eva's impulsiveness and Henni's newfound desire to "put in an appearance" at Hitler's tea party. All things considered, embarking from the teahouse site would entail even more uphill climbing than leaving from the guest dormitory.

I concluded that a delayed departure would allow extra time to savour the wonderful scenery, drop off Henni *and* make the acquaintance of Herr Brandner at his mountain studio; I hung around the dormitory clicking a few shots until the whole hillside sprang to life.

I glimpsed the group gathering below the new stone steps below the patio, and before long Hitler appeared wearing a muted lounge suit, tie and trilby, twirling his walking stick impatiently as the bevy of "traditional" mountain maids approached. Eva darted ahead to give a little curtsy before bending down to pick up a throwing stick for the two Alsatians, only to be stopped dead in her tracks by a harsh word from the pack leader. We were all reminded there and then that no one, not even the kennel master, was allowed to feed these dogs or even throw sticks while the "Alpha Male" was in attendance.

Bormann handed the Führer his rhinoceros-hide whip and he immediately brought the dogs to heel. The beautifully marked bitch, "Blondie", fell on her belly and crawled slowly towards him, ears flattened and whimpering softly. Although the pack leader did not raise the whip, as he bent forward to pat her ears she cowered lower, involuntarily urinating on his patent leather pumps. It was pretty obvious that she was as terrified of her master as everyone else.

It would be several more months before Hitler finally relented and presented Eva with Negus and Stasi, her very own pair of "hand-lickers" as he called them, black Scotch Terriers that never did learn the meaning of obedience.

Chants of "We want our Führer" were growing louder, drifting up through the high wire boundary fence holding back the adoring crowds of pilgrims, many of whom were bedecked in period costume and loaded down with produce marking the annual Harvest Festival.

Setting off at a jaunty pace, the Führer was in his element, preceded by a half dozen armed SS men with several more bringing up the rear; the remainder of the walking party was strung out in between.

As we approached the gate the crowds pressed forward, before parting like the Red Sea before Moses in awe of the great man walking among them. There was joyous applause, weeping and wailing; I observed several swooning females being dragged away from the front ranks when trying to kiss his already sullied, tear-stained boots.

"Some of them actually strip slivers from the railings he leans on and gather up jars of gravel from the path after he passes," Henni sniffed. "The fools! It's hard to believe he was an ordinary man in my house growing up."

I swallowed hard. This was no adoring and submissive "sweet little sunshine" talking; she had dropped back to join me at the rear.

The Führer was saluting and nodding left and right, without lingering too long in any one place. Several girls broke ranks and bared their breasts at the last moment, but he simply gave a funny little twitch of his schnurrbart, a slap of the dog whip against his thigh and continued on down toward the open meadows.

I took several excellent rear shots of the tiny figures appearing to hover over the vastness of valley and lake below, and through my viewfinder noticed splashes of red, green and blue dirndls popping in and out among the leaders. With the SS bringing up the rear, I felt somehow safer with Henni for company, who turned out to be a veritable fount of knowledge regarding Nazism in general and the Obersalzberg in particular.

"They've started running special trains down from Munich at weekends, you know. Whenever Onkel Adi is in residence the tourists are greeted by brass bands and all the pomp inside the station. It stands to reason why locals are only too keen to cash in on all this curiosity," she said wryly, "that is, the few remaining who've somehow avoided Bormann's heavy hand; a far less forgiving hand since he bumped Hess aside. You've seen how many heritage buildings have been razed and grassed over; I hate him, and so does Eva. I just can't imagine why Onkel Adi lets him get away with it." She sounded genuinely puzzled. I felt it best not to comment.

"Take poor old Herr Buchner, host of the Platterhof for decades; I'm sure he'll be next. He took me under his wing as a child and gave me the run of the place; now I hear he's being offered a pittance for his wonderful establishment," she said, waving toward the high slopes. "They say he is being more or less 'encouraged', Bormann's word not mine, to pack up and move on. I find it hard to accept all this horrid upheaval being meted out in Onkel's name."

"Well, I guess your Onkel Alf has plenty on his plate just running the country; but he does seem to want to make every decision for himself," I offered, raising my camera to take another shot.

As we slowed for the last hundred yards, the rear-guard strode forward and barred our way. One of them spoke to Henni and the other levelled his machine pistol at my navel. "Frau Schirach, proceed. *You* remain; papers, now!" He seemed to be ignoring my prominent yellow press card and brushed aside Henni's protestations that I was a Studio Hoffman employee.

My chest tightened and I suddenly became aware of the many hazards that lay ahead. "You may join the group, Frau Schirach, but your friend will remain here with us. I fumbled in my pack for my library card and motorcycle rider's licence, which upon examination almost satisfied his suspicions. He motioned me to join his companions under a nearby shade tree, where they appeared to be settling in for the duration. None of them had heard of my brother.

Two handlers had set up a series of high jumps for the dogs, and everyone turned to watch the Führer put Blondie and Wolf through their paces, over hurdles and fetching sticks.

"No photos!" barked one SS man as I removed the lens cap to snap the gathering. "Fraulein Braun will take any photographs the Führer deems necessary." I could see Eva darting about trying to catch Hitler off guard while he passed around a large tray of sandwiches, commencing with his personal staff and bodyguards, then the ladies, before heading towards our shady Yellow Birch.

Hitler had taken but a few steps before Eva took one elbow and Henni the other, both chatting together and nodding in my direction as the SS guards snapped to attention with arms outstretched.

His eyes settled on the sandwich already in my hand, coldly searching; I knew instinctively that I must not avert my eyes for a moment. Suddenly, his gaze passed right through me into the distance, and as the previous occasion, when we'd briefly locked eyes, I felt that somehow I had survived yet another terrible assessment.

Exchanging pleasantries with the SS guards, he proffered a cucumber sandwich which I gingerly accepted, struggling to ensure that my trembling fingers did not betray a thumping chest.

"Herr Hahn," he spoke in a slow, guttural voice, and his bad breath nearly curled my eyebrows. "You've certainly made something of an impression on the ladies," he said, watching me like a hawk.

Nodding crisply, I uttered, "Danke schön, mein Führer."

"It seems Hoffman and his wife also have a soft spot for you, correct Frau Schirach?" Henni was once more his "Little Sunshine".

Can this really be happening? I thought to myself in a fearful rush, wondering if he really could see into my mind and read those unkind remarks I'd made behind his back.

"Yes, my Führer," she answered and gave a little curtsy.

"I've heard stories of Hahn Enterprises flying the Imperial flag in far-off Brazil; you must tell me all about it sometime." Again I nodded, this time clicking my heels, causing my ankles to collide painfully.

"SS mannen, at ease!" he snapped, before turning away to rejoin the walking group. It's fair to say that at that moment I'd never known such pride.

Hitler's apparent humility had swept away all my doubts in an instant, leaving me quite lightheaded. I could barely wait to share my encounter with Tante and Onkel.

Now I could hear him addressing his entourage in a rambling monologue, "… the absolute aim of female education must be with the view to future motherhood." From my vantage point, I saw Eva smiling in concurrence and caught further snatches about the dangers of interbreeding and femininity in general.

"The German woman is knitting again," he proudly exclaimed, "after all, most women desire little more than becoming the envy of their female friends." There was some hand-clapping among the menfolk. "There are now two million girls in the League of BDM, with those as young as five years already knowing how to salute properly. As for my young men, knowledge is ruin to them: I will have no intellectual training."

Occasionally, he smoothed back his forelock with the fingers of his right hand.

"My teaching will be hard, and all softness will be knocked out of them as you shall soon witness, Frau Schirach," he said upon learning of Henni's proposed visit to the nearby youth camp. He was now standing with arms outstretched and a messianic look in his eye, as if he were addressing thousands. "I want a violently active, dominating, brutal youth; swift as greyhounds, tough as leather and hard as Krupp steel; that is what I am after. Youth must become indifferent to pain."

I wondered if I should mention the "Gloves of Happiness".

"They shall learn to overcome their fear of death; this is the true heroic stage of Youth. Out of it will emerge the creative man, the God-Man of Nietzsche." His eyes shone and he seemed transfixed by the vision; I too held my breath.

Just as suddenly he became aware of his surroundings. Calling the dogs to heel, he cast a final glance over the granite teahouse foundations and started back to where several cars were waiting, leaving everyone else to scramble behind. Henni skipped Schreck's invitation to jump aboard and opted to join me on foot.

"Come on slowpoke; this will be good practice. Race you to the top of the hill."

50

Early next morning as our feet hit the road, soft mists were stirring in the valleys and the surrounding peaks were brushed with soft pink.

For the first half hour, the going was easy, allowing time to measure my thoughts. We were making good progress and I was holding my own beside Henni, when out of the blue she charged. "Onkel Adi says that children of great men often turn out to be imbeciles. What do you think?"

"Er, I don't know many great men, nor their offspring I'm afraid," I foolishly opined to Henni's blank face, "… present company excepted, of course."

Her face didn't soften. "I've also heard that certain party doctors are sterilising anyone deemed unfit for breeding," she persisted, but before I could respond we rounded a corner at the edge of the woods and beheld an amazing sight.

A hidden valley opened into a sea of tents and flags, from which the strains of the "Horst Wessel Song" rose up to greet us. Younger Hitler Youth members were practising each verse of the new anthem, while older boys rode up and down the slopes on each other's shoulders, challenging other teams of gladiators to combat.

More squads engaged in games of hide and seek, hurling each other to the ground at every chance and whooping triumphantly whenever the opposing team was routed. I imagined this bivouac looked something like the Sparta of old, busily preparing the warrior class of the future. Within minutes Henni pointed out her man and we made our way briskly toward the reviewing stand.

"This time next year we will have completed a 500-bed Youth barracks down on that flat," Schirach was saying, pointing to the valley below. He was addressing a select group of Hitler Youth Leaders in his squeaky voice, not noting our approach or acknowledging his mail-order bride until we were

448

almost on top of him. I had a few moments to observe his pasty, shapeless legs protruding from a well-worn pair of lederhosen.

"Henriette! What are you doing here? Can't you see I'm busy?" He was clearly rattled by our unannounced arrival. Nearby, another group of fresh faced recruits was gathered around a small bonfire, reciting out loud one of the Hitler Youth's many mantras. I was impressed by the power of their affirmations, repeated three times over until all voices spoke as one.

> "ADOLPH HITLER is our Saviour, our Hero.
> HE IS the noblest being in the whole wide world.
> FOR HITLER we live, for Hitler we die.
> FOR HITLER is our Lord."

I could but marvel at the necessity for such blind obedience and potentially terminal oaths coming from mere youngsters via their comical-looking leader in his leather bib and braces; I wondered how many of them knew that Baldur, like Putzi, was only half-German anyway.

Indeed, how many even knew or cared that their beloved Führer, for whom they were apparently ready to lay down their lives, wasn't even a German at all?

Schirach, turning his attention back to the troop at his feet, puffed himself up for our benefit and said, "In conclusion, the Führer wants to see again in the eyes of our youth the gleam of the beast of prey! Adolph Hitler, you are our great Führer. Thy name makes the enemy tremble. This is our God-given task, now and forever, Heil Hitler!"

"Heil Hitler!" joined the full-blooded response.

I had seen enough and was keen to be on my way. Henni was led off by two eager lads to "freshen up" in her husband's hastily vacated quarters, where several older boys were busy beneath the tallest tepee carrying out bedrolls and suitcases. I felt a little unsettled leaving Henriette behind in such fraught and outlandish surroundings; but after all, they were married.

For the remainder of that day I fired off shot after shot at every turn. The unfolding panorama was, as we sometimes say in the studio, a photographer's dream. And in between flashes of recent events, I scrambled onto every ledge and vantage point along the crooked way, having no doubt that my postcards would soon be gracing the newsstands of Munich.

Now and then a horse-drawn wagon overtopped with household furnishings plodded by, heading downhill with silent ashen-faced family members strung out behind; none raised a glance in my direction.

As the sole ascending hiker I gained a second wind and settled into a comfortable pace for the last couple of miles. The drowsy autumn afternoon drew my eye back and again to the viewfinder; all around, the freshly snow-dusted peaks ducked in and out of the cloud.

From the valley below Berchtesgaden beamed back, seemingly unruffled by the frantic overhead activities. A keen breeze hurried the fallen leaves, pressing them in orange windrows against fence and bush. I began to be excited at the thought of Tante and Onkel snuggled up in front of their cosy fireplace, awaiting my overdue knock at the door. The last swallows coursed and darted through the golden twilight of a rising moon, when finally I glimpsed the lights of Chalet Hahn in the distance.

Dragging my heavy feet onto the porch, I discovered I was nearing exhaustion; both grateful and surprised to see Tante Gretel throw open the door before I could reach for the bell. My smile froze on my lips.

Her face was pinched and gloomy, as if all worries had descended at once. With a brief hug, she ushered me into her studio, piled high with part-filled packing cases.

Flushed from my day's exertion, at first I barely noticed the frosty atmosphere and darkened hearth. Through a doorway I glimpsed Onkel Fedi seated at a fresh-laid table, head in hands, sobbing quietly. Upon hearing my voice, he looked up with pleading eyes, wringing his hands.

"Those bastards! … Sitting up there on the mountainside as if their shit didn't stink. After all, I've done for the Party and this is the thanks I get."

Tante stared down at him in grim exasperation. "Oh, for God's sake Frederick, if indeed there is a God. Just light the damn fire. I asked you to do it an hour ago so the house would be snug for Klaus."

Her impious command surprised me and set Onkel Fedi fussing at the hearth in slow motion, he wasn't used to this new assertiveness that threatened to overturn the entire Nazi pecking order.

Silently and stoically she commenced to load the table with my favourite sausage rolls and strudel with fresh cream, as if nothing was amiss; no one spoke until the familiar flames had crackled into life, restoring something of the old atmosphere. Little did I know this would be the last fireside we shared together.

From my pack I produced a chilled bottle of Blue Slate Riesling from the cellars of Hotel Zum Tuerken, which Onkel Fedi dismissed as "lolly-water" with the wave of a hand, preferring instead to open a bottle of his home brew.

"Well, I can't cart the whole bloody batch down to the lake house, can I?" he responded when Tante chided him for lack of gratitude.

"Gratitude? There's no such bloody thing as 'gratitude', if you ask me." I noticed he was swearing a lot and his uniform looked untidy and soiled, but decided to hold my tongue. Pouring two glasses I sat opposite Gretel and listened stunned to her recounting the horrors perpetrated upon them and their neighbours by Mountain Gauleiter Bormann.

The Hahns, like dozens of other residents, suddenly found themselves "illegally occupying" the Führer's newly gazetted "Exclusive Private Space". Bormann himself had even dropped by personally to deliver the demolition notice.

"When your Onkel Fedi, to his eternal shame, saw the Brown Eminence step down from his shiny black Mercedes outside the front gate and run his eye over our beautiful home – go on, admit it Frederick – he couldn't imagine what *we* had done to deserve such a high-profile visit from the big man himself. He raced inside to straighten his uniform and strode down the path to greet Bormann – couldn't even wait for the knock of doom at the front door, could you? – so sure you were in line for another Nazi trinket, another so-called 'exemplary service' medal."

I'd never seen her so worked up, or Onkel Fedi so cowed.

"Nothing could have prepared us for what was coming," her voice steadied, "although Bormann's initial expression should have dispelled any illusions. It was not until the bastard barged into our kitchen and ran his gloved finger tactlessly along the mantle, every stone of which was laid by Aunt and Onkel before the Nazi Party was even thought of, that your brave Onkel Fedi finally stuck out his Iron Cross Second-Class and found his voice, 'What's this all about?' 'It's about the sale of the house,' Bormann pronounced matter-of-factly."

She said that they both stood dumbfounded and that he sneered when he asked what they wanted for it. They had paid over 48,000 marks for it many years ago, but he gave them fourteen days to pack up and arrange a title transfer. It was that or suffer the same as their neighbour's. Workmen were already tearing their place apart.

"At this your fearless Onkel Fedi went to pieces, begging shamefully on his knees for mercy or exemption; but that was a lifetime ago."

Her voice sounded measured but resigned, "At least I was able to hold my head high. Just look out the window for a reminder; the concrete foundations are all that remain. In another 24 hrs there will be just a patch of fresh laid turf. It's an incentive to get cracking and keep packing if we hope to be out of here in time; but we wouldn't have missed your visit for all the tea in the Führer's new teahouse, eh? We do have to look on the bright side … if indeed there is one."

I guessed that this was her way of putting on a brave face and felt my chest tighten in sympathy.

"All in all," she continued, "a total of 27 farms and 650 acres have been gobbled up in the Führer's landgrab." She choked back a sob, "Our whole community had begun the year with such high hopes."

Over breakfast the next morning I dared not mention the brief exchange I'd had with Hitler, belatedly recalling the boss' last-minute instructions. Turning to Onkel, who poked listlessly at his eggs and sausage, I relayed Hoffman's greetings to "most venerable Party Comrade Hahn" before expressing my hope, that above all others, Hoffman alone may yet be able to bring pressure to bear on their behalf.

Slowly, Onkel lifted his head and fixed his beaten eyes on mine, struggling to place the name. "Hoffman. Hoffman? … Oh him! I wouldn't spit on the man. He's no better than the rest of the so-called impresarios making a fortune off the back of untold misery, without having to get their hands dirty.

"As for yourself, obviously up to your neck in the thick of it, don't make the same mistake I did by pretending that in the end everyone will walk away with a smile on their faces. It's high time you grew up and began asserting your own independence from the whole rotten system."

His outburst took Tante and I both by surprise but she quick as a flash shot back. "It's a pity your Onkel didn't display such fighting spirit before Bormann when he had the chance."

"Oh, for Christ's sake, Gretel don't start up again; haven't I been through enough already?"

"Enough? Enough?" She spat out the words like bullets. "Do I recount how you and all those other loyal Party Members were so easily flattered at the thought of their almighty Führer coming to reside among them? Of how the humbug flew through the district like wild fowl, honking over the prosperity and prestige that was sure to accrue. Bah! You can stick your Nazi Party. Come on Klaus, I could do with some fresh air before I return to my packing." With that, she moved to the door and pulled on her knapsack, and me trailing along uncertainly behind. As I glanced back over my shoulder, poor Oncle was sitting confused and shocked, "… and see that a few more of those boxes are filled when we return."

I had a job keeping pace, as Tante strode off with head down, ignoring both me and the electrifying scenery. When I eventually did set my Leica around my neck and caught up, puffing little dabs of steam, her usual composure had returned and she forced a light smile, even commenting affectionately on my healthy flush.

We stood for a time looking down at Chalet Hahn with its forty immaculate acres. "Ah, this place, where shall we ever find another with views like this? We were eagles," she sighed, waving her arm and allowing her eyes to drink in the familiar surroundings. One by one she pointed out the lonely copses, where farmhouses, barns, lumber mills and Churches had recently stood.

Strolling on in silence we rounded a corner and came upon a low stone wall upon which had been scrawled in bold letters: "Down with Hitler!" The exclamation mark had been formed in the distinctive double-star shape of the Mountain Edelweiss flower. Contrary to my startled reaction, Tante didn't seem at all surprised. Narrowing her eyes, she asked in a soft voice if I'd heard of the "Edelweiss Pirates"?

"Er … not exactly, but I have heard of Austria's National Flower being pirated in regard to certain other Resistance activities," I replied evasively, not wishing to betray Claudia's confidence.

"Well, this looks like their handiwork. 'Pirate' is certainly a fitting brand for these bands of brave warriors. They often bail up hiking groups of Hitler Youth and beat the stuffing out of them, before melting away into the mountains. Schirach is dashing about like a chook with his head cut off." I gave an involuntary twitch. "Mercifully, there are still some young people who have the moral courage to stand up for free speech."

"And not only here" I added, reminding myself of Claudia's friends in the Edelweiss Orchestra; for a brief moment I missed her terribly.

"And we mustn't forget there are also many womenfolk among their ranks, doing what they can behind the scenes," Tante enthused, "… brave souls who thumb their noses at Nazi strictures, wear western-style clothing and dance to Jazz and 'swing' music when they can. 'Nigger music', Bormann calls it!

"They are becoming quite a headache for the Party Machine and growing in popularity as more and more stories leak out. Regrettably and predictably, the Gestapo is now rounding up anyone even faintly suspected of 'disloyalty' and packing them off to Dachau.

"Hullo! I don't like the look of this," she stopped suddenly, before cautiously approaching a cluster of partly demolished shop fronts, one of which belonged to a small barn.

A wooden shingle, "Hansel Brandner – Photographer", hung askew above the side entrance but there was no sign of Herr Brandner or his equipment. From among the tumbled timbers, two middle-aged women tottered straight out into Tanti's arms, each striving to be first with details of their beloved brother's arrest.

"Oh, Frau Hahn, our beautiful Hansi was taken in the dead of night and all his equipment was smashed, dragged off to some place called Dachau. We swear on the Holy Mother that he has done nothing wrong."

Their "beautiful Hansi" was the very person with whom I'd hoped to share a few tips on excessive ultraviolet light in the high country.

"All he did was write a letter to the Führer and hand it to him personally on the railway platform," one sister explained in hushed tones, "politely drawing attention to the shameful way our family has been treated and seeking justice.

"None of us want to leave home; Hansel had not long set up his new darkroom and renovated the studio, and business was starting to boom with the hiking trails growing in popularity. Then, the notary arrived at the farm and valued it at 25,000 marks," she paused for a painful moment. "Gauleiter Bormann arrived just one hour later and in the blink of an eye offered us 1,500, turning all fifteen of us out into the street as beggars. On top of this, our baby brother has been taken God-knows-where."

Neither Gretel nor I could think of any sensible response other than to keep hugging.

"At first he thought he'd been well received," the second sister continued through her grief, "and we saw Hitler pass his note to an SS man and heard him issue the order that 'this man needs special treatment'; we heard the Führer say those very words, didn't we sister? Our Hansi returned home on top of the world."

Each spinster took turns filling in the details of the unfolding disaster that had befallen the family, continually dabbing at their eyes. We didn't have the heart to tell them about all the others, or explain why Chalet Hahn was still standing.

"That very night the Gestapo just barged in and arrested him in the clothes he was wearing, without even giving him time to pack a bag," the first resumed, fumbling in a large apron pocket to produce a dog-eared portrait of the missing photographer. "Look, young sir," she pushed the print under my nose, "the good Lord knows our Hansi wouldn't hurt a fly."

I looked at the frank, open face in the picture, a robust young man wearing traditional embroidered Bavarian jacket and breeches with a felt hat sporting pheasant feathers cocked jauntily to one side. I felt immediately that we would have been friends.

"Oh, Lord Jesus, what is to become of us? What have we done to deserve this?"

"But surely the Führer must know of your eviction Fraulein Brandner, with what you've told me. After all, you are his neighbour," I foolishly commented, handing the photo back. Gretel shot me a dark look and offered a few more soothing words of her own before we turned to leave, assuring them that we would do everything in our power to look into Hansel's whereabouts.

Fraulein Brandner's parting words haunted me for weeks afterwards, a portent of Tante and Onkel's own ordeal. "But it is already too late Frau Hahn; by the time a possible resolution is found, every last building will be gone."

As we walked resignedly towards home, Gretel pointed out a field of grazing red-poll cattle where only two days earlier had stood the farmhouse of an old couple in possession of a rare "lifetime" lease.

Apparently, after a visit from Bormann, they agreed to sell and move out within the space of 24 hours. The roof was being torn from their house while they were still packing. And in the depths of winter! She shook her head in a daze. "To whom does one appeal when it's the Government destroying the lives of its own citizens? What sort of government is that?" she said bitterly, to which I had no reply.

"Hitler is giving the majority just what they secretly crave; assurance of their own superiority! I see clearly now that it was Bourgeois impotence and conceit that caused them to elevate this wicked man. Those on the fringes like us and the Humps and Brandners are simply trampled underfoot," she added bitterly, without looking up.

"I don't know what to think, Tante. As you know, my friends Ernst and Marty were murdered in cold blood. Since then, nothing surprises me," I added gamely.

"Make no mistake, Klaus, this is only the beginning. Onkel and I are fortunate we have the boatshed to move into while we try to pick up the threads of our lives. If you have any sense, get out of Germany while you can. You do still have a Brazilian Passport, don't you?"

"W … Well, yes and no. Hoffman took it away the day I started working at the studio. I can never leave without his say-so. As for escaping, to where? You two and Robert are the only family I have in the world. Somehow, I just have to try and make the best of my situation. I really am much better off than most, you know."

Gretel looked at me and shook her head. "How often have I heard that same pathetic rationale from others with their heads in the sand? 'When they came for the Communists I didn't speak up, because I wasn't a Communist. When they came for the Jews I didn't speak up, because I wasn't a Jew. When they came for the homosexuals and Jehovah's Witnesses I didn't speak up either. Now they're coming for us and there's no one left to speak up.'"

I gulped and tried to avoid her eyes. "W … What about your collection of Modernist paintings? Couldn't you return it for safekeeping to somewhere like the Bauhaus, until you find somewhere larger?"

"The Bauhaus? That's a laugh. Much of their collection has already been destroyed and many of their brightest lights have fled overseas. Dr Goebbels has seen to that. I'm afraid Modern Art has no place in this New Order; it will take more than a few roving bands of artists and freethinkers to halt the juggernaut now." She paused at the front gate and ran her fingers thoughtfully along the railing, before turning to scrutinise the scene below through half-closed lids.

For long minutes we stood side by side watching the last rays of thinning sunlight crawl up the Untersberg opposite to mark the close of another dismal day. We found Onkel sitting where we'd left him, before the cheerless embers in the fireplace; his eyes were ringed and darkened with uncertainty.

Tante made no further effort to intrude upon his gloom as we nibbled disconcertedly at our meal of leftovers. No amount of prattle could defuse the bomb that had landed on Obersalzberg.

The next morning Gretel and I made our way down to the Berchtesgaden Bahnhof, where the festive atmosphere gave no hint of the dramas unfolding on the slopes above.

Eager pilgrims poured from the Munich Special Express. The Führer was now in residence and a Brass Band announced the fact to newcomers, many decked out in dirndls and lederhosen, despite the brisk air. Everything and everyone appeared to be orderly and clean.

At the last minute, my dear empty-eyed aunt pressed a heavy brown package into my hands and looking back from the near-empty carriage as it pulled away, I could see her still waving and wiping a tear.

Whatever would become of them? I asked myself over again, a whole community of the very folk the Nazi Party claimed to represent, just wiped off the map.

With fumbling fingers, I peeled off the parcel wrapping to reveal a leather-bound Folio of Shakespeare's Plays in Old English, something I'd only ever dreamed of owning. Written inside the cover:

> K. You may need your English before you're finished. This greatest of Englishmen will improve your knowledge of Human Nature.

> Love, G.

As the "Führer special" clattered through the narrow cuttings toward Munich I tried immediately to lose myself among the well-thumbed pages, which I knew would have to be kept out of sight upon my return. I became aware for the first time that the entire alpine adventure had brought my delusions into focus.

51

"No more prints will be made from the pre-chancellorship period without my express permission," Hoffman barked before departing in late October for the opening of his new Berlin studio. He was responding to requests I'd received from a list of overseas publications seeking "early and informal shots of the Führer".

"That's it! You've been told. If I can't be reached you will submit all such appeals to the Press Room."

I paused with the top drawer of the filing cabinet still open. "Well boss, there aren't that many celluloid negs in the files anyway, and these are always referred to you before being printed," I responded, thinking of the chuckles Claudia and I had had over those early photos of the Führer posing in the snow in his punitive lederhosen.

Come to think of it, I'd never yet seen a grown man entirely comfortable when strapped into a pair of these quaint but no doubt practical leather breeches, and Hitler in particular did not suit the garment. With his wide hips, formless legs and smooth white knees all competing with the familiar piercing glare for the viewer's eye, I sensed that such moments had revealed too much altogether of the man.

Hoffman's private collection preceded Hitler's rise to power by a decade or more and was nowadays eschewed by any unauthorised eye. "And that shot with the jackdaw on his shoulder should have been destroyed years ago," Hoffman added, "but I just couldn't bring myself to do it. On some roadside picnic, we were feeding luncheon scraps to the birds, when much to the Führer's surprise a jackdaw landed on his shoulder looking for crumbs. I alone caught that flush of pleasure softening his features; for a few moments, he looked almost childlike. It's a look I've never seen on him before or since."

457

"Now Adolph's forbidden it to be printed again and has ordered the negative destroyed. See to it while I'm gone. Oh, and don't forget to clear the decks ready for the Parade of the Old Fighters and the Blutfahne ceremony next month."

The boss rarely had time for small talk these days; I'd heard that the Berlin studio was to be run even more efficiently than Munich, using Henry Ford's latest ideas on time and motion to streamline the operation. Apparently, there is even a portrait of the great American innovator in his new Berlin office, with another in the Chancellery itself.

"Meanwhile, you stay with the postcards; Iris will let me know if you fall below 500 per day ... And start wearing a Party armband when you go out on assignment."

"B ... But Boss, you know I'm not even a member ..."

"Just keep your mouth shut and do as I say. The swastika offers more protection and will open more doors for you. After all, that is our duty is it not?"

I nodded dumbly in response, tucking the proffered phylactery into my pocket.

"At least it's only when I'm on official assignments," I reasoned, having always felt I'd achieved more spontaneity by *not* drawing attention to myself. Wearing such patent propaganda on my arm may well open more doors, but it certainly would not endear me to the few friends I did have. What would Claudia think, for one?

But Hoffman was in no mood for backchat at the thought of a long drive ahead. Hitler's pilot Bauer had just phoned to report that the "Führer Plane" had been grounded because of bad weather.

Between my workload and the plummeting temperatures, few opportunities arose to wander Munich's open spaces. Ever inquisitive, I was led to frequent those art galleries still open but soon discovered that without the nascent smattering of modern Expressionism, the truncated and sanitised collections looked grubby and stale.

It fell to my Shakespearean Folio, and a neverending stream of art books from the nearby Bibliotech to provide the inspiration to stay afloat amidst the wreckage of my former delusions.

Huge parades and official occasions came and went with unmissable regularity, as Studios Hoffman groaned under their workload. Hugo Jaeger now sought and obtained one darkroom exclusively for his increasingly popular colour processing. I had to admit we were all inspired and impressed by his breathtaking "Official Colour Experiments" inside the new Berlin Chancellery.

Eva, meanwhile, ever more adept at dodging her parents' controlling tendencies, managed to squeeze in a quick visit to this monstrous, intimidating structure, completed by Albert Speer in record time.

She complained to me that while in Berlin, Hitler had taken little to no notice of her whenever she attempted to ask questions, and she overheard him commenting that he "detested women who dabble in politics".

It was obvious that Eva was fast becoming "sick of playing salesgirl", and that February 6, our joint birthdays, marked a real turning point in her mental outlook. She had waited in vain for a puppy, disdainful of her office overflowing with flowers; pining for a kind word from the one person who now seemed to matter.

Herta Schneider, sensing her friend's distress, dropped by the studio in the late afternoon to take both of us for a low-key, high-tea at the Carlton Hotel, an act of kindness that sadly backfired and plunged Eva into yet more gloom. There in the next aisle, with his back to us, sat none other than her elusive man, who according to the head waiter had been engaged in lively banter with a rising actress named "Ondra" for the past three hours.

None of us had heard of her, prompting Eva, rather than walking out in a huff, to remain seated and attempt to catch his eye on the way past. Nearby, sat three SS bodyguards who immediately noted our arrival and handed a slip of paper to the Führer.

Sure enough, when he rose to leave, Hitler passed right by our table without a word, pausing just long enough to thrust an envelope into Eva's trembling fingers. Flabbergasted, she gathered her wits and tore it open while fighting back tears. "No note, no word," she exclaimed, holding up 50 marks. "Oh Herta, I can't take much more of this."

Later, when walking back to Schellingstrasse, she stopped at the first jewellery store and selected a dress ring, chain and earrings, before stuffing them abruptly into her Italian leather handbag. "If he doesn't like them he can choose something himself," she sniffled.

A long-faced Herta farewelled us at the studio door when Eva expressed her intention to sit by the phone in her office "until daybreak if necessary".

Later, when I dropped by to present my gift, a royal-blue leatherette photo album with acid-free pages and tissue interleaves, there was no sign of her: a diary lay open on her desk.

Placing my gift carefully, I succumbed to the temptation to peek, if only at last night's entry, and immediately felt a pang of guilt. "Am I being too selfish?" it began with a scrawl. "I should never want to be blamed if he stops loving me."

She didn't disclose if Hitler did indeed phone, but the next morning Hoffman presented her with an album twice the size of mine, handmade from cream calf vellum, also featuring acid-free pages and tissue interleaves.

Not long before departing for Obersalzberg, she confided that her 23rd birthday was the most disappointing she could remember.

"At least up there, putting finishing touches to our new darkroom I carry some authority, whether Adolph is in residence or not," she said hopefully. Frau Schaub had filled her room with birthday gifts mostly from people she didn't even know, probably, Eva said, from those trying to keep in good with "The Chief".

Then, her return to Munich involved more bad news, conveyed this time by Frau Hoffman: the Führer had on more than one occasion been seen dining quite openly with Unity Mitford at the Café Ostaria Bavaria. Nonetheless, on February 18, another quick peek further revealed a glimmer of hope that temporarily appeared to lift her out of the darkness.

"Adolph came yesterday. He's thinking of taking me out of the studio and buying me a little house. I'm just so sick of bowing and scraping to strangers. I do so hope this time he keeps his word."

Predictably, Eva's hopes were short-lived, plunging her once again into deep despair. Whenever I had the chance I took a peep at her latest tear-stained entries.

> March 4, 1935. "Mortally unhappy. Last night I was with Him at Hoffman's until midnight, when he gave permission for me to use my Munich Ball Loge ticket for two hours. Hopes were dashed when chaperoned by Frau Schwartz. Breaks promise to see me Sunday morning.
>
> I've had enough. Klaus drove me to Munich Bahnhof in his sidecar, to confront him over not even saying goodbye. I was determined to have it out on the railway platform, if necessary. Too late, we arrived in time to see the tail lights of his train disappearing in the distance. Why?"
>
> March 11. "I'm going to buy sleeping pills."
>
> March 27. "I know now he only keeps me for one thing."

Meanwhile, beyond the studio walls, events were proceeding with lightning speed: Hitler announced that military conscription, specifically banned under the Versailles Treaty, was being re-introduced effective immediately. A half-million young men were being called up in the first wave. Some of us wondered why the so-called victors were allowing this to occur; there could be but one possible reason for compulsory military service.

On April 10, all Germany paused for the spectacle of Fat Herman's Berlin wedding to Emmy Sonneman, a well-known opera singer with a flair for publicity equal only to her corpulent new husband.

Hoffman was furious that he had been engaged only for official portraits and candids after the event, whereas British Pathé Pictorial had been hired to make a full-length documentary. For the first time, Studio Hoffman stringers had to compete with a truly international press contingent containing many excellent photographers.

When I got to develop the negatives I had a birdie's eye view of the entire proceedings. Once again I could see that Hitler was the best man, while Emmy was attended by two Hitler Youths in short pants carrying her ten-foot train. Later on, during the formal portrait session, a rather dour-looking pair of bridesmaids in clashing outfits that I thought looked more like curtain material arrived out of the blue. The bride herself looked none too moved by Hoffman's jokes, or by being posed beneath a life-size oil of Frederick the Great.

Earlier, given the perfect "Führer Weather", bride and groom arrived together in a black, open-topped tourer, from which the Reichsmarschall alighted first to cross the street and receive well-wishes from his troops. Movie footage showed Emmy alone floating up the Lutheran Cathedral steps like a Rhine Maiden, followed at a discreet distance by the best man.

Hoffman's pictures seemed to be composed less carefully than usual; as a result, he later complained of "dozens" of other photographers getting in his way. When the happy couple emerged from the ceremony, dozens of right arms shot out from the SS Honour Guard, *and* from a bevy of beaming clergymen.

Frau Göring, staring straight ahead, stuck out her right hand to return the salute in like manner, while the Reichsmarschall lifted a hand to cap in a more traditional fashion. Behind them, hanging back in the doorway stood the best man with his bodyguard, eyes fixed firmly on the horizon.

The groom was resplendent in full-dress uniform, specially designed for the occasion; across his right breast flowed a wide ribbon of unknown significance, while the left sported his Pour le Mérite. An assortment of service medals and a cluster of five large stars almost obscured his paunch, while a woven, three-stranded belt held up his elephantine striped trousers and ceremonial sword.

Beaming from left to right, the groom offered his arm and the newly married couple descended through an archway of ten drawn swords to the open tourer waiting below. Hoffman had managed to catch the rumps of several other photographers, some in uniform, others in trench coats, who had leapt out in front of him onto the lower steps.

In the movie footage, I noticed the cheer that went up for the Führer's descent was much louder than that for the bride and groom.

I later learned that some 33,000 Brownshirts and Wehrmacht soldiers lined the route to the wedding breakfast, quite aside from the tens of thousands of curious onlookers. For the first time ever, I had to erase our competitors' backsides from official wedding photos, using ferricyanide in the darkroom. The reception candids showed a stoic bride seated between her Herman to the left and her stone-faced Führer to the right.

Hoffman himself insisted on vetting the negs, editing out every one that showed Hitler blinking, eating or half-smiling, which in the latter case wasn't very often. Those few remaining showed him staring off into space, or off to one side when being addressed by the bumptious groom.

"Oh, Klaus, you are going to get the shock of your life next visit. The darkroom is just the way you wanted; with one or two minor adjustments. Unfortunately, many of the staff still have not yet realised the significance of my position, even since I moved next door to the Führer. Don't worry; they'll soon get the message."

When developing Eva's latest snaps of the Berghof, I was staggered by the pace and scale of Bormann's "renovations". Although she still had to use the back stairs when dignitaries were in attendance, she showed a picture of her quarters on the newly completed upper floor. Her spartan room was dominated, like most of the other guest quarters, by a 16" × 20" framed portrait of their scowling landlord.

Spread across Eva's work desk were swatches of colour for choosing the outdoor patio furniture and sun umbrellas. She never again mentioned the plight of Hitler's homeless neighbours, now facing the fiercest winter in years.

Despite her patently shallow efforts to radiate good cheer, I could tell without reading more of her diary that she was teetering on the brink of a nervous breakdown. When we spoke briefly in the corridor her eyes were red and her hands trembled.

"I've sent him a deadline letter, Klaus; I cannot bear the thought of another three months without a kind word. Here I am alone again at Easter, the sweetheart of the greatest man in Germany and all the world. Is this the 'mad love' he promised? … I'm not to blame; you do know that, don't you Klaus? Who else would put up with his stinking breath and constant farting? I'm certain Dr Morell's anti-flatulence pills only make things worse."

April 28, 1935. I have decided on 35 pills.

April 29, 1935. Things are tough. Debts are piling up. I'll start selling some of my jewellery and clothes. Tomorrow will be too late.

Later that day, Ilse Braun found her sister unconscious on the bedroom floor; she didn't appear to be breathing and an empty pill bottle lay nearby.

Again the news flew around the studio like wildfire, and for a time many were sceptical. Ilse almost compounded the problem by summoning Dr Marx, her former Jewish employer who still possessed a stomach pump and other tools of the trade, despite being banned from practising. The usual tearful reunions ensued, but this time, in the absence of blood, Eva's family were angry rather than surprised. They set out immediately to cover up the whole incident, with an agreed diagnosis of "overwork".

Hitler, on the other hand, seemed baffled and even flattered by this second suicide attempt: he rushed to Eva's side and immediately agreed to the purchase of a tiny red-roofed villa that Hoffman had sussed out on Wasserburger Strasse, just over the Isar in the district of Bogenhausen.

Apparently, sales of *Mein Kampf* and Bormann's postage stamp royalties had turned him into a multi-millionaire almost overnight.

He told her in hushed tones that her new home boasted a large living room fireplace with a People's Radio on the mantle. She could decorate the whole place as she wished, and choose from any number of Hoffman's "borrowed" artworks. Why not sunbake in the private garden with Gretl, Negus and Stasi as often as she fancied?

From now on she could be assured that he was taking her "seriously", and by way of confirmation assigned her two SS bodyguards and made permanent the arrangement with the chauffeur-driven limousine.

Fritz Braun, however, was not so easily mollified, firing off yet another three-page salvo at Hitler, via Hoffman, voicing his objections to Eva becoming "anyone's mistress". For months the fearless Führer had shied away from further confrontation with Eva's prying parents.

"I want my daughters at home until they marry," Fritz blustered, now powerless to prevent Hitler's late-night visits to his daughter's new bagnio. This letter too was deftly intercepted before reaching its target and Eva's life slipped back imperceptibly into its former uncertainty.

Soon after, Hitler began appearing more often in a simple brown tunic bearing only his Iron Cross and swastika armband. In case anyone had forgotten, he was after all the Reich's Soldier Number 1.

As for Eva, she selected a whole new wardrobe, dyed her hair with a cheap-looking blonde perm and returned to part-time work, trying to ignore the newspaper headlines appearing nearly every day: "Führer attends concert with English Girlfriend by his side" and "Führer dedicates new Autobahn under the watchful eye of English Girlfriend."

Apparently, Unity Mitford had arranged for her own Baby Austin sedan to be shipped over from England, which threatened to turn more heads than Eva's sleek six-wheeler. Mitford had already obtained a German driver's licence, allowing her to get around Munich on the "wrong side of the road". She began turning up everywhere the Führer was due to appear.

Gossip columns reported that the Baby Austin's distinctive little bonnet was decorated with a Union Jack and swastika flying side by side, "as a symbol for our joint futures", Unity confided to one journalist. Being alongside Hitler was "exciting and fascinating; like sitting next to the Sun".

Unashamedly, given the Leader's constant extolling of her "perfect Aryan proportions", Unity dared see herself as future consort, even "Queen of Germany". After all, wasn't her sister Diana engaged to marry Oswald Mosely, head of the British Fascists back home?

She often started her mornings alone at a table in Café Ostaria, intending to catch the Führer's eye; if successful he would leave his frustrated retinue to loiter about aimlessly looking at their watches.

One morning, Eva dragged me downtown again for a covert peek through the picture window abutting the restaurant gardens, but it was difficult trying to see much in the candlelit gloom. That very morning it was reported that the Führer had presented Unity with a specially designed Gold Party Badge, personally signed, which no other foreigner was ever allowed to wear.

"Valkyrie! She's calling herself now. Can you believe it? Flat-chested, unwomanly, no hips and those Amazon legs ..." Eva spoke half to herself, "... and all that makeup he so despises; I honestly don't know what he sees in the pretentious bitch. Ages ago, Adolph went out of his way to inform us that French lipstick is made from fat skimmed off the Paris sewers ... oh Klaus, first Geli and now this. What am I to do?"

I thought for a moment. "They say it's easier to catch the jaguar in his lair; or the Caiman when asleep."

"What's that supposed to mean?"

"I mean up there on the mountain, where you have him all to yourself. *You* can be number-one hostess and escort; at least when he's in residence."

"And when he's not? How about when he's off somewhere with the likes of her, or that porn star, Jenny Jago, or any one of a hundred others; what then? Up there, he doesn't even allow me to go skiing in case I break an ankle or something. I feel trapped."

At that moment a waiter passed by the window holding aloft a steaming tray of blood sausages shaped like swastikas; Germany's newest fare to feature the ubiquitous icon. Nowadays, it was not uncommon to see young and old alike devouring the sacred symbol in one form or another, such as bon-bons, fruit drops and even children's ice blocks, much like a heretical consumption of the Eucharist.

Walking back to the studio I made a point of scrubbing my toe over every painted swastika on the footpaths, keeping one eye open for the Special Police. I would never understand why Eva continued to torture herself so.

No event in 1937 brought such gratification to Adolph Hitler and frustration to Heinrich Hoffman as the grand, three-day opening of Munich's much-touted neo-classical masterpiece, the Haus Der Kunst (House of German Art) which had taken a thousand workers over four years to complete.

As Curator of the inaugural "Great German Art Exhibition", Hoffman discovered that even though he now had the space to exhibit hundreds of purloined pieces side by side for the first time, he'd been given little more than a month to put the whole show together.

Propaganda Minister Goebbels also fancied himself as a spokesman for Germany's re-awakened, pristine tastes in art, badgering Hoffman with unwanted recommendations as he struggled with his final choices. Almost as debilitating to the boss was the continual interference from Gerty Troost, wife of the original architect who had died partway through the project.

At Hitler's behest, the widow Troost stepped in to finish the task and impose her own forthright tastes upon the final collection. She was a cruel critic of those who stood in her way, as Hoffman soon discovered.

"That bloody woman has the Führer's ear and the whole show is turning into a dog's breakfast," he complained when more of his choices were rejected in favour of Frau Troost's grand vision. I already had more than enough nudes. It seems that some have begun calling it 'The House of German Tarts' behind my back."

Night after night I saw lights burning in the boss' office as he pored over the prints of possible contenders, troubled doubly by the threat of a "Führer Veto".

Since his appointment as Reich Art Curator, he cleverly redirected those acquisitions even slightly controversial or adventurous onto the walls of his own Schnorrstrasse Villa or sold them on to black-market collectors.

Hitler wanted no delays in his first grand building project designed to showcase his own impeccable artistic taste and a further slap in the face to all those blowhard critics with "modernist tendencies".

Nonetheless, on opening day I was there in the crowd early when the official party, guided by Frau Troost, mounted the red carpet between the mighty columns fronting Prinzregentenstrasse to settle back and watch the two-mile-long parade celebrating some two thousand years of "German culture".

Tens of thousands in traditional garb lined the route, waving flags to cheer on a real-life Charlemagne, and a Frederick Barbarossa, both Hitler's boyhood heroes. Each was splendidly mounted, leading brigades of historic Prussian uniforms through the ages.

Close behind came squadrons of Hitler Youth, also in period costume, and farmer's carts piled high with rural produce; all saluting fervently with a loud Sieg Heil. Coveys of cross-bearing priests wore their swastika armbands proudly as they shuffled by the command podium, lending a divine touch to the proceedings.

Undoubtedly, the loudest cheers were saved for the float of topless "Amazonian Warriors" and buxom "Valkyries", some on ersatz horseback brandishing spears with others wearing only scant metal breastplates. On and on it wound, until the ominous ranks of goose-stepping Army and SS units delivered their earthshaking climax.

Everyone I spoke to later said that Munich had never seen anything like it. Newsreels showed the Führer with arm outstretched and admiring the swastika mosaics in the ceiling panels above his head; a last-minute personal touch from Frau Troost. Above the main portal, his immortal thoughts were chiselled in stone:

ART IS A SUBLIME MISSION
DEMANDING FANATICAL DEVOTION.

I suspected that this prescient revelation was well off the mark from Tante Gretel's discerning theories and those of many other modern art lovers. One thing I did know, however, was that for the next three days and nights, our darkrooms ran hot as Hoffman pumped out his copyrighted images by the tens of thousands, not to mention the international royalties.

When it came time for speeches a hush settled over the crowd, until eventually, it came Hitler's turn to officially declare the gallery open *and* to inaugurate the exhibition in one fell swoop.

Caesar firmed his shoulders and stood gripping the lectern, surrounded by all the colourful pageantry of modern Germany; as usual, he waited for silence. He was not only the master of the Nation but the final arbiter in Aryan artistic taste; at that moment seemingly just one hop away from becoming Master of the Universe.

He began in soft tones lauding Paul Ludwig, Gertrude's deceased husband, for commencing this "First great task of Cultural Purification", before laying into Weimar architects and "those small-minded 1918 criminals who spewed the flood of slime and refuse onto the surface of our lives".

"*This* 'immortal achievement' puts an end to the chaotic, bungling attempts at construction I have left behind. It was only through defeat that our thoroughly rotten body first experienced the full extent of its inner decay and its impetus for cleansing; this implies to me that to be German means to be clear and logical; above all to be true against a world of adversaries …"

Returning to the Studio with several urgent rolls, I joined those now gathered around the Siemens radio with greedy ears. I wrote down a few key phrases, in case I was quizzed later by Lothar on my recollections.

Hitler's thoughts on the alternative exhibition of so-called "Degenerate Art", to be opened nearby on the following day, July 19, were particularly revealing.

After all, I'd previously seen and heard I was not particularly surprised by the venom and fluency of his derision; Tante said later that it sounded like the subliminal baggage of a failed artist.

"It is my immutable resolve to do for German Artistic Life what I have done for political confusion; to purge it of empty phrases and of people to whom God has denied real artistic talent. Such works by Jewish Bolshevists and other foreign scribblers and dabblers will no longer find their way to the German people. *We* are all much less interested in so-called *intent* than we are in *ability*!

"We are turning away from the spawn of an impudent, shameless arrogance, and the truly frightening incompetence of those who see our people as 'degenerate cretins', forced to experience meadows of blue, the sky as green, and clouds as sulphurous yellow, and so on.

"We utterly reject the stilted, stammering degeneracy of so-called Cubism, Dadaism, Futurism and Impressionism; they have nothing to do with our German people. Our Nation will no longer be bothered over the humbug of these miserable scoundrels who sit cackling over each other's eggs. Every person or thing participating in this perversion should realise that his elimination is at hand."

I gulped; the threat was clear.

"I know that when the German People walk through these halls they will also acknowledge me as their spokesman and guide; a stroll through this exhibit will reveal much again that is beautiful, and above all, respectable ..."

As if to drive home his point I learned later that he'd instructed Hoffman to purchase an uninspiring traditional landscape, "Cattle Drive in the Alps" by Rudolph Scheller, though I never did find out the price paid.

"... I hereby declare the Great German Art Exhibit of 1937 in Munich, open!" he rounded his diatribe with a flourish.

We were all in shock as someone reached over to turn down the volume, and for the next several days I would relive the whole event via graphic stills and snippets of colour movie footage which contained all I needed to know. Fascinated, I watched newsreels of the official party moving through, with Frau Gerty's white satin suit gleaming like an angel's wings. Her floppy, matching beret quivering with conviction as she explained to the Führer the importance of this or that piece.

Dozens of leading Nazis in full-dress uniform straggled along behind, cocking their heads knowingly and straining to endorse her comments. I could see the jilted curator was struggling to keep up, falling farther behind with each refill of his silver goblet. Goebbels attempted to sidle up beside Frau Troost and throw in one or two observations of his own but he too was ignored by the only pair of true connoisseurs in attendance that day.

Hitler seemed particularly taken by a large "Leda and Swan", framed in heavy-gilt, pausing only to comment on the necessary contortions required for copulation to occur between that unlikely couple. Then he lectured the group briefly on "Man in Golden Helmet" by Rembrandt, claiming the subject, mistakenly, to be Mars, God of War. He drew attention to the steely resolve in the sitter's eye.

However, even I knew that most art experts had long since attributed this work, depicting an ordinary Dutch night watchman, to one of Rembrandt's pupils. Slowly but surely, the official Party gravitated toward an aggregation of oversized marble nudes, peeking discreetly at their compact if reposing genitalia. The Führer was clearly disappointed that these splendid Aryan specimens had not been better endowed.

It was all here in my developing dish; the expressions and pretences of those exposed for the first time to an entire range of "Germany's Greatest artworks". At a glance, I could tell these monoliths lacked either the simple grace of Greek originals or the energy of Roman copies. On every side, huge combatants, heroic workers and fertile female nudes stretched, crouched and reclined ready to slay or seduce the viewer. Given all the head nodding and banter it was clear that this new "German Heroic Style", depicting purest Aryanism, was hugely popular with both Führer and retinue.

As for the paintings, when I finally did get away to see the Great Exhibition for myself, I found some traditional oils, such as "Cattle Drive in the Alps", indeed tolerable; most of the remainder were merely pretentious and predictable, stressing the hackneyed Nazi theme of "Blood and Soil".

A few noteworthy pieces from Holbein, Runge and Casper Friedrich I recognised from books and gallery visits, but mostly the entire collection comprised edifying still-lifes, idyllic landscapes and portraits of proud peasants. The only obvious curse I could see resulting from the "shattered hammer" incident was mediocrity itself.

Predictably, there was no sign of the True Moderns, some of whom, thanks to Tante Gretel, I'd come to appreciate and even admire. The reason soon became apparent: across the street, just a short distance away in the Hofgartenarkaden a second exhibition was preparing to open its doors. Minister Goebbels, along with the President of the Reich Chamber of Arts, Adolf Ziegler, one of Hitler's favourite living painters, had brought together all the "Degenerate Art" they could lay hands on, plundering hundreds of private collections and thirty public galleries across the country. Each piece was gleefully chosen with the sole intention of publicly denouncing its "blatant shortcomings".

From the estimated thirty thousand works so far acquired, just 650 of the "very worst" including Picasso, Kandinsky, Beckmann, Klee, and my new favourite, Vincent Van Gogh, among others, could be squeezed into the available space.

Advertising posters stuck on every lamppost hinted at the revelations to come: "Haus der Kunst" proudly featured nudes in heroic poses, whereas the "Degenerates" emphasised violent colours and contorted shapes. In fact, the sculptor Otto Freundlich, whose carved "New Man Head" had featured nationwide on one poster, was hunted down and sent off to a concentration camp in '43, to be killed on the day he arrived.

I gasped upon browsing the catalogue, which ridiculed most of Tante Gretel's favourites as examples of those same "very deviant dabblings" spoken of by the Führer in his speech, "… standing in defiance of everything it means to be truly German."

Unbeknown to Hitler, during his own whirlwind tour of the "Rejects", and in order to drive home the Nazi viewpoint, Minister Goebbels had cleverly sewn the collection with a sprinkling of "similar" works from Munich mental asylum inmates.

Painted captions on the walls, such as "This is how a deranged mind looks at nature" were designed to assist the viewer in forming the proper opinions. At first, it appeared that "dabblers and tinkerers" had been outed once and for all as a "public disgrace". Hoffman was disgusted to learn that almost three million visitors flocked to see the degenerate display that contained several "marginal" works he'd been forced to divest from his own hamstrung exhibition up the road.

Both exhibitions were eventually dispatched on an "educational" tour of twelve major German cities, before many of the "very worst" were sold overseas and the remainder burned in Berlin.

Hitler's attempt to glorify Nazi Art had backfired spectacularly.

When Yuletide decorations went up in that freezing winter of '37, Eva invited me, quite unexpectedly, to act as her chaperone for the much-feted Studio Hoffman Christmas Party at the boss' Schnorrstrasse Villa.

She had already dropped tentative hints about 'catching up' on The Mountain for the New Year celebrations, but I was reluctant to accept having already arranged with Tante and Onkel for a visit to their renovated boatshed on Lake Königssee. Moreover, I wouldn't put it past Eva to try and evoke a jealous response by arriving on the arm of a common printer; I smelled a rat. For someone like me, such a misstep could spell disaster.

Yet I need not have worried. As Yuletide arrived we turned up a half-hour late as usual, thanks to Eva changing outfits several times before settling again on the ink blue satin polka dot.

By then, celebrations were already in full swing and hearty renditions of "Silent Night" floated out through the doorway; no one could yet know that this and other Christmas Carols would soon be banned by Dr Goebbels. Inside I glimpsed a few familiar faces, Henni, Gretl, and even Iris, amidst a sprinkle of SS uniforms. Rising starlets chatted nervously with each other and hoped to be noticed.

Frau Hoffman with impeccable charm hastened to greet us. "Heini and Adolph have been delayed by the atrocious weather; come in and join the fun. I'm sure you know everyone, Eva," she bubbled. I suddenly felt very small in a large roomful of important people.

Trying not to stare I took in my surroundings using peripheral vision, but my attention was quickly drawn to the dance floor.

From the moment we'd arrived, Eva and Gretl were swept up by the SS security detail, sweeping past time and again on a cloud of air as they laughed and flirted shamelessly in the immaculate black arms of their dance partners.

Once or twice Eva cast her funny little gummy grin in my direction and drained another flute with a toss of her new perm.

Chastened, I found a quiet place in the corner chatting with several regular stringers, none had been permitted to bring along their cameras. Without my Leica in my hands, I felt at loose ends and self-conscious around the extravagant Yuletide gaiety, while trying to avoid direct line of sight with Iris.

Almost immediately, one fellow had the cheek to quiz me on the contents of the boss' private files, which I avoided answering by moving away to inspect the candlelit shrine beside the hearth.

Bending over in search of familiar holy themes, I overheard one SS man joking above the strains of "Silent Night" that there would soon be more people going *up* the chimneys than coming down, but only his fellow officers caught his meaning and sniggered.

Like in millions of dedicated German households, the Hoffman Yuletide shrine comprised a framed postcard of St Nicholas on one side and an 8" × 10" of Hitler on the other: no sign of the Baby Jesus or Blessed Virgin Mary that Mam had forced us boys to kiss each Christmas morning. In this part of the world, it seemed a new god was rising.

At last, the clatter of jackboots and loud voices in the lobby; all leapt to their feet, saluting wildly with cries of "Heil Hitler" toward the guest of honour who was being ushered in alongside a tipsy Hoffman.

The Führer was berating his political opponents as "sissies" and "snivelling gentlemen" loud enough for all to hear. Then, casually, he nodded for all to be seated and the music to strike up again, momentarily locking eyes with those he recognised en route to the women's corner to kiss a few hands.

Passing my chair his gloves brushed lightly past my shoulder, and to this day I swear that something akin to a thunderbolt shot down my spine. Perhaps, as Claudia said later, it *was* merely static electricity, but I never believed it. No one seated nearby seemed to notice.

As Hitler and Hoffman stood admiring the oversized and over-decorated Spruce tree, two astonishing incidents occurred without warning to irretrievably sour the evening. Eva, by now almost delirious with happiness was unable to restrain herself; she tore away from her partner's arms and pounced on her lover, attempting to drag him onto the dance floor. With a hiss, Hitler wrenched himself free, pushing her away with such force that she fell backwards against the Spruce, squashing several gaily-wrapped packages. Before either could recover from the shock, a young starlet whom I'd not noticed before, took two steps forward and planted a bold kiss on Hitler's tight lips, before stepping back innocently with a little giggle, pointing to the sprig of mistletoe dangling overhead. "You see, my Führer," she cheerily recited her rehearsed lines, "it is a lady's prerogative to take the initiative under such circumstances ..."

"Madam! You call yourself a lady?" he bellowed, wiping his mouth on his sleeve and shooting daggers at the SS men now tearing themselves away from their dance partners. "Get her out of here, now!"

Then he turned seething towards Eva, who was being helped back to her feet, looking dazed, "And you, Fraulein Braun will kindly remember that I do not dance. Nor do I kiss any woman in public."

He spat little flecks of spittle down the front of her party dress.

From outside, a lone wail floated up past the perimeter guards, all now on full alert: "... but it's a ladies' prerogative ..." as the poor girl was bundled into a waiting SS vehicle. We heard the car door slam shut and a squeal of rubber in the distance.

Frau Hoffman was the first to speak, clapping her hands imperiously and commanding the three-piece band to resume. "The Führer will accompany my husband and I to the next room to freshen up," she informed the guests, who were already attempting awkwardly to pick up their threads of conversation.

"I've never been so humiliated in all my life," Eva complained when steered into the ladies' corner, trying to put on a brave face. "He treats his staff better than he treats me," she sniffled. "I ... I'm going to give him an ultimatum, and he's not going to like it." Now Henni was beside her, offering comfort.

"Otherwise, I'm through. I really mean it this time; six years, Christ!" This was the first time I'd ever heard the convent-educated girl swear. It seemed to me that her behaviour had started this ruckus after all, but she couldn't see it. I moved closer and sat down.

"A hard heart, that's what's needed ... And a thick hide," she slurred her words slightly. "And I have neither," she wailed again into a silk handkerchief, not wishing to face the piercing rejection she felt at that moment.

"Now now, Fraulein Eva; you caught the Führer off guard, that's all. I'm sure you are imagining the worst," Frau Hoffman said, drifting past. "This is no time to be wearing a long face, you're among friends here."

When Henni was called away to oversee the sauce for her famous Spaghetti Bolognaise, the two of us were left alone on the sofa. Eva's tear-stained face turned and sniffed that she didn't know why she felt compelled to share all her personal feelings with someone like me.

"I'm not going near the dance floor again. He tells me nothing and treats me like dirt in front of everyone. Every time I open a magazine there he is escorting one fancy woman after another. 'Just work', he says. I can't believe he's at it again. Oh Klaus, shall I never be rid of this feeling of loneliness?"

Without thinking, I placed an arm around her shoulder, too shaken to talk further or even look around. I don't remember much of what happened later that night after Eva blotted her copybook, only that I made my apologies and left early with Dante's phrase of "Having Lucifer by the tail" ringing inside my head.

As things turned out, that whole Yuletide season produced several other memorable moments. Using a studio voucher, I'd managed to obtain reservations for Robert and I for lunch the next day at the Carlton Tearooms. We had not exchanged more than a few words in many months and I anticipated lots of reminiscing, being especially eager to throw in a certain surprise for dessert.

"Did you see me riding on that gun carriage?" he began, typically talking about himself as we were shown to a corner table, "I mean, in the Riefenstahl movie of Nuremberg, dummy. Oh, forget it."

I vaguely recalled the dusty spectacle of SS Cavalry Divisions thundering around the arena in "Triumph of the Will" with teams of splendid war horses towing heavy Field Howitzers into mock battle.

"I ... er, I sort of remember that part, but it was hard to see anything much through the dust."

He grunted, rolled his eyes and proceeded to inform me that as one of the newer recruits he'd been granted the dubious and thrilling honour of holding onto the back of a speeding gun carriage as it hurtled in and out among the Wehrmacht's canvas decoy tank columns.

Now though, he looked positively splendid in his SS uniform. I felt compelled to move his cap with its grinning silver death head out of sight to a nearby chair. "You're gunna have to toughen up soon, liddle brudder; there's major plans afoot for all non-Aryans. Some of the tricks they're getting away with nowadays are even causing me to shy off," he said, eyes narrowing.

I had chosen the Carlton Tearooms in the hope they would provide a quiet, more relaxing venue for our long-overdue rendezvous. The place had lately regained something of its original ambiance since being boycotted by the rowdy stormtroopers in retaliation for management's refusal to have patrons stand and applaud during the Führer's frequent arrivals and departures.

Maybe, I hoped, our meal together could revive something of Mam's Christmas table traditions, when her ceramic Virgin with Child had taken pride of place in the centre of the table amidst the riverine largess.

"My, my ... from Baby Jesus to a Death's Head in just a few short years; whatever would Mam think of her bairn now?" I provoked, but Robert was already tucking into his Glazed Turkey Drumstick before I had a chance to say a quiet Grace or raise a toast to departed friends, of which there were growing numbers.

Between mouthfuls, it was impossible to resist his colourful tales of adventures past and present, as always enhanced to play himself as hero. He claimed to have been in the Honour Guard of Hitler's first-ever diplomatic mission abroad when he met with Mussolini in Italy. He even attended Hindenburg's funeral but neither contention was verifiable. "You'll just have ta take my word for it!"

I foolishly imagined we could compare notes over Röhm's death, which I considered as nothing less than cold-blooded murder; but for Robert, this was old news. "The S.A. is full of 'losers'; they've had it. From now on the SS will oversee Germany's future. The Führer says there will be no need for further revolution for a thousand years!"

"B ... But, I don't believe Ernst or Marty would ever have lifted a finger against him; you know how Ernst was always shooting his mouth off over one cause or another when he'd had a few drinks. To see our friends and so many others shot down like that; surely, it's enough to cause reflection of your own position?"

"Not if I'm to survive. Or you either, for that matter." He clicked his fingers for another stein of lager, "Come on matey, drink up. You never could handle the grog." He motioned towards my half glass of red wine. "And toss another couple of those drumsticks on our plates, will you Fraulein?" he said, slapping the waitress on the backside as she passed.

"Where was I? Oh yes, anyone not on the winning team will find many obstacles in his way. If I've learned one thing it is the futility of swimming against the tide. Sooner or later everyone will have to get used to the new Reich and its methods. You only have to look around to see the scope of change. All these massive building projects, motorways and the like don't just happen; they are part of a commanding vision. And I must say I'm proud to be part of it." He took a gulp of beer and burped loudly, causing some to look around and just as quickly turn away on spying the black uniform.

I tried to recount details of Aunt and Onkel's eviction, and the other ham-fisted horrors unfolding on the Obersalzberg, but he merely waved me off. "Bad luck for them, I'd say; being in the wrong place at the wrong time. You can't make an omelette without cracking a few eggs, eh? Anyway, they're not my relatives, they're yours. I have no soppy ties impeding my advancement and I intend going all the way.

"If you must know, it's Hitler's sheer audacity I admire, and I enjoy the companionship I've found in the SS; they're certainly a cut above those Brownshirt oafs." As he spoke he leaned forward, causing his scars to glow and the veins to stand out on his neck; he flaunted his scars as badges of honour from his "duelling days", and had almost convinced himself.

"And the girls, ooh la la. They go crazy over the uniform," he confided, adjusting his cuffs. "Jesus, last week a party of Bund Maidens arrived at the Brown House to take tea with the Führer, all in their hand-stitched dirndls, mind you; you'd think butter wouldn't melt in their mouths, gooing and cooing before their hero. One or two of us helped to requite their inflamed passions later on," he smirked. "Talk about hot! Did you know they are actually calling themselves 'Führer Brides' while trying to fall pregnant with SS studs?"

"Good Lord, you must be kidding. What happens to all the babies?"

"Lebensborn Homes! They book in a few weeks before they're due and Bob's your uncle; the cannon fodder of the future is farmed out among respectable German families to be raised as their own. Mind you, it's only the best SS stallions that get to enjoy these sorts of fringe benefits," he puffed himself up and waited for my further response. Such barracks language always made me squirm, and I refused to meet his eye.

"I prefer to express my physicality with someone I really like as a person," I replied, touching a nerve in the process.

"Balls! I bet I could count all your conquests on the fingers of one hand," he scoffed. "I assume you're referring to your imaginary love affair with Claudia? Don't worry, she's told me all about it," he let slip, relishing my discomfort.

"I can't deny it's you she wants," I responded, "but for the life of me I can't see why. Did you ever repay her your gambling debts? That money was supposed to be for a trip to Poland. It seems you've gone out of your way to treat her like … like scheisse." I was beginning to lose patience. "I can't understand how anyone could behave with such disrespect toward a woman of her calibre."

"Is that so? Have you also shared these feelings with the great Professor Hoffman? After all, he's the one who brought her into existence to share among his Party comrades. At least with me, she knows where she stands."

"Why don't you at least give her a chance? After all, you seem to have no problem charming the socks off everyone else …"

"In case you haven't noticed liddle brudder, that's a far cry from committing to the deep and meaningful entanglements you and so many women hunger after. Anyhow, what's it to you? Come on, everyone's motivated by self-interest."

It was exasperating that this arrogant belief in himself never faltered.

He leaned close again. "Well, old boy, in a sentence I've grown tired of her. As far as I'm concerned she's all yours; I've no intention of getting further entangled for that matter. My life is heading in a whole new direction …" His expression brooked no comeback and his eyes, which had dominated me throughout, suddenly flicked up.

"Well, of all the …"

"Season's Greetings and a merry Christmas to my two favourite boys."

I was jolted; having completely forgotten my planned surprise of inviting Claudia to join us for drinks after work. Given our earlier fraught exchanges I immediately regretted the decision, having naively imagined that it would be more honest, even cleansing, for the three of us to sit down and share a little Yuletide cheer over a festive drink together; but I hadn't been prepared for Robert's intransigence.

We both rose as she seated herself between us at the round table, immediately jumping up with a little squeal, clutching the SS cap with its glittering skull and crossbones. She tapped it lightly against the edge of the table, polished the peak with her sleeve and placed it carefully over the back of his chair. "There we are Robert, all good." She seemed in amazing good spirits.

For once, my brother looked a bit sheepish, avoiding Claudia's eye when I called for the wine list which she merely waved away, opting instead to join him in a stein of lager. I had to make the most of it, in the hope we could settle into some kind of mutual amity; a family arrangement of sorts.

If only Robert could understand how much we both craved his patronage and affection, ever ready to put aside the violent madness that had seized him in the past. Was there any chance we might yet make it through these curdling times together? Even emigrate somewhere?

Poland? Brazil? Australia? Anywhere! Just so long as it's not the Third Reich! For a moment, he looked puzzled. "I'll pretend we never had this conversation. I have my whole career ahead of me now, just when we are breaking free from the hated Versailles Treaty. You are sounding like those pigmies who imagine they can stop with a few phrases the gigantic renewal of a people's life: they're the Führer's words, by the way. Wake up to yourselves! The Fatherland is the new jungle, with new rules. Either adapt or go under, the choice is simple."

He had regained his composure ... "I'm not going anywhere, and if you know what's good for you this better be the last time your half-witted escape plan is ever raised." There was an awkward pause ...

"Well, that's good to hear, Robert," Claudia spoke again; leaning close and placing a live white hand on his forearm.

Her gaze was unwavering. "I've just found out I'm pregnant!"

BOOK ALPHA

52

The year 1938 came and went in quick succession, under a garnering cloud of repressed hopelessness and fear.

While I prayed for equanimity, milestone events in Nazi life flew by in a blur of printed images and fragmented memories, almost too numerous to recount. New laws carrying heavy penalties popped up like poison mushrooms, despite Hitler's oft-stated contempt for "artificial notions of law". These were aimed squarely at suppressing "malicious gossip, discussing murder with another person, wearing uniform without permission" and even "making fun of Party Leaders", each framed so broadly as to sweep up anyone straying from the Party line.

Inexorably, the screws continued to tighten on work-shy non-conformists and misfits who had evaded earlier dragnets. For ordinary Germans, perhaps tempted among friends to make light of the New Order, the thought of being carted off into "protective custody" without even a court hearing was striking dread into all but the stoutest hearts, particularly given the Gestapo relied almost entirely on informers and disgruntled citizens to provide grist for their insatiable penal system.

A formerly friendly neighbour suddenly filled with grim envy, or the work colleague passed over for a promotion may at any moment decide to settle old scores in the blockälteste's ear. Everyone now feared the crunch of jackboots on the stairs and the pounding of fists at the door in the early hours.

Many Volk looked the other way and put their hands over ears as their Jewish neighbours were booted into the street and led away in terror. Those remaining behind quickly fell upon the valuables and furnishings so hastily abandoned and some even moved holus-bolus into the vacant spaces thus created.

Anyone thus forcibly removed was automatically presumed guilty unless vouched for by the Nazi blockälteste; many of the older Jews had their beards hacked off, or even set on fire prior to their disappearing altogether.

Progressive towns and villages boasted their own Adolph Hitler Plaza, Street or Square, and schoolchildren saluted their Führer's portrait upon entering the classroom. "Führer, we belong to you!" cried the little ones in unison, to the growing dismay of many parents.

Even at home, older siblings saluted each other at the dinner table in the modern way. "Guten tag" was out and "Heil Hitler" was in, along with absolute obedience to any superior in uniform. Church Christenings were suddenly declared "unnecessary". Henceforth, swastika-draped fonts would suffice for newborn "Naming Ceremonies".

Hate-filled speeches now blared non-stop from People's Radio receivers in workshops, private homes and loudspeakers in public places; there was no way to escape the Party propaganda.

Thanks to postage stamp royalties and rocketing sales of *Mein Kampf* the Führer lost count of his personal riches. His turgid tome, which I'd forced myself to read from cover to cover, urged readers to "annihilate Bolshevists and Jews, punish France and grab Russia", among other equally grandiose pipe dreams.

Newlyweds were mandated to keep a copy beside the nuptial pillow and read a page or two together before turning off the light. Many Protestant church leaders openly advocated substituting *Mein Kampf* for the Bible. A national amnesia was gripping the Fatherland.

They say that no man is a hero to his own butler, and that might just as well apply to his personal photographer.

Heinrich Hoffmann, like Ernst Röhm before him, had been by Hitler's side through thick and thin and wasn't fooled for a minute by his pretence at divinity. Hoffmann masked his cynicism by praising his chief's "phenomenal knowledge of arts, history and finer military details" when in company.

The Führer was now riding the wave as the Number One Citizen *and* foremost Reich Art Connoisseur, honing his instinctive ability to size people up and know just what he could get away with.

He continued to jolly Eva that he was "nothing but a drummer and gatherer awaiting Christ" which of course, was music to the ears of the former convent schoolgirl who nearly swooned every time she heard this and other pithy axioms rolling off his tongue, hems such as "Words open the gates to a Peoples heart, like blows of a hammer" and "When people adore a genius, they release their inner strength". She often repeated these quotes word for word in the darkroom, closely watching for my reaction under the safelight. Certainly, she exuded more confidence these days, despite the slights and disappointments that kept coming.

Propaganda Minister Goebbels too, now reached his apogee of eloquence. His incongruous baritone pounded the airwaves by night and day, laying it on thick over the Führer's countless achievements, while warning of the growing threat from Jewish saboteurs and other parasites.

Gone was the need now for tens of thousands to pack into Circus Krone and similar spacious venues for their regular doses of enlightenment; the People's Radios were performing the task far more effectively.

"The longer one knows him, the more one admires him," gushed the Black Dwarf into his microphones, "he is a good man by nature, kind and modest; a friend to his comrades, having no vices. His capacity for work is extraordinary …"

Listening to these repetitious rants at work and on every street corner set my blood boiling. I felt sick at heart remembering Ernst, Marty and the hundreds of other "comrades" who had died so horribly on the orders of this same exalted genius; I knew I was trapped.

I was still churning out postcards from the '36 Berlin Olympics, which had stopped the nation and stunned the world with Germany's "astonishing regeneration".

Many international critics were soothed and reassured by the enticing propaganda campaign that had played out inside the 100,000-seat, purpose-built arena, while others were awed by the sheer scale of the event.

Having just received a 98% plebiscite approval from the German Volk, the Führer had arrived to a thunderous eruption of applause during his lap of honour in an open-topped tourer, dispelling any doubts as to his popularity. After all, had not he overseen Germany's miraculous economic revival?

News footage from the Games showed the adulation rolling on long after the Great Leader had climbed the steps to take his seat in the V.I.P. box. In his opening address, aimed jointly at the gathered ranks of army conscripts and the international audience, Hitler spoke of the "senselessness of war" before going on to exhort his budding warriors. "One can serve God only in the garb of hero. This glorious army is not dead; it has only slept and has risen again in *you*."

Those of us stuck in Munich had to rely on news bulletins, publicity photos and eyewitness accounts; all agreed, however, that one sour note occurred when Hitler had refused to shake the hand of Jesse Owens, the American negro victor in the 100 m and 200 m sprints *and* the long jump finals; trouncing his Aryan rivals in front of the world's media.

The new Germany had striven to put her best foot forward; swastika daubs and other slurs had been hastily removed from Jewish-owned store windows and the wave of evictions was halted. Malingerers, bums and beggars had simply vanished from Berlin's spotless streets.

Mercifully, our Munich studio had been spared the brunt of the printing avalanche, since Hoffmann had channelled his considerable Olympic output through the newer and larger Berlin establishment.

During those weeks of frenzied international activity, the boss and his band of stringers were shunted, blocked and scooped by dozens of alien cameramen daring to jostle for the best vantage points; only his access to the private box and after-hours activities kept him one jump ahead of the pack. Often fuming, he could sense the International Royalties slipping through his fingers.

Eva too, had set off for the Olympics in high spirits, hoping to make her first public appearance by the Führer's side. Instead, from the many press releases I saw, she was barely visible six rows back in the stand, lost among the secretaries and Nazi wives.

Upon her return to Munich, I'd pressed for more details, but at first, she wouldn't be drawn. Such snippets as did leak out smacked entirely of her personal frustrations, rather than any professional satisfaction. When handing over three rolls of 36 black-and-whites, she'd said little, merely asking to be notified when the proof sheets came off the dryer.

At first, I thought her camera must have malfunctioned; many shots were blurry, as if she hadn't been able to hold steady. One frame after another revealed only the back of Hitler's close-cropped neck surrounded by black uniforms and honoured dignitaries out of focus.

Only then, had I noticed the distinctive outline sitting beside the Führer: it was none other than Unity Mitford; in one frame leaning close to whisper something in his ear, and in others howling hysterically at his throwaway observations. Eva must have then descended the steps in frustration, catching a side-on shot of her love gleefully slapping a programme against his thigh while barracking for the home team.

Not once had he glanced in her direction.

"That was not a happy time for me, Klaus," she finally admitted when thumbing hurriedly through her proofs. "I might as well have stayed up on the Mountain; having to suffer that hard concrete seat for days on end while watching that gold-digging bitch pee her pants every time Adolph opens his mouth ... not to mention that herd of other bumkins attempting to touch the hem of his garment as they pass," she sniffed.

"Oh, I could just scream. That snooty *Unity* has the hide of a rhinoceros! Now she's ingratiated herself into Hoffmann's circle after Hitler made him supply a brand-new movie camera for her use during the Games. It's 'Heini this and Heini that', every time the boss turns around. Am I the only one not fooled by this ... this big horse, daring to pass herself off as a perfect specimen of Aryan womanhood?

"And then, to top it off, I find out that Henriette has been sharing her opera box with both the English interlopers, then has the nerve to tell *me* not to worry, that it's Unity who's jealous of *my* relationship with Adolph. Humph!"

Eva's insecurities were never far beneath the surface. "He just fobs me off when I try to share certain home truths about her Royal Highness *and* Leni Riefenstahl; that other skinny contortionist he so admires! May the Devil strike their names from my tongue?

"When I bring up sweet Leni's fling with Udet, Adolph's favourite combat pilot, right under his nose, he accuses me of 'gossiping'. Yet, *I'm* not even allowed to go skiing, or anywhere socially without a chaperone. Oh, Klaus, it's just so hypercritical and unfair."

Under the bright lamp that day I could see that Eva's "chocolate-box prettiness", as the boss once described it, was under strain.

Despite her film-star façade of never appearing twice in the same outfit or with a predictable hairstyle, there was loneliness in her eyes when she spoke, especially when affecting those "butter wouldn't melt in my mouth" gummy half-smiles. She seemed resigned to her role as mere material witness; while dreaming and scheming of how she might forever draw her elusive lover closer. Her denial of reality was almost complete.

During that hectic five-year period of "recovery and expansion" in the Munich Studio, my own routine had withered under the numbing pace of the Press Department, yet I seemed to be printing more postcards of Hitler than ever while the Regime was riding high. The world still clamoured for informal images of the enigmatic German Leader and even Gretl Braun had one or two personal candids published under the Hoffmann logo.

Notwithstanding, I did manage to squeeze in a riverbank picnic or two between my regular and Obersalzberg rosters, where the darkroom workload was much lighter. During such Alpine assignments, I was free to savour the surrounding snow-capped peaks and suck in the cool clean air, even wangling a night or two with Tante and Onkel at their Königssee boathouse. But oh, how my heart still ached for the fragrant symphony of a Jungle sunset.

Eva too, was spending more and more time at the Berghof, usually accompanied by her sister Gretl, a bevy of girlfriends and of course her two black Scotch-terriers Negus and Stasi, "hand-lickers", as Hitler called them.

Often her parents Fritz and Fannie accompanied her on weekends when the Führer was in residence, but despite her father turning out in a brand-new, custom-made Nazi uniform, Hitler remained polite but distant. Eva confided later that her parents felt "a little claustrophobic" in the guest quarters, and that Papa was already eyeing off the nearby chalets under construction for Göring, Bormann and Speer.

Sometimes, I would catch sight of the Brauns tagging along on Hitler's daily downhill stroll to the newly completed teahouse, which, with its tiny windows and two-foot-thick stone walls, looked to me more like a prison-fortress jutting out over the doll's houses in the valley below.

Here, a variety of herbal teas, cream cakes and other delicacies were served on the finest Dresden china featuring swastika motifs, being downed with solid silver cutlery purloined by Himmler. For a good half-hour after Blondie's jumping performance and obligatory Führer monologue, guests were required to talk in whispers while their host slid low in his comfy lounge chair for a customary nap.

Like their leader, few chose to tackle the return journey on foot, preferring to ride back aboard the growling fleet of armour-plated, open-topped tourers with their 400HP six-litre airplane engines.

Eva was particularly proud to show me her blue leatherette album of the recently completed Berghof interiors, all 30 rooms and three storeys (not counting the motor garage and darkroom) of Bormann's ham-fisted "renovations".

There was the 60' × 40' dining room and its stunning picture window, reportedly the largest in Germany, overlooking the Untersberg resting place of the great Barbarossa himself. In one corner Hitler could be seen cooing before his aviary of exotic birds, the squawking of which, Eva complained, "made normal conversation impossible".

One by one I turned the album pages to view the fourteen individual guestrooms, each featuring a Dürer or similar etching on one wall and the piercing portrait of Hitler over the dresser.

Eva's own "suite" was connected to Hitler's spartan quarters by an adjoining doorway and she took great pleasure in pointing out his brown satin bed quilt and matching silk pyjamas, with a bathrobe featuring embroidered swastikas hanging nearby. She confided that no photos were allowed in the Planetarium above, where the Astrologer Karl Ossietzky had supposedly designed a ceiling of dark blue glass, across which the Zodiac signs and planets slowly revolved at the touch of a button.

In the years I poked around Obersalzberg I was never once able to verify the existence of such a space. Indeed, each room appeared pretty much the same as the others, given Bormann's insistence on uniformity. A petite fifty-seat movie theatrette on the first floor boasted décor by Eva and featured nightly screenings of those latest Hollywood blockbusters banned elsewhere in Germany.

I'll never forget the excitement when Goebbels announced he had arranged a subtitled copy of *Gone with the Wind*, which played to packed houses. For weeks afterwards, Eva and her girlfriends responded to each other's questions with, "Frankly my dear, I don't give a damn," followed by side-splitting bouts of laughter. She seemed besotted by Scarlet O'Hara's sumptuous outfits and confident manner, apparently reviving her own on-again-off-again desire for stardom on the big screen.

"I have to admit, Klaus, a full moustache does look more appealing on Clarke Gable. Oh, what I'd give to play his leading lady," she commented blithely soon after its third showing in as many days.

"Well, I just can't see Clarke Gable with a schnurrbart," I replied without raising my eyes from the developing dish, "... and I think you would make an excellent Scarlet O'Hara, but seeing it's already been done in such grand fashion perhaps you would be wiser to stick to Tarzan's Jane."

"Well, tosh to you, Jungle Boy," she spoke to the back of my head. "I've already had sketches sent off to my dressmaker, so there! Adolph will fall off his chair when I do a full 360 twirl in all those petticoats," she responded light-heartedly before letting herself out.

During some sessions Eva managed to insert her own silent movie footage between the official newsreels, as a warm-up to the main feature, but was disappointed by the lack of enthusiasm: Braun family members, Eva's girlfriends and off-duty SS guards were shown clowning around, pulling faces or tipping each other into Lake Königssee's chilly waters.

Other clips had her contorting around tree branches in a swimsuit or performing reverse pushups by the water's edge; hardly nail-biting stuff for those waiting on Clarke and Scarlet. But despite her brief flurry of renewed interest, the driving ambition to play a leading lady on screen was no longer there.

Strangely enough, she rounded off the blue "Berghof" album by using Pressroom snaps of the Führer turning the first sod of a proposed dual motorway linking Salzburg to Vienna; and a group of Jewish women in fur coats being forced to scrub Berchtesgaden's sidewalks with their own toothbrushes. The third photo showed two policemen standing over the kneeling women and urinating on their heads.

Eva explained that she had merely wanted to fill the last page with something "less formal".

Little did we realise the reasoning behind this slick interstate artery until mid-March of '38, during the "Anschluss" takeover of Austria.

After that brazen and momentous event, no one in the newsroom was left in any doubt about Hitler's expansionist intentions.

Weeks earlier they say he'd worked over the Austrian Chancellor Schuschnigg after he reluctantly climbed the front steps of the Berghof, seeking a "peaceful way forward" for the two neighbouring countries.

The dictator met him in a dark mood, dispensing with all the usual niceties accompanying state visits. Hitler made it clear that the Anschluss *would* take place and demanded the chancellor's immediate resignation to make way for his National Socialist rival in waiting, Arthur Seyss-Inquart. His team would oversee all the arrangements, Hitler told Schussnigg, effective immediately.

The brow-beaten chancellor was then left alone to ponder his options, and when Eva returned from her Mountain excursion she relayed details of the poor man's second failed attempt to engage the Führer in a "civilised discussion".

"He was left for hours without food or drink, and it was finally up to me to order refreshments; I insist that all guests at the Berghof be treated properly," she reported, inhaling deeply and increasingly confident of her position.

Henceforth, she added, the Obersalzberg Guards had been ordered to salute her passing with the greeting "Heil, Kind Lady" anywhere within the sprawling compound, further infuriating Bormann and the housekeepers.

She further reported how the hapless Austrian Chancellor, when confronted by General Keitel looking like the very God of War came clattering into the conference room in full battle armour, including sword and spurs, grew faint when Hitler turned to his toady.

"Are my generals ready for war?"

Upon receiving a noisy stiff arm and Sieg Heil, the Führer proudly announced, "The whole operation will be directed by me!"

The gutted emissary scuttled back to Vienna in shock, not really grasping the inflexibility of Hitler's demands, and then had the cheek to call a plebiscite of the Austrian people in order to settle the question "once and for all". He was no doubt mindful that his predecessor, Engelbert Dollfuss, had been shot dead during an attempted coup by the Austrian Nazis in 1934.

Suddenly, newsreels across Germany were proclaiming the triumphal entry of the Wehrmacht into Vienna: crowds in the millions screamed their gratitude at once more belonging to a Greater Reich and Fatherland. Their prodigal son had returned home triumphant, with an army at his back, to absorb his long-abandoned homeland into the Reich with hardly a shot being fired.

Hysterical Austrians pressed against the barriers and spilled onto the roadway, leaving barely a car's width for their new Führer's motorcade to pass. Countless thousands more hung from trees and lampposts lining the parade route. Two days later, footage emerged of Hitler visiting his mother's grave in Leonding and even poking his head into his old classroom filled with barefoot urchins.

After all of Life's setbacks, Providence had come full circle.

Simultaneously, orders were issued for the immediate round-up of all Austrian Jews and other "traitors" who had resisted the Nazi takeover; Schussnigg himself was placed under house arrest.

International dailies trumpeted their approval.

There was a great commotion in the boss' office that day before Eva came pelting down the stairs barking orders right and left.

Her limousine would be arriving in five minutes, with Fritz and Fanny already on board for the trip to Vienna. All we heard was that she and her parents were being driven down to witness Hitler's "official" arrival in the Austrian Capital for "the biggest parade ever".

When her black Mercedes slid to a halt outside Studio Hoffmann we could see the rear luggage rack was already full. It seemed Fritz and Fanny would have to endure the long journey with Eva's suitcases piled up on the rear seat between them.

When they returned to Munich after several delirious days of wining and dining they were hoarse, having vehicle and chauffeur all to themselves for the return journey. Apparently, Eva had been invited to join Hitler's flight from Vienna to Berlin at the last minute.

"You'll manage!" she had rejoindered flippantly when Fritz and Fanny protested at not being invited, or even consulted.

Eva later boasted that Berlin's streets, including the New Reich Chancellery and her own quarters, had been a sea of flowers, with its Great Hall a veritable forest of exotic palms and pot plants.

Hitler's return to Munich was hardly less dazzling. Servants waited at the airport wearing magnificent uniforms with silver lanyards and medals on their chests. Tens of thousands lined the road into town, bands played "Deutschland, Deutschland Uber Alles", "Horst Wessel Song" and Hitler's favourite piece, the "Badenweiler Marsch".

The next morning, at his Prinzregentenstrasse apartment for the first time Eva could remember, he rose at 8 am on the dot. She noted him lingering before a full-length mirror, adjusting his gold-embroidered cap and brown tunic with the Iron Cross First-Class, seeming pleased with what he saw. Straightening his tie one last time and wiping back his drooping forelock, the triumphant Führer settled the cap squarely on his freshly scissored cranium and descended into a forest of stiff arms and hearty Heil's.

Fawning felicitations followed from a long line of Party Grandees and chastened commanders who'd been proven wrong once again by their Führer's audacious victory. They grovelled shamelessly.

At their head stood Göring, proud from head to dainty toe with a chest full of medals and ribboned crosses. A thick gold chain, a gift from the King of Sweden, was draped over one shoulder and the Order of the Golden Fleece, awarded by Franco for the help accorded by Göring's "Condor Legion" against a resurgent Spanish Republic, gleamed at his throat. Heavy artillery and tanks roared past outside and a squadron of the latest aircraft not previously seen in all of Europe droned overhead.

That evening Hitler received a final conga line of well-wishers, after which Eva hoped to have him to herself when the tempo subsided. At first, things seemed to be going according to plan, when out from the crowd stepped none other than Leni Riefenstahl, whose star Eva had figured was on the wane. The multi-award winning director stopped a few yards away, staring at her Führer with wide-eyed steadfast gaze, before suddenly from her livid lips came a piercing shriek. Quickly covering her face with her hands, she composed herself and stammered in a scarcely audible voice, "My Führer ..."

Then, to Eva's disgust, she launched herself tearfully at her idol and thrust an enormous bunch of carnations toward him with both hands. A stone-faced

Hitler took the flowers and passed them to an aide, before offering his arm to lead her into the music room filled with well-wishers.

In the crowd that night was the Party's newest convert, a dashing Fritz Braun who'd realised that he was being outsmarted on all fronts. He had spoken resignedly to Fanny during the long ride home from Vienna, "It's too late now, Mutti, the Bratwurst is out of the bottle and our baby girls are in the hands of Fate. We can be thankful that two out of three, at least, are well connected to the Regime; and of course, with the Führer guaranteeing our pensions for life."

Since joining the Party, Fritz had received an unexpected promotion. "Things could be a lot worse, Herr Headmaster," Fanny purred, settling down on the limo's generous backseat with her head in his lap. Soon they were both snoring.

53

I occasionally took the mail train down to Berchtesgaden, at other times in one of the sleek official limousines that plied the round trip, sometimes lucky to catch a lift back to Munich along the upgraded route above Lake Chiemsee, where five thousand bare-chested "volunteers" had been slogging away with pick and shovel for many months.

On the outskirts of Seebruck and Obing, I'd noticed fresh signs announcing "Jews not wanted here", and one new warning at the winding section: "Drive carefully, sharp curve – Jews 75 M.P.H."

I was also surprised to find the quaint Berchtesgaden railway station had been remodelled almost overnight, with the addition of an exclusive "Führer Platform" to handle the *Amerika* and the other Nazi private trains.

The swelling numbers of sight-seers were being diverted via separate gates, where those with binoculars could check and see if the giant swastika flags were flying over the Berghof; a sure sign that their beloved Führer was indeed at home.

In record time the Mountain retreat had been converted into a third seat of Government, nick-named the "Grand Hotel" by Eva, towards which most of the top Nazis were now beating a path. Someone whimsically suggested that "Temple on the Heights" may be more suitable. Renovator Bormann's sole sensitive architectural achievement up to that point was the aforementioned retention of Hitler's time-honoured den, the "Dietrich Eckhart Room" in the demolished Platterhof Hotel. The more the Mountain Gauleiter gratified his master with such thoughtful and expensive gestures, the greater his powers and the hatred of the other staff grew.

Adding insult to injury, Eva was often required to enter the dining room on Bormann's "fat brown arm", as she described it, while the Führer chatted breezily with one or other of the Nazi wives.

489

The Mountain Gauleiter habitually butted in on private conversations and made clear attempts to steer Hitler in certain directions. He craftily employed a team of readers to keep him abreast of the latest publications, which he could then recommend over dinner.

"My Führer, you really must read so and so; it accords perfectly with your own designs."

Hated by most he may be, but Hitler marvelled openly at Bormann's seeming infinite capacity for work and thought him a genius. After 1936, the powerful Party Secretary took the bold step of banning most other leading personalities from uninvited visits to the Berghof.

When Eva refused to partake of the Führer's unappealing vegetable diet, claiming to be already sufficiently "trim and healthy", the Mountain Gauleiter went a step further by announcing that henceforth he too, would share his Führer's fare of broth and dumplings.

Behind the scenes, however, the catering staff soon discovered the rotund martyr helping himself to huge servings of cutlets, chops and sausages smothered in beef gravy from the kitchen; although not one dared breathe a word of this to the Führer.

Despite the carefully vetted menu and his bevy of "tasters", Hitler began to suspect he was being poisoned. His stomach troubles grew steadily worse, much to the discomfort of bystanders, and even Dr Morell's "anti-gas" pills seemed to be losing their efficacy.

Yet, it would take a brave soul indeed to suggest opening a window or wiping a watery eye in his presence.

Eva, like everyone else gathered before the evening hearth, had no option but to ignore the sounds and smells, laughing it off when her man cast blame on one or other of the German Shepherds stretched at his feet. She wondered if he allowed himself such liberties when in the company of Frau Wagner, or Lady Mitford's circles.

The good Dr Morell had been summoned down from his Kurfürstendamm V.D. Practice to treat Hoffmann, a long-standing patient who had fallen gravely ill with an unknown ailment. When Hoffman's life was miraculously and suddenly restored, Dr Morell was conscripted immediately, along with his many potions, to remain at the Führer's side until further notice.

For a while, it seemed "Professor" Morell's concoctions (for the job came with a promotion), did put a spring in the Führer's step, allowing more enjoyment of his diplomatic triumphs and a boost in energy for the daring moves that lay ahead.

The professor and his wife soon began appearing together on the Berghof terrace and became regular fixtures. Other staff members were encouraged to seek Morell's potions and rejuvenating injections for all manner of ailments, while Frau Morell, who was not quite so portly as her horn-rimmed husband, was still feeling her way in the rarefied atmosphere, conscious of being surrounded by numerous lithe figures in swimsuits who lolled about in deck chairs and chatted easily among themselves.

Now and then one of Eva's friends would comment on the physique of a white-uniformed SS waiter, loud enough for all to hear. It seemed to Frau Morell as if Eva's companions spent their days working through the strapping SS staff and guard units stationed nearby, so she certainly wouldn't be taking any lip from that quarter.

Then, out of the blue, I was instructed to retrieve the "Gruhn" dossier, which had been ticking away in the boss' Private Archive.

For those of us keeping an ear to the ground, rumours abounded that a major shake-up of the armed forces leadership was afoot.

Following the nationwide conscription of young men, the eviscerated Reichswehr had quickly blossomed into a fully-fledged Wehrmacht Army of several hundred thousand, led by the lachrymose General Blomberg.

Concurrently, Göring's freshly blooded Luftwaffe was already honing its next generation of pilots in secret, both at home in so-called Gliding Academies, and in the skies above sympathetic Spain and Russia. His "Condor" Legion was perfecting its tactics above the battlefields of Spain's Civil War, drawing worldwide condemnation for its merciless bombing of the tiny Basque town of Guernica during a "training" sortie.

At that time Hitler notoriously took a keen interest in the married lives of his associates, matchmaking or undermining according to his fancy. For starters, he ordered his new driver Erich Kempka to divorce his wife if he wished to remain behind the wheel of the growling six-wheeler, simply citing her "unacceptably loose morals".

We found out later that the formerly happy couple did pretend to go through the motions while seeing each other in secret. Conversely, the Führer forbade Joseph Goebbels from divorcing Magda, the "Official Reich Hostess" who had already presented the hobbling minister and nation with six delightful blond children in rapid succession.

In this case, dissolution was unthinkable, given all Magda's hard work earning the Nazi Party's highest female honour; a golden "Motherhood Badge" bestowed only on those women bearing six or more children.

Despite this admonition from above, the "Goat of Babelsburg" as he was now known, remained distracted elsewhere, foolishly stepping out in public several times with one Lidar Baarova, a Czech actress who had recently graduated from the casting couch with flying colours.

Following Magda's tearful pleas, Hitler was adamant: The wayward Minister would return to the family home and the would-be usurper was sent packing back to whence she came.

During all this meddling, nowhere did the beam of intrigue focus more acutely than on War Minister Blomberg and his new bride, Erna Gruhn, some forty years his junior. When tying the knot with full military honours on January 12, 1938, General Blomberg had chosen Göring to be the best man and Hitler as a witness. The bride's name rang a bell and I recalled printing up two sets of 8" × 10" glossies for Hoffmann; startling images that had until that very hour remained under lock and key. It was soon revealed that the new Frau Blomberg had a long police record for prostitution, not to mention selling pornographic postcards of herself.

Iris instructed me to deliver the Gruhn file immediately to Gestapo Headquarters in the Wittelsbacher Palais, from whence they would be forwarded to Himmler in Berlin.

Later that month, when the deliriously happy General Blomberg returned from his cruising honeymoon, looking fresh and youthful when fronting up for his new orders, an infuriated Hitler laid out the whole sordid collection of prints before him.

His beloved Führer demanded that in view of the Army's impeccable moral standards the marriage must be annulled immediately.

When the stunned groom refused he was relieved of his command on the spot. Folding and pocketing the evidence in silence, General Blomberg spun on his heel to leave. They say he walked right past the open door of his car in a daze.

His replacement, General von Fritch, fared little better, being also removed soon after appointment by yet one more Gestapo sting. This impeccable career officer was flabbergasted to find himself falsely and publicly accused of a homosexual encounter in a city lavatory with one "Bavarian Joe". By the time fellow officers cleared his name, General von Frisch's reputation and career, like his predecessor's, had been eviscerated.

These manoeuvres left the way clear for Hitler to appoint himself Commander-in-Chief to exert absolute authority through the mouth of his frontman, General Wilhelm Keitel.

Long considered a fool by many in the army leadership, no one was more surprised than Keitel himself when Hitler named him Supreme Commander of the Wehrmacht, second only to the Führer, a move that infuriated far more competent career officers who promptly nicknamed the obsequious officer, "Lakeitel" (Hitler's lackey).

Many questioned how a Great Leader could even consider, let alone tolerate, an apple-polishing "advisor" such as Wilhelm Keitel in constant proximity. But it was soon apparent that Lakeitel's speedy promotion to Generalfeldmarschall and "Chief Enforcer" effectively allowed the dictator a completely free hand behind the scenes.

Throughout peace and war by his master's side, Keitel dispensed the Führer's heinous commandments for seven long years, without fear or favour, bowing and scraping his way towards a Nuremberg scaffold.

Nowhere did the pair sink lower than in their drafting of Hitler's infamous "Nacht und Nebel" (Night and Fog) decree of WW2, which stated that all known political activists and resistance fighters in occupied territories were to be immediately imprisoned, killed or simply made to "disappear".

Keitel was hanged for war crimes in October 1946, after unsuccessfully pleading that he had been "merely following orders".

But to return to Obersalzberg: thanks to Reichsleiter Bormann's brutal efficiencies, most of the "renovations" had been completed by 1938, including the "Leader's Exclusive Territory", now comprising 650 acres of upward rolling meadows dotted with ancient Linden copses, all contained within two encircling rings of steel mesh fencing and anti-aircraft artillery.

Sprawling barracks now stood where flocks of sheep once grazed, behind an outer radius of approximately twenty miles in length and an inner of two, encompassing the former expanse of a once contented and self-sufficient community. No signs of prior occupation remained inside the wire and concealed minefields ruled out cross-country incursions; occasional explosions marked the passing of an unsuspecting deer.

Tante Gretel was attempting to keep me up to date via a series of letters hand-delivered to the front desk, with coded instructions to burn them immediately after reading. At first, she fearlessly recounted details of the former mountain villagers' fate, and of the photographer Brandner's "special handling" in Dachau after he'd dared approach Hitler. She said that all told, Bormann had overseen the removal of 35 private homes besides Chalet Hahn, 18 farms, 3 inns, 6 B&B, several hotels and local businesses including Herr Brandner's Photo Studio.

If this could happen to Hitler's own neighbours, she lamented, it could happen to anyone. After numerous appeals and written apologies from Herr Brandner's 13 sisters and a family doctor, the young photographer was eventually released from Dachau after two years, with his head shaved and front teeth missing; a mere shadow of his former self.

His siblings had to promise that they would help their brother "turn into a useful German citizen". Tante wrote that young Hansi was now a broken man living in Berchtesgaden with his family, not daring to speak of his ordeal. Above the dining table in the Brandner lodgings hung a small plaque: "Walls have ears."

"So much for all the hoo-ha over so-called Aryan Values. Even your Onkel Fedi has come to realise the extent of Nazi hypocrisy since we were booted off the mountain." She enclosed a local newspaper clipping which was brief and to the point: "ANYONE SPREADING GOSSIP about Obersalzberg evictions will be declared an enemy of the State."

On a lighter note, she included a snap of Onkel Fedi in lederhosen with his "goose in a suitcase" being fattened for our next get-together, which she hoped would be soon, "or Onkel will have to find a larger suitcase." Apparently, several times each day he would move the contented goose to fresh pickings, where its long neck could reach out and browse through a small hole in one corner, without exerting a single fibre of its coddled flesh. A second convenient opening at the rear end provided a space for waste to shoot out and fertilise the freshly nibbled patch of grass.

She explained that this was an old Bavarian custom to tenderise and fatten festive geese, and added that Onkel Fedi was almost back to his old self since resigning from the local branch of the Party. She hoped the photo would give me a laugh. She was concentrating on her painting and not missing the high meadows as much as she thought she would.

Despite having witnessed the forced evictions of the entire community, Tante Gretel expressed disgust that local members of the Obersalzberg Shooting Club still gathered at the Führer's gate on New Year's Eve to discharge their blunderbusses across the valley.

"Have they no shame? We can hear their racket bouncing along the entire length of the lake, but now for the first time it feels so threatening; like Odin himself belching thunder from the clouds.

As you know I don't go along too much with all that mythical warrior twaddle.

Do try and come down as soon as you can.

Love, Tante and Onkel XXX (one kiss from the goose!)

As instructed, I kept the pictures and burnt the text.

The year 1938, however, was far from over. No sooner had the dust settled in Vienna than Hitler began agitating for the return of Czechoslovakia's German-speaking minority in the Sudetenland, along the joint border, which if granted, would mean the effective dismemberment of that proud tiny nation.

He launched vitriolic calumnies during the Nuremberg Rally in September, declaring the Czech Government to be an "illegitimate construct of the hated Versailles Treaty", and of subjecting the Sudeten Germans to "unbearable pressures in their daily lives".

A series of realistic war games, interspersed with countless thousands of Jung Bund Madels in white smocks holding hands while performing their predictable gymnastic routines, played out before the besotted multitude. As part of the myth-confirming machinery, the sacred Blutfahne was once more trotted out to inspire new military formations, confirming that communal identity had been consolidated at last. Nonetheless, Propaganda Minister Goebbels cynically muddied the waters with his speech reiterating that "Germans want only peace".

But most galling of all from Studio Hoffman's perspective was his rival Hugo Jaeger setting up a team of photographers from *Life* magazine, who stunned the world daily with their spectacular full-colour images. Colour movies had also come into their own, flooding international newsreels with footage from every conceivable viewpoint.

Team Hoffman had been dealt a crushing blow.

That summer, Czech President Hacha was summoned to the Berghof and subjected to an unusually violent tirade; only this time Hitler's victim fainted clean away and had to be revived with an injection from Dr Morell.

Like Schussnigg before him, the diminutive Czech Chancellor foolishly believed that Britain and the European powers would not stand by in the face of German hegemony. Like the former Austrian Chancellor, he was wrong.

I was required to develop Hoffman's photos of the occasion. They clearly showed Hitler's outrage at the turn of events, and after forcing Hacha to sign the secession document the Führer again spurned the advice of his generals and took another leap of faith.

On September 15, 1938, at 5 pm, British Prime Minister Chamberlain climbed the Berghof's steps with cap in hand and umbrella hooked over one arm, still light-headed following his first-ever airplane flight.

No matter his private thoughts on meeting the dictator – "Hitler was 'the commonest little dog' I ever met," he confided later – the British Prime Minister was here to do a deal.

After all, the several million Sudeten Czechs in question *did* speak the German tongue and mostly "saw themselves as German" anyway. Both the Prime Minister and French Premier, Daladier, were war-weary, quickly agreeing that Czechoslovakia was hardly worth doing battle over.

There followed several more flights across the channel before the infamous "Munich Agreement" was signed; ceding vast swathes of Czech land without so much as a nod toward President Hacha and his horrified Government. Former agreements guaranteeing Czech sovereignty were simply brushed aside.

Mussolini arrived just in time to affix his signature to the document and reinforce Germany's demands. Hermann Göring turned up as "Master of the Hunt", in full accoutrement, hanging around to see ink on paper and rubbing his pudgy fingers with glee. The corpulent "Hunt Master" bore little resemblance to photos I'd printed of that former steel-eyed aviator of the Great War.

Newsreels worldwide showed Chamberlain's return to England, holding his scrap of paper high before a grateful British public. "I have here Chancellor Hitler's signature guaranteeing that our two nations will never again go to war against each other," he bleated into a keen wind whipping off the tarmac.

It seemed that almost everyone in Britain, except Winston Churchill, breathed a collective sigh of relief. In the Studio Press Room, stories and photos emerged of Sudeten Jews being beaten up and dumped at the Czech border, forced to crawl across on hands and knees and warned never to return to the Reich.

The Peoples' Radio announced that Germany's remaining Jews were forbidden henceforth from driving on any motorway "built by German hands", and compelled to add "Sarah" or "Israel" to their given names on all written documents.

Hitler, of course, was jubilant, conquering yet more territory and millions of loyal followers without firing a shot. His contempt for his timid generals knew no bounds. "I could see Chamberlain was shitting his pants! … If I took your advice we'd never have seen an end to this business. No longer does a German have to be ashamed of being German," he stated gleefully.

The Studio was abuzz with excitement. Adolph Hitler began appearing on magazine covers worldwide and was about to be chosen *Time* magazine's "Man of the Year".

Also seizing the moment, Unity Mitford set off with her sister through the conquered territories in her imported Baby Austin, flying her trademark Nazi swastika and Union Jack side by side. She spoke publicly of a "Grand Alliance between Germany and Great Britain", sharing her dream of "an impregnable alliance between the ruler of the seas and the Lord of the earth".

The Führer, impressed with this initiative, now referred to the Britisher as "Lady Mitford", mollifying a miffed Eva by confiding that she alone had been elevated to "first in his Will".

After all, hadn't he issued Fritz with a rare "Green Card" that allowed him to socialise with the Old Fighters?

When Eva arrived at the studio loaded down with gifts from Mussolini, she was astonished that he'd guessed her shoe and jacket sizes perfectly; she threw me a surplus alligator skin wallet which I carry to this day. Most items had been monogrammed EB, using a design by Dr Brandt, Hitler's surgeon, who fancied himself as creative.

She further implied that Adolph was merely being "sarcastic" over Lady Mitford, as "he would do anything to gain more information on England".

She spoke of her first visit to "Eagle's Nest", the Mountain Gauleiter's latest adjunct to the mountain fortress, in the company of Hitler and the French diplomat François-Poncet. This creation was all part of the miniature castle-fortress designed and erected at enormous cost and effort as a 49th birthday gift to the Führer.

While there she'd learned that German troops were marching into the Sudetenland, formerly Czechoslovakia, and expressed delight that Adolph had at last freed even more German Volk from their "unbearable oppression".

She raved over the elevator that whisked twenty persons at a time up through the granite massif to alight in a semi-circular dining hall with a view like no other and went on to describe in great detail the 360-degree panorama. She showed me photos of her bedroom behind its metre-thick walls, confiding that it would be "far too spooky" to ever stay up there alone.

"Naturally, Bormann took all the credit," Eva sniffed, "… but at least I got to choose the curtains."

54

I n far-off Paris, a Jewish teenager whose parents had been brutalised by the Gestapo was apprehended soon after gunning down the German Ambassador.

This was the moment the Propaganda Minister had been waiting for. He whipped up the Brownshirts and the general population to a level of fury against Jews and Jewish businesses not seen before. Newspapers and radio announcements incited the Volk to take the law into their own hands; within hours a thousand synagogues were torched across the land and their sacred contents trampled underfoot.

Jewish homes were plundered and countless store windows were smashed. Jews caught outdoors were severely beaten and over four hundred were kicked to death in the streets. Tens of thousands more were rounded up and packed off to concentration camps, where they were made to run brutal welcoming gauntlets under the new SS administrators.

For good measure, Göring levied a collective fine of one billion Reichsmark on the total Jewish population, to pay for the clean-up and for "defiling German blood". Following this unprecedented wave of destruction, most of us in the studio were walking on tenterhooks, particularly after Claudia came under suspicion on the street.

She had been saved only by her Press Card bearing Hoffmann's personal signature and told how she had been photographing street clashes on her way home, managing to evade the Gestapo pimps who scoured the crowds looking for Jewish sympathisers.

She said a Jewess being dragged along by the hair suddenly tore free and pointed her out, crying, "She's one too! I swear I've seen her in the synagogue. Why should I be taken when she's free to walk the streets?"

"I tried to explain that I didn't know her but at that moment she was felled with a rifle butt and dragged away. A Gestapo agent in a hat and trench coat appeared at my side, demanding to see my papers. I tell you, Klaus, it was a near thing. They're no longer running just a cursory eye over us; they mean business. It took them long enough to verify Hoffmann's signature.

"That woman was mistaken, but for the first time I felt afraid for my life; that same bottomless dread being felt by all those stripped of their homes and dignity, deracinated on the streets before gawping mobs. Whatever is to become of the children? At least I get to catch some of it on film; who knows what justice such photos may deliver down the track?"

I agreed to stash her negatives secretly in the boss' Private Archive, where the Gruhn file used to be.

Despite the smoking ruins, the broken glass strewn from one end of Munich to the other, and the countless photos taken nationwide, both Eva and Hoffmann denied that anything too drastic had occurred, passing off the rampage as a "storm in a teacup". Eva had recently returned from Obersalzberg, where she'd been thrilled to sit beneath a full moon at Hitler's side on November 18.

Earlier that morning there had been an eclipse, which she took as a good omen, but no one had been game to awaken the Führer.

"What was it old Ernst used to say? 'You can't make an omelette without cracking a few eggs,' eh!" the florid-jowled Hoffmann chortled.

"You just do your work, that's all, and let the Führer worry about what's going on in the streets. No one will dare touch *my* staff."

During the ensuing mayhem, Hitler did give a long speech that failed to mention "Kristallnacht" at all, a name already coined to describe the sea of broken glass littering city streets. The photos we developed showed only too clearly the extent of the damage.

"The Jews have only themselves to blame. All of us can only survive if we do not let the world see our mistakes. No one who went through war wants to repeat the experience," the Führer said evasively, sidestepping any mention of the nationwide upheaval. "Now I am ice cold. I am totally indifferent to what the future thinks of the methods I've had to use. I am committed by duty to my people alone, to nobody else."

When the full extent of destruction and injuries became known it was clear that we had turned an ominous corner.

"The man is a vulgar demagogue, Klaus, nothing less. He'll bring suffering and grief to all before he's through," Claudia was really bagging Hitler in the privacy of the darkroom. "I've observed him for hours on end; that pimp's forelock, the hoodlum elegance, the interminable speechifying complete with wild gesticulations, his foaming at the mouth and those shifty, staring eyes … I could go on and on.

"Perhaps worst of all, the Hitler Youth has a stranglehold over the youngsters, teaching them to hate their parents if they are not loyal Nazis. 'Your child belongs to us already,' he boasts.

"It seems to me they've taken a leaf straight out of Lenin's cookbook. 'We must hate! Hatred is the basis of Communism,' Lenin said and I can see now that National Socialism is no different. When will Germans wake up to what's really going on? He's sent in his army to take over the rest of Czechoslovakia and who is there to lift a finger? Dear God, I fear my own beloved homeland may be next."

Sissy was agitated spouting her heartfelt views, and I warned her about thin walls. "Hah! At least they won't get my dear flesh and blood; that abortion was probably the best and worst decision of my life.

"I should have known your libertine brother would sidestep his responsibilities when the time came. 'Just sign into the Lebensborn Clinic,' he said. 'Lie back and take it easy. Let them take care of everything. How do I know it's mine anyway?' he had the nerve to ask. I told him we girls just know such things.

"It was a boy, by the way," she added matter-of-factly, looking away, "… imagine what would have happened had they pried behind my married name? As if I would feed the Nazi beast with Schicklegruber flesh and blood, just to provide one more little bastard to dress up in their dog-shit-coloured uniform.

"Well, I was having none of it and it's broken my heart ever since. No girl should ever have to face such choices." This was the first time she'd opened up about the pregnancy and its aftermath, and I could clearly see the anguish in her once-bright eyes.

Come January, when Robert left town with a hundred other professionally trained speakers on an SS recruitment drive – their program touched upon, I later learned, "The Jewish Question: How they lied; how they deceived" – she cursed him to the heavens. Perhaps for the first time, my friend was seeing him for what he was. That must have been the final straw in her making the terrible decision to seek out a potion from Dr Morell.

I sighed and caught her lowered eye, feeling that now the time was ripe to lay my cards on the table. "Beloved Claudie, can I call you that? I want nothing more than to enjoy these times we have together. I want to protect you, and I promise to never make you feel uncomfortable. I don't care about all that other stuff Hoffmann makes you do, but it won't be forever. He used to be my hero too, but now I see only his pact with the Devil. Soon our turn will come to make a fresh start and put all this darkness behind us."

She looked incredulous. "Oh dear, dear Klaus. That sounds quite like an unwanted marriage proposal. Can't you see? This *is* the way things are now, and if Hitler gets his way it will be for the next thousand years. It's becoming ever harder for my friends in the Orchestra to make an impact. When the time comes, each of us must be prepared to lay down his life for freedom."

I gulped, unsure whether I'd ever have the courage to go quite that far.

"Meanwhile, we must each in our own way cater to these pigs and hope to Heaven that we may be of service to the Great Cause when called upon. You're right! You and I should spend more time together. Robert has made his bed and he can damn well lie in it. He tore the very skin off my grief, accusing me of having bad breath and thick ankles; you know that's a lie, don't you Klaus?"

I felt proud that she really was confiding in me and replied that her breath was sweet and her ankles had always looked just fine to me. She hinted that I'd been right about Robert all along.

"When I demanded to know what other women had to offer, he merely replied that we all look the same with our faces unwashed. It's just so infuriating. He'd better not come crawling back to me when things go awry.

"If I go down, he goes down; and I'll make damn sure everyone knows he's been consorting with the enemy. It seems every woman but me is now his 'darling'. He can go on playing cops and robbers with his new pals for all I care. And there'll be a few red faces among the boss' high-falutin cronies, too."

It was as if the floodgates had opened and she'd finally let out years of painful memories. I remembered the quote that "fascination does not reside in formal beauty" and drank in her new sagacity, hoping to consolidate my gains.

She returned my earnest glance for glance; this troubled Polish beauty who had simply wanted more and had found out the hard way what it took to survive in Nazi Germany. I knew not to comment further. In this case, Goethe was wrong: her mystery was also a miracle. I would never forget that glorious surprise she had sprung on me beside the Isar.

Two weeks before Hitler's 50th birthday in 1939, all Germans were exhorted to decorate their houses in readiness; woe betides anyone not displaying at least one swastika in his window.

Closer to the day, colour prints showed thousands of huge banners dangling from tall buildings in every town and city, like portentous sails dipped in blood, gestating their white eggs filled with spinning embryos that threatened to burst out and engulf the world.

Goebbels took to the airwaves on April 19, asking the Nation to join him in a prayer to Almighty God. "May He grant the German peoples' deepest wish to keep the Führer in health and strength for many more years and decades," before issuing specific instructions on how the church bells were to be rung.

At midnight, the mountain of "Führer gifts" began to be unwrapped, including a two-metre-long birthday cake baked in a specially constructed oven, but nothing could compare with Architect Speer's scale model of "Germania's" (for such was Berlin to be renamed) proposed 117-metre "Arch of Triumph", a structure to dwarf anything left behind by Napoleon or Roman Emperor.

Hitler stood glassy-eyed before the plywood and papier-mâché city laid out on a huge tabletop, bending down and around to examine it from every angle. Sometime later, when Speer showed off the completed model of Germania to his father, a noted architect, the old man just shook his head and declared them all "stark raving mad".

Following two full days of pomp, flag waving and special events, including Berlin's biggest-ever parade over five hours long, Hitler retreated to the Berghof for the remainder of the summer, secretly mustering his generals and planning for war. After fifteen years of groundwork, he was ready to mount his chariot of fire and lead them into Hell.

On the other hand, Eva and her coterie believed that Germany's rush of blood to the head was over, and we were looking forward to "at least twenty years of peace".

Indeed, the Führer actually declared himself "Dictator of Peace", enjoying "the happiest time of my life".

"We move through the world as a peace-loving angel, but one armed with iron and steel," he added menacingly. "So far, Germany has engaged only in 'flower wars'."

All the while he whipped up the nation with delusions of grandeur.

While Eva busied herself in her expanded "hostess" role, she inevitably incurred the envy of those other petty despots with a stake in the Grand Hotel. Bormann, together with Dr Morell, hatched a plan to knock her out with an injection and give her a "thorough examination" for her own good. This humiliating proposal was only thwarted at the last minute by the chambermaid, Ada Hocher, who happened upon the unconscious and partly undressed patient just as the private examination was getting underway.

Alerted by the ensuing racket, Dr Brandt rushed in and prevented things from going further without Hitler's express permission. He saw at a glance that the interest of the pair was impertinent and indecent rather than medical.

When Eva came round she was appalled to think that the two men she most despised had come so near to unlocking her closest secret. She never again consented to treatment at Dr Morell's hirsute hand, and Bormann fired Frau Hocher.

For weeks afterwards, Eva crept about the place like a wounded animal, keeping to herself. She chose to persevere with Negus and Stasi's "obedience" training, despite her empty expression betraying the degree of trauma with which she was wrestling.

Eventually, she sidled up to me in the darkroom and following a few halting false starts, opened her heart with all its bruises, beginning with archrival Unity Mitford.

"I suppose you heard about the big Amazon coming down with double pneumonia at Bayreuth? It's a pity they didn't let her die. Apparently, while all the bigwigs were up there for the opera season, Magda decided to engage in a half-baked romance with Karl Hanke; if you ask me it was just to get back at the Black Dwarf. She made a real spectacle of herself sobbing uncontrollably through 'Tristan and Isolde'; everyone noticed.

"This is one and the same 'Official Hostess' Adolph chooses to oversee his Berlin soirees. I'm just so sick of playing second fiddle at one boring parade after another; they all look the same to me. We're supposed to be approaching a 'war footing'; war against whom I might ask? Surely Adolph's already achieved more than anyone thought possible?

"Worse still, Goebbels is talking of banning electric hair dryers, colours and permanent waves for the duration; I've never heard anything so ridiculous. He keeps repeating that French lipsticks are made from the fat scooped off the top of Paris' sewers but of course that just makes us girls all the more determined to use them.

"It seems that German women wearing trousers are out! And Hoffmann insists we hold the staff picnic this year on the slopes above Eagle's Nest, where there's no opportunity for a dip and the wind plays havoc with our hair. He says he prefers us with our clothes on, at least in public. Ha, ha! Very funny, I don't think.

"Don't worry, I'll soon talk Adolph around when he sees me fresh out of bed without lippy and a perm. If you ask me, such restrictions are totally unnecessary for the leading Nation in Europe; war or no war. Even the three secretaries feel Adolph's gone too far this time; Christa as good as told him so. She's the only one game enough to openly disagree with him but even she had better watch her step; I've heard him chastise her more than once over her 'dangerous opinions'.

"I must show you the newly completed bunkers below the royal mountain suite: all six rooms can be accessed only via Adolph's private elevator. Did I tell you I now have my own quarters in the Berlin Chancellery?" she gibbered. "In reality, it's lonelier up there than the Berghof. Sometimes I'm allowed to accompany Herr and Frau Speer on short skiing holidays, but no amount of distraction makes up for *his* interminable absences."

On and on my colleague rambled in this fragmented vein, I was beginning to wonder if she'd learned anything at all from her years of disappointment.

At that time it was impossible to suppress rumours that Poland would be the next domino to fall, and during my stay on the mountain, I had plenty of opportunities to witness for myself the ten-car convoys disgorging German generals and their staffs in rapid succession.

The secretaries were flat-out taking dictation into the night, and what I could see of the Führer screamed "man on a mission". He barked orders in rapid succession and harangued his generals with a two-hour speech, none of whom seemed gung-ho to tempt fate much further.

There followed a tea break of caviar and fine wines before they were lectured for a further two hours. "This time we won't bring it off without violence," the warlord conceded. "France and Britain are too weak to object; we've already seen their 'limp-wristed gentlemen' in action."

Göring warned that this time around, the masses were far less enthusiastic over the prospect of another war, and cautioned against "going for broke". It was only two decades since the unspeakable slaughter on the battlefields of the Great War and many families had long memories. Things were finally starting to look up for most Germans, especially those who had demonstrated their ongoing loyalty despite the fate of their neighbours.

The Hunt Master felt that even Goebbels would have a hard time preparing the people to fight, and he for one could see no need to rock the Ship of State when he barely had time to count his plunder.

Nonetheless, as September drew near we could hear the Führer's tone hardening. "German sons must fight stubbornly and die laughing! Close your hearts to pity and act brutally," he urged his reluctant generals.

Excitement and anxiety crackled together through the air, stirred on by non-stop radio exhortations. Hoffmann departed on "the most secret mission of my life", a marathon flight beside Foreign Minister Ribbentrop to, of all places, Moscow: the Great Satan!

I had packed a variety of cameras and lenses for the boss, and ten rolls of Agfa 400 ASA black-and-white for the expected low light in the Kremlin.

"Keep your eyes peeled Heini, and report back to me personally with your opinion of Stalin. Without a doubt Ribbentrop is the greatest statesman since Bismarck," Hitler chortled, "although I find his hatred of England a little misplaced. We Aryans should stick together."

Given his grievous aversion to "Jewish Bolshevism" and all things Slavic, this extraordinary volte-face stunned the world. The signed and sealed "German-Soviet Non-aggression Pact" was described by Hitler for a while as "the greatest Diplomatic Coup ever!"

Upon their return the two emissaries and their pilot Bauer basked in the Führer's praise; he could be seen prancing about on the Berghof sundeck, slapping his knees and demanding to hear every detail of the meeting repeated.

Not without trepidation I was assigned the important task of developing Hoffmann's film, which among other captured moments revealed Stalin and Molotov appearing to down huge volumes of Vodka after the sealing of the deal.

The formalities were followed by an enormous State Dinner featuring every delicacy. I later learned from Hoffmann that the crafty Stalin had substituted water in his own glass all evening, and that amidst the apparent bonhomie an agreement had been struck with Ribbentrop to carve up hapless Poland between the two conniving neighbours.

Miraculously, at the stroke of a pen the former contestants had papered over their irreconcilable political differences, allowing Hitler a free hand to invade Poland without risking war on two fronts.

Goebbels, however, having been forced to watch on from afar with the rest of us, was not nearly so flattering towards the Foreign Minister's lauded diplomatic coup. "He bought his name, married his money and swindled his way into office," ranted the propaganda chief when news of the successful foray came through.

"This is *your* war!" he screamed over the phone days later in Ribbentrop's ear. "Well, you've got what you wanted! To begin a war is easy; to end it much more difficult." After all his fiery rhetoric, Goebbels too was getting cold feet at the last minute, forced by events to keep on churning out positive news items intended to deceive the world in general and the German Volk in particular.

But nothing could stop the wheels of Fate from turning.

Fifty-three divisions were deployed for battle; one and a half million Wehrmacht soldiers moved up to jumping off points along the Polish border. General Guderian's thirteen new, radio-controlled tanks stood ready to smash down enemy defence and Göring's Stuka pilots were studying maps of key bridges, railway yards and cross-roads earmarked for destruction. Two and a half million more infantry reserves were honing their battle skills behind the lines.

All in all, five German Armies stood poised for a quick victory, hopefully before France and Britain could launch a two-pronged attack from the west. Nothing like this had been seen before in the Press Room.

"The English will leave the Poles in the lurch as they did the Czechs," Hitler confidently predicted, and at 12:30 on August 31, he issued "Directive Number 1 for the Conduct of the War" which was brief and to the point:

1. Now that all political possibilities of disposing by peaceful means a situation which is intolerable for Germany are exhausted, I have determined a solution by force.

2. The attack on Poland is to be carried out.

Date of Attack: 1 September 1939

Time of attack: 04:45

The sword of Damocles was dangling from a fraying thread.

But first a plausible excuse to launch the invasion was needed by the Chancellery in Berlin, and it wasn't long in coming. A stop-press announcement flashed across the Press Room: IT'S OFFICIAL!

"Operation White" had begun. Printers were to remain on constant standby. "Just after midnight," it continued, "Polish partisans attacked a number of customs posts along the border and overran the German Radio Station at Gleiwitz. Several of the attackers have been killed after broadcasting inflammatory anti-German messages in Polish. German forces have retaken the radio station and are firing back."

I rushed across to Framing and Finishing clutching a copy of the cable. "Claudia; please drop what you're doing and step into the darkroom," I whispered.

Minutes later I had her to myself. "There's no nice way to say this, but it looks like war with all its tears! Just as you feared and predicted; well, almost as you predicted. It's the Poles who attacked German positions first, it says so right here."

She reached trembling for the cable and read it without comment, before tearing it up and casting it to the floor. "Bullshit! Every word of it. Nazi lies! My friends in the Orchestra will know what's really going on," she said, picking up the pieces to leave.

True to her promise, later that evening she knocked softly on the darkroom door, waiting for the safe light to go off before relating her version of events.

"It was a setup, just as I thought. The attack on Gleiwitz had been planned for weeks, not by the Poles but the SS; those photos of the dead attackers were staged. My friends reported that the so-called Polish soldiers were really concentration camp prisoners dressed in Polish uniforms and labelled 'canned goods' before they were shot dead by the SS and left behind as 'evidence'. As they say, dead men don't tell tales … and Hitler's bodyguard has suddenly been issued with submachine guns; it's diabolical and unbelievable."

One by one, she filled me in on the final details in an agitated state.

"It was the Kriegsmarine who broke the Treaty of '34, firing the opening salvo from the battleship *Schleswig-Holstein* into Danzig's very heart. Of all the treachery! She was supposed to be in port on a 'goodwill' visit.

"As I suspected at the time, Hitler's non-aggression pact with Poland was not worth the paper it's written on; mark my words, he'll do the same to Russia. They have already stopped the Polish Jews from driving and placed them under an 8 pm curfew, supposedly 'to prevent further molestation of Aryan women' But of course, that's just an excuse to get them off the streets.

"Other laws carrying the death penalty are being posted up around the city, directed at anyone caught listening to any but the three 'official' radio stations beaming from Berlin, Munich and Hamburg; and especially toward anyone tuning into the 10 pm BBC short-wave broadcast. You can't tell me all this hasn't been in the planning for months." She added that most of her friends were stunned and appalled by the turn of events. "How can a country go to war with a population so dead against it? Good people are asking each other."

Soon after, Hitler addressed the Reichstag in the Kroll Opera House building to announce that the invasion had begun. He wore his custom-made Nazi uniform of field-grey army material, which he vowed to remain wearing until the conclusion of hostilities. "Polish troops of the regular army have been firing on our territory during the night. Since 05:45 we have been returning fire," he perjured excitedly. As the falsehoods continued to flow, the members hooted and stamped their frenzied endorsement.

Within hours he'd boarded his newly configured command train, christened *Amerika*, and set off for the front, firing his aide-de-camp upon arrival for failing to provide his favourite mineral water.

Two days later, on September 3, 1939, to Hitler's great surprise, France and Great Britain declared war on Germany, a move which not only infuriated him but brought Unity Mitford's dreams for a "Grand Alliance" crashing down around her ears.

Having failed to obtain an urgent audience with Hitler, Lady Mitford finally realised that she had been shamefully used, and given the addition of new laws threatening "immediate arrest for anyone weakening the war effort", was immediately suspected by Hitler's inner circle of being a spy. Placing her signed photo of the Führer and other Nazi memorabilia in a large envelope she approached Gauleiter Wagner in a hysterical state, only to be told bluntly, "You should go back to your own country."

Later that day when Claudia and I were making our way from the Isar back home through the English Gardens, we perceived a flurry of excitement up ahead. Observing from a safe distance we saw a crowd milling about calling for help, with a woman slumped over on the park bench with blood streaming from a head wound; some were trying to staunch the bleeding. Two medics soon arrived to lift the limp body onto a stretcher, and we both strained to identify the victim.

"I'd know those long legs anywhere," said Claudia, "Can it really be her?"

"It's the Englisher; she's shot herself, twice!" someone in the crowd observed loudly. A sigh went up when the lifeless-looking form was whisked away.

As it turned out, neither shot was immediately fatal; Hitler dispatched a team of doctors and a bunch of flowers to the clinic. Somehow, Lady Mitford's life was saved. "Poor thing; she takes it so much to heart that England and Germany apparently do not hit it off," he told his aides.

Soon after Unity regained consciousness, several friends appeared at her bedside with another signed, framed photo of Hitler and a brand-new Nazi badge in gold, the latter immediately grabbed by the deranged patient, stuffed into her mouth and swallowed, forcing Professor Magnus to save her life a second time.

Thus it came to pass when Unity had recovered sufficiently, Eva and Dr Morell loaded the disillusioned invalid onto a train for Switzerland, much to everyone's relief, especially Eva's.

Some months later we read in the Press Room that Lady Unity Mitford had passed away on Lord Redesdale's Estate in Britain from complications of a brain infection.

"Well, that's two down and two to go!" Eva boasted rather callously to me in the darkroom, obviously referring to her remaining rivals, the "Official Nazi Hostess", Magda Goebbels, and the acclaimed Director, Leni Riefenstahl. "Given Magda's marital turmoil and successive pregnancies," she added, "I can't see her retaining that title much longer, can you? If there's one thing the Führer can't stand its women appearing at official functions in maternity wear."

Although I did not reply, in a way I was pleased for Eva, who seemed to be outlasting or outliving at least some of the competition. It's well known that most of us are concerned about things to the extent we don't have them; and Eva was no different.

If only she could forbear a little longer, Adolph might yet be hers. "One by one the general staff are coming round to accept my true status," she went on haughtily.

"I want nothing more than to spend time at the Berghof beside the man I love. I now have Negus and Stasi for company, who by the way, are undergoing 'obedience' training so they can be allowed back inside near the fire."

<h1 style="text-align:center">55</h1>

Just two weeks later, the international press announced Russia's invasion of Poland from the east, with 1.5 million men, 6,000 tanks, 1,600 aircraft and 9,000 assault guns; all under the pretext of protecting their own ex-pat population from the Germans.

Suddenly, the Polish defenders found themselves under attack on three sides, fighting back bravely against overwhelming odds. By month's end, nearly three quarters of a million of their soldiers had been killed, wounded, or taken prisoner, and some 30,000 civilians had been slain in the air raids and cross fire. Claudia was distraught.

With the Russian Bear now at their backs, further resistance was futile. On October 5, we received film of Hitler in Warsaw reviewing a march-past of his victorious troops and claiming the conquered territories to be long overdue Lebensraum for the new Reich.

Elsewhere, in the eight months leading up to the invasion, a mild-mannered Munich cabinetmaker had been preparing to give an emboldened Herr Hitler the shock of his life.

One Georg Elser, a patriotic German deeply troubled by the slaughter and aftermath of 1914, had been secreting himself after hours in the Burgerbraukeller, painstakingly chipping away at the plastered column behind the speakers stand. Inside this hard-won hollow, Elser had secreted his homemade bomb.

As per protocol, Hitler's appearances were thoroughly checked over in advance by the SS, who then ringed the speaker's platform in an armed cordon. And so it was on the evening of November 9, 1939, when the Führer alighted outside a packed Burgerbraukeller in Munich, scene of his ill-fated Putsch in '23. He returned religiously each anniversary to address those Alter Kämpfer who had marched beside him on that fateful day, and this was to be the final occasion of honouring that milestone event from his early career.

In the eyes of the world and his followers, the new chancellor appeared ubiquitous and invincible, regularly changing his schedules and route maps at the last minute to avoid any possibility of an ambush.

Only later, amidst flying press room speculations, did we learn details of the mighty explosion that brought down the whole upper balcony of the beer hall, killing fourteen in the audience and seriously wounding dozens more. According to the press reports pouring in, Elser's planning had been meticulous, right down to his escape. However, call it Fate or as Hitler said, "Providence", no one could have imagined the guest of honour departing the hall thirteen minutes earlier than usual that evening, just before the bomb went off.

The brave but luckless Elser was picked up trying to cross the Swiss border and whisked off to Mauthausen concentration camp, there to be mercilessly tortured for the names of his accomplices.

Neither Hitler nor the Gestapo could believe that that such a carefully planned attack did not have the backing of the British Secret Services. It took nearly five more years before anyone even came close to killing the great dictator. The courageous lone assassin was held in solitary confinement as a "Führer Private Prisoner" before being murdered at Dachau in April '45.

With Claudia's underground connections and my own access to the Press Room news releases we were able to keep abreast of unfolding events. There was no doubt in our minds that the inevitable declaration of war by the Allied powers would impose added burdens on every German.

In the darkroom we enjoyed a certain degree of privacy and, despite winter's onset, managed to exchange wild ideas around our campfires by the river. Sometimes she arrived alone, and at others accompanied by a member of the Orchestra who instructed me on compiling records of the worst atrocities being committed against Jews and other minorities. Clearly, everyone was on tenterhooks but there was no denying their commitment to the cause when we repeated our oaths of secrecy.

Word spread around the studio that Hitler had appointed Henni's husband, Baldur, to the plum job of "Gauleiter of Venice" but when his "Little Sunshine" personally intervened to have her husband's title embellished even further, the Führer flew off the handle and summoned Schirach to the Brown House. Upon arrival, the unsuspecting and hopeful new Gauleiter received a severe dressing down instead, being warned not to send his wife to plead his case in future.

Hitler ordered Schirach to have Henni remove her "war paint" of silver eyelids and false eyelashes before she approached him again.

This incident particularly gave Eva quite a chuckle. In between visits to Italy with her mother and sister Gretl, she had expressed the view that Henni was getting "too big for her boots", and even seemed pleased that Hoffmann himself was gradually being eased out of his unquestioned position of dominance by photographers like Walter Frenzl who worked almost exclusively in colour.

When I stuck my head into Eva's office that afternoon, I wasn't surprised to see the loot from her latest shopping spree spread out across the floor and furniture. She was leaning back in her chair smoking a cigarette, admiring a pair of pretty red flatties propped up on the desk.

"Oh, Klaus, what do you think? I couldn't make my mind up between the red and the blue; Signor Ferragamo insisted I have both. These days Adolph just tells me to go ahead and buy whatever I want, look!"

I slowly counted thirty-six more pairs of ladies' shoes lined up neatly behind her chair, in all styles and colours.

"Of course they all fit perfectly, but I've no idea when I shall get a chance to wear them. Gretl says I just can't say No as if *she* should talk. Adolph agrees that colour photography is the way of the future, and the boss is going to have to lift his game; he's had things all to himself for far too long," she opined, reaching for Frenzl's latest folio of prints showing the completed Chancellery in Berlin.

She pushed the set of sparkling 8" × 10"s across the desk toward me, but I was yet distracted by the stunning array of ladies' footwear and the six or so open suitcases brimming with fashion items.

Noting my interest, Eva added with an affected sigh. "You have to take your hat off to the Italians when it comes to style; especially now that Hollywood is off-limits."

Thumbing through Frenzl's prints I could only gasp in wonder at the enormous scale of Berlin's palace chancellery, lined with pink marble blocks and erected in record time by Albert Speer.

Hitler's sole stipulation to the young architect required the Grand Gallery of his Chancellery to exceed the hated Versailles' Hall of Mirrors in length and height. "On the long walk from the entrance to the reception hall they must get a taste of the power and grandeur of the German Reich," he'd stressed. Frenzl's coloured folio had certainly captured both scale and detail of the magnificent interior perfectly, but I thought better than to share these impressions with the boss.

Only recently I'd discovered by chance that my name did not appear anywhere in the pay-office records, nor did Claudia's; I had to make do with an occasional bundle of Reichsmark and Café Stefanie vouchers poked under the broom-closet door by an unseen hand, while a ripening Claudia was dependant entirely on the gratuities she could wheedle from her various Nazi consorts.

When we caught up to exchange these unsettling revelations it was agreed that Hoffman would try every trick in the book to hang on to every penny of his extracurricular activities. She repeated her belief that the current hierarchy was an "administration of cowards", with each rank bowing and scraping to its superiors while mercilessly lording it over those below. "Even cowards with unlimited power like Hitler's often seek excuses for their acts," she informed me.

I ventured the opinion that, with one or two exceptions, brave souls like Ernst who'd shown exemplary courage in standing up to the dictator had paid with their lives during and since the "Night of Long Knives".

"I'm afraid courage is a scarce commodity these days; there are times when I think I would be better off facing the onslaught back home, side by side with my family, instead of here and now consorting with these swine. Oh Klaus, my parents are frail; terrified of the typhus and dysentery already running wild through the camp. They think I've abandoned them. I must find a way to return and somehow ease their suffering; I'm nearly out of my mind …"

Only later did I remember the old saying "Be careful what you wish for" as the two of us stood whispering together in Framing and Finishing. I could not have imagined what was about to happen. A commotion at the doorway caused all heads to turn. "Where is the Jew?!"

We looked up to see an SS captain pushing forward, backed by a squad of foot soldiers. During the present period of uncertainty and terror, emissaries of this kind were only too frequently the messengers of death and we both knew it.

"Over here! This way, Herr Captain," a hand-wringing Iris leapt forward, almost spreading her cloak at his feet. She stopped before Claudia, rose to her full height and thrust an accusing finger into her chest. "The Jewess you seek, Herr Captain."

"What do you know? Hiding here among decent Aryans all along."

Icy fingers gripped my gut and I stopped breathing. Claudia stood tall and silent. The SS man snapped to attention and stuck out his right arm: "Heil Hitler!"

For a long moment there was strange silence: I too held back when I saw my friend's steadfast, even serene refusal to return the hated salute. He seemed not to notice me, untying a small scroll to address her directly. "Sarah Schicklegruber, alias Fraulein Claudia or Fraulein Sissy?"

She remained impassive.

The SS captain looked a little awkward, before clearing his throat to continue. "It has come to the attention of Reichsführer SS Himmler that you have been in the care and employ of Heinrich Hoffmann and have carried out your duties faithfully. Herr Hoffmann has been duly advised and notice is hereby given to you to accompany the officer under guard. You have been chosen for a mission of special importance and will now take all orders directly through the Reichsführer's Office."

She stood her ground; was it a trick?

The Nazis were notorious for hoodwinking their victims into thinking all was well before the doors of double cross slammed shut. She knew their ways well.

"Do you really require an armed squad to take me?" she looked the captain dead in the eye without flinching. "Am I not here at the Studio or dancing in your own officers' club on weekends? Why have none spoken up before?"

"I have my orders, Frau Schicklegruber, and you have yours," he replied with a wave of his arm. The double rank stepped forward and without further ado marched Claudia away to the waiting vehicle.

I was almost beside myself but tried not to let it show when I confronted the boss, who dismissed my concerns out of hand.

"Grow up lad! I'm sure we'll see her around from time to time on assignment, but she'll soon be dancing to the beat of a different drum, ha-ha! Get it, Jungle Boy? Different drum?"

Hoffman could be quite sarcastic after a few Schnapps, which was most days, and behind the scenes was now labelled as "Germany's biggest art thief".

But today he was basking in the success of his new illustrated hardcover, *With Hitler in Poland*, which added up to the dozen picture books already published under his name. He had also just released a collection of Hitler's Vienna watercolour facsimiles, which on the whole was well-received.

However, my poor heart would not be stilled, and the animal in me continued to rage unseen and unheard. When alone beside the Isar I often wept hot tears when thinking of our special moments together.

Every week or so, after carefully checking the street for would-be informers, I briskly mounted the steps to Claudia's apartment and knocked hopefully upon her door, rousing only the tiny mongoloid face in the tenement opposite.

"Sissy not home. Mutti say bad men take Sissy away" came the plaintive lament. After several such attempts, a haggard woman's face appeared behind the boy, flashing fearful eyes in my direction.

"Pauli! Come inside this minute. How many times must I tell you not to open the door when strangers are about?" But the child pulled away and emerged fully. "Man not stranger, Man Sissy friend. Pauli see Sissy kiss man." His mother took another step forward and searched my face imploringly.

"Please stay a moment," I entreated. "Have you heard anything of her at all?"

I could see Frau Falkenhorst was ill, almost doubled over in pain. "I am a friend of Claudia's, a good friend; Pauli knows, don't you, little mate? Are you in trouble, Frau? Is there something I can do to help?"

She flashed another glance in each direction along the corridor and without a word took me by the elbow into her own tiny flat. Silently she motioned me to a rather lumpy chair beside a burning gas ring and settled herself with a groan onto a spotty mattress opposite, pulling a thin blanket up under her chin.

Without waiting to be asked, the child shape flung itself into my lap and gently stroked my chin. "Man kind to Pauli, man Pauli friend too."

I began hesitantly but hopefully, "Dear Frau, my name is Klaus Hahn, and I swear on the Holy Mother that Fraulein Claudia is my best friend. You are obviously in need of medical attention."

"No!" she hissed, half-rising on one elbow before sinking back with a little whimper. "No doctors. They told me if I said a word to anyone they would put my Pauli into Hadamar and send me to Dachau."

"What is Hadamar? … And you are not to say a word about what?"

Again, her plangent eyes searched my face for any hint of infidelity, until she could stand it no longer.

"My womanhood. Oh! My motherhood, they've taken it away," she blurted, before attempting to staunch her flow of tears with a once white lace handkerchief. Pauli, upon seeing his mother's distress, gave a loud wail and buried his face into my chest, continuing to sob silently.

"Sissy come home soon. When Sissy come back see Pauli?"

Slowly, gasp by gasp, she related how one of her neighbours had reported her mongoloid child to the Gestapo and how they'd come to sterilise her soon afterwards, without anaesthetic.

"'Unfit for the responsibility of Aryan motherhood,' they called me. If I hadn't consented, they said they'd do it by force anyway; and take away my Pauli there and then. Oh, Herr Hahn, what's to become of us? Pauli used to play outside with the other kids until the new blockälteste got wind of his condition. He's been locked inside all day every day, for fear they'll snatch him off the streets. Dear sir; can't you take him with you and find a place of safety? Now Fraulein Sissy is gone I've no one left to turn to."

I looked blankly back at her as I dandled Pauli's curls, much as I'd seen Mam do with Robert. "B … But Frau Falkenhorst, I have no place of my own; I live beneath the staircase of the studio," I mumbled evasively. "My Boss assures me that Sissy Claudia will return at the completion of her training; please don't give up hope. I'll … I'll bring some pain relief, an … and a toy for Pauli, I really will. You hear that, Pauli? I want you to stay inside and look after Mutti until I return with a new toy. Deal?"

His narrow eyes began once more to sparkle, and his lips parted in a smile, revealing two tiny rows of yellow teeth. *And I know what else,* I thought to myself as I closed the door gently behind me and tiptoed out onto the street.

Next afternoon, true to my word, I tapped softly on Frau Falkenhorst's door and pressed two boxes of double-strength aspirin into her grateful fingers. For Pauli, I brought a bag of building blocks and a small rocking horse from the studio's ample collection of children's props, which eased slightly my feelings of guilt and inadequacy.

From the rocking horse's mane protruded a brand-new toothbrush and his squeals of delight brought a tear to both of us, quickly wiped away.

Sometimes, after a big night, Herr Hoffman would send me down for a shift to photograph the endless stream of lower-ranking Nazi officials and families booked in for a genuine "Photohaus Hoffman" likeness. This allowed me to play around with the lighting to my heart's content.

Despite the boss' heartfelt losses, no respectable National Socialist would dream of going elsewhere for his "Official" head and shoulders, or even a family portrait; and luckily for me, most sitters liked the strong side lighting I favoured to accentuate their features; especially those in uniform.

I soon discovered there was a method in the boss' seeming trust, as the Hitler Youths turned out to be particularly troublesome.

Both large and small boys ruined many poses by refusing to take instructions from either myself or their parents; they were just as likely to jump up at the last minute and shout "Heil Hitler" into the lens as I released the shutter. Nonetheless, anything was better than being locked away day and night in that stuffy darkroom.

Behind the scenes, Adolph Hitler had bigger fish to fry.

On May 9, 1940, Hoffman and the generals were summoned aboard the *Amerika*, his private train, for the overnight trip to his brand-new "Felsenest" headquarters in western Poland. The all-conquering Commander-in-Chief was readying himself to invade France and the Low Countries, drawing closer every moment to launching his largest offensive yet. As usual, he would rely on deception to blindside the enemy.

Without any declaration of war, the speed and ferocity of the initial German blitzkrieg swept all before it, threatening to cut off an entire Allied Expeditionary Force moving up into Belgium for a rerun of earlier battles.

Within a few weeks, we were receiving orders for thousands of reprints of Hitler inspecting the Eiffel Tower with the ever-bashful Albert Speer, Dr Brandt and a handful of others at his side. It was reported that during this moment of triumph, he confided to Speer, "All Paris may have to be destroyed, but anyway it will only be a shadow of the New Germania."

Even Hoffman seemed stunned by the sudden turn of events, noting the "abysmal despondency" of the current mood compared with 1914. "This time", the boss lamented, "there is no excitement, no hurrahs, no cheering and no throwing flowers, no war fever and no war hysteria." Hitler too, was taken aback by the public's lack of enthusiasm but cheered up quickly in the wake of the Wehrmacht's swift military advances.

By Yuletide, however, increased rationing was beginning to bite. Half the German population was already freezing owing to the shortage of coal, and income taxes had increased by 50% to finance the war effort. For the first time in living memory, no church bells welcomed in the festive season, having been melted down to make bullets.

Robert Ley, bibulous head of the German Labour Front, made his usual Yuletide proclamation: "The Führer is always right ... Obey the Führer."

Before the war began, Ley had overseen a massive network of Nazi holiday adventures titled "Strength through Joy", which enabled pure and worthy Nazi Party workers to partake in low-cost vacations by land and sea. Ley had been forced to watch on helplessly while his beloved Führer drooled over his own demure new opera-singing wife, Inge, stooping to kiss her hand at every opportunity and engaging her in long conversations. Hitler made no secret of his infatuation with this exemplary blonde specimen of German womanhood, admiration which only increased when Frau Ley bore four perfect, blond Aryan babies in quick succession; becoming a morphine addict in the process.

Some said she only married Robert Ley, twenty-odd years her senior, in order to be close to Hitler; but then again, the same thing had been said of Magda Goebbels and several other Nazi wives.

One funny incident involving Inge Ley saw Hoffman temporarily regain his place in Hitler's esteem: several magazines had recently printed a Walter Frenzl rear view in colour of Hitler conversing with Inge at some official function or another.

Apparently, the Führer was congratulating her on being well on the way to receiving her gold-plated Motherhood Badge while still managing to retain her figure.

The moment I saw this photo I rushed to show the boss, who snatched the article from my hand and gave a little whoop of joy.

"Ja, ja! That's Adolph's corset all right; showing through the back of his tunic as clear as day. This sort of faux pas would never have slipped through at Studio Hoffman; wait until I point out Frenzl's blunder, the Führer will be furious." Picking up the phone, he demanded to be put through to Bormann, and within minutes was on his way to the Brown House, clutching the offending publication.

Sure enough, Hitler *was* ropeable, and Frenzl's editor was lucky not to have been whisked off to Dachau. All remaining copies were quickly removed from the bookstands, but the Führer's pot belly was no longer a secret.

In little more than a year later, in December '42, Inge Ley, like so many of Hitler's other female devotees, would be found dead with a self-inflicted bullet wound in her flawless forehead, following which Eva breathed yet another sigh of relief.

It seemed to those of us watching events unfold via photographs and newsreels that a quite unbelievable sequence of conquests was undeniable. If so much of Western Europe could be conquered so quickly, given the bloody battles of attrition just twenty years earlier, that had drained dry so much of the world's manhood, anything was possible under this great German Leader.

In awe we watched footage of the panzers bursting from the narrow Ardennes forest roads to take the allies in the rear, coming within a whisker of wiping out the retreating Allied armies huddled at Dunkirk.

General Keitel repeated his claim that Adolph Hitler was the "Greatest Military Leader of All Time", completely overlooking the fact that it was Hitler himself who ordered Guderian's thundering panzer divisions to stop short of their coastal objective, fearful that his supply lines were being over-extended.

This extraordinary lack of judgment was the first of many occasions when Hitler intervened to overrule his generals while a battle was in progress, allowing almost the entire French First Army and British Expeditionary Force of 300,000-odd fighting men to be evacuated safely back across the channel to Britain.

General Guderian, the very architect of blitzkrieg strategy in concentrating his panzers to smash through enemy defences, was fuming, having pleaded in vain that if given just one more day moving forward, he could have wiped out the invasion force entirely.

But Hitler and his officers were flattered and distracted by the Allied casualties and the tremendous volume of perfectly sound equipment left behind on Dunkirk's bloodstained sands. Goebbels' headlines trumpeted the rout as a "Complete Wehrmacht Victory" and a "Total Defeat" for the Allies.

In shock, we watched the Führer dance his little jig of joy beside the railway carriage in Compiegne, before overseeing France's humiliating surrender. This was the same carriage into which the defeated German generals had shuffled on November 11, 1918, to sign their own surrender documents: now the tables were turned and the world looked on with bated breath.

More ominously, Göring's Luftwaffe had lost control of the skies over Dunkirk during the evacuation, a portent of the looming Battle of Britain to come. Without air supremacy over England and the Channel, Hitler knew his plans for Operation Sea Lion, the invasion of the British Isles, would have little chance of success.

We heard that he had already jumped the gun in drawing up a hit list of names and addresses of those to be shot immediately following the landing, and day after day we saw footage of Heinkel bombers almost blacking out the sun on their way to bomb R.A.F. airfields across southern England.

During August and September of 1940, the nation was confounded to hear rumours of its decimated Luftwaffe formations limping back to their bases in conquered France. Once again, Hitler had reportedly intervened in the battle plans, ordering his battle-scarred squadrons to blast English cities instead of airfields; starting with London. He mistakenly believed that the spirit of the British people would be more easily broken when their cities were reduced to rubble.

It was no surprise to learn that heading his hit list was Prime Minister Winston Churchill who, unlike his well-intentioned predecessor, would be no pushover. When the British leader gave the order to bomb Berlin in retaliation, Hitler exploded in fury. "Doesn't he realise we have once again become a world power? For every tonne of bombs the drunken Churchill drops on us, we'll drop ten, twenty and a thousand tonnes on him," he raged. "Our duty is to teach men to see whatever is lovely and truly wonderful in life."

Goebbels backed him up by releasing a series of cartoons showing the cigar-munching bulldog as some kind of Frankensteinian buffoon created in a laboratory, but not everyone laughed when air raids across Germany stepped up in frequency and tempo.

The Supreme Leader soon turned on Göring and accused him of being a 'braggart, a drug-addict and a failure,' blaming his own Reichsmarschall rather than the indomitable R.A.F. for his reversals over England.

I almost felt sorry for Göring, who had wanted first to wipe out all the R.A.F. airfields and hence Britain's ability to respond, *before* unleashing the blitz on populated areas. Notwithstanding such outbursts, Hitler remained buoyant, even bragging that "Britain's position is hopeless" and "this war is already won by us."

He gave another long-winded speech to the bankrupt Reichstag, "not as the leader of a defeated people standing cap in hand, but as a conqueror making a final appeal to this 'Nation of Shopkeepers' to come to their senses and see reason".

Of course, Churchill would have none of it and replied with a series of rallying cries to parliament; speeches that would ring out through the pages of history: "We should get no worse terms if we went on fighting, even if beaten, than are open to us now …We shall go on to the end defending our island, whatever the cost may be. We shall fight on the beaches, we shall fight on the landing grounds, we shall fight in the fields and in the streets, we shall fight in the hills; we shall never surrender."

Lord Halifax also gave an upbeat radio broadcast on the BBC, stating among other things that "Hitler has prostituted the gift of oratory" and "it is a noble privilege to be defenders of things so precious".

Thus the British people knuckled down to preserve their homeland and repel the enemy while across the channel, Marshall Pétain, France's much-decorated septuagenarian "Hero of the Great War", took his chance to impose Nazi rule across the southern half of his conquered homeland as a figurehead of collaboration; at least for the time being.

While Germany pulled the strings of the naive old warrior and his puppet government in Vichy, Pétain oversaw the continued smooth running of the French public service and civil authorities, thus freeing up many thousands of German soldiers from occupation duties.

The southern French "protectorate" now boasted its own ruthless Melice, a political police force answerable only to Nazi authorities through the venerable Marshall himself. With few exceptions, French men and women were encouraged to open their hearts and homes to the invaders, in the misbegotten belief that they would be "treated kindly" throughout the occupation.

Indeed, at first, those German soldiers returning home on leave loaded down with plunder had nothing but kind words for the French population, especially the Paris brothels, until many respectable German Frauen suddenly found themselves stricken with V.D., now spreading like wildfire across the Fatherland. Rotating occupation units were instructed to wear "muzzle protection", and wash their mouths and private parts out regularly with Borax or Eau de Cologne.

"For the life of me, why don't the Brits just make peace and be done with it?" Eva declared one day on the Berghof sundeck.

Usually, all talk of war was forbidden within the private circle, but now it was a forgone conclusion and only a matter of time before Germany occupied the whole of Europe, including Great Britain. Hadn't they already overrun most of the continent and scared off the puny English defences from the Channel Islands closest to France?

"Have you heard the morphine addict Morell has been despatched with a team of his special pox doctors, to 'clean up' the French brothels…" she added, "starting with the Madams? That's right up his alley.

"He's already declared Polish women are mere 'objects', and rightly so. He's blamed them for the outbreak of the 'you know what', and forbidden them to work as prostitutes with the soldiers.

"Papa's really no different when it comes to the Polacks but admits that at least they are Catholic 'Christians', while the Brits are true Aryans, just like us. He can't see why they won't accept that they are beaten. He says they should throw out that drunken old lecher Churchill and accept the Führer's generous terms. Vati thinks it would have been much better for Germany if King Edward VIII had remained on the throne. He and his American wife Mrs Simpson came all the way to the Berghof to visit Adolph, you know? … Although I was furious not to be introduced when they were right there in the house.

"Now, that's what I call true romance; when a great leader walks away from his power and glory to marry the woman he loves. If only my Adolph could find it in his heart to make such a commitment. I suppose a girl can always hope …" She rolled her eyes in a futile flutter and sat up straight on the deck chair to face me. Both of us were hoping for a bit of a tan during that long, late summer of 1940. I gingerly slipped off my shirt for the first time in front of her friends, most of whom were wearing Italian one-piece bathers despite there being no pool, to a wolf whistle or two and suggestive observations.

"Don't take any notice of them," Eva said, "they are used to admiring the strapping SS hunks; one doesn't need big muscles to be the best printer in Munich."

I blushed slightly and gave a little stretch of my arms above my head, ignoring muttered comments that sounded like "knots in cotton".

"Don't laugh," I heard another say behind her hand, "they say he knocked that brute Lothar out cold soon after he arrived, unlikely as it seems …"

Given Eva's earlier comments, I decided to probe a little deeper, heartily sick of her girlfriends' persistent persiflage and suggestive comments about men in general. I leaned closer so the others wouldn't hear, and caught her heavy fragrance. "Are you sufficiently calm to indulge in a little philosophising?" I ventured.

She bent down to lift the squabbling Negus onto her lap and returned my question with a glance entirely vacant of thought.

"Nose to nose leads to blows; nose to bums ends in chums, see?" she recited to no one in particular while soothing the terrier. A long pause followed, before she fixed her whimsical eyes on mine.

"Philosophy? Good God, girls," she exclaimed in a phony Hollywood accent, "he wants to engage lil ole' me in philosophy. Well, all right, if you must; shoot away, Jungle Boy, ha-ha."

I could see Fanny Braun, now also one of "the girls", prick up her ears on the fringes, and try to ignore the background chatter before continuing. "Well, you shared your father's opinions on the British Monarchy and the state of the war, and I must say he seems to have his finger on the pulse. However, I have a slightly less sanguine view …" The buzz fell silent.

"Papa? You must be joking! He thinks by wearing that silly uniform day and night and puffing on his pipe that he looks like one of the generals; it's as if he seeks the Führer's praise by undertaking this series of petty transformations. He's even attempting to grow a little schnurrbart of his own, much to Mutti's disgust. Adolph says he's proud to have actually created a fashion …"

"What's that, dear? Did I hear my name mentioned?"

"Papa's schnurrbart, Mutti; Klaus hasn't noticed it yet. I told him you certainly have, ha-ha."

I didn't want another "round robin" and leaned even closer to her pearl-studded ear. "That may be so, Fraulein, but from what I've seen in the darkroom, Operation Sea Lion may not be the only campaign failing to unfold according to plan ..."

"Don't you presume, Klaus Hahn," she hissed back. "Adolph says that if the Brits persist in fighting on against all odds he may well leave them to it, and turn his face eastward to the unimaginable acres of fertile Lebensraum awaiting us there. He says it's only a matter of kicking in Russia's door and the whole rotten structure will come crashing down. Plainly, he belongs by nature to another species and would prefer not to see anyone suffer."

"I wouldn't be so sure about that," I ventured foolishly. "What about the phoney non-aggression pact signed just months ago? Anyhow, I thought you took no interest in political matters?"

"Well, what of it? Who are you to dare question the Führer's predictions; everyone can see the Russians are a nation of illiterate mouth breathers *and* that the British are a spent force ..." Her eyes narrowed angrily.

I decided there and then to push my point. "Russia covers a mighty big area, and it doesn't look to me like the Englishers are quite finished yet ... at least, not according to the photos coming across the news desk, which are being immediately censored by the way. It appears the British Navy has inflicted a catastrophic defeat on the Kriegsmarine off Norway ..."

"Norway? Why, that's impossible! Aren't they a Neutral Country? I sailed past there on a cruise with Mutti and Gretl; I think it was Norway. All those rocky cliffs look the same to me; it was so dashed cold and cloudy we couldn't see much anyway. I'm sure I showed you the footage ... although some of it was a little underexposed."

"That usually happens with snowy scenes and automatic light meters," I opined.

"Anyhow, I overheard Adolph saying that it's land armies that matter most in Europe, and we seem to have plenty of those from all accounts. This offensive has become a matter of national honour, designed to restore Germany to her rightful place in ..."

"But, Eva! You may not be privy to all the latest news from the front ... er, perhaps we should no longer be hiding the truth ..." I blurted a little too loudly. "I've seen the foreign news reports."

"How dare you repeat such slander; Bormann would have you shot for less," she cried aloud, drawing everyone's attention, including the guards.

I turned pale, realising I'd gone too far. There was no shaking Eva's conviction that the war would soon end, and there was little point in my rocking the boat of negativity. In a moment she had reverted to the restless emotions of her lower mind, becoming unstable as mountain water.

"Oh, just be gone! All this so-called philosophical discussion leaves us cold, doesn't it, girls?" Herta's small daughter, sensing my plight, ran over to grip my knees, allowing me briefly to run my fingers through her hair.

"Don't worry, Ushi, the big bad wolf is just leaving until he learns a few manners." Eva petted the little one, feigning concern.

Wounded, but not surprised, I pulled on my shirt and began to walk away, coming face to face with Gauleiter Bormann who had just emerged from the newly completed air raid shelter, alerted by the racket.

"Last I heard *you* were hired to work in the darkroom, isn't that so?" I returned his hard gaze without answering, conscious that Hoffman had specifically instructed me to answer only to him and Eva while thus engaged at the Berghof.

Just look at the man, he has slime written all over his face, I thought to myself, taking an involuntary step backwards.

"Well? Puppy got your tongue, Jungle Boy?" he sneered.

"Herr Mountain Gauleiter; I am well aware of my position and my duties. I was invited onto the sundeck by Fraulein Eva her—"

"Then why is she ordering you to leave?"

There was no avoiding his bulk planted atop the stairway, it was hard to suppress my disdain for this vile man with unlimited access to the Führer's ear.

"Actually, Herr Gauleiter, I'm all caught up down below and was just about to visit my relatives on Lake Königssee ..."

"Hahn ... Hahn? Oh yes, now I remember; they were the last to be resettled. Frederick is one of our founding members, though I suspect that wife of his could be a real handful. Neither of them was prepared to go quietly for the greater good, until I relieved him of his marvellous collection of Party memorabilia. Those items are much better off on display in the Brown House in Munich and he'll get over it. Give Herr Hahn my compliments and tell him I hope he's settling into that roomy boathouse by the water."

I did not dare mention that Onkel had resigned from the local in disgust and was agitating behind the scenes for the return of all lifetime leases on Obersalzberg. I wondered how long his snub would go unnoticed and unpunished by Herr Bormann.

Breathing a sigh of relief to be temporarily free of restrictions, I stuffed a few clothes into my backpack and set out for the shimmering lake shore below, a good two hours' walk away, not entirely able to free my mind from suspicion.

Like so many other top Nazis, Bormann exuded a philosophy of "Do as I say, not as I do"; whether regarding his so-called conversion to vegetarianism or in his relationship with Frau Bormann.

This wasted, brow-beaten woman had already received her Golden Motherhood Badge with six healthy children to her credit, and was well on the way to a total of nine.

Rather than being outraged when her husband proposed moving his new mistress, the actress Manja Behrens, into their brand-new chalet with her and the children, she stunned everyone by welcoming the thought of a ménage à trois with a younger woman.

"My Martin is too racially pure not to father as many children as possible," Gerda boasted to raised eyebrows, apparently even suggesting he "see to it that Manja bears a child one year and her the next".

"That way," she told him, "you can always have one of us around in good shape."

Frau Gerda's father, Walter Busch, a Justice of the High Court, was far from pleased by his daughter's free-wheeling proposal, and at the first opportunity lodged a complaint with Hitler, who predictably set off down the mountain to have it out with his impudent underling.

Early that summer I found myself with more time on my hands, free to wander Munich's many parklands and swim in the Isar's biting pools, where for a few hours each week I could immerse myself in the cool breeze of freedom.

Photohaus Hoffman now oversaw so many studios and employees that we almost lost count. Only through constant assembly line upgrades and the speedy embrace of every new invention did he have any hope of keeping his finger on the pulse, and then somewhat sketchily.

Fortunately, my hand-printing skills were still in demand for "special orders" and "special clients", most of which were, as always, extremely revealing of human nature. Many of the other manual printers had been "promoted" to machine operators.

During this time I fancied myself drawing closer to Eva, partly through our shared loneliness and partly because of misguided compassion. We often found ourselves together late at night, at the completion of my shift, when she sat drinking champagne in her Munich office awaiting her regular 10 pm phone call from Hitler.

Not once did she express any interest or concern over Claudia's absence, and given her earlier assessment I thought it wise not to raise the subject.

I spent many lonely hours beside a campfire by the river, missing my best friend while chanting softly Sister Klara's vowel sounds at the swirling current and striving for perfect equilibrium. "Whenever you take a step towards God, He takes two towards you." Her words rang in my ears.

I sometimes glimpsed the broken limbs and body of Maya among the willow branch reflections. At other times I felt the happiness of birds after rain, especially when emerging aroused from a swim when I could not take three steps upon the sand without feeling Claudia's hot mouth close over me. In those moments I was once more the eternal lover, for whom the whole world was insufficient.

Poking at the embers I pondered the influence of these remarkable women in my life, each connected by an unbreakable silver thread of understanding. At other times I succumbed to darker memories, unable to concentrate at all and plagued by a sense of hopelessness. No roads led me toward Rome, merely horizons of menace and uncertainty.

Returning to the Studio I often sought out Eva, who seemed happy to indulge in conversations of a lighter vein.

"The only time I see Adolph lately is in photos. I can tell at a glance if he's unhappy, you know?" she began, returning to her favourite topic. "He just can't seem to sit still; always on the move.

"Everyone knows his stomach troubles are getting worse, the flatulence is almost unbearable. For someone usually so polite and well-mannered in front of ladies, he just lets rip these days without restraint, in any company. It seems Morell is the only one he'll let near him for injections, and poor Dr Brandt is tearing his hair out. He claims Morell's potions contain arsenic among other things and may cause long-term harm, but Adolph won't listen to such talk. 'You just keep yourself at the ready in case of car accidents or assassination attempts,' he scolded Brandt in front of everyone."

"I thought you and Bouhler would have your hands rather full with the T4 project," I said although Eva later admitted she didn't know what that entailed.

I dared to suggest that from my observations her beloved Adolph lived by the doctrine of "Divide and Rule", most recently evidenced in France where it was intended to keep his respective factotums off balance. "I also find it hard," I added, "to identify any original thoughts in Nazi political doctrine, aside from the effectiveness of the Führer's leadership style, of course, which cannot be disputed."

She gazed back uncomprehendingly through half-closed eyes and drained the remaining champagne from the bottle. "Did I show you that footage of Gretl and I with the SS detail at Lake Königssee?" she asked, changing the subject.

Having previously sat through many reels of her home movies I settled down reluctantly to watch her latest projected onto the office wall. Right from the start it was clear there was nothing new.

First up, there was Fanny, Fritz and Gretl frolicking on and off their blow-up air beds in some lake, repeatedly pulling faces and hamming for the camera. Might I say here and now that few activities look more foolish than grown-ups like Fritz and Fanny Braun in swimming trunks feigning high spirits while splashing water over others.

Then followed scenes of naked children making mud pies at the water's edge; several of Eva's married friends encouraged such free-spirited self-expression. After changing spools there appeared several lily-white male buttocks, obviously SS by their firm sinews, charging into the lake with much splashing and shoving, to swim out and climb onto an off-shore pontoon and proceed to jig about shamelessly. It was obvious from their words and gestures that they were calling for Eva and Gretl to strip off and join them.

"That's Gretl's new friend, Herman; the one with the big … the big muscles on the left. I believe he has also been keeping an eye on your elusive brother."

"Well, I'd know my brother's backside anywhere and that's definitely not his."

"Herman cuts a fine figure in his SS Cavalry uniform," she continued unfazed. "He's been pestering Gretl and I for ages to go horseriding, of all things; actually, I think she's falling for him."

Eva was clearly titillated by the bold exhibitionism and attempted to pilfer my thoughts. "See, there's nothing wrong with having a bit of fun with the guards, is there? Nor with male nudity if filmed tastefully," she slurred slightly, rewinding the reel.

"Or, from a respectable distance," I added.

"Oh, if only Adolph could let himself go like this; he's such a prude. I've even suggested he take a ten-minute clip of me with him on tour, doing my special dance on his coffee table. I thought it may help him drop off to sleep more easily. Oh Klaus, I've tried everything to keep him interested, but he says if he can't watch the real thing he's happy to wait."

Eva picked up the champagne bottle, then squinted ... realising it was empty.

"Wait? He says? It's me who does all the waiting, and even then he's usually too tired to comment on my exertions," she added, flashing another of her gummy little smiles.

I am relating these words just as they came out of her mouth, leaving me not a little unsettled. Surely, if the Führer ever got wind of her semi-secret romps I may be asked to explain why I didn't lift a finger to confiscate the offending footage.

She lit another cigarette off the butt of the last and leaned back with feet resting on her desk. She began caressing one of her many butterfly brooches with her free hand. "Adolph thinks Gretl and I are 'tomboys', can you believe that?" she asked offhandedly. "I'm not quite sure whether to be pleased or offended."

"Tomboy? I ... er, I wouldn't say that at all, Fraulein Eva. I've always known you as the very essence of femininity, particularly in your blue dirndl. Do you remember that time when we printed up the 8" × 10" for the Führer's birthday ...?"

"Please do not presume to know me, Klaus, I'm far more complex than you ever imagined. All I can say is clothes may well maketh the man but they don't necessarily make the woman, especially when it comes to the big fish I'm trying to land. It's just so damned frustrating having a mouse's ear; otherwise, I'd really be able to show Adolph a thing or two."

I cleared my throat, feeling a little lost for words; the last time we'd shared such intimacies I was convinced she'd sealed up her heart, lest love should break forth anew against perpetual disappointment. But here she was, ready to throw herself down again at the Führer's feet and probably suffer more rejection. I simply couldn't keep up with these mood swings of hers.

"There are other ways to please a man, Fraulein Eva," I ventured, blushing slightly at the recall of my exquisite moment by the Isar, "perhaps you could obtain a book outlining such techniques from the Bibliotech?"

"Oh, Klaus, you are such a sweetie but ..." she screwed up her nose as if wrestling for the right words, "... there is something else I haven't mentioned about Adolph; you must swear never to tell anyone."

"I'm all ears, Fraulein Eva ... except perhaps for a mouse's ear, ha-ha," I foolishly threw in. She glared back impatiently. "Or, perhaps I should have said that between the two of us, we're all ears, eh?" I cackled, slapping myself on the thigh and unable to speak for a moment; buoyed by my own little pun.

"This is no time for your smutty jokes, Klaus Hahn. Please try to be a little more sensitive when I'm trying to share something so important."

"I ... er, yes, of course; I swear on the Kaiser's left elbow I won't breathe a word. What is it?"

"I wish you wouldn't use that stupid saying. Well, it's something very personal. It's ... it's just that Adolph has only one ball." She stopped midway through the sentence upon noting my look of bafflement. "Ball, nut, testicle, silly! Adolph has only *one*, and he's quite embarrassed about it. He says that unlike other boys reaching puberty, his second one never descended. I've tried telling him that it doesn't matter to me, that his impoten ... er, inability, is all in his head. We really are a great pair, aren't we?"

What could I say in reply?

"By the way, the staff picnic has been brought forward owing to the war. The boss has agreed to hold it on the slopes above Kehlstein but, of course, everything depends upon the weather at that altitude. I can't really say I'm looking forward to it this year, given Adolph's vanishing acts to his so-called forward bases. Oh Klaus, just wait until you see the view from my bedroom window up there."

I could see Eva was getting back to her old dizzy self.

56

Having been thwarted at the last minute during my previous attempt I had been hoping to spend a few days in the boathouse with Tante and Onkel before the cold weather set in, but before I knew it, the whole team was gathering outside Berchtesgaden Bahnhof for the scenic drive up the mountain.

Soon, our convoy passed through the required security checks and wended its way up the impossibly narrow access road built by Bormann's army of workers to the base of the cliffs.

After passing through a series of tunnels and corners so tight as to require descending vehicles to pull off the road altogether to let us pass, I glimpsed my excited workmates leaning out to grab shots of the valley below. But these scenes were nothing compared to what lay ahead.

Eventually, the lead car spun about and we were ordered to alight at the entrance to an even longer tunnel in the mountainside, the entrance to which I could see was usually secured by two huge metal doors.

Hoffman and Eva led us forward into the gloom, illuminated by a row of candles along each wall; I could hear Eva's excited voice up ahead, reverberating off the granite casing. Immediately, my thoughts flew to the Rainbow Cave, where so many of my ideas and insights had come to light.

After about two hundred yards we halted before an extraordinary sight: there, cut into the rock face sat a pair of polished copper elevator doors gleaming in the soft light. Noiselessly, they opened wide to swallow the first group of twenty staff, while the rest of us milled about in the cold, speaking in hushed tones. A few minutes passed before it was our turn to enter and admire the amazing polished mirrored trims. Surely the only elevator of its kind in existence? No one spoke as the floor lifted gently beneath our feet. Perhaps like me, the others were contemplating the huge cost of such an undertaking.

But no! The moment the doors slid back my workmates poured out into a semicircular dining room to gather at the windows. "Oh look, there's the Berghof down below; it looks like a doll's house."

"I can see a toy train pulling into the station downtown," cried another. The view was just as Eva had described it.

"Yoo hoo, Klaus, where's Klaus?" I heard her voice calling from a small doorway on the left. "Oh, there you are. Come on in, I want to show you my room." At the sound of her voice, I snapped out of my reverie and slowly moved to take her proffered hand.

"Mind the steps, I've not long finished decorating."

Her much-touted bedroom was located on a slightly lower level than the main hall, and as I stepped down into it I was taken by the cosy family of stuffed toys adorning the window sills and other flat surfaces.

Several oversized teddy bears sat propped against her pillow beneath a scowling 16" × 20" black-and-white of Hitler.

"I've hardly any wardrobe space, thanks to Bormann. He says I should only need to bring up one or two outfits at a time. Oh, how I'd love to wring his fat neck, if only I could get my hands around it … Well, what do you think?"

I had already noticed her obvious frilly decorations clashed with the knotty pine wall panelling. A rather gloomy choice, I thought, for a lady's bedroom. "I guess wood panelling is suitable for chalets, hunting lodges and the like, but it's not really that feminine for someone like you …"

"Exactly! That's just what I told Adolph and I'm glad you agree. Apparently, Bormann had great difficulty obtaining sufficient sheets of plywood to finish off the whole interior. Adolph agreed that nothing looks worse than a patchwork of different colours; so much for my suggestion of soft pastels in all the bedrooms."

"What do you do for heating? It must get pretty cold at this altitude."

"Oh, when I'm up here alone, and that's not very often, I have my hot water bottles and my puppies to keep me warm. There's always a skeleton staff on duty and it's not as spooky as I'd feared. On the rare occasions when Adolph sleeps over he insists on the fireplace in the main room burning day and night. It is quite cosy if I leave my door open."

One could hardly miss the massive hearth of plum-swirl marble upon exiting the elevator; it dominated the main hall beside a stack of logs requiring two men to lift. Unlike the many fireplaces scattered about the Berghof, this one was particularly impressive, given the relatively small size of the room. I could only imagine the lonely pleasures to be had sitting before it during a winter storm, with the alpine winds screaming fit to tear the entire fortress from its foundations.

At that moment, Frau Hoffman appeared from the kitchen, ringing a brass dinner bell. "Come on, you two, the others are gathering outside on the patio for a bowl of Henni's Spaghetti. You're missing the best part of the day."

"Be right there!" Eva responded, before muttering something inaudible under her breath. "This way, kind sir," she said cheerily, skipping ahead up the steps onto a covered patio, the roof of which was supported by overly sturdy stone pillars, "… the views are better this side and we'll avoid all those horrid kitchen smells."

Together we hurried across the windswept deck, high above the picture book scenery. Up ahead, tables with bright umbrellas had been erected in the sun, protected from the nipping mountain Zephyrs in the lee of the building. Otherwise, the weather seemed perfect, with only a few unseasonal snowdrifts remaining in the shadows higher up the ridge. Uniformed SS waiters were busy filling glasses and placing baskets of buttered bread rolls in the shade thus created. A crescendo of happy banter filled the air.

Soon, a bowl of steaming Bolognaise was placed before me and a champagne cork popped at the next table. Again, I had to take my hat off to Frau Hoffman for overseeing every detail of our sumptuous fare. Despite the isolated location, this staff picnic contained just as many dainties, if not more.

Eva and her girlfriends had claimed a table for themselves, which I thought a little strange given it was supposed to be a staff picnic. I'd come to recognise most of them hanging around the front counter at work, where they somehow considered themselves an indispensable part of Eva's coterie. Shallow stone retaining walls prevented careless or drunk diners from plunging into the valley below; overhead the snow-capped peaks protruded through the whipping mists.

Swiftly devouring my bowl of Spaghetti I could remain seated no longer and rose to take a few snaps. The views were everything Eva had said they were, and more.

Tiny farmhouses and curling knots of smoke dotted the lush canvas beneath our feet and in each valley nestled a village postcard. I attempted to pick out Tante's boathouse on the shores of Lake Königssee but without success. From up here they all looked the same. I think it was third from the end.

Above us loomed walls of grey granite, surely more formidable than any landscape I'd ever encountered. Once or twice I thought I heard moaning, but it was only wind on the Watzmann. Again, Frau Hoffman rang the dinner bell, this time for silence, and the boss rose to give his annual speech to the staff. He looked more than ever like a uakari monkey with his blood-flecked eyes and florid features; his pants seemed set to burst.

I found a flat surface atop the retaining wall and allowed my eyes to wander, settling on the farthest table which I had been avoiding for obvious reasons and nearly fell over the edge in shock. There, sitting opposite Iris' brown bun and Lothar's bull neck, a vaguely familiar face was staring back: Claudia?

Could it really be *my* Claudia, here in this unlikely setting? Why had I not spotted her earlier? From this distance I could see she looked different, with hair pulled back and scant makeup she looked drawn.

But after all, it had been many months.

I turned away with clammy palms and a surging heart, not wishing to draw attention. It just couldn't be. When I gathered the nerve to check my peripheral vision she was gone, the boss' speech was over and people were applauding. A small group were on their feet carrying hampers, about to head higher up the mountain path and conclude with a picnic. Cautiously, I made my way towards the vacant table amidst a flood of memories. Then, a soft touch on my elbow. "Hello, stranger. I've been trying to catch your eye ever since we sat down." That voice, her voice; it hadn't changed at all.

"It *was* you! Oh, Claudia …"

"Dear Klaus, don't get too carried away in front of all these people; I'll grab a hamper and you choose a bottle of wine. We'll tag along behind the picnickers until 'you know who' is out of sight."

Most of the others had spread out their coloured cloths close to the trail but we pushed on up the hill to the first real snowdrifts. I was determined not to show any sign should my asthma intrude on that day.

After much puffing and panting on my part, she took my hand and steered me between a clutch of large boulders, to where the cliffs fell sheer away beneath our feet and I could see almost to infinity.

Without another word, my friend had spread a rug and emptied the hamper onto it, while I sank the rosé into a handy snowdrift. Almost instinctively we nestled side by side, gazing over the storybook scene; this time she didn't pull away.

For a few long minutes, neither of us spoke although my head was buzzing with a hundred pressing questions. Claudia was the first to break the silence. "Does this remind you of somewhere else we used to sit and swim together in another life?"

Blushing involuntarily, I stammered out a reply. "How could I forget those hours spent with you, m … my love? They are among my happiest ever since … But for now, I'm desperate to know what has happened to you; where have you been? I want to know everything. I felt sure you'd been swallowed up in Dachau, but try as I may no answers ever came …"

"Sweet Klaus, I'm sure you don't really want to know what it's like in Hitler's Citadel of Horrors, you'll find out soon enough. Anyway, for your own good, I'm not authorised to tell you everything."

"Jeez, w … what do you mean by 'everything'?"

"First things first: do you think our wine will be chilled yet? These local cheeses smell delightful and the rolls are fresh out of the oven."

We both chewed thoughtfully and sipped our wine. "But, I must say it did seem strange hoeing into a bowl of pasta as an entrée. Good old Hoffman never misses a chance to extol Henni's many talents. I should have thought Daddy's little favourite would have all the hired help she needs these days to produce Bolognaise by the bucketful, at the click of a finger, being married to the Gauleiter of Vienna and all."

I wanted that meal to last forever. Far below, tiny figures were hard at work in the meadows, felling the autumn fodder in a slow rhythm of sweeping scythes. Swarms of blackbirds wheeled overhead, waiting to pounce on displaced grasshoppers. We clinked glasses as a Golden Eagle circled above in the updraughts, until suddenly, with a screech, the great bird shot up vertically, folded its wings and dropped like a bomb into the scattering flocks below.

"Wow, just look at that; I do believe it's an omen," Claudia gasped. "Like the Nazi Eagle plunging into a peace-loving population; yet still missing its target."

"On that occasion, at least," I observed wryly.

"Oh, I do so hope we all come through this next phase unscathed. Do you remember that time the fortune teller revealed how Robert and I would surely end up together when this business is all over? Including you too, of course. It's a hope I shall cling to until …"

"Robert bloody Robert, why does our conversation always turn to Him? You know full well he moves in grander circles these days; he has little time for you or me," I snapped back.

"Now, now, settle down, don't be such a pessimist; we're probably the only real friends he has. There will never be anyone else for me but Robert; surely you can accept that by now? He'll come running back when things don't go his own way, just wait and see. He's still our best chance of getting out of this mess *if* we can negotiate the next phase successfully. As you know, I am a very patient …"

"What's this next phase you speak of? Can things get much worse than this? Does it have anything to do with your absence?" My heart and mouth thundered on, "I feel like our friendship is going around in circles … we once agreed to be honest with each other; surely we still have that to cling to?"

My moment of jealousy had mastered my judgment. She turned to face me, furrows gathered on her brow as if wrestling with a great dilemma. "When everyone lies, truth is lost," she said slowly, "and without truth we are all lost … Should I start from the day I was taken into 'protective custody'? That too seems a lifetime away." Her eyes glimmered as she fought back a tear.

"From the studio, I was bundled downtown to Gestapo Headquarters, there to be presented before Heydrich himself. Of all the leading Nazis I've confronted and comforted, he is by far the most menacing. When I was shoved into his office he didn't even look up for some minutes, leaving me to wrestle with my fears. Then, slowly he raised his great beak and fixed me with those ice-cold eyes, I knew immediately my fate hung in the balance of my answers."

In his hand he held a list of names. "'Which Schicklegruber are you?' he asked offhandedly. 'Oh yes, Hoffman's little plaything; he took a risk harbouring a Jew all this time. You must realise he has been toying with you, merely playing cat and mouse until you were needed elsewhere for a new role assignment. Now that time has come,' he said, pushing a photograph across the desk and watching my reaction. I could hardly believe my eyes; it was an 8" × 10" of my beloved parents, wearing striped uniforms and a Star of David on their chests.

"'You recognise these Jews of course. If you ever wish to see them again, you will do exactly as Commandant Biebow instructs you. I won't beat about the bush, Fraulein: your parents, like all of the other Jews in Lodz, have been confined to the ghetto where I'm sure the conditions are adequate. Following a period of training, you will be despatched to join them, with one important difference. Your mission will be undertaking surveillance of certain individuals on behalf of the Gestapo, of which you will breathe not a word to anyone, including your parents. In the meantime you will retain your status as 'privileged Jew' and they too will be given special treatment with a room of their own; all provided you continue to carry out your new duties exactly as instructed. Do I make myself clear?'

"That's more or less the way he put it; I assured the vile bastard I would stop at nothing to protect my parents and only then did he fill me in on the details: I was to set up and operate a photo lab inside the ghetto, recording all new arrivals and undertaking 'special assignments' as required. And just between us, it seems my real mission will involve obtaining evidence on Chaim Rumkowski, the Nazi-appointed Jewish Overlord suspected of having his hand in the till as well as his fellow Judenrats in compromising situations. Anything untoward is to be reported back to SS Commandant Biebow, stationed downtown.

"When I read the brief this Rumkowski sounded like a pretty distasteful fellow, selected by the Germans last October to implement Nazi rule over all the Ghetto Jews. On the surface, he has set out to more than please his new masters, even at the expense of turning in his own people. Three weeks after appointing 31 prominent fellow clerics to the Judenrat Caucus, he had 23 of them executed for refusing to 'rubber stamp' his policies. No one knows what happened to the rest."

I was silenced by this sobering resume of her unseen boss.

"I've had scant news of my parents since the invasion, and the Germans have now sealed off the Lodz Ghetto, cramming tens of thousands of Jews into a few square miles of brick walls and barbed wire. The stories coming out are appalling, with talk of *nine people* per room! Surely, no one can live on these rations. Poles receive 634 calories per day, Jews just 300, while the guards stuff themselves in excess of two thousand.

"Mama says they call the evening meal 'sand soup' as it comprises unwashed potatoes and carrots boiled up with one or two cow heads containing hair, teeth and eyes.

"Rumkowski has complainants of both sexes beaten and his political rivals have been threatened with denouncement to the Germans. It seems he is in control of all the workshops and presses the workers every day to do more on their starvation rations. His latest motto is 'To be at least ten minutes ahead of every German demand' and he's even printed up his own currency, the 'Rumkin'.

"They tell of striking ghetto workers handing out flyers that rail against this 'Accursed Parasite' and his family, for enjoying all the choicest plunder. The special Sonder Jewish Police are loosed against those dissenters who defy his policy of total collaboration. Rumkowski believes that only by absolute commitment to the production of useful goods and clothing can the Jews stay alive and prove themselves indispensable to the Germans; what a joke!"

She was fired up. "I'm glad to be called upon to help take him down. Don't worry, I've been thoroughly briefed on how to handle myself; his reputation for perving on and molesting 'his girls' is widely known among the captive population and he is hated for it. Herr Heydrich assured me that as long as I fulfilled my obligations my parents would continue to receive 'special treatment'.

"Can't you see, Klaus? It's my one and only chance to do something meaningful at last, to ease not only Ma and Pa's suffering but maybe certain others among those tens of thousands slaving under Rumkowski's heel. I shall be close to my parents and among my own people. I'm not doing this for Heydrich and his Nazis; I'm doing it for myself and those poor bastards locked away in the ghetto."

"B ... But 'special treatment' doesn't mean what you think it means, your survival will hang by a thread ..."

"I have no choice. I'm assured that I'm doing the right thing by my people, a service only I can render: to identify those abusing power and holding back a slice of the workers' efforts for themselves. Chaim Rumkowski is at the head of that list.

"The Gestapo suspects that all his seeming compliance may be a ruse, to distract from a potential uprising. My friends in the Orchestra want me to go; it's only a matter of time before my cover here is blown. Don't forget Iris still knows my secret." She leaned closer though no one was in sight. "They say Hitler is on the cusp of invading Russia, can you believe that? If it's true then surely this madman will *never* stop until every last one of his 'inferior' neighbours is 'annihilated', to use his own words. When he alone will stand crowing on top of an extirpated world in flames."

"Yes, but even the mighty Frenchman was no match for Russia's General Winter."

"Ha! Do warlords ever truly learn from history? Hitler's convinced if he goes in quick and hard, the troops will be marching into Moscow while the sun's still shining. Look how he walked all over Austria and my own beloved Poland."

"Well, I guess we'll soon see. When must you leave? How long will you be away? Are you free to return to Munich when you choose? You will send me photos won't you, perhaps even a roll or two of ghetto life?"

"Please! Not too many questions at once. Until the call comes I'll simply be enjoying myself around the Munich hotspots, as usual with my ear to the ground, and put in my spare time at the studio.

"The boss thought that by keeping up my rent during my absence he could retain his former grip on my old ways. 'My friends will be so disappointed,' he wails, but you should have seen his eyes pop when I handed him Heydrich's letter of intent. I'm beyond the reach of even the biggest wigs, at least for the time being. Anything would be better than having to face another of those grinning Nazi jackasses with their reeking breaths and beer bellies. At least in Lodz, I can almost be myself, among my own kind, wherever that path may lead.

"If fate serves me true and the fortune teller is correct I have no doubt Robert will find me. He is the only one able to save us from this unfolding nightmare … By the way, I want to show you something when you return from visiting your relatives; I have obtained a very special gadget."

As I was about to accept her invitation, a vigorous pealing of Frau Hoffman's bell warned that we had fifteen minutes until the last elevator descended: otherwise, stragglers would need to descend one thousand feet on foot via a narrow winding path in order to reach the carpark and ride back to Munich. The staff picnic was as good as over and it seemed our exchange of ideas had barely begun.

Hurrying down the ridge, I snapped a bank of clouds breaking up the distant sky, causing a lone shaft to pick out the Steeples of Salzburg in the distance. I also persuaded Claudia to pose for a silhouette against the sunset, which as it turned out would be the last photo of my friend I would ever take.

In the elevator, our fellow travellers huddled together in their thick garments, complaining of the cold, while I gazed at our joint reflections in the polished copper walls and mirrors, convinced that this had been the best staff picnic ever.

In that spirit I was able to get the picnic printing completed and distributed to each participant by lunchtime the next day, being thus free to take up my knapsack and set out downhill on foot for a well-earned break beside the silver lake.

As I walked, my mind was troubled, at other times receptive to the freedom and beauty all around. The network of paths ran on through checkpoints in the perimeter fence, down through a sprinkle of resorts and a more or less "normal" small-town lifestyle.

Of course, swastikas fluttered from every lamppost and building around Lake Königssee, but so far the valley population appeared to have been spared the worst of Bormann's heavy hand.

Arriving at the water's edge I was again overcome by the beauty of that spectacular reservoir, walled in by sheer cliffs of grey granite. I could see smoke rising from the deck of the farthest boathouse, with Gretel waving and Onkel puffing away contentedly in his wicker easy-chair; theirs appeared to be the only shingled cabin with a pot belly stove outdoors, so I hurried toward it.

"Well, dear boy, they say absence makes the heart grow fonder, and this has been one heck of an absence," said Tante, crushing me to her bosom. "Come on through. Frederick insisted we put the Christmas decorations up early to make you feel right at home. What do you think?"

I could see a tree dripping with red candles beside the indoor fireplace, sprigs of holly and coloured streamers dangled overhead.

Instead of St Nicholas, a huge rosy-cheeked "Father Christmas" beamed down from the top of the tree.

The renovated boatshed was long and narrow, with several hand-painted screens dividing the space into separate areas.

"You can sleep on this settee closest to the deck; it offers the best views of the lake. Elbow room is a little tight, but we don't get many visitors these days," Onkel said, fussing about placing a glass of water and a gift pack of family cookies on the table next to my bed, before removing his cap and looking me up and down.

"Well, well, let's have a good look at you. There's been a lot of water under the bridge since last we saw you, or, should I say, under the deck, ha! Come on outside and take a look, we spend most of our time out there," he said, throwing wide a large sliding glass door that opened up the whole end of the building.

"Give him time to catch his breath, Frederick, that's some hike down from the Berghof, the poor boy must be starving."

"I never say No to your homemade cookies and a cuppa, Tante; at least the walk this time was mostly downhill," I replied, settling into a prepared wicker chair before the crackling stove on the deck.

Onkel sat down and re-lit his briar pipe, looking as if a great burden had been lifted off his shoulders. His bristly grey hair no longer stood up aggressively, but clung to his skull in uneven tufts; his nicotine-stained moustache drooped down on one side. Despite this rather careworn appearance, his mood was bright and upbeat, the only sign of his former affiliation that I could see was a tiny swastika flag fluttering from the deck railing. From this area the boathouse enjoyed a panoramic view along Lake Königssee in one direction, and a full view of the ferry terminal surrounded by its souvenir shops almost opposite.

With a squeak of steam whistles, several launches were embarking on the afternoon cruise to St Bartholomeus and Obersee; the "Horst Wessel Song" was blaring over loudspeakers.

"Just look at that bevy of stuck-up Nazi bitches in their latest fashions," Onkel muttered under his breath, as one of the launches passed dangerously close. "Don't they think they're something? We can't be too careful; the skippers are rewarded if they report anything amiss around the shore, hence my one remaining symbol of 'loyalty' out front," he added, gesturing toward the drooping swastika.

Tante chuckled. "I'm afraid the Christmas goose has long been eaten, but I've kept you some Foi Gras," she said before taking her seat and placing a rack of toast and glazed pot on the table before me. "The poor goose outgrew his suitcase and there were scant pickings in the shade of the boatsheds.

"Believe it or not, we've settled in quite well, given all the upheaval. With Onkel's Nazi memorabilia now gone I've just enough room for my easel and paints, and sufficient wall space to hang a handful of modern masters. 'Better a hovel in paradise than a castle in hell,' I remind Onkel Fedi, and as you can see we keep to ourselves since he resigned from the Party.

"It's not so easy maintaining the pretence of 'gratitude'; everyone is just so suspicious of everyone else, looking to settle old scores by ratting on their neighbours. We do our best to keep up appearances: I attend the Frauenschaft group every Wednesday and we both wander over for the Gauleiter's speech on Thursday nights. That's about the extent of our involvement; just enough to keep them off our backs, we hope. We sing a few songs thanking the Führer for the weather and for awakening our love of nature. It's quite pathetic.

"Did I tell you that 'Silent Night' was composed near here, just over the Austrian border, a few short miles away? It's one of the last Christmas songs still being heard in public these days. Next thing you know it'll be banned too."

Before I could answer, Tante leaned closer, glancing around to ensure no vessel was in earshot. "You must have seen for yourself: all Germany is silent, nervous, suppressed. It speaks in whispers, there is no public opinion, no discussions of anything. Even your Onkel is being accused of 'left-wing sympathies'."

"It's true boy," Onkel concurred, "being a loyal Party Member since the Putsch didn't help me one jot in the end. This little strudel here ..." Fedi smiled affectionately and draped an arm around Gretel's shoulder, "... saved me from being sucked irretrievably into Nazism's ever-deepening black hole; how could I have been so stupid and blind?" His words were pensive and measured.

"Most of them will never see the light, my dear, yet this boy sees only too clearly ... By the way, whatever happened to that girlfriend of yours who was living the high life?" Onkel Fedi changed the subject upon receiving a glare from Tante.

"Which one, Onkel? There's always Eva moping about the darkroom, of course, but then there's my … well, she's not really *my* Claudia. She still believes she loves Robert, despite his oft-stated indifference; but I don't wish to speak ill of my brother, he's steeped in all this up to his neck."

Fedi stroked his chin thoughtfully.

And so the conversation wandered as always, from one interesting topic to another; we sipped on our Pilsener and emptied the cake carousel twice. One by one, the immaculate little launches putted past with blasts on their air horns, all to demonstrate, Tante said, the remarkable reverberating qualities of Königssee's sheer granite walls.

A few tourists waved approvingly toward our cosy setup as the last gilded sun rays crept up the tree-spattered cliffs opposite, and apart from a fisherman casting his fly in the distance, the scene fell still. My soft chanting slipped away with the mist, accompanied by the song of a river warbler. That night I slept on a pillow of "Peace Profound" with no sign of a wheeze.

The next morning, the first beam brushed the treetops high above before slowly dripping down into the boathouse. Gretel was already out on the deck and had the stove alight; the waterway was stirring with small craft.

"Welcome aboard nephew. When I looked in, you appeared to be sleeping the sleep of the dead. I had hoped to take the launch up to Obersee and maybe have a picnic beside the falls, but it may be wiser to keep our heads down. We have so much to discuss and only this day to do it. Tomorrow you will be back in that horrid darkroom with all its toxic vapours."

"Oh Tante, there's so much I want to share with you: the things I see and realise, the current dull directions in art. Your letters have brought me such pleasure; a glimmer of hope that we may not be stuck forever with this boorish brood of demons."

"Good Heavens, boy! You could have your tongue cut out for even thinking such thoughts," Fedi chipped in, "but good on you anyway."

Lapping trusses of froth broke against the gravel shore and the autumn sun stirred my inner eye. A whole day and night yet lay ahead. While Fedi read and re-read his illustrated magazines, Gretel and I pored over art books and her eviscerated collection of modern originals. She said that space constraints had allowed the retention of a mere handful of her very best pictures.

"This here is what painting is about: part poetry, part philosophy," she mused, turning the light onto a small Picasso drawing in the corner that I fancied. "And then there's our very own 'Blau Ryder' movement, stunning the world with its bold colour compositions," she added with a flourish, pointing to a Klee squiggle hanging beside a bright Marianne von Werefkin.

"I must admit that's more my style," I responded knowingly, "I so loved Franz Mark until they pulled his works from the gallery walls …"

"And here's my Russian baby," she added, ignoring my interjection, "a cartoon by Kandinsky, perhaps the most exciting of them all. Can you detect his perfect tensions between colour, line and form? Oh, I do so long for the day when fine modern art will be welcomed again."

As I stood staring she moved on. "Now here's something completely different: Gericault, same century," she enthused, rolling out a poster of a sword-wielding Napoleonic Hussar on a rearing grey dappled steed. "Nonetheless the rules remain the same: it's all about Life Force energy! Without that, no piece is worth framing. Just look at this explosion of vigour, possibly the greatest horse painter of all time; with the exception of Leonardo, of course. This is a mere print but as you can see, the best painters know how their subjects *behave*, not just where every muscle and sinew is located. All Jungvolk should be introduced to fine art and only the best literature, which is why I passed on my library to you; although Heaven only knows what's happened to it now."

I squirmed slightly in my seat but she didn't seem to notice; at that moment I felt I detected a weakness in her argument.

"I'm not convinced your analogy stacks up, Tante; when we look at the ancient Greeks or a sculpture such as Michelangelo's 'David', for example, where is the evidence of your energy explosion?"

Gretel seemed taken aback; for a long moment, she perused my face closely before speaking. "Ah, yes. I was wondering when you would get around to the *latent* forces residing in a great piece like 'David'. Michelangelo, like the Greeks, had surpassed himself in restraint, merely *implying* in his subject's demeanour the tremendous event that was about to unfold across the pages of history.

"It's true; no muscle ripples in readiness, and no pre-emptive snarl mars the slinger's lips, but somehow, deep within this mighty block of marble, every atom stands eternally poised to deliver Divine Retribution ..."

"Oh, Tante; I'm not so sure my own appreciation of art will ever extend to such insights; remember, it's not so long ago when I was utterly repelled by Picasso's revolutionary dabs. One has to learn a whole new language." She nodded.

We then proceeded more comfortably to reinforce each other's opinions of the lacklustre "Great German Art Exhibition" which we both felt had contributed nothing whatsoever to the advancement of fine art, when a cacophony of gunshots erupted from the hills above, reverberating down the cliffs and through the village. A pair of startled grey herons took off and a nearby kingfisher gave an angry squeak.

"It sounds like great Thor rattling the storm clouds overhead, we are getting used to it now. Actually, it's Göring and his band of Junker cronies," she said, without looking up. "He's taken possession of a huge area in the high country and released dozens of ibex and grouse to blast away at. One would think that given we are at war he would have more pressing responsibilities."

"And save ammunition for what lies ahead," Onkel added.

"There seem to be just so few birds remaining in Germany, at least in Munich," I rejoined. "Sadly, even now there are those who would reduce their numbers further. Oh, Tante, how I miss that jungle glee club at sunrise. Once upon a time, I knew each call by heart … and every bird by the sound of its wingbeats."

"Jungle? Jungle? Well, you're in a very different jungle now, young Klaus," Onkel said, looking up from his newspaper. "Our erstwhile Führer seems hell-bent on turning the whole world back into one big jungle, where only the strong survive and the rest of us will never feel safe again. Although, to be fair, I do subscribe to the theory that Darwinism supports German racial superiority …"

"Nonsense Frederick, Darwin's Theory of Evolution makes no such distinctions between Homo sapiens. 'Every race and nation has greater and lesser beings than thou,' to quote the Dalai Lama. You of all people should only need to take a good look at the physiognomy of Goebbels and the other leading Nazis, including Hitler himself, to discount that perverse heresy once and for all."

Onkel snorted surrender and returned to his reading.

"Now, where were we?" Gretel asked, flicking through her pile of prints and canvases.

I sat up straight. "I guess I was trying to say that my acquired skills are now being applied mainly to the subjects in my developing dish, rather than outside, in the real world."

"Don't be too sure. You are in a unique position to observe much of what is going on at the highest levels. Photography may in the end be capable of bringing many of the perpetrators to justice. 'As in Heaven, so on Earth' like the fearless Pastor Niemoller preaches. I have some of his printed sermons here if you're interested. There's not much in his words to find fault with; not every clergyman has buckled under to the great lie, you know?"

"'As above, so below.' Sister Klara too expressed the belief that certain basic truths run through all religions, beginning with the Rainbow Serpent of the Australian Aborigine and Isis of Egypt. It's getting harder these days to discern much truth or wisdom in National Socialism …"

Onkel grunted, pretending to read.

"Don't confuse the boy, Frederick. You know as well as I that National Socialism is shaping up as a failed experiment, benefiting only those who are prepared to bow down before the leader in absolute submission. It's no different from any other form of tyranny. We are better off right out of it. Klaus already has a clear idea between right and wrong. If you won't listen to Pastor Niemoller it would do no harm to heed more closely what the boy has to say; in the end, we all have to face our Maker with a clear conscience."

"Bah! Don't talk to me about conscience and clerics. Even Pope Pius has rolled over before Hitler's black angels. I guess he's more fearful of Bolshevism than of Moloch himself. Gone are the days when common Volk feel understood by their leaders; those with a different view run the risk of being hung out to dry. I hardly think classical religion has any answer to the horrors we are facing."

"But Onkel, I can only refer you back to the 'Law of the Triangle' as espoused by Pythagoras. Surely you can see that the Universal powers of Creation, whatever name men choose to give them, manifest as Light, Life, and even Love far beyond our puny earthbound comprehension? 'As above, so below', this is the Great Secret; open to all yet realised by few."

He stared back, dumbfounded.

"Can I put it this way, Onkel? Mother Nature will not be thwarted in Her forward thrust towards fulfilment for all sentient beings, at least, that's what I've come to believe …"

"Twaddle boy! Pythagoras? You are indeed drawing a long bow. Didn't your time in the jungle teach you that many of your so-called 'sentient beings' will have to submit to stronger and smarter predators? In other words, some of them are surely born to be eaten!"

Tante Gretel cleared her throat.

"Well, I suppose I could be referring to humans at the top of the food chain, blindly grasping at the two-edged sword of free will," I added. "Surely, Nazism is the very opposite of this, designed to crush individual expression."

"Mein Gott, my nephew's become a philosopher overnight. I told you already, I want nothing more to do with the whole rotten system. I've seen the last of 'em …"

"Oh, yes dear, but have *they* seen the last of us?" Aunt interjected. "We both know that it's only a matter of time until the Party starts poking into every last bedroom; none of us can remain forever immune from their meddlesome surveillance. Even our local officials have long memories and good filing systems."

She turned back to me and lowered her voice, "Thus far, they've contented themselves with banning Fedi from his old haunts, which in one way has been good for our marriage, hasn't it dear?"

"Eh? I suppose so. Well, whatever God there was is now dead. It's going to take a lot more than the churches to save us; that's all I'm sayin'."

I felt responsible for stirring up this angst between them. "Sister Klara had a way of forming parables that made sense in simple terms. With hindsight I see them holding deeper meanings, going back to the roots of all Creation and our part in it. She taught us to see ourselves as single raindrops, sometimes seemingly separate, yet always part of the same element, water.

"Raindrops often gather together in puddles and streams, at other times going home to the clouds and oceans; but always they remain water. H_2O! Doesn't it follow that our palpitating earthly existence always remains a part of that very infinite Life Force that brought all of Creation into being?"

Onkel Fedi peered at me hard over the top of his glasses, before returning to his sports page, sensing the conversation was going nowhere. Tante brought the discussion to a close.

"Well, I can't see too much wrong with your ideas, dear boy; German brains are being swamped with pre-determined thoughts, while drained of all hope. Onkel and I can go on wishing for a miracle, but either way, we've come to realise that Life itself is the greatest gift and Freedom the True Garnish."

Thus we filled our short hours with speculation and supposition, feeling closer than at any time.

It was with a heavy heart that I crunched my way next morning through the splintery crystals of hoar frost, toward Berchtesgaden Bahnhof; pausing only long enough to glance up at Bormann's forbidding transmutation.

There were whispers that the sister of the Belgian King, Princess Marie-José, would be arriving shortly for an audience with Hitler. Early-bird "Führer Tourists" already had their binoculars trained on the high slopes, where one or two lights yet twinkled.

It was later revealed that during this royal visit, the princess had burned her mouth on a hot teacup, causing Hitler to lay into the staff before offering profuse apologies. During the train ride home, I was too preoccupied to open my book.

It seemed like no time before the first ten rolls were coming out of the fixer. It was as if I'd never left.

57

At the first opportunity, I made a beeline for Claudia's apartment, bounding up the flight of steps to be confronted by a scene of sorrow.

Frau Falkenhorst stood in the corridor sobbing uncontrollably, her face buried deep over Claudia's shoulder. "Oh, my baby, what is to become of him? He's so frightened of the dark."

My friend motioned me to go on inside, and she followed with the weeping woman clinging on.

"Perhaps it's as they say it is at Hadamar, Frau Falkenhorst. The children will be given a thorough check and special treatment if needed," Claudia cooed. "Why, my own family in Poland also receives special treatment and Pauli may even enjoy spending time with the other special kids; I wouldn't be worrying too much just yet. Dr Brandt himself, one of the Führer's leading physicians, is in charge of the children's facilities and has been overseeing their care personally."

I could hardly believe she was mouthing such platitudes; yet again, the poor woman was in no fit state to hear the likely truth.

Slowly, the distraught widow pulled herself together and cast a more suspicious eye on both of us. "Why then do the transport orders always come in the middle of the night? Tell me that. Watching those terrified little ones being herded onto the grey bus was enough to break any mother's heart; even the healthy children label them 'death wagons'. Oh, my dear little lost Pauli."

I could tell that Claudia was nowhere near as unconcerned as she made out, and in the weeks that followed, she went out of her way to comfort her desolate neighbour. Apart from that brief official notification of the child's whereabouts, no further information concerning Pauli's welfare was forthcoming.

As forewarned, Claudia knew that she would soon accompany a trainload of German Jews being "resettled" back to Poland and that the Party would continue to pay rent on her Munich apartment. Her inner struggles were clearly visible. "I know nothing more than that!" she snapped at me one day in Framing and Finishing when I pressed for more details.

"I'm torn between leaving that poor woman and being with my family, I know not what will become of her when I go."

After several more weeks without news, the broken creature was almost ready to limp down to Gestapo Headquarters and demand answers, hang the consequences, when a small metal urn turned up one morning on her front doorstep.

To her horror and that of everyone on the first floor, the accompanying death certificate stated that the urn contained the ashes of Patient No. 13587, one P. Falkenhausen, who had died of "appendicitis". For "hygienic reasons", the body had been cremated immediately. When I pressed her through her tears, she eventually pulled herself together and gasped out the terrible truth.

"M ... My Pauli had his appendix removed years ago when he was only three," she wailed. "Liars! ... Filthy Nazi liars."

Weeks later, when I arrived outside Claudia's empty flat, I found the babbling woman propped against her doorway, clutching an identical urn to the first. Taking the supposed death certificate from her trembling fingers, I noted that Patient No. 13587, P. Falkenhorst, had regrettably passed away from "Double Pneumonia".

A handwritten addendum across the bottom of the page warned that under no circumstances should any relative of the deceased attempt to contact the above facility. Soon after, it came as no surprise to learn that Frau Falkenhorst had been consigned to a mental institution, where her own fate would have been sealed.

To say I was devastated by the unfolding events of early '41 would be to downplay their combined impact, but there were many more public crimes conspiring to sour the scene.

First of all came Rudolph Hess' harebrained "peace mission" to Britain in a "borrowed" fighter plane, which made headlines worldwide. Quite off his own bat, and following a session with his astrologer, Deputy Führer decided to cross the channel in person to discuss teaming up with Churchill against Bolshevism.

After somehow avoiding Britain's coastal aircraft defences, Hess bailed out over the Scottish estate of his onetime acquaintance, Lord Hamilton, allowing the plane to crash in a nearby field. Upon being taken into custody by a startled farmer, Hess was soon labelled insane by the British authorities, who not only denied him access to the Prime Minister but threw him into goal.

Hess' misadventure came as a huge shock to Hitler, who joined forces with his Propaganda Minister to spread the word that his erstwhile Deputy had clearly suffered a "total nervous collapse".

Little did we know that final preparations for Operation Barbarossa, the foreshadowed invasion of Russia, were in their final stages, and Hess' misguided peace feelers inadvertently threw a spanner in the works.

A flamboyant Mussolini, fearing he might miss out on a share of the spoils, launched out of the blue his own pre-emptive foray into Ethiopia. German generals watched on in dismay as the Italian forces almost immediately got bogged down and grounded to a halt, throwing the momentous German timetable into disarray.

For days after learning of Hess' defection and Mussolini's ill-fated invasions, Hitler stormed about roaring like an animal, ordering the immediate arrest of all and any of Hess' staff who could possibly have had prior knowledge. The sudden necessity of coming to his Italian allies' aid delayed Operation Barbarossa by several crucial, and as it turned out, fatal weeks.

"Get me Bormann now!" his cry thundered. "That pompous fool waited until he could see we were winning before he had the balls to fire a single shot!" Hitler pilloried the Italian leader to his sympathetic Gauleiter and anyone else who'd listen.

After finally calming down, he admitted that Hess really had no case to answer; there was "no question of treachery".

Bormann, however, not nearly so forgiving, had the bit between his teeth and moved swiftly to fill the vacuum, expunging all traces of his former superior from Party and public memory.

He issued orders for the immediate removal of Hess' photographs, printed articles and even school book references, a monumental task in itself. Within a week, all traces of the former Deputy Führer had vanished and Bormann had secured his grip on power.

Anyone who retained a lingering fondness for the old leadership style, or did not bow down to the new, was quickly shunted aside in a spiteful flurry of efficiencies.

Still not content, the newly appointed Personal Secretary then changed his son's name from Rudolph to Gerhard, and nominated a new set of Godparents for the boy, before going on to convince Hitler to get rid of his former Chief Adjutant, Bruckner, now in his 50s, as being "too old" and altogether too close to the former Deputy Führer. Naturally enough, the Mountain Gauleiter now assumed all outstanding responsibility under his own iron-fisted aegis, while choosing several extra mistresses from the catering staff.

Soon after that turbulent distraction, I received my first note from Claudia in Poland, hidden in an empty film canister among a collection of black-and-whites, detailing life in the camp.

It was brief, to the point and deeply troubling, warning me against Dr Brandt and his murderous campaign against so-called "Unproductive members of the National Community" in the gas chamber at Hadamar and elsewhere.

I guessed she had somehow tracked down little Pauli's movements, coming across the ghastly details of the Nazi's T4 euthanasia programme. She further noted that Dr Brandt was busy performing "hundreds of abortions" on "unsuitable" women and that high-ranking Nazis seeking exemptions for their family members could apply only to Dr Brandt himself.

It seemed Claudia was not the only one warning of "defective" children being disposed of in the very institutions designed to keep them safe.

Munster's popular Bishop von Galen delivered several sermons over the summer, denouncing the disappearance of mentally and physically handicapped inmates, the arrest of Jesuits and the confiscation of Church property. His audacious filing of murder charges against the Nazi authorities under long-standing German Law caused Hitler, who feared a backlash from his vast Catholic following, to blink.

In the future, such cleansing of the National Soul would take place in a far more subtle and decentralised fashion, while a dark undercurrent of suspicion continued to lurk.

Eva too, felt compelled to add her voice to the growing controversy, but in the end could gain no backing. When she finally did pluck up passable courage to inform Hitler he told her tersely "not to bother him with gossip".

But in raising the matter behind the Mountain Reichsleiter's back, she'd been brought into even greater conflict with Bormann, who was now confirmed leader of the Nazi Party *and* Private Secretary to the Führer.

Bormann, having completed his Obersalzberg transformation, now turned his considerable attention to yet another seemingly impossible task: the removal of all outward signs of orthodox religion in Germany. Crucifixes were to be removed from school rooms and nuns were banned from teaching. No house of worship was safe, even those flying the "Führer Standard" alongside their red-velvet pulpit Baldachins with the gold tassels. It seemed the Party Secretary's hatred of religion in general had been granted free reign.

Henceforth, there would be but One God for Germany, Adolph Hitler, and his choir of brown angels of which he, Martin Bormann, was now the principal conductor.

58

Operation Barbarossa, when it came in the early hours of June 22, was almost an anti-climax for those of us in Munich.

We learned that three and a half million men were already pouring across Russia's borders in the greatest land invasion in history. Newsreel footage showed the commander in high spirits, emerging from his tri-motor behind the frontlines to congratulate his generals on their initial successes; surely, this was the biggest and most exciting gamble of his life. His first target was the ruling Communist Elite and his second was Soviet Jewry.

At long last, Adolph Hitler was poised to establish a true "Garden of Eden" in the East and promised great rolling victories to come.

"Stalin is sick in the head," he assured his generals. "The original inhabitants are to be treated like red Indians," he instructed, "Victory and Glory awaits our invincible army! It's good if terror leads the way."

Indeed, for a while it seemed as if all these predictions *were* coming true; perhaps the five-week delay in bailing out Mussolini didn't really matter too much after all. On that first day, 1,800 Russian aircraft were destroyed, mostly on the ground, while hundreds of thousands of Soviet footsloggers were surrounded by the swift-flowing Panzer divisions and taken into captivity.

From the skies overhead, 2,700 Luftwaffe combat aircraft strafed and bombed stubborn strong points out of existence. Over the People's Radio came news that Stalin had fled to his Dacha, in a state of nervous collapse.

However, as more and more pictures came across the press desk a very different story began to emerge: it seemed many of the officers carried 35 mm folding cameras of their own and some of the images now emerging could only be described as criminal.

Some showed Himmler, as head of the SS, swiftly following up the advancing Wehrmacht on an inspection tour designed to streamline the killing process. The task of the newly-fashioned Einsatzgruppen murder squads was to eliminate anyone superfluous to the war effort, which in Himmler's estimation amounted to some thirty million Slavic souls. Grainy images of these SS killing units going about their grisly work began turning up at the studio where I was soon instructed to create a separate "Ostlands Private" file.

Day after day in the darkroom, I was confronted firsthand with what it meant to be conquered by Germany: whole villages going up in flames and fresh-dug ditches overflowing with bodies. Rows of unarmed civilians lined up against walls in the blood-black snow, waiting to be shot.

I wondered to myself if it really were possible for war to be this simple and absolute. The boss had other ideas about my distraction with certain press releases, literally bombarding me with undeveloped films of his latest escapades, more rightly called orgies. By now I was relatively inured against the goings on of him and his bevy of hangers-on of both sexes. I churned out series after series of tradeable postcards in a variety of Bacchanalian settings. It seemed such uninhibited romping was becoming commonplace across Nazi high society.

Out of the blue, I received a visit and a roll of 35 mm to develop from Herman Fegelein, Robert's supposed guardian angel from the 2nd SS Cavalry Division. The pair was in town for a final bender before they and their horses were shipped out to the Eastern Front by rail.

"Keep these beauties safe until I return; Bobby said I can depend on you. From time to time, you will receive films from our assault on Moscow, which I'm led to believe will be all over by Yuletide. You will develop them for your eyes only, until we return from our mission, understood? Heil Hitler!"

While Robert's best mate clicked his heels and looked every inch the conqueror, my big brother wasn't looking too confident at all, given his stated aim was to kill as many enemies as possible in the shortest time. When they lurched out to continue their pub crawl, I overheard mention of "Operation Typhoon", the great thrust toward Moscow by Army Group Centre, which did not mean much to me.

Meanwhile, Hoffman's chain-smoking, puffy features and flabby midriff broadcast the apogee of his excesses, while his cynical blood-flecked eye-slits hinted at many more. One wag noted Hoffman "had more Chins than a Chinese phonebook", and was increasingly being disparaged as "The Reich Drunk". Though able to steal everything he wanted, including alcohol, it was impossible to resist with the world's finest wine cellar right under his nose.

His earlier charisma had long since crumbled beneath Hitler's beck and heel, as bit by bit he was reduced to the role of court jester.

Between assignments, which could come at any moment of the night or day, he could be seen wandering the hallowed halls of Nazidom with glass in hand, offering wisecracks and cutting observations.

He was too drunk to oversee our move into larger premises in Frederickstrasse, only recently confiscated from its Jewish owners, let alone his far-flung empire of studios across Europe. A certain laissez-faire attitude began to take hold.

Then, in a seeming act of Divine Intervention, he was again struck down by severe illness which was quickly diagnosed by Bormann and Morell as "suspected Typhus". This powerful pair, for years chafing at Hoffman's unrestricted access to Hitler, saw their chance to enforce his banishment from the inner circle until further notice!

From that day on, Himmler and Bormann cemented their friendship, with the former enemies now greeting each other with double-hand clasps and flowery compliments. Any further attempts to bring Hoffman's exonerating paperwork before Hitler was nipped in the bud, and for the first time ever, the "Official Photographer" lapsed into resentment.

"It's my damn portraits that made him what he is today. He took advantage of my Henni and then insisted she marry that pansy, Schirach. This is the thanks I get for giving my life to one man," he grumbled to no one in particular.

New alliances were emerging, and Hoffman was rattled by his ongoing exclusion. Worse still, Walter Frenzl's colourful images were coming more to the fore, gracing yet more international magazine covers with a natural charm that all photographers aim at but seldom convey; and we all knew it.

Despite the successful release of his newest black-and-white illustrated book, *The Face of the Führer*, and the acquisition of two brand-new Volkswagens exclusively for studio use, Hoffman remained at arm's length and his depression only deepened.

It seemed like knowledge of the power he wielded over us served only at such times to sharpen his contempt for our efforts.

However, for the one printer already in possession of a driver's licence, these two bright orange "People's Cars" implied the possibility of a whole new era. Despite the poor wages, fractured work schedules and excessive Party deductions, there now appeared this glimmer of hope.

For the time being, I was instructed to remain on call in my old lodgings in Schellingstrasse, until the latest time and motion methods across town had been implemented fully. A second team was busy in the Press Room, modifying all our old-fashioned routines into promptitude itself.

Occasionally, the phone in the empty foyer rang and I was ordered to collect a "special order" from Frederickstrasse. At other times, whenever I had processing to drop off, I was able to keep the Volkswagen overnight; I found myself with more time to explore Munich's galleries and parklands, besides catching up on my reading. When out and about it was impossible not to observe the almost endless troop convoys passing through town with little cheering.

Later in 1941, when the cold weather really began to set in, first reports emerged of whole trainloads of German wounded freezing to death while en route home from the Eastern front. When one trainload of walking wounded pulled in beside Hitler's *America* outside Berlin and pressed their noses against the frosty glass for a glimpse of their Commander-in-Chief, apparently Hitler ordered his blinds to be drawn.

And strangely enough, newspaper headlines continued to trumpet confidently: "Russian soldiers, kaput! Moscow, kaput!"

About that time I first noticed Jews of all ages wearing yellow stars on their chests; that is, on those remaining few who dared to show their faces in the street. Hitler's "Nacht und Nebel" (Night and Fog) decree was already a terrifying reality across the Fatherland and conquered territories, not only for Jews but other "useless eaters" swept up into indefinite confinement, or worse. Once under arrest, the Gestapo saw to the swift disposal of "troublesome" prisoners.

To everyone's dismay, Hitler's favourite fighter pilot, Ernst Udet, long a hero of the Great War and favourite at court among Eva and friends, shot himself through the head while on the telephone to his girlfriend, Inge, after contumelious attacks on his character and competence by Hitler and especially Göring, who'd tried to blame the flying ace for the Luftwaffe's failure to annihilate the R.A.F. and crush British morale. Udet strongly believed Hitler's decision to switch the attack from England's fighter bases to her big cities was the turning point of the air battle, and he went to his grave cursing Göring for having acquiesced.

Notwithstanding, in a perfect propaganda campaign, his actual suicide was concealed from the public, and Udet was lauded as a hero killed in flight while testing a new weapon. The great warrior was laid to rest with full military honours. Eva didn't attend.

Yet more unsettling was the first Allied bombing of Munich in September, causing minimal damage but widespread panic. All this and more was covered by a Press Room run off its feet, forced to suppress as much as it released.

Between mid-October and November 11, at the start of the worst winter in a hundred years, twenty trainloads of German Jews were crammed into cattle cars under appalling conditions and despatched eastward to the ghetto at Lodz. Other trains loaded with Gypsies headed toward the gas chambers of Chelmno Concentration Camp.

Nazi social cleansing was just hitting its straps, and there was ever more talk of finding a Final Solution to the "Jewish Problem".

"All Germans feel this fear, it has suddenly become *their* fear; most conceal it behind a mask of busyness," Claudia warned, summing up the wider mood before the rest of us had fully woken up to the unfolding horrors.

There seemed no use in my attempting to plan ahead for Christmas, with Munich now on a war footing facing serious disruptions and a shortage of essentials like butter and darkroom supplies. Somehow though, despite cardboard rationing, Hoffman managed to secure his monthly allocation of four tonnes of printing paper. All across town, blockältestes had become air raid wardens, with ever more intrusive powers. For a while, it seemed I'd been left alone to face the gathering storm.

Well, not quite alone. Our great rival, Walter Frenzl, accompanying the invading forces on the long road to Moscow, stumbled across a mass execution of civilians outside Minsk by one of Himmler's murder squads. Greatly distressed, he rushed back to Germany to show his colour footage of the Einsatzgruppen's methods in all their graphic detail, believing his favoured status would ensure swift action by Hitler.

Formerly an avid fan of colour photography in general and Frenzl in particular, the Führer was forced to backpedal, not inclined to be pleased when actually confronted by the reality of his "Nacht und Nebel" decree. He stormed out of the screening, leaving Bormann to make a final pronouncement that it was "unsafe" for ordinary Germans to see execution pictures before "strongly advising" a dismayed Frenzl to "get rid of it and don't poke your nose into matters that don't concern you".

Like me, many Press Room colleagues were clearly shaken by Frenzl's footage, showing something of the true cost behind the "statistics of conquest" being fed to the public every day. A mood of uncertainty began to settle over Studio Hoffman.

Then, I received my first ever letter from Robert, postmarked "Field Hospital bon Bock, Mozhaisk". It was hidden among the press releases from the front, which I soon discovered to be within a stone's throw of Moscow. I'd often imagined my brother immersed in the miseries of an approaching Russian winter, bereft of adequate clothing; my hands trembled as I tore the handwritten note from its stained and crumpled envelope.

> Dear Liddle Brudder, [it began shakily]
>
> I never thought I'd say this, but I do envy you sitting there in your warm studio, playing with your cameras and you know what, ha-ha, only joking. Life in the East is proving far more taxing than imagined.
>
> Food is scarce and we have received no supplies of winter clothing, despite the sub-zero temperatures. Our well-bred horses stood no chance and have had to be eaten; we were forced to replace them with rugged little local ponies that could survive on birch twigs and thatched roofing.

Frostbite has already taken a terrible toll on the toes and fingers of my comrades but censorship is very strict; the Propaganda Dept. doesn't want you to know what's really going on out here, which is why I've concealed my letter among these photos. If intercepted, I can only hope no penalties ensue at your end. This fellow Zhukov is no pushover, despite the best efforts of our mechanised forces.

As for myself, I'm really past caring. I've lost an eye and two fingers from one hand. They say I'll be sent home on light duties when I'm well enough to travel, which brings me to the point of the letter: I know you have a key to Claudia's flat, which she's not going to need for some time. I want you to have the place ready for my recuperation when I get there. I'll tell you all about it then. R.

Communications of this kind were risky and I tore it up after reading it through a second time. However, my musings didn't last long. News of Japan's surprise attack upon America's Naval Base in Pearl Harbour flashed around the world, closely followed by President Roosevelt's declaration of war against Germany's Axis partner.

Not to be outdone, Hitler took the absurd step of declaring war on the United States, ensuring that we now faced enemies in all directions. This was it! We were effectively plunged into yet another World War.

News reports from the Eastern Front spoke of "temporary setbacks", and of Hitler sacking the Field Commander responsible. Seemingly unfazed, he had millions of leaflets printed to be dropped to his beleaguered forces in the East:

"Soldiers of Germany, forward to Moscow! Kill as many Russians as possible; they are a lazy, eternally drunk and corrupt people, incapable of managing the riches God has given them. This wealth rightly belongs to the German People; forward to Moscow, where victory and glory await you."

For good measure, every frontline soldier was given a copy of *Mein Kampf* to browse between battles. Despite such stirring incentives Yuletide was soon upon us, with gloomy news reports of Army Group Centre being in full retreat across the frozen steppes.

Word flashed through the newsroom that the invasion had already sustained over one million casualties, and lost 14,000 heavy guns and 4,000-odd trucks. Simultaneously, the official *Glockenshau* newsreel declared with a fanfare of trumpets that in a stroke of military brilliance, the Führer had miraculously halted the rout and was regrouping his forces, "Turning them about to await the spring offensive", all the while reiterating they were "close to victory". In that same newsreel, a repeat of scenes from late summer showed smiling, triumphant troops surging forward, even skylarking.

Robert's arrival in Munich came as a shock in more ways than one.

I saw him through the studio window, standing on the footpath in his SS uniform, obviously thrown by the empty display windows.

I could see at a glance the injuries spoken of, yet the face with the black eye patch lit up as I stepped onto the street and reached for his suitcase. "Ach! It is you! I'm fine, I don't need any help," he said tersely, in heavily accented but greatly improved German.

"Don't worry, I'm the only one here," I chirped, "and there's a sofa in the waiting room if you feel like a lie-down." I locked the door behind us and tried not to let my eyes wander to the partial thumb protruding from his coat pocket.

"I won't stay long," he said, looking about suspiciously. "I'll be getting on to Claudia's place as soon as you feed me and fill me in on the latest." He seemed unsettled by the silence, even dazed. "It's like I've been on a different planet, where all the normal rules are left behind ..."

"What rules? It's not been much fun for us here in Munich either, you know?" I responded defensively. "It's surely not a matter of *me* filling *you* in. Your letter hinted you'd tell me all about Operation Typhoon. *You're* the one who's been in the thick of it. Make yourself comfortable while I rustle up something to eat ..."

"And a couple of beers while you're at it," he called towards the staircase, where I was rummaging through the little larder I kept for emergencies.

"The beer's not icy but it's wet" I ventured optimistically after a few minutes of watching him tuck into the plateful of sausage and cheese. Before serving, I carefully sliced the mouldy ends off the Knackwurst.

"Cripes!" he finally exclaimed with mouth half-full. "It's been a while since I've seen this much fat at one time. Do you remember how Mam could always rustle up a feed out of nowhere? Never thought I'd be pining for the old Fazenda ... but out there in that God-forsaken wasteland all I kept thinkin' of was Alois' Sunday chickens, ha! That's what kept me smilin' through the pain."

After a second tepid beer, he gave a loud belch and settled back with his boots up on the settee, looking more relaxed. "I can see you are bustin' to know how I did on my first combat mission. I can start by sayin' that it was bloody hell on earth; no more, no less."

An involuntary shudder ran through his body and his good eye clouded over as he proceeded. "First up, I couldn't wait to shoot my first Bolshie. The whole adventure seemed like fun; we caught 'em off guard and shot 'em down like rabbits. Bock executed huge double envelopments that trapped entire Soviet armies. We razed the last villages still standing, which weren't many, and shot all their livestock, supposedly to allow a fresh start for the hordes of German settlers expected to arrive chasing their own cheap little slice of Lebensraum. We captured so many prisoners we didn't know what to do with 'em. Yet, strangest thing of all, we found the Russians didn't seem to know that they were already beaten."

He noticed me staring at his bandaged hand.

"Oh, this? I got off lightly compared to many of the poor buggers in my regiment." He then lifted his eye patch to disclose a pinkish muscle squirming in the empty socket. "What's the matter? Too confronting for you, liddle brudder? I can tell you Herman would have been blown apart if my horse hadn't taken the full force of that mortar round. It just caught the side of my head and my hand of course."

He let the eye patch snap back against the empty socket with a plop.

"Bloody fools should have seen the folly of expecting horses or men to be in any sort of fighting condition after covering such mind-numbing distances," his voice trailed off and he stared at the floor.

"When not fighting, the troops were putting in up to forty miles a day. The first snow fell on October 6, before a temporary thaw turned the roads into quagmires. Little did we know that this was just the beginning of the freezing cold and drenching autumn rains; 'Rasputitsa', they call it.

"In the days following that first downpour, things went from bad to worse: ditches overflowed into the fields and in no time the roads were churnin' axle-deep in one vast, impassable bog; our supply trucks ending up hopelessly stuck by the roadside when tryin' to go around. Not even our few remaining Panzers could get through. Men had their jackboots sucked clean off their feet performing simple tasks, and the rain came down so heavy they couldn't see their 'ands in front of their faces.

"Our Cavalry divisions got hopelessly bogged down and were soon surrounded; it took up to ten horses to drag one light field gun into position, through mud up to their bellies. Long before the ground froze over we ran out of fodder and were forced to eat the lot of 'em. To our amazement, such hellish conditions didn't seem to slow the Bolshie counter attacks ..."

"You said that in your letter. It must have been a shocking decision to make. I mean shooting and eating your own horse; how did you keep going under such conditions?"

He paused again, briefly. "You can't do much without food in your belly, brudder. And a big thanks to the man who invented Pervetin, the new miracle drug that kept us goin' for days on end. What's more, it suppresses the appetite, so I guess they were able to kill two birds with one stone, or should I say, with one pill? None of us had heard of it until we learned how the Panzer crews stayed awake for three days straight when they tore across France.

"Following our unexpected feast of horsemeat and Pervetin we were set to work laying miles of corduroy road surface, using tree trunks, but this was backbreaking work in the driving sleet and biting winds."

Robert then recounted the first time they came up against Russia's new tank, the T-34. It had wider tracks and "ran rings around us" in the snow and mud, while German advances were delayed by weeks. It took ages getting Panzers just to move, ruining days of road repairs within minutes.

"We knew Bock was faced with the terrible dilemma of trying to fight on without sufficient fuel or ammunition or choosing to dig into the rock-hard ground and ride out the gruelling winter. Either way, the casualty numbers could no longer be suppressed. As usual, the Führer stepped in to override the Field Marshal's decisions, demanding that not one inch of captured territory be surrendered. That was the death sentence for countless brave soldiers who didn't have to die." He watched keenly for my reaction with his good eye.

"B … But, the newspapers were saying nothing of the sort, I read for myself. And the newsreels are already calling it a great victory: 'Moscow Kaput!'"

"You know that's bullshit, brudder o' mine … I fell for it too in the early days. In my experience old Russia's not beaten by a long shot. 'Just kick the door in,' Hitler said, 'and it will be all over before Christmas.' Hah! 'This little affair of operational command is something anybody can do,' Hitler boasted. One thing was certain; he didn't take into account the thousands of brand new T-34s coming off the assembly lines every month, did he?"

Robert swung his feet to the floor and rested his elbows on his knees, before taking a series of deep breaths and suddenly looking up. "You insist on knowing what it's really like; certain things happened out there to change my way of thinkin' forever.

"I guess my first doubts arose in Ukraine when I saw a collaborator dancin' a jig atop a pile of Jewish corpses he'd just beaten to death with an iron bar; in front of a cheering crowd, mind you. Petrus Zelionka was his name and I'll never forget it; he announced it proudly enough.

"For the first time, something snapped inside me and I realised the monstrous injustices we were not only inflicting but encouraging others to perform. I should have shot the bastard there and then but he was, after all, supposed to be on *our* side.

"Anyway, the crowd would have turned on me too; they were all for it. Suddenly, someone throws him up an accordion, and Petrus, natural as you like, starts waltzing back and forth across the pile of bodies, singing the Lithuanian National Anthem. Some people are just doomed; a waste of space, I heard one bystander observe. After all, they were only Jews."

"I'm telling you, Klaus," he said, his eye glittering, "I've seen enough killin' to last a lifetime. Drivin' those women with babes into the marshes and then havin' to shoot 'em when the water ain't deep enough to drown 'em … Christ!" He paused, dropping his gaze again, "And, to top all that off, we burned down every barn and village, didn't we? Shot every animal we couldn't eat.

"And, lo and behold, this short-sighted policy left our own army trapped by the Russian winter, didn't it? … without even a hole to crawl into. If truth be told, it's those 200,000-odd horses I really feel sorry for; bein' flogged to death on a one-way journey across the wilderness, dragging impossible loads.

"First came the dust, then the Rasputitsa, and finally sub-zero starvation; you can't imagine the condition they were in after ten weeks of that, and when they can pull no more they're eaten. All that effort, with no hope of ever retiring to lush pastures … it's criminal, that's what it is."

This was the first time I could remember him ever expressing concern for any cause other than himself or Mam, let alone a horse.

"Then there were those columns of Ivan prisoners being marched away from the front into damnation, which brought little comfort to me. They were a reminder of what lay ahead, if and when the boot was ever on the other foot.

"Poor bastards! Never thought I'd hear meself sayin' that; without food or medicine and eatin' only snow, they're dropping like flies. Still, they've managed to slow our advance by choking the roads with the sheer weight of numbers … The retreating Russians stripped the countryside bareback then, just as they're doing now, and shipped off to the east anything of possible value to us. All they had to do was await reinforcements from General Winter before striking the fatal blow."

I nodded resignedly.

"Following our first retreat, the Russians stepped up their counter-attacks and we first heard the name Zhukov. He brought in fresh Siberian Ski Troops who could strike out of nowhere during the worst blizzards, and immediately we noticed their thick, quilted uniforms; a far cry from our own threadbare rags.

"'Uri, Uri, Uri'; I still can't get those bloody battle cries out of my head."

"Me neither," I blurted. My head raced. He looked puzzled.

Where had I heard that sound before? In a nightmare?

"First up, Zhukov starts forcing six- and seven-year-olds from nearby villages to advance across the open ground ahead of his troops; just one more barbarous tactic designed to trigger our landmines and reveal our strong points. 'Reconnaissance through combat,' he calls it.

"As soon as we open fire we reveal our positions to those coming behind and bring down a rain of shrapnel on our heads. No matter how well we dug in or how many we shot, those brown uniforms just kept on coming. 'Uri, Uri, Uri,' the damned sound mingled with a chorus of legless kids still haunts my sleep. Seeing little ones getting blown apart does something to your head after a while, that much I can tell you. I never dreamed I was joining up to kill goosens, did I?

"When does a child become a man?" I pondered with closed eyes and growing sadness, not daring to imagine the scenes this stranger was describing.

"When he's big enough to shoot straight or stuff a grenade down his shirt, I suppose," he answered with a faraway look, before clearing his throat to continue.

"Believe me, Bro, that cold set in with a vengeance, bringing a whole new set of problems. I remembered snow from the Old Country, even used to play in it as a kid; but those Russian winds could blow a man off his feet and burn exposed skin like fire. Just the slightest exertion can cause a man's lungs to form ice crystals in his chest. How can any soldier fight on with frozen cartridges and firearms? Some of the truck engines froze solid as they sat idling, including those using anti-freeze. I wouldn't believe it myself if I hadn't been there.

"Come November, the landscape was shrouded in thick fog 'till about 9:00, and by 3:00 in the afternoon, dusk was already settling in. An hour later we found ourselves facing one more interminable terrifying night at 20-below. I tell you, kid, cold like that cannot be imagined when you haven't lived through it. Everyone at the front was asking, 'How can the Bolshies see *us* through the blizzards and get *their* guns to fire?'

"When we finally did beat the secret out of a P.O.W. it didn't help us one little bit, did it?" He paused to increase my curiosity. "It turns out that Russian weapons are lubricated with *walrus* blubber. Ha! Who'd a thought of that?" Robert chuckled with undisguised admiration. "And there aren't too many fucking *walruses* around Moscow, are there?!"

I listened to his for once unvarnished tale with growing sadness, not wanting to imagine some of the scenes he described.

"Fighting on home soil does have its advantages," I offered. "By the sound of things, Operation Typhoon has not turned out quite as expected. Was I right to be sceptical? The Press Room saw only parts of certain stories from the front before they were hushed up; please do go on, what happened then?"

He paused for a moment as if unsure of my purpose.

"Well, we had to keep fires burning under the panzers day and night to stop the engine blocks from cracking wide open. There was just enough space for a few lucky men to crawl under between the tracks and huddle next to the flames, like dogs.

"One night, not far from me, five hundred Wehrmacht soldiers froze to death. We were forced to use up our precious grenades tryin' to blow foxholes in the solid ice. The body parts of our comrades clinked together like porcelain when we threw 'em into heaps awaiting the thaw. And spring was still a long way off.

"Meanwhile, we were tortured by the very idea of the Führer snuggling up on his mountaintop with his girlfriend and hot water bottle. Surely, someone has to oversee the entire operation, don't you agree?" He threw a sideways glance and continued unabated.

"Seein' your mates covered in blisters like that from exposure; it's enough to change your mind in a hurry and put the wind up you good and proper. And then, just when we thought things couldn't get any worse, the Russian people showed what *they* were really made of; even prepared to torch their own humble shanty's in order to deny us shelter. We were soon faced with the reality that the landscape had already been plundered twice, and everything of value had long since been removed or destroyed.

"If anything, the Russian peasant seems enlivened by the onset of winter. At any hour of the day or night, hordes of illiterate townsfolk might hurl themselves upon us armed only with pitchforks; dying with that same fearsome war cry on their lips. At first, it was just the Russian frontline soldiers carrying rifles. When they're shot down, the weapon is picked up by those coming behind, and so on. Oh, how I've seen such bravery and such suffering on both sides."

"I ... I'm shocked. What you're telling me has been only vaguely hinted at in the newsroom, and never in the papers," I stammered, trying to reconcile Robert's version of frontline conditions with the buoyancy from other sources.

"I tell you, I've seen it with me own eyes, when I 'ad two that is!" he quipped, looking for a moment as mischievous as the Robert of old. "When we finally did get to see Moscow's spires gleaming in the distance, it was too late. The great warlord suddenly grabs half our panzers to send south to Stalingrad, after declaring that the battle for Moscow was 'as good as won'.

"From where we were sitting the situation didn't look at all like a fait accompli; quite the opposite, in fact. It beats me what Hitler was thinking, knobbling our advance just as winter tightened its grip. Many in the frontlines had already frozen to death in their summer uniforms ..." he paused for a moment with a far-off look in his good eye, no longer fiddling with his eye patch or concealing his bandaged hand.

"Mark my words, kid, Russia's just too bloody big to conquer. Normal distances don't mean anything out there. Tryin' to supply several armies at once over thousands of miles is ridiculous, especially after we'd lost the element of surprise. Many of our panzers wore themselves out racing back and forth between Moscow and Stalingrad, rather than doing any actual fighting."

His full lips twitched involuntarily. "Anyone daring to mention 1812 gets a bullet in the head, make no mistake. We are bein' blown back to where we came from ... and, worst of all for morale, we had to leave many of our wounded behind; so much for a thousand years of Prussian military tradition!"

"Luckily not you among them," I ventured.

"You can shout that out! I've had a gutful and so have those poor bastards still out there tryin' to hold back the tide, prayin' for a miracle to save their frozen arses."

Again, he seemed to look through me, as if struggling with some inner demon. It was as if the floodgates had opened and he needed to cleanse himself of the nightmares bottled up within.

"Right from the start we missed a golden opportunity to get the natives on side. At first, the cheering crowds welcomed us with open arms; peasant girls showered the soldiers with flowers. It was pretty obvious that they hated Stalin and everything he stood for. So, what do we do? We kill 'em anyway, and rape their womenfolk in front of the men. Then we have the nerve to call *them* 'subhumans'."

One small victory Hitler was particularly proud of during the early days of the invasion was assisting in the capture of Stalin's eldest son, Yakov Dzhugashvili, who was considered a potentially invaluable bargaining chip.

"The whole forlorn incident went something like this, as best I remember: Yakov was Stalin's only biological son from his first marriage, and had achieved the rank of Artillery Lieutenant just before Smolensk was overrun by Operation Typhoon. At first, he was a minor celebrity whom the Nazis were certain could be traded for one of their own high-ranking officers; but Stalin would have none of it.

"Had not he issued the order that no Russian soldier was to be taken alive? Any whoever did so, including Yakov, were branded cowards or traitors, threatened with execution or exile to Siberia upon their return."

Robert and his comrades were stunned by Stalin's callousness, perhaps more understandable when it became known that following his mother's death from typhus years earlier, Yakov had been virtually abandoned by his father at eight months of age and subsequently raised by his maternal aunts.

Nonetheless, the Nazis lived in hope that a deal might yet be possible farther down the track, and Yakov was hastened off to Sachsenhausen Concentration Camp for the next twenty-one months. His incarceration was marked by constant bickering with the other prisoners, where he regularly picked fistfights with British airmen who, after all, were supposed to be his allies.

In April 1943, following a final, failed attempt to swap him for General Paulus, it emerged that the fractious Artillery Lieutenant had been put out of his misery with four shots to the head, after throwing himself against an electrified fence in Sachsenhausen. It was suggested that this could be seen as an early birthday present for the Führer.

Robert gave a long sigh, and appeared to talk to himself. "Sure, I started out keen enough, but I'm still waitin' for someone to point out what's actually the point of it all. 'Kill or be killed,' that was the code we lived by. Why? And for what? That whole friggin' wasteland hasn't got a decent feature in it."

He looked over to address me more directly. "I reckon I was startin' to go outa my mind havin' to gun down so many of those defenceless poor bastards day after day, not one of 'em wanted to 'arm a hair on my head. It's no wonder some of the Einsatzgruppen troops are already drinkin' 'emselves to death; it gets to a man, bein' splattered with blood and brains all day long. And then comes Hitler's September Directive: 'If you retreat, you'll be shot! If you advance you may save your skin.'

"In the end, it was hopeless tryin' to fight on … our flasks and even the water wagons froze solid. Frostbite crippled thousands of men each day and the last of the horses starved to death. Anyone caught outdoors after dark stood little chance. We fought like tigers, but it wasn't enough. No running water, no toilets and no proper rations. When push came to shove, most of the men spent all day huddled in their foxholes, outgunned and outmanoeuvred. The weather just kept getting worse.

"We are facing a mighty defeat. *Do you hear what I'm sayin?* It's the Wehrmacht and not Moscow staring 'Kaput' in the face!" Robert's voice now betrayed a hint of desperation.

"So, where does that leave the rest of us?" I asked thinly.

Even allowing for his usual embellishments, the future according to Robert looked dark and uncertain; I was relieved that he'd turned up at just the right moment, but he rolled his eyes in frustration.

"Us? … Us? You must be joking. Now it's every man for himself. I intend to see out the rest of the war as a camp guard or something cushy; I reckon I've earned it and the SS always looks after its own …"

"B … But, you didn't finish the story; however did you make it home in one piece?"

"Oh that? I suppose it turned out to be an anti-climax. They packed me into a trainload of wounded where the stink and suffering was even worse than at the front. If I didn't have this splitting headache every night to remind me, it would be like the whole bloody shebang happened to someone else."

For a while, he sat nursing his head in his hands before picking up the tale of woe. "Eventually, Hitler halted the rout by ordering the men to dig in for winter where they were, to await the coming spring offensive. Like yours truly, most of the newer conscripts were already having second thoughts. Only by shooting deserters on the spot along with their families back home did the Commander-in-Chief regain control over the ranks.

"I was one of the 'lucky' few with a ticket to ride, tanks to dis." He wiggled his purple trigger finger protruding from the bandage.

"As for you civvies, I'd be stayin' as close to the border as possible in case things really do go pear-shaped. I suppose we can always continue to hope for a ceasefire …?"

"Ceasefire? When? We've just declared war on America, the most powerful country in the world; what borders did you have in mind? I've been hoping that you might be ready to reconsider Clau … Sissy's plan to escape the country altogether? I've always believed the three of us could pull it off with access to the right paperwork," I said, almost pleading.

He flicked the fingernails on his good hand and stared at them lovingly. "See? It's amazin' what I can do with 'em already; it's only a matter of practice, huh?" His ears pricked up. "What plans?"

"Why, yours, of course! She told me you had connections in the Vatican who could get us safely back to South America; I've never questioned her further about it …"

"Hold your horses, liddle brudder. The three of us together? That would never work. I haven't given the idea a second thought," he said as he attempted to stroke his chin with the bandage. "Then again, maybe she is onto something? What does she know that I don't?"

"I know only that she seems safe enough for the time being; she's doing some sort of undercover work in Poland. The Gestapo have just shipped her out to the Lodz Ghetto with 40,000 other German Jews …"

"Sissy Schicklegruber working for those bastards? I guess she's always been one to play with fire … You know what women are like?"

I ignored the invitation. "I don't think she had much say in it; she was promised special treatment for her parents."

"Jeez, special treatment in Lodz? Don't hold your breath. I've heard all about that place. As far as I know they're gearing up to murder the lot of 'em in the gas chambers at Chelmno. Ninety-nine percent of those Poles arriving at the railway station are dead within an hour of arrival. You said you've heard from Sissy? Does she realise the danger she's in? How does she manage to get letters out of Lodz? You really should try and warn her before it's too late."

For a long moment I wrestled with the guilt I knew would follow my divulgement, and once more see her beholden to the very person who'd trampled her down in the past; my broken brother, Robert Hahn. Yet, somehow, he still seemed our best and only hope.

"She … she photographs her letters using a macro lens and sends Hoffman the undeveloped film in a locked bag. They are explicitly marked 'Private Files' and can be processed only in our darkrooms; it's very ingenious."

"What happens if someone else prints the negatives?"

I gulped, "But I am the only one authorised and Claudia has a special way of marking the canisters. So far, her eye for abnormalities and freaks has been of great interest to Hoffman, though wrenching to print. Her position in charge of the Ghetto Photo Register, under the very noses of the ruling Judenrat I may add, allows her far more freedom to move about the city beyond the wire. She's always reported directly to Biebow and by the sound of it has him wrapped around her little finger. If anyone's job is secure it should be Clau … Sissie's …"

"You fool! Can't you get it through your thick 'ead that no one's safe anymore, especially in Poland? They've been under the conqueror's heel for the longest.

"When the Bolshies were our allies at that time, they grabbed the Eastern 'alf of the country for 'emselves and set to murderin' the Polish intelligentsia even more efficiently than our SS, and that's sayin' somethin'. An' before you could say 'Jack Robinson', here we are invading *their* country, an' tryin' to wipe *them* off the face of the Earth. I couldn't see an end to it and still can't. It looks to me like war for the sake of bloody war.

"Believe me, nowhere will be safe from our excesses; they will reshape the future *and* the past to suit the whim of one man, when he himself doesn't know what he wants, and probably never has known." The veins in his forehead stood up for a few moments and he reached absent-mindedly for his medals with the missing fingers, before taking a deep breath and closing his good eye.

With a barely perceptible quaver, he continued. "From the moment we marched into Belarus I started having second thoughts; I should have realised sooner that killing isn't so much fun when it becomes a chore. But, getting out of SS clutches requires more luck than management, and in my case I can hold up my 'good luck' for all to see.

"If I needed any further proof, it came during a stopover on the tedious train trip home, when the Reichsführer himself was due to land beside one or other of the numerous P.O.W. camps, on a guided tour of the killing fields. As our train came to a standstill in a nearby siding I couldn't help overhearing part of his speech to a battalion of Order Police, wherein Himmler admitted for the first time that Russia, like Poland, would soon become one gigantic work camp. He expressed his deep concerns for the mental health of his Einsatzgruppen shooters. 'Those dedicated warriors stepping up to do the dirty work on behalf of the whole Nation.'

"He proudly disclosed that a far less messy, 'absolutely final solution', was almost 'shovel ready'. 'I am resolved that no more suffering should accrue to noble German blood in the process of destroying this subhumanity. Our new gassing facilities mean my SS guards will never again need to soil their hands.'

"'What's even better,' Himmler had added, 'is that these prisoners are building the death camps themselves, with their own hands ... before they go up their own chimneys.' At this thought he gave a high-pitched little bray and a ripple ran through the ranks, before the pep talk concluded with one last chilling observation: 'It is the curse of greatness that it must step over dead bodies to create new life.'

"At that very moment, a volley of shots rang out and another row of prisoners tumbled into the pit nearby. When we turned back to Himmler he was pale and cross-eyed, gasping for breath, engrossed by what appeared to be a snot of brain matter or skull dangling from the peak of his cap. I saw him go weak at the knees and clutch at his throat; it seemed the Reich's chief executioner wasn't so cocky when up close to the real action. A couple of his bodyguards had to sponge him down before he cut the tour short.

"Mark my words, Bro, the world ain't seen nothin' yet. Wait till Action Reinhardt *really* gets goin'. Our half of the Lebensraum is not called 'Poland' anymore, but 'General Protectorate'. If you ask me, it's all very confusin'. Hitler doesn't seem to know when to stop and you could say I'm a bit muddled meself. 'Just follow orders,' they say, 'and everything will turn out fine.' Well, now I'm not so sure. But at least I've learned a thing or two along the way.

"Didn't Mam always read to us from her bible? 'Those who are first will be last' and vice-versa? Back then I just couldn't see what she was on about; you bet I can see it now though. After a nice spell of R and R, I'm hoping to see out the war from the rear. I think it's fair to say my fighting days are over, old chap," he said, throwing off his Gaelic jargon.

"By the sound of things, the war may be over sooner than you think. Will you at least promise to revisit the idea of ... you know, getting the hell outa here?" I probed optimistically, knowing full well he would probably never look down a barrel or pull a trigger again. Hard experience had apparently taught him carefulness and diluted his impulsiveness.

Robert rose, gave a painful stretch and tossed Claudia's keys into the air, before snatching them back again with his good hand and taking up his suitcase. "Well, I'm not making any promises. If you want to save that girlfriend of yours, I wouldn't leave it too much longer. I'm glad it's you and not me, that's all I'm sayin'."

In the days and weeks that followed I stewed over his words. How could he know so much about conditions in faraway Poland?

Nineteen forty-two brought little good cheer. By late summer, Rommel's much-lauded Afrika Corp had been defeated at El-Alamein and in November the Allies landed an invasion force in Tunisia. Besides Dachau, Chelmno, and a sprinkling of others, more death camps were brought online in quick succession: Mauthausen, Sobibor, Treblinka and Auschwitz were names that soon became familiar to us in the Press Room.

Word leaked out that Jews, Gypsies, and other "space-wasters" were being murdered at these camps in their tens of thousands, but the average man in the street refused to believe such stories.

From Czechoslovakia came news of Heydrich's assassination by partisans supposedly parachuted in by the British Secret Service. Hundreds of innocent villagers in the nearby town of Lidice were slaughtered in a ghastly reprisal.

Yet, slowly and surely the tables were beginning to turn; so much now depended on the successful investment of Stalingrad. A rattled Führer despatched "Travel Master Schaub" and Dr Brandt by air, for a firsthand account from someone he could trust.

Grimly, they reported back that fighting and medical conditions on the ground were "horrific": some twenty-two divisions were completely tied down in the bombed-out city ruins, about to face a second winter of ferocious counter-attacks and crippling temperatures. It was clear to both that Göring's bold commitment to supply the frontlines from the air was nothing more than hot air! A mere fraction of the promised supplies was getting through and the Sixth Army was slowly starving to death; some 12,000 men in the outer suburbs had already died of exposure.

Upon receipt of this grim news Hitler was apoplectic, having previously rejected General Paulus' plea for a strategic withdrawal to withstand the expected winter counter-attacks. Poor Paulus, like so many of his officers and men, was racked with dysentery, which made concentration, let alone initiative, all but impossible. He was to receive no comfort from his Führer's reply: "Retreat is out of the question; you will resist to the end and will not, repeat will not, under any circumstances take a single step backwards. Sixth Army will fight to the last man and go down gloriously into the annals of Reich Military History." The Order was signed 'Adolph Hitler' in his usual savage scrawl.

That was it: the fate of three million men had been decided from afar, in petulance. Sixth Army was surrounded and could expect no further relief. With a tirade heard all over the Berghof, the Führer excoriated Göring personally, tearing off the Air Marshall's shoulder boards and hurling them at his feet. "You are a disgrace to the Reich and a … a drug addict!" He spat out the words.

"But, my Führer; am I not still Deputy Führer? Your designated successor?" the Reichsmarschall pleaded earnestly, but this time he had no leading Ace to blame for the Luftwaffe's failures. Hitler had by now perfected the shattering effect of his rages, and when Schaub accompanied Göring down the Berghof steps for the last time, the once mighty airman was in tears.

However, it was for the hapless General Paulus that the warlord saved his bitterest invective and sweetest bribe. At the battle's lowest ebb, the skeletal general suddenly found himself promoted to "Field Marshal", with a reminder that no German officer of that rank in the whole history of warfare had ever surrendered; and none ever would. Suicide was the only honourable way out for any Wehrmacht Generalfeldmarschall, after he'd discharged his penultimate round toward the enemy, of course.

That December, the Führer again appeared on the cover of the *Illustrierter Beobachter*, in a folksy snow scene near the Berghof, far removed from the travails of his far-flung forces. Photos inside showed him throwing sticks for Blondie while pondering ever more effective ways to crush his many enemies.

He had noticed the absence of adoring crowds outside the front gates. "One of these days I'll have only two friends left, Fraulein Braun and my dog," a weary Führer lamented one afternoon upon rising, before going on to praise Fraulein Braun's devotion as an example for any staff member feeling overwrought.

At other times black rages precluded all hope of meaningful dialogue. Battlefield commanders were often forced to sit twiddling their thumbs for days on end awaiting an audience to approve some minor field adjustment.

Otherwise, the Commander-in-Chief remained out of sight, plagued by worsening flatulence and insomnia. Only Dr Morell and Martin Bormann now enjoyed exclusive, almost unrestricted access, which true to form, each manipulated to consolidate his own powers.

As Secretary to both Party *and* Führer, Bormann now ensured that nothing and no one entered his master's orbit without *his* knowledge and approval whereas the ebullient Dr Morell, a closet morphine addict himself, had become Hitler's virtual shadow, poised to administer some twenty-eight injections daily into his master's flabby backside. The unhealed scabs on Hitler's forearms had long since rendered them unusable.

Dr Morell's closely guarded "Satchel of Happiness", as he called it, reportedly contained 88 different concoctions necessary to keep the Führer going, including Opiates, Barbiturates, Cocaine, Methamphetamine, anti-gas pills containing Strychnine, Glucose, Oxycodone and, of course, "Orchikrin", the wonder-cure for Führer depressions containing pulverised bulls' testicles.

"He does ease my pain and I feel so wonderful after his injections," Hitler tut-tutted blissfully one evening when Eva expressed concern at the possible side effects of shooting so many different substances into one's body. Ever since Morell's crafty attempt to examine her "mouse's ear", and his phony diagnosis of Hoffman's "Typhus", Eva and her coterie had steered well clear of him, preferring instead to run their issues by Dr Brandt.

Only recently labelled a "Sacred Healer" by Hitler, this bright young Specialist was quickly inserted to oversee Germany's entire health network, a move bound to ruffle establishment feathers. Brandt's first act was to join forces with Eva and Speer in expressing concern over Morell's methods, which all three considered "dangerous" at very least.

But "Patient No. 1" was having none of it, refusing to hear an unkind word against his alternate "Sacred Healer".

Soon after an initial unpleasant confrontation, Morell, now seemingly untouchable, began meddling in Hitler's diet; striking pork dumplings from the menu and steering him onto more of his next favourite dish of vegetable pudding with sauce.

The good doctor had by now become a fixture at meal times, rarely straying far from his number one patient. Afterward he could sit back in one of those comfy lounge chairs and down a port or two, even getting away with nodding off beside the fire to the familiar drone of his master's voice. Often, upon awakening, Morell would appear sufficiently refreshed to recount his own fruitful adventures as a young shipboard doctor in Africa.

Furthermore, he began turning up at mealtimes wearing a military-style uniform with a cap of his own design. Like it or not, the Morells had become part of the permanent evening charade, much to Eva's disgust. It was around that time in early '43 when poor Henni, for so long Hitler's "little sunshine", broke the cardinal dinner rule of the Berghof and raised a forbidden topic during the evening meal.

She had not long returned from visiting friends in occupied Amsterdam and while there witnessed several Jewish families being beaten and dragged onto trucks in the street below. Immediately upon returning, she made her way straight to Hitler to report what she had seen.

"Frau von Schirach, you are sentimental," Hitler replied menacingly, rising to his feet and gripping the table edge.

"My Führer," she continued enthusiastically, also rising to her feet, "you ought not to be doing that. Our own soldiers pointed out that we are making enemies of the Dutch in using such brutal methods. With my own eyes I witnessed innocent women and children being treated appallingly, and realised you could not be aware of such goings on ..."

"Enough!" Hitler bellowed, with flecks of spittle forming in the corners of his mouth. "Frau von Schirach; every day, ten thousand of my best men die on the battlefield, while these people go on living in the camps. You know nothing of the disciplinary requirements in occupied Europe and will kindly refrain from raising such matters in—"

"But, my Führer, surely these methods are unnecessary under the circ—"

"Enough, I said!" His knuckles were white and the veins stood out in his neck. "Frau von Schirach, you will vacate this table at once and Gauleiter Bormann will escort you to your vehicle. Do not return unless specifically invited, is that clear?"

"B … But, I came straight here to warn you of—"

"Get out! Do you hear me?" Hitler screamed, his face was beetroot purple as he spat out his words. Bormann had already gripped Henni in a bear hug and was frog-marching her toward the door.

As things turned out, neither Henni nor Baldur was ever invited back to the Obersalzberg. The unexpected confrontation soured the rest of that meal, and Hitler remained sullen and withdrawn for the evening; or so Eva confided in me, word for word, just after it had all happened. She alone seemed buoyed to see one more long-standing rival sidelined for good.

The Führer, weighed down daily by bad news and betrayal, embarked on a program of short naps, sticking to his vegetable pudding and sauce with lashings of his favourite apple cake. Under Eva's watchful eye he found his appetite returning, and once again second helpings became the norm.

Throughout his convalescence, Eva had taken the chance to strengthen her own authority, while walking a fine line between Bormann and the head housekeeper. Once or twice I noticed her attempting to dominate the female staff. Was she coming out of her shell at last?

One day, when we were alone in the darkroom, I began to relay some of Robert's observations of the soldiers' suffering at the front.

She turned on me with eyes flashing. "Suffering? Suffering? What do those incompetents at the front know of suffering? My Adolph carries the weight of the world on his shoulders and I for one am determined to protect him against further unpleasantness. It is better that ten thousand others die than a single hair on his head is harmed." There in the red safelight her face was contorted and she was half crouching, daring contradiction. In that moment it was clear that for Eva, there would be no turning back.

He had impregnated her with his own contempt for humanity at large. Neither of us moved. Her eyes glowed red and the top lip curled back in a snarl; a belch of foul air came up from her stomach into my face as her mouth opened and closed wordlessly.

My head spun in disbelief: there was Moloch, horns and all, reaching into my very soul.

"Klaus, Klaus? Wake up, wake up!"

It was a concerned Eva, sweet as ever, bending over and wetting my lips with champagne from her finger. "You fainted clean away while I was speaking. Are you all right?"

"Eva?" Thank heavens it is you after all"

"Silly Billy … who did you *think* it was?"

"I … er, my mind was elsewhere."

"I'll say it was. You slumped down like you'd seen a ghost, and I'm very much alive, which is more than can be said for my poor neighbours who got bombed out by the Americans. Actually, Adolph's insisting on Gretl and I having our own bomb shelter in the backyard. Construction has already started and everything's such a mess. All I seem to do is sit around and eat. You can't tell, can you Klaus? That I've been pigging out, I mean?"

"I, er, it's difficult to tell from this angle, Fraulein Eva."

"Fraulein? … Eva will do, thank you. There's no need to rub it in. Anyway, I'm as good as married. Mutti will be joining me for Chri … Yuletide at the Berghof. It's tipped to be a great ski season if I can sneak away. Have you heard? The Platterhof has been turned into a hospital for the wounded? Looks like farewell to our favourite dance floor. Oh well," she said with a sigh, "there's always the Officers' Club. … By the way, did you know that the Black Dwarf is gearing up to announce 'Total War'? Whatever that means."

The forsaken fiancée had now to find her thrills among her girlfriends and attending endless SS parties in Munich and the mountaintop barracks, where predictably the ladies were danced off their feet and received many proposals.

I believe it was that Christmas when the Party Secretary announced the banning of "Silent Night" entirely from the Reich's Yuletide repertoire. Once again, the Führer spent the festive season alone, taking long walks with Blondie.

Those unfortunates summoned to join Hitler for the evening meal were assailed with the same repetitious and boring monologues that extended into the early hours; no one else could get a word in. "Listening to his table talk," someone confided, "you'd think we were on the cusp of victory."

He refused to attend a luncheon arranged by Eva, or any of the nightly screenings, shunning the latest *Glockenshau* newsreels with their upbeat messages of immanent glory.

He scoffed at reports that Russia's new T-34 tanks were rolling off the assembly lines in their tens of thousands.

When the final collapse of the Sixth Army came, Germany's newest Field Marshal Paulus, gaunt with dysentery and despair, dragged himself into Chiukov's headquarters in Stalingrad and laid his pistol on the table. German troops were everywhere falling back across the frozen wastes. Operation Barbarossa was hanging by a thread.

Of the several hundred thousand invaders, less than half remained functional. To the cries of their wounded comrades being bayoneted where they lay, 91,000 prisoners who could still walk, including 24 generals, were soon lining up for the long march to Siberia.

Most would never return to their homeland, either succumbing to the bitter cold or being worked to death in the gulags. The Russian High Command had yet more pain and revenge to inflict before they were through.

Paulus, however, ended up in far more comfortable surroundings, after seeing the light and broadcasting radio appeals on behalf of his captors, that urged all German soldiers to lay down their arms.

Despite his earlier apparent revival, Hitler began again to deteriorate, almost never being seen in public. As Allied bombs rained down on German cities, the Army faced crippling reverses on all fronts: Hamburg was flattened with 40,000 casualties; more deaths than reported across the whole of Britain. Once again the Führer had been betrayed by his "spineless commanders".

"Just think," he was heard muttering to himself, "that a woman had sufficient pride to shoot herself after receiving a few insulting words, yet the leader of a whole army can't even pull ..."

Those who caught most of the sentence were unsure of his meaning. Bad news was pouring in from all quarters, gradually exposing the German populace to the dreadful realities of war.

After much soul searching I plucked up sufficient courage to write to Claudia, and as arranged concealed my heavy news in an empty film canister. For sad indeed it was, which I'd struggled to convey rightly.

Darkroom, Munich. March 1943.

My dearest C,

Please find enclosed ten pkts. Grade 2 printing paper and the rolls of 35 mm film as requested, I'm afraid this is the best I can rustle up at the moment.

It is with a heavy heart I report the shameful murder of your friends Hans and Sophie Scholl in Stadelheim Prison. While not wishing to add further to your difficulties, I felt a word of caution may be in order now that news of the "White Rose" has been splashed across the front pages.

Your orchestra too may be imperilled. The pair was apprehended on February 18 by one Jacob Schmidt, the University Custodian, while distributing flyers condemning the regime, from an upstairs balcony.

They were tried four days later in Judge Freisler's notorious "People's Court" and both guillotined within hours of being found guilty.

Many other sympathisers from Ludwig Maximillian have also been rounded up. It may be some comfort to you, knowing that brother and sister died bravely. It seems just a handful of the educated have the courage to speak out. Please take care of your health and let me know if you are lacking anything I can fit into the locked bag.

With undying affection,

Your K.

Darkroom, Lodz. May 1943.

Dear K,

Your news came as one more blow in a long list of reversals. My friends in the Orchestra had already relayed news of the beheading of my dear Hans and Sophie, forever Martyrs in the cause of Freedom.

I have so much to tell you; conditions here in the ghetto are appalling and terrifying, no one is safe from the constant selections. Chaim Rumkowski, the head Judenrat of whom I spoke, draws up periodic lists of those unfortunates he alone earmarks for "resettlement".

As I write, 10,000 more "useless eaters", mainly children and elderly are being weeded out this week; of course, my own parents are at greater risk. All Lodz lives in constant fear, given the rumours that those sent away to Chelmno are being murdered, which seems inconceivable.

As a "privileged Jew" I answer directly to Commandant Biebow, who seems satisfied so far by my reports which have cut down on corruption in the Judenrat, although my resurrected Catholicism doesn't cut much ice with him.

I draw daily comfort from the golden cross you so carefully placed around my neck; I guess I'm not likely to come across another like it in these parts, especially one with a Ruby chip in its centre representing the unfolding red rose. You never did tell me the story of how you came by it.

During that horrific train ride to Poland, it brought me continual comfort. Four days packed into a cattle car without food or water, being forced to sit upon the corpses of our fellow travellers and slide around in each other's faeces. It's only now I can bear to talk about it. As we neared our destination Polish kids threw rocks at the wagons, chanting slogans: "Jews, Jews, you'll soon be turned into soap" and that sort of thing. To those of us who survived that nightmare, Lodz at first appeared almost welcoming.

During my Dachau training, I was instructed to stay close to Rumkowski and report to Commandant Biebow weekly. Thus far my job as ghetto archivist provides more security and relative freedom of movement. My arrival in a cattle car dispelled all suspicion among the so-called Council of Elders; my parents and I have been allocated a small room of our own on Rybna St without arousing too much resentment. I'm expected to gather evidence against the Council members in general and Rumkowski in particular; who is a real sleaze as I may have hinted previously.

"King Chaim" homes in on all the new girls for their "medical examinations", and corrals the orphans to one side as personal belongings.

Although rumoured to be impotent, his favourite plaything is a dwarf by the name of Bronia, whom he regularly locks in his office and forces to stand on the desk and spread her legs for his delectation.

All the attractive young girls get their turn, aware that resistance means certain deportation. At the first opportunity, he tried groping me and shoving my hand inside his trousers. "Make it work, make it work," he grunted, and I still gag at the thought of his slobbering lips and putrid breath, before he pushed me away roughly when I failed to achieve the desired result. Fortunately for me, he only tried that once, preferring younger girls without family connections.

As the Nazi-appointed all-powerful "Elder", Rumkowski doesn't shrink from selecting "non-productive" and "troublesome" fellow Jews for "resettlement" in the East; 3,000 here, 5,000 there, and just yesterday an additional 10,000 was demanded by Biebow.

These will include many children between two months and ten years, all of the sick and adults over 65. I watch him through the window during these selections, listening to his harsh, metallic laugh. He stands there between the doctors in his polished jackboots motioning quaking inmates to the left or right using whips and snarling dogs.

Everyone knows that those in the left queue are loaded onto lorries, never to be seen or heard from again. Those on the right, many of whom desperately pinch a little colour into their sallow cheeks, force their aching bodies to stand upright a little longer before scuttling back to the factories for a brief "reprieve". King Chaim is hated by the many and envied by the few. Notices bearing his signature are posted all over the ghetto.

"The only way is work. These are my five mottos: [1] Bread [2] Work [3] Care for sick [4] Care of children [5] Peace within compound."

Some posters contain an extra footnote: "I will remove all troublemakers from the workshops."

To his way of thinking, the community's preservation will come only if every Jew gives his all: anything less will result in even worse deprivation and deportations.

"Labour is our only way" is the ghetto mantra. This sounds like just one more cynical Nazi slogan to me; much too similar to the gates of Dachau. He not only threatens the starving prisoners but insists on daily quotas, always ready to dish out beatings personally when the mood takes him. I want you and the whole world to realise what we Jews are up against.

"Here in the ghetto we are all equal …" we hear ad infinitum, but then comes the hypocritical addendum, "… but some must make way for the good of the community."

His family and friends are allowed to help themselves to any little delicacy they desire from the abundance of confiscated goods in his special shop fronts. For the rest of us, the only legal tender is his phoney paper money, the Rumkin, trading at a rate of ten Rumkies per Reichsmark; to discourage smuggling through the fence, so they say.

I know you will forgive me for rambling on, but I have nowhere to turn; this environment is simply terrifying and I cannot burden my dear parents. I might as well be hanged for a sheep as a lamb, as they say.

At this moment the ghetto operates over one hundred factories, reaping huge profits for the Nazis making furniture, rugs, officer's uniforms, saddles, ladies' corsets and even kids' toys for the garrison guards to take home on leave. Some SS guards arrive from Germany with written lists, amazed at the luxury items being traded for a crust of bread. Prisoners can't eat a silk blouse or an alligator skin purse, and they know it. Most have been stripped of everything but their memories.

I watch the bastard bowing and scraping before Biebow, in stark contrast to the arrogance shown to his slave labourers. He thinks nothing of calling in his special Sonder Police Force to root out anyone suspected of complaining.

A few brave souls attempted to hand out flyers denouncing his entire family as "parasites", and calling for a general strike. Needless to say, they were brutally suppressed and denied further work; families without work or protection are doomed to be next aboard the transports.

"If I can eventually save just 10,000 in the ghetto it will have been worthwhile," our high and mighty Elder declares. What a joke! Some 18,000 have starved to death in the past 12 months alone. Bad luck for the other 140,000 huddled ten to a room, trying to survive on a crust of bread and a bowl of watery "soup" each day.

Rumkowski claims the Germans could not continue to thrive without his Jewish craftsmen putting in their twelve-hour shifts on 800 calories. He boasts that they are considered a real "gold mine" down at Nazi Headquarters, where he showers Biebow with all manner of gifts and favours.

Now I can only blanch at Jesus' words: "Do good to those who hate you; pray for them who despitefully use you …" Perhaps in any other universe only He could imagine such forgiveness could bring about the desired result, but not here. Clearly, the Nazi beast is implacable and insatiable.

Oh dear friend, I've never felt so alone among so many; there is no one here in whom I can confide. Both my parents are resigned to their fate, but still better off than most. I long for the tenderness of true friendship before I go crazy, but not for you to worry; I'm managing to keep my act together, even under constant scrutiny. Everyone fears being accused of something or other.

Here behind the barbed wire, I imagine I'm taking on the people's pain. Hunger rules their lives and remains their sole focus of existence. Dysentery is everywhere rampant and the afflicted often have to descend multiple flights of stairs to use the outdoor toilets. Needless to say, the stench inside the corridors and stairwells is almost unbearable.

Children loll about listless and hollow-eyed; since the last influx of 20,000 Jews from the west, Rumkowski has reduced the daily bread ration from 33 to 28 gms. He accuses the German Jews of being "too slow", and only those with a job get an additional bowl of watery noonday soup. In this place, Iris would look like a choir girl.

I do feel better getting this off my chest.

Your Friend, C.

Just one week later I received a shorter follow-up note containing a glimmer of hope.

Dearest K,

I've come to realise that terror is a solitary thing, insulating each of us from the suffering of others. Hitler knows that all too well, it is at the root of all Nazi culture.

Of course, I'm mad with worry when each deportation list goes up. Is this selfish of me to hope that someone else's parents will get shipped off to Chelmno rather than my own? I'm afraid Gestapo assurances don't hold much water in Lodz.

National Socialism exercises a frightful power of corruption against which it is difficult to guard oneself. Then again, I'm not convinced that *any* religion has been able to make men more compassionate over time.

Enough of my philosophy for now, I know you'll excuse my babbling; it feels good to share my pain and you've always been such a good listener. I hope the boss is pleased with the unusual subjects I've chosen for his "special collection". Please let me know if there are any particular abnormalities. Does he still have Hitler's ear these days? I want to ask a big favour.

Perhaps he could find it in his hard heart to request my transfer back to Dachau by intervening with the Political Dept.? I'm already familiar with the system there and I know you will put in a good word for me if my case comes up. But who am I kidding?

I can never abandon my parents; even swallowing my pride and approaching Dr Brandt during his recent inspection tour of the Ghetto; I've heard he is undertaking certain experiments in Dachau. I told him I could keep an eye out for anything unusual if it means his chosen "patients" are getting away from this hellhole to the relative luxury of that place. Did he need decent photos? Did he need someone who knew the ropes in both organisations? Have you heard anything of this?

Something about twins, I think. He said he remembered me from earlier times and promised to look into it, but he's a cold bastard and I don't like my chances. I do so long to be human once more. Here in Lodz, the step from an initial monstrous accusation against any Jew to his annihilation seems but the blink of an eye. Three thousand years of history and tradition crammed into a freezing lice-infested slum, shows just how fragile is the veneer of so-called civilised society.

Do stay safe. Who knows? If I can swing a transfer back to Dachau, we may yet enjoy another picnic together by the Isar.

Your friend forever, C.

Receiving these lengthy shared confidences from Claudia was both depressing and exhilarating at once; the faintest possibility of her returning to Dachau set my mind racing. Of course, the knowledge of Robert's recent transfer into the SS Deaths Head Division and transfer to Dachau sat a little uneasily. Nonetheless, the warmth and intimacy of her letters brought some hope that she may gradually be heeding my entreaties.

Lurching into yet another year of shortages and aerial bombing, unrest grew among the staff, particularly when we heard whispers that Hoffman was already making plans for his own escape. For those of us who caught a glimpse of the shuffling Führer around that time, an end to Germany's ghastly ordeal seemed more likely than ever. His shoulders were slouched and perpetually dusted with dandruff; his face appeared a blotchy blue-grey. His once-proud schnurrbart barely clung to his lip as a pale ginger smudge.

At regular intervals, he appeared to lose all self-control, railing at and cursing his hated lieutenants in absentia. Overall, discipline in his presence had noticeably dropped off and many staff no longer sprang to attention or even rose to their feet when he entered a room, continuing to carry on conversing.

Eva, however, appeared to be trying to step in and fill the social vacuum while struggling to dominate those she considered of weaker character. Hitler's Munich housekeeper, Frau Winter, now labelled her "high-hatted" but the die was cast; she had leapt into the moral void that most Germans could never tackle alone.

Hence my surprise when she barged into the darkroom one morning and blurted out two items of astounding news in the same breath.

"Gretl's Hermann has been appointed Himmler's liaison officer to Adolph, and he's finally proposed; not before time in my opinion! That means he will be Adolph's brother-in-law and I will be Fegelein's sister-in-law; can you believe that? He actually asked Papa and Mama for Gretl's hand in marriage, all very proper, and naturally they agreed.

"I'm to be bridesmaid and I've already told the boss I want you to do the reception candids; nothing too posed. I do so want everything to go perfectly and I don't have much time to make all the arrangements. Dear me, where shall I begin?"

"Naturally enough, given Fegelein's reputation for corruption and lechery, we were all taken aback at this news, and that's saying something. Within days I was on my way to Berchtesgaden in the orange Beetle, and during the drive down I had time to ponder Fegelein's on-again-off-again association with my brother and the SS Cavalry."

On June 3, 1944, just three days before the Normandy landings, Gretl and Hermann were married in a civil ceremony at the Mirabel Palace in Salzburg, followed by a three-day reception at Eagle's Nest.

Gretl and Eva wore sumptuous satin gowns and bold permanent waves, despite Goebbels' ban on the latter. Each carried an oversized bouquet of fresh roses. The glabrous-cheeked groom wore a full-dress SS uniform, adorned with, among other citations, an Iron Cross with Oak Leaves. He wore his dark hair slicked back off a high forehead and behaved every bit towards Fritz and Fanny as the doting son-in-law, being attended predictably by Hitler and Himmler as witnesses, with Bormann as best man.

During the formal portrait session at Mirabel Palace, I noted Hoffman carefully placing Hitler between the two bubbling Braun sisters for the group shots, while the Bride's father, Fritz, in his ersatz Nazi uniform, jockeyed to position himself alongside the senior officers. The boss even managed to squeeze himself into at least one group photo with the aid of a long cable release, while Fanny, wearing a huge orchid corsage, kept popping up between the younger girls. At one stage she was captured holding both bouquets aloft, with her proud nostrils quivering as if she were about to gobble them down.

Since reconnecting with Fegelein, Robert had been given the day off from Dachau to celebrate his old mate's big day, arriving replete in his SS Guard uniform, black leather mitten and eye patch. After the photo session, he wedged himself into the front seat of the leading Mercedes in the official motorcade, with my Beetle bringing up the rear.

We did not stop in Berchtesgaden or at the Berghof, climbing straight up the tight mountain road towards Kehlsteinhaus, now officially dubbed "Eagle's Nest". The bridal party had already alighted in near-zero visibility, the surrounding crags having been shrouded in cloud and mist for much of the day.

I was instructed to park the Beetle several hundred yards downhill, as the tiny Kehlstein carpark was already jam-packed with six-wheelers. Panting heavily, I made it back up the steep incline clutching my Leica, just in time to see the bride make a dash from the car wearing a sumptuous mink stole about her shoulders, just one of many "acquired" by Hoffman in recent months.

Outside the tunnel entrance, I was stopped by SS guards who phoned ahead to verify my press card number. Belatedly, I entered the frosty silence just in time to see the polished elevator doors glide shut on the last group of guests. Impatiently, I sprinted forward and pushed the button.

After what seemed an interminable delay, it returned containing just one SS operator who stared straight ahead during the smooth ascendance. What a scene greeted me as I stepped from that shining capsule into the curved dining space of the Führer's Fortress.

Schaub and Bormann had transformed the utilitarian Aerie into a wonderland of candles and fairy lights, with two lavishly decorated "official" tables almost hidden by the crowd. The bridal table itself was oval-shaped and oversized, laid out for the official party and inner circle with SS cutlery, crockery and fine crystal. Nearby, a small rectangular drop-leaf was set for Bormann and the "elders", for the moment various groups just stood around chatting awkwardly, awaiting a word or a smile from the bride. Clearly, Hoffman was not happy at the lack of space available for his lights and informals.

I soon spotted Robert surrounded by a group of SS, none of whom seemed interested in the drawn-out preamble. Amidst the hand-kissing and well-wishes the crowd suddenly parted to allow one of Bormann's nine children, a three-year-old girl dressed in full fairy garb with wings, to approach the bride and groom waving a tiny bouquet above her head before attempting to read a trite love poem from a note in large print.

At once, Eva fell to her knees and smothered the child with kisses, completely throwing her off the planned recital. A beaming Fanny leaned over from behind so as not to miss a single word, while Herman and Gretl feigned delight. Nonetheless, later on, everyone agreed that the little one had indeed stolen the show.

A three-piece SS ensemble struck up and the brooding granite walls reverberated with music for the first time; the drinkers fell back to make room for the dancers, thanks to Eva's tearful entreaties Hitler had consented to lift the ban on dancing just this once.

An announcement was accordingly made and the bride and groom, renowned for their grace and precision when treading the boards during courtship, led off with a slow waltz, soon followed by a brisk fox-trot at the urging of Eva's girlfriends. They were then joined by the parents and several Nazi dignitaries, but not unexpectedly, Hitler again refused to be coaxed from his seat. This left Eva sitting alone wearing a forced smile until she was eventually serenaded by two violins and a piano accordion.

Not wishing to be partnered by either Himmler or Bormann she hung back with hope fading, until being swept into the arms of Dr Brandt for a barn dance. Under Hitler's gaze, she dared not linger in any man's embrace for too long, choosing rather abruptly to flit from partner to SS partner while feigning gay abandon. I was undecided whether to approach Dr Brandt with mention of Claudia's plight, but thought better of it.

Gretl Fegelein was clearly flattered by all the attention, dancing and hand-kissing, almost swooning when her new husband began referring to her loudly as "my love" in front of other guests, having hitherto called her "Goose" since their first meeting.

Following a sumptuous wedding breakfast, all the more surprising given the nationwide food shortages, the bride's father gave a rambling speech in which he announced how proud he was that his youngest daughter had actually tied the knot … "Not before time, either; with my other two hopefully soon to follow," he added between muted sniggers and while casting a glance in Hitler's direction. Fortunately, Fanny was able to pull him back into his seat before the inference was widely noted. Eva flushed visibly and slid a little lower in her chair.

Following the toasts and cake-cutting the band picked up the pace again, even daring to pump out one or two of the latest "swing" numbers, for so long odious in Nazi circles; but certainly none of the young ones objected. As the tiny dance floor rustled with uniforms, laughter and swirling gowns, I noticed Hitler becoming more and more uncomfortable when unable to make himself heard above the racket.

In fact, the whole day had seen him stilted and awkward, and when his stooped figure rose to leave early, there was an audible sigh of relief across the room. Clearly a little unsteady on his feet, the Führer was escorted to the elevator by Eva, the newlyweds and of course an omniscient Bormann. Some in the room gave a half-hearted salute from afar, impatient to resume their repartee and dance the night away.

When driving back to Munich the next day with Hoffman's film in the satchel by my side, I nearly ran off the road twice through exhaustion. Nonetheless, his instructions were clear: no rest until the final roll was on paper. When the first proof sheets rolled off the drum dryer I immediately saw that the group portraits looked hurried and cramped. I could not rid myself of the concept I'd read somewhere about re-arranging deck chairs on the Titanic.

Just three days later certain news items on the Peoples Radio confirmed my apprehensions: the first announcement advised that Pastor Niemoller's remaining clergy were being drafted en masse to the Eastern Front, the next warned that homosexual liaisons within SS ranks would henceforth be punishable by death. Way down the list came a mention that a decoy landing of Allied forces had occurred along the coast of occupied France; it had long been expected and was being contained.

If this landing was expected, some wondered, why then had Field Marshal Rommel, who was in charge of the coastal defences, been on leave in Germany that very day? Worse still, it seemed that no one had dared awaken the Commander-in-Chief for instructions before his usual rising time of 11 am, some six hours after the first invaders had hit the Normandy beaches.

But by then, the bratwurst was already out of the bag.

"Good. It's finally happened," were Hitler's drowsy first words, before he reiterated his belief that the main attack would surely come in the north, near Calais, where he'd cleverly positioned his main Panzer force in readiness.

Subsequent Radio broadcasts assured us that the Allied landing force was "being driven back into the sea".

59

D arkroom, Lodz Ghetto.

My dearest K,

My whole world has collapsed in a few short weeks, this may well be my last letter. Despite our best efforts, the ghetto has been "liquidated". Barely a handful of those, like me, who are under the control of the Political Police have been left behind to "tidy up"; in other words, to remove all remaining traces of the former administration.

Biebow is refusing to say whether we too shall be returned to Dachau, or most likely Auschwitz, where 160,000 of my fellow Jews have just gone up the chimney; I've never felt so useless and despondent. My dear parents were aboard the last train, along with Rumkowski and his extended family. No amount of pleading on my part could save them; damn the Gestapo's empty promises.

Mercifully, Mama and Pappy dealt with the parting more gracefully than I. In these last months, the Nazis have really tightened the screws; it became clear that no group, however talented, would be spared in the end. Now, I see that those remaining 160,000 poor souls were doomed from the start; as perhaps am I.

I cling to the hope that Hoffman may yet intervene on my behalf; the thought that all this suffering may never come to light is gut-wrenching, I repeat Sister Klara's admonition several times daily about Life *never* ceasing to have meaning if we trust in God.

Rumkowski had become more urgent and depraved towards the end, grooming the orphans with hard sweets, soft words and sleepovers in his office. The prettiest one of all, called Mania, was delighted to ride in his horse-drawn Droshky and to sit on his knee. Soon after that "privilege" he took her into his office and forced himself upon her. Her screams could be heard on and off for half an hour before he opened the door and shoved her out sobbing hysterically. No one could comfort her and there was no other authority where we could complain. Right to the end that cursed man held absolute power in the ghetto; only Biebow could countermand his orders. I feel so helpless at the mercy of forces beyond my control; I remember what you said about sitting quietly and concentrating on the small, still voice within, rather than my black whirlpool of thoughts right now. Rumkowski must have known what was coming, yet for weeks he was determined to weed out the weak and powerless: 2,000 one week, 3,000 more the next, every one of them sent to feed the beast and save the best for just a few moments more.

Finally, and I can hardly speak of it without weeping, it came time for the remaining children to go. He went before the ghetto parents with a stultifying request that I am including in its entirety, in the hope that one day you may reveal what happened to those thousands of innocents. What am I saying? We're all innocent.

A GRIEVOUS BLOW has struck the ghetto. They are asking us to give up the last best we possess; the children and the elderly. I was unworthy of having a child of my own, so I gave the best years of my life to children: I've lived and breathed children. I never imagined I would be forced to deliver this sacrifice to the altar with my own hands. In my old age, I must stretch out my hands and beg: brothers and sisters hand them over to me. Fathers and mothers, give me your children.

What terrible choices we are forced to make. I shall never forget the hopeless wailing of the parents that night; but in the end, they did hand the children over. What choice did they have?

No one who wasn't there could ever imagine those scenes. That supreme act of cruelty. In fact, all of the preceding selections merely delayed the inevitable. The ghetto cemetery has long since filled to overflowing; some 10,000 are now buried beneath the walking paths.

Nothing could compare with the imposition of that final 7-day "Sperre" when all remaining 160,000 prisoners were locked down under house arrest with little food or water. Suddenly in the dead of night seven the Germans came in force, illuminating the entire ghetto with spotlights and filling the air with sounds of savage dogs, screams and shouts of "Raus! Raus! Everyone out and onto the trucks."

Armed soldiers went through every room in every building; I and a few others could only watch on horrified from our quarters. That silver-haired Judas could be heard pleading with the guards in one final futile gesture, "… if I can save just 100 Ghetto Jews everything will have been worthwhile."

Days later, we received word from the commandant that Rumkowski and his wife had been murdered by the other prisoners within minutes of their arrival in Auschwitz; all his conniving and betraying counted for nothing in the end.

Apparently, several bone-grinders have been rushed to the camp in an effort to obliterate all traces of the Polish Jews. The enclosed film shows the Baluty Quarter in Lodz old town as it used to be, almost as if the Ghetto never existed. I've included a head and shoulders of Mania and Bronia from the files, so at least these two may not be forgotten. I want you to know every detail of the suffering I've witnessed here. Sadly, the remaining Poles don't waste any time claiming the leftovers, all of which has left me more disgusted and at loose ends.

By a strange twist of fate, "King Chaim" had sidelined me only the week prior to the final transport, for "asking too many questions", and this may well have saved my life. He had been trying to sack me since the day I arrived and I'm glad to have helped bring him down.

Do you still have that photo of me by the river? I'm afraid I don't look anything like that now. Life here is balanced on a knife edge, with no reason to expect I'll be treated any differently from the others. I'm aware that only God can save me now. Please know I don't feel quite so alone when sharing my fears with you.

Again, all my love, C.

Midsummer found me spending more time at the Berghof, where I often accompanied Eva and Herta on picnics to Lake Königssee. Usually, I wandered around with my camera while they splashed about in the shallows or performed gymnastics on the grass.

On one particularly balmy day in July, the three of us were stretched out sunbathing side by side on a pontoon, some fifty yards offshore. From their conversation, it was obvious that each of us had retained very different impressions of Gretl's wedding day.

"There's no denying it, Eva, Herman has a real reputation among the ladies; let's hope he settles down, if she is indeed pregnant as claimed …"

"Well, pooh to you, Hertchen! As if Gretl would pretend over something so important as that. I just know Captain Fegelein is fully committed to this marriage and what's more, loves the idea of being Adolph's 'brother-in-law', so to speak."

"Apparently, the SS men are giving him a real ribbing anyway, he wouldn't dare step too far out of line knowing Himmler is looking over his shoulder".

I kept my head buried in my elbow as the pair bantered overhead.

"Are you sure about that? Or Gretl's phantom pregnancy for that matter? Have you forgotten that Hoffman accused *you* of 'play-acting' both times you tried to kill yourself, didn't he? Yet, *you* got what you wanted out of those two charades, didn't you?"

There was an ominous silence before I heard Eva puffing herself up to fire back across my sizzling loins. "You know damn well I wasn't faking either of my suicides, Herta Schneider. Go on, say it to my face why don't you?"

Unable to withstand the searing sun on my buttocks any longer, I chose this moment to roll over and attempt to intervene with a soothing word, covering my lower half with a towel. Eva was dabbing her crocodile tears, flustered, before reaching for the movie camera and pointedly gazing off into the distance.

"I'd just like to say how happy I am," I began graciously, "to be here in this wonderful setting with two beautiful women enjoying the—"

"Oh, do shut up, Klaus. Even my Uschi understands that we girls like to get down and dirty sometimes. It's alright for you sitting up there in your ivory tower moralising on how things should be done while the rest of us have to live in the real world, which at the moment is not very promising for my little schapperl, is it darling?"

Eva gave a little sniffle and softened. "I like to deal with things in my own way, tit for tat, you know that. Hermann's promotion to Chief Liaison Officer at headquarters has filled him with a whole new sense of responsibility, he's told me as much himself."

"That may be so but it's *your* future I'm more concerned about," Herta responded. "All those lies you keep telling Fritz and Fanny about 'being on the road' with Hoffman. Surely, Vati Braun will come around now that *your* ultimate happiness is at least a possibility?"

Eva stared back as if struggling to avoid another argument. "You *always* do this to me, raising doubts and confronting me with my own failings …" She gave a little whimper and leaned over to kiss her best friend lightly on the lips.

"For goodness' sakes, Eva," Herta continued advisedly, "surely, you must keep on pushing yourself forward with Adolph, before he turns in on himself altogether; he's clearly not a well man. You live in perpetual terror of being supplanted by some more fortunate rival, while the reality of your own marriage plans seems, dare I say, more remote than ever …"

"Don't you lecture me, Herta Ostermayer; Adolph will get around to it when we win this bothersome war, and not before," the irrepressible Eva shot back.

I again turned over and buried my head in my hands while the pair tussled overhead. "I know he hates new faces in his presence and I shall do whatever it takes to lighten his load. He has already told me he can no longer satisfy my needs and that I should find a younger man; how would *you* feel if Erwin said that to you? I can only hope this phase will pass."

I thought Eva might again dissolve into tears and at that moment I felt real sadness for her situation. After all, what teenage shop assistant could have resisted, or even wanted to resist, the country's most powerful man sending daily bouquets and chauffeur-driven limousines to her home and workplace?

Yet, after all that not to be permitted to appear alone with him in public; was it any wonder that her emotions were in turmoil? At that moment from behind the boatsheds came speeding one of the motor-pools' black Mercedes, tyres screeching to a halt beside the pier. Out leapt Captain Fegelein in full battle dress, quickly espying us bobbing on the pontoon offshore. "Fraulein Eva, you must come at once. There's been an attempt on the Führer's life. I want you to know he's almost uninjured," Fegelein yelled through cupped hands.

At this, Eva let out a shriek and looked at us both. "Almost? What does he mean *almost* uninjured? I want to go to Adolph, immediately …" At that she dived into the icy water and with a few frantic strokes reached the shore, leaving her movie camera to be returned in my waterproof satchel.

"I'm afraid that won't be possible, Fraulein Eva," I heard Hermann trying to explain, "there's been a bomb blast in the Wolf's Lair, many hundreds of miles from here. I am instructed to advise you that the Führer is alert and uninjured. Dr Goebbels is already rounding up the traitors responsible. I am to handle the investigation on behalf of Reichsführer Himmler and keep you fully informed."

Herta too had now reached the sand, gathering up their discarded clothing before shepherding her hysterical friend onto the back seat of the gurgling tourer. Once again, I had been left behind to tidy up and see to the equipment.

After side-stroking to shore with my precious load and placing the waterproof bag on the back seat of the Beetle, I drove slowly up the winding black ribbon to a chaotic Berghof and slunk off to my quarters; it seemed the whole Mountain was in turmoil.

Of course, for weeks after, Operation Valkyrie proved a topic of conversation and people everywhere speculated over how such a thing could have happened. While all evidence pointed to a "clique" of disgruntled army generals, Hitler unequivocally blamed Winston Churchill and was hot for revenge.

"We will pay those Allies back a hundredfold," he raved to his surviving generals, but his words lacked conviction.

Subsequent press photographs of him and Mussolini inspecting the damage showed wads of cotton wool protruding from his burst eardrums. Fegelein carried a wad of postcards showing suspected conspirators being hanged in Plötzensee Prison.

The next morning at the Berghof, a delirious Eva Braun unwrapped a special delivery package that contained the Führer's shredded trousers, upon which she fell sobbing. "Oh, no, no, no, this can't be happening; without Adolph, we are all lost! How could he have survived such a blast? Just look at these bloodstains, his blood," she wailed, holding up the tattered garment for all to see.

Indeed we all agreed that anyone else should have been mortally stricken and that Hitler's survival was another Providential Sign that his mission on Earth was not yet complete. She would not settle until a telephone connection was established with the far-flung scene of the crime. Then, clutching the trousers under her chin, she poured out her heart into the mouthpiece: "My dearest schapperl, I promised to follow you even unto death, and I am ready."

There followed a few moments when he attempted to reassure her that he was in no further danger. "If anything happens to you I shan't go on living; you do know that don't you?" she wailed.

Slowly, after listening intently, she seemed to regain her composure and began breathing more easily, eventually blowing a series of kisses and replacing the handset. She turned back to us with red and rolling eyes that stared into space.

"He told me he has only a few cuts and bruises and will remain in bed for a few days with jaundice. Woe betides those cowardly generals who attempted to carry out Churchill's orders. We will be receiving movie footage of the executions as soon as they have been duly convicted by Judge Freisler.

"Those … those bastards who dared threaten a single hair on Adolph's head; how I'd love to get my hands on them …" Her voice displayed an unusual icy calmness. Eva now blamed the British Prime Minister for every mishap, since learning that he'd labelled her beloved an "abortion of hatred and defeat".

Within hours Eva had summoned her favourite fortune teller to the Berghof, there to be reassured that she and the Führer would be "linked together for all eternity", which settled her nerves right down. She smiled thinly at the group of concerned friends, among whom I was the only male, remonstrating that she attributed all our fuss to ignorance rather than ill intention.

In no time she appeared never to have suffered a single hour of disappointment, let alone ongoing rejection and heartbreak. "Adolph wants me to remain at the Berghof until it's safe to return to Munich; he says the bombing of the city has been heavier than expected."

We heard later that Hitler had put on a brave face during Mussolini's visit to the shattered Wolf's Lair but from the photos, it was clear that the Deuce too was rattled by this latest turn of events.

Many low-ranking Wehrmacht officers were hauled before firing squads before they had a chance to implicate their terrified superiors who were scrambling to cover their own tracks. After a brief appearance in the People's Court, a dozen or so of the main conspirators were dragged off to Plötzensee Prison and strung up six at a time, reputedly from meat hooks by piano wire nooses with their trousers pulled down around their ankles as a final humiliation.

The whole ghastly spectacle was captured on film by the SS, with copies being rushed by courier to Wolfschantze and the Berghof, where I walked out during the first screening.

Conversely, Hitler watched the execution footage over and over again, applauding loudly at the condemned men's prolonged death throes and involuntary ejaculations. Not yet sated, he turned on Field Marshal Rommel, his most highly decorated battle commander, who had probably known of the vague plans but failed to denounce the plotters.

Rommel was given the unenviable options of being shot by firing squad alongside his wife and family, or taking cyanide and being given a State Funeral with full military honours; allowing his family to live.

The lionhearted Rommel chose the latter, and once more Goebbels' propaganda machine sprang into action, cloaking the vile deception with fine words and crocodile tears. Of course, at that time, none of us had an inkling of the *real* cause of Field Marshall Rommel's demise, believing that he had died of battle injuries.

Meanwhile, the heavy hand of revenge reached out across the land in search of anyone remotely connected to the failed assassination attempt. Some two hundred had been rounded up and executed within days and ultimately thousands more by association. I doubt if anyone knows the actual total.

We did not then realise that Hitler had already spent his last hour at the Berghof. Henceforth he would be consumed with repelling Germany's invaders on all fronts, from beneath fifty feet of concrete in the Nation's capital. The twice-daily situation briefings became increasingly gloomy; desertions were out of control and many high-ranking officials were committing suicide.

He gave a long-overdue speech on the People's Radio: "I'm the only one who sees the danger and the only one who can stop it," which no one but Eva really fell for. "The Russians will suffer their bloodiest defeat ever before the gates of Berlin. The good and best of us have already been killed. In these three decades, I have been actuated solely by love and loyalty to my people, in all my thoughts, acts and life."

Other news flashes told of the hated Russians chaining prisoners together in lots of ten and putting out the eyes of all but the frontman, in preparation for their long march to captivity in Siberia.

This was an unmistakable message to 80 million adrenalised Germans back home. But as yet, few believed these stories.

Darkroom, Dachau.

My dearest K,

Thank you, thank you! How can I ever express my gratitude for your efforts in bringing about my miraculous reprieve? I have been plucked from the jaws of death by Dr Brandt at Dachau, and given the task of streamlining their whole photo I.D. filing system.

And, joy of joys! I've seen R here in camp, which you probably know already. Despite his ghastly injuries, he's still the same old Robert to me, and I feel further blessed to be working at something I know and having him in close proximity. Right now, stop what you're thinking! I want you to put all those jealous thoughts out of your head; there will never be another best friend for me, but *you*.

He, of course, remains aloof as ever, but I'm sure that even he was pleasantly surprised by this unexpected turn of events. I know your brother looks upon me only as an inconvenient sister figure and for the time being I have to be contented with that. Have not had a chance to speak to him yet about the "you know what", but I can't imagine he'd want to hang around Munich any more than we do, given the widely reported bomb damage and imminent invasion. Has the Studio escaped a direct hit? How about Hoffman and Eva's houses? I hear she has a bomb shelter. I'm back doing mug shots and recording Dr Brandt's experiments on the inmates; I must say they are pretty gruesome, will fill you in later.

Do write and tell me you are pleased, who knows, we may be able to squeeze in a visit or picnic nearby? I feel like I've been born again.

Your friend always, C.

Darkroom, Munich. October 1944.

Dear C,

I am thrilled by your deliverance; not sure how much my argument influenced Hoffman to step in, but thank God he did. At this end, Brandt cannot hide his disgust at Morell's treatment of Patient No. 1. They clash ever more frequently over the sheer volume of drugs being jabbed into the Führer's rump, which Brandt claims contain lethal doses of strychnine.

I've only glimpsed H briefly and must say something is clearly wrong. Since the assassination attempt, which I assume everyone has heard of by now, he regularly stays in bed all day. Eva's snapshots show him as a mere shadow of his former self, from which all life, fire and flame have long since departed. His schnurrbart is faded, limp and lop-sided and her movie clips show him humped over and shuffling; she confessed she's never before seen him like this.

Brandt stepped in to give a pep talk to the staff, urging us to "be faithful to oneself, faithful to the people and most of all remain faithful to the Führer" which, as you'd be aware, is quite laughable.

Rumour suggests that he and Albert Speer are planning to gang up on Hitler to "prove" that he is being poisoned by Morell's cocktail of drugs. Hoffman too, is more weighed down than ever by excess; he's grossly overweight, always drunk and nowadays shunned by H; it's a minor miracle he was able to intervene for you at all. I fear he is going senile, refusing to emerge from his bunker at the villa until long after the all-clear has sounded. The costive Iris and Lothar the bully have taken over the day-to-day running of the Studio, resulting in many resignations. I would be resigning too if I had somewhere to go. Eva is spending more and more time in Berlin, even preparing the Führer's meals since his vegetarian cook was "regretfully sacked" upon Himmler's discovery of her Jewish ancestry. It just never stops.

During Eva's visit, she related how Hitler had been pleasantly distracted by the mating of Blondie with Gerti Troost's splendid male Shepherd, Harras, and was keen to find out how Blondie had "performed" during the actual affair. As you know, he's leery about the copulation business in general but seemed eager to learn the details of Blondie's brief encounter with "the big boy".

Eva confessed to having to "jolly the Führer along" in the hope that he will regain his old sparkle, but from what I've seen he's already passed the point of no return.

He's sacking people left and right; poor old Rochus Misch, his longest-serving bodyguard, has been demoted following a "moral lapse" with Frau Mumme. And now, in a last-ditch effort to enforce discipline, the Hitler "salute" is being demanded right across the board.

Apparently, there have been more casualties in the last six months than in the first three years of the war. There are lots of stories about entire families of army deserters being imprisoned. The nightly air raids on Munich continue to cause extensive damage; some staff are whispering that these are the "chickens coming home to roost" and I have to agree. You would be aware that the ringleaders of the "Edelweiss Pirates" have been publicly hanged. I do hope the trail doesn't lead back to your friends in the Orchestra. STOP PRESS: Dr Brandt has just been fired as Führer's "personal physician", effective immediately. That quack Morell has triumphed over a mountain of professional opinion. It appears that Hitler will continue to receive his bulls balls injections and gas pills, no matter what anyone thinks.

"Dr Brandt has outlived his usefulness and will be returning to carry on his important medical work at Dachau," the news release stated, so I guess you'll be seeing a lot more of him. Do take good care of yourself and my big brother. See? I'm not really jealous at all.

Love always, K.

Darkroom, Dachau. Yuletide, 1944.

My dear K,

I've stepped from one hell into another; Dachau is now chaotic and grossly overcrowded, a place of unimaginable suffering.

In a monstrous betrayal of their Hippocratic Oath, the camp doctors are now actually involved in selecting those to be killed on arrival, including the sick and disabled. Don't ask me why, but despite the approach of the Allies and the writing on the wall, Dr Brandt and his murderous team continued to inflict horrific medical experiments upon the remaining inmates, which I'm required to document in detail.

The gas chamber is flat out night and day; flames and black smoke belch from the chimney of the crematorium. The townsfolk are complaining of the stench and tufts of singed hair are falling from the sky. With access to Brandt's files and being so close to Munich I'm revolted by the extent of the cruelty being inflicted, merely to test the efficacy of one drug or method or another; e.g. healthy men and women having body parts removed and inserted into others, all without anaesthetic. Some are deliberately infected with typhus while others are immersed in freezing water with their bodily functions being monitored right up until the moment of death.

This particular "experiment", nothing but calculated murder in my opinion, is supposed to inform the Luftwaffe of how much time downed pilots can survive in the freezing ocean. This ignores the fact that the Luftwaffe has few serviceable planes or pilots, and no fuel stocks.

Make no mistake: our once revered Dr Brandt is in the thick of the suffering. On his desk sit glass specimen jars filled with different coloured eyeballs; talk about kinky. Worst of all is having to photograph before and after results of healthy shin bones being smashed with hammers and infected with mustard gas, supposedly at Himmler's behest, to test the dubious healing effects of various sulphonamides.

The agony of these human guinea pigs is unimaginable and indescribable; I am enclosing close-ups of the wounds in the hope you may be able one day to show the world. Brandt's files reveal that even now he continues to perform hundreds of abortions using various experimental techniques, none with anaesthetic.

"No child is to be born in the camps", the signs are everywhere. Following the failed prisoner uprising at Treblinka in August, Deputy Commandant Kurt Franz, nicknamed "Doll" because of his youthful complexion, was brought across to Dachau by Brandt in order to demonstrate the efficacy of his crowd control techniques.

Apparently, the pair had worked together setting up the T4 "euthanasia" program. Franz's reputation in Treblinka for kicking babies to death and throwing others into the furnaces alive is probably a carry-over from that time.

Franz disembarked at Dachau railway station, from whence accompanied by his dog, Barry, he took to horseback for the short ride to the quadrangle, where all the inmates had been turned out to watch.

His ponderous St Bernard was infamous for latching onto the buttocks and genitals of any prisoner who caught his master's eye.

After one or two rounds of the assembled prisoners, Doll reined in his horse beside the whipping table, where a group of new arrivals were being forced to witness one of their number receiving a "welcoming 39" on the backside.

Dismounting, Franz pushed the Dachau guard aside and announced that there was a better way to do it. "Let's see, where are we up to? Best if I start over again. One ... two ..." – he brought the Ox pizzle down across the angry buttocks with a whistling crack – "… three." Then, slowly and deliberately he stopped to light up a cigar and take a few puffs, before continuing. "You see, you fellows are too soft, rushing the whole process. I like to be sure the prisoner will always remember my name is Kurt Franz … four … five …" He paused to take another puff and blow smoke rings toward the quivering sinciput strapped to the bench before him.

Long before the final blow fell the body had ceased to buck and moan, merely twitching at each stroke. With stops and starts and little tips in between, Doll slowly counted out the "full 39", after which the prostrate body had to be revived with a bucket of ice water.

"Remember, give them a welcome they'll never forget," he repeated, handing the whip back to its chastened owner.

Then, the guards were treated to a demonstration of Barry's unique skill set: at his master's command, "Man, grab that dog," the shaggy beast responded in an ironic role reversal by leaping to fasten its fangs into the nearest striped crotch. Sometimes, it was rumoured, Barry had been known to chew a set of male genitals clean off.

In a flash of surprising energy for a big dog, and before the horrified inmates, the skeletal victim was knocked off his feet and mauled beyond recognition. The work-Jews were forced to watch on and listen to such screams during his daily "demonstrations".

"Franz is a pure Nazi beast, the most calculating and terrifying I've come across since Heydrich; and I've seen plenty. They say he carries a hunting rifle in Treblinka and is liable at any moment to pick off one of the prisoners in the compound. He likes to single out newly arrived Jews with beards and force them to hold up glass bottles for "target practice". "If your God indeed exists then I will hit the bottle, and if he does not exist then I will hit you," he tells the terrified newcomers. Sometimes, he shoots the bottle from their hands, at others he sends a bullet or two whistling past their ears before dropping them with one between the eyes. He maintains that this keeps everyone on their toes, never knowing if their own head, or that of the person they are talking to, will suddenly explode.

Being handy with his fists, Franz proudly boasted of certain other fatal tricks he enjoys playing on the prisoners; such as challenging one of the few brawny Jews to a "boxing match" with the promise of "special treatment" should the other win.

The surprised opponent is given one boxing glove "for maximum fairness", while Franz pulls on the other. At his command the hopeful pugilist takes up his stance, before Franz pulls a small pistol from his glove and shoots him dead. They say not a single day passes without him murdering someone. I'm telling you all this because the world needs to know.

Yet, to look at him you'd think butter wouldn't melt in his mouth. When noting the paucity of children in Dachau he told of Treblinka Commandant Schwartzhuber's mistake in allowing his own son to play with the condemned Jewish kids behind the wire. How one day his precious boy was rounded up by the over-zealous guards and marched off toward the gas chambers, only to be miraculously snatched aside at the last minute. Now all the guards' children are required to wear bells around their necks.

Franz lectured the Dachau guards daily on "the futility of pity", how in Treblinka he'd come across a female guard who'd attempted to save a child from the selections by hiding it in her own quarters. He dragged the child from its concealment and forced the woman to carry the wailing infant personally to the crematoria and fling it into the flames, supposedly to dissuade others being tempted by such sentimental lapses in judgment.

That such a person remains best friends with Brandt shows how we were sadly mistaken about the good doctor living among us. Since gaining access to Brandt's Hadamar dossier, which makes for chilling reading, it's clear he was involved in the murder of crippled and retarded children ever since the start of the war. It's all here in black-and-white. Even before 1939, he was advocating the "mercy killing" of institutionalised children, many of whom were disposed of by exhaust fumes in specially constructed vans.

As soon as war was declared, Brandt and the other "carers" wasted no time installing larger and more discreet gas chambers behind the high walls of Hadamar and other institutions. No matter the killing methods, bodies have to be disposed of, and the crematoria were soon operating day and night. There were complaints from townsfolk over the smell of burning flesh coming from the chimney.

Earlier in the T4 project, as it was first called, phenol injections were the preferred method of "humanely" killing crippled children. It's all here in detail; how they experimented with the dosages and deceptions to be used.

These unsuspecting youngsters, along with a selection of older "useless eaters" were told they were being "vaccinated". They were required to sit on a chair and bite down on their right hand thumb while the doctor stood behind and stretched back the patient's left hand to expose the chest. Then, in a swift, smooth movement, he reaches over and plunges a 6" hypodermic into the unsuspecting rib-cage, between the fifth and sixth ribs, causing instant heart failure and death within 15 seconds. For a while they tried injecting the phenol intravenously but the victims took too long to die. Other "lives unworthy of life" are forced to drag the bodies away to the crematorium, where at the conclusion of each session, their own luck runs out.

I've searched through the many thousands of "patient" names listed there until I found a record of our friend, Pauli Falkenhorst. As I suspected he did not die of "appendicitis" or "pneumonia" like the death certificates stated.

For a whole day afterwards, I remained in my quarters, weeping.

I cannot take much more of this hellhole; I'm finding it impossible to look Brandt in the eye and I feel sure he suspects me of snooping. You know what that means?

R too is appalled by the lack of direction and order. For the first time, we have actually discussed the "you know what". Have you had any further thoughts on the matter?

I remain always your dear friend, C.

60

Nineteen forty-five was upon us with feeble celebration: there was nothing to celebrate. In early January came the heaviest air raid on Munich so far, which I had to admit put the wind up me and many others. Now, it seemed nowhere above ground was safe from the British bombers by night or the American planes by day.

Eva was increasingly holed up in Berlin, where Hitler had just issued orders for the Gestapo to shoot looters, deserters and other rabble on sight. Later that month, he too moved permanently into the Führer Bunker beneath the Chancellery, where Eva was busy trying to pretty up her stuffy quarters buried under fifty feet of concrete.

While thus occupied she was visited there by her elder sister, Ilse, who did not hold back in blaming Munich's destruction on Hitler.

When Ilse realised the magnitude of Eva's decision to defy Hitler and return to the bunker in Berlin she was flabbergasted.

Nonetheless, they soon kissed and made up, after Eva assured her that "everything is going to be fine". Some short time later, Eva made her farewell visit to Munich, to give away her dogs and attend her belated 33rd birthday party among her few remaining family and friends; I was not invited, however.

The next day, inside the old studio at Schellingstrasse, she tearfully reminisced with Herta. "We had such a lovely time together, didn't we?" she said before handing over what I imagined to be her final roll of 36. She ran her fingers lovingly along the countertop.

"Do you remember, Klaus, how Herta and the girls sat together here, on this very spot, and begged you to tell tall tales of your life in the jungle? How you used to blush when they asked about those scary initiations you'd undergone? Well, that's all over now."

For a few moments, she searched both our faces affectionately. "We *shall* get through this, you know, if we all stick together behind the Führer. You've heard? I will be staying with Adolph to the end," she stated again, putting on a brave face. She had outstayed all her rivals and we could only nod dumbly, almost too sad to reply.

But I couldn't let this moment pass. "Fraulein Eva, I … er, couldn't you think about getting away to Obersalzberg where it's still safe? My Aunt and Onkel live nearby; you are still young with your whole life ahead of you," I pleaded. "You're not implicated in any of the nasty stuff, are you? When things settle down you may yet pick up a starring role in the movies; you know, with Tarzan?"

But I blushed at the hollowness of my own words.

Herta too, knew it was all over.

"Just stop it!" Eva snapped. "Thirty-three is hardly 'young' … you're no better than that snivelling Ribbentrop, who's also been pleading with me to convince Adolph to flee to the mountains. What good would that do? Merely postpone the inevitable. I've made my mind up to die beside the only man I've ever loved."

We could see she meant it, and that was that.

Hitler gave his final speech to the Gauleiters, reminding them that there had been no foreign troops in Berlin since 1806. News footage showed a trembling wreck emerging from the bunker to bestow bravery medals on a group of Hitler Youths commemorating his 56th birthday.

We heard that Eva, after returning to Berlin, had arranged a modest celebration for him underground, attended by a handful of the Party faithful. Göring managed to bluster his way down to the inner sanctum, wearing an American-style general's uniform, only to be relieved on the spot from his duties as head of the lame-duck Luftwaffe.

Speer too, turned up at the "Isle of the Departed", as he called it, to inform his Commander-in-Chief that he had failed to carry out the widespread "scorched earth policy" so vehemently insisted upon.

He went on bravely to inform a stunned Hitler that at the "cessation of hostilities" Germans would need their remaining infrastructure intact to rebuild the shattered nation. Unsure of the likely repercussions of such admissions, Speer was greatly relieved when, instead of being taken out and shot, his despairing leader merely sank into a chair and mumbled a chilling brief reply.

"Rebuild? Rebuild? The German people are too weak; they don't deserve to rise again. They have shown themselves incapable of ruling and unable to follow a great leader when they had the chance. They deserve everything that's coming to them …" he said before waving him away.

With a final backward glance, Speer turned silently to leave the room, passing briefly and easily among the subterranean and calmly lingering to embrace Eva and the secretaries. As Hitler's favourite, he felt himself lucky to escape a death sentence, as pronounced a day earlier upon Dr Brandt, for "treason" no less.

What followed the next day, April 21, came to me second-hand, and I shall here attempt to relay events as told to me by those who were there.

In a flood of tears, Dr Morell was ordered to remove his uniform and leave Berlin by a hysterical and paranoid Hitler, convinced that his long-term, half-Jewish benefactor had been about to drug him and hand him over to the enemy, "to be paraded through the streets of Moscow in a cage, like an animal …"

Moments after Morell's departure, the Führer reportedly broke down and wept uncontrollably.

Speer later revealed in his memoirs something of the seemingly carefree final fling unfolding deep underground, including drunkenness, hysterical laughter and swing dancing. Eva had monopolised the gramophone, playing her favourite "Blood red roses spell happiness for you" repeatedly, while swigging French champagne straight from the bottle.

He had been further deflated to overhear the bunker conversation centring on the best and least painful way of killing oneself when the moment arrived.

The next week brought a chain of unrelated events triggering yet more calamity in the smoke-filled Führer Bunker. As Russian artillery shells thudded into the gardens above, radio operators underground picked up the nightly 9 pm BBC broadcast from London, announcing that Himmler had approached Swedish diplomats with an offer to exchange several thousand Jews for clemency for his family and a position in the upcoming administration.

Upon receipt of this formerly forbidden news source, Hitler summoned up his last vestiges of frothing rage in total disbelief that "Loyal Heini" would ever dare to launch such despicable overtures.

In the next breath, he demanded that Fegelein, Himmler's liaison officer, be brought before him to explain. Unbeknown to the Führer, Fegelein had already contacted Eva by telephone, when she'd refused point blank to even consider joining his escape group; she was heard screaming into the mouthpiece that he was a coward and a traitor to Gretl.

A thorough search of the Chancellery turned up no trace of him and a city-wide manhunt was launched; Gestapo agents finally tracked him down and found him blind drunk in bed with a prostitute.

When his dishevelled brother-in-law was hauled before Hitler, Eva refused to offer a single word in his defence. Fegelein was court-martialled on the spot and found guilty of desertion and treason, before being marched out into the Chancellery garden and shot in the back of the head.

Meanwhile, Hanna Reitsch, Hitler's favourite female test pilot, had at great personal risk flown into Berlin on April 26 to offer her final farewell "on the altar of Nazism" and to "receive orders from the very top" as she said later.

She had set out flying low-level in a tiny Fieseler Storch, piloted by her partner Ritter von Greim, using the ruined buildings for cover. When Greim, Hitler's choice to take over leadership of the eviscerated Luftwaffe, had his foot blown to shreds by Russian ground fire, Hanna took over the controls herself and skilfully guided the aircraft down onto the bomb-pocked Tiergarten, taxiing almost right up to the Brandenburg Gate.

After a tearful reunion with Hitler, during which Greim lay in agony on a bunk nearby, Hitler issued his new string of orders: Greim was to take over command of the Luftwaffe, effective immediately, and commence his promotion by bombing those Russian forces already streaming over the Elbe River into Berlin. Additionally, the crippled Greim was to track down and punish the treacherous Himmler, who'd been fired in absentia by Bormann.

Under normal conditions this would have been mission impossible; now it was but a final fleeting fantasy in Hitler's mind as he thrashed about issuing orders to phantom armies that no longer existed.

When the two aviators took off on the final flight to leave Berlin, they were again raked by ground fire from Russian commanders who were convinced that Hitler was escaping; but aside from their impossible mission, Reitsch and Greim managed only to carry Eva's final letters to Gretl and her best friend Herta. In shaky handwriting, Eva confided for the first time that "death matters little to me", although she was "terribly frightened and it was difficult maintaining self-control".

Nonetheless, she went on to state that she would remain at the side of her beloved "until the very end", certain that this was the "right and proper way" for her to die. Lastly, she bequeathed her bulky fur coats and other clothing to the secretaries.

One other precious item was also left on Hanna's final flight; an undeveloped roll of 35 mm film which was delivered to me at the studio the next day by a tearful Gretl.

"These are Hanna's own photos of Eva's wedding; I don't have to tell you how precious they are. She insisted they come to you as proof of her final triumph and wants them shown to the whole world." Gretl seemed strangely proud of her sister's achievements throughout the Reich's twelve years in power, while avoiding mention of her own recent traumas and late husband.

"I'll do my best, Gretl, you can be sure of that. I'm keen to see them myself. Part of the darkroom is blown away and I have a blanket covering the hole in the wall. Tonight I will try to put them through; I have just enough chemical to develop your film and possibly a single proof sheet, which I shall carry on my person to the outside world."

She seemed greatly relieved, happy to relay Hanna's impressions of the ceremony itself and Eva's fleeting radiance on finally landing her man.

"I have a copy of the marriage certificate right here, for safekeeping," she confided, unrolling a small scroll from her coat pocket. "See, see here, how she's started signing her name 'Eva Br ...' before crossing it out and signing 'Eva Hitler'. Oh, how I'm dying to see how she looked; I do hope she didn't overdo it on such an important day. It's a miracle she managed to obtain fresh flowers.

"Please call me the moment you have something, I'm staying in Vati's bomb shelter under the house. He's been shattered, but Mutti's still holding out hope. They'll never understand how her love for Adolph has driven her to this 'Wagnerian sacrifice', as he sees it ... I alone can understand, as only a sister can who knows betrayal ..." She stopped herself and touched her tiny bulge, turning to wave from the footpath.

I locked the front door and hurried to my shelter beneath the stairs, relieved to find the electricity still working. Thought after thought raced through my head. *Would Munich's power grid survive the night? Would the pathfinders come again and light up the night sky with their "Christmas Trees", a sure sign the bombers were close behind?*

Without power there could be no darkroom. *What would I see on this single roll of black-and-white film? What sort of photographer was Hanna Reitsch anyway?* I longed for the darkness to come, so that any leakage of light would be less damaging. Here in my hand I held probably the only photos taken of that forlorn, world-shattering occasion, and Gretl had left them with *me* rather than at the new premises.

If only I could locate Hoffman should I even tell him of their existence? Perhaps he was now beyond all help and caring? Maybe he'd have me shot for not speaking up earlier?

If these pictures were as exclusive as hoped, and that was a big "if", should I make a copy for myself while the chemicals and power hold out, or return the original set of negatives and proof sheet to their rightful owner? They could well be my ticket to fame and fortune.

As the hours ticked by there were occasional air raid sirens going off and the thud of distant explosions. Now and then the front door knob rattled, but I did not make a sound. What would I find if everything went well tonight? Too excited to read, I tossed for a while on my bunk and must have slipped into a fitful slumber for I know not how long. I was there again in Hitler's private quarters at the Berghof, with Eva as my guide, confronted with his mother's framed photo and her arresting eyes.

"Isn't she beautiful?" Eva had purred at the time of my grand tour. I only wish I'd come to know her; she held a special place in Adolph's heart.

But even that first glance told me something wasn't quite right. In the many prints of his mother Klara I'd made over time, at least one for each desktop or dresser where the Führer had ever spent a night, his Mutti was never too far away.

That one photo captured her haunted, desperate plea with eyes of ice, which I recognised at once as Adolph's own. In that same dream, Frau Hitler reached under her skirts and brought forth a squirming, pink hissing thing, which she lifted triumphantly above her head, never for a moment averting her gaze from mine. Her drooling lips opened and shut wordlessly, as if trying to warn me to flee; I found it impossible to look away and woke unnerved, in a cold sweat. To this day I wonder about the effect that dream had on my deplorable lapse of concentration in the darkroom.

Again, I'm being long-winded and getting ahead of myself; so much happened in those final days that I struggle to recount them in some order.

In the week prior, when Vienna fell to the Russians, I could see an air of gloomy resignation settling over the German population.

Blindly, mechanically, a few of us yet manned Studio Hoffman, awaiting orders from Lothar and Iris in the vain hope they knew what they were doing. Photo supplies were almost exhausted and there was little petrol available for the Volkswagen, which I was hoping to make one final trip to Lake Königssee.

Terrible reports and movie footage began pouring in to the news desk from all fronts: endless columns of German refugees fled westward ahead of the Russians, some riding on overloaded horse-carts with the vast majority strung out behind on foot. Small children struggled under huge burdens, past roadside ditches dotted with strafed vehicles, dying people and screaming horses. Young and old alike wore masks of terror, causing me to almost choke on my own apprehensions.

It seemed that town after town besides Munich were now helpless beneath the deadly hail of high explosives falling from the skies.

Everyone forgot about me as soon as I'd delivered my allotted reports to the Press Room; otherwise, various "special orders" with return addresses were continually being poked through the slot in the front door on Schellingstrasse. In between bombings, it seemed some petty tyrants still prioritised their perversions over my safety but, of course, without sufficient chemicals my hands were tied.

Unexpectedly, Hoffman took himself off to Berlin with fifty documents to prove he did not have paratyphus, but neither Eva nor Bormann could procure him an audience with Hitler. He returned looking deranged, spreading wild rumours of "Secret Weapons", including "Death Rays", that would once more turn the tide in Germany's favour.

Early one morning, a mysterious package containing strips of negative was dropped through an aperture in the front door by an unseen hand. No attempt had been made to conceal an envelope lying nearby, which I hastened to tear open/

Dachau Barracks A.

Dearest K, I must be quick. I have been assigned to a work gang cleaning up bomb damage in Munich; we pick up broken glass, masonry and splintered timber with our bare hands.

We women had to run naked past the camp doctors in order to prove our fitness for the task; even now they are keeping an eye out for abnormally shaped skulls. Those who failed to make the work detail were marched straight off to the gas chambers.

R says the Americans are less than a week away from liberating Dachau and then the shit will hit the fan when they come across the piles of rotting corpses in the camp.

Thousands of inmates who could still walk have been marched away in appalling conditions to God-knows-where; we could see them dropping like flies before they'd made it up the first hill. And then, it's into Munich for me, so you must be prepared. During the next air raid, I propose to "disappear" and remain out of sight in my old flat.

R plans on meeting us there before April 25, when I'm hoping the three of us can finally slip away together. He has a plan to get us into Italy through Austria: if we can make it as far as Rome, the Vatican will send us down the "ratline" directly to South America; I can hardly believe this moment is finally upon us.

Come as soon as you can in the next few days and carry only a knapsack; Robert says we *must*, repeat *must*, be out of Munich before midnight on the 25th. Please hurry, I have lost all track of time and am delirious at the thought of the three of us being together again. Robert knows I have no intentions of leaving you behind.

Yours Always, C.

This letter from the blue threw me, as I was on the verge of one last departure to Lake Königssee via the Berghof darkroom. I quickly figured I would have sufficient fuel and time to make it there and back by the deadline; maybe even find time to help Tante and Onkel tidy up their affairs, if indeed they intend fleeing. Fedi had always said they would stay where they were and take their chances.

After I'd processed Gretl Braun's precious canister I would be free to leave, hoping that a plausible excuse and a yellow press card would see me through the roadblocks one last time. I was charged with removing the remaining negative files from the Berghof darkroom and returning them to Munich for disposal.

Over in the newsroom, images came through of Mussolini's execution in front of an Italian firing squad of Partisans, after which he was strung upside down from a petrol station awning in Milan, alongside his long-time mistress Clara Petacci.

Misch's radio messages continued to crackle out from the Bacchanalian bunker. That's how we learned the official dog handler had himself gone insane and committed suicide, after being forced to shoot Blondie's puppies and test out a cyanide capsule on their mother. Brandt's replacement, Dr Stumpfegger, demonstrated how to crush the glass vial of poison between Blondie's teeth and watched her collapse with barely a whimper, happy to report back to Hitler that the capsules being distributed were indeed suitably lethal. The Führer's greatest fear remained being drugged and handed over to the enemy as part of some armistice arrangement.

Terrible descriptions emerged of buckets of blood and body parts lining the bunker corridors; those of us frequenting the news desk watched on ashen-faced from afar. Surgeons there were working in the most appalling conditions, unable to empty operating room detritus into the gardens above because of the relentless artillery barrage. Reports came in of top Nazis and public officials shooting their whole families and then themselves.

"The Germans must stay on their feet, no matter how," said the Propaganda Minister in a defiant radio broadcast. "Just stay on their feet, and then the moral and historical superiority of the German people can manifest itself ..."

By contrast, the Führer's moods were oscillating wildly between hope and indifference as he issued frantic orders to ghost armies. Some infantry units arrived on the crumbling frontline just in time to retreat, while Göring's paratroopers had fled the field altogether.

Aside from Hitler, it seemed that Youth Leader Artur Axmann was the only person who still believed in victory, forming up a double rank of his uniformed youngsters in the adjoining waiting room, whom he assured his leader, were "ready and willing to fight".

Touched and re-invigorated, the Führer dispatched Keitel in person to turn about General Wenck's vestigial army and disrupt the Russian thrust at the heart of Berlin. Wenck's orders were nothing if not Homeric: "Free Berlin. Rescue your Führer. His fate is Germany's fate."

The capital's battered and scattered defenders had few tanks and no heavy guns, rendering fanciful the likely success of any such mission. Worse still, given Hitler's misplaced notion that Zhukov's forces would wheel about at the last minute to take Prague, he brushed aside the bedlam in the bunker and penned a direct order to General Wenck's wounded warriors on how salvation might yet be snatched.

Soldiers of Army Wenck.

An order of great importance has caused you to turn east. Your duty is clear. Berlin remains German. The goals ordered for you *must*, under all circumstances be achieved.

On other sides, operations are in progress with the goal of dealing the Bolsheviks a decisive defeat in the battle for the German Capital and thus fundamentally altering the situation in Germany.

Berlin will never capitulate before Bolshevism. The defenders of the Reich Capital have taken fresh heart with the news of your fast approach, and fight with obstinacy and doggedness in the belief that soon the thunder of your guns will be heard.

The Führer has called you. You have, as in old times, started on the road to victory. Berlin waits for you. Berlin yearns for you here with warm hearts.

There was a jagged signature in the lower right-hand corner.

That night with trembling fingers I removed the roll of 35 mm film from its canister, wound it into the stainless spool and added the remaining developer; so far so good. It was hard to shake the memory of that slithering, evil thing being held up by the heels and I found it difficult to concentrate on the task at hand. Even now the contents of the light-tight container seemed to exude a potent energy: Eva Braun finally married; it seemed barely possible.

Slowly, impatiently, I waited for the timer to ring; when it did I nearly jumped out of my skin. The responsibility of the moment almost took my breath away. I reached for the last remaining swig of fixer, hoping there was enough in the bottle to cover a single roll.

Minutes passed and the bell rang again; I popped the lid and nervously held the cellulose strip up to the safelight, straining my eyes to make out the first image: a faint group around a plain wooden table with a single light globe overhead, just as Gretl had described.

That tall man sitting in the centre with his papers spread out must be Herr Wagner, the Berlin notary who'd been snatched from his ruined office to oversee the most important and momentous task of his long career: a legally binding marriage of the Führer to his paramour of nearly fifteen years.

Although the images were black-and-white, I instantly recognised Eva wearing Hitler's favourite dress; the black silk taffeta with the wide skirt sprinkled with tiny embroidered stars which I too had admired on previous occasions. Two golden clasps secured pink shoulder straps, with an identical third clasp steadying Eva's permanent wave.

On her tiny feet, she wore comfy black suede flatties and on closer inspection I noticed she had on the stunning Mikimoto pearl necklace gifted by the Japanese Ambassador, as well as her platinum watch with the diamond numbers which I thought tended to overdo the whole effect.

Still, it was *her* wedding day, towards which she had been striving and fighting an uphill battle for more than a decade; under the circumstances, it was perfectly understandable she wanted to appear as august as possible.

Standing to one side and looking on were the two witnesses, Bormann and Goebbels, with Frau Goebbels and her six children gathered about the bride in a semi-circle. Each of the Goebbels' girls wore a white dress with flowers in her hair. I could see that Hanna had moved in to get a close-up of Eva signing the marriage certificate, but the poor lighting only accented the dark bags under her eyes and threw her half-smile into shadow.

More informal candids followed, showing the hunched figure of Hitler kissing the hands of his two secretaries and shaking hands timorously with his adjutants; one shot caught him wearing a wan smile surrounded by all six Goebbels' children and certain front-on poses showed what appeared to be food stains down the front of his tunic.

Linge, Hitler's long-term valet, could be seen handing out liverwurst sandwiches and pouring champagne; image #36 showed a rear view of Eva walking arm-in-arm with the groom and Frau Goebbels on the other into Hitler's private apartment for a last supper of spaghetti and salad.

Keen for a better view and frustrated by the poor illumination I stretched the film strip across the lightbox to apply my Agfa Lupe for closer inspection. As the light flickered on, calamitous, irretrievable disaster struck: before my eyes, the celluloid strip began to darken, and within seconds turned solid black. Images 1 to 36 were gone forever.

The fixer! That last cup or two I'd been saving had been diluted down over recent weeks to stretch it out and had obviously ceased fixing altogether.

Of course, I panicked and even wept a tear of bitter regret while fumbling to kill the white light and scrambling to locate a last dribble of chemical; but there was none. By failing to check properly I had ruined possibly the most precious roll of film ever to pass through my hands.

What could I tell Gretl? That the whole film had turned out to be underexposed? She would want to see *something*. My heart pounded as I struggled to come up with a plausible excuse. Time and again I moved the black strip of celluloid back and forth on the lightbox, searching in vain for a contrast; any image.

Badly shaken, I knew the time had come to leave for Obersalzberg.

Mumbling self-recriminations, I threw a few things in a bag and stumbled through the garage door to climb into the Beetle, sensing I just had to get the hell out before it was too late. Obersalzberg was after all one of my favourite destinations; perhaps I could clear my head and settle on a plausible excuse?

Pulling out into the hell of Schellingstrasse, I was confronted with abandoned cars and piles of smouldering rubble strewn across the roadway. Here and there flames spurted from open windows and a brick wall opposite had tumbled into the street; smoke and dust reduced visibility to a minimum. I could not help noticing white sheets fluttering from many of the public buildings, which only weeks before had boasted rows of bright red swastika banners.

Bang! Someone hurled himself onto my bonnet with a contorted face against the windscreen, screaming to be taken along.

Instinctively, I swerved wildly, flinging the fellow to one side and tearing off a wiper blade in the process. Perhaps the brute would have dragged me out of the driver's seat and hijacked the vehicle? I told myself I simply couldn't take the chance and risk my mission.

Hoffman's final instructions, written out and signed on the back of a Carlton Hotel menu, clearly stated my mission: "Burn all files, prints and negatives remaining at Berghof. Burn all files, prints and negatives remaining in Schellingstrasse Private Collection." The handwritten order was signed "Heil Hitler" and the adjacent Deaths Head hinted at the cost of non-compliance.

Stopping and starting in frustration I drove by dishevelled citizens digging through the rubble with bare hands, searching desperately for loved ones trapped in once-safe cellars. More white flags appeared in upstairs windows and one hastily scrawled sign said: "Heil General Patton and U.S. Liberators."

Swerving and honking, my little Beetle finally shook loose the smouldering suburbs and turned her nose towards the Alps, only to run headlong into formations of walking wounded. Stalled and confounded, my mind mulled over the disaster of the wedding photos.

How could I possibly explain the loss to Gretl?

What should I have done differently? Maybe smelled the fixer to ensure its integrity? Was it possible that Lothar had deliberately sabotaged the remaining chemicals, in order to bring discredit upon my final assignment? With the benefit of hindsight, all scenarios seemed possible; my conscience insisted it was too late for useless speculation.

The deed was done.

Hemmed in by refugees and wounded soldiers, a journey that should have taken two hours, took six. When finally I nosed my little wagon up the narrow Obersalzberg bends, I was soon overtaken by a convoy of black limousines bearing Berlin SS licence plates, conveying passengers in leather jackets up the chaotic mountain road with air horns blasting; an indication of what was to come.

On all sides in full view, Nazi uniforms with rank and decorations removed, scurried about clutching papers and shouting orders. Abandoned vehicles stretched higgledy-piggledy from the foot of the Berghof steps back down the driveway, forcing me to park the Beetle in behind Zum Turken.

Nearby, a crowd of bewildered locals, fugitives from the law of averages, stood with their noses pressed against the wire fence, anticipating a glimmer of hope that never came. Clutching dry kindling and matches I made my way discreetly across the meadow and through the yawning garage doors toward the darkroom, pausing only long enough to exchange snippets of gossip with a group of motor pool drivers just arrived from Berlin.

"From that moment on …" I overheard one of them saying, "… the Führer has been in a state of total collapse but, more importantly for the remaining staff cooped up in the bunker, he's finally given permission for those wishing to abandon their posts to do so … and not before bloody time!"

Upon reaching the relative safety of Berchtesgaden the drivers did what any self-respecting escapee from that cauldron would do; they got stuck into the world-class wine cellar, visibly relieved that their official duties were at an end. Given the chronic petrol shortage, it appeared that whatever lay ahead could be best tackled from within an alcoholic haze.

Nonetheless, they all seemed happy to see a fresh face, eager to compare the situation in Berlin with that in Munich and keen to sort fact from fiction. Yes, they all knew that Hitler was planning on marrying Eva Braun at the eleventh hour, and that the leading Nazis were committing suicide in droves. Some were placing bets on when, and even *if* Hitler and his new bride would jump together, or indeed even jump at all, given the persistent rumours of a "Werewolf" redoubt being established by rumps of Hitler Youth in the mountains behind Obersalzberg. From there the great struggle could continue under the enervating eye of Barbarossa himself.

"I'm afraid the Führer is stubborn on that point," Bormann had assured Kempka, even as he pleaded with his doomed master to flee.

Taking advantage of the mood in the garage, I sought and received permission to drain a few cups of gasoline from the discarded jerry cans in the corner, which I stashed away gratefully for my return journey. Someone wondered out loud if any photos from the actual wedding ceremony existed, but I pretended not to hear.

Rumours flew that three whole Russian fronts, comprising two and a half million men, were converging on Berlin's suburbs in an orgy of rape and summary execution. Predictably, the mighty Red Army was unleashing its own wave of terror upon its tormenters in ghastly retribution for Russia's long years of suffering under the German heel.

Drunken troops could be seen going from cellar to cellar, "Woman, come cook for us," in thinly disguised coercion, while other soldiers didn't bother with such pretences at all, raping young girls and old women on tabletops in front of their horrified families. Each one of the drivers had a different story to tell: of how hunger and fear had combined to strip away any last vestige of human dignity which, up until that moment, German society had held most dear.

They told of one middle-aged housewife being dragged out from beneath her grandchildren, crying pitifully to her husband to step up and save her. Instead, he gave her a push, "For God's sake, go with them woman, you are going to get all of us all into trouble."

Had not the Führer warned that old men and children would be murdered by the Ivans out of hand and that women and girls would be reduced to barrack-room whores? Several told how they'd been lucky to escape with their lives, sickened to see so many broken and bleeding women left lying in the gutters, if alive at all unable to ever face their loved ones again.

Another driver with a bandaged head gave a frightening account of the Führer's final breakdown and the subsequent turmoil that followed, including details of Göring's eleventh-hour visit. Apparently, the flustered former Reichsmarschall had undertaken one final errand in an attempt to kiss and make up with his contemptuous and cornered Führer; a mission doomed to failure from the moment he caught sight of Hitler's sour mien.

Following that gruelling encounter, the big man fled hastily to the temporary safety of his chalet at Obersalzberg, with Hitler's oft-repeated threats to "hang the entire Luftwaffe staff" ringing in his ears.

Once safely settled in the bracing alpine atmosphere, the Hunt Master fired off a carefully considered letter to Hitler, the contents of which soon became general knowledge given the explosive reaction it triggered deep underground.

Allegedly, Göring had wrestled long and hard with the wording, before being rattled by a secret radio message from Bormann that raised suspicions that he, Göring, may be planning to usurp power prematurely.

"If I act, he will call me a traitor. If I don't, he will denounce me as having failed at this most critical moment," the flustered former Reichsmarschall moaned. With much stopping, starting, and amendment, he eventually settled on an authoritative, yet respectful tone, which I hereby reproduce more or less verbatim.

My Führer,

Is it your wish, in view of your decision to stay in Berlin, that
I take over complete control of the Reich in accordance with
your two official decrees of June 29, 1941, with full powers in
domestic and foreign affairs? If no answer has been received by
10 pm tonight I shall have to assume that you have been deprived
of your freedom of action, and I will consider the terms of your
decree as being in force and will act for the good of our people
and Fatherland. You must realise that I feel for you in this most
difficult hour of my life and I can find no words to express myself
adequately. God bless you and speed you here as soon as possible.

Your most loyal, Hermann Göring.

For those awaiting orders in the bunker anterooms, perhaps believing that the
Führer's tantrums were long spent, what then occurred struck fear into every
heart thereafter: for a few moments Hitler stood mute, staring at the piece of
paper in his hand.

Then, his head began to jerk uncontrollably and his face turned crimson
with fury. Breathing heavily, he uttered curses in a tight, hoarse voice while
lurching around the room waving his right arm wildly, the left flopping
uselessly by his side as a result of the assassination attempt.

With flecks of foam flying from the corners of his mouth he screamed that
he was "surrounded by traitors and liars, all of whom were too low and mean
to grasp my great purpose". He accused everyone of deserting him and gasped
that he was the victim of "spineless treachery", and that the war had been
forced on him by an "Anglo-American, Marxist-Jewish conspiracy".

When finally regaining control he ordered Bormann to draft his reply
which, after some amendment, was despatched straight back to the crestfallen
"Führer in Waiting", who had just learned that he no longer held the post of
Reich's Chief Game Warden.

Your assumption that I am prevented from carrying out my
own wishes is an absolutely erroneous idea whose ridiculous
origin I do not know. I request that this be strongly countered
immediately, and I shall, by the way, only hand over my power
to whom and when I consider it to be right. Until then I shall be
in command myself.

The note was unsigned.

Unbeknownst to his Führer, Bormann issued a simultaneous order to the SS Commandant at Obersalzberg to arrest Göring for high treason. Hitler's absolute dependence on his omniscient secretary suggested it would more likely be Bormann than Göring in a position to betray the sinking ship.

Soon after, small groups began slipping away upstairs from the Führer Bunker, while others awaited the cover of darkness to break out of the Russian encirclement and run the gauntlet of burning buildings, snipers and Gestapo patrols.

One fellow revealed how he'd personally seen Hitler kiss Eva on the lips for the first time, in front of the small group remaining, before shuffling off to dispense cyanide capsules among the secretaries.

Elsewhere, men in uniform were advised that it was probably best to "shoot oneself in the mouth as it shatters the skull". The same man saw Eva place a cyanide capsule in her pocket, stating that she, for one, wished to remain a "beautiful corpse". "If it's good enough for Romeo and Juliette, it's good enough for me!" she quipped, trying to fashion a little laugh.

To a man the drivers were saddened by the condition of their once hard-hitting employer, whom they reported as "off-balanced, with head sunk down like a turtle; unfocused bloodshot eyes peering out above dark bags". No one in the bunker dared mention the uncontrollable tremors in the chief's left arm and leg; or his drooling lips, yellowed teeth and foul breath.

The final "Führer handshakes" were limp and unresponsive, lacking eye contact. "So much for the Thousand-year Reich," they whispered.

Before fleeing Berlin, however, Kempka's drivers had been ordered to collect all remaining jerry cans from the motor pool and place them outside the escape tower in the Chancellery gardens. Little did they know then the purpose for which these 170 litres of precious gasoline was intended: the cremation of human corpses; one male and one female to begin with, each wrapped in a simple brown blanket with the larger one dripping blood from its head.

As Russian shells exploded overhead and nearby, both bodies were carried by the valets a short distance to the nearest shell crater and thrown in, before being set alight. No fanfare, no prayers, just one or two stiff arm salutes from the bunker doorway to farewell the defeated dictator and the beautiful corpse of his bride.

For the next few hours, Eva sizzled away beside her new husband, together at last in a puddle of fat and flames; the only woman I ever heard of who managed to commit suicide three times!

At regular intervals, Kempka and Linge reportedly dashed out to throw more petrol on the blackening remains.

These and other details from the Führer Bunker were confirmed by the drunk and distressed bodyguard, Rochus Misch, now reduced to last-ditch Radio Operator. His patchy transmissions were being picked up by the SS detachment on Obersalzberg and also by Göring's home receiver.

Stories emerged of the difficulties in cremating fresh bodies using only petrol and green garden waste, but most of the Berghof staff dismissed Misch's ramblings out of hand, preferring their People's Radio version of the Führer's final moments. This proudly proclaimed that their indomitable Leader had "fallen at the head of his troops, fighting to the last bullet".

Were even part of this true, it still lay in the future, six days in the future to be precise, when I for one would be facing certain repercussions. My mind churned over the narrowing options while I coasted the Beetle downhill towards the tranquillity of Lake Königssee. Away in the distance, the splash of silver offered no hint of the deadly drama already playing out by her shore.

Drawing close I pulled up beside a noisy crowd surrounding Onkel's humble boatshed and spilling onto the roadway. Out back, I could see a white sheet fluttering from the deck railing.

"Liar. Traitor! I say string him up now!" the taunts flew past the car window unexpectedly. I slithered lower in my seat. "You're a coward, Hahn! You'll stand and fight like the rest of us, or else."

"He's done all the fightin' for the Führer he's going to do, you, you Ship of Fools!" It was Tante, standing defiant on the top step, head and shoulders above the angry rabble. "You know damn well my Fedi is no coward. You've known him for thirty years. He and his brother fought side by side in the Great War and distinguished themselves for the Fatherland. Have you forgotten all that?" The crowd fell silent.

I squeezed my way carefully from my seat and closed the car door with a soft push from my behind, trying to move toward her without drawing attention.

"Fine words indeed, Frau," said the local Nazi Commandant stepping forward to take hold of the rope binding Onkel's wrists and pulling him savagely to his knees. Another Brownshirt emerged from the house.

"Here it is," and hurled a Siemens radio over the railing, where the metallic cloth covering the speaker burst open and two knobs fell off on the ground. The trooper looked triumphantly toward Onkel Fedi and back to the crowd. "Take a good look, comrades. This set has been modified to pick up Churchill and his BBC lies. You all know the penalty for tuning in to foreign broadcasts. How much do we really know about this man who chose to turn his back on the Party?"

"Think you're too good for the rest of us, eh, Hahn? And all the while living under the Party's protection after all it has done for you and the rest of the useless eaters!" One or two onlookers glanced at each other. "He refused to contribute to the last *two* Winter Appeals for our wounded comrades and has spread defeatist propaganda saying the war is lost; that's the thanks we get for our protection, comrades."

"I say we make an example of him to anyone else thinking of betraying the Reich." With that, he flung the rope end over a lamppost and fashioned a noose around Onkel's neck while he slumped on the ground.

"Over my dead body," screamed Tante Gretel, and flung herself into the crowd. By now I was out of the car and pushing my way forward; both Tante and Onkel saw me at once. "They're going to hang me, boy. Have you ever heard of such a thing? Me? Despite all I've done for this stinking country over the years … the *real* Germany, I mean."

"There! You've heard him yourselves, insulting the Party. What more do you need?" said the commandant. With one swift movement, several burly Brownshirts hauled on the rope and yanked poor Onkel Fedi off his feet and into the air, where his face began to turn purple.

"No! I say No, you swine. He's never done anything to hurt …" but Tante was felled to the ground by a blow and Onkel was hoisted even higher; several in the crowd chanted "death to traitors" while poking fun at their gasping neighbour. "If he's so clever, let him save himself … always sticking his nose into people's business. Thinks he's better than the rest of us; well, look at him now."

I was pushing futilely against the crowd, aghast at the speed of events; watching on helplessly as Onkel slowly danced his way into heaven. The big Nazi, having noted my unorthodox arrival, stepped back and caught me by the collar.

"What's the matter, boy? Nazi justice a bit much for a weak stomach, eh? Why don't *you* go over and pull on his legs to put him out of his misery?"

I turned a desperate eye towards Tante, who remained out to it on the grass. "It's better for her this way," someone muttered.

Could this be really happening? I struggled to free his iron grip.

"Like this!" the big man grunted, releasing his hold on me and stepping forward to pull down on Onkel's knees with all his strength, causing Fedi's neck to break with an audible crack. A half-hearted cheer floated out over the lake and the fellow dusted off his hands. "Death to all traitors is my motto," he repeated once more, to convince himself as much as the onlookers.

By now I was at Tante's side, patting her cheeks as she came around and trying desperately to protect her from the terrible sight overhead.

"You're coming with me to Munich …" I gasped, half-lifting, half-dragging her towards the Beetle, "… there's nothing for you here now."

Delirious and uncomprehending, she kept trying to look back, while I tried with equal vigour to steer her into the passenger seat.

"Fedi. Oh my prince, my dear sweet Fedi, what have they done to you?" With difficulty, I bundled her in and locked the door, before striding back to the porch to collect her single suitcase. Some were already drifting away, second-guessing the wickedness of the event in which they had so eagerly joined. A voice rang out. "What about her? She's no better than him, swanning about with her nose in the air and acting arty-farty all the time."

Unperturbed, the big Nazi pulled up a chair at the foot of the steps and took a swig from a bottle of Schnapps, seemingly well-pleased with his afternoon's work. Tanti was never a full Party Member.

In the background I observed two Hitler Youths in uniform untying Onkel's rowboat and pushing it out onto the Lake; one pulled at the oars while the other rifled through the fishing tackle.

Sensing Gretel's peril I moved quickly past a smaller mob forming nearby and leapt through the driver's door, slamming the Peoples' Car into first gear and accelerating away.

We were finally together at last, and for a while neither spoke, assured by the steady whining of the rear engine and smooth click of the gearbox. The nearer we came to Berchtesgaden Bahnhof, the greater became the flood of fugitives fleeing the town by rail, road and on foot, I could only hope we had sufficient fuel to negotiate all the stops and starts we could expect along the way.

Buses and open trucks crammed with luggage and sobbing families were departing from outside the station at regular intervals, most heading south into Austria. Ours seemed to be the only vehicle attempting to go against the tide and into the eye of the storm.

At that moment a series of loud crumps came rolling down from Hitler's alpine fortress, panicking the crowd. Pulling over, we heard the drone of airplane engines above and saw plumes of building parts, glass and smoke rising into the air above Obersalzberg.

It appeared that several structures including the Berghof itself were already on fire. "It's the R.A.F," someone screamed. "Run! The town will be next." Now, the squadrons of bombers could be clearly seen, with a second wave already closing in to dump its lethal load on the hallowed heights: Thump! Thump!

This time they made no mistake and within minutes the whole compound erupted in clouds of dust and flame; surely, no one up there could still be alive. Tiny figures could be seen scurrying like ants across the grassy slopes to the stutter of Mustang fighters strafing the few limousines that had disentangled themselves to make a break for the valley.

"Where is *our* Luftwaffe? That fat bastard Göring should answer for this?" someone else yelled. "Fancy allowing them to even get this far and bomb us in broad daylight …"

Tante let out a deep sob and appeared to be struggling for breath.

"Dear God, the world is coming to an end. My Fedi will be all right, won't he, Klaus?" She croaked. As I sped away from the melee trying to dodge the traffic snarls ahead she asked me for the umpteenth time. "Do you still believe in Heaven, Klaus?" Forgetting my earlier assurances, she seemed unable to grasp either the severity or speed of events.

"Dearest Tante, try not to think about Onkel's last moments; what's done is done. It's a shameful act, no matter how you look at it."

Listening to my own pathetic platitudes I thought, *Is this the best you can do?* and further surmised that we were both still in shock, trying to come to terms with that terrible vision of Onkel Fedi swinging from a lamppost with a sign pinned to his chest: "I am a traitor to my Volk and Reich!"

Sure enough, the road to Munich was ever more choked with refugees heading south. Often we were brought to a halt by the sheer press of bodies and stalled vehicles, as I leaned on the horn and tried to force my way through. Now and then, Aunt tried looking back through the tiny rear window, until the flaming mountaintop vanished from sight and I could distract her with talk of our immediate plans.

"Firstly, Tante, I have unfinished business at Studio Hoffman. Tonight I'm planning to meet up with Robert and Claudia, about whom you've heard so much, to see if we can't shake loose this horrible place once and for all. My wily brother has an escape route through Italy all mapped out. I'm sure he won't object to one more coming along."

There was a long silence as we crawled around corners and climbed hills at a snail's pace. Between carts, horses, and faceless herds of foot traffic, I noticed the recommended sharp bend speed sign for Jews had been torn down.

"Didn't you tell me he was now SS?" she asked vacantly, and I nodded. Occasionally, tears started in her eyes as she tried to put her deeper thoughts into words for the first time.

"Ah, my dear boy. What a terrible thing you've had to witness; this is what our beautiful homeland has become. I feel the pit of destruction yawning beneath the feet of the German Volk; surely, not one of them will escape the coming flames of retribution …"

What could I possibly reply?

We chugged forward in fits and starts towards yet another glowing skyline, changing gears gently to conserve petrol with each lost in our own thoughts. Eventually crossing the Isar at Ludwigsbrucke we passed jammed, abandoned vehicles and hollow-eyed women pushing their worldly possessions along in baby-carriages.

Here in the city centre, the damage was more concentrated with gangs of prisoners in striped uniforms struggling to fill fresh bomb craters and keep even a single lane free.

As I was about to turn towards Amalienstrasse, Tante suddenly cried out, "No! Turn left! I just can't do it." The shock caused me to stop dead with a screech of brakes. "I'm so sorry, Klaus; I'm going to take my chances on the railway and head west. I never did like running with the herd, you know that; three's company and four's a crowd, or something like that. I would only slow you down. Please, dear boy, drop me as close to the Bahnhof as you can.

Wherever God leads me I will put down roots and try to make a new life for myself in the coming Germany …"

"B … But Tante …"

"Hush, Klaus, my mind's made up. You've brought me this far and I love you for it. I'll take my chances with the Americans, just as Onkel Fedi wanted. I'm sick to death of hiding; *Germany* is where I belong and with God's help shall remain. There must be places in the Fatherland where I'll be safe; somewhere I can thumb my nose at all the Reichs to come; those shatterers of dreams. Can't you see? This is my least bad option; I'll leave you young ones to do the escaping and can only wish you safe passage."

Tante now seemed much refreshed and seized with a new resolve to strike out on her own. After some minutes of tearful exchange and fruitless promises, she alighted from the running board clutching her suitcase and plunged into the crowd without a backward glance.

Lost to me forever.

61

I knew there was no time to lose. Numbed by the shock and speed of events, I turned toward the Studio, forced to park in a side street and walked the remaining distance. I figured I had time to carry out my final fateful mission, gather my belongings and be at Claudia's apartment by 9 or 10 pm, with time to spare.

Instead, I was greeted by apocalyptic scenes of burning buildings and vortexes of swirling flame among the fleeing inhabitants as they stumbled frantically through the rubble piles; one woman screamed in terror as she tried to extricate the wheels of her baby stroller from the melting asphalt. No one seemed to know which way to turn; ahead loomed only flame and crashing walls.

With great difficulty, I forced my way through to the seeming safety of Amalienstrasse and was surprised to find a broken lock on the Studio's front door. Probably looters, some of whom could be seen darting in and out of nearby buildings carrying everything from mantle radios to vacuum cleaners that they had little hope of ever plugging in.

Beneath the main staircase, my padlock was intact and nothing in Hoffman's office seemed disturbed. Someone had covered the hole in the darkroom wall with a sheet of corrugated iron, but light still filtered in about the edges. I quickly emptied the boss's private filing cabinets beside the woodstove and was soon feeding in multiple strips of celluloid. The pungent vapours given off confused my conflicted brain.

How could I be doing this thing, to destroy such history en masse? Was it anathema to wipe away the work of so many capable professionals, rather than enhance their images as was my forte and vocation?

Suddenly, I recalled the Death's Head on the Hotel Carlton Menu and doubled down, feeding roll upon roll of film into the roaring flames.

A loud crash followed by a string of oaths alerted me that someone else was in the building; the creak of jackboots could be heard on the stairs.

"It's you!" we both said together as I came face to face with Lothar in the doorway, who was in no mood to exchange pleasantries.

"Where in the fuck have you been, Jungle Boy? I've been looking all over for the getaway car …"

"That's none of your business. The boss sent me here on an important mission and I intend to carr—"

I didn't get the words out of my mouth before a slap from his open palm sent me reeling backwards: "Today, *I'm* the boss, got it?" I could smell the liquor on his breath and saw his eyes were flecked and cloudy. Clearly, this time the boot was on the other foot.

"As soon as it's dark I'll need a lift out to the American lines, where I intend for the two of us to surrender together. I've no doubt you'll be a hit with the Yanks, just like you've been around here. I'm relying on you to tell them how I always defended the workers against Party excesses."

I was so dumbfounded by this suggestion that no words came.

"Well, haven't I?" He took a step forward and poked an accusing finger in my chest. "You've only got a few hours to get your story straight. Now, what was your position in relation to Herr Lothar Schultz? Are you prepared to swear Herr Shultz was not acting on behalf of the Nazi Party? Yes! Yes! Of course, you will swear that to the Americans, boy, and anything else I tell you to say …"

"B … But you don't understand, the car is nearly out of petrol," I lied, feeling for my fat lip. "I'm afraid you'll have to plead your own case with the Americans and I wish you every …"

"Just shuddup and do as you're told. This is not a request, it's an order!" At that, I found a Luger pointed at my middle. "Today, I am boss! Got it? And bosses know how to get petrol, right? Problem solved." Without waiting for my response he placed the pistol back in its holster. "First of all, where is the damn thing parked so I can have my boys top up the tank?"

"I … er, I'm not quite sure. Most of the street signs are down, but I could show you when I'm finished here. He took two steps forward and banged his rhino-hide whip on the mantle, sending several of Hoffman's trophies flying; the veins in his neck popped out with repressed anger. "*You* don't seem to understand simple instructions: you and your press pass are working for me now, for as long as it takes; isn't that clear enough?"

I muttered something about an important delivery I had to make before midnight and turned my mind over frantically for any sign of weakness in his plan. Claudia had promised to wait for me, but now it would be touch and go to arrive on time. To go with Lothar would mean the end of everything I'd dreamed of, and all to save his lousy hide. The Americans would never fall for his cock and bull story and I would probably be held as an accomplice.

No! I would somehow try to find a way to join Robert and Claudia for a chance to get away down the route they'd been planning so long.

But before my task was half-complete I was being forced to accompany Lothar and his offsider into the rear garage, where they proceeded to throw back Hoffman's car cover and milk a jerry can of gasoline from his mothballed limousine. "Right, let's go, you lead the way," the big man said impatiently, as his offsider struggled along behind carrying the petrol can.

Try as I may, the Beetle could not be found, and while my kidnapper's patience quickly faded I began to wonder if indeed the vehicle had been stolen. Both men were perspiring heavily from climbing over the rubble mounds, while I attempted to explain the improbability of any thief wanting to steal my little VW when there were so many other bigger and flashier vehicles for the taking.

"Other than fuel consumption," mocked Lothar, pointing to the burdensome jerry can.

In desperation, I turned back to the Bahnhof, and from there attempted to retrace my route to Studio Hoffman, The pair struggled along behind, taking turns with the jerry can and cursing ever more volubly.

Darkness had developed from the gloom and the flickering orange light of burning buildings created a ghostly spectre, confounding my sense of direction. Now and then dark shadows stumbled through the flames and rubble, intent upon saving themselves.

Suddenly, there was the Beetle, right where I'd left her, covered in dust and surrounded by fresh-fallen rubble, just a block away from our earlier search area. The Brownshirt and I were ordered to clear a path forward, while Lothar struggled to fill up the tank without the convenience of a funnel. Eventually, we three stood gasping before our handiwork, but Lothar did not intend to procrastinate. "Come on, we've wasted enough time; let's get out of here before another bloody wall falls on our heads."

"Not you!" he barked at his offsider. "You will deliver this letter to whoever is in charge at the Brown House, explaining that I am on my way to surrender what's left of Hoffman's Studio equipment to the Americans, including *all the remaining files*." He emphasised these last few words while glaring pointedly at me. "Now get in and drive west as if your life depended on it; and believe me, it does."

"As far as I can tell, the invaders should be about *here* by now," he said, pointing his pudgy finger to a spot on the map, near Dachau, in almost exactly the opposite direction from my own planned escape route. I felt like throwing up; every minute behind the wheel carried me away from my rendezvous with Claudia, and even farther from freedom. The hour was fast approaching when I was meant to be joining Robert and Claudia for the breakout. At this realisation, my breath began to come in short gasps as I struggled to breathe clean air in the choking smoke.

The Beetle's feeble headlamps barely illuminated a few yards ahead, as Lothar yelled instructions with his head out the window.

"Go right … now turn left … look out for that wall, it's about to come down; not that way, you bloody fool!"

And so we crept northwest toward Karlsfeld, often having to back up half a block to find a way through. Clearly, Lothar's map was of little use given the seeming realignment of Munich's bombed-out thoroughfares. In the flickering yellow glow, I could see beads of sweat glistening on his brow.

Gradually my asthma worsened and I felt at any moment I could pass out through lack of oxygen. As I huddled over the steering wheel fighting for breath, he noticed my distress. "What's wrong with you, for Christ's sake? Watch what you're doing; do you want to get us both killed?"

"I … I think it would be … better if you … took the wheel," I wheezed, as we approached the outer city limits and the going became less exacting. He merely stared dumbfounded and his face was frozen in fear; up until that moment, I hadn't realised the real reason he'd forced me to go along. Just like most of the other studio employees, Lothar Schultz hadn't learned to drive, and now the panic froze his features in a half-snarl.

"I … I must stop in a quiet place to do my vowel exercises … that might help," I gasped. In an instant, he drew his Luger again and pressed it to my temple.

"The moment you stop this vehicle you're a dead man," he said threateningly.

My mind raced. "*Then* how do you think you'll make it to the American lines?" I replied with a sudden burst of bravado. He slowly lowered the pistol and I could see his face wrestling with the implications of either choice.

"Vowels? What in the Kaiser's name do you mean by making vowel noises? How long will it take?" He continued fingering the Luger, cocking and uncocking it on his lap. "Well, pull over here then, if you must. You've got five minutes, not a moment more; do you understand? … And I'll be watching your back in case you try any funny business."

I slid the Beetle to a halt beneath one of the only few large trees still standing by the roadside and tumbled out onto the leaf-strewn verge. The bomb damage here was less noticeable and most of the fires had been extinguished. Silent figures hurried past with heads down, some pushing overloaded hand-carts and strollers.

I dragged myself over to the tree trunk and propped against it, the exertion of which almost prevented the first rousing sounds from escaping my constricted airways. "Ahh-umm, Ahh-umm, Maa-th-Raaaa, Maa-th-Raaa …" and so on through the series I went, humming and chanting; beginning to feel stronger as my mantra grew purer. My mind grew steadily clearer and I knew what I must try and do if the chance arose.

"On your way, Jungle Boy, your pantomime is over," Lothar called acidly through the open window, shattering my serenity; yet, somehow I felt ready and my thoughts were sharp.

As we resumed driving towards Dachau, he settled down and became less jumpy; the goal was almost in sight. "Once we cross the Amper we'll be home and hosed, and after you've assured the Americans what a good fellow I am you can run along and do as you please … Though if you ask me, anyone wanting to go back into that inferno must have rocks in his head. Have *you* got shit for brains, Jungle Boy, eh?

"In case you don't know, more Germans have died in the last twelve months than during the first four years of the war. What's so precious back in Munich? Do you think that brother of yours will save your scrawny hide?

"I'd bet the Kaiser's left elbow that the Gestapo is already on his tail. Nonetheless, only I have certain information the Americans might find useful and I'm expecting to blend into the new administration with a minimum of fuss: a sort of personal Gleichschaltung with the conquering armies, eh?"

By now we had reached the banks of the Amper and were making good time towards the Furstwegbrucke, where he hoped to hand himself in. He gave a whoop to see an illuminated U.S. flag flapping above the pylon on the far side; just a few more turns and he'd be on the road to freedom.

"B … But what about me? I don't want to surrender yet," I said firmly enough to make him sit up straight and the Beetle lurch violently. "How do I know the Americans won't lock me up too? Or at least steal my vehicle?"

"Your vehicle? That's a laugh. I'm the one in charge of all Studio assets now, and this car is a studio asset …"

"Perhaps, but what good is it to you or anyone else who can't drive? The boss specifically authorised me to use the Company vehicle for special orders."

"Well, I'm the one giving the 'special orders' now and you'll continue to do exactly as you're told. Hullo, what's going on here? Some kind of stoppage up ahead; looks like a roadblock"

"They're searching all vehicles; I have my press pass ready," I said with growing trepidation.

Lothar pulled a small pair of binoculars from his pack and began scanning the bottleneck, giving a little whistle. "Gestapo, the bastards," he said before exclaiming, "Bugger me, just look who's calling the shots? That fool of a woman was always too big for her boots; we'll soon see just how much authority she *really* has."

With that, he hauled himself out of the Beetle and strode purposefully towards the clandestine group of agents surrounding Iris Bumke, wearing a full-length leather coat and black beret. My supervisor detached herself and stepped forward to greet her old partner-in-crime, looking very much in charge.

I turned off the motor and shrank down to observe the bottleneck of vehicles. Lothar took a few more steps, but before Iris had finished her acknowledgment, demanded to be allowed to pass over the bridge. There followed an animated discussion before the big man lost patience and began yelling and waving his arms about, accusing Iris of being "out of her depth and drunk on power".

Then, in a fluid and barely perceptible movement she drew her pistol and before he could blink had it pressed against his forehead. When he opened his mouth again to protest she pulled the trigger, blasting a hole through the back of his head and sending a spray of blood and brains as far as my windscreen.

At once adrenalised yet frozen in place I watched Lothar crumple to the ground as Iris calmly placed her weapon back in its holster.

The group of agents again went into a huddle, and through the spattered windshield I saw one of them heading in my direction.

In a split second, I started the motor and jammed the Beetle into reverse, barely able to steer a straight course using the rearview and side mirrors. The Gestapo man too started running, as I sped backwards weaving wildly from side to side down the narrow roadway. At times he appeared to be gaining.

Smack, smack: a bullet pierced the windscreen and another banged into the bonnet where the engine should have been. In any other vehicle, I would be a goner; luckily the shooter was unable to see me properly through the gore. With the engine screaming and bullets whistling past, my head bobbed up and down like a target in a shooting gallery.

Suddenly, there in the rearview mirror, a figure in a leather coat stood barring my passage, waving a pistol and yelling "Halt" at the top of her lungs. Could it really be Iris? I thought I'd left her behind.

I had no idea how she had suddenly turned up to my rear; in a split second, I pulled down on the wheel to avoid her. With a loud bang and a sharp cry, the figure disappeared beneath the rear window and my little Beetle bucked once or twice in the air before a bloodied leather lump popped out from under the front wheels. When relying on my rearview mirrors I had swerved in the wrong direction.

Though battered and bruised, Iris showed great courage and resilience in attempting to pull herself along using only her elbows, felled with what appeared to be a broken back, all the while hurling curses in my direction.

To this day I don't know why I then did what I did. Slamming the Beetle into low gear I pitched forward and ran over her for a second time. Again all four wheels jumped off the ground, leaving only a torn and bloody heap of leather in the middle of the road. Stifling a cry I took several deep breaths to still my racing heart, knowing Claudia's secret would never have been safe while Iris Bumke lived.

I was temporarily euphoric at having seen off both Lothar *and* Iris in the one manoeuvre. A howl went up from those manning the distant roadblock.

"Did you see that car swerve to hit Obersturmbannführer Bumke? Don't let it get away. Stop him, I say!"

Almost delirious, I spun the wheels and turned towards Munich. Had not Sister Klara taught that lethal force was acceptable to God when protecting one's own life or the lives of one's family?

One or two shots whistled past, but there was no further sign of pursuit. Perhaps I was the only driver with fuel to spare? The gauge read just under a quarter, hopefully enough to carry me safely to my Munich rendezvous. I was woefully late, but Claudia did promise she would wait; I could believe this of her but not of Robert.

One's own promises are hard enough to live up to, let alone those of a brother, which too often in the past had proven hollow. Notwithstanding Claudia's intentions, in his rush to get moving, Robert would probably prefer that I didn't turn up at all.

With no thought now of saving petrol I ripped through the gears, my dribbling headlamp beams failing to illuminate obstacles until I was right on top of them.

It was early morning when I again drew near the English Garden, where an acrid smoke swirled about. I had but one thought in mind: Claudia's apartment! Would she delay her departure and possibly risk everything?

Inching forward I cursed the rubble piles and fallen power poles, swerving first one way and then another, ignoring the growing dangers. Oh, how I'd dreamed of this moment. Delirious with anticipation I accelerated wildly around the corner into Hohenzollernstrasse, just as the pavement fell away into a huge bomb crater! For a terrifying moment my trusty Beetle flew through the air and landed nose first, giving up the ghost with a splash and a sputter in a puddle of grey mud!

For minutes I sat stunned, feeling a warm trickle of blood run down and drip from the end of my nose; cold water swirled around my ankles.

I had banged my head against the steering wheel and was unsure of where I was.

Feeling myself all over I determined there were no broken bones. Winding down the window I could have been on the far side of the moon. I don't know how long I lay there, partially stunned, before gaining sufficient presence of mind to push my knapsack through the window and lift it onto the sloping roof.

Painfully but surely I clamoured outside and leapt onto the crater wall, dragging my pack behind. Climbing up to the rim I peeped over, hoping that I could probably cover the remaining distance on foot.

On all sides, multi-storey buildings lay pancaked, while the one next door or across the street had been left miraculously unscathed.

It was clear, however, that there were few miracles left to celebrate in Munich.

Weaving carefully, I limped across the broken ground towards Claudia, keeping one eye peeled for roving killer squads of Gestapo. Despite the sombre surroundings, my excitement rose to a fever pitch as I took the debris-spattered stairs in her building two by two, pausing only when I reached the first-floor landing, there to be confronted by Frau Falkenhorst's door hanging off its hinges.

Claudia's too, had been kicked in. With heart in mouth, I blundered down the corridor, finding not a soul. Meals remained half-eaten on kitchen tables as if the occupants had dropped everything and left in a hurry.

Returning to scrounge through Claudia's flat I found a man's sweater and several items of clothing stuffed behind the settee and signs of hurried departure, but no Claudia and no Robert.

As arranged, I fumbled under the toilet seat and found a note securely taped, safe from prying eyes. With trembling fingers I began to read …

> Dearest K, I'm afraid that when R said midnight, he meant it; we have it on good authority that the building is to be raided in the early hours. It was either leave on time or be swept up with the others in the final dragnet, of which we'd been warned not to speak beforehand.
>
> We plan on crossing Max-Joseph-Brücke and turning south. R says we shall remain under cover beside the Isar and avoid most of the roadblocks that way; it's this route you should follow. We will conceal ourselves for a further 24 hours near the Golden Angel and keep an eye out for your arrival, God willing.
>
> Robert says more and more roadblocks are going up and you may find all the remaining river crossings sealed off by morning. Do be careful! What I have heard of his plan sounds very exciting. I pray you are safe and will join us soon. Love always, your C.

This note naturally raised my spirits, and by the time I'd covered several blocks through the ruins of Prinzregentenstrasse, dawn's harsh glow was by now defining the few skeletal trees still standing.

Cautiously, I hugged the English Garden and made a dash for the riverside foliage, arriving just in time to see a roadblock going up on the far side of Prinzregentenbrücke, behind which a group of Volkssturm carrying Panzerfausts were taking up positions.

Keeping cover I crawled down the embankment on hands and knees, finding passage through the tangle of low branches and onto a familiar sandbank, hoping earnestly that the others had made it safely across. From behind came explosions and the occasional rat-a-tat of a light machine gun; there could be no turning back. I felt trapped.

From here it appeared I would have to swim for my life to avoid the roving armed patrols.

Not having eaten for many hours I became aware of just how spent was my poor body. Was it worth risking a small campfire and a mouthful of nourishment, or should I plunge straight into the freezing current? Opting for the former, I figured I would need all the strength and wits I could muster before tackling the Isar's tumid springtime whirlpools.

Within minutes I had erected a wall of green branches and coaxed a welcome flame to life at my feet, over which I skewered and scorched my last two slices of ham and the stale bread roll. Few meals ever brought more joy and I washed it down with a cupful of melted snow from the Isar, even allowing myself to savour a glimpse of the Friedensengel, that was now just a short swim away and almost within shouting distance.

Safely tucked behind the curtain of green I was tempted to pat myself on the back, if I hadn't felt so sore and sorry. Peeping out occasionally to study the currents and pick the least dangerous crossing point, I observed a bundle of colourful clothing floating past in the green waves, like a partly deflated beach ball, followed soon after by several similar items strung together.

When one such appurtenance became caught in a nearby whirlpool so I decided to wade out and investigate. Round and round the deflated bags of fabric slowly swirled until I caught hold of one with a stick and dragged the bobbing flotilla into the shallows at my feet.

At the very moment I identified human remains protruding, a stench burst forth that sent me reeling backwards. Each bundle contained a human corpse, roped by the waist to other family members in a final act of defiance: I counted two adults and three children.

These loving, yet suicidal adults must have plunged themselves and their wretched offspring into the icy Isar, rather than face looming captivity. Rumours of Bolshevik atrocities and Gestapo retribution were unhinging even the most cohesive thinker, pushing sound families units to commit the unthinkable. These were the Volk no longer prepared to entrust their future lineage with the wagging finger of fate.

The full import of each floating clump suddenly took on new and ghastly meaning; entire families who would never again share a Yuletide pudding or salute their Führer driving by. Those who only a few short months ago were screaming slogans at their Saviour.

I stood mesmerised by a young child floating face-down, with a golden halo undulating gently about its head. Despite the gagging stench I mumbled a few words of prayer and shoved the terrible flottage back out into midstream. The Isar would never again hold for me the charms of earlier days, just the unforgettable stink of rotting flesh; yet the worst was yet to come.

Overcome with panic to put this ordeal behind me, I stripped off and stuffed my clothes, except the undies I stood in, into the watertight knapsack, wanting only to be gone from here and take my chances with the current.

Holding my nose with one hand and slinging my knapsack over one shoulder I waded out to begin dog-paddling toward the far bank, stunned by the icy grip on my body and not really caring if I was spotted or not. My airtight bag proved as much hindrance as help, catching every breeze and eddy as I attempted to dodge the otherworldly bundles drifting past.

I had underestimated my ability to gain the far shore with a single energetic burst. The Golden Angel was fading in the distance and up ahead I was greeted with a daunting sight: arrayed on the Max-Joseph-Brücke was a boisterous group of Hitler Youths, one of whom was shooting into the water below to the cheers of his comrades.

He seemed to be picking targets at random, and every so often a bloated corpse up ahead would explode like a blown car tyre. Inexorably, I was swept into their path beneath the bridge, not daring to flinch or bat an eyelid. I clutched my pack and held my breath. My knapsack!

The shooter was aiming at the plumpest targets, hoping for yet another vile bull's-eye, and my pack sat high in the water. Should I cast it adrift to save my life and lose everything I needed for the journey ahead? Realising how much I wanted to stay alive I let it go.

Bang! Hiss … another corpse popped loudly and a cheer rang out overhead. Blue in the face I maintained my "dead man" pose until safely beneath the protective concrete arch. For the moment I was out of danger, but if I didn't make landfall soon my next great peril would be the roaring weir, where I knew I'd be done for.

As the bridge faded into the distance, the roar of the weir swelled up ahead. Only with great exertion did I manage to grab the very branch that had snagged my pack previously, and clamour ashore a mile or more downstream from my intended tryst, a move that would involve a long and dangerous hike. The howl of distant sirens rent the air; my chest felt constricted and my breathing was laboured. Slowly, I pulled on my set of dry clothes and set out towards my last chance for freedom.

Staying within the thin line of riparian foliage where possible, I was torn between forcing the pace or taking a few minutes of relative seclusion to vent my vowels and calm my laboured breathing. I was troubled by thoughts of Lothar's planned route over the Amper; perhaps Tante and Lothar were right after all? Try as I may to concentrate, this plan niggled the back of my mind. What if one could avoid the roadblocks, swim that narrow river and surrender directly to the Americans?

Tucked between the willows at the water's edge I soothed my frazzled nerves and steadied my breathing, feeling almost strong enough to make the final dash.

At last, a burnished gleam through the tattered treetops: my goal, our goal, the Golden Angel in all her glory, the harbinger of freedom, resonating in the setting sun.

Suddenly, came the voice I'd been longing to hear. "Klaus, is that you?"

I spied her sweet face through the undergrowth … "It *is* you," she gasped, "thank the Lord, we'd almost given up hope …"

Claudia! My Claudia, turning up at the very moment I needed her most. My mouth fell open and in a flash all doubts were dispelled.

"Claudie my dearest," I croaked, as she took both my hands and stared deeply into my frightened eyes. "Robert said I'd find you hiding somewhere in the bushes. We saw you being swept away downstream and I've been praying ever since that you would somehow make it ashore … Oh Klaus, how I too have hoped for this moment …"

"B … But, where's Robert? Isn't he supposed to have the escape plan all figured out?"

"Just shoosh up and listen to me, there have been changes owing to the number of patrols combing the rear for deserters. He's been negotiating with a group of Hitler Youth to see us safely across the Austrian border; they seem to be the only ones with knowledge of the paths less-travelled through the mountains these days."

She settled down beside me with a sigh. "There's no need for us to rush back; it's far too dangerous to leave before dark, anyway."

"That's just what I'm trying to tell you; I think I've found an easier and less dangerous way out, and much closer …" – her face brightened quizzically – "… simply by crossing the Amper at Dachau and surrendering to the Americans. The camp has already been liberated. Allied aircraft are dropping leaflets saying that all who surrender will be treated well …"

For a few moments she looked stunned, as if betrayed. "Are you mad? You seem to be forgetting that Robert is not only SS but we've both been employed at Dachau? The very suggestion of surrender is preposterous. He's been working on this plan for months. If we make it through Austria with the H.J. we should have a clear run to the Italian border. Once in Rome, the Vatican will arrange safe passage on the "ratline" to South America. Most Nazi officials and SS Officers have already left; surely, nothing could be simpler than that? Have you forgotten our dream of starting a new life together?"

"B … But, that's hundreds more miles on the run, dangerous miles; the Americans are just an hour away to the North …" She hesitated. "I tell you I saw their flags flying right there; they even sent across balloons filled with lollies for the kids. I feel sure you and I would be treated properly; neither of us has committed war crimes … we're ordinary Studio employees."

"Ha! Are you kidding? Anyone connected to the camp has a target on his back and …"

"I … I could say up front that you and I are married and have lost our papers. By the time they find out any different the worst should be over?" I could hardly believe the words had popped from my mouth.

She snapped out of her daze. "And where does that leave Robert? High and dry, I suppose? Do you think I'd abandon him now, after all we've been through together? And just supposing your plan did have merit; any SS man carrying his injuries would be a sitting duck …"

"But don't you see? Robert has more connections than the Munich telephone exchange," I interjected. "He's always preferred doing things his own way. He probably regards us as little more than millstones around his neck. Dearest Claudie, it would only be for a little while and perhaps we could all meet up later in Australia, or somewhere else, when things settle down," I pleaded.

"Ha! Talk about a long shot … with him back in Brazil and us in Australia taking wedding photos? Anyway, we don't know anyone in Australia."

I tried to ignore the jibe and persevered. "With a bit of luck we could make Dachau on foot in a couple of days; and then no more hiding, ever!"

I could sense her firming dubiety. "How do I know I wouldn't be shot on sight? I'm well-known to every camp guard and prisoner, all of whom will be hell-bent on revenge; and rightly so," she replied, face twitching.

"Stop right now! You are missing the point. You've done nothing to hurt anyone simply by taking their photographs, have you?"

Her eyes flashed green like the Claudia of old and a single tear ran down her cheek, to be quickly wiped away. I knew my argument was sound, and in reiterating it had firmed up my own convictions.

"I told you; I can vouch that you never left Hoffman's employ and that you and I are, er, you know, together. Just think, 48 hours from now we could be tucked up together enjoying one of those big American beefsteaks. What do you say?"

She did not respond.

"Robert is more than capable of taking care of himself, you'll see … Just a chance to make you happy, that's all I ask." I felt I was making real headway.

"That's enough!" she stamped her foot. "Don't you think I can see what you're up to? … Trying to come between me and a wounded warrior whose never needed me more than he needs me now. My heart is not free and never will be; my destiny lies with him, can't you accept that?"

"Surely you and I can still love each other? I want to be more than simply 'best friends'."

"Maybe that will happen someday. Have you forgotten the fortune teller's prediction that Robert and I would spend the rest of our lives together?"

"B … But, you know me better than that, my dearest: I'm the one who's bent over backwards to make you happy. I'm the one who saw to it that both the Berghof and Hoffman's private collections were burned; at least most of them. And I saw Lothar do the same with the staff records, if only to cover his own arse. He and Iris are both dead, so your secret is safe with me."

"My secret? To which secret of mine could you possibly be referring, that has not already been laid bare? Just because great grandmutti fell pregnant to her Jewish employer in the distant past, generations of Schicklegrubers have been hounded and vilified. How many times have I tortured myself over how life might have turned out without that one simple dalliance? … But of course, such speculation now seems pointless … that the hatred of a single man could reach so far and wide to exact such terrible revenge will no doubt seem fanciful to future generations. Had Herr Hitler triumphed it would have been only a matter of time before every last one of Abraham's heirs were tracked down and murdered."

I could feel her slipping away.

"Despite mountains of undeniable evidence there remain those still wedded to his perverted doctrine …" she hesitated and gave a sigh. "Look … this is my last chance to start over with the man I love, and given time I know Robert can learn to love me, too."

It was hopeless, so I reluctantly changed the subject. "Hoffman will soon have more than that to worry about. He's been unable to find safe havens for all his plundered artworks." But she wasn't listening. "I daresay you heard that Eva got her wish in the end? Bloody terrible business, being coerced into ending her life that way."

"Bullshit!" Claudia responded savagely. "You know as well as I that she made up her mind long ago to do it. If you ask me, she was nearly as bad as *him* towards the end … As an excuse, ignorance soon wears thin."

"Aren't you being a bit harsh?" I asked. "No one got to know her better than I. That poor girl went through hell so many times during her 'fairy tale', or was it 'fairy floss', courtship? She remained a frustrated actress right up until the end, sustaining herself through the whole cursed affair on hope alone. Eva died as she lived for the past dozen or so years, clinging to the vain hope that things were about to get better. Just like our mighty Führer, she was destroyed by her own creation."

In a flash of inspiration, I said, "But then again, aren't we all in the end?" She looked puzzled; clearly not convinced.

"As for our would-be Messiah," I continued, "I don't believe that in his case suicide was that same 'honourable option' he so freely espoused for others. Most likely it was to avoid public humiliation and the hangman's noose. Sister Klara once told me Karma has a long memory.

"I'd have thought most Germans would be relieved by his ultimate demise, but not so it seems our beloved Christian clergy. The Propaganda Ministry is urging everyone to read Cardinal Bertram's Solemn Requiem Mass held in the Breslau Arch Diocese following news of Hitler's suicide. This misguided Sadducee implored what remained of his flock to 'Pray to the Almighty in accordance with the Liturgy, that the Almighty's son, Adolph Hitler, be admitted into Paradise …' How's that for wishful thinking?"

She went quiet for a while and her face clouded over. "I'm not surprised: all moral authority has collapsed. Did you hear anything from Berlin about Goebbels and the children? It's just too terrible to contemplate."

I said that I'd heard from one usually reliable source that the Goebbels' family had moved into Hitler's Bunker some weeks prior to Eva's demise; whispers over their ultimate fate kept surfacing. I felt a growing sense of dread as Claudia touched on the timeline with a voice showing little emotion. "Don't ask me how I know these things, I just know …"

"Please tell me those gorgeous children were evacuated in time …" I asked anxiously.

"*Dead!* All of them, from Helga to Heidrun, poisoned by Dr Stumpfegger at their mother's behest."

I felt suddenly bereft; even now barely able to recall the details of that terrible event without breaking down. Apparently, Magda helped knock out her babies with a morphine cocktail. Then, a reluctant Dr Stumpfegger crushed cyanide capsules between their perfect little teeth while they slept.

On emerging from the death chamber, a distraught Frau Goebbels announced to the remaining staff: "Living in a world without Hitler would be no life at all. Better that the children should die pure so they could reincarnate more fortuitously."

"It seems Helga the eldest did wake up to their terrible intentions and had to be forcibly held down to administer the draught. It was an act that caused even the bodyguards to weep. Both parents were shot in the garden upstairs soon afterward by the SS, at their own behest. Last I heard, they were incinerated in a shell hole next to Hitler's."

"Oh, God no …" I groaned. "I've not long printed up their Yuletide cards using the last family portrait; let's see, Helga, Hildegard, Helmut, Holdine, Hedwig and Heidrun; how's that? Hoffman makes me memorise all client names before each sitting. In this case, it's not too difficult given they each begin with the initial of their revered Godfather."

I realised I was babbling while inside trying to process an enormity of evil exceeding even Medea's own timeworn retribution.

I recalled certain aspects of that final Goebbels' family sitting in December '44, when Joseph and Magda had dragged all five down to the Studio for yet another updated shot of the family group, including baby Heidrun.

By then the stresses of the times were clearly evident in the faces of both parents as they fussed about changing the children into white smocks. Magda carried dark bags under her eyes that no amount of makeup or low lighting could disguise and Minister Joseph was fidgety and brusque. Hoffman managed to grab just three exposures before he jumped up and left "to oversee the Volkssturm defences", or so he said.

"Dear God, I'll never forget the purity of those innocent angels in white that day, laughing together and even singing a Yuletide Carol or two for

Hoffman while he worked. After their father's early departure, I was permitted to help out with individual poses and, as usual, the children were a delight to work with. Each looked after the one below and all looked out for the baby.

"I … I simply can't grasp what you are telling me. That day their mother fussed over them like a clucky hen, giving no hint of the steely resolve she was planning to bring down on their heads. Would a real clucky hen take the lives of her own chicks, or threaten the life of an adamant Doctor Kunz who couldn't be convinced to carry out the dirty deed?"

In an emotionless monotone, Claudia relayed details of those last days and hours deep underground in Berlin, while I sat staring at the river.

"Magda had read out a final letter to her eldest son, Harald Quant, whose timely absence had saved him from joining the Götterdämmerung." Claudia repeated the scribbled message to Klaus. It was short and to the point:

My Dear Harald,

Mother is about to join her babies in Paradise. Be true to yourself, true to Mankind, and true to your country in every possible way.

With undying love,

Mutti

There followed a long silence before Claudia spoke again. "All that now remains is for us to slip through the net and start a new life on the other side of the world. It doesn't sound all that difficult when I say it quickly, does it?" She gave a strange laugh.

But I wasn't listening; a terrible cramp was tearing at my stomach and my forehead was feverish. She sensed immediately that something was wrong; far more than mere reaction to her tale of woe.

I dry-retched once or twice, before sending a jet of vomit into the water.

"Good God, food poisoning!" she exclaimed. "Whatever have you eaten?"

I gasped out that I had indeed taken a mouthful or two of river water before noticing the floating corpses. Moments later, I was again racked by wrenching cramps and bouts of vomiting that left me exhausted. Then, for the first time in two decades, I did something shameful and embarrassing: I filled my trousers.

"Don't move from here, I'm going to fetch Robert. A right pickle this is turning out to be. I'll leave you my water bottle; don't drink anything else, understand?"

I nodded dumbly, feeling yet another stab of pain rip through my gut.

"Oh dear, I don't think I'm going to be able to walk very far …" I mumbled at her vanishing rear end through the leaves.

I guess I lost track of how long I lay there, throwing up and soiling myself at regular intervals until my stomach muscles cried out. Across the river, I thought I saw a zebra grazing on the grassy bank and moments later a lioness stalking through the bushes. Clearly, I was hallucinating from the pain.

"This way, Robert." It was Claudia's voice. "Thank heavens you're still here; we heard the zoo was bombed and all the animals are running free ..." She was at my side in a flash, stirring a spoonful of charcoal into a cup of water ... "Here, drink this."

Through a cloud of pain, I looked up to see my brother's black eye patch and before he opened his mouth I could read his mood.

"I ... I saw them, I tell you, over there on the opposite bank. A lioness and a zebra, I thought I was going crazy," I exclaimed.

"So long as they stay over there. That's all we need, a fucking lion on the loose," he answered, loosening up. "Just look at you: a physical wreck covered in your own scheisse. For Christ's sake, clean 'im up Sissy. I want to be on my way by dark and am yet to finalise the scouting party to see us safely over the border. Jeez! Take a good look at yerself, liddle brudder, yer in no shape to be setting out for *any* border, let alone crossing da bloody Alps ..."

"I ... I'm not going with you; I've found an easier way ..."

"What? Easier? Easier for whom? Sissy and I could have been away last night if we hadn't hung about waiting for you, see?" Robert cursed, turning with clenched fists.

"What did I tell you, woman? He was always going to be a bloody hindrance." His face glowed and the weals on his neck stood defiant. "There is no other way out for SS personnel, get that through your thick fucking skull. I've spent months arranging supply drops and safe houses; all we need now are reliable guides to get us over the shepherd's track as far as Salzburg ..."

"You, not we; my mind's made up," I stood firm, drawing on every ounce of courage for my final appeal. "If you really cared about Sissy you would allow her to come with me and surrender to the Americans. You know she's done nothing wrong. I feel sure they will treat us wi—"

"I'm not stopping her, am I?" he blurted, fixing his singular gaze on Claudia's tear-stained cheeks. Time stood still.

"Well? What'll it be?"

"I've already told Klaus I'm going with you. Why do you have to throw it back in my face every time there's a minor hiccup?"

"Minor? Pull the other leg, will yer! I should have been looking after Number One all along; just like always. Nothing's ever minor when it comes to you two ..."

"You are so mistaken, my love! How long must I beg? I've said over and over that I'm coming with *you*, and I mean it ..." Claudia gasped.

On hearing these words, my heart sank to a new low, but by now he was in one of his tempers. He rose to his feet and pushed the conflicted girl roughly away with his good hand.

"Why don't the two of you just fuck off! I let myself be talked into something *he* had no intention of going along with, and now I find *you* having second thoughts," he spoke directly at Claudia through clenched teeth.

"You know where I am if you come to your senses; it doesn't bother me either way," he added, refusing to make eye contact before storming off.

I moved closer to put an arm around my friend's sagging shoulders, hardly daring to believe my good fortune. "Don't worry, Claudie. He's always treated both of us like scheisse, and this time is no different. I promise to … to lay down my life for you until we are safely in American hands. What do you say? C'mon, let's dry those sad eyes. We can be on our way before anyone even notices."

"Get right away from me," she screeched like a harpy, pushing me off and burying her face in her hands. "You smell like spew!"

I fell back stunned removing my shirt and trousers mechanically, before rinsing them in river water and airing my thoughts just loud enough for her to hear. "I … er, I just feel you'd be happier living in peace on a little farm somewhere … I've always known it. Do I need to remind you of the many times you cried yourself to sleep in my arms over him, huh? Anyhow, I'm starting to feel a little better now; just think, the Americans are only hours away …" Although at that moment even a short journey seemed beyond me.

Claudia pulled herself together and was digging around in my knapsack for a set of clean clothes. "Trousers, clean shirt, Homer, what's this?" she exclaimed, peering into the brown envelope left behind by Lothar. Before I could respond she tipped the contents onto the grass and gave a low whistle.

"There's over $5,000 U.S. all up," I proudly announced," more than enough to see us safely settled a long way from here … it's part of Lothar's stash if you must know."

"B … But how did *you* come by all this? It's a small fortune."

I riffled the wads in my fingers with growing confidence. "It's a long story. Suffice to say neither he nor Iris will be needing money. By the way, how much does Big Brother have in *his* kitty, eh?"

There followed a dismal pause.

"But Klaus, this is all so sudden, I'm now confused. How do I know you won't change *your* mind in a new country? How could you ever settle down knowing *my* heart wasn't in it?"

"I'm prepared to take that chance. Are you certain you can trust Robert not to dump you as soon as he's safely over the Alps? It wouldn't be the first time he's left you in the lurch, if you know what I mean …"

"I bet he would think twice if he laid eyes on my five big ones," I said offhandedly, borrowing a phrase from Bormann, "… just stop worrying about what may or may not go wrong and you'll soon get over him." She stopped crying and gave a sniffle.

"Perhaps you're right. There's so much more to consider. Why don't I return to the Freidensengel and have things out with him once and for all? When daylight fades I know he won't stay a minute longer than he has to."

She turned to go, then stopped. "Oh, and Klaus, I know he didn't mean those things he said earlier ..."

"You will come back to me, won't you Claudie, with or without Robert?"

"Of course, silly; I just want to get a few things straight, that's all," her brow creased and she leaned closer. "Promise me that if I'm not back a half hour after nightfall you will go on without us ..."

When I opened my mouth to protest she placed two fingers firmly on my lips and gazed into my eyes. "You *must* promise me. There are too many chiefs and not enough Indians gathered around the Golden Angel; the Gestapo are combing the back streets for deserters."

Now it was my turn to look miffed.

"And Klaus: do me a favour and stop calling me 'Claudie', will you? If we ever did find ourselves shacked up together that would surely drive me mad."

I swallowed deep with her censure ringing in my ears and watched her scramble into the riverbank foliage for a second time. Above the treetops, the Freidensengel glowed forth from its mighty Corinthian column. From the same general direction came a muffled hubbub of some kind and the rattle of gunfire.

I looked at my watch: two hours to go. Make no mistake, I would depart on the appointed hour as fast as my tottering legs would carry me, alone if necessary; knowing further delay would be suicidal.

Now decked out in clean clothes I was able to keep down a dry biscuit with a sip of clean water. Still thoroughly drained, I started up each time I heard gunfire nearby.

"Surely Robert would have things in hand by now," I told myself, peeping at my watch: one and a half hours to go.

Despite my resolve, I could not quell a growing anxiety, still giving myself a better-than-even chance that Claudia would indeed return: 30 minutes to go.

I washed down another half of the dry biscuit with a sip from her water bottle. Really, there could be no other sensible option if she took the time to weigh up my proposal. What girl in her right mind would walk away from someone who loves her, and five thousand U.S. in his pocket? Eight minutes to go.

I stuffed the last items of wet clothing into my knapsack and made ready to leave, feeling hurt and angry. Good riddance, the two of them deserve one another. Twilight was settling fast.

After taking a few steps my conscience began to get the better of me. What if they had been detained unavoidably? What if Robert had put his foot down to prevent Claudia from returning alone? Perhaps they did need my assistance after all, or some cash for bribes?

Swearing under my breath I stopped dead and turned around; I would never rest until I heard that final decision from her own lips.

Up until that moment I'd been wrestling with wrong answers, more of which were not long in coming.

Emerging from the riverside vegetation I immediately saw that something momentous was occurring at the base of the Angel's column.

A tight-knit crowd of onlookers, twenty deep, pressed against the monument and others packed the staircases on both sides. Unable to penetrate the wall of bodies I climbed a low tree for a better view and what I saw made my blood run cold: of the three high arches in the marble façade, two were already occupied by grizzled Volkssturm corpses, swinging on ropes suspended from the balustrade above. Around their necks were signs I could not read.

Most shocking was the sight of Robert and Claudia standing in stark relief on stools beneath the centre arch. Their necks too wore nooses. My heart stopped for a moment and my tongue stuck to the roof of my mouth, but no sound came.

Claudia lifted up her face and appeared to be praying, Robert was arguing with the Gestapo officer, who was egging on the group of Hitler Youths to get on with it. They and others in the crowd were baying for my brother's blood and that of his "Jewish whore".

Predictably, Robert was giving as good as he got, "Garn, the lot o' yer. There's not a man among you who could beat me in a fair fight. Take a look at this then!" he exclaimed, waving his shattered hand in the air and with the other lifted his eye patch to reveal its gemless socket.

"Comrade?" he spoke directly to the officer in charge. "You know me, we fought side by side in the Brownshirts …" A murmur ran through the crowd and the man appeared to falter.

"That was a long time ago, comrade, things are different now. You have been found with false papers; a deserter. We have our orders, the matter is no longer in my hands. The youths are particularly anxious to get their hands on deserters."

"At least I'm only partially blind. Take another look at me: one eye missing and half a hand blown off in the service of the Reich. And deep down Oim still a proud Oirishman, can't yer tell by the accent?"

"There's nothing further we can do; you and your whore are both on the list."

"He's probably a Jew himself by the look of 'im," someone called from the crowd, "it should be easy enough to prove; let's pants him!"

"I'm no Jew and I'm not droppin' my tweeds for anyone," Robert protested, "You'll just have to take my word for it." But grasping hands soon had his trousers down around his knees and the evidence was there for all to see: circumcision, the sure sign of the Jew.

"I'm tellin' you those South American savages did this to me with a rusty razorblade, no bull; and I didn't bat an eyelid. It's not at all what you think."

From my vantage point, I could only cling on, frozen with fear that in speaking up or making any false move the mob would do the same to me. It was far and away the worst moment of my life and I would have to live with the guilt forever. How could I hope to save them against such overwhelming odds?

"If you've got anything to say, say it now, before the boys start hauling on the ropes …" I heard the Gestapo man call out.

"To Hell with the lot o' ya," Robert cried in a loud voice, "and remember, everyone picks 'is nose when no one's lookin'. That's it, do your damnest." He was standing straight and proud and Claudia was staring ahead with a slight smile flicking across her proud features.

The whole scene slowed down like a twilight ballet as she reached out and took Robert's hand to the roll of a kettle drum. The stools were kicked away and I watched mesmerised as my last two guiding lights were despatched with their fingers tightly entwined. A cheer went up from the mob as I diverted my eyes and clung sobbing to the branches, wracked by a terrifying loneliness.

Dimly, I was aware of the erupting crowd and the H.J. youths whooping like savages around the base of the Angel. In a flash, they reminded me of certain warriors in a far-off land.

As they rounded the column for the third time I heard a voice call out, "Over there in that tree, he's one of them; I've seen them together. Get him, quick!"

I'd been spotted, but before my accusers could push through the crush I made the decision to jump, hitting the ground heavily. Instinctively, I headed for the riverbank downstream, my left ankle stabbing pain with every yard. In the distance, the troop of uniformed youths could be heard baying for more blood, my blood.

I paused only to stuff my knapsack under a tangle of willow roots and Lothar's bundle of notes down my shirt. Then, taking a deep breath I plunged once more into the putrid Isar, heading straight for the bottom. As before I was bowled along by the swift current and each time I surfaced there were fewer of the Brownshirts in pursuit.

Freezing and spent I could hear the roar of the weir ahead, spelling calamity if I did not act fast. In a desperate cast, I grabbed at a waving willow finger and hung on against the current, fighting to keep my head above water.

I know not how long it took to pull myself ashore, but by chance, I emerged beside my very footprints in the sand where the whole harrowing episode had begun. No food, no dry clothing; just a rioting mind and a fresh stab of pain in the gut. Aware that I'd certainly swallowed more of the tainted liquid, I had to get as far away as possible from that river of death.

Overhead, a ghastly moon was pulsing through Munich's shroud of grey and orange, altogether lending the scene a Dantean tint.

An open path through the tree-lined parklands stretched away to the north, but it too was threatened by distant flames on both sides.

Across the river came the roar of big cats and the panic-stricken trumpeting of elephants. Hobbling from cover to cover with chattering teeth, I feared the end of the world was upon me, but determined not to go down without a fight. My last chance for deliverance lay beyond the open space ahead. With my head pounding and my lungs close to bursting I knew deep down it was hopeless.

Without warning a huge spotted shape sprang from the shrubbery with fangs bared, but this time I was ready. In a flash, my Master within raised his fist and struck a mighty blow at its head: Bam! "Klaus, wake up!" My wife was shaking me gently. "It's just a dream, you're having another one of your nasty Nazi nightmares."

I rubbed my eyes … trying to figure out exactly where I was.

"Come along, you have an interview with the bride and groom in an hour. Every second couple these days wants to get married among the grapevines."

I lifted my head from the waiting room sofa and swung my feet to the floor; squinting at the sunshine coming through the window, I was gladdened by the familiar cackle of Kookaburras in the big gum tree outside. As I dressed, I found myself softly humming the "Horst Wessel Song"…

FINIS.

www.ingramcontent.com/pod-product-compliance
Lightning Source LLC
Chambersburg PA
CBHW032025180726
48283CB00008B/2825